BLOOD AND BONE

www.transworldbooks.co.uk

BLOOD
AND BONE

A NOVEL OF THE MALAZAN
EMPIRE

Ian C. Esslemont

BANTAM PRESS

LONDON · TORONTO · SYDNEY · AUCKLAND · JOHANNESBURG

TRANSWORLD PUBLISHERS
61–63 Uxbridge Road, London W5 5SA
A Random House Group Company
www.transworldbooks.co.uk

Published in Great Britain
in 2012 by Bantam Press
an imprint of Transworld Publishers

A CIP catalogue record for this book
is available from the British Library.

ISBNs 9780593064467 (cased)
9780593064474 (tpb)

Addresses for Random House Group Ltd companies outside the UK
can be found at: www.randomhouse.co.uk
The Random House Group Ltd Reg. No. 954009

The Random House Group Limited supports the Forest Stewardship
Council (FSC®), the leading international forest-certification organization.
Our books carrying the FSC label are printed on FSC®-certified paper.
FSC is the only forest-certification scheme endorsed by the leading
environmental organizations, including Greenpeace. Our paper procurement
policy can be found at www.randomhouse.co.uk/environment.

Typeset in 10½/12½pt Sabon by
Kestrel Data, Exeter, Devon.
Printed and bound in Great Britain by
Clays Ltd, Bungay, Suffolk.

2 4 6 8 10 9 7 5 3 1

This novel is dedicated to the memory of my father,
John Roy Esslemont, 1934–1989.

You are greatly missed.

ACKNOWLEDGEMENTS

It is with gratitude that I acknowledge my time at the University of Minnesota, where I was encouraged to pursue my interest in nineteenth-century travel writing, colonial texts, and the myths of imperialism. I hope to return to this rich material some day. Truth is indeed stranger than fiction.

DRAMATIS PERSONAE

Thaumaturg Villagers
Saeng   A descendant of local priestesses
Hanu   Her brother

Himatan Villagers
Oroth-en   Village headman
Ursa   A female warrior

The Mountain Bandits
Kenjak Ashevajak   The Bandit Lord
Loor-San
Myint
Thet-mun

Of the Thaumaturg
Golan   Commander of the Army of Righteous Chastisement
U-Pre   Second in Command
Thorn   Principal Scribe of the army
Waris   An officer of the army
Pon-lor   A newly trained Thaumaturg
Tun   An overseer of the army (similar to a sergeant)
Surin   The Prime Master of the ruling Circle of Masters

Servants of Ardata
Rutana   A witch
Nagal   A warrior

| Citravaghra | The 'man-leopard' |
| Varakapi | The 'man-ape' |

Of the Tribes of the Adwami
Jatal	A prince of the Hafinaj
Andanii	Princess of the Vehajarwi
Ganell	A chief of the Awamir
Sher' Tal	Horsemaster of the Saar
Pinal	Horsemaster of the Hafinaj
The Warleader	A mercenary commander
Scarza	His lieutenant

Of the Crimson Guard Avowed
K'azz D'Avore	Commander
Shimmer	A captain
Gwynn	A mage, once of Skinner's company
Lor-sinn	A mage
Turgal	
Cole	
Amatt	

Of the Disavowed
Skinner	Captain
Jacinth	Lieutenant
Mara	A mage
Petal	A mage
Red	A mage
Shijel	Weaponmaster
Black the Lesser	
Hist	
Leuthan	

Of the Malazan Mercenaries
Yusen	Captain
Burastan	Lieutenant
Murk	A mage
Sour	A mage
Ostler	A soldier
Tanner	A soldier
Dee	A soldier
Sweetly	A scout

Others

Ardata	Also known as the Queen of Witches
The Queen of Dreams	Also known as the Enchantress, T'riss
Ina	A Seguleh, of the top thousand fighters, the Jistarii
The Witch Queen	Also known as the Queen of Monsters, Ardata
Old Man Moon	An elder
Ripan	One of his offspring
Sister Spite	Daughter of Draconus
Osserc	A Tiste Liosan, worshipped by some as a sky god
L'oric	Son of Osserc
Gothos	A Jaghut

BLOOD AND BONE

PROLOGUE

In the third moon of the third year of the Great Drought, we put out to sea from the estuary of Holy Ubaryd. On the fifteenth day of the third moon we arrived at an island of the barbarian Falarese. From then on, we were harassed by contrary winds, which delayed our arrival. Further, we encountered treacherous fields of ice that could only be navigated with the greatest care. It was not until the eleventh moon when we finally dropped anchor at the mouth of a great river. Certain it is that so short a visit cannot encompass all the customs and peculiarities of this country, yet we may at least outline its principal characteristics.

Ular Takeq
Customs of Ancient Jakal-Uku

GHOSTS RULED THE JUNGLES OF JACURUKU. SAENG REMEMBERED staying awake through the night as she strained to understand their whispered calls. Somehow their murmuring beckoned so much more seductively than her own dreams. One of her earliest memories was of walking alone through moonlit leaves hunting for the source of the jungle's voice. She'd been utterly self-composed and without fear – as only a child could be. Long into her wandering she distinctly recalled a hand taking hers and guiding her through the dense fronds and stands of damp grasses back to the village. Her mother swept up then, her face wet with tears, to squeeze her to her bony chest while Saeng calmly explained that everything was all right. That there was no need to cry. That a friend had brought her back.

And of course later everyone swore to seeing her wander in from the dark alone.

Since then the leagues of impenetrable jungle surrounding the village had held no fear for her. A dangerous and, she could admit, rather reckless attitude in a land where flower garlands and prayer scarves festooned trees in honour of countless spirits, restless dead, ghosts, lost forgotten gods, and far too many missing children and adults.

Growing up she continued to steal away into the woods whenever she could. And there among the hanging vines and leaves dripping night-mist the old spirits of the land came to her and she learned many forgotten things. In the morning she would return from her wanderings through the jungle tracks, her legs and feet sheathed in mud and grass and webs tangled in her hair. At first her mother beat her and twisted her ears. 'You are no low-bred farmer's daughter!' she would screech. 'We come from an ancient family of priestesses and seers!'

And often, during the midday meal, her mother would take her hands and always it would be the same story: 'Saeng,' she would begin, as if so disappointed in her. 'Our family has kept the old faith. Not like these ignorant fools surrounding us with their grovelling to idols, charms and amulets. All these superstitious mouthings to earth goddesses, or beast gods, or the cursed God-King, or the Witch – all of these empty words. Or worse. Our family, we women, we descend from the original priestesses of the Sky and the Sun! We worship Light. Remember that! The Light that gives all life!'

Her mother would try to capture her gaze as if pleading with her to understand but she would glance away, mouthing, 'Yes, Mother.' Eventually her mother gave up even these exhortations and she was allowed to continue her wanderings in pursuit of the voices that whispered from the great green labyrinth that surrounded them.

As she grew older, and her mastery of the whispered teachings grew more assured, she found she could summon these ghosts, which she now knew as the dreaded land and ancestor spirits, the Nak-ta. And as her skills advanced these spirits and shades came to her from ever further into the ancient gulf of the land's past. And each commanded greater and greater puissance in the manipulation of their talents. In the murmurings of these restless dead she learned how to bind the will of animals, how to interpret the voices of the wind, how to trick the senses, and how to tease knowledge from the earth itself. As she drifted, half asleep, it seemed to her that they stole close to her ears where they whispered of darker secrets. Of ancient forbidden charms, of lost deadly wards, and how to dominate the recesses of the human mind.

At first she thought nothing of this, even as the shades crowded ever nearer and proved ever more difficult for her to dismiss. Until one night the tenebrous clawed hand of one clutched her arm. Its voice was no more than the sighing of the wind through the leaves as it hissed, *'The High King will be well pleased with you.'*

She remembered her shock at its frigid touch. 'All that was dust ages ago.'

'Nay, 'tis of the moment. No more foolishness from you.' It began to sink into the wet ground, yanking her down by the arm.

A yell shocked her even more then as a branch swung through the shade, dispersing it. She lay staring up at her elder brother, Hanu, while he glared about, branch readied. Strangely, all she felt was outrage. 'What are *you* doing here?' she demanded.

He pulled her up. 'You're welcome. I've been following you. And thank the ancestors for it, too.'

'What?' She danced away from him. 'For how long?'

He shrugged his broad shoulders in the shadowed darkness. 'Whenever I can. Someone has to keep an eye out while you offer yourself up to these feral spirits.'

'I can control them.'

'Clearly not.'

'That one surprised me, that's all.' A sudden thought occurred to her and she drew closer, biting her lip. 'You're not . . . you're not going to tell Mother, are you?'

'Great Witch, no. She's worried enough as it is.'

'Well . . . you can't stop me.'

'That much is clear as well,' and he crossed his thick arms, peering down at her.

She raised her chin in defiance and saw how the sweat of the humid night ran in streams down his face and neck. Through her skills she sensed his drumming heart and rushing blood and she realized: *He is terrified. Terrified of the night – just like all of them. Yet he is here. He came to protect me.*

His breathing was heavy as he scanned the deep forest shadows. 'At least promise me that you'll wake me, yes? That you won't go out alone.' His gaze swung to her, pleading. 'Yes?'

And how could she refuse? Her own defiant front melted. 'Yes, Hanu. I promise.'

For another year the nights passed in this fashion; she waking her brother and the two stealing out to where she communed with the wild Nak-ta ghosts that haunted the jungle. And with far older spirits of stone, stream and wind. Night after night she sat for hours under the wary gaze of Hanu and spoke to things he could not see nor sense. It was then she realized that while he might protect her from any physical threat, he remained susceptible to their compellings and charms, and so she surreptitiously cast over him protections and guardings against such magics.

'Who are you talking to?' he would sometimes ask from where he squatted under a tree.

'The old dead,' she'd answer.

'Aren't you scared?'

'No. They're dead.'

Befuddled, he'd throw up his hands. 'Then – why aren't they gone?'

'Because they're angry. Only anger is strong enough to keep the feet of the dead to the ground.'

Then he would glower because secretly he was afraid. And as the months passed he began to pester her. 'It isn't safe,' he'd say. 'We shouldn't be here.'

And he was right. But not in the way either of them imagined.

One night she sat on the edge of a choked swampy depression. She was speaking with the shade of a woman who'd been drowned here in what she claimed had once been a great reservoir. In those days, the spirit asserted, its waters had been clear and deeper than a tall man. Among the trees behind her, Hanu pretended he was one of the ancient warrior-kings as he swung a heavy branch.

'Drowned?' she asked. 'What do you mean you were drowned?'

'*Heavy rocks were tied to me and I was thrown in,*' the shade replied.

Saeng resisted the urge to curse. Sometimes the dead could be so literal. 'I mean *why* were you drowned?'

'*I was a priestess of the old faith.*'

'The old faith? You mean—' and Saeng lowered her voice, 'the damned God-King?'

'*No,*' came the uninflected voice of the ghost. '*Not him. It was at his orders that the temple was burned and I was slain. I speak of the ancient old religion. The worship of Light. The Great Sun.*'

Saeng leaped up from the edge of the swamp. For the first time something said by one of these shades seemed to touch her very heart.

Hanu appeared at her side. 'What is it?' he demanded.

Saeng's hand had gone to her throat. 'A spirit,' she managed. *By the ancients! Could Mother have been right all this time?* 'She claims to be a priestess of an old faith.'

20

Hanu waved his contempt. 'Which? They're like flies.'

But she held his gaze long and hard and eventually his brows crimped. 'No . . .' he breathed, and she nodded her certainty.

'Oh, yes.'

'The one Mother goes on about . . . ?'

'The same faith that runs in your blood,' came the shade's voice from behind and Saeng jumped once again. She turned on it. 'What do you mean?'

'Who's that?' Hanu demanded, peering about.

The ghost raised an arm, pointing off into the jungle. *'And now comes your time of trial and your time to choose. Remember all that we have taught.'*

Saeng stared her confusion. 'What? Taught? What do you mean?'

The woman clasped her hands before her and it seemed to Saeng that she was peering down at her as if she were her own daughter. *'Really, child. You did not think that you were called for no reason, did you?'*

'What is it?' Hanu whispered, insistent.

'*Called?*' But the shade dispersed like smoke. Saeng turned to her brother. 'It seemed to suggest that something is coming.'

Hanu frowned, considering. 'The Choosing is approaching,' he murmured.

Of course. The Choosing. Suddenly her heart tripped as if a grip were attempting to stop it. 'You mustn't go.'

He snorted. 'It's required, Saeng. We'll all be arrested if I'm not seen. Ancients, all our neighbours will see to that!'

Saeng knew what he meant. It was an ugly truth, but better one of another family be chosen than one of theirs.

A month later the great travelling column of the ruling Thaumaturgs swung through their province. And eventually a representative arrived even at their insignificant village. He came escorted by twenty soldiers and carried in a great palanquin of lacquered wood shaded by white silks.

Saeng watched from next to her mother among the villagers crowded together by the sharp proddings of the soldiers' sticks while the menfolk of age lined up for the Choosing. She was apprehensive for Hanu, but not overly so, as it had been years since any son of the village had been selected for service.

The palanquin was lowered and the theurgist stepped out. He was dressed exquisitely in rich layered silks of deepest sea blue and blossom gold, and was rather fat about the middle, and short. Yet

21

he held the all-important ivory baton of office, which he carried negligently in one ringed hand, swinging it back and forth.

It occurred to Saeng that the man was bored with his task and was merely going through the motions for the sake of ritual. A great churning hatred for him overtook her – a hatred she imagined just as strong as his for their downtrodden poverty, their mud-spattered cheap rags, and the responsibilities that took him away from his scheming at the capital deep in the heart of their nation.

He paced a quick inspection of the assembled menfolk then headed back to the cool shade of his palanquin.

Saeng eased out a taut breath of relief; yet again no one had been chosen. Once more their distant dreaded rulers had come, collected their taxation and tribute, examined the males of the village, and marched on never to be seen again until another year turned upon the wheel of their grinding fate.

The representative paused, however. He swung the baton up to tap upon one shoulder next to the fat folds of his shaven neck. He turned and padded back to the assembly where he slowly retraced his steps, once more passing before the men, one by one. When he came abreast of Hanu he paused. The ivory baton, gold-chased, bounced heavily upon his shoulder. He leaned forward as if sniffing her elder brother, then suddenly rocked back as if thrust.

His head turned and his black narrowed eyes scanned the crowd of villagers, Saeng included. Then his thick jowls bunched as he smiled with something like cruel satisfaction and he thrust out his baton to touch Hanu upon the chest. Their mother lurched forward crying out but Saeng caught her arm and held her.

Hanu's stunned gaze found hers. As the soldiers closed in and tied his arms, he stared, silent, until they urged him onward. Then he twisted to peer back over his shoulder. 'Don't worry – I'll protect you! I swore! I swore!' he called over and over until the soldiers yanked upon his fetters.

Their mother cried into her arms, but Saeng watched while the soldiers prodded her brother off. She had to watch; she owed him that. The theurgist, whoever he was, some minor bureaucrat of their ruling elite, had returned to his palanquin. Saeng finally lost sight of her brother as he was urged up the track to disappear with the column into the hanging leaves of the jungle as if swallowed whole.

At that moment, as she stood supporting her mother, she vowed her revenge upon them all. Upon their crushing rule, their contempt, and upon the blood-price they exacted from their own people. Who were they to make such demands? To impose such suffering and misery?

She would see them burn. So did she swear.

Yet all the while a quieter voice whispered a suspicion that burned like acid upon her soul: *Would he not have been chosen but for your own castings upon him? Was not this all your fault?*

*　　*　　*

Shimmer happened to be at the waterfront when a battered vessel came limping up to one of the piers of Haven. She sensed something unusual about it, though she was no mage with access to any Warren. Nevertheless, she was of the Avowed of the Crimson Guard, and more than a hundred years ago she had sworn to oppose the Malazan Empire for so long as it should endure. And over the years it seemed that this vow had caused preternatural instincts and strengths to accrue to her. She could now sense things far beyond what she could before. Such as this modest two-masted ship; or rather, those it carried. Something was there. No mere lost coastal traders, or fisherfolk thrown off course. Power walked its deck. Despite wearing only a loose shirt over trousers, belted, with a long-knife at her back, she went down to meet the vessel.

They were certainly foreign. Of no extraction she was familiar with: hair night-black and straight; squat of build, close even to her own petite stature. And dark, varying from a fair nut hue to a sun-darkened earthy brown. Their vessel flew no sigils or heraldry. It appeared to have had a very hard crossing of it. The crew busied themselves readying for docking and though no sailor herself she thought the ship's company quite lacking in hands. The various lads and lasses who hung about the Haven waterfront took thrown lines and helped in the placement of a wood and rope gangway.

First down was an arresting figure of a woman: shorter even than Shimmer, and painfully lean. Her hair blew in a great midnight cloud about her head and she wore a loose black dress that obscured her feet. Some sort of binding encircled her arms and from each hung bright amulets and charms. More amulets hung on multiple leather thong necklaces to rattle like a forest of baubles.

After running a sceptical eye up and down Shimmer she announced in passable Talian: 'You are no customs official.'

'And you're no ship's captain.' Another figure stepped up on to the gangway, yanking Shimmer's attention away from the woman: a towering man in layered shirts, a curved dirk at his side. He too was dark, like the woman, as the Kanese can be, skin the hue of ironwood rather than the black of Dal Hon. He too wore his hair long, but gathered atop his head by some sort of carved stone clasp. The thick timbers of the gangway groaned and bounced as he descended.

After looking Shimmer up and down, he rumbled, 'She is of them.' His gaze was not challenging, yet something of his eyes made her uneasy: the irises glittered as if dusted in gold.

The woman's gaze sharpened, a sudden wariness touching it. 'Ah. I see it now. I was fooled – no Isturé would have deigned to appear so . . . informal.'

Shimmer frowned, and not only at being discussed as if she were not standing right before these two foreigners. *And that word . . . why did it grate like a dull blade across her back?*

Yet with Blues gone north she was the acting governor and so she inclined her head, all politeness. 'I'm sorry, but you have me at a disadvantage. What was that you said?'

'Isturé. It is our word for you in our lands.'

'Us . . . ?'

The woman did not even try to disguise her distaste. 'You Avowed. It translates as something like "undying fiend".'

Shimmer reflexively retreated a step and her hand went to her long-knife at her back. 'What do you two want here?'

The woman opened her hands in a gesture of apology. 'Forgive my ill-temper. I have been set a task that finds in me a reluctant servant. We come with an offer for you Crimson Guard.'

Shimmer relaxed her stance a touch. Behind the two foreigners the sailors climbed the rigging to prepare the ship for the repairs of a port call. They worked barefoot, the soles of their feet black with tar. 'An offer?' she answered, doubtful. 'What would that be?'

'Employment.'

She understood now, and she shook her head. 'We are no longer accepting contracts.'

'Well, perhaps that is for your general to decide. K'azz.'

'He's not . . . seeing potential employers right now.'

'He will see us.'

'I doubt that very—'

'There is an inn, or hostel, here in this hamlet?'

Shimmer gritted her teeth against her annoyance at being interrupted. 'Perhaps it would be best if you stayed on your vessel . . .'

'I think not. I am quite as sick of it as they are of me.'

That I can well understand. 'If you insist.' She invited them onward. 'We have an inn with some few plain rooms . . . but I cannot guarantee they will take you.'

The woman's smile was a wolfish flash of needle ivory teeth. 'Our gold is good, and innkeepers are the same breed everywhere.'

As they climbed the gentle slope up to the hamlet Shimmer introduced herself.

'Rutana,' the woman answered. She gestured back to the man who followed with slow deliberate steps. 'This is Nagal.'

'And where are you from?'

She snorted a harsh laugh. 'A land close to this but of which you would never have heard.'

Shimmer's patience hadn't been tested like this for some time. 'Try me,' she managed to offer lightly.

'Very well. We come from the land known to some as Jacuruku.'

Despite her irritation Shimmer was impressed. 'Indeed. I know it. I haven't been there, but K'azz has.'

'So I have been told. You will take a message to K'azz for us.'

Shimmer's irritation gave way to wonder at the woman's breathtaking imperiousness. 'Oh?' she answered. 'Will I?'

'Yes. You will.'

'And what is that message?'

Rutana stopped. She scowled, as if only now noting something in Shimmer's tone. She tugged on the tight lacing of the leather straps cinching her left arm and winced as if at an old nagging wound. Shimmer noted that the amulets knotted there were small triangular boxes each of which appeared to contain some sort of tiny carved figurine. 'Skinner walks our land,' the woman finally ground out. 'Tell him that, Isturé. The curse that is Skinner walks our land.'

Later, Shimmer summoned Lor-sinn and Gwynn to discuss their visitors. At table Gwynn maintained his grim and dour demeanour, dressed all in black, saying little and smiling even less. His newly grown shock of white hair stood in all directions. Shimmer could very easily imagine the man spending even his free time sitting stiffly while he glowered into the darkness rather like a corpse presiding gloomily at its own wake. The second of her company mages present, Lor-sinn, was still obviously uncomfortable sitting so close to Shimmer among the seats normally occupied by Blues, Fingers, Shell, or the recently departed Smoky. Having the opportunity to study her more closely now, Shimmer thought that the woman was slowly but steadily losing the plumpness that had endeared her to so many of the company's males.

25

As servants brought soup Shimmer turned to Lor. 'You are continuing to attempt to contact the Fourth in Assail?'

'Yes, Commander.'

'Shimmer will do.'

'Yes, ah, Shimmer.' She leaned forward over the table, ever eager to discuss her work. 'My last effort was last week. I could try opening a portal if you wish . . .'

'I would not risk that, Lor. Not into Assail. Nothing so drastic as yet. We will see what K'azz thinks.' She turned to Gwynn. 'And our friends the First?'

The humourless mage – who only seemed to be getting even gloomier – studied his soup as if it were something unrecognizable. 'As our visitors claim. Jacuruku still, Commander.'

'Just Shimmer, please.'

Gwynn bowed his head, then, as if reordering his thoughts, he set down his utensils, sighing. He cradled his chin on his fists. 'This Rutana is a servant of ancient Ardata. Whom some name the Queen of Witches.'

Shimmer nodded. She tasted the soup and found it pleasant. She set down her spoon. The servants slipped the main entrée of roasted game birds before them. She inhaled the steaming birds' scent then sat back to meet Gwynn's glistening steady gaze. 'Yet you assure me they are enemies of Skinner.'

'They are.'

'Then your point?'

'They are here to draw us into their war. And, Commander, I have been there. I have seen it. And I strongly counsel against this.'

'I see. Thank you for that blunt appraisal.' She turned to Lor. 'And you?'

The mage shrugged her still-rounded shoulders. 'It remains academic. No one even knows where in the interior K'azz has disappeared to.'

Shimmer lowered her gaze to the small baked game hen. She plucked at the crisp skin. 'I will send the message through our dead Brethren. They will find him.'

'He may not bother to reply,' Gwynn added.

A touch too blunt, Shimmer thought, her lips tightening in irritation. 'We shall see.'

Much later, Shimmer stood in the centre of her chambers. It was the set of rooms which had once belonged to the old lord and ladies of the dynasty that had ruled this province as one of the petty kingdoms of Stratem before the arrival of the Crimson Guard. Officially it was Blues', as it was his rotation as governor, and it would be K'azz's should he be visiting. Not that whichever of the Avowed occupied the room would have altered anything. The furnishings remained sparse: a cot for a bed and a desk for paperwork. That was all. And a travel chest containing Shimmer's armour. As for her whipsword, it hung in the main hall downstairs.

Studying the empty room, its walls of dressed stone, the dusty old tapestries that dated back to the original dynasty, that hung rotting where the Guard had found them, her thoughts returned to her irritation at dinner. It was not Gwynn and his clumsy manners; no, it was K'azz's absence. The man was avoiding *something* and what that might be worried her. At times what personal vanity she had left fancied he was avoiding her. At other times she cursed the man for running away from his responsibilities. It was damned hard work struggling to build a unified nation from the ground up. Roads had to be surveyed, bridges built, settlements planned. Things couldn't be allowed to fall out haphazardly. And the man had walked away from the dull dreariness of it all – leaving others to clean up the mess. That irresponsibility had lowered her estimation of him a fair bit. She shook herself, frowning at the dark. In any case, he had to be contacted. She summoned the Brethren to her.

Shortly, a ghostly shape coalesced within the room, lean, bandy-legged, right arm gone at the elbow: Stoop, their old siegemaster, recently lost to them. The shade offered a slight inclination of his head. '*Shimmer,*' he breathed, and she was surprised to actually hear the word pronounced.

'Stoop. I have a message for K'azz.'

'*I can deliver it,*' the shade of the old man drawled. '*But I can't say as whether he'll respond.*'

'I understand. The message is that visitors have arrived from Jacuruku. Skinner has returned there and they appear to be implying that he is our responsibility.'

'*We sensed those two,*' Stoop murmured. '*Hardly human, them.*'

Shimmer frowned at the observation. 'You will pass on the message?'

'*Course. Get right on it. Good to see you again, Shimmer.*' The shade headed to the door as if it would open it to exit but passed right through the adzed planks instead. His presence left behind a cloud of dust that wafted to the stone floor.

Puzzled, Shimmer knelt to run a hand through the dust, then straightened, studying her fingers. The man had acted almost as if he were still alive. And never before had she seen one of them gather dust to their form. But then, Stoop quite often appeared as spokesman for the fallen Avowed. She wiped the powder from her hands and returned to the desk.

Shimmer frankly expected no response. K'azz had disavowed Skinner and those who chose to follow him. Thrown them from the ranks more than a year ago. The man's actions were now his own. The company was in no way answerable for them . . . no matter what others might insist. These visitors could linger as long as they liked. They would get no satisfaction. Over the next few days she ignored them while approving requests from the local merchants regarding expenses for repairs to their vessel.

Four days later she was therefore quite surprised when Ogilvy, one of the regulars, a recruit of their Third Investment, knocked and entered, pressing a scarred and battered knuckle to an equally scarred, hairless brow. 'K'azz, ma'am,' he announced in his hoarse gravelly voice, bowing as if she were some sort of nobility. Countless times she had told him a salute would do, but it seemed the man's manners were ingrained as he bowed and ma'amed even as she told him not to. Now she just endured it.

Nodding, she dismissed him. She set down her quill and rose to come down. She took a moment to pause before a mirror of polished bronze next to the door and examine herself. Short and dark, her long black hair braided. She happened to be wearing a full-length gown of brocade, slit and laced at the sides, tight across her chest and narrow at the arms all the way down past her wrists where the cloth flared. It hadn't occurred to her before, but she seemed to have taken the role of acting-governor rather seriously in setting aside her usual plain leathers and quilted aketon. *But that face! Always so severe, lass. Nose flattened like some brawling barroom wench, and lips too damned thin.*

She scowled at her reflection. *Still, not exactly something to run from howling into the night.*

And anyway, who gave a damn? She threw open the door, yanked the sheathed dirk hanging there from its peg, and shoved it through the back of her belt as she descended the circular stone staircase.

She found him at the stables running a hand over one of their few mounts. His leathers were travel-stained, with tall moccasins wrapped tight up to his knees. Seen from behind his hair hung wild and unkempt, touched with streaks of grey.

He turned before she reached him and she paused. Again the shock of this man, this youth of her own remembrance, now an old man. He must've been living very hard recently as he'd lost even more weight. His keen eyes were sunken and his cheekbones stuck out as sharp as blades. And he'd grown a beard, also touched with grey.

Old. Prematurely old. Prematurely? We're all old, girl! You're over a hundred and twenty! Shaking herself, she closed to take both cool hands in hers, giving a light kiss to each cheek. 'Welcome! What have you been doing?'

'Picking out routes to Lake Jorrick.'

'You're really going to name it after him?'

He smiled behind his beard. 'Why not? He's a hero in Genabackis.'

'Well . . . I suppose so. Here to stay?'

The bright eyes, which had been searching hers, edged aside. 'Perhaps. My apologies for leaving all the paperwork to you.'

'You left it to Blues.'

'Ah! No wonder he fled. Then I don't apologize. Any word on them?'

'They may have reached Korel by now.'

'So . . . they merely have to find Bars and rescue him from the Stormwall – should it even be him. They ought to be back soon.'

'I should've gone.'

'Blues can take care of himself. He's the best of us.'

'Well, I miss him. As I miss you . . .'

The dark wind-burnished skin about the man's eyes wrinkled then and he glanced down. 'I miss all of you as well – so, what of these visitors?'

Shimmer headed for the open fortress gates. 'Gwynn names them servants of Ardata.'

K'azz walked at her side, hands clasped at his back. 'Yes. I can feel their presence. No doubt they rank among her most powerful. She's telling us that she takes their message very seriously. Unfortunately, we can't oblige . . .'

'Such was my answer.'

'But they want to hear it from me.'

'Yes.'

'That's why I'm here . . .'

Shimmer's questing gaze fell to the gravel road that wound to Haven Town. *And when they go – so too will you? Off into the wilderness again? Do you not worry about the effects of these long absences? The rumours and disquiet? Not among us Avowed, of*

29

course, but the regular troops and the lay people. Some even claim you died long ago and we merely rule in your name.

Still, she mused, it was just like the old days when so often they laid false rumours of his presence or absence . . . *Blues and others even masquerading as him . . . all as precautions against the ever-present threat of those damned Claw assassins . . .*

Blinking, Shimmer came up short, realizing that they'd reached the town already. The long descent down the rear of the cliff seemed to have passed in an instant. They must have spent the entire walk in a long mutual silence.

And ahead, down the main strip, the two emerged from the inn, no doubt just as aware of their proximity as they of theirs. The big man, Nagal, was forced to duck quite low to manage the small doorway. From windows and open doors curious locals watched as they closed upon one another. None of the four of them, Shimmer noted, carried a blade longer than a dirk. A deliberate wariness?

The dark woman offered the sketch of a bow. The forest of amulets upon her breast rustled and clattered. K'azz answered the bow. 'Duke D'Avore,' she said. 'Or is it Prince?'

'I have held many titles,' he answered easily enough. 'I suggest the one of which I am most proud – Commander.'

'Very well . . . Commander. I am Rutana and this is Nagal.' The huge fellow, who appeared to have been suppressing a crooked secretive smile the entire time, also bowed.

'Greetings and welcome to Stratem. How may we be of service?'

'You have my message,' she snapped. 'You should know how you may be of service. Your vassal, Skinner, has returned to Jacuruku and would make war upon us. It is your responsibility to come and rid us of him.'

'He is no longer my vassal. I am no longer answerable for his actions.'

The woman was undeterred. She raised her chin, her mouth twisting into something even more sour. 'What then of reparations for his crimes in our lands during the time he was your vassal? His elimination would perhaps be just blood-price for those!'

Again, the woman's imperiousness stole Shimmer's breath. *Gods above! She stands in K'azz's lands and denounces him for crimes committed by another – and all in a distant kingdom?* It was too much to tolerate. She would have sent them off that instant.

K'azz, however, seemed to possess inhuman patience. The man merely tilted his head as if considering the woman's point from all possible angles. Then from behind his beard he allowed a small considered frown. 'It occurs to me, Rutana, that Skinner entered into vassalage to your mistress when he first arrived in Jacuruku, did he not?'

The woman clutched the leather bindings of her arm, twisting them savagely, and rage darkened her features. After a moment she mastered her emotions enough to answer: 'There was no formal agreement as such. For a time my mistress and he merely struck up a relationship.'

K'azz's shrug announced he considered the subject closed. 'Be that as it may, Skinner has long gone his own route and I am in no way answerable.'

'Yet even now the Vow sustains him,' Nagal suddenly broke in, his voice low and melodious. 'Your Vow, K'azz.'

Something like pain clutched at the prince's features. 'I would revoke that if I possessed the power,' he answered, strained. 'As it is, I have disavowed him.'

'That is not enough,' he answered. 'Still the Vow encompasses him. Our mistress knows the mysteries of it, K'azz. Are you not curious?'

Shimmer felt a profound unease. Through these two servants she was aware of the influence of this mistress of all witches, Ardata, stretching out to touch them. The sensation made her queasy and her flesh crawled as if befouled. K'azz, she could see, was shaken by what could only be taken as an Ascendant implicitly offering to examine something entwined with his very identity.

Tentatively, he began, 'I do not question your mistress's wisdom and power. Perhaps, in the future, I shall take advantage of her generous offer.' He inclined his head without taking his eyes from the two. 'But until such time I bid you a safe return journey.'

He turned and walked away, rather stiffly. Shimmer followed, backing away, unwilling to take her eyes from the two.

The big man, Nagal, simply raised his voice to call: 'Yes, some time in the future, Prince. For do we not possess all the time in the world, yes?'

That checked K'azz for a moment but then he moved on.

'One last thing!' Rutana shouted.

Sighing, K'azz turned. 'Yes?'

'As you are uncooperative, my mistress has empowered me to reveal one last point.'

'Yes?'

'You know my mistress's powers as seer and prophetess. She has foreseen that soon there shall be an attempt upon the Dolmens of Tien. What say you to that, K'azz? Can that be allowed?'

31

At first this obscure warning meant nothing to Shimmer. Then she remembered where she'd heard that odd name before: the very locale where K'azz had been imprisoned in the lands of Jacuruku. Her attention snapped to him and she was shocked to see his reaction: he had gone chalky white and his shoulders visibly bowed as if beneath a crushing burden. He shook his head in denial. 'That mustn't happen,' he finally grated, his voice thick.

Rutana's smile revealed a hungry triumph. 'My mistress is in agreement with that, Prince.'

'You've made your point, Witch.' He turned to Shimmer. 'Summon the Avowed. I sail for Jacuruku.' And he walked away.

Shimmer stared after him in stunned amazement. *Just like that? One vague threat or hint, or whatever that was, and he agrees?* She glanced back to the two but their avid gazes ignored her, following instead the rigid, stick-like figure of K'azz as he appeared to drag himself, painfully, up the road.

*   *   *

The vessel's bow slid up the strand with a loud scraping of wood on sand. At the bow its master stood scanning the dunes and scrub stretching inland. All the crew and the assembled warriors awaited his command, for though cruel and harsh he had led them on many successful raids and they trusted his leadership in war. His long coat of grey mail hung to the decking, ragged and rusted. His hair and beard hung likewise grey and ragged. The Grey Ghost, some named him – in the faintest whispers only. He preferred the title Warleader.

With a savage yell he vaulted the side, landing in the surf in a splash. His crew followed him, howling like wolves. Of them, if any one might be named second in command, this was Scarza. A great hulking warrior who some whispered possessed more than a drop of Trell blood. He came now to the Warleader's side, noting, in passing, how the rust of the man's armour left a great blood-like bloom trailing behind in the surf.

'No shaking of the earth, Scarza,' the Warleader observed, shading his gaze upon the scrublands. 'No pealing of trumpets. Not the end of the world.'

'What is this you speak of, Warleader?'

The man's aged sallow eyes flicked to him, then away. 'Nothing, my good Scarza . . . It has just been a great many years since I last walked these shores.'

32

'And what are we to do in this wretched land that reminds me too painfully of my own?'

The deeply furrowed lines of the ancient's face darkened as he smiled; he seemed to enjoy his second in command's caustic vein of humour. 'It's not these lands I want, Scarza. It's the neighbouring kingdom. It's ruled by a complacent set of self-aggrandizing mages who style themselves master alchemists and theurgists. *Here*, however, are ragged bands that make their living raiding the Thaumaturgs. *These* we will take under our wing and show what rewards a sustained campaign can bring.'

'Their deaths, you mean?'

The lean man's lined mouth drew down as if in mild disapproval. 'Well,' he admitted, 'eventually.'

The Warleader turned to the surf where the rest of the fleet of ten raiders now came grinding up on to the strand. 'In the meantime send out scouts and see to the unloading, then dismantle the ships for their timber, yes?'

Scarza bowed. 'At once, Warleader.'

The grey man returned his attention inland, shading his gaze once more. 'So,' he breathed. 'I'm back, you wretched circle of mages. What will you do? Yes . . . *what will you do?*'

CHAPTER I

The voice of an old friend hailed me, when, first returned from my Wanderings, I paced again in that long street of Darujhistan which is called the Escarpment Way; and suddenly taking me wonderingly by the hand, said, 'Tell me, since you are returned again by the assurance of Osserc, whilst we walk, as in former years, towards the blossoming orchards, what moved you, or how could you take such journeys into the Wastes of the World?'

Chanat D'argatty
Journeys of D'argatty

S AENG POUNDED MORTAR WITH PESTLE, GRINDING THE SAUCE FOR the midday meal. In went nuts, young crayfish, greens and peppers, all to be mixed in with sliced unripe papaya for a salad. She worked on her knees, bent over the broad stone mortar, her muscular forearms clenching and flexing. Her long black hair stuck to her sweaty brow and she pushed it away with the back of a hand.

All the other women her age in the village were performing the same task in their family huts, yet with the all-important difference of fixing the meal for husbands and children. Saeng had neither. She prepared meals and cleaned house for herself and her aged mother, who, to Saeng's continual annoyance, never missed an opportunity to criticize her efforts, or to wonder pointedly why her daughter was on her way to an early spinsterhood. *How could it be otherwise, Mother? With you dismissing all our neighbours' religious festivals as superstitious cowshit, their household shrines as false idols, and their faiths as ignorant childishness? No wonder Father disappeared. And no wonder we stand as the village pariahs.*

She dished the meal on to two banana leaves then squatted cross-legged, frowning. Not that her own habits helped. Everyone named her a witch. A servant of the Night-Mother, Ardata. In the past some had even secretly approached her asking that she curse a rival, or strike down a neighbour's buffalo. And their indignation when she refused! It would be laughable if weren't so sad.

As it was, the village had their scapegoat for every stillborn calf, every sick child, and every poor harvest. And she herself was heartily tired of it. But Mother – who would take care of Mother? Yet again she wished Hanu was still with them. How she missed his quiet strength. *He* should've married and *she* should've moved in with him to rule it over his wife, leaving her free to escape all this. Instead, the unthinkable had happened and he'd been taken by the Thaumaturgs.

And she supposed she should be thankful. For that fact alone – the prestige accruing from their sacrifice and the relief of all her neighbours that such a price fell to another – allowed them their tenuous grip here on the very edge of the village.

She took up a pinch of rice with the salad and chewed without enthusiasm. And soon Mother would arrive fresh with gossip from her morning round. So-and-so is expecting another grandchild! And so-and-so's nephew has a cough! Saeng hung her head. *Gods deliver her!*

And here she comes up the path. Saeng took a steadying breath. 'So,' she welcomed her, 'what news, Mother?' After some moments she peered up, a pinch of rice in one hand. Her mother watched her, quite uncharacteristically silent. 'Yes? What is it?'

Her mother stood just before the open front veranda. She twisted her hands in the cloth of her mulitcoloured wrap. 'News? Yes – real news this time, Saeng. Refugees passing the village. Fleeing the west. And Mae's relations have arrived with nothing more than the clothes on their backs.'

Saeng sat back, frowning even more than usual. 'What is it?'

'An army comes, littlest. Our lords the Thaumaturgs march to war and they come impressing into service everyone they find.'

Saeng popped the ball of rice into her mouth and chewed thoughtfully. 'Well, what is that to us? *We've* already paid.'

Her mother shook her head. 'I don't think that will count any longer. And—' but she stopped herself.

'And what?'

'Saeng,' her mother began again, reaching out a hand, 'the old faith is explicit! In times of war the priestess must be in the temple . . .'

'*Please*, Mother . . . don't go on about that.'

Her mother clasped her hands, shocked. 'Do not blaspheme! Your great-grandmother was unswerving in this – you must seek out the Great Temple.'

Saeng could hardly find the words. 'Mother . . . the old faith is long dead. No one even knows where the temples are!' She laughed a touch nervously. 'Really – you're being . . . silly.'

But her mother's face eased into her usual disappointment and she shook her head. Clenching her lips, Saeng looked away and finished her meal.

That night she couldn't sleep. The Nak-ta called to her louder than they had in many years. No matter which way she tossed or turned she couldn't shut them out. And even more distantly, when she concentrated, she thought she could hear the crash of great shapes lumbering ever closer through the jungle.

Then a voice called even louder than the wind rustling the palm leaves and shaking the rattan. Wordless it was; no more than a moan that sounded like someone gagged or wounded. Never before had she heard such a thing. And the voice – a man's. One of the villagers? Occasionally some fool would stagger drunk or sick off the paths only to be taken. If she got to them soon enough she would try to intercede, but when the shades had claimed their victim it was almost impossible to retrieve him. Only once had she exerted the extra, and very perilous, effort necessary – and that had been for a child. She threw on her wrap and padded out past their cleared garden patch into the wall of trees that was the verge of the trackless jungle that stretched from one coast to the other of her land, Jacuruku.

Once within the darkness between the tall trunks she paused, listening and sensing. She reached out, extending her awareness in an ever-broadening circle. She felt the footfall of the many night creatures surrounding the village, from a small family group of snuffling peccary to the nosing of a tiny shrew. Pushing even further she sensed the hot watchful presence of a night-hunting cat high in its perch, and on the far side of the circle of huts a troop of monkeys scavenged a meal – as far from the cat as possible.

Strange. Was there no one? Usually those who left the paths at night crashed blindly about as hard to miss as an elephant. So much for the flesh. What of the discarnate? Perhaps—

A footfall sounded. Close. Heavy. Far too heavy to be that of any villager. Then another. And a shape emerged from the deeper darkness, a monstrously huge figure, tall and broad. It crossed an errant beam of the green-tinged moonlight as it approached and

Saeng's breath caught as she recognized one of the Thaumaturg's giant armoured soldiers. The yakshaka.

So – they were here already.

She calmed herself and knelt, head bowed, awaiting the arrival of its master, who could not be too distant. These indestructible giants guarded the Thaumaturgs and were the backbone of their armies. *So it is true. They march to the eastern highlands.* An advance upon the true source of the wilderness's lurking dangers: the vast primeval tracks of the Demon-Queen's demesnes. The jungle of Himatan, half of this land, half of the spirit realm.

Yet I sense no others nearby.

A strange grating noise raised her attention to the yakshaka. Wary, she peeped up. It was doing something at its neck with its heavy armoured hands. Perhaps adjusting the great full helm. The mosaic of inlaid stones that covered its armour glittered as it moved. To Saeng's horror the helm lifted off revealing a head beneath, the scalp shaved and horribly scarred. Dark eyes – human eyes – blinked, wincing even at this unaccustomed dim light, then peered down at her with a strange gentle intimacy.

She stared, terrified, and irrationally all she could think was: *They'll blame me for breaking it!*

Then the mouth moved soundlessly, forming a word. A word she couldn't believe such a creature would know. Her name, Saeng.

And her flesh prickled in shocked recognition. She knew that face, disfigured though it might be.

She answered, hardly daring to breathe: 'Hanu . . .'

The yakshaka nodded, its mangled lips rising in a travesty of a smile.

She came close and pressed a hand to its chest, then recoiled at the cold rigidity of the armour. 'What happened? Why are you here? What's going on? Oh, dear Hanu – *what's happened to you?*'

The smile fell from her brother's lips and his gaze fell. Taking a deep breath he touched a finger to his lips then opened his mouth. Puzzled, Saeng looked, then felt the strength leave her knees and darkness take her.

His tongue had been sliced away.

She came to, finding herself propped up against a tree. Hanu stood over her, his gaze on the surrounding woods. She peered up at him for a time, enjoying the old familiarity of his presence.

Guarding me still. But you should not be here. What's going on?

'Hanu,' she whispered, 'why are you here?'

He turned, peering down. With one gauntleted hand he made a shape and Saeng recognized it as one of their old hand-language signs, part of a system they had invented for silent communication.

'*Promise.*'

'Promise? Whatever do you mean, promise? Your promise to protect me? *That?*'

'*Coming,*' he signed.

'Coming? So – they *are* coming.' She stood, brushed the damp rotting humus from herself. 'Well . . . what's that to me?'

'*Danger.*'

'Danger? Why? Who am I—' And she understood. The Thaumaturgs' long hatred of their neighbour extended to denouncing and drowning any considered under *her* influence. No doubt she would be killed out of hand as a suspected witch and servant of the Demon-Queen. 'So you—' She cut herself off again, staring anew. 'All the lost gods . . . you've run off . . . You deserted to warn me!'

'*Quiet.*'

'You great fool!' she yelled. 'How does this help? Now it's *your* head they'll want!'

He winced, signing again, '*Quiet.*'

'Well this is just wonderful. Now we're *both* fugitives.'

'*Yes.*'

'Perfect.' She set her fists on her hips, eyeing him. She watched while he began refitting his helm. 'Fine . . . we'll need food. I'll go find what I can.'

'*Hurry.*'

'Yes, yes.' She padded back to the hut. Here she set to filling a sack with rice and collected all the preserved fish and vegetables she could find. Through it all her mother lay breathing wetly in her cot. For a moment Saeng considered waking her to say goodbye, but only for a moment. She'd make too much of a fuss.

Well . . . I yearned for this moment for so long and now that it's here I don't want it. I'm finally getting out of here but this is surely not the way I dreamed of it.

She threw together a bag of the sturdiest clothes she could find, plus sandals and bedding. From outside the hiss of a light rain brushed against the grass walls. *Wonderful. And in the rainy season, too.*

She collected an umbrella of thin wood and set off into the mist.

Hanu joined her in the dark. He pointed then signed a question, indicating obviously enough, '*Which way?*'

Under the umbrella, Saeng clutched her bag to herself and bit her lip. *Yes, which way?* Steeling herself, she extended her awareness outwards farther than she ever had dared before. It expanded to encompass the village, its surrounding garden plots, and the outlying fields and further fallow wildlands that constituted their outlying holdings. It swept onward over neighbouring villages' wilds and fields, then the modest hamlets themselves. Like thinning ripples its furthest leading edge now brushed up against something far to the west – a sizzling unfamiliar power that repelled her mild questing like a thick wall of dressed stone.

The army of the Thaumaturgs. And not just passing by in their litters or carts on their mysterious errands. Marching with defences raised and powers unfurled.

'North, I think. We can let them pass by, then return.'

Hanu simply peered down at her, signing nothing. She felt his mute scepticism. Irritated, she scanned the dense fronds and hanging vines while the light rain pattered down around them as the faintest hint of the downpours to come. She waved him to follow. 'This way.'

*　　　*　　　*

Murken Warrow, known in Untan black-market circles as 'Murk', narrowed his already unusually thin eyes on the coast of desert dunes and the forest of strange pillar-like stone markers, then shifted that dubious gaze to his partner Hint, known as 'Sour'. Together, the duo had achieved a level of notoriety unhealthy in their line of work. They had even come to be pointed out in the streets of Unta as . . . well, as Murk and Sour. By then it was long past a prudent time to leave the city – as their arrest proved.

'I don't like it,' Sour said.

Hands stuffed into the pockets of his vest, Murk rolled his eyes to the overcast sky and let out a great sigh of long-suffering and annoyance. 'Why am I not surprised?'

'Got a bad feeling 'bout this contract.'

'No kidding.'

'Gonna end in tears.'

'As always,' Murk answered beneath his breath as he squinted to the stern deck where the sponsor of their current contract was speaking with the ship's captain.

'Miss Nibs is gonna be the death of us,' Sour continued, aware of his partner's shift in attention.

'Only if you keep makin' passes at her.'

'It's those legs o' hers. They just go on forever.'

Murk grunted his agreement at that. The woman wore the

most amazing outfits: tall leather boots as high as her knees, tight trousers, a shape-hugging leather hauberk over a lacy white silk shirt. She looked like someone's fever dream out of a bordello. But the sword strapped to her belt was well worn, and early in the voyage a single punch from her had floored one of the mercenaries for some suggestive remark, real or imagined.

Most oddly, she insisted on the name Spite.

Murk smiled now in remembrance of Sour's remark when she'd given that name. Sour had screwed up his frog eyes and asked, "Would that be Miss or Mrs Spite?" Sometimes the squirrelly guy really did crack him up.

Orders sounded and the crew began readying the launch and unstowing cargo. 'Something tells me we're gonna earn our pay on this one,' Sour said. Murk let a breath hiss between clenched lips. 'Gonna be hairy.'

'*Enough!* Would you just – keep it to yourself for a change?'

Sour pulled at the tiny tuft of a beard he kept on his chin, frowned while he eyed the coast. 'Might not make it out.'

Murk clenched the railing and hung his head in defeat.

The mercenaries went first to secure the landing. They were a scruffy lot Spite said she picked up on the southern coast of Genabackis. Pirate territory, that. None of them admitted to taking imperial coin. But he could tell they had served their time – though he had yet to call any of them on it, as the same could be said for him and Sour. Their leader, Yusen he gave as his name, smelled especially of officer material. Had that demeanour: that old familiar *you're an idiot* look he gave them whenever they had anything to say.

Reminded him of their days as imperial mage cadre.

Not much later the scouts returned to the shore to sign the all-clear and the unloading of equipment began.

They watched the ship's crew and the mercenaries busy unstowing the crates and sacks, lowering them to the launch, and arranging them in the bobbing craft.

Some time into the process Murk became aware of the tall slim figure of their employer, Spite, at his side, her arms crossed and her eyes, an amazing rich golden hazel, on them. He nudged Sour and they touched their brows. 'Ma'am.'

'Things would go much quicker if everyone lent a hand.'

'Just keepin' an eye out for trouble,' Sour volunteered.

One shapely eyebrow arched. 'Really? When I hired you – or should I say rescued you? – from certain arrest and imprisonment in

Unta, I was under the impression that you were *not* a mage of Ruse. Are you a mage of Ruse?'

Sour lowered his confused gaze and kicked at the decking. 'No, ma'am.'

'Then tell me – how could you be any help here at sea should there be any . . . trouble?'

The squat mage raised his head, his mouth open to speak, paused, frowned as he reconsidered, and scratched his scalp instead.

Spite continued: 'I want you two to go ashore and reconnoitre.'

'Yes, ma'am.'

'And do *not* enter the circle of the dolmens, yes?'

'Dolmens?' Sour asked. 'Is that what them pillar things is called?'

'Yes,' Spite answered as if addressing the village idiot. 'That's what they're called. Don't enter their formation. Range around. I want to know who's in the immediate vicinity. Do you think you two can manage that?'

'Oh yes, ma'am.'

'Well and good. That is something at least.' And she turned away.

They watched her walk off; Murk could swear she put an extra swing in her hips as she went. At his side Sour gave a heavy sigh.

'They just go on and on . . .' he murmured.

Irritated that this sweaty, unwashed, bow-legged fellow should be giving voice to his own thoughts, Murk elbowed him none too gently. 'Let's go.'

They waited until the launch was completely loaded then climbed down a rope and wood ladder. Sour carried down a chicken in a wicker basket that he handed to a sailor. 'There you go.'

The man grabbed it from him while mouthing something under his breath. The two lay down on rolled tent canvas near the bows, crossed their arms, and shut their eyes. The sailors and mercenaries readied the oars.

As the bows ground up on the beach a light misting rain began to drift over them. Murk and Sour jumped down to the wet sands and walked up the steep shore. More of the crew of mercenaries, who numbered about fifty in all, wandered down to help unload. Yusen appeared and waved the two over to him. When they reached the man in his leather and mail hauberk, mail skirting, iron greaves and vambraces, helmet under his arm, Murk fought an urge to salute.

He looked them up and down with barely concealed distaste on his lined mouth and in his slate-blue eyes. 'What do you two think you're doing?'

'Reconnoitring,' Murk supplied.

'I have scouts out.'

Sour made a show of touching a finger to the side of his nose. 'Not like us.'

The man rolled his eyes to the thick cloud cover; then, peering about, he allowed, grudgingly, 'Well, from the looks of this place I'd be right careful, if I were you.'

Murk almost saluted at that, murmuring instead, 'Our thanks . . . Cap'n.'

The man's gaze hardened and he dismissed them with a jerk of his head. 'Get going.'

'Oh, aye aye.'

They left the sands behind to enter a forest of trees the likes of which Murk had never seen before: some held wide leaves almost as broad as shields, others thick waxy ones like hard bullets. 'What d'ya think?' Sour asked as they walked. 'Fourth Army?'

'Naw. Seventh.'

'Maybe. Long as he weren't Fifth. Anyways . . .' Sour sniffed the air. 'What d'ya think?' he repeated.

Murk shrugged, wiped the misted rain from his face. 'Hardly anyone. Just a few fisherfolk.'

'Yeah . . . I think so.' Sour sat against the base of a tree and stretched out his legs. 'Is it noon?'

Murk eyed the other forest just to the north: a forest of grey pillars, dolmens, darkening in the gathering rain. 'See the ruins when we came in?'

Sour's eyes were shut. 'Yeah. Damned big city.' His eyes popped open. 'Say! Think there's treasure 'n' such there? Maybe we should have a poke around.'

Murk favoured his partner with his most scornful glare. 'There's no treasure lying around ruined cities. All that's just silly troubadour's songs. Naw – it's all gone. Just dust and rot and dead spiders.'

Sour shuddered. 'Gods, spiders. Did you hafta mention spiders? I got feeling all shivery when you said that. Don't like it at all.'

Murk's attention had remained on the dolmens. 'I know what you mean.'

Sour cocked his head, one eye screwed up shut. 'But maybe there's tombs 'n' such. Buried loot. How 'bout that?'

'Buried?' Murk continued to study the maze of stone pillars. 'Yeah. That would be a whole 'nother question, wouldn't it . . .'

Sour's gaze followed his partner's. 'Aw, for the love of . . .' The crab-like fellow gave a great shiver. 'Bad news that. Knew it the moment I clapped eyes on it.' He bit at a dirty fingernail. 'Has to be it, though, don't it? Any other place and I'd jump right in. But there . . . what a damned shame.'

Murk spat aside. 'Aye. Gonna be keep-your-bags-packed scary.'

'You're startin' to sound like me,' Sour complained.

Murk grimaced. *Great gods, now there's reason enough for me to jump right in.*

It was dusk when Murk tapped a snoring Sour to wake him. He motioned aside, mouthing, 'Here she is.' Sour nodded. He smacked his lips and stretched. The two shadowed their employer, skulking from towering dolmen to dolmen. The woman was pacing a slow encirclement of the entire installation. As she walked she held a Warren open and the two mages had to glance away wincing and shading their eyes from the powers summoned and manipulated in her hands. The sculpted energy remained behind as a flickering and pulsing wall of power.

They followed, peering round the pillars, which consisted of stone blocks fitted one on top of the other, tapering to a blunt tip.

'You see what I see?' Sour fairly yelled to be heard.

Head turned away, eyes slit, Murk answered, 'Cutting it off from everything! Nothing's getting past that wall o' wards and seals!'

Together, the two suddenly glanced aside where the rippling barrier of folded Warren-energies stood between them and the outside.

'*Shit!*' they mouthed as one and both pelted for the opposite side of the maze of standing stones. As he ran past row after row of the columns, Murk noted how they appeared to possess a slight curve, and he realized that they inscribed immense nested circles, one inside the other. Sour was ahead, his worn shoes kicking up sand, only to stop so suddenly that Murk almost ran over him. Righting himself, he saw what had put a halt to his partner's flight. It was an open circular court or plaza, empty and utterly featureless, lying at the centre of the dolmens, made of what appeared to be raked gravel.

The shortest way was straight across, but one glance was all Murk needed to see that that was no option. His mage-sight revealed an entirely different version superimposed upon the apparently empty plaza. Something writhed and coursed under the surface just as a monstrous sea-serpent might thrash beneath ocean waves. Murk hit his partner's shoulder and gestured aside. Together they took off round the plaza's border. They reached the opposite side of the massive ruin long before Spite appeared, tracing her ward. They watched her complete the intricate and blindingly powerful ritual while they lay flat behind a dune.

44

Sour slid further into cover and wiped a sleeve across his slick face. Murk joined him. 'So . . . maybe we should just save time and run off now?' Sour asked.

Murk rested his arms on his knees. 'Naw. I'm kinda curious.'

Sour's gaze slit almost closed. 'Curious? *You're* curious. You mean your wretched Shadow patron's all curious, ain't that what you mean!'

'Oh, and you're sayin' little Miss Enchantress ain't!'

Sour blew a nostril to empty it. 'Don't need to be a fortune-teller to know where this is gonna end. With us handed our heads!'

Murk looked to the darkening sky, now clearing of the thick clouds. 'You know – when you predict the same damned thing over and over it kinda loses its credibility.'

'Call for rain long enough and you're bound to be right.'

Murk threw open his arms. 'Now that doesn't even make any goddamned sense!'

Sour's wall-eyed gaze shifted to right and left. 'It will . . . eventually.'

'Would you stop that!'

'You lovebirds finished your little spat?' a new voice asked from the cover of nearby brush.

'Whosat?' Sour called, sinking even lower.

A fellow straightened from the thicket and approached to squat next to them. It was one of Yusen's scouts. The man wore leathers, long-knives at his sides, and a plain and battered Malazan-issue iron helmet that brought back plenty of memories to Murk. None of them happy. 'What're you doing here?' he demanded – he was of the opinion that when caught off guard an aggressive front can often compensate.

The scout shifted a twig from one side of his mouth to the other while eyeing them. 'Cap'n wants your report.'

'What report?' Sour asked.

'On what you've sniffed out.'

'We ain't seen nothing,' Sour answered, crossing his arms.

The man removed the twig from his mouth, studied it, then tucked it back in. 'Yeah. I see that.'

Murk wanted to slap the damned thing from the fellow's mouth. 'Listen, merc. What's your name?'

'Sweetly,' the man answered, his face flat of any emotion.

'Sweetly,' Murk echoed. 'What's your name – Sweetly?'

The scout glanced about the darkening shadows of the dunes and pockets of low dry brush. His gaze returned to them. The twig sank as his mouth drew down. ''Sright. Now c'mon. You two got a report to make.' He jerked his head towards the coast and started off.

Murk and Sour followed along. 'Oh look at me,' Sour grumbled sotto voce as they walked. 'I'm a tough guy. I chew twigs. Look out for me.'

'You just don't like meetin' someone named Sweetly,' Murk told him, smiling.

Sour's grumbling descended into dark mouthings.

They found a camp pitched just inland, sheltered from the winds by a high dune. Pickets led them to a central tent, currently more of a simple awning as its canvas sides were still raised. Yusen ducked from beneath. Sweetly gave a tilt of his head then ambled off.

The mercenary captain regarded them from within the deep nests of wrinkles surrounding his eyes then drew a heavy breath and crossed his arms.

'What?' Sour said, bristling.

'Let's have it,' the man sighed.

'She's interested in the dolmens,' Murk answered.

'Dolmens?'

'The standing stones. That's why we're here.'

Yusen got a pained look on his face. He lowered his eyes to study the ground for a time. 'Damn. I was hoping that wasn't the case.'

Sour glanced to Murk. 'Now what?'

'Now you two stay on her good side, that's what,' Yusen answered.

Again, Murk almost saluted. 'Yes, Cap'n,' he said. The man shot him a searching sideways glance then grimaced his impatience and waved them away. They ambled off.

After searching for a while Murk stopped a mercenary and asked, 'Which one's our tent?'

'That one,' the woman answered, pointing to a pile of poles and bundled canvas. Then she walked away.

'Yeah, very funny,' Murk called after her. He waved to Sour. 'Looks like you'll have to put it up.'

'Me? Whaddya mean, me? *You* put it up.'

'No, you.'

'You.'

'I ain't.'

'Well, I sure ain't.'

'Both of you put it up!' a mercenary bellowed from the next tent. 'Or I'll put them tent-poles up where they don't belong!'

Both offered choice gestures towards the side of the tent then knelt to the damp canvas. 'Just like the old days, hey?' Sour murmured.

'Yeah. Unfortunately.'

K'azz, it turned out, fully intended to go alone. He only acquiesced to a token guard when Shimmer told him flat out they would come regardless. In the end she chose two of the remaining Avowed mages, Lor-sinn and Gwynn, and three of their best swords: Cole, Turgal, and Amatt.

Tarkhan, captain of the Third Company, would be left behind to command Stratem. Shimmer was not happy with this arrangement as the Wickan tribesman, a formidable knife-fighter, had been among the top lieutenants of Cowl's 'Veils'. Though, she could admit, the intervening years of commanding the Third through various contracts across the world did appear to have tempered the man. And K'azz had every confidence in him. But then, that was one thing K'azz always did well – give and instil confidence.

Seeing the surviving Avowed gathered together in Haven was a pleasure for Shimmer – and at the same time a melancholy reunion. A pleasure to see old friends; heartbreaking for all the absent faces and the painful thinness of the ranks. Her count put the total number at less than seventy. Yet that number varied as the occasional lost Avowed would suddenly appear in Stratem, having made their way from imprisonment, service to some patron, or from simply being stranded in this or that land. And there was always Cal-Brinn's Fourth Company as well: gone missing in Assail lands but possibly still surviving if Bars' reappearance was any indication. Of the near forty Avowed who chose to follow Skinner into exile, well, they would meet them soon enough.

A week later, the foreigners' vessel, the *Serpent*, was readied and fully victualled. When all had been stowed away and the vessel started south under quarter-sail, Rutana turned to K'azz and growled resentfully, 'I was expecting some sort of an army yet here you come nearly alone. This is an insult to my mistress. Better not to have answered at all.'

Again, to Shimmer's eyes, K'azz displayed remarkable forbearance in merely quirking his lips. 'I understand your mistress is something of a seer – surely then she knew this when she sent you . . .' and, bowing in the face of the sour woman's mutterings, he added, 'I will be in my cabin.'

Alone with Rutana at the vessel's side, Shimmer offered no comment. The woman wrenched angrily at the bindings on her arm, shot her a hot glare, and grumbled, 'And I hate all this damned water.' She marched off. Shimmer leaned over the side to watch the foaming wake. She rather enjoyed being at sea.

Exiting the Sea of Chimes, they headed west round the desolate coast of the Grey Lands. This desert wasteland supported only the thinnest scatterings of scrub and stunted twisted oak and pine. Shimmer had heard the mages discussing whether its barrenness was due to natural unproductive soils and lack of rainfall, or whether the ruins of ancient K'Chain Che'Malle citadels hinted at another possible cause. In either case it was a forbidding peninsula of windswept semi-arid desert, scrubland and broken rock.

Once past its horn, which the Guard had named half jokingly 'Cape Dire', the Jacuruku pilot sent them more or less on a due west heading out into the rough waters of what some called the 'Explorers' Sea' and others the 'White Spires Sea', named for the hazards of its many floating ship-sized mountains of ice. Indeed, it was even speculated that an immense floating field of ice blocked passage between these lands and those to the immediate west – Jacuruku itself. Yet this vessel had slipped through as, Shimmer knew, another ship bearing Crimson Guard deserters had as well: Kyle and other Bael land recruits who then went on to rescue K'azz from the Dolmens.

And now he leads us back to this land. Why? What is so pressing at these Dolmens of Tien? K'azz spoke little of his time there though it had changed him profoundly: before, like Shimmer, he'd not shown his age but when he returned he looked every one of his hundred plus years. From Rutana's words, and her commander's reaction, she gathered that something inhabited the Dolmens. Something that he agreed mustn't be disturbed.

The crossing was for the most part boring. Rutana and Nagal kept to their cabin, as did K'azz. The dull repetitive drone of shipboard routine would only be broken by jolting periods of sheer terror when the call 'Ice spire!' rang from the lookouts. Then all aboard ran for the sides while the crew scrambled to the sails and the pilot rammed the tiller aside. Shimmer and the other Avowed watched fascinated as the emerald and white glowing floating sculptures edged past. They looked to her to have been made by the gods, so otherworldly and beautiful were their curving blade-like lines.

Now that they had entered the corridor of ice crags, the captain ordered the sweeps unshipped and their progress slowed to a tentative crawl. Crew and Avowed passengers alike watched from the sides, long poles at hand. Two observers occupied the crow's nest at all times. Yet despite all these precautions one night Shimmer was thrown from her hammock as the ship rocked and shuddered beneath her like a hammered child's toy. She lay stunned on the timbers while around her everyone groaned, rousing themselves. The sound of something scraping the ship's planking tore at her ears and ran its jagged clawed nails down her spine.

'Ice crag!' came the panicked yell from above.

Pretty damned late! Shimmer grabbed her gear and ran for the deck. Up top she found open panic as the sailors ran about, yet the captain was calmly shouting and pointing: 'Shanks, inspect the damage! Why aren't the pumps sounding? Stow that cargo!'

She crossed to the slim figure of K'azz, peering over the side. 'What happened?'

He shrugged. 'Some sort of submerged ice mountain no one saw. Sideswiped us.'

'Bad?'

'We'll see.'

Everyone took a hand at the pumps. A bucket line was organized. All the while the ship's carpenter and his apprentices were below inspecting the damage. Finally, Shimmer was waved to where the captain, K'azz and Rutana were speaking with the carpenter, Shanks.

'Not at sea,' the carpenter was saying as he shivered, sodden, his lips blue.

'No choice,' the captain growled.

'Something temporary, perhaps?' K'azz suggested.

'Land!' came a shout from the lookout, startling everyone.

The captain scowled behind his beard. 'Are you daft, man!' he bellowed back. 'There's no land here!'

'Ice!'

The captain and the carpenter shared a wary glance.

'What is it?' K'azz asked.

'The floating ice field,' Rutana answered after neither of the sailors responded. 'Haunted. No one goes near it.'

'No choice, I should think,' K'azz said. He gave the captain a speculative look. 'We'll heave up and repair on the ice.'

The captain waved his dismissal. 'This is no slim galley. We don't have enough hands to heave up on to the ice.'

'We have enough mages – isn't that so, Rutana?'

The woman's hard gaze narrowed, perhaps at the implied challenge, then she sneered her answer. 'Of course!'

~

The captain ordered a narrow set of sail and they limped slowly towards the distant white line to the west. They slipped under high clouds and a snowfall began of thick huge flakes that Shimmer could almost hear hissing as they touched the wood of the ship. The captain knocked the snow from his shoulders and tangled hair as if it were some sort of contagion. Watching Shimmer's amusement at the man's antics, Rutana crossed to her side to explain: 'Many name this the Curse of the Demons of Cold. The Jaghut. Somewhere within, a shard of their frozen realm, Omtose Phellack, endures. It is the cause of this. And it hates us – all who are not of their kind.'

'Or perhaps it is we who hate all others who are not of our kind,' K'azz observed from nearby.

The Jacuruku envoy appeared surprised by the suggestion – and she startled Shimmer by nodding even as she scowled. 'You are right to say so.'

Once the ship came close to the edge of the vast plain of ice, a party containing the Avowed mages Gwynn and Lor-sinn, together with Rutana and Nagal, disembarked to prepare a surface for the vessel. Shimmer watched from the railing while some sort of chute was melted in the jagged shore. Then the crew fixed lines and almost everyone disembarked. With the aid of the mages and Nagal and Rutana, the *Serpent* was slowly eased up, stern first, on to the carved chute of gleaming ice.

That night they camped on the ice. The captain and crew jumped at every crack and rumble and shot anxious glances to the tall mounds of jumbled shelves that looked to Shimmer like a giant's heap of carelessly piled timber. The captain had even insisted that pickets be posted, though the waste appeared devoid of all habitation. K'azz acquiesced, murmuring to Shimmer that in fact there might be carnivorous beasts about.

Shimmer agreed to the pickets, but she did not think anyone at risk, what with the Avowed present, plus the Jacuruku emissaries. That night, while doing a tour of the perimeter, she found K'azz out on the ice with Turgal. The latter still preferred heavy armour, as had been his habit. He now wore a cuirass of banded iron with mail skirting and a large shield on his back, all beaten and badly scraped. The long grip and pommel of a hand-and-a-half blade stood tall from the sheath at his side. The two stood staring off to the west across the ice field. She joined them to scan the plain, which was brilliantly lit by the Great Banner arcing high like a sickly bruise across the night sky.

After seeing no movement at all among the ink-black shadow and nauseatingly green snow, she asked, 'What is it?'

'Do you not sense it there?' Turgal asked, his voice hoarse, as if from disuse.

'Sense what?'

'The shard our Jacuruku emissary spoke of,' K'azz explained.

'Shard?'

'Omtose Phellack,' Turgal added, his breath pluming. 'The ice-magery of the Jaghut. Don't you sense it there?'

'No.' Shimmer almost added *I am no mage*, but snapped her mouth shut, realizing *and neither are they. How then . . . ? Well, K'azz invoked the Vow after all. Perhaps that gave him some sort of privileged insight. But Turgal? Why should he possess such an awareness?*

And yet . . . there were times when she sensed people nearby before seeing them; and the Jacuruku emissaries – their potency buzzed at her awareness like two distracting flies. So, perhaps she should not be surprised.

'A danger?' she asked.

K'azz shook his head. 'No. It is fading. In a hundred years, who knows? All this may be gone.'

A wind sharp with cold blew particles of ice into Shimmer's eyes and bit at her naked hands. 'Yet to have endured for so long . . . Why now?'

The snow crackled beneath K'azz's boots as he shifted his stance. 'It seems that perhaps we live now in an age when the old is passing away.' He cocked his head, thinking. 'Yet does it seem this way to us merely because we are living now? Or does every age feel the same to those who live through it? Every age, after all, is an age of transition from what came before to what will follow.'

Turgal gave a soft laugh in appreciation of the point. 'A question for the cross-eyed philosophers of Darujhistan I think, Duke.'

'No. Let us have mercy upon them. They are cross-eyed enough.'

'Come,' Shimmer urged, motioning to the tents. 'This inhuman cold grips my bones.'

K'azz eyed her, surprised. 'You are cold?'

All the crew and the Guard lent a hand to the repairs, which were completed in less than three days. Their fourth and last night, Shimmer suddenly awoke in the utter darkness. She knew that something powerful was approaching; she did not know how she knew, but she was certain of it. In the dark she pulled on her long mail coat, belted on her whipsword, and ducked out of the tent.

Outside it was quiet but for the snow and ice particles hissing wind-driven against the hide tents. That and the stentorian snoring of a few of the sailors. And it had to be the sailors, for Shimmer saw that her fellow Avowed were awake already. Like ghosts summoned to some haunt, the figures of her companions walked silently among the tents, tying their last knots, adjusting belts, gathering to the west where they formed line – all without any given order.

She joined them next to K'azz. 'What is it?' she whispered, her breath steaming.

Without shifting his slit gaze from the darkened ice field he answered, 'Not certain yet. But close.'

Shimmer signed *'Ready'* to the left and right. Turgal unsheathed his massive hand-and-a-half blade and raised his shield. Amatt drew his heavy broadsword and likewise readied his wide infantryman's shield. Cole, who fought after the two-sword style, stepped aside a way for room to slide free his twinned longswords. Lor-sinn and Gwynn took up positions behind the line.

'Ware!' Gwynn warned, his voice taut with anticipation.

Shimmer scanned the snowdrifts and gleaming wind-bitten ice shelves, seeing nothing. *Damn, it was strong!* She felt it now: a terrible potency. In fact, she'd not felt anything like it since—

Dust or some sort of wind-lashed dirt spun upwards like a wave from the snow. While they watched it merged, solidifying to reveal a single figure wrapped in ragged furs. It stood on legs of naked bone stained brown. A fleshless face stared at them from beneath the ridge of the bone helmet fashioned from the skull of some prehistoric beast. An Imass.

K'azz stepped forward, raising a hand. 'Greetings, Elder. We of the Crimson Guard salute you.'

The undead's jaws worked, the sinew creaking, and a word whispered across the ice, 'Greetings.'

'To what do we owe this honour?'

'Your presence here . . . drew me.'

'Are we trespassing? If so, we apologize and will leave at once.'

The great width of its robust shoulders rose and fell. 'We are all in kind trespassers here.'

'You mean the Jaghut . . .'

'Yes.'

'Is this why you are here?'

'No – none remain. I merely pass by. I follow the call to the east. All are gathering. A Summoner has come to us.'

K'azz bowed his head. 'Yes. I heard. Go with our best wishes. But before you go – may you honour us with your name?'

'I am Tolb Bell'al, Bonecaster to the Ifayle T'lan Imass. And long have I been absent.'

'Our thanks, Tolb Bell'al. I am K'azz D'Avore.'

'We know you, K'azz.' Tolb inclined his head a fraction. 'Farewell. Until we meet again.'

Shimmer drew breath to ask what the creature meant but the Imass slumped into a scarf of dust that the wind snatched away. K'azz turned to her and they shared a wondering glance. 'What did he – or she – mean by that?'

K'azz shrugged. 'I've no idea. Perhaps it meant in the afterlife.'

'Afterlife?' Cole growled, coming up. 'What afterlife? They're already after life.'

K'azz waved to close the subject. 'It's gone now. And with the dawn so too shall we.'

'Following its call,' Cole mused.

K'azz frowned at that then signed: *Stand down.*

* * *

The capital of the kingdom of the Thaumaturgs, Anditi Pura, possessed no walls, fortress, or defensive works. At its centre lay the sprawling complex known only as the Inner City. Here could be found the centralized administrative offices, the dormitories, and the training academy of the Thaumaturgs who served both as rulers and bureaucrats of the state.

The generalship of the Army of Righteous Chastisement fell to the next in line to join the Thaumaturg ruling Circle of Nine, Golan Amaway. The Grand Masters of the Mysteries judged the position – correctly – all too demanding in its duties and thus too much of a distraction from the continued pursuit of their one and only obsession: penetrating the secrets of life, and of death.

As the lowest ranked of the Adepts, and thus not sworn into their highest mysteries, Golan had been sanguine in the assignment. He bowed to the assembled Nine Masters, accepted the proffered Rod of Execution, and exited to make ready.

After all, he told himself in solace, it was not as if the Nine Masters would remain behind in idle meditation. They would follow the march at a convenient distance. For as soon as the forces penetrated Ardata's territory – what the ignorant peasants invoked in superstitious dread as the spirit realm of Himatan – no doubt all would be needed to keep at bay the worst of her attacks.

His bodyguard of ten yakshaka fell unnoticed into step about him.

He tapped the heavy rod of blackwood chased in silver in one palm, already considering plans of how best to ensure that their untrustworthy foreign allies, these Isturé, might be manipulated into bearing the brunt of every engagement.

Now, after months of exhausting preparation, they marched east for the mountain highlands, the Gangrek Mounts, that divided the as yet untamed borderlands of Thaumaturg territory from the deep jungle of Ardata's haunts. A land quite thinly populated where, their own peasants believed, continued existence could only be assured by pacts and deals with elder spirits, demons and monsters of the world's youth.

A version not too far from the truth should their Isturé traitors' intelligence be accurate. In any case, they should know soon enough.

Golan travelled in a large covered litter born by four yakshaka. Normally he would travel to war by elephant. However, painful experience gathered through the many – unsuccessful – punitive campaigns against Ardata had demonstrated the limited effectiveness of their war-elephant columns. The dense jungle impeded their progress, they became mired in the deep swamps and they sickened in droves from the raging clouds of insects and thick miasmas. Those few that remained were driven mad by the terrors of the night. And so this army was carried forward by human feet and bent human backs alone.

It was also his habit to travel far closer to the front lines than his predecessors judged prudent. Yet he felt himself to be at no risk. Not only did he enjoy the protection of his bolstered bodyguard of twenty yakshaka soldiers, he also stood at the centre of an encircling crowd of his staff of regular army officers, messengers and ordinary soldiers. Not to mention yet a further army of clerks and scribes travelling with their own logistical support of reams upon reams of records listing everything carried and worn by the army entire. He would not even be surprised if there lay within the clerks' long train of paperwork a sheet reading *General of the Army: one*.

His second in command, U-Pre, edged close to the open side of the rocking litter, bowed for permission to speak. 'Yes?' Golan said, and waved a switch to brush away the plaguing flies.

'The leader of the foreign mercenaries wishes to speak, Master.'

'Very well, U-Pre.'

The man bowed again and jogged off.

Golan rocked with the motion of the raised platform. A light rain, no more than a mist, masked the distant green line that was the highlands where they appeared now and again through gaps in the surrounding forest canopy. The swaying helped Golan maintain a meditative calm despite the horrors that, as earlier campaigns reported, awaited beyond that ragged mountain range.

Heavy armoured boots thumping into the dirt of the track next to his litter announced the presence of this Skinner, commander of the Isturé. 'You wish to speak?' Golan asked without turning to look.

'Yes.'

'The slow progress of our advance still troubles you, yes?'

The long silence following that observation told Golan that he was correct in his prediction. After marching for a time the foreign mercenary, once an aristocrat within Ardata's demesnes, and, it was rumoured, so much more than that, cleared his throat to speak again.

Golan slid his gaze sideways to the man: tall helm under an arm, long coat of armour glittering darkly like a curtain of night, wide brutal face so unlike the properly symmetrical rounded features of those of Jacuruku. And, unusually, a long mass of pale hair the colour of sun-dried grass. Was this the feature that had caught the eye of Ardata herself?

'Yes,' the man admitted, 'the slow pace remains an irritation. Allow my command to travel ahead to scout the way and to evaluate the character of the resistance.'

Golan edged his gaze away. 'No, Isturé. We shall all stay together. Present a strong united front, yes? Like any good artisan I wish to keep all my tools with me so that I may respond appropriately to whatever situation may arise. As a skilled craftsman yourself, you understand this, yes?'

The foreigner's answering smile was thin. 'Of course, Master Thaumaturg. How could I possibly argue with such sound reasoning?' And he bowed to take his leave. 'If I may?'

Golan waved his switch to indicate his permission. The man tramped heavily off. From the edge of his vision Golan watched him go. *As if I would allow you to travel alone in the land you once ruled! Perhaps to meet clandestinely with representatives of Ardata. Who knows what trickery may be hatched against us! No. I shall keep you close, traitor or failed usurper that you are.*

He noted the emaciated reed-thin figure of Principal Scribe Thorn hurrying up to the litter. The shoulder bag at his side bulged with paper sheets, his inkpot swung on its leather strap round his neck, and Golan sat back with a suppressed groan. He waved the switch across his face, eyes shut. As he heard the man's sandals slapping the churned dirt next to his litter he said, loudly, 'Yes? What is it, Principal Scribe Thorn?'

'Amazing, Master!' the man squawked in his hoarse buzzard voice. 'Your powers astound us mere mortals. How could you have ever known it was I?'

The carrion stench, perhaps? No, that is not fair. The man is merely doing his job. With the meticulousness of an ant building a mountain out of sand – one grain at a time.

Eyes still closed, Golan sighed, 'You have something to report?'

'Ah! Yes, Master. The manifest of our honoured yakshaka, sir. A routine recount has recently been completed and it would seem, contrary to all expectations, that we are short one.'

Golan's eyes snapped open. He turned in his seat to peer down at the scrawny man. *Long curved neck just like a buzzard as well.* 'You are saying that we are missing a yakshaka?'

The man jerked his sweaty shaven head, his prominent Adam's apple bobbing.

'You have rechecked the count?'

Now the man flinched, offended. 'Of course, Master! It is my duty to be absolutely certain before bringing such an incongruence before you.'

'Perhaps one has been mislaid . . . like a broom or an umbrella?'

Thorn's gaze fell and he fiddled with the leaf-green carved jade inkpot hanging from his neck, his badge of office. 'My master is demonstrating his sense of humour?' he murmured.

Golan arched a brow. *Was that sly mockery?* Well, the man would hardly have achieved his vaunted office without some measure of guile. Golan made a show of sniffing a great wad of catarrh then spat over the side of the litter. All the minor officers nearby mouthed sounds of admiration for such prodigious capacity.

'Good health, Master,' Thorn added, admiringly.

'My thanks. And no, Principal Scribe. Merely exploring all options. I applaud your thoroughness. Send Cohort Leader Pon-lor to me.'

The man jerked a bow. 'I will order a messenger at once.' He hiked up his robes and ran off bandy-legged through the churned-up mud and trampled grasses.

Golan fell back into his padded seat. Through slit eyes he watched the dense forest pass on either side. Screens of infantrymen walked in a broad arc among the tree trunks while the main column, consisting almost entirely of file upon file of impressed labourers burdened beneath the materiel and supplies of war, kept to the trampled path. A few carts followed far behind, drawn by oxen or water buffalo.

These carried the field hospital and various smiths and armourers. All rumbling and tramping east. *And what awaits us there? What will we find? Will we be able to scavenge enough food to support our numbers should we run short of supplies? Will we even be able to find Ardata's centre of power, this fabled city in the depths of the jungle, Jakal Viharn?* The Isturé, of course, were sure that they could find the way – after every prior Thaumaturg expedition had found only failure and madness, none even to return from that green abyss.

Cohort Leader Pon-lor arrived next at the litter and bowed, smoothing his robes. From beneath heavy lids Golan's thin gaze appraised him. Apprentice Thaumaturg of the Seventh Rank. A promising junior officer. 'Cohort Leader,' Golan began, brushing his switch before his face, 'One of our yakshaka has had the poor grace to go missing. No doubt it has sunk into a bog. However, I am charging you with ascertaining its fate. We cannot have them blundering about knocking down peasants' huts, can we?'

The lad raised a hand to push back his long straight black hair, but stopped himself, clasping his hands behind his back. 'No, Master.'

Golan had hoped for at least a flicker of a smile at such an image, but the young man was too conscious of rank. He waved the switch to send the officer on his way. 'Very good, Cohort Leader. Take twenty men.'

Pon-lor bowed again and hurried off.

Now, if only I could dispatch these foreign Isturé in such a manner!

*

That night in the encampment of the Thaumaturg army, Skinner's High Mage, Mara, prepared for her evening meditations. She arranged the parchment, inkpot and stylus on a low enamelled table then sat cross-legged before it. She tied a black silk scarf across her eyes, set her hands on her knees and worked to calm her mind. The noises of the surrounding camp distracted her at first but she was no stranger to such sounds and so slowly, in stages, she managed to relegate all to the background. After achieving the necessary inner calm, she began to sketch.

A knock sounded at the front pole of her tent.

She let out a thin hissed breath, stylus poised, then set down the copper instrument. After one calming breath she pulled down the scarf to study the incomplete sketch before her. Simple flat lines hinting at a bare landscape, and amid this desolation a tall robust spar or boulder.

Obelisk. All that is past. Yet here it stands before me.

Disquieting. She did not like her past.

The knock sounded again. She carefully replaced the cap on her iron inkpot and rose to cross the tent. She thrust aside the hanging to surprise a Thaumaturg army officer who jerked, startled, then bowed – but not before his gaze slid down the wide curves of her silk shirt and sashed trousers. Mara was of pure Quon Dal Honese descent, and as black as all from that land could be: she knew the men here found this exoticism . . . fascinating. And she also knew all men everywhere were dogs. 'What is it?' she demanded, deliberately pitching her voice as seductively low as possible.

The officer worked to clear his throat. 'We have captured a man who claims to be a monk—'

'What of it?'

The officer paused, offered a thin smile. 'He also claims to have a message for you.'

'Couldn't it wait until the morning? I ought not to be disturbed while communing with demon spirits.'

The man's alarmed gaze flicked past her to the darkness of the tent and he hastily bowed again.

That's better.

Head still lowered, the officer said, 'He claims the message comes from his, ah . . . god.'

So. I see. 'Very well. You may bring him to me.'

'Yes, Isturé.'

Mara turned away and let the tent flap fall closed. She dressed in her robes then waited, gathering her powers to her until she could feel the very edges of her D'riss Warren sizzling about her.

Another knock and an old man was thrust into the tent. He stood blinking in the relative dark. Even from this distance she could smell the filth of his tattered robes. 'You have a message for me?' she demanded.

An unnerving grin climbed the man's cracked lips. 'Indeed, Isturé. My master grows impatient. Pacts were made. Agreements were reached between your master and mine. You have your mission. When can we expect fulfilment?'

'Soon.'

'*Soon?*' the man echoed scornfully. 'We tire of this "soon". We demand action. Events unfold. The need grows ever more dire.'

'I will press for action.'

The man tilted his head in slight concord, his eyes glittering bright and black across the tent. 'Let us hope so . . . for your sake. My master does not take betrayal lightly. When you find your courage I will be nearby, with instructions.'

Mara answered the slight bow in kind. The man thrust aside the heavy cloth and exited. Tentatively, Mara reached out with her senses and flinched from the lingering moil of Warren-poisoning that was the unmistakable sign of the Shattered God.

That stupid Kingship of Chains. What need have we for it? Yet perhaps Skinner sees some hidden way it could aid our final goal . . .

Mara pushed back her robes and sat once more before the table. She raised the scarf to her eyes and attempted to ease her breathing. But the requisite centring would not come. Her thoughts were too disturbed.

And through that disequilibrium the ghosts returned. She saw them suddenly standing before her light-starved eyes. The wavering presences of her dead brothers and sisters, all the Brethren of the Crimson Guard. Their relentless demanding voices whispered once more in her ears.

You swore . . . Always remember . . . Remember your Vow . . .

An arm of dried skin stretched across bone gestured, inviting. Lacy.

'*Walk with me, sister,*' the corpse murmured. '*Our path ever remains. It is unavoidable. Why this obstinate lingering? It shall ever lie before you . . .*'

'No!' She yanked the scarf away and drew in a ragged breath. Her flesh prickled cold and damp with sweat. Her gaze found the sheet with its sketch of the Obelisk before her. Snarling, she crumpled it and threw it on to the brazier of coals at the centre of the tent where it burst aflame.

*   *   *

Jatal, prince of the Hafinaj, rode with his escort into the encampment of this foreign Warleader to find it much larger than he had anticipated. In truth it was not one encampment at all, but a conglomeration of lesser compounds each the province of one of the tribes, Greater and Lesser. Offhand, Jatal recognized the standards of the Awamir, the Salil and the Manahir, plus many of the Lesser families. This self-styled Warleader appeared to have succeeded in his bid to interest the tribes of the Adwami, the People, in a major punitive campaign against the cursed Thaumaturgs.

Hardly a month ago an emissary of the Warleader had arrived at their camp offering word of a negotiated collective truce among all the tribes. A concord during which all families were invited to discuss the assemblage of a great force to strike deep into Thaumaturg lands. Such raiding was of course nearly an annual ritual: small bands sneaking across the bordering canyon lands, looting villages, stealing crops and taking captives. Now this foreign Warleader promised a raid such as had not been seen in a generation. Entire caravans of riches and an army of slaves to be won.

At the head of his column, Jatal eased his mount into a gentle walk as he parted the assembled fighters and camp followers. Talk died away and heads turned and Jatal felt reassured for this was as it should be – the Hafinaj being the largest and most powerful of all the Adwami. Foreign warriors pointed him on towards the main tent at the centre of the assembled compounds.

His father, patriarch of all Hafinaj, had been dismissive at first. Who was this outlander to speak to them of war? Such effrontery! Had the man no respect or manners? He would have nothing to do with such foolishness. Then word came of the crushing of the Fal'esh and the Birkeen and the subsequent rounding to the man's standard of the majority of the Lesser families.

This and the promised riches brought in a few of the Greater houses. And once this was accomplished, Jatal knew, none other of the Adwami could risk the loss of prestige and gold that standing aside would bring. So it was that shortly after the news broke he was summoned before his father: the lesser son of a lesser concubine.

'Jatal,' his father had brusquely welcomed him from where he reclined on the cushions of his raised platform. And Jatal knelt before him on the ground, head bowed. 'Remember that you are a prince of the Hafinaj! As such, you must not arrive like some tattered beggar. Therefore I send with you fifty of our knights, plus seven hundred men at arms. The largest of all the contingents, I'll wager!' and he laughed at that, anticipating the envy and gritted teeth of his rivals among the other families. 'Yes, very good. Do not shame us,' and he waved him off.

'Father,' Jatal had murmured respectfully, and backed away, head lowered.

Now, as he approached the great tent surrounded by its foreign guards, a man emerged. Tall and thin as one of the tent-poles themselves. He wore a long coat of mail, bore a grey beard and had a face as lined as a desert draw. But the eyes! Such lofty arrogance in their washed-out paleness. It was as if the man were looking down upon him, though he now had reined in at his side. 'You are this Warleader?'

Something like a smile tightened the man's thin lips. 'I am. You must be a son of the Hafinaj.'

'Prince Jatal.'

'Welcome, Prince Jatal, to my humble encampment. You honour us with your presence. My men will show you a place for your lancers. No doubt you wish to refresh yourself. May I expect you this night for an assemblage of families?'

'You may.'

'Very good.' The man bowed though his eyes held no deference in the least.

Vaguely irritated, Jatal answered with the curtest of nods.

That night, with the help of his retainers, Prince Jatal dressed in his best silk shirt and trousers and thrust through his waist sash the most jewelled of his ornamental daggers – all because his father had warned him not to shame his family. He ate first before going to the dinner so as not to be distracted by his hunger, or the carnality of eating itself.

Foreign guards opened the tent flap at his approach. Entering, he paused to allow his eyes to adjust to the greater brightness of all the torches and braziers. Low tables encircled the walls at which all the guests were seated on carpets and cushions. Opposite the entrance sat the Warleader, cross-legged, incongruously still encumbered by his mail coat. From one side a huge bear of a fellow lumbered to his feet and swept up to Jatal, arms out. He recognized the man as Ganell of the Awamir, longtime allies of the Hafinaj.

'Prince Jatal!' the fat man boomed. 'How you have grown!' He made a show of looking Jatal up and down. 'How the ladies must have swooned at your departure! You are every inch the prince now.'

'Ganell.' Jatal greeted the man with a hug that could only embrace a portion of his bulk.

'Come sit with me. I insist! We of the Awamir welcome the Hafinaj!'

'You honour me.'

Sitting, Jatal noted across the way the glowering bearded face of Sher' Tal, Horsemaster of the Saar, their traditional blood-enemy. Jatal chose to merely glance away to their host, the Warleader. The man nodded his welcome.

Servants came and went carrying platters of steamed cracked wheat, entire roasted lamb and goat, fruits and decanters of wine. Jatal allowed a plate to be set before him but partook of none. He lifted a bronze wine goblet to his lips but did not drink.

Meanwhile, Ganell, next to him, consumed enough for two or three, laughing and entertaining everyone with a story about one of his sons, whom he considered a gaggle of empty-headed smoke-addicts good only for spending his gold.

'Not like you, Jatal!' he boomed, slapping him on the shoulder. 'Poet and philosopher, I hear! Just like the princes of old!'

'Yet they honour you, I'm sure,' Jatal murmured.

'What? By their fornicating? Their dissipation and squandering? In that I suppose they honour me.'

'For myself,' began Sher' Tal from across the tent, 'I did not come to hear stories of the consequences of inbreeding.'

'Breeding?' Ganell responded, peering about and making a show of being puzzled. 'Speaking of breeds, I hear the braying of an ass!'

Sher' Tal lunged to his feet.

'*Gentlemen!*' the foreigner shouted, also rising. 'Gentlemen – and ladies,' he added, nodding towards the women who had come as representatives. 'Let us not forget we are here to discuss cooperation.'

'And why should we listen to you?' one of the crowd called.

The man paced to the centre of the tent. His mail rustled like the stirring of dry leaves. He made a show of frowning as if deep in thought. 'Good question. First, I am, as you say, a foreigner. And a mercenary. I fight for gold. Assemblies of tribes such as these have been attempted in the past, yes? Is that not so?' The man circled, searching for confirmation. Many nodded their agreement. 'Just so,' he continued. 'Yet they failed. They could not hold together and so they fell apart before they could achieve anything of any significance. Why?' He searched among them again.

Jatal noted how almost all the representatives present shot accusatory glances to one another. Even Ganell leaned close to murmur, 'Because they all have the brains of water buffalo.'

The Warleader nodded as if what he saw confirmed his thoughts. 'They fell apart because none could agree upon who should lead. The Vehajarwi would not listen to the Hafinaj. And the Saar would not follow the Awamir . . .'

'Never!' Sher' Tal called.

Grinning, Ganell tossed a handful of cashews into his mouth, muttering aside, 'Buffalo.'

Jatal worked hard to suppress a laugh.

Circling, the Warleader raised his lined hands for calm. 'Just so, just so. It is understandable. I, however, am an outsider. A professional. War is my calling. My men and I fight for payment alone. I will favour no tribe over any other. And when the campaign is finished we will simply take our share and go . . .'

'And what would be your share?' Jatal asked.

The old man's brows rose in appreciation of the question. 'Prince Jatal wishes to dispense with the airy assurances. Very good. For the services of my tactical and strategic leadership and the blood of my fighting men I ask one tenth of all spoils.'

Ganell choked on his cashews. 'Outrageous!' he spluttered.

Everyone objected at once. 'Would you beggar us?' Andanii, princess of the Vehajarwi, called out.

The Warleader had raised his arms again, beseeching silence. His huge second, or lieutenant, Jatal noted, sat unconcerned throughout, gnawing on a lamb haunch and drinking. Normally, it seemed to him, the discussion of fees for services ought to interest such a one.

Jatal raised a hand for quiet. Slowly, one by one, the representatives ceased their objections. Once silence had been regained he began, 'Warleader, what you ask is not our way. Traditionally, the band that defeats an enemy, or takes a village, is due all the glory and spoils accruing from the victory . . .'

Nods all around. 'Rightly so!' Ganell called.

'However,' Jatal continued, 'a wise man might agree that nine-tenths of a meal is better than no meal at all . . .'

Ganell chortled and slapped a wide paw to the table. 'Haw! The prince has the right of it!'

'. . . and so perhaps we should measure the size of the meal before we turn our nose from it.'

Princess Andanii rose from her seat and threw down her eating knife so that it stuck into the table. 'Speaking for the Vehajarwi, we have heard quite enough.'

'If you would *allow* me to finish.' The Warleader spoke through gritted teeth. Clearly he was not used to being dismissed, or even petitioning, for that matter. He seemed unable to blunt a habit of prideful high-handedness. An attitude, Jatal reflected, that was hardly helping his case here among so many likewise vain and bloated personages. And in the figure of Princess Andanii the man had quite met his match in blind overweening conceit.

The girl, one of the deadliest living archers, it had to be said, pushed back her long braid of midnight hair and raised what to Jatal was a perfect heart-shaped chin to command scornfully, 'Speak, then . . . I give you leave.'

The old man's stiff answering bow was a lesson in suppressed bile. 'My thanks . . . Princess. What I propose is that our combined forces sack the Thaumaturg southern capital and ritual centre of Isana Pura.'

The outrage that had heated the air before was as nothing compared to the howls of protest that met that announcement. Even Jatal sat back, shocked by the daunting scale of such a proposal. *Like no raid in over a generation. Dread King . . . in living memory!*

Next to him Ganell bent to the right and left, spilling his wine, 'Can it be done? Could we do that?'

So stunned by the scheme was the princess that she sat quite heavily. His gaze unfocused, Jatal pressed his hands together, touching his fingers to his lips. *A quick dash in. Surprise. Swift flight before any response could be organized or brought to bear. It may work.*

'You will face the Thaumaturgs,' a new harsh voice cut through the din.

Jatal did not look up. *But what is the garrison? And what of the yakshaka guardians? We will need intelligence.*

A pall of quiet spread through the tent as one by one those present fell silent.

'Many Thaumaturgs in the great ritual centre of Isana Pura,' the grating voice continued.

Frowning, Jatal peered up to see all eyes turned to the opening where a newcomer stood. What he saw squeezed the breath from him in distaste and a shudder of dread. It was a shaduwam dressed in the traditional rags of his calling. His torso was smeared in layers of dirt and caked ash painted his face white. His hair was a piled mane of unwashed tangled locks. He carried in his hands the traditional accoutrements of his calling: the staff and begging bowl. But in this one's case, the begging bowl was an upturned human skull.

Everyone lurched to their feet in disgust, alarm, and, it had to be admitted, atavistic fear. 'Who allowed this abomination among us!' demanded Sher' Tal. 'Guards!'

'Iron and flesh are no barrier to me,' the shaduwam grinned, revealing teeth filed to fine sharp points.

The guards came rushing in, only to flinch in loathing from the holy man. 'A curse comes to any who dare touch me!' he warned.

'Curse wind and wood, then, dog,' answered Princess Andanii, and she turned to her guards: 'Bring me my bow!'

'Would you strike down your own beloved mother and father, Princess?' the shaduwam challenged. 'For that is what will happen should you slay me. They too shall die . . . and not quickly.'

Andanii paled yet her dark eyes glared a ferocious rage.

'What is it you wish?' the Warleader called, breaking the silence.

Ganell waved the question aside. 'Nay! Do not invite this one into our congress, stranger. Do you not see the skull in his hands? He is no normal holy man. He is an Agon. He has enslaved his spirit to dark powers: the Fallen One, and the Demon-King, the infernal Kell-Vor.'

'Kell-Vor?' the Warleader echoed, and his lips quirked up as if amused.

The shaduwam had been staring avidly at the foreigner all this time. His own mouth tilted as if sharing some dark secret with the man.

The Warleader broke the gaze and shrugged his indifference. 'Yet it seems to me we should fight sorcery with sorcery. Is that not so?'

Sher' Tal clawed his full beard as he examined the priest the way one would a diseased animal – with disgust and wariness. 'If these dark ones will slay theurgist mages then it is about time they did something useful . . .'

The Agon smiled, baring sharpened teeth that looked to Jatal as if eager to sink into the man.

'Then it is decided,' the Warleader said. 'When—'

'It is *not* decided!' Princess Andanii called, interrupting him yet again. She faced the priest while making a great show of her loathing. 'You offer to help us . . . yet you speak not of any price! What is it you would demand of us?'

Many of the assembled tribal chiefs murmured in support of Andanii, including Jatal, despite their families' traditional antipathy. He called: 'Aye. We would have it now.'

The priest drew himself up tall: easily as disdainful of them as they of him. 'Gold and jewels are as coloured dust and dirt to us. Our price is one quarter of all captives.'

'Blood rites!' Ganell spat. 'Unholy sacrifice!'

'Never!' Andanii swore, and she yanked her belt knife from the table.

Jatal stood as well to show his support of the princess. His own father had always carried a particular hatred of the shaduwam Agon priests and forbade any to enter his lands. Ganell surged to his feet also and with that all representatives waved the priest from the tent.

The priest's seething slit gaze shifted to the Warleader, who remained silent. The foreigner offered a small pursed frown of regret as if to say: *I am very sorry, but there is nothing I can do . . .*

The priest bowed to the Warleader and backed away. Yet it seemed to Jatal that the mocking smile remained, half hidden, as he ducked from the tent.

Across the way, Princess Andanii offered a pleased nod in acknowledgement of Jatal's support. He bowed then sat, as did all. Ganell called for another round of sweetmeats and wine, 'To clear this gods-awful taste from all our mouths.'

After the cups had been refilled the Warleader raised a hand and conversation died away. 'My lords and ladies,' he began. 'Have I your answer, then?'

Peering about the circle of tribal representatives, Jatal saw in the eager faces that most appeared convinced. He cleared his throat and eyes shifted to him. 'Warleader,' he began, and gestured in an arc to everyone assembled, 'I see some twenty tribes and families of the Adwami gathered here this night. Each of which, myself included, expect no more than our fair share of any spoils.' He opened his hands. 'All things being equal, that should come to one twentieth share each. And so I ask myself . . . why should your share amount to twice that of all others?'

'By all the demon gods!' Ganell exploded. 'You have the right of that, Jatal!'

Most of those present joined their voices in support of the point. 'Well?' Andanii demanded.

The Warleader offered Jatal a slit of a smile that eerily echoed that of the Agon priest. 'Prince,' he began after the calls had died down, 'your wisdom is unassailable. However, I bring to this raid my experienced fighting men—'

'Are you claiming ours are inexperienced?' burst out Sher' Tal. 'Are you saying that we of the Adwami know nothing of fighting?'

The Warleader offered a stiff sitting bow, hands on knees. 'Not at all. I merely . . . misspoke . . . However, I am a *very* experienced commander in matters of tactics and strategy—'

'Then you may serve as a valuable adviser in this endeavour,' Princess Andanii cut in, decisive. 'And no servant should expect a share larger than that of any of the Adwami.' She cocked a brow to Jatal, inviting his reaction to her judgement.

He offered a deep bow of respect. At his side, Ganell sighed admiringly, 'Such a spirited mare . . .' Jatal, however, now studied the Warleader. The man's jaws worked behind his thin iron-grey beard while his eyes held an unspoken fury. Yet somehow the man mastered himself and slowly inclined his head in concord. 'Very well,' he ground out. 'One twentieth share. We are in agreement.'

Many in the assembly raised their cups, cheering. Ganell slammed his goblet against all he could reach, all the while offering up his great belly laugh. Jatal noted the hulking lieutenant of the Warleader. The

66

man now frowned at the gnawed bone before him and shot narrowed glances to his superior. It appeared to Jatal that such cavalier halving of his expected proceeds did not sit well with him. And Jatal had to agree: it seemed to him that for a mercenary who fights for gold the Warleader acquiesced to the loss of rewards far too easily.

Negotiations finished, calls arose for more drink and for entertainment, musicians and dancers. Ganell launched into an old story of a legendary hunt he and one of Jatal's uncles went out on only to become lost and nearly shoot each other. It was a story very familiar to Jatal and he listened with one ear only, already thinking ahead to the problem of intelligence-gathering.

A challenge. The Thaumaturg had always been very effective in intercepting their raiding parties. Their mage's arts, no doubt. He believed there were one or two among his family's men-at-arms who bore the scars of Thaumaturg shackles upon their wrists and ankles. He would interview them. He also possessed among his documents accounts of travels through their neighbours' lands. Had he brought them? He clasped Ganell on the arm, murmuring, 'A pleasure, my friend. But I must clear my head.'

The big man squeezed his hand, laughing, 'Of course, of course!'

He stood, inclined his head to the foreign Warleader, now their Warleader, who answered the gesture, then departed for his tent. He did not see the gaze of Princess Andanii follow him as he left.

After searching among his possessions Jatal found that indeed, no, he had not brought the relevant documents; one can never anticipate everything. Irritated with himself and unable to sleep, he set off on a walk round the sprawling encampment. His wandering brought him to a darkened edge where a picket faced away over the brush-clumped hillsides. He paused here for a time and listened to the insects whirring through the night air, and watched the flitting of the bats feeding upon them.

It occurred to him then that a strange glow lit the dark far out across the rolling low hills. 'Is that a fire out there?' he asked a near-by picket.

The young man bowed. 'Just a reflection, no doubt, noble born.'

Jatal studied the guard: of a Lesser house, the Birkeen, and very young. 'You have not investigated?'

The guard appeared stricken and wet his lips, smiling his apology. 'My post is here, noble born.'

Jatal bit down on his cutting response; it would be of no use. And no sense wasting even more time berating the lad. The Birkeen were among the poorest of all the families. No hired tutors for this one.

He was like the majority of the Adwami: superstitions ruled his world. Jatal went to where he knew he would find those willing to walk out into the night – the foreigners' compound.

After calling for the officer in charge he waited and was quite surprised when the broad hulking shape of the Warleader's lieutenant came lumbering up.

'Yes?' the fellow rumbled – the due honorific forgotten, or ignored.

'A light out amid the hills. Thought you'd want to investigate.'

A wide blunt hand rose to rub equally wide jowls where pronounced canines, tusks almost, thrust. 'That I would.' He turned to a guard. 'Gather a team and follow me.'

'I will show the way,' Jatal said.

The lieutenant's brows rose in his own surprise. 'Very good. Lead on.'

While they walked Jatal eyed the fellow: quite tall, but much more markedly broad – like an ambulatory shack. 'You are . . . ?'

'Scarza.'

'Prince Jatal.'

The man eyed him up and down. 'Prince, hey?' Jatal heard the deliberate lack of respect but let it pass – perhaps where this man was from the title was unknown, or was considered just plain silly. The fellow was only a benighted foreigner, after all.

Before they reached the border of the camp Jatal had described the situation and Scarza had ordered his mercenary team to encircle the area while he and Jatal approached openly. Walking, Jatal rested his hand on his curved sword's grip. 'Hardly a spy,' he murmured aside to Scarza as they entered the dark.

'A very poor spy?' the big foreigner supplied, arching his brows.

Jatal allowed himself a wry smile; while the character of the Warleader left him feeling uneasy, he suspected that he might just come to like his lieutenant.

The faint dancing light led them to a depression and a stunted nearly dead tree, half bare of bark, limbs twisted and gnarled. Set before the tree and in its branches glowed a great number of candles. Some had burned down, or been blown out. Amid the candles lay tatters of torn cloth and coconut-shell bowls containing dark fluids, and symbols of some sort had been slashed into the dirt and daubed in powders. Jatal smelled old blood. He and Scarza stood peering down for some time, then the lieutenant crouched for a closer look.

'Dark magic,' Jatal said, warning him.

'The work of our shaman friend?'

'Shaman? Ah – shaduwam. Yes. He is a practitioner of Agon.

Sacrilege and desecration. Note the cloth. I see the weave of the Awamir, Manahir, Vehajarwi and my own Hafinaj. Curses upon all our heads.'

'Not a man to be denied.'

'No.'

Scarza's mercenaries emerged from the dark to shake their heads. Scarza stood, brushing the dirt from his knees. 'Well, he's long gone.' He waved a hand, indicating the evil makeshift shrine. 'You believe in any of this?'

'They have power, these shaduwam. And they are immune to punishment or threats.'

'Immune?'

'It is their religion, you see. They worship pain and violation of the flesh.'

The man grunted his understanding. 'Not immune to a plain old beheading then.'

'No. But such a one would probably embrace that fate. He would be considered a holy martyr.'

The lieutenant appeared to be staring at the candles yet again while he rubbed his jowls. 'Have to punish him with forced feeding then,' he mused, his thoughts seeming elsewhere. 'And dancing girls.'

Jatal smiled his appreciation. 'Yes. A fate worse than death.'

Scarza half reached out for one of the candles then reconsidered, lowering his hand. 'Burn this down,' he ordered his men and turned away. Jatal followed.

*   *   *

The throne room lay empty but for the shifting shadows cast from the dim flames of lamps hung on chains that climbed disappearing into the gloom. Footfalls on the polished stone flags announced the entrance of a man, tall and powerful, his hair a mane of white. Crossing to a wall, the man studied the shelves of artwork and scrolls. He spared a glance to the tall wooden throne where it stood enmeshed in shadows then lifted a scroll and opened it, reading its contents. 'Just what effect are you trying for, Usurper?' he asked, still studying the scroll. After a time he raised his head to the throne. 'Well?'

'God-like patience, I should imagine,' a reedy voice answered from the gloom.

The man narrowed his eyes, which glowed a molten gold. 'I don't see it.'

'You are *quite* finished, Osserc? I would have you know *I* am very busy.'

The man returned the scroll then lifted a vase from another shelf. 'Then you need not follow me about like an anxious shopkeeper.'

'Ha!' A finger pointed from the murk obscuring the seat of the throne. 'You'd like that, wouldn't you? Then you'll try . . . whatever it is you mean to try, then . . . won't you!'

Osserc turned a rather puzzled glance upon the throne. 'I'll do . . . what?'

'Exactly!'

The tall man frowned and cocked his head, attempting to work his way through that. Shrugging, he replaced the vase. 'Well, you need worry no longer. I am finished here.'

'You most certainly are!'

'I go to speak with another.'

'Another? Who? Who would you speak to?' Osserc ignored the question and walked up a darkened hall. The murky transparent figure on the throne leaned forward as if listening. 'Where are you going?' The flickering light in the main hall changed, dimming even further. 'Osserc? Hello?' He leaned back. 'So . . . gone! Ha! Drove him off, the fool!' A fisted hand banged from one armrest. 'But where has he gone?' Hands flew to a head cowled in shreds of shadow. 'Gaa! I must know! I must know everything!'

A tiny monkey-like animal came waddling from a corner. In one hand it turned something bright which glimmered and flashed. 'You!' the figure on the throne yelled. The monkey whipped its hands behind its back and peered about innocently. 'You! Do something!'

The animal's expressive face wrinkled up with something resembling determination. It sat on one of the steps leading up to the throne and proceeded to stare off into the distance. It stroked the tuft of hair at its chin as if deep in thought.

'Oh, you're a big help.'

CHAPTER II

There are many tattooed men and women. Tattoos are often religious incantations or symbols. They are held to offer protection against illness, curses and to ward off the attention of ghosts. The more superstitious the person, the more tattoos they are apt to have. Since tattooing is very painful, the victim chews mind-dulling leaves or inhales stupefying smoke, without relent, for the days of the operation.

Matha Banness
In Jakuruku

THE FIRST SIGNIFICANT ATTACK UPON THE ARMY CAME ON THE fourth night of the march through the border region of jagged limestone mounts, sheer cliffs and sudden precipitous sinkholes, the Gangreks. Golan had fallen asleep at his travelling desk. Long into the night he'd been reading U-Pre's disheartening progress reports while the candles burned out one by one around him. Screams and shouts from the edge of camp snapped his head from among the sheets of cheap pressed fibre pages. The candles had all guttered out. Wrapping his robes about himself, he stepped out of the tent and met the messenger sent to bring him word of the disturbance. He waved the man silent and set off.

His yakshaka bodyguard fell in about him, swords drawn, and Golan sourly reflected that this was hardly where their swords were needed. Still, they were not to be blamed. It was not their job to patrol the camp perimeter. He found most of the troops and labourers up and awake. They murmured among themselves and strained to peer to the south. The whispers died away as Golan and his escort passed. He felt the pressure of countless eyes following him from the dark, all glittering as they reflected the dancing flames of the camp torches. He recognized the gathering panic fed by the darkness and their destination – a smothering animal coiling itself about everyone.

The south was a trampled battleground of torn tents, overturned carts, slaughtered men and animals. The butchery appeared indiscriminate, savage. Corpses lay where they had fallen, sprawled, revealing hideous wounds, and Golan gritted his teeth. Where was U-Pre? He expected better than this of the man. Droplets of blood and other fluids spattered the grasses and slashed canvas. Here and there limbs lay completely torn from torsos. He studied the corpse of a labourer eviscerated by a ragged gash across his stomach. Blue and pink-veined intestines lay thrown like uncoiled rope. Someone wearing sandals had walked across them. As reported: a fanged monstrosity emerging from the forest to rend men limb from limb. What else but an opening move from Ardata?

He sighed, and, chilled by the cool night air, slid his hands up the wide silk sleeves of his robe. Thankfully, a cordon of troopers had been organized and these, with spears sideways, held back the curious.

Yet even so, stamped on the faces of those survivors, in their wide staring eyes and sweaty pallid features, lay their obvious terror and near panic. *Must separate these from the rest; such fear is contagious and grows in the recounting.*

Walking unconcerned through the muck and steaming spilled viscera came the equally fearsome apparition of the Isturé Skinner himself. His ankle-length armoured coat glimmered like mail, though Golan knew it was actually constructed of smooth interlocking scales. As he stepped over the sprawled corpses his coat dragged across staring faces and slashed wet torsos. It shone enamelled black except where spattered fresh gore painted it a deep crimson.

'And where were you and your people during the attack?' Golan demanded.

'Elsewhere,' the foreigner responded, unconcerned. He clasped his gauntleted hands behind his back to study the field of dead. Golan strove to shrug off a feeling of unease at such a blasé attitude to this bloody business. 'Well . . . now that you are here it is time you were useful.'

The foreigner, so tall as to literally tower over Golan, cocked a blond brow. 'Oh?'

'Yes. Track down this servant of Ardata. Slaughter it.'

In a scratching of scales Skinner crossed his armoured arms. 'It is hardly a servant of Ardata.'

Golan waved a hand, forgetting momentarily that he wasn't carrying his rod or fly-whisk. 'What more evidence is necessary? It is a monster! It attacked us! We are entering Ardata's demesnes!'

'I would suggest that what we have entered is this thing's hunting grounds.'

Golan eyed the man more narrowly. 'Regardless. You have pledged certain obligations to the Circle of Masters.'

The foreign giant waved a hand in its banded, articulating gauntlet. 'Yes, yes. You have in me a partner for the campaign.'

'Very good. Your first task awaits.'

Turning heavily away, the foreigner murmured, 'For all the good it will do . . .'

Golan followed his retreat to the dark forest verge. *All the good? Well, yes, Ardata's servants are no doubt many. But that is your half of the bargain, foreigner. The throne of Ardata's lands could hardly be won so easily. And if you should destroy each other in the process . . . well . . .* Golan shrugged, then waved away a swarm of flies drawn by the spilt warm fluids.

In the woods Mara awaited Skinner. With her stood Shijel and Black the Lesser, younger brother of Black the Greater, who had remained with K'azz. 'Well?' she demanded as her commander appeared.

Skinner gave a slow shrug of disgust. 'Our noble ally wants it killed.'

'Ridiculous! In a few days we'll be out of its territory.'

'Regardless . . .'

Mara kicked the ground. 'Damned useless . . .'

'Who's coming?' Black asked.

Skinner studied them. 'We should do it. Mara, tell Jacinth she's in charge until we return.'

'Very good.'

'The trail?' Skinner asked Shijel.

'A blind tinker could follow it.'

'So be it. Let us track it down. I'd like to be back by dawn.'

Shijel did the tracking. He wore light leathers and gloves on his hands, which were never far from the silver-wire-wrapped grips of his twin longswords. The trail, obvious even to Mara, led them on. The nightly rains returned, thick and warm. Mara's robes became a heavy encumbrance that she cursed as she stumbled over roots and through clinging mud. The possibility of returning by dawn slowly slid away as they failed to reach the creature's lair until a feathering of pink touched the eastern sky. The four gathered short of a jungle-choked opening in a tall cliff face and Mara cursed again. 'Could go on for ever,' she muttered, keeping her voice low.

Their commander pulled on one of the hanging vines as if testing its strength. 'Yes,' he agreed. 'I do miss Cowl.'

Mara flinched at that mention of her old superior, now dead. 'Meaning *what*?' she demanded.

Skinner turned to her, frowned his puzzlement, and then nodded his understanding. 'Ah. No slight intended.' He drew on his helm. 'I simply meant that I could just have sent him in and wouldn't have to go myself.' He waved them on.

Mara followed, stepping awkwardly over rotting logs and fallen rock. *Well, there was that,* she admitted. Cowl *would* actually have gone in alone. And no doubt Skinner did miss his old partner in scheming. Together they'd proved a formidable team. Always it had been just the two of them hammering out stratagems and tactics. Now that Cowl was gone Skinner was well and truly utterly alone. And it seemed to her that the man was even less human because of it.

She knew this cave was just one of the countless sinkholes and caverns that riddled this mountain border region. Over the millennia rains had rotted the limestone into a maze of grottoes and extended underground tunnels where one could suddenly find oneself exposed in open sunlight yet lost hundreds of feet below the surface. Some argued this was the true face of Ardata's realm. As if she were some sort of queen of the underworld. But Mara knew this to be false. The Night-Queen's demesne was open countryside. Yet likewise over the millennia, her presence had altered the entire jungle until it too resembled this border region where the unmindful traveller could suddenly find himself wandering half immersed in a Warren-like realm: the legendary enchanted forest of Himatan.

They pushed through the hanging leaves and vines then paused to allow their vision to adjust, and to become used to the stink that suddenly assaulted them: the overwhelming miasma of the layered urine and guano of untold thousands of bats.

'You have the sense of this thing?' Skinner asked Mara.

'Yes. Downward and to the right.'

'Very good.'

Shijel led. Mara summoned her Warren to improve her vision. The swordsman was on his way across the main section of the cave when she sensed a shimmering of power there on the floor – which to her vision seemed almost to seethe. 'Halt!'

Everyone froze. 'Well?' Skinner murmured.

'The floor of the cave. Something strange there . . .' Mara summoned greater light, then selected a stone that she tossed on to the oddly shifting floor. The stone disappeared as if dropped into water. The surface burst into a flurry of hissing and writhing. It seemed to boil, revealing a soup of vermin: centipedes, ivory-hued roaches, white beetles and pale maggots. Amid the slurry of legs and chitinous slithering bodies lay bones. The skeletal remains of animals. And of humans.

'Strip you of flesh in an instant,' Mara commented.

Shijel peered back at her, unconvinced. 'They're just insects.'

'There is power there.'

'D'ivers?' Skinner asked sharply.

Mara cocked her head, studying the pool more closely. 'Not as such. No. They are . . . *enchanted*, I suppose one might call it.'

A disgusted sigh escaped Skinner. 'Himatan already . . .'

Mara nodded. 'Under here, yes.'

'No wonder the thing fled this way. Very well . . .' Skinner gestured to Black the Lesser. 'You lead. Mara, follow closely.'

Black unslung his broad shield and drew his heavy bastard sword. Mara fell in behind him, directing him to keep to the walls and to watch his step. They descended in this order for some time; Skinner bringing up the rear, perhaps as a precaution against their quarry's attacking from behind. The route Mara dictated narrowed and they slogged on through knee-high frigid water. From somewhere nearby came the echoing roar of a falls.

Mara sensed it as it happened: she opened her mouth to shout a warning even as a shape lunged from the dark water to latch itself upon Black and the two went down in a twisting heap. From the slashing water rose the monstrosity to launch itself upon her. She had an instant's impression of a glistening armoured torso like that of a lizard, sleek furred arms ending in long talons, and a humanoid face distorted by an oversized mouth of needle-like teeth. Two swords thrust over her shoulders impaling the creature in its lunge and it shrieked, twisting aside to disappear once more beneath the water. Black emerged, gasping and chuffing. His right shoulder was a bloody mess. He cradled the arm. Mara nodded her thanks to Shijel, just behind her.

'It went for you,' he said.

'It knows who's sensing it,' Skinner rumbled. 'I believe you wounded it, Shijel. Mara – is it far?'

Still shaken, she jerked her head. 'No. Not far.'

'Very good. Black, fall in behind Mara. You lead, Shijel.'

They found it close to an underground waterfall. It lay up against rocks, half in the water. Blood smeared its chest and naked torso. Its dark eyes glittered full of intelligence and awareness, watching them as they approached, so Mara addressed it: 'Why did you attack us?'

Its half-human face wrinkled up, either in pain or annoyance. '*Why?*' it growled. 'Stupid question, Witch.' It gestured a clawed hand to Skinner. 'You are a fool to return, Betrayer. She will not be so patient with you a second time.'

'We shall see,' he answered from within his helm.

'Again I ask,' Mara said, 'why attack? You are no match for us.'

It bared its teeth in something like a hungry grin. 'No. But our mistress has spoken. You are no longer welcome and I honour our mistress. You . . .' it gestured again to Skinner, weakly, 'Himatan shall swallow you.'

Mara frowned, troubled by what seemed a prophecy, and she crouched before it. 'What do you—'

The heavy mottled blade of Skinner's sword thrust past her, impaling the creature. Mara flinched aside. 'Damn the Dark Deceiver, Skinner! There was something there . . .'

'Well,' the giant observed as he shook the dark blood from his blade, 'there's nothing there now.' He turned away. 'Bring the body. The damned Thaumaturg might yet demand proof.'

At the cave entrance Skinner paused, raising a gauntleted hand to sign a halt. He regarded the wide cave floor, now as still as any placid pool. He then went to the body, which Shijel and Black had dragged all the way. Grunting with the effort, he gathered up the muscular corpse and heaved the carcass overhead and out on to the floor. As it flew Mara flinched to hear it give vent to one sudden despairing shriek, cut off as it disappeared beneath the surface. The pool of vermin foamed to life in a great boiling froth of maggots, beetles, writhing larvae and ghost-white centipedes.

Mara turned away, nauseated. Skinner watched for a time, motionless, then headed for the surface. Passing Mara, he observed, 'You were right – stripped in an instant.'

*   *   *

Saeng woke up feeling worse than she had in a very long time. She was shivering cold and her clothes hung sodden and chilled. Her hair was a clinging damp mess, her nose was running and her back hurt. Early morning light shone down through the thick canopy in isolated shafts of gold. She stretched, grimacing, and felt at her back;

76

she'd slept curled up on a nest of leaves and humus piled in a nook between the immense roots of a tualang tree. Her umbrella stood open over her, its handle jammed into a gap between the vines that choked the trunk. Hanu stood to one side, his back to her.

Standing, Saeng adjusted her shirt and skirts and brushed ineffectually at her matted hair. She pulled the umbrella free and closed it. Hanu turned to her.

'Thanks,' she said, indicating the umbrella. He nodded within his helm, which glittered with its inlaid jade and lapis lazuli mosaic. A suspicion struck her. 'You stood there all through the night?' Again he nodded. That struck her as inhuman, which made her rub her arms and look away, an ache clenching her chest. 'Don't you need to sleep . . . any more?'

'*Little,*' he signed.

'I'm sorry.'

'*Don't.*'

Deciding not to pursue that any further, she scanned the jungle. 'Hear anything in the night?'

'*Many things come.*'

'What's that? Many things? What?'

'*Night animals. Wild pigs. Monkeys. A fire cat hunting. Ghosts.*'

'Ghosts? What did they look like?'

'*Dancing balls white light.*'

'Oh, them.' Wanderers. Spirits doomed to search eternally for some lost or stolen thing. People greedy in life. Sometimes, though, she knew it could have been a sad affair with one hunting a lost love. 'Any hint of the Thaumaturgs?'

'*No. But close. Must move.*'

'Yes. But first we must eat.' She sat on a root and dug in her cloth shoulder bag. 'We have rice for two or three days only. After that, fruit and anything we can catch, I suppose.' She held up a ball of rice. He worked at his helm to open it. Saeng studied her brother as he popped the rice ball into his mouth and chewed, his gaze searching the woods. So much a figure from her youth. How she could still see the smiling child in his face. *Oh, Hanu . . . what have they done to you?*

'More?' she asked.

'*No.*' He closed his helm.

No more? For such a large fellow it seemed to her that he ate like a mouse. She packed up the bags and wraps and they set off.

Pushing through the wet leaves she was sodden again almost immediately. She brushed at her skirts in irritation. Hanu, leading, did what he could to break trail. Towards midday the clouds began thickening as the evening rain gathered itself. They exited the tall old forest to enter a broad meadow of dense grass stands reaching higher than either of them.

'An old rice field,' Saeng said, wonder in her voice. 'We must be close to Pra Thaeng, or Pra Dan.'

Hanu signed for silence, now tensed. He motioned Saeng back and drew his long broad blade. She at least knew enough not to say a thing, and backed away quickly. She then heard it: something large approaching, shouldering its way through the thick stands. *Great Demon-King! Not another yakshaka! I must help.* She summoned her power from within.

An immense monster suddenly crashed through the stand immediately before Hanu, who went down beneath its charging mass. Saeng had a glimpse of a dirty white juggernaut, beady fear-maddened rolling eyes and a curve of flashing horn, then it was gone.

She ran to Hanu and threw herself down at his side. Her brother was climbing to his feet, rather unsteady, giving vent to a strange noise. She helped him stand and realized that the sound he was making was laughter distorted by his helm. She let go her own worry and laughed as well.

'*More scared us,*' he signed.

Saeng nodded, smiling. *Yes. A great white rhino – more scared than we.* She shook her head, almost silly with relief. 'Just having lunch, then we come along.' She invited Hanu on. 'Some sort of a lesson there.'

They found a path through the fields and glimpsed in the distance the steep thatched roofs of the village houses, tendrils of white smoke rising. Hanu stopped here and motioned aside to the thick grasses. Saeng frowned for a moment, then comprehension dawned and she nodded her fierce agreement, waving him into hiding. She continued on alone. The quiet and stillness of the village struck her immediately. Where was everyone? Surely the Thaumaturgs hadn't swept through already . . .

Someone stepped out of a hut ahead. He was dressed as a peasant: a colourful wrap over his head against the sun, a loose blue shirt of coarse material, short pants tight at the calves, and barefoot. But the broad curved blade thrust into his waist sash was most unpeasant-like. He froze, seemingly quite as startled as she. Then a very savage grin climbed his unshaven face and he advanced, swaggering.

'Where have *you* been hiding, pretty bird?' he called.

Saeng's first reaction was to flee, and she did back away a few steps.

'No running!' he shouted. 'We have everyone. Don't want them to get hurt, do you?'

Saeng stilled and was surprised to find a calm resolve take hold of her. 'No,' she answered, firmly, 'I do not.'

The fellow rested a hand on his sword grip. 'Good. Come along then.'

As she walked next to him she asked, 'You are bounty men collecting people for the army?'

He eyed her, his gaze evaluating. 'That's right. Coin for every hale man and woman.'

'Labourers?'

The man shrugged his indifference. 'Labourers, workers, haulers, spear-carriers, shovel-carriers, cooks, launderers, carpenters. Or . . .' and he looked her up and down, 'other services.'

He brought her to the temple, the main structure of any village. Here more armed men and women guarded the villagers who knelt in the dirt of the central square. He led her up to another armed fellow, this one quite young, in a long hauberk of overlapping leather scales set with blackened iron rivets that hung to his knees. With this presumed leader stood an old woman, possibly the head of the village.

The leader eyed Saeng then turned an angry glare on the old woman. 'You gave me your word there was no one else!' The old woman merely hung her head.

'I'm not from here,' Saeng called.

The leader turned his attention to her. 'What is your name?'

'Ahn.'

He snorted his disbelief. 'Well . . .' gave her a long lazy-eyed study, 'the name doesn't really matter, does it?' Saeng saw how he eyed her long unbound hair. 'You're unmarried.'

'Yes.'

'Why so old yet unmarried? What's wrong with you, Ahn?'

Stung, she raked a clawed hand at his face but he flinched aside, catching her wrist. 'Now I see why,' he laughed. 'Too much of a temper. Well . . . we'll see about that.'

She wrenched her hand free – or he allowed her to. 'What are you going to do?'

He ignored her, gestured to one of his men. 'Have them prepare a meal for us.'

'Yes, Kenjak.'

Saeng stared anew at the fellow – hardly older than she. 'Kenjak Ashevajak? The Bandit Lord?'

He smiled, clearly very pleased. 'Ah! Heard of me, have you?'

Saeng looked away, damning herself for the outburst. 'I have heard stories.'

He brushed errant strands of her hair from her shoulder. 'You can tell me them all – tonight.' She slapped his hand aside but he walked off, laughing.

Saeng caught a pitying look from the old woman. 'I'm sorry, child,' she murmured. 'There is no succour here.'

'I'm no child,' Saeng growled, pulling at her tangled hair. She eyed the surrounding huts and fields. *Hanu, wherever you are, stay hidden! I'll handle this.*

Under the watch of the bandits the villagers prepared a meal first for them, then for the roped gang of captives squatting in the square. Kenjak had Saeng sit next to him in the largest of the village huts. He offered her food pinched in his fingers, which she refused, much to his amusement.

As the evening darkened and the rains began, the young man turned to her again. He leaned back on an arm, saying, 'So . . . tell me these stories,' and he chewed on coconut meat, watching her steadily.

'I could tell you what I have heard of your past . . .' she began, slowly, 'or I could tell you your future.'

The bandit leader stopped tossing pieces of dried coconut into his mouth. The talk around the low table among the man's lieutenants died away. His gaze narrowed and Saeng was shaken to see for the first time true cruelty in someone's eyes. 'You are a witch?' he asked, his voice flat.

She shrugged. 'I have some small talents.'

Kenjak peered around the table, a mocking smile now on his lips. 'This one claims to be a witch,' he said, chuckling. 'She is trying to scare us, I think.' The gathered men and women eyed one another, laughing uneasily. 'Go ahead. Read my future. Don't you need a chicken? Or prayer sticks, perhaps?'

'No. Nothing like that. I simply need to concentrate on the night.'

'Be my guest, little witch.'

Saeng settled herself and stared out the door to the dark where the captives still squatted, hunched and wretched, in the now drumming rain. Peripherally, she saw the bandits' hands sliding across their laps to the wood and bone grips of knives in their sashes. Kenjak, next to her, had not moved and she realized that they were now locked in a game neither could back away from: he displaying his fearlessness and she – to his mind – attempting to terrify everyone. She had no doubt he was not bluffing; he would kill her if he so chose. But what he did not understand was that she was not bluffing, either.

Saeng now attempted something she'd never dared before, and reached out to her brother. '*Hanu,*' she called through the arts taught her by the shades. '*Do you hear me?*'

'*Saeng? Is that you?*' came his astonished reply.

'*Yes. Do not show yourself! Leave this to me.*'

'*I am watching. If anyone—*'

'*No! They mustn't see you.*'

'Well?' Kenjak urged. 'We're waiting.'

'I see your death,' she announced, proud of the steadiness of her voice.

'I am grey-haired and between the legs of my favourite concubine, no doubt.'

Saeng tilted her head, squinting into the night. 'No. You—' She broke off then, her voice catching in surprise as an image did suddenly come to her. Kenjak in darkness, a cave, or underground, the mark of death upon him. 'Fear the underground, Kenjak. You will die there.'

For an instant the man's face drained of all blood. He leaped to his feet, drawing his knife. 'Who told you this, whore?'

Screams sounded from the darkness and the hissing curtains of rain. Kenjak waved out two of his men then returned his attention to her.

Saeng knew what lay behind the screams. She had sensed them gathering: the Nak-ta. '*Go away!*' she ordered.

'*You summoned us . . .*' came the cold reply.

'*I did not!*'

'*The violence of your thoughts did. We come to serve. Give them to us . . .*'

'Look!' one of the bandits called, pointing to her. Saeng looked down at herself. Blue ghost-flame flickered upon her lap and arms. 'Kill her!' the man shouted, terrified.

Kenjak thrust. But it seemed to Saeng that she merely touched his arm and he flew in an eruption of the ghost-flame to crash into a wall. The table, everyone else, all were flung backwards to strike the walls in a storm of writhing fire that lashed about her while she stared, dumbfounded, at her flaming hands.

81

Everyone scrambled for the door and windows, crying and screaming their terror.

'*They are ours!*' came the savage cry of bloodlust from the gathered
Nak-ta.

'*Touch them not!*' Saeng demanded. '*Obey me!*'

She felt a slow reluctant acquiescence chill her. '*We . . . obey.*'
Beneath the admission she sensed the unspoken *for now . . .*

Heavy steps announced Hanu's arrival into the swirling storm of
blue flame. Stooping, he scooped her into his arms.

'*I told you to stay away.*'

'*I guess your methods are just too subtle for me.*'

She almost laughed but sudden exhaustion settled her head against
his chest instead. He carried her out into the rain, past the gaping
captives struggling with their bonds, tramping on into the dark
woods, pausing only to open the umbrella above her.

Dimly, as she rocked into sleep, she was aware that her brother
was walking past and through the flickering pale flames that were
the assembled restless ghosts and spirits of the land – none of which
he seemed able to see.

*   *   *

During their voyage west Shimmer came to the opinion that K'azz
was avoiding her. It took almost an entire day to finally catch the
man leaning against the ship's side. An achievement on his part,
considering the restricted size of the vessel. She rested her weight
on her forearms next to him while the blustery contrary winds of
this stretch of frigid ocean lashed their hair and clothes. Among the
rigging the sailors shouted back and forth in a constant panic to trim
the canvas.

'A stormy crossing,' she offered her commander.

His gaze on the white-capped waves, the man nodded his assent.
'I'm told it is the steep temperature change from the ice fields to the
warm coastal waters.'

'Jacuruku *is* warm then?'

'Yes, just as all the stories say. Like Seven Cities, but with a long
season of rains.' The man raised his chin to the western sky. 'Which
we're entering now.'

Shimmer glanced up past the foredeck. A front of dark clouds
marred the horizon. 'Dangerous?'

'Just unrelenting.'

'And these Dolmens? What of them?'

K'azz's tanned leathery features clenched and his pale gaze returned to the waves. 'Yes? What of them?'

'What is there?'

Her commander brushed his hands on the cracked paint of the rail. Shimmer felt a chill as, for an instant, the slim hands appeared skeletal. 'A wild power that mustn't be disturbed. That is all anyone need know.'

'How do we know Ardata isn't lying about all this?'

'She would not lie about that.' He leaned more of his weight upon the rail. 'Not that.'

But you are, my commander. Lies of omission. What more might this Ardata be lying about? 'You were at these Dolmens, weren't you?'

The memory of something that might have been pain furrowed the man's brows and he lowered his gaze. 'Yes.'

'So . . . what did you learn?'

He laid a hand on her arm in a gentle touch. 'That that is enough to know. Do not worry yourself, Shimmer.' And he gave her what he must have imagined was an encouraging smile but struck her as a death's head stretching of skin across his jaws. He walked away, leaving her at the ship's side.

Rutana joined her where she stood peering after the man. 'You and he,' the witch began, tentatively, 'you are lovers?' Utterly taken aback, Shimmer slowly turned her head to meet the woman's frank direct gaze. Her thick mane of kinked black hair blew about her face, the amulets and charms tinkling.

'No.'

She nodded. 'Ah.'

Shimmer could not help herself: into the long silence that followed she had to ask, 'Why?'

'My mistress is . . . interested in him.'

'The way she was interested in Skinner?'

A savage scowl twisted the witch's face and her eyes blazed almost amber. 'Her offer was genuine! He betrayed her.'

'And what was the offer?'

The scowl slid into dismissive scorn. 'That would hardly be your business, would it?'

Shimmer stared, quite bemused by the vehemence of her reaction. Before she could frame a reply a panicked shout sounded from the lookout high on the main mast: '*Sea serpent!*'

Shimmer scanned the waves. Her brother Avowed boiled up from below, barefoot, yet readying crossbows and bows.

'Where 'bout?' the pilot called.

'Off the larboard bow!'

Shimmer pushed her way closer to the bow. Searching among the tall waves she spotted a great ship-like girth, snowy pale and stunningly huge, mounting just beneath the surface. Calls went up as others saw it as well.

Cole lowered his cocked crossbow, taking aim.

A thick arm swatted the weapon up and it discharged into the straining shrouds.

Amatt and Turgal turned on the hulking Nagal, who described a slow arc, facing all in turn.

'Hold!' K'azz ordered. He pushed his way to Nagal. 'What is the meaning of this?'

'Isturé fools!' Rutana called from the side. 'Would you anger our sea-guardians?'

Shimmer exchanged wondering looks with Cole, Lor and Gwynn. 'Guardians?'

'Lower your weapons,' K'azz ordered. Turgal and Amatt reluctantly lowered their bows. Rutana sounded a high cackling laugh into the silence. She was leaning over the side as if meaning to embrace the great beast, clapping her hands and gesturing to the water, perhaps inscribing something. Shimmer edged her way to her.

'What is this?' she demanded.

Straightening, Rutana laughed her savage glee, revealing her oddly needle-like sharp teeth. 'Our sea-guardians. Servants of our mistress. Just as Nagal and I are so honoured.'

'They serve Ardata?'

The witch peered up at her slyly. 'They answer her call. They obey her commands. Is this service, or is it . . . worship? Who is to say?' And she laughed again, brushing past.

Shimmer remained at the ship's side, as did all the Avowed. Out among the waves immense girths broached the waves, humped and glistening and mottled and as broad as the flanks of whales.

Cole murmured, 'In Seven Cities those are called dhenrabi. Any one of them could crush this ship.'

'Then let's be glad they're on our side,' Shimmer answered, not bothering to hide her sarcasm.

Cole's answering look told her that he fully understood her message.

Three days later they sighted land. The shore, if it could be called that, lay invisible beneath a thick forest of tangled trees, the roots of which stood from the water like a crazy maze of spider's legs.

'This is Ardata's land?' Shimmer asked Rutana.

'The border of it.'

'Where do we put in? Is there a port?'

Again the witch gave the knowing superior smile that so annoyed Shimmer. 'No port, Isturé. We travel upriver.'

'I see. So, the settlement is inland.'

The woman turned away, smiling still. 'Settlement? Yes, far inland.'

This half-admission troubled Shimmer like few other things on the voyage. While she scanned the swamp-edged jungle, the ship's pilot pushed the stern-mounted tiller to swing the vessel aside and they struck a course following the coastline south. As the day waned it became obvious that they skirted an immense delta of twisting channels. Some coursed a mere few paces wide, while others passed as open and broad as rivers in themselves. All debouched a murky ochre water to churn and swirl with the darker iron-blue of the sea. Towards evening they came abreast of what Shimmer imagined must be the main channel. So wide was it that she could hardly see the opposite shore. The low tangled jungle edge stretched up the river's length. Large dun-hued birds scudded over the muddy water; their harsh calls sounded a cacophony of noise. Shimmer saw no signs of settlement, or even of any human occupation.

The order went out to drop anchor. Lor came to Shimmer's side. She gestured to the nearby swampy shore. 'Look there. See those?'

Shimmer squinted, not sure what she was looking for. Already in the deepening light the tangled depths of the forest were impenetrable to her vision. 'What?'

'Standing from the water.'

'Oh.' What she took to be dead stumps resolved into carved wood signs, or totems. They stood at odd angles, rotting and grey with age. All were carved in fantastic shapes, half animal, half human. A snake-human, a half-leopard. Staring closer now, she noted tufted round objects hanging from them, and it took her a time to recognize them as human heads in various stages of decay.

Peering around she found Rutana and crossed to her side. 'What are those?' she asked, gesturing to the shore.

The woman glanced over, her gaze half-lidded, disinterested. 'Hmm?'

'Those carvings.'

'Ah.' The sharp-toothed smile returned. 'Warnings against trespassers. Bandits and pirates.'

'Pirates?' Shimmer waved a hand to the shore. 'There's nothing here . . .'

'They go upriver to raid for captives. And perhaps they are drawn by the old stories and legends.'

Shimmer nodded. *Ah yes. Legendary Jacuruku. The great city in the jungle. Jakal Viharn. City of gold. Paved in jewels. Immortality and inestimable magical powers to be won.* She leaned against the side. 'Those are just stories.'

'Yes, but as with all such legends there resides a kernel of truth in it. Jakal Viharn is real, and it is a very magical place. It is simply . . . very hard to find.'

'But you can bring us to it.'

'Yes. Nagal and I are your guides.'

'And without you – we would never find it.'

The witch shrugged. 'It would be most difficult. Yet you Isturé are perhaps resourceful enough . . .'

'As Skinner was?'

Rutana's face closed up once more, her mouth snapping tight. Walking away she said over her shoulder: 'Tomorrow we start upriver. Prepare yourself for such a journey as you have never known. We enter the world of my mistress's dreams.'

*   *   *

The assembled army of tribes that was the Adwami's raid into Thaumaturg lands made very little headway. Oh, Prince Jatal could admit that the noble cavalry of each house made a pretty enough pageant charging back and forth along the order of march, their polished spearheads gleaming and the colourful tassels of their long caparisons kicking up and whipping as they flew past. But when the dust settled from all that patrician display, the main body of infantry with its carts and wagons of materiel trudged along in a disordered and rather neglected mess. Only the intervention of the Warleader and his officers kept the columns moving along: disentangling a crossing of columns here, or settling an order of march there.

And judging from the old man's stinging rebukes and even saltier language, the outland general was rapidly loosing his patience with it all.

To Prince Jatal's disgust the traditional scheming and internecine jockeying that was the curse of the clans of the Adwami began even as the army took its first steps into the maze of bone-dry canyons and buttes: the Saar would not ride alongside the Awamir; the Salil refused its posting and instead filed up next to the Vehajarwi; while he, it had to be admitted, nearly trampled several minor families as he manoeuvred his forces to claim the head of the main column. Of course, as the largest of the contingents present, such placement was his by right in any case.

The Warleader and his mercenary army, some two thousand strong, rode as well. Such was the first of the foreigner's requirements, and fulfilled readily enough as the Adwami counted their wealth in horses – all held against restitution from his twentieth share, of course. The infantry column marked the main body of the army. The mounted noble Adwami contingents surrounded this, riding dispersed, scouting and screening.

Jatal and his fifty loyal retainer knights had the van. As they walked their mounts through the stony valleys and washes – sodden at night but bone dry by midday – representatives of the various families joined him under pretexts of social calls and honouring distant blood-ties. Ganell was of course the first, thundering up on his huge black stallion. The man was nursing a blistering headache which did his notorious temper no favours.

'I cannot believe these Saar fools are with us!' he announced, wincing, and holding up a fold of his robes to shade his head.

'The Warleader welcomes all who would contribute.'

The man's mouth worked behind his great full beard. 'Well . . . I'd best not catch sight of them after the fighting is done, I swear to that by the Demon-King!'

True to the lessons of the many tutors his father had inflicted upon him, Jatal decided to remain the diplomat. 'We shall see if they honour their commitments.'

'Ha! That will be a first. Well . . . I'll be there to urge them along with the flat of my blade. I swear to that as well!' And he kicked his mount onward. 'Fare thee well, O great Prince!' he laughed as he rode off.

Representatives of Lesser families came and went, joining him at the van for a time. Families his had allied with during various vendettas and feuds of the past. All pledged their support against the certain treachery to come. Jatal thanked them and pledged his own of course, as honour required, but inwardly he could only sigh as he imagined the very same assurances being offered to Sher' Tal, Horsemaster of the Saar, or Princess Andanii.

As the day waned he became impatient with the army's slow progress – so contrary to their lofty aim of a lightning-quick raid. How typical of any concerted effort from the Adwami! When the order went out from the Warleader for a cease to the day's ride, Jatal could contain himself no longer. He turned to Gorot, his grizzled veteran master-at-arms. 'I will scout ahead,' he said, and kicked his mount onward even as the first objections sounded from the man.

He rode hard at first in order to put as much room as possible between himself and the encampment with its great swarm of Adwami warriors. As evening came he continued at a more leisurely pace. The route he chose was one of the most direct; it had no doubt already been scouted by the foremost outriders, but that was no concern. The excuse alone was enough to quit the column with its dust and endless bickering and childish rivalries and ages-old grudges. These last months the lurid emerald arc of the Scimitar brightening across the sky had made such night travel far less of a danger for horse and rider. However, to Jatal's mind the benefit of the greater light was offset by the confusing twin shadows as the moon's silver light warred with the Scimitar's jade. He eventually gave up and found a narrow gully in which to throw down his blankets and hobble his mount. He rolled up in the blankets and went to sleep.

In the morning he awoke to an enormous passing of gas from someone. He pulled down his blanket, blinking in the light, to see the hulking shape of the Warleader's second, Scarza, sitting opposite. The man had a cactus leaf in one hand and had frozen in the act of eating it.

'Sorry,' the fellow said, and took a bite of the thorny green bud. 'Strange diet lately.'

'They say eating charcoal helps,' Jatal offered.

The man raised one tangled bushy brow. 'Really? Chewing on a burnt stick? You're having me on.'

'Not at all. Our old healers swear by it.'

'Old healers? Why, the force of my eruptions alone would slay them.'

Jatal cocked his head, considering. 'Well . . . I'll just have to take your word for that.'

'You are wise to do so.'

Surprising himself, Jatal found that he was warming to this hulking lieutenant. 'The Warleader sent you after me?'

'Yes. He is understandably concerned regarding the safety of a prince of the Hafinaj.'

Sitting up, Jatal rested his arms on his knees. 'Let me tell you about the so-called princes of the Hafinaj . . .' He stirred the embers

88

of the fire. 'First, there are over twenty of us. Sons of wives and of concubines. I am nearly the youngest. Among all the Adwami, princes number as many, and are as common as, grains of sand.'

Scarza grunted his understanding, appearing even more broad and stump-like sitting hunched as he was. 'Good. Then you won't be expecting me to make you tea or any damned thing like that.'

Jatal grinned and blew on the fire. 'No. I prefer to prepare my own tea – just as I like it. And you?' He studied the fellow: his dark cast, the wide face, prominent canines – almost like tusks – heavy brows and thick pelt-like brown hair. 'You are of the Trell, or legendary Thelomen kind?'

'Legendary here only, Prince. As I understand, your ancestors killed them all.'

Jatal set his small bronze pot on the fire. 'The Demon-King was responsible for that. And the gods dealt with him for it.'

'Cursed to wander eternally.'

'Yes. And his kingdom swallowed in a rain of fire.'

Scarza eased himself down further into the sands. 'I don't know . . . wandering eternally doesn't sound like much of a punishment to me.' And he laid an arm over his eyes.

Jatal fixed his tea and chewed on a stale flatbread. After his tea he cleaned the tiny thimble-cup and went to see to his toilet. Returning to their camp it occurred to him that the only horse present was his, Ash, named for his colour. Having readied the mount for the day's ride he stood over the apparently sleeping half-breed. 'Scarza . . . you have no horse?'

'No.'

'Then . . . how do you propose to keep up?'

'I can keep up with any horse over the day. Especially in country as rough as this.'

'So . . . I should simply go on ahead?'

Arm still over his eyes the half-giant answered: 'Aye. I'll find you. And must I point out just how easy it is to spot you, mister not so discreet at scouting. What with you riding a horse and all.'

Jatal smiled. 'If I wished to go on more circumspectly, I could simply send him back.'

Scarza moved his arm to blink up, puzzled. 'Send him back? How?'

'I would merely tell Ash to return to his friends and relatives among the Hafinaj.'

Scarza eyed the horse, impressed. 'Truly? What talented animals. Myself, I've never seen their use. Eat far too much, as, now that I think of it, has been said of me.'

Jatal mounted, chuckling. He nodded his farewell. 'Until later, then.'

'Yes. Until later, Jatal, prince of the Hafinaj.'

The canyon lands took all of the next day to cross. Swift scouts of various families came and went, saluting him. Not one subject of the Thaumaturgs, guard or picket, was evident among the draws and cliffs. As Jatal expected. For these subjects were farmers all, none rich enough to own a horse, even if their Thaumaturg masters allowed it. Late in the day he crested a shallow rise to look down on the vista of the broad plateau of channelled rivers and farmlands of the southern Thaumaturg lands. A land, if poor in portable riches, at least rich in population and fertility. To the north clouds gathered and the slanting darkness spoke of rain approaching.

Studying the countryside, Jatal nearly fell from Ash's back when a woman's voice called out, laughing: 'Hail, Jatal, prince of the Hafinaj!'

He flinched and turned to see Princess Andanii come walking her horse. 'What in the name of the ancients are *you* doing here?'

'Same as you,' she laughed. 'Scouting a best approach for our army.'

'This is no pleasure outing, my princess.'

She lost her smile and her eyes narrowed to slits in sudden anger. 'I had hoped for better coming from you, Prince Jatal.'

He raised his hands in surrender. 'My apologies. I am aware that you have gone on raids and bloodied your sword. It is just . . . this will be different.'

'It will be the same. Only differing in scale.'

He tilted his head in acceptance. 'Let us hope. Yet I have my reservations.'

As she drew close he dismounted so as not to tower over her. For while they might carry titles of equality among the Adwami, Jatal knew of their differing status: he was one prince of many, and the least, while she was the one and only princess of the Vehajarwi.

Close to her now, and they all alone – a scandalous breach of decorum – Jatal could not help but notice the heady smell of her sweat mixed with jasmine perfume, her proud chin, and the dark eyes which held the teasing knowledge that she too understood the complexities of their . . . predicament.

'I have heard much of you, Prince Jatal,' she said, the teasing even more pronounced.

'And I of you, Princess.'

She laughed. 'How I bedevil my father and am the weeping shame of my family, no doubt.'

'Not at all. I hear how every family envies the Vehajarwi for the strength, bravery and beauty of its daughters.'

Now she laughed in earnest, waggling a finger. 'I was warned against you. They say you are so learned and cunning you could talk a lizard out of its tail.'

'Yet I doubt anyone could outwit you, Princess.'

'Poet and diplomat they say, as well. Is it true you had outlander tutors?'

He bowed. 'Yes. Travellers and castaways from other lands. As a lesser son, it was the wish of my father that I gather knowledge to serve as adviser to my elder brothers.'

'As if they would listen to any younger brother – hmm?'

Jatal cocked a brow. No one had ever put it quite so bluntly to him before. 'Well . . . yes. There is that.'

'I do apologize, Jatal. But I've met some of them. And so, as I said . . . I am very glad you were sent.'

Jatal had to clear his throat. 'Princess . . . you honour me to no end. And perhaps you had best ride back before we are seen.'

Andanii swept her arms out wide and turned full circle. 'But why, after I have gone to such trouble to meet you alone?' And she laughed again, a hand at her mouth. 'If only you could see your face right now!'

For his part Jatal was struggling to think. Trouble? To meet *him*? Whatever for? What could she want? Were they not enemies? The Vehajarwi were the only extended clan that could rival his. For generations they had taken opposing sides in all the standing vendettas and feuds. 'I am sorry, Princess,' he finally managed, 'but you have the advantage of me.'

Eyes downcast, Andanii brushed a hand through the leaves of a nearby sapling. 'You or I could never truly meet or talk there within the column, could we? We are both bound by tradition and history and the confines of our roles. I watched while the cringing Lesser families approached you swearing their loyalty. I know because they came to me as well. As if they could make a gift of what is owed to us in any case!'

Jatal disagreed with the sentiment but nodded his understanding anyway. 'It is an old story.'

'Exactly! I almost cry my frustration to think of it!' She stopped then, as if reconsidering saying more, and instead mounted her handsome pale mare. 'All I ask, Jatal, is that when this tradition-breaking raid is done and the rewards apportioned, you consider what more could be yours – should you and I agree to put aside even more of the traditions that have hobbled our two families.' And before he could close his gaping mouth she snapped her reins to urge her mount into motion. His parting vision was of one last look backwards, her hair streaming about her face like a scarf, and the teasing smile once more at her lips.

Jatal stood immobile for a very long time indeed. A scattering of sand announced a spiny lizard scampering over one of his boots. He'd heard the foreign word 'poleaxed' and now he believed he finally understood. What Andanii proposed – *proposed!* – amounted to nothing less than the union of their two families. A union through their betrothal.

Now a strange dizziness assaulted him, and not just from the consideration of her obvious charms. Should they succeed in such a plan all the Adwami lands would be theirs. Only the total combined forces of all the rest of the families could possibly oppose them. And knowing the Adwami as he did, the possibility of such a grand alliance was virtually nil. As his foreign tutors had taught him of realpolitik: in such cases what usually happens is that a third of the remaining families will come out against, justly fearing the looming hegemony; another third will temporize, waiting to see which side appears to be gaining the upper hand; while the remaining third will overtly oppose yet at the same time send secret envoys pledging their loyalty in return for positions of preference in the coming hegemony. Apparently, such a sad tally was how things shook themselves out everywhere, not just among the patchwork of traditional hatreds, alliances and ongoing feuds that was Adwami politics.

He mounted absentmindedly, almost blind to his immediate surroundings, and urged Ash back south. As the shadows gathered among the walls of the canyons around him a further insight from Andanii's words struck him like a wash of cold rain.

His brothers. She said she'd met a few and was glad *he'd* been sent.

Meaning . . . what? That he was unlike them.

Meaning that . . . she might have made the same proposal to one or more of them.

And they had turned her down.

He reeled in his saddle then, fighting the revolted convulsion of his stomach. *Gods of our ancestors! Was that the way of it?* Who was in the right? Were his elder brothers correct to have spurned her as an enemy? Was he the weak-willed puppet to deliver the Hafinaj into the hands of the Vehajarwi?

Or was it the reverse? They the mulish slaves to tradition, blind to daring new opportunities?

Ash, his favourite, sensed his inattention and slowed to a halt. Jatal pressed a sleeve against his chilled sweaty brow. *Ye gods . . . that is the problem, isn't it? How can one ever be certain which is the case?*

*   *   *

In the dim light of the morning Murk warmed his aching bones at one of the driftwood fires the mercenary troops had thrown together. From his years of travel with an army it occurred to him that these warm lands always had the coldest nights. That just wasn't fair at all. A passing mercenary pressed a stoneware mug of steaming tea into his hand and this small act confirmed his suspicions regarding this band: imperial veterans all, cashiered or deserted. The experienced troopers always took care of the mage cadre. That, he realized, was his and Sour's position once again. Back to their second career. Such regard came with obligations, though. Always an even trade. Maybe this lot were Fourth or Eighth Army. If they'd been Fifth he'd know them. Or they'd know him.

Sour appeared, groaning and snuffling. Another mug of tea appeared for him. Their employer walked up soon after. To Murk's satisfaction she looked rather less elegantly made up today. Her long dark hair was braided and pulled back tight. And she now wore a much more functional leather gambeson. Her tall leather boots had lost their polish. The labours of yesterday also showed in the dark circles under her eyes, her lined brow and her squinting pinched expression.

With typical imperiousness she curtly waved them to her.

'Bad feelings 'bout this,' Sour murmured under his breath.

'You know,' Murk answered, suddenly sick of his friend's constant single note, 'one of these days – why don't you try surprising me?'

That silenced the squat bandy-legged fellow for a time. Until he rubbed dirty fingers on his brow leaving a long soot smear and cocked his head, puzzled. 'Like how?'

Yusen joined them, and again Murk had to suppress an urge to salute. The captain wore an iron helmet complete with nasal bar and a long blackened camail that hung to his shoulders. A banded iron hauberk, mail skirting and greaves completed his gear. The shaded pale eyes holding on Spite did not appear pleased. She nodded to him and he raised a hand in the Malazan sign: *move out*.

The troopers all about grunted, rising, and heaved up their packs of gear. Murk noted that almost all were accoutred as heavy infantry, with large shields, short thrusting weapons and crossbows. They appeared to move together as an experienced unit. A mercenary troop of cashiered vets all from the same division? What was the likelihood of that?

Their employer motioned for him and Sour to accompany her.

'What's up, Miss Spite?' Sour asked.

Her smoky gaze slid sideways to the poor fellow and Murk winced at the heat of that glare.

'It's what's *down*, actually.'

'Oh?' Murk asked, as if disinterested. 'What?'

'Us.'

Sour's face wrinkled up all puzzled once more. Then he scowled. 'I don't like the—'

Murk threw up a hand for silence. 'We didn't sign up for some sort of tomb robbery.'

The dismissive gaze shifted to him and Murk was startled to glimpse for an instant how the pupils churned like liquid magma only to flit to black once again in a blink. 'You signed up with me, little man, and that is that.' She smiled a straight savage slash. 'You do as I say or I'll hunt you down and slit you open like a pig, yes?'

He inclined his head in acceptance of the warning. 'Yes, ma'am.'

Sour shot him his *I told you so* look.

As they tramped between the rows of stone pillars, the barrier Spite raised yesterday hove into view flickering and shimmering ahead. Sour's gaze moved significantly to the mercenaries following along. Murk knew the Warren-laid barrier of wards and snares was invisible to them and that without warning they would walk right into it: to their deaths if Spite had woven it so. Of course, she wouldn't have brought them all this distance only to slay them, but still he couldn't help holding his breath and stiffening as they all passed through the barrier. Within lay the inner ring of the standing dolmens and the flat central plaza of featureless white sand and gravel.

She turned to Yusen. 'Start your soldiers digging around the bases of these pillars.' He nodded and went to organize his troop. 'You two. You're with me.'

'Yes, your Spitefulness,' Sour answered.

Her response was a humourless predatory smile. She led them aside then snapped out an arm to indicate the plain of coarse sands. 'You two are supposed to be thieves – find me a way into that.'

'Yes, ma'am,' Murk answered before his partner could come out with something else.

She stalked off. Murk sat himself down against a dolmen. Sour took another one, grumbling under his breath. 'Knew we shouldn't a taken the damned job.'

'Kind of late now, mister prescient.'

'You want my help or not?'

'You know the drill.'

Sour kept grumbling but crossed his legs and rested his arms on his lap, squinting his eyes closed. Murk drove himself to likewise relax, though it was a forced sort of poise, the kind that usually accompanied the tension of battle. 'Forced calm', the magery schools called it. An acquired skill necessary for any battle mage. When his mind had stilled sufficiently he summoned his Warren and opened his eyes to regard the location through Meanas.

And almost walked away right then and there.

'*Queen's tits!*' Sour grunted next to him.

Murk growled his awed assent. Before them the inner circular plaza of sand was not the flat calm it appeared in the mundane world. The pit, for it was a pit – a hole that opened on to the bottomless Abyss itself – roiled and stirred, agitated by something contained within. But that was as nothing compared to the storm of Warren-energies that lanced and flickered about the construct in a near-constant release of deadly charges. Coiled lightning-like ropes sizzled and whipped, anchored from each and every standing dolmen, and converged on whatever lay ensnared, imprisoned, at the very centre.

'Do you know what this is . . .' Sour murmured beneath his breath as if afraid to mention it aloud even here within a Warren.

'Yes.' Neither of them had ever seen one, of course. But among mages they were legendary. What they were looking at was a Chaining. A prison constructed by an assemblage of the world's most powerful practitioners of any one age: Ascendants, mages, some say even gods themselves. All to contain the various scattered fragments of the Shattered God – not coincidentally also known as the Chained God.

'We ain't up to this,' Sour hissed, and for once Murk heartily agreed. 'We are pissing in too many ponds.'

'Yeah . . . I get it.'

'Gonna get our—'

'*Yes!* All right! Trying to think here.' *Could just sneak in and out. No need to broadcast. These constructs ain't made to keep things out. Rather the reverse, in actual fact.* 'What does the queen of soothsayers say?'

'Doesn't like me being here.'

'That's it? Nothing stronger?'

Vexation glowed from the presence of his partner. 'What'd you mean? We're all free to do as we choose! None of us is slaves. What about Ammanas?'

'Same,' Murk answered, his thoughts elsewhere. 'Could put the boot to this right now if he wanted . . . so, either he approves, or, like you said . . . we really are free to choose . . .'

'I think your boy just plans for everything,' Sour grumbled, 'that's what I think.'

'As if yours doesn't.'

'I think she just makes it her business to know the players and follows the odds.'

'That doesn't sound so reverent.'

'She never asked for no worship.'

Murk grunted his assent then cleared his throat. 'Well, that's enough hemming and hawing, don't you think?'

Sour stood, stretching. 'Yeah, s'pose so . . .'

'Let's have a look.' Following the paths of Shadow, Murk stepped into the construct. As was their usual arrangement, his partner monitored his progress by way of the Warren of Thyr. Murk carefully edged between the twisting coiled power 'chains' where they spread to be anchored at each dolmen. Touching one, he knew, would diffuse him into nothingness. He walked a full circuit of the construct.

For an instant he froze as a new vision out of Meanas superimposed itself upon the scene before him: that of another, similar construct, its enormous fetters lying shattered before dissolving to be swept away as if by some unseen wind. It took a moment for him to gather his composure after that, but eventually he managed to calm his pulse enough to continue on.

He returned to Sour and the two shared a nod of understanding. They lowered their Warrens and went to find Spite.

She was squatting, her back to them, next to a pit dug around one of the dolmens. Murk heard a whimper from Sour where he stood with his knuckles jammed into his mouth. Murk resisted elbowing the man: the sweeping double curve presented *was* breathtaking.

She straightened, facing them, brushing the sand from her hands. 'Well?'

'You can get in,' Murk said, 'but can you get out?'

'You leave that to me.'

'What's with the digging?'

'Have to break the bindings.'

Murk shook a negative. 'No. It's suspended over the Abyss. Break the bonds and it's lost for ever.'

The rumbling growl that escaped Spite did not sound human. Murk felt the tiny hairs of his forearms straightening in atavistic fear.

'It's like one of them trick musical instruments,' Sour said.

Both Murk and Spite eyed the squat fellow with his matted unwashed hair, scrunched-up frog-face, and one squinted eye higher than the other. 'A what?' Murk asked.

'A conun-drum,' he said with a grin.

Murk stared anew, studying the man. *By all the gods . . . sometimes I wonder, I really do.*

Spite's eyes seethed now, almost roiling with a deep crimson glow as she regarded the plaza. 'What if we left two in place? I might manage against two.'

Murk tilted his head, considering. 'Maybe. Opposite tendrils.'

'Yes, good. Can you break the bonds?'

'Have to give a look. Sour here might be better at that than I.'

Her scepticism couldn't have been more obvious. 'Really? Well, get to it.'

'Yes, ma'am.'

After Spite stalked off Yusen approached. 'What's the word?'

'Sour and I are gonna give the dolmens a poke.' The man's frowned disapproval vexed Murk. 'What did you expect? You took the job.'

'I'll earn my pay, mage. Don't have to like it.'

'Yeah, well, life's tough all over.'

A ghost of a smile flitted across the officer's face. 'That's my line.' He gestured to nearby troopers. 'Ostler, Tanner, Dee . . . you're with these two.'

That's better. We ain't dead yet.

*   *   *

The view from one of the windows of the Dead House offered a prospect on the harbour and the dark waters of Malaz Bay beyond. Osserc preferred this view. Such a preference was, he could admit, all too human of him. He had slipped now into his elder, slimmer version of the Tiste form. He allowed himself such an indulgence, for, having succeeded in one long-blunted ambition, that of penetrating the Azath, he now felt another all too human emotion . . . that of a vague troubling dissatisfaction.

He let out a long breath, sending cobwebs fluttering across the glazing. Now he must face the mountain of smugness waiting downstairs and sit himself before him and endure the predictable ritual of the petitioner before the possessor.

It was, to be frank, all too exquisitely distasteful. And he would rather die. Almost.

His mouth hardening, he turned. Enough. The inevitable awaits, as it so prosaically does. And he would face it. Was that not his strength? Accepting what must come – what cannot be avoided? So he had thought . . . once.

The stairs creaked beneath his feet. In the main hall the only source of light was a fire burning in a stone hearth at one end. At the long battered main table waited the House's current . . . what? Resident? Custodian? Curator? Curse? Or just plain servant? He did not know, not having been accepted among the Azath in the usual manner. As was his manner. Not the usual, that is.

All the appearance was, of course, an illusion – only the inner essence being real. He regarded the fellow hunched at the table, amber firelight flickering from coarse iron-grey hair, lined green-tinged skin and prominent thrusting tusks. A Jaghut, and not just any Jaghut. Gothos himself, hoary old teller of tales and self-appointed judge of all. Once known, appropriately enough, as the Lord of Hate.

He sat opposite. The figure did not stir, though Osserc glimpsed the shimmer of light within the eyes hidden by their cascade of wiry hair. Osserc crossed his legs, set one hand atop the other on one knee, and exhaled a long tired breath.

The two regarded one another in silence for some time after that exhalation. The fire continued to burn, though neither stirred to feed it. At length Osserc inhaled through his nose and plucked a bit of dust from his trousers. 'Is this all there is, then,' he offered as a statement. 'Disappointing.'

Gothos' habitual sour expression deepened even further. '*You* disappoint *me*. How conceited to think that existence should arrange itself merely to be interesting to you.'

Osserc clenched his teeth so tightly he heard them creak. After a time he managed to loosen his jaws enough to grate his answer. 'Such was not my expectation, I assure you. Yet still. One must admit to the . . . mundaneness of it.'

Now the wide hunched shoulders fell even further and Gothos slouched back against the high-backed chair. He shook his head in exaggerated frustration. 'The mere fact that you sought does not somehow call into being that which you sought. Or imply that there should be anything *to* seek at all. Typical backwards thinking.' A clawed hand rose to wave as if dispersing smoke or fumes. 'Positing a question does not magically create an answer.'

Lips tight, Osserc snapped his gaze to the murky ceiling. His entwined clenched fingers shook until they became numb. Eventually he mastered himself enough to clear his throat and say, slow and thick, 'You try my patience, Gothos.'

Now a one-sided smile crept up the Jaghut's lips and the hidden gaze seemed to sharpen. 'Really? I rather hoped to break it.'

'Break it? Or exhaust it?'

A slow shrug of the shoulders. 'The choice is yours – as the way out is through me.'

'Through you? You mean that to leave I must twist your arm, or some such childishness?'

Gothos inspected the blackened nails of one hand, each broken and striated. 'If that is the best you can think of . . . but I'd rather hoped for more from you. But be that as it may. The way is open. You may go whenever you should choose. As has been the case since you entered, of course. However . . .' and he shrugged again.

Osserc's answering smile was as brittle as old dead branches. 'I see. I may go . . . but without any answers.' Gothos merely stared back. Osserc settled into his chair. Once more he eased his hands one on the top of the other over his crossed legs. 'I understand. We must face one another until you relinquish what you know. Very well. You were foolish to enter into this with me, Gothos. The will of any other you would crush. But not mine.'

To this Gothos, as was his wont, gave no answer.

The fire continued to burn though neither stirred to feed it.

*   *   *

The great lumbering beast that was the army of the Thaumaturgs lurched onward, threading east through the jagged mounts that stood like rotten bones from the forest canopy, and Cohort Leader Pon-lor watched it go.

After the ordered columns of soldiers came the roped human chains of bearers, their feet great lumps of black mud, hunched almost double beneath their massive loads, hands clutching the cloth bindings that supported the fat baskets and boxes and ran round as tumplines to their heads. Then came the supply train of carts and further bearers and labourers, all conveying the necessary materiel and services of an army on the march in hostile territory: the small portable smithies, the various messes, the infirmaries, and behind them yet more tramping bearers bringing along even further materiel and supplies. With this sauntering mass came a second army – the camp followers. Wives and husbands and children of officers and soldiers, and surgeons and clerks and tradesmen. Plus their mistresses and prostitutes. And their soothsayers, petty traders and merchants, unsanctioned private healers, minor apothecaries, arrack and palm-wine tappers, professional gamblers, singers, dancers and thieves.

Last to disappear up the broad mud-churned track to be swallowed into the jungle's hanging fat leaves went the great groaning siege wains, oxen-pulled, their tall wheels of solid wood levered along by hunched slaves and labourers, mud-smeared, straining and chanting in unison.

For the first time in his life Pon-lor was left entirely in charge. It struck him as exhilarating and terrifying all at once. Exhilarating to finally be out from the suffocating fist of his superiors; to have the opportunity to prove his competence or perhaps, more important, his reliability. Terrifying for the now very real prospect of failure and disappointing said superiors.

He drew his robes about himself and nodded to Overseer Tun to see to the arrangement of his troops. The overseer bowed in his iron-studded leather armour and set to kicking and cajoling the soldiers into column. Pon-lor took his place at the centre of the column. The train of his troops' bearers followed at the rear beneath their loads of equipment and supplies.

For three days they backtracked the route the army had hacked through the jungle. The way was a mire of trampled paths. They filed through abandoned villages where all was ghostly quiet but for the calls of birds and the hooting of monkeys, the inhabitants having fled with food and valuables to avoid confiscation and impressment.

On the third day word came to him from Overseer Tun at the van: a civilian had approached wishing to speak to him and was being brought. Pon-lor cast about and spotted the impressive broad trunk of an ancient kapok tree from which vines hung like a collection of ropes and whose roots gripped the jungle floor like the fists of giants. He chose to receive the fellow while standing beneath it, his men arrayed around him.

Tun pushed the fellow down on to his knees and he bowed, head lowered, arms straight forward in obeisance. 'What is your name, peasant?' Pon-lor asked.

'Jak, Great Lord Thaumaturg.'

'And you would speak with me?'

'Yes, Great Lord.'

'You realize that if you are wasting my time you will be killed.'

'Yes, Lord Thaumaturg.'

Pon-lor was intrigued to see that this pronouncement had not evoked the usual shudder and tightness of voice that it did from other peasants. He stepped closer and saw that the fellow was young, probably new to his twenties – much like himself. He also noted that the man's shirt and trousers betrayed the wear pattern of having lain under armour; that the man's belt was scraped where a sheath would hang; and that his hair was pressed and rubbed away in places as if habitually beneath a helmet.

'You are a deserter.'

This evoked a satisfying squirm and abject writhing in the rotting humus and mud. 'No, m'lord. A private guard and bounty man.'

'You have papers?'

'Yes, m'lord.'

The man reached for his neck but Tun slapped the hand away and yanked free the pouch that hung there, snapping its leather thong. He knelt, proffering it in both hands. Pon-lor opened the pouch and studied the cheap reed-paper certificates. Water-smeared and half rotten, they might have been valid, years ago. He handed the documents to Tun. 'These have long expired. Private guard, you say? For whom?'

'Khun-Sen, lord.'

Pon-lor was quite surprised. 'Khun-Sen? The warlord? He is still alive?'

'Yes, lord.'

The news seemed hard to credit; that old general had been exiled in his grandfather's time. Some sort of political falling-out among the Circle of Masters. He'd fled to the border region and claimed an outpost in the mountains. 'You are far from Chanar Keep and Sen has no business interfering in Thaumaturg lands.'

'He does not seek any influence, m'lord.'

'Yet here you are – with a band of men, no doubt. Taking advantage of the army's passage to raid a few villages?'

'No, lord. We are collecting recruits for the army.'

'To sell to the army, you mean. Very well. Have you a message from Sen?'

'No, lord. But—'

'No? No message? Then you *are* wasting my time.' He waved for

101

Tun to take the man away. 'This one will now follow all those whom he has sent ahead into the ranks, Overseer. No doubt they will be pleased to see him.'

'Yes, lord.' Tun yanked the man up by his shirt.

'We were attacked by a witch!' the fellow gasped, now upright and glaring furiously. 'A servant of the Night-Queen.' Remembering his place he quickly lowered his gaze.

Pon-lor stepped even closer to peer down at the much shorter young man. *A witch. So that's what this is all about. They have some poor village woman they hope to sell as a witch.* He made a show of sighing his utter lack of interest and clasped his hands at his back. 'Believe me, fool. If you had met a servant of the demoness you would be either dead or insane. I do not have the time for a court of inquiry. You'll just have to let the old woman go back to selling her moss-unguents and d'bayang tea.' He waved to Tun, who smacked the pommel of his sword across the man's head, sending him face first into the mud.

He stopped short as the fellow spoke from the muck. His voice was slow and tight with suppressed rage. 'You will be interested in this witch, I think . . . Magister.' Pon-lor turned: the man was actually levering himself up to his hands and knees. Tun stood over him, sword raised, a brow cocking a question.

Pon-lor raised a hand for a halt. 'Very well. You wish me to ask . . . why?'

'Because this one,' the man coughed and brought his hand away from his head, red and wet with blood, 'has enslaved a yakshaka soldier.'

After a long pause Pon-lor said, 'That is impossible.' Tun swung the sword up to finish the man but another curt sign halted the execution. 'You realize that if you cannot support this claim you will be slain?'

'Yes, lord.'

'And so what happened?'

The man straightened, wincing and touching gingerly at his head. 'The witch escaped us through the use of her arts and her yakshaka guard.'

'I see. She escaped you. How unfortunate. Is it too much to expect that you can produce witnesses to these events?'

'There are witnesses, Magister. I can lead you to where it happened.'

'Very well. You will do so. And if I find that you have lied I will have you beheaded. Is that understood?'

102

The man bowed even lower. 'Yes, m'lord.'

Pon-lor turned away. Tun grabbed the fellow's arm and pulled him aside. The man kept glancing back, his gaze hardly that of a browbeaten peasant or servant, but Pon-lor did not notice. He was barely aware of his surroundings, hands clasped behind his back as he walked. His thoughts were a roil of unease. The yakshaka captured? How unlikely. Yet, if this so-called witch should succeed in fetching it to the Demon-Queen's court, all the alchemical secrets and rituals of their creation could be penetrated. This was the most deadly threat the Circle had faced in generations. If it should be true *. . . Ancient Ones, let it not be true.*

As he was being pulled along, Kenjak kept his head low and worked hard to keep the satisfied smirk from his mouth. Yet he could not help sneaking quick glances to the retreating back of this young Thaumaturg mage. He'd given his name as Jak, the true nickname of his youth, but until most recently he'd been known as Kenjak Ashevajak, the 'Bandit Lord' of the borderlands. At least until a damned witch showed up and destroyed his authority and scattered his men to the seven winds. But he would have her head and a fat bounty for it. And this upstart Thaumaturg would not come between him and any bounty. He did not fear the yakshaka: he could easily outrun those lumbering elephants. This was his gods-sent chance to avenge the insults his family had so long suffered at the hands of these self-appointed nobles and rulers. And if the witch were to die along the way, well, no matter. Imagine what the demoness Queen of the Night herself would pay for a trussed-up yakshaka warrior.

CHAPTER III

When the functionaries of this nation [the Thaumaturg] go
out in public, their insignia and the number of their attendants
are regulated according to rank. The highest dignitaries are
protected by four parasols with golden handles, the next,
two parasols with golden handles, and finally there are those
protected by a single parasol with a golden handle. Further down
the line come those permitted only parasols with silver handles.
Likewise so with their rods of office, and their palanquins . . .

Ular Takeq
Customs of Ancient Jakal-Uku

FOR SHIMMER, IT DID COME TO SEEM AS IF THEY MOVED WITHIN A
dream as the changeless days of travel upon the river slipped
from one on to the next until all became one. The unruffled
earthen-brown waters flowed beneath the ship as smoothly as if they
traversed a slide of mud. Not a breath stirred the leaden air between
the walls of verdant green where flowers blazed bright as flames.
The sails hung limp, damp and rotting. Yet the vessel moved upriver
against the sluggish current. As the days passed, the crew came to
huddle listless and dozing in the heat on the deck. They watched
with fever-glazed eyes the vine-burdened branches brushing overhead. All came to speak in hushed whispers as if afraid of breaking
the spell of stillness that hung upon the river.

As evening came on, clouds gathered as predictably as the sun's
own setting and a torrential downpour would hammer them
through the night. So dense was the warm rain that it seemed that
they had sunk into the river. Nothing of either shore could be seen
through the solid sheets. To be heard one had to press one's mouth
to another's ear. Figures would appear suddenly from the roaring

downpour, emerging like ghosts. Come the dawn the clouds would be gone as if they'd thrown themselves to the ground and the day's heat would gather like a sticky tar. Heavy mist arose to smother the river. To Shimmer it appeared so dense it could actually snag and catch at passing branches and hanging vines. Her sodden clothes gave off a vapour as if she were boiling – and she had long given up her armour as a useless rusted heap.

Throughout, she kept a wary eye on the vessel itself. At times it appeared terrifyingly derelict, as if everyone had been snatched away, or become ghosts. Its shrouds hung in loose tatters. She couldn't remember the last time she'd glimpsed a sailor among the spars or in the rigging. Yet it continued to move, silently gliding. In the dawn and dusk it resembled to her nothing more than a mist-cast shadow, or their own ghost.

One dawn she emerged from below to find the crew sprawled asleep and no one at the tiller. Of the Avowed, Cole was on watch and she spotted him standing near the bow. 'Cole,' she called. The man did not answer. 'Cole!' Still he did not respond. She crossed to his side and leaned close; he was staring down over the side at the passing blood-hued water. She reached out and gently touched his shoulder. The man slowly blinked. 'Cole? Can you hear me?' He frowned now and his gaze rose to her; for a moment he stared as if not recognizing her, then he drew a sudden breath, as if broaching a great depth.

'There are *things* in the water, Shimmer,' he pronounced as if imparting a profound secret.

'Where's the pilot – what's his name? Gods, I can't even remember his name . . .'

Blinking heavily, Cole peered about, frowning. 'I'm sorry, Shimmer – it's morning already?'

She squeezed his arm. 'It's all right. I feel it too.' She headed for the afterdeck. 'Captain! You are needed! Captain!'

The men and women of the crew stirred yet none moved to set to work. Shimmer took hold of the tiller arm. The captain arrived, unshaven, in a stained shirt that hung to his knees. He was followed by Rutana and K'azz. 'Where is the pilot, Captain?'

The man rubbed his jowls, his brows rising. 'We'll have a look for him,' and he lumbered off.

'Shimmer,' K'azz said, 'what happened?'

'I found the tiller unmanned.'

Rutana snorted at that, as if scornful.

'You have something to say?' Shimmer asked.

The woman nodded, her gaze defiant. 'We may have had a pilot, Isturé, but another has been in control of the vessel for some time.'

'Another? Who?'

Rutana smiled as she squeezed the bands indenting her upper arms. 'Ardata, of course.'

The captain reappeared. 'He's not on the ship. Must've fallen overboard. We'll have to go back to look for him.'

'We are not going back, Captain,' Rutana announced without breaking gaze with Shimmer.

'Yes, we are,' K'azz said. He motioned to Shimmer. 'Turn us round.'

She clasped both hands on the long arm of battered wood and pushed. The broad tiller swung but somehow the ship did not respond. It continued its slow sluggish advance.

Rutana's contemptuous smile climbed even higher. 'There is no turning back now, Isturé.' And she walked off.

Shimmer's gaze found K'azz, who was eyeing the tiller arm, his mouth sour and tight. 'What now?' she asked.

He drew breath to answer but a shout went up from the crow's nest. 'A village ahead! People!' The crew surged to the larboard rail. Even the crewman from the crow's nest came swinging hand over hand down the ropes. The Avowed gathered at the stern with K'azz. Banners of mist painted the river's surface and coiled along the jungle shore. Through them, Shimmer glimpsed a clearing dotted by leaf-topped huts standing on tall stilts. Figures lined the shore. Most were in loincloths and bright feathers decorated their hair and hung at arms and legs. The crewmen and women waved, shouting. 'Hello! Help! Help us! We are ensorcelled!'

'Back to work, damn you all!' the captain bellowed in answer.

'We're cursed!' one shouted and jumped overboard.

'Not a good idea . . .' Rutana warned.

The rest of the crew followed in a surge, as if terrified they would be held back. They jumped, arms waving, and splashed into the murky water to emerge blowing and gasping. The captain managed to catch one woman by the arm only to be smacked down for his trouble. He lay holding his head and groaning. The entire crew swam for the shore. Shimmer shot a questioning look to K'azz who motioned a negative. 'Let them go,' he murmured. 'Perhaps they will find their way to the coast.'

'Or perhaps they will all be eaten,' Rutana offered, laughing her harsh cackle.

K'azz faced her. 'Then see that they are not . . .'

Her hands, closed about her neck, seemed to squeeze off her laugh

106

in a hiss. She jerked her head to Nagal at the bow. The big man climbed up among the loose rotten rigging and yelled to the shore in a language Shimmer had never heard before. A banner of mist wafted across the river and the bank and when it had passed the figures were gone, disappearing as if they had never been.

'Thank you,' K'azz said.

But Rutana only sneered and turned away.

Through the scarves of fog Shimmer caught glimpses of the crew dragging themselves up the muddy shore and running into the jungle. Then a curve in the river's course carried them from sight. She turned to K'azz. Their commander had a hand on the tiller arm, which jerked this way and that, yet to no apparent shift in the vessel's course. 'What is it?' she asked.

He shook his head as if awakening from a reverie and his gaze jerked from hers – as if terrified, she thought. *Terrified of what? Our situation? Or of what he may reveal?*

'A lesson here, Shimmer,' he murmured, his mouth tight. 'One can squirm and fight against it, but everyone is drawn inexorably along to the fate awaiting them.'

'I don't believe in that self-serving predestiny justification that religions flog.'

He nodded his understanding and she was struck by how skull-like his features appeared. 'Well, let us call it a natural proclivity then,' and he offered a smile that struck her as heart-achingly sad. 'No one's alone from now on,' he called, raising his voice. 'Watches at all times. A mage on each watch.'

Shimmer saluted. 'Yes, Commander.'

Yet the spell that clung over the river and surrounding impenetrable walls of forest somehow made the distinction of being on or off watch irrelevant. Shimmer, and, as it seemed, the rest of them, found it increasingly difficult to sleep. She would lie only to stare at the damp mouldering wood unable to slip into any dreams. And so she would arise and go above and here she would find the majority of the party, eyes on the river or passing shores, silent and watchful, like a standing troop of mist-shrouded statues.

She saw, or thought she saw, bizarre creatures among the branches of the trees: enormous vultures and bats the size of people, hanging upside down. On the shore one of the long-snouted alligator-like creatures that swam along pacing the vessel heaved itself up on the mud slope and she was only mildly surprised to see it stand erect on two thick trunk-like legs, a wide pale belly hanging over a bare crotch. It followed them with its unblinking baleful eyes.

At one point she found herself next to Gwynn, the one-time mage of First Company, Skinner's command, and she asked him, 'Was this how it was when you were last here?'

The man shook himself, rubbing his eyes and frowning. 'We weren't here, Shimmer. We stayed on the south coast. It was pleasant there – much cooler.'

'You didn't travel through the countryside?'

The man laughed and waved to the shore. 'Gods, no.'

'Not to Jakal Viharn?'

'No. Never been.'

The news startled Shimmer so much that she had a hard time comprehending it. She felt that it ought to alarm her, but for some reason all she could summon was a vague unease. 'You haven't . . . But I thought . . . I'm sorry. I thought you had.'

'Skinner has.' Then Gwynn ran a hand over his sweat-matted pale hair and frowned as if chasing after a thought. 'At least he was gone for much of the time . . . We simply assumed he was with her.'

'You never asked him about it – about the city?'

'No.'

Shimmer found that difficult to believe. 'Really? No one asked about Jakal Viharn? Not even once?'

Gwynn cocked his head, the edge of his mouth quirking up. 'One does not ask personal questions of Skinner.'

Ah. There is that. She knew that some people were just naturally less forthcoming or prone to talk about themselves than others. And Skinner even less so than most. He'd always been silent regarding anything other than the business at hand. He'd become utterly closed to her before the end.

Now Shimmer frowned, thinking, for it seemed so very difficult in this choking thick air. 'Well, then, why don't we travel by Warren?'

Gwynn rubbed a finger along the knife-edge bridge of his great hooked nose. 'Jakal cannot be found via the Warrens. Ardata has seen to that. She *allows* you to enter. This time she sent a boat.'

'Why?'

'I do not know. A demonstration, perhaps?'

'Perhaps.' Shimmer tried to think through to the hidden motive behind the choice but couldn't come up with any definitive possibility, and so instead she let it lie to be answered later and returned to watching the thick reddish-brown flow coiling and ribboning beneath them.

What she did come to understand was the spell, or sensation, she and her brother and sister Avowed were experiencing. She wasn't certain where the answer came from; perhaps from a waking dream she had when the deck appeared populated by all the fallen Avowed brethren interspersed with the living, all journeying to their unknown destination on the river. And it struck her that this *timelessness* was a sensation she'd known before. Over these last few years it had been growing, ebbing and waning, yet always abiding just beneath the surface of her awareness. It was – perhaps – an artefact of the Vow they had all sworn together.

And now this land, Jacuruku, seemed to somehow intensify it . . . or perhaps the word she was looking for was exacerbate. Or aggravate? In any case, it was not entirely imposed from without and so she tried to let slip away her almost constant state of heightened anxiety.

She was, unfortunately, premature in that choice.

It began as a noise, a loud thrumming or hissing. It seemed to be coming from all around. Rutana, Shimmer noted, ran to the bow to stand tall, peering to the right and left.

'What is it?' K'azz called to the woman.

She shook her head. 'I cannot be sure . . .'

'Look there,' Amatt called, pointing ahead upriver.

A cloud was approaching, skimming the dark bronze surface of the river, stretching from one shore to the other. Within the haze of the cloud a blinding iridescent storm of colours flashed and glimmered. Shimmer winced, shading her gaze. 'What is it?' she called to Rutana, just as K'azz had.

The woman just shook her head as she stepped down from the railing as if retreating. 'I do not know.'

The cloud engulfed them, flowing around the vessel. Her vision of either shore was lost in a hurricane of lustrous rainbow-like flashing. Blinking, Shimmer was astonished to find herself surrounded by hundreds of darting and rushing hummingbirds. The blinding colours came from their feathers, which held a metallic iridescence of every hue.

They hove in close to her face as if inspecting her. Their wings churned as near invisible blurs. She didn't like the glow of their tiny red eyes and she gently waved them aside. 'What is this?' she called to Rutana. She had to shout to be heard above the combined roaring of the thousands of whirring wings.

The woman might have answered but Shimmer did not hear as one of the hummingbirds suddenly darted forward and thrust its long needle-like beak into her neck. She flinched and reflexively grabbed hold of the tiny bundle of feathers and threw it to the deck. 'The damned thing stabbed me!' she yelled, more surprised than hurt.

Grunts of shock and annoyance sounded all around as the Avowed waved their arms through the eddying clouds of birds. Then, all at once, as if at a given order, the birds crowded close all about Shimmer, jamming so tight they blotted out the day. Stiletto beaks thrust for her eyes, her neck, and clawed feet scratched for purchase on her ears. She covered her face to spin left and right but the mass of birds followed, stabbing her. She ran into someone, his face a steaming wet mask of blood, who howled. A scream sounded and a splash as someone fell or jumped into the river. She heard Nagal's bull voice shouting in that strange language, then K'azz bellowing: 'Gwynn!'

An eruption of power swiped her to the slick decking where she slammed into the side. Groggy, she fumbled for a grip to pull herself up. The hummingbirds were gone, as was what was left of the sails, and even the upper masts had been sheared away. On the deck only Gwynn and Nagal remained standing; all others had been pushed to the sides in a circle outwards from the mage in black. Something hit the deck at Shimmer's feet. A dead hummingbird. It lay dull and lustreless now, so tiny. She peered up. Others fell all about. A pattering rainbow deluge of dead birds. Most struck the river, slightly behind, as the vessel continued its unhurried advance. She limped to where Rutana was straightening to her feet.

'And just what in the name of Hood was that?' she snarled.

The woman gave another of her uncaring shrugs. Shimmer noted that she was completely untouched; not one cut or jab marked her face or hands. 'An inhabitant of Himatan, like any other.'

'D'ivers?'

Again the indifferent shrug. 'Of a kind. The forest is full of many such creatures. Here you will find all the old things that once walked the earth before you humans came.'

'Well . . . you could have warned us.'

She laughed, waving a hand to dismiss her. 'Even I have seen only a fraction of that which exists within these leagues,' she said, and walked away.

Shimmer cast about for K'azz, to find him at the stern where he and others had thrown a rope to Cole, who had jumped overboard and now swam after the lumbering ship. Beneath the tiller arm lay the captain, dead, his eye sockets bloody and empty, his throat a torn gaping wound.

K'azz joined her to regard the captain. He motioned to Turgal nearby. 'Find some cloth.' He saluted and headed for the companionway.

Sighing, Shimmer raised her gaze to the shore. Hidden animals still roared and hooted in the distance in answer to Gwynn's great blast of power. Masses of strange birds churned, flapping their huge ungainly wings over the ragged treetops. *You humans*, the woman had said. *You humans.*

Shimmer drew a hand down her slick hot face; it came away wet with blood that dripped from her palm to the decking. She felt a terrible foreboding that somehow they were never going to get out of this jungle.

*   *   *

Of course a Hood-damned storm would gather as he and Sour unravelled the last of the chains coupled to their dolmen anchors. Only four now remained, each at a compass point, and beneath the centre of the plaza the *thing* this entire installation was constructed to contain jerked and struggled like a gaffed dhenrabi the size of a war galley. Murk gestured his disgust to the massed black clouds blotting the night sky as the wind, the discharge of thunder, and the combers crashing into the shore made conversation almost impossible. From where he crouched next to the dolmen, Sour caught the wave and answered with the expression he was named for. Rain pelted down but at least it was warm rain, not like the freezing sleet of north Genabackis. Yusen emerged from the sheets to lean close to Murk.

'Now?' he asked.

Murk nodded and raised a hand in the *mount up* sign. Yusen gave a curt jerk of his head and went to his men, signing orders. Murk found Sour's squinted gaze and they turned to where Spite sat cross-legged facing the plaza, her back blade-rigid. Sour gestured him over and now Murk gave a sour look, but he went.

Kneeling next to the woman the first thing he noticed was the heat. The great fat raindrops actually hissed to steam as they touched her shoulders and hair. Her gaze was locked ahead, the eyes an eerie all-carmine that churned like flame. 'Which one next?' he shouted.

The eyes did not shift, did not so much as blink while Murk waited. Silent, the woman extended an arm to point opposite. Murk grunted his understanding and retreated to Sour.

'Across the way,' he told Sour, then signed to Yusen.

Sour packed up his sodden leather satchel of shells, bits of wood,

111

and other found bric-a-brac that he used to somehow 'read' the maze they faced. A team of five mercenaries led by the three big swordsmen Ostler, Tanner and Dee jogged up to join them, plus the silent scout Sweetly and the lieutenant, a Seven Cities native, to judge by her sharp coffee-hued features beneath a bright domed helmet woven round by a cord of yellow silk.

He and Sour started tracing the border of the plaza. The team spread out round them. When they reached the dolmen Sour clambered down into the excavation pit and laid out his satchel. Murk crouched, peering down. The rain dripped from his nose and snaked down his ankles. The squat little fellow studied the base of the dolmen for a time. He picked up the bits and pieces he'd gathered together and let them fall on the soaked leather. This pattern he studied for a while. Then, as before, he raised his Thyr Warren and reached in towards the pulsing cable of power wound about the stone to manipulate it as one might a knot or trick puzzle. Murk had no idea how the unimpressive fellow managed it. He definitely was no bright spark; wordplay blew right past him; and he could be as slow as the son of the village idiot. It must be instinctive – that was the only explanation Murk could think of. A freak talent like that old man he'd heard tell of that the prince of Anklos kept in his court who could give you the day's date in any calendrical system you would care to mention.

Murk had his own Warren at his fingertips and so he saw when the bound energies tore free of the dolmen like a whip and snapped Sour backwards with a crack that echoed from every stone. He ran to where the fellow lay immobile, his chest steaming in the rain, and tapped one unshaven cheek with the back of a hand. 'Sour? You with us?'

The fellow coughed and Murk caught a whiff of rotten breath and turned his head aside. He stood and prodded the man with a toe. 'You all right?'

Sour nodded, blinking as the rain pattered down into his eyes. 'Got a kick like a mule.'

'Yeah, well. You should stop getting intimate with them.'

The fellow peered around confused then screwed up his eyes to squint. 'But I never have . . .'

'Never mind.' He reached out a hand and Sour took it. Murk pulled him upright. 'Last one.'

Sour frowned, then brightened. 'Oh, yeah.'

Murk signed to their bodyguard mercs. Sour went to collect his gear.

This time either Sour got it just right, or was more careful. In any case the sizzling band of power slipped away as easily as a released fishing line and he grinned up at his partner like the naughty boy who'd let it go. 'Damn good,' Murk said, hands on his knees. 'Let's see Miss Nibs.'

Spite was standing when they found her in the sleeting rain. A steady pounding announced the surf crashing on to the nearby strand. Something seemed to echo that pulse from within the roiling gravel of the plaza. 'You will aid me,' she told them without so much as turning her head.

'Yes,' Murk answered – though he didn't think they could contribute much of anything.

Spite simply stepped forward to sink straight down into the gravel as if it were a pool. In a panic, Murk struggled to follow her through his Warren. He found her approaching the small object at the centre of the installation where it jumped and kicked very much like that proverbial hooked fish; except that the power this captive bled would've boiled off any lake. Held only by the remaining two chains of woven potency it swung wildly now, hissing through the gravel as if the tons of stone did not exist. Spite closed warily, her hands raised.

Murk had no idea what her plan was – but he most certainly did not expect her to simply snatch out and grab hold of the thing as it swung by. The resulting explosion of energy tore through the plaza. In that curious double image available to a mage viewing a scene through both his Warren and his mundane vision, Murk watched the underside of the gravel plaza sear and boil even as the surface erupted upwards, sending the mercenaries running and ducking under their shields.

Murk reduced his Warren-sensitivity against the roaring forge-like energies. He saw that whereas Sour had applied an uncanny delicacy of manipulation to undoing the bonds, Spite was all pure force and overwhelming power. Spite, it seemed, possessed no subtlety whatsoever. The rock-grinding might being brought to bear made Murk's teeth ache.

'Like some damned Ascendant!' Sour yelled next to his ear. Murk nodded his appalled agreement. 'Ever hear of any one of these Chainings being broken?' Murk shook his head.

Then with a crack as of a stone cleaving, it was done. The two remaining bonds sizzled, swinging and snapping loose like whips. Spite weakly churned a path through the gravel, making for them. She held something that was painful to look at through his Warren.

An arm broached the surface of the heated stones where the rain hissed and misted, then a head. Spite drew back her arm and heaved something towards them. Appalled, Murk watched it arc through the air. *Shit*, was all he could think. '*Don't touch it!*' he bellowed.

But everyone was half deaf from the cracks of thunder, the pounding rain and the blasts of power. One of the mercenaries reached for the object, and screamed – briefly. Murk and Sour ran for the fellow. They pushed through the gathered bodyguards to find a blackened corpse, ribcage curving up through crisped flesh, arms ending in white sintered bones, yet head and face completely unmarred. The moustached fellow looked as if he'd merely closed his eyes in sleep. The object lay within the seared carcass: a smoking casket of black stone, chased and edged in silver, like a lady's jewellery box.

'Get a pack,' Sour ordered.

Two mercenaries ran to obey. Murk noted that the man's armour was torn. *Consumed the flesh only. Gods, man, will it even be safe to carry? How to touch it?* 'Get some sticks,' he told Sweetly, who nodded.

'Murk!' Sour called from the plaza.

Standing, he told the female mercenary: 'Make a stretcher!' In the panic of the moment the woman gave a quick Malazan salute. Murk ran to his partner.

Spite lay hugging the stone lip, only her head and shoulders above the gravel. Sour knelt next to her but wasn't helping. There was something in his gaze – wonder and perhaps even a wide-eyed dread. The woman fairly glowed with power, her flesh steaming and hissing. Murk thought he caught a glimpse of rough dark-scaled features, and hands misshapen taloned claws. The eyes burned like pits of melted stone. 'You have it?' she grated.

'Yes.'

'Get me up.'

Murk held up his hands. 'We can't touch you yet . . .'

'Oh, for the love of Night! Get a sword or something!'

'Right.'

Spite jerked then, sinking to her open, surprised lips. For an instant those formidable eyes, so superior, so scornful, widened in unguarded panic. '*Oh, no . . .*' she whispered, and then she disappeared as if snatched back by some giant.

Murk switched to Meanas to see what was going on. The chains of puissance, loose and unbounded, had flailed about seeking something to latch on to, anything, and had found Spite. She fought now, caught between the two lashing tendrils of punishing powers. Even as Murk watched, she was weakening. She kicked ineffectually and struggled to summon the streams of her own Warren-energies. But she was already exhausted and now she hung limp, her arms loose and drifting.

'Overcome,' Sour murmured, awed. 'What're we gonna do?'

'You're going to untie those last two bonds! Let's go!'

'Can't . . . she'd just fall into the Abyss and that'll be the end of her.'

'Well, then – we'll pull her up!'

'Can't yank on those chains, man. Use your head.'

Yusen came to their side. 'What happened?'

'Trap's closed on her,' Sour answered.

The man wiped the rain from his face, scowling. His disgusted expression seemed to wonder why nothing ever went right. 'Can't hang around here. We have to disappear.'

'The captain's right,' Sour told Murk. 'You have any idea what's on its way right now?'

'I know, I know,' he answered, thinking furiously. 'Is the stretcher made?'

'Yes. But we haven't touched the . . . thing.'

'All right. Let's pack up. Come back later once the dust has settled out.'

'Right.' Yusen jogged off. Murk waved for Sour to follow him to the body. Here their escort waited while through the rain the rest of the troop could be glimpsed withdrawing to the coast between the dolmens. Murk motioned Sour to the pack laid next to the corpse. Sweetly tossed down two broken sticks. Murk took them up and bent over the body.

'Poor Crazy-eye,' one of the mercs said, and he made a sign to D'rek, goddess of rot and rejuvenation.

'Always actin' before thinkin',' added another.

Murk, who had been bent over the seared torso, now leaned back to blink up at them. 'You finished?'

They frowned down at him, puzzled, drops falling from the rims of their helmets. 'Yeah,' one said, shrugging. 'I s'pose so.'

'Fine. Thank you.'

Sour laid out a sodden blanket. 'Put it on this. We'll wrap it.'

'I'll try.'

He used the sticks to feel about. He dug against the curve of the blackened pelvic bone. Turning the box vertical he managed to get a good grip and he lifted it from the still-smoking cavity that once held Crazy-eye's viscera. He laid it on the blanket and used the sticks to roll it over and over, then picked it up and slipped it into the pack which Sour was holding open.

Sour set the pack into the stretcher and tied it down with rope.

Murk motioned to the mercenaries. 'Who's got it?'

Their guards all backed away, hands raised and open.

'Oh, come on! We're not . . .'

'Yes, you are,' the Seven Cities woman answered.

Murk waved to Sour, impatient. 'Fine. Let's go.'

Sour struggled with the stretcher's spear hafts, grumbling, 'Not bloody fair . . .'

Murk waited a moment for Sour to ready himself then jogged for the shore and the waiting ship. Their guards spread out around them.

They found the crest of the strand lined by the troop, all crouched down in the rain. They crab-walked, hunched, to Yusen who alone was standing, scanning the storm-lashed seas. 'What's going on?'

'Boat's not here,' the man answered, almost in a lazy drawl.

Murk eyed the white-capped waves as they crashed the beach. 'Well . . . they must've just withdrawn.'

'Oh, they've withdrawn all right.' And the officer pointed out to sea.

Murk squinted into the overcast pall. Far towards the steel-grey horizon he could just make out the pale smear of sails and darker shadow of the hull. 'What? They've abandoned us?'

Yusen regarded him through a half-lidded gaze. 'What goes around comes around, hey?'

Murk adjusted his grip on the rain-slick spear hafts. '*Shit*. Well, now what? We follow the coast? Find a port?'

'You see any ports on the way in?'

Murk shook his head. In fact, the coast had been completely un-inhabited.

'No. If we want to get lost there's only one place for us.' The officer raised his chin to the south.

Murk followed the man's gaze and his shoulders fell. The jungle. The damned jungle. He heard Sour cursing away under his breath.

Yusen signed the *move out*, indicating the south. He stopped suddenly and eyed Murk and Sour and the burden between them, then turned on the Seven Cities woman. 'What's this, Burastan?'

The woman saluted. 'Sorry, Cap— Sorry.' She gestured curtly and Ostler came and took Murk's place, as Dee did Sour's. After one last warning glare Yusen turned away.

Had the woman almost said 'Captain'? And was her name really

116

Burastan? But Ostler and Dee took off with the stretcher bouncing between them and Murk had to run after them shouting: 'Hey! No. Take it easy, damn it!'

*

With the evening, the low oppressive massing of clouds of the wet season announced their nightly downpour. Skinner, dressed as always in his blackened shimmering coat of armour, his barrel helm pushed back high on his head, stood at the open cloth flap of his tent where he appeared to be watching the descending curtains of rain. Within, Mara and her fellow mage Petal leaned over a tabletop cluttered in maps and documents of rotting woven plant fibres.

Sighing, Mara picked up a glass of wine. She eyed her commander's scaled back. That armour. Gift of Ardata, he called it. Everyone else had abandoned their metal armour as useless in this constant damp. Now heavy layered leathers couldn't be purchased for anything less than their weight in silver. Yet no rust or stain marred that blackened scale coat. And it seemed nothing could penetrate it. Perhaps that's why Ardata had been unable to retrieve it when . . . well, when they parted ways.

'Our Master of the Inner Circle remains committed?' Petal asked in his slow and deliberate manner.

'Quite,' Skinner answered, keeping his back to them.

Petal pursed his thick lips, nodding. He tapped a blunt finger to the documents. 'I calculate this force to be a full third of the entire Thaumaturg military. Their only currently assembled field army. Leaving but scattered garrisons across their lands . . .'

Mara lifted the glass, saluting. 'To its success, then.' She cocked a brow and offered a mocking smile. 'May it advance far indeed.'

Skinner returned and picked up his glass to answer her toast. 'As far as it is able.'

'To the very end,' Petal added.

Mara's raised senses detected a familiar, and unwelcome, arrival. *The insolent one has returned.* She swallowed her wine while lifting a hand for silence. 'Our would-be master approaches.'

Skinner grimaced his distaste. 'Again? He is most insistent.'

The three faced the tent portal where the dusk was obscured by a shadow and the ragged figure of a beggar or itinerant monk slipped within. He glared as if enraged, his eyes black and wide behind the strings of his matted hair. 'Your cowardice and delay have cost us dear!'

Skinner's frown deepened. 'What is this?'

117

'While you have sat upon your hands others have moved against us!'

'Clarify . . .' Skinner ground out, his voice low and menacing.

'My lord demands you accompany me now.'

'Where?' Petal asked.

'To where you should have been and gone had you any shred of initiative.'

'Explain—' Skinner began.

But the priest gestured and the interior of the tent seemed to blur. 'Enough! We go.'

It seemed to Mara that the tent spun while the damp earth of the floor grew soft. They sank as if through a slew of mud, the soil tinged by a hot acidic burn of chaos. After a sickening plunge and twist they emerged into rain. Petal straightened nearby, slapping at his robes and snarling his outrage. Mara leaned over, her stomach roiling from the obscene touch of raw chaos, and vomited violently. A hand in an iron gauntlet steadied her: Skinner. She straightened while wiping the bile from her mouth.

Beneath massed clouds a plain of standing stones surrounded them. Lightning illuminated the scene, slashing almost continuously. It seemed to be concentrated . . . sizzling energy overwhelmed her groping senses. Its waterfall coursing blinded her and drove a spike into her forehead. She turned away, gasping her pain, to face the scowling priest of the Crippled God, who glared, free of any sympathy. Through the stars flashing in her vision Mara blinked at the man and grated: 'Do that again and I will kill you.'

He ignored her. 'Know this place, King of Chains?' he demanded, sneering.

'The Dolmens of Tien,' Skinner answered, his voice oddly hollow.

The Dolmens! Mara turned to him but his back was to her. *Where he and Cowl imprisoned K'azz. With, some whispered, Ardata's connivance.*

'Yes! Where what lies within ought to have been ours by now!'

Skinner adjusted his full helm and advanced into the forest of standing stones. Mara and Petal followed. The priest trailed in a curious hopping and jerking walk. Soon a shimmering wall of Warren-magics came into view. 'Hold!' Mara called to Skinner.

'I see it,' their commander answered, sounding annoyed.

She and Petal exchanged a wondering glance. *He sees it?*

'Can it be breached?'

'Perhaps,' Petal answered.

While Skinner waited, arms crossed, she and Petal examined the layered warding. 'Kurald Galain,' she opined. Petal gave a ponderous nod of assent.

'And more. Something very rare. Something I haven't seen since . . .' His gaze flicked to Skinner then held hers. 'Starvald Demelain.'

That most ancient Warren! Some said progenitor to all magics. And one accessible to . . . Ardata. She nodded in answer to the man's silent message. She knew she was out of her depth here in any case; stone and earth were her strengths. Petal was the researcher into the ways of the Warrens. Was this *her* work? If so, it had come too early. Their plan called for a much later confrontation – if any at all. 'A slide?' she suggested.

Petal nodded again, his chins bunching. 'Yes. It appears to have been woven to allow passage . . . we merely have to find the correct . . .' He hissed a breath between clenched teeth as he worked his Warren manipulation: a personal admixture of elements of Thyr and Mockra. The borderlands of both, he'd once told her '. . . the correct . . . *note* . . . and we may pass as well.' He grunted then, and wiped the rain from his face with a sleeve just as sodden. 'There we are. Safe enough.'

She eyed him, as did Skinner. Neither moved. Petal smoothed his robes down the broad slope of his stomach and sighed. 'Very well . . . if I must.' He stepped through in his ungainly rocking gait then turned to them and described a mocking bow.

Skinner gave a laugh of appreciation. 'Well done, Petal.' And he stepped through. Mara followed. The priest hopped past, flapping his arms as if he could push the churning energies aside. Skinner led them to the edge of a central circular marshalling ground or plaza. Here he stopped and crossed his arms, seeming to survey the scene.

To Mara at first it appeared completely still. Then she noted how the stones shifted and humped as if something beneath were heaving or turning. *Like the surface of a lake where huge creatures swim. And just what creature might this be?*

Aside, she noted the many impressions of footsteps. *Most of similar kind: heavy boots. Uniform. A military force? And recent excavations around the inner stones. These pits now pooled in rainwater. Come and gone, in any case.*

Something punched through the surface of the fine white gravel and Mara jerked, startled, a hand going to her throat. She immediately pulled the hand down, growling her anger at the instinctive reaction. Skinner had knelt to one knee. The black skirting of his armour rustled and spread about him like a pool of glistening night.

It was an arm, human, seemingly, and it scooped at the stones as a swimmer might pull at the water, making for shore. Another hand appeared and as they flailed closer Mara came to doubt their humanity. The fingers appeared more like bird's claws, the flesh scaled and ending in amber talons. Scraped and raw, they dug at the gravel, making a slow advance towards the stone ledge of the field.

Mara cast an uncertain glance to Petal whose brow was furrowed as he studied the amazing demonstration. Skinner, his back to them, had tilted his head aside as he watched, neither shrinking away nor offering aid of any kind.

In time a scalp of grimed long black hair broached the surface and was thrown back with an exultant yell and gasp of air. It was female, whatever it was. Her eyes blazed in the night like twin flaming suns.

'*Get me out of here!*' she demanded.

'Where is that which was within!' the priest yelled, now daring to dance in closer.

The woman ignored the priest: her gaze was fixed upon Skinner. She threw out an arm, reaching for him. 'Take my hand! Break the bonds . . . you can do it.'

Their commander did not move. 'What happened here?' he asked gently.

'Pull me out and I'll tell you,' she snarled as she dug at the stones like a drowning swimmer.

Skinner straightened. He shook his helmed head. 'Nothing better than that?'

'Damn you to the Abyss,' the woman growled. With an immense surge of effort she managed to lurch forward and slap one hand on to the cut stone ledge. Her thick talons scraped and gouged the stone.

Skinner continued to shake his head. 'No. I think it best you re-main out of contention for a time.' And he drew back his armoured boot then swung it forward, kicking the woman across the face.

She slewed backwards into the wide field of stones. If her gaze had been furious before it now fairly crackled with dazzling insane fury. She drew a hand, all sinew and amber talons, across her bleeding mouth as she was dragged backwards, sinking, and she yelled: 'Jacuruku will consume you, Skinner!' Then she disappeared once again as the stones hissed and collapsed in a smoking slurry.

Skinner turned away, murmuring, 'As has been prophesised.' He now regarded Mara and Petal from behind the slit of his helm. 'Well? Which way have they gone?'

Mara started, jerking a quick bow. As did Petal. 'Yes – of course. Right away,' she said shakily, still rather shocked by the brutal – and audacious – act. They headed off, following the trail.

The priest came along hopping and jerking at Skinner's side like a mongrel dog. 'You were too hasty,' he complained. 'We could have questioned her . . .'

'Shut up or I will cut your head off,' Skinner told him.

The man's mouth shut with a snap.

The trail led Mara and Petal to a shore cluttered in wave-wrack, the aftermath of the storm. Mara cast her awareness out to sea, seeking a vessel, but discovered nothing. However, by the light of the Jade Banner, as some named it here, it was clear that the party had not entered the surf. Rather, they had milled about for a time then headed south.

She and Petal followed for a few leagues just to be certain. They stopped before the seemingly impenetrable jungle wall at the base of the peninsula. The priest hopped from foot to foot in his impatience. 'Well? What are you waiting for? Go, now. Retrieve it!'

Skinner shook his head. 'They have entered Himatan. There is no finding them now. The jungle will deal with them. We will wait. Your treasure will be found among their bones.'

The priest grew still. He gnashed his yellowed rotten teeth. 'What? You refuse? Very well then. I demand you accompany me to another! Now. Immediately.'

Oh no. Mara threw out an arm. 'No! Not like that.'

'Your master demands fulfilment of your terms, Disavowed.' The air about them grew opaque, tearing into streamers of sickly grey roiling power.

Mara clutched her head and the nauseating agony swelling there. Petal grunted as he fell to his knees. The obscene oily touch of raw chaos enmeshed them and the dune shore, the massed clouds, all disappeared in a snap of displaced air.

*　　*　　*

Saeng warmed herself over a meagre fire of wood scraps and dry moss. She squatted near the vine-choked mouth of their cave on the floor of centuries of rotting leaves and droppings. Her outer clothes hung on branches over the fire, drying. She'd stink of smoke but that would be better than dying of the wet-lung. Hanu stood just within the opening, keeping watch.

While she rubbed her hands over the weak flames a spider emerged from the moss seeking escape. Its bulbous red body announced to all its poison. She used a twig to flick it aside. On another side a snake squirmed out from under dead leaves, attracted by the heat. Its glowing yellow and orange bands shouted its deadliness. She scooted it aside as well. *Spiders, snakes, bats, rats, tigers, rhinoceroses, ghosts . . . ye gods. Everything under the sun and those that avoid it into the bargain!* It was a miracle they were still alive and not stung, bitten or sickened unto death. *Well, me at least . . . Hanu seems impervious to everything.*

'I think we should return,' she called to him. 'They've moved on by now, surely.'

He turned his helmed head, gave a slight nod.

He's not enthusiastic about returning. What does he expect to find? She's just an old lady! What would they do to her? She must be fine. And speaking of fine . . . She eyed the glimmering opalescent blues and emerald greens of her brother's armoured back.

'What will you do?' she called. 'You cannot return . . . can you?'

'No,' he answered with his thoughts. '*I must leave this land or be hunted down.*'

She wanted to dispute that assertion but knew it to be true. She stared at the licking flames. 'Where will you go?'

'*Somewhere – it matters not where.*'

'Well . . . what will you do?'

'*I will easily find employment as a guard to some rich merchant or noble. Or I could join a travelling freak show as a living statue.*'

Her gaze snapped to him to find his helmed head tilted her way. 'I'm serious!'

'*As am I. An income will be no issue.*'

'Perhaps I could—'

'*No. You must remain. You belong here.*'

'So you say. I—' A deep growling roar from the jungle interrupted her. It shook the ground like a minor earthquake. The hanging vines vibrated, pattering down droplets.

'*Your friend wants his cave back.*'

'Well, he can wait,' she grumbled. 'I'm not spending one more night out in this damned rain.' She cast outwards for the beast and found the bright spark of its awareness. She urged it to curl up elsewhere. A throaty rumble answered that, as reluctant as she. Yet the crashing of undergrowth and the shuddering of nearby trees announced the great animal's capitulation. Hanu, at his post, visibly relaxed. His hands encased in their armoured gauntlets eased from his belt.

'Tomorrow, then,' she said. 'We might make it in one day if we push it.'

'*Very well.*' Hanu's response was just as reluctant.

That night she dreamed, as she almost always did now. This time she was not fleeing the bony reaching hands of the Nak-ta. Rather, she found herself wandering the deep jungle. It was day, the sun high and hot as it beat down upon her between gaps in the upper canopy. A troop of monkeys scampered about the treetops. They seemed to follow her wandering, curious perhaps. After a time she somehow came to the realization that what she walked was not some empty wasteland, but that the steep hillocks she passed were in fact tall sloping structures, human made, all overgrown and crumbling beneath the clutching roots of the jungle. And likewise, that the broad flat floor of the forest here was in fact a stone-paved plaza, the great blocks heaved up here and there by the immense trees.

So, she walked one of the ruins that she knew dotted the uncounted leagues of Himatan, which featured so prominently in her people's ghost stories.

Some time later she paused, sensing that she was being watched. Yet she saw no one. After she cast about at the shadows and great tumbled heaps of stone, a figure resolved itself out of the background of a root-choked staircase leading up the side of one of the great hillocks. It was a crouching man, mostly naked, wearing the headdress of a snarling predatory cat, a tawny leopard, some of which still haunted Jacuruku lands, occasionally dragging off the unwary.

'Hello?' she called.

The man stood, or rather, he uncoiled; his legs straightened and his arms uncrossed, all in a smooth grace of muscle and lean sinew. He came down the jumble of broken stone stairs in an easy, confident flow and Saeng had to admit that he was the most amazing example of male beauty she'd ever come across.

Closer, however, her breath caught as she saw that the headdress he sported was none such: the man's upper torso and head *was* that of a golden leopard. Her instincts yammered for her to run but she was frozen, unable even to scream. He stopped before her and eyed her up and down. Those eyes were bright amber slit by vertical black windows into deep pools of night. His black lips pulled back over jutting fangs, grinning perhaps.

Exhaling, Saeng managed to force out: 'Who – *what* – are you?'

'You know my brothers and sisters,' he answered, his voice appropriately deep and smooth.

'Brothers? Sisters?'

The monster nodded, perhaps grinning even more. 'Boar, tiger, bull, wolf, eagle, bear . . .'

'The beast gods. The old gods.'

The creature gave an all-too-human nod of assent. 'Yes. Some name them Togg, Fener, Ryllandaras, Fanderay, Argen, Tennerock, Balal, Great-Wing, Earth-Shaker . . . their names are too many for anyone to know them all.'

'There is no leopard god among all those names.'

The man-monster closed the distance between them in a blur. Its black muzzle brushed across her face as if taking her scent. 'You have the right of that, Priestess. I am the one none dared worship. And do not mistake me, child. I am not a scavenger. I never skulked about your villages. To me *you* are the beasts. *You* are just another kind of pig. I am the reason your kind fear the night.'

Saeng turned her face away from the stink of its hot damp breath. 'What do you want from me? You name me priestess. I am no priestess.'

'You are that and more. Priestess, witch, mage. All we possess, all we know, has been poured within you.'

'Poured? What do you mean?'

The creature tilted its head as if considering its words and paced off a distance. 'The future, child. Any one point in time leads off into a near infinity of choices. Yet a blight sits astride an entire span of these. A catastrophe is threatening. Some of us see its approach. Others . . .' his voice hardened to a snarl, 'those who would stand aside, choose to ignore it.'

'What does this have to do with me?'

'It is possible that you may either ensure it or avert it. The choice is yours.'

Saeng found that the edge of her terror had eased. In fact, she was becoming rather irritated. She threw out her arms. 'I have no idea what you are talking about!'

The creature turned its feline head to face her. 'Really? You do not recognize where you are? Where I have brought you?'

'Not a damn bit of it.'

Gesturing, the man-leopard invited her to approach the hillock. 'Examine the façade.'

Saeng approached warily. She edged around the creature, giving it a wide berth. Next to the extraordinarily steep staircase the wall of the hillock, or temple, or whatever it was, held a wide band of sculpted figures. Vines and leaves obscured them, but they appeared

124

to be walking in some sort of grand procession. They wore archaic costumes of short pants tight at the calves and their chests were bare – both men and women. All carried goods such as sheaves of grain or baskets of produce; some led buffalo, others pigs. She followed the processional along one side to where it ended at some sort of stylized tall shape: perhaps this very building itself. Some sigil or glyph stood atop the building and Saeng had to pull off the clinging vines and brush away the dirt and mat of roots to see revealed there the squat rayed oval that was the ancient sign of the old Sun god.

She flung herself from the gritty stone wall, nearly tripping on the many roots that criss-crossed the bare ground. She glared about for the creature but he was gone. Standing some distance off was a new figure, this one unmistakable as a Thaumaturg in his dark robes and gripping his rod of office.

As she watched, terrified, he raised his face and thrust the veined black and white stone baton skyward. The light dimmed as if dusk were gathering with unnatural speed and the colour of what light remained took on an unnatural emerald tinge. The disc of the sun itself seemed to diminish as though another object were swallowing it. Saeng had seen the sun eclipsed before but that event was nothing like this. The darkness deepened into a murky green as the object loomed ever closer. It was part of the Jade Banner, now descending, and it seemed as if it would swallow the sky, the world, entire.

'And behold!' the Thaumaturg bellowed into a sudden profound silence. 'The sun is blotted from the sky!'

Now a roar gathered so loud it deadened her hearing. A mountain of flame fell upon them. It obliterated the trees, the man, the ground, herself, even the enormous mass of stone behind her as if it were no more than a clot of dirt.

Saeng awoke gasping and clutching at the dry leaves beneath her. In a quick step Hanu was next to her.

'*What is it?*'

She forced her hands to relax, eased her taut jaws and exhaled. 'Bad dreams.'

He answered with something like a mental shrug of understanding. '*Yes. But now that you are awake we should go.*'

'Fine!' She pushed back her hair and suppressed a groan; it was hardly dawn. She broke her fast with cold rice. Their supplies were getting low. Another day, perhaps, then they would be searching for mushrooms and roots.

They climbed down the overgrown rocks just as dawn brightened the eastern treetops. Beneath the canopy it was still dark and Saeng struggled to keep up with Hanu. Off a way through the trees an immense shape reared, easily three times the height of any man, and Hanu froze in his tracks. A great black muzzle turned towards the cliff outcropping and sniffed the air.

'*Back to your home!*' Saeng urged the huge cave bear. '*We will trouble you no more.*'

A growl of complaint rumbled their way; then the beast fell back to his forepaws, shaking the ground and sending a shower of leaves falling all about, and lumbered off. Hanu turned his helmed head her way as if to say: that was too close for comfort.

She waved him on, dismissing the entire episode.

Their return route was much more direct than their way out. They found the countryside deserted. Thin smoke rose from the direction of the village of Nan and this troubled her more than seeing villages merely abandoned. Were the Thaumaturgs burning as they went along? Yet why do that? To deter desertion? She hurried her pace.

It was past twilight when they entered familiar fields. Hanu motioned aside to the woods where Saeng most often used to hide to confer with the ghosts of the land. She went on alone. At least the village hadn't been burned, yet most of the huts were dark where usually one or two lamps would be kept burning against the night. Their family hut was dark as well. Trash littered the yard and the reed door hung open.

'Mother?' she hissed. 'Mother? Are you there?'

Inside was a mess. Looters, or soldiers, had come and gone. Anything of any possible value had been taken, as had every scrap of food. Through a window she saw that the small garden had been dug up and that the chickens and pigs were gone. Saeng searched her own feelings and found that she really didn't care that the hut had been ransacked, or that her few meagre possessions had been taken. All that concerned her was her mother. Where was she? Was she all right?

She headed to the nearest light and found Mae Ran, one of the oldest of her neighbours, sitting on the wood steps leading up to her small hut. 'Who is this?' the old woman asked in a fearful quavering voice as Saeng came walking up. 'Are you a ghost to trouble an old woman?'

'It is Saeng, Mae. What has happened here?'

'What is that? Saeng, you say?' The old woman squinted up at her. 'Janath's daughter?'

'Yes. Where is she?'

'Saeng? Back so soon?'

'Back? What do you mean – back?'

'Janath said you'd gone on a pilgrimage to some temple or other . . .'

Saeng pressed the heel of a hand to her forehead. Gods! *Mother!* 'Well . . . I'm back. What happened?'

'What happened?' She waved a shaking hand to encompass the village. 'The Thaumaturgs came and took what they wanted. Food, animals. The hale men and women. Only we elders and babes left now. Every decade it is so. It is as I have always said – no sense gathering too much wealth to yourself, for the gods will always send a plague to take it from you. If not our Thaumaturg masters, then locusts, or fire, or flood. Such is the lot of humanity . . .'

Gods, old woman! I did not ask for a sermon. 'Thank you, Mae – yes. I agree. So, where is my mother? Is she well? Where did she go?'

Mae blinked up at her, confused, and Saeng saw her eyes clouded by the milky white of cataract and her heart wrenched. *Ah! Ancients! I am too harsh. Who remains now to look after this elder? Or the others? Could they labour in the fields? Harvest bark from the trees to boil to quell the pangs of starvation? And the infants? Who shall mind them? The army of our masters obviously judged them too much a burden to be worth their effort. How dare I denounce them for it yet prove as heartless?*

'Go?' the old woman repeated as though in wonder. 'Why, no-where. She is with Chana, her mother's brother's youngest.'

'Ah! Aunt Chana. Thank you. You take care of yourself, Mae. Take care.'

The white orbs swung away. 'We must hold to what we have, child. It is all there is.'

'Well – thank you, Mae. Farewell.'

Saeng backed away from the hut and made for her aunt's house across the village. It seemed strange to her that her mother should have gone to Chana's – ever since she could remember the two had only bickered and argued. Nearing the dwelling she found light flickering within and she stopped at the steps up to the front porch. 'Hello? Auntie Chana? It's Saeng . . .'

Thunder rumbled in the distance while she waited, and a thin mist of the last of the evening rain brushed her hair and face. Clouds appeared from the east, massing for another downpour. 'Saeng?' a voice called, her mother's. 'Is that you?'

She appeared on the veranda, a young child at her shoulder. 'What on earth are you doing here?'

Saeng nearly gaped. '*Mother,*' she answered, outraged. 'What kind of welcome is that? I was worried sick about you. I came to check—'

Her mother waved a hand. 'Oh, I am fine. I'm helping Chana.' She indicated the child. 'Look, little Non.'

Saeng frowned her puzzlement. 'Non?'

Her mother rolled her eyes. 'Chana's husband's sister's son! You know! Non.'

'No, I don't – I mean, I know the name,' she finished lamely.

'Oh, and old man Pelu? Next door?'

'Yes?'

'He's dead. His heart gave out when the Thaumaturgs came through.'

'Ah. Thank you, Mother. I really needed to know that.'

'Well, I thought you'd be interested. You liked him. He always gave you candied pineapple. Remember when you were four you ate so much you threw up?'

'*Mother!* Our house has been ransacked!'

She pressed a hand to Non's head. 'Quiet! You'll wake him. Yes, they came stomping through in their muddy sandals.' She looked to the lad nuzzling her neck. 'But we'll clean it up, won't we, Non? Would you like to help your auntie?'

Saeng took a step backwards to steady herself. She felt outraged. *Didn't her mother care?* Yet here she was busy and needed – getting on with her life. *Holding on to what she has.* 'I was worried about you . . .'

Her mother smiled warmly. 'That is sweet of you, Saeng. But worry about yourself. They asked about you, you know. Questioned everyone. They claimed you were an agent of the demoness! What silliness! No one said anything, of course.'

Now Saeng thought she was dreaming still. *No one said anything?* Her thoughts must have shown on her face as her mother tsked and said, 'Saeng, really . . . you're related to half the people here. And everyone's proud. You've kept the Nak-ta quiet for more than ten years now. No one's been taken in that time. Not like Pra-Wan. What a terrible time they've had of it there!'

Saeng felt like sitting down to steady herself. Was this really her village? And what of Hanu? Should she tell her? Perhaps not – she would want to see him and that would be too cruel.

Her mother reached out to smooth her hair. 'Poor Saeng. You always held yourself apart. You spent more time with those awful spirits than the living.'

Saeng bit back her argument that it was *her* beliefs and manners

128

that had held them apart – wasn't it? Yet it was too late to revisit such ground. Gently she removed her mother's hand. 'Well, I know what to do now, Mother. You were right. There is somewhere I must go.'

'Of course, Saeng. I knew it would come to you. You are the eldest daughter of the eldest daughter going back generations. It has always been so.'

'Goodbye, Mother. Take care of little Non.'

'Of course. That is also how it has always been.'

Saeng kissed the palm of her mother's hand and turned away. On a path east of the village Hanu fell into step with her. Other than the firmness of his footsteps only the deep green glint from the inlaid stones of his armour revealed his presence in the absolute dark of night.

'And Mother?'

'She is safe, Hanu,' Saeng sighed. 'She is safe and well.'

*   *   *

When the door to her private chambers was thrown open, Hannal Leath, abbess of Tali's monastery of Our Lady of the Visions, threw the covers over the naked body of her latest lover and glared at the offending acolyte. She wanted to say something properly majestic and abbess-like, such as: *What is the meaning of this intrusion?* But what slipped out was a high-pitched: 'What do you think you're doing?'

The young acolyte stood blinking at the bed, wide-eyed. Hannal followed her gaze to the impressive tenting of the sheet over her lover's midsection. She slapped Javich's thigh and he rolled on to his side. 'What is it?' she repeated.

The young woman swallowed, flushed. 'She's on her way, m'lady.'

'What? Whatever do you mean?'

'The contemplation pool. It's glowing. She's coming. Now.'

Hannal leaped to her feet on the bed, naked. '*What?* Now? Great impotent gods! You,' she kicked Javich, 'get out of here! You,' she pointed to the acolyte, 'collect my clothes.'

'Yes, Abbess.'

Hannal paced the bed. 'Of all the shrines and temples and schools . . . she has to come *here*?' She clutched at her neck. 'What have I done? Have I displeased her?'

Javich opened his mouth to say something but she pointed to the door. Bowing, he backed out, a sheet gathered at his waist. The acolyte handed over her clothes and she hurriedly dressed.

Ahead, up the hall of the monastery, a silvery light played among the pillars and stone arches. It rippled over the marble flags, the domed roofs and wall niches making it seem as if the entire building were underwater. As Hannal approached the inner sanctuary, she saw that the light spilled out of the doors to the central cynosure. She paused at the threshold, hands on the tall door leaves, already short of breath, and took in the milling crowd of nuns, guards and acolytes. She snapped a finger. 'All of you – *out*. Now!' She stood aside and they hurried past her, robes hiked up, feet slapping the polished marble floor. She took hold of the leaves. 'No one enters,' she told the guards. 'Is that understood?'

'Yes, Abbess.'

'Good.' She slammed shut the doors.

Oh, gracious goddess, what am I going to do? She ran to the stone lip of the central reflecting pool. Its quicksilver liquid rippled and shook as if agitated by her own anxieties. *What am I to do? One touch and I'll burn to ash!*

The surface of the liquid metal bowed upwards in a wave as if disturbed from below and she hissed her uncertainty. *Tongs? A fork? No – anything would burn. Centuries of Warren-ritual have gone into this instrument and I don't even know how it works!*

A hand emerged through the surface. The quicksilver beaded from it, running between the fingers. Hannal gaped, then thrust up her sleeves. *Well – only thing for it.* She reached out and clasped the hand, then gasped her exquisite pain as she found the flesh beyond frigid cold.

The hand tugged, almost heaving her over the raised lip of the pool. But Hannal had been a soldier before answering the call of the Queen and she had strong thighs. She braced herself against the ledge, pulling back just as insistently. An arm emerged – and not a shapely dancer's arm: a thick muscled limb, and quite hairy. *My goddess has the arms of a washerwoman!*

Hannal yanked even more strongly despite the fact that the skin of her palm and fingers was cracking and the blood was hissing and smoking as it dripped to the pool's juddering surface. She slapped her other hand to the wrist and hauled. A scalp emerged bearing straight brown hair. Another arm splashed up from the pool spraying droplets that burned where they touched, but Hannal clenched down on her agony and heaved with all her considerable muscle and heft.

Something gave, or a tipping point was reached, and the figure

130

slipped towards Hannal as if down a slick chute to flop over the lip of the pool and fall to the stone floor in a slapping of limbs and grunts of pain. The quicksilver liquid ran over the marble, hissing and eating into the surface until it dissipated into mist.

Hannal got down on to her knees and lay prostrate on her stomach before her goddess.

'Oh, just help me up,' the Queen of Dreams croaked.

Abbess Hannal threw open the doors to the cynosure of the monastery. Beyond, the gathered acolytes and guards stopped their whispering and hushed arguments. She knew she appeared a fright in only her thin shift scorched and burned through, with further red burns down her arms. 'Bring warm water, towels and clothes,' she ordered, then slammed shut the doors.

Much louder murmurings resumed out in the hall.

She hurried back to where the Enchantress now sat on the lip of the pool, wrapped in her outer robes. She was examining her arms, pinching the flesh of her hands. 'It has been . . . a very long time,' she said to herself.

Hannal knelt before her once more. 'You honour me, my goddess.'

The Enchantress shook her head. 'I am no goddess.'

'Your capabilities, your various manifestations, are godlike to us. Therefore we choose to name you such.'

'Well . . . you are free to do as you choose.'

'Have we displeased you? Have you come to censure us?'

'Censure you?'

Hannal wet her lips. 'The . . . lesson of Kartool . . . is never far from mind these days.'

'Ah. No, nothing like that.' She shook her head again, smiling, and Hannal lowered her gaze, for unworthy thoughts played across her mind. Thoughts of how in person the Enchantress was far from the beauty she projected to her penitents. She was in fact a middle-aged woman with unruly mousy brown hair, short, a touch on the heavy side, with facial moles and – *forgive me, Goddess!* – the dark dusting of a moustache.

When Hannal glanced back she saw the smile had broadened into something that appeared self-deprecating. 'The actual truth, Hannal,' the Queen of Dreams murmured, 'is always far from pretty.'

The abbess ducked her head once more, shamed. 'You honour me.'

'I offer you the truth. Call that an honour, if you choose. Most prefer to have their expectations fulfilled with lies.'

Quiet timorous knocking sounded from the doors. Hannal

131

bowed, backing away. She opened one leaf a crack and snatched the proffered clothes, towels and bowl of water from the acolytes who struggled to peer in past her, then slammed it shut. While the Enchantress washed herself, Hannal faced away, asking, 'May I ask, then, why you have come here to Tali?'

A throaty amused chuckle answered that. 'I suppose again I should say something flattering but I will not patronize you. I did not come because of the strength of your devotion, or the purity of your spirit, or any such thing. I came because this is the closest centre to where I wish to travel.'

Hannal frowned, puzzled. 'Travel, my goddess? Surely all the world is open to you. You may travel as you wish.'

Again the husky barmaid's chuckle. 'Ah, Hannal. I suppose that would be true were I a goddess. But in fact there are many places that are closed to me. And it is important that I travel to one such now. The time has come.'

Such words drove Hannal to abase herself once again upon the polished marble floor. 'Enchantress! Perhaps such knowledge is not for me.'

The Queen of Dreams paused in her dressing. 'Now I am the one distressed to hear such words. Are you or are you not an abbess of my calling? Knowledge is neither good nor bad – it is what you choose to do with it that matters. What you should know is that an opportunity is approaching . . . a rare chance to pose challenges where none have dared do so for a very long time. And to demand answers that have been avoided for far too long. Now, Abbess, stand – if you would.'

Chastened, and rather terrified by the sharing of knowledge that could be mortal for her, Hannal rose to her feet and dared a glance to her goddess. The woman now wore sandals, trousers of some sturdy weave, and a loose shirt beneath layered open robes. A long white silk cloth wrapped her head and a veil hung over her features leaving her eyes alone uncovered. And those dark eyes seemed to possess a startling allure now that all else was hidden.

'So, has my champion arrived?' the Queen asked.

Hannal blinked her uncertainty. 'Your . . . champion?'

'Well, let us say . . . my bodyguard, my spokeswoman.'

'Who – who would that be, my goddess?'

The Queen of Dreams crossed her thick arms; above the veil her dark brows wrinkled. 'The woman would be wearing a cloak no doubt, and keeping her face hidden.'

'Ah . . . But, my lady of prescience, I assure you there is no one here who answers that—' Hannal clamped shut her mouth. 'There is an odd itinerant who has slept on the steps of the monastery these last few days. We have been feeding her. She keeps herself wrapped in a filthy cloak.'

'Has this one spoken to anyone?'

Hannal cocked her head in thought. 'Not that I know of. No, I believe not.'

The Queen of Dreams smiled behind her veil. 'Very good. Have her brought to me.'

Hannal bowed and returned to the doors. All became quiet again as she pulled open one leaf. She paused, blinking, as it appeared that the entire constituency of the monastery was gathered in the outer vestibule: every acolyte, nun, priestess, guard, cook and groundskeeper. A sea of faces stared back at her, expectant. 'Get that itinerant,' she hissed to Churev, the highest ranking priestess nearby.

'Who?' the woman answered, trying to peer in past her.

'*The one outside on the steps!* Is she still there? By the Deceiver, you haven't driven her off, have you? Get her. Bring her!'

Churev bowed. 'At once, Abbess.'

Hannal slammed the door and leaned against it. *Goddess forgive us! Well, now I suppose I could just ask . . .*

Not too long after a knock sounded and Hannal heaved open the leaf. The cowled and cloak-wrapped beggar faced her, Churev at her side. Hannal motioned in the silent woman, while at the same time throwing an arm across the open portal to block all the others surging forward. She managed to urge everyone back far enough to press shut the door. Meanwhile, the homeless beggarwoman had walked on alone to stand before the Queen of Dreams.

Hannal hurried to her side to hiss: '*Bow before our goddess!*'

The beggarwoman merely turned her hooded head to cast her the briefest of glances. Hannal caught nothing of what lay within that hood.

'Thank you for answering my call.' The Enchantress addressed the figure. 'And thank you for tolerating such shameful disguise. The time for it has passed – you may cast it aside.'

The figure seemed to merely shrug and the heavy travel-stained cloak fell away revealing a sturdy woman in travelling leathers, twin narrow swords at her sides. But what drove Hannal back one step was the nearly plain white mask at the woman's face.

Nearly plain! My goddess! I know what that means!

'Now we can go. Ina, you may lead the way. We must go straight to the harbour.' She directed what appeared to be an amused smile at Hannal. 'As they say – my ship is about to come in.'

The Seguleh woman immediately turned to the doors. Hannal jumped from her path. 'And I? Shall I come?'

The Enchantress waved a hand, unconcerned. 'You may arrange an escort, if you must.'

Despite her light leather armour, her weapons, the Seguleh champion crossed the polished stone floor soundlessly to pull open both leaves of the portal. Priestesses and acolytes who had been pressed up against the doors listening fell in a tumble at her leather-wrapped feet. The entire jammed crowd of the vestibule gaped at this sudden masked apparition, until, in a rush of feet, they frantically scrambled to either side.

Ina advanced and the veiled and robed figure of the Queen of Dreams emerged.

For a moment the assembled priestesses and staff of the monastery stared, taking in this new arrival, then thoughts turned to the awakened portal within, for it was known to all that no other entrance existed, and one by one, then the rest in unison, they knelt and bowed their heads.

Abbess Hannal emerged last. She grasped the sleeve of the nearest priestess, hissed, 'Assemble the guards, get torches, surround them! Let none approach!' She swallowed her panic, caught sight of the folds of the thin slip she wore. 'And get me some damned clothes!'

That night what appeared to be a bizarre religious procession tramped through the streets of Tali. Those few citizens awake during the third hour before sunrise, these being the night watch, city bakers and their apprentices, wandering drunks, and some few others whose business brought them out at such an hour – the nature of such business precluding them from ever admitting to being abroad at that time – later swore to hearing and catching glimpses of a torchlit convoy that wound its way down out of the temple district and on towards the waterfront. The mother of a family that slept on the street near the broad arched gate to the temple district, ever hopeful for alms, swore that the coin she used to pay for a room in a tenement house came from a priestess in that very procession. It was her opinion that they were of the hidden temple of the Shattered God escorting a human sacrifice to her doom.

At the waterfront the cordon of guards and priestesses spread out surrounding Hannal, Ina and the Queen of Dreams. By this time

Hannal was frantic. Did her Queen expect her to have contracted a ship? What was her intention? No one was even up – how could she negotiate for a vessel? She was considering sending runners to all the nearby ships to bash on the decks or sides when she felt at her side the presence of her goddess. She bowed.

'Do not worry, Hannal. Transport has been arranged.'

'Of course, my Queen. Which one?'

'None of these. I've . . . *negotiated* . . . to borrow a very special vessel.'

Hannal could not help but cast a quick glance to the quiet harbour. 'And it will be arriving soon?'

The goddess smiled behind her veil. 'Very soon. I merely have to call it . . .' She advanced towards a section of empty wharf and Hannal waved to clear the priestesses and guards from her path. At the timbers' jagged ends the Queen gestured out over the water below then crossed her arms. She looked to be waiting. Hannal dared to step up next to her. She peered down. The murky darkness of the harbour waters beneath the wharf appeared unchanged. She glanced to the Seguleh woman, Ina: she was looking behind them, back across the wharf front, ignoring anything that might be happening on the water. *Of course, any threat would rush them from the streets, wouldn't it?*

A flickering from under the wharf snapped her gaze down. A silvery light rippled from the water beneath the floating sticks and refuse. The rotting timbers of the wharf juddered under her feet as if kicked. The surface of the harbour waters swelled.

The escort of priestesses and guards backed away from the edge of the wharf leaving Hannal, Ina and the Queen alone.

The swelling domed like an enormous bubble. From within this bulge a vessel's bow arose to breach the surface in a great hissing and slither of water. What appeared to be the most alien ship Hannal had ever seen emerged. As long as a war galley it was, with a series of oar ports, dark and empty, lining its side. Yet it was completely closed across its top as if sealed to all access. A tall stern rudder was the last of it to heave into sight and the bow eased down into the water with a gentle sigh. No colours or sigil marked the dark polished planks of its sides and stern.

'Who,' Hannal stammered in wonder, 'whose vessel is this?'

'Mine, temporarily. It has been lost in the Shoals since the magus who built it died – slipped in a bathhouse and cracked his skull, rather ironically. I've been keeping an eye on it.'

Hannal's mouth had dried. *The Shoals? Isn't that some sort of*

135

gyre of trapped ships? Some say Mael's own purgatory for lost sailors . . . She cleared her throat. 'And who . . . who is the captain?' *Hood himself?*

The Queen regarded her, amused. 'No captain. No crew. You could say the ship is – enchanted.' She headed for a wooden ladder down from the wharf to the pier that the nameless vessel rubbed against. Ina quickly stepped ahead to lead the way, which she did smoothly, landing like a cat.

Hannal gripped the rough wood of the top rung. 'Where are you headed, my goddess?'

The Queen of Dreams raised her veiled face from the dark where she stood on the wave-splashed floating pier. 'For a chat. A long-delayed chat with an old acquaintance.'

No gangway or opening was in evidence along the side of the vessel. Yet the Seguleh swordswoman somehow vaulted atop the planking of the flat deck. Kneeling, she extended an arm. The Queen took it, and in this rather awkward and undignified manner scrambled her way up the slick side and on to the deck.

Old acquaintance? Hannal was thinking. *Who* . . . *?* For the life of her, she had no idea who that might be. *Something for the cult archivists and researchers to sink their teeth into* . . . *And we, of course, out of all our rivals, possess the best of these.*

Her last sight of the goddess and her champion was of two small figures painted in the sickly green tinge of the Visitor standing atop the long sweep of the vessel as it made its grave and stately way out of the harbour. Driven by no means discernible to her.

*   *   *

. . . *and farther along the river we did come upon numerous populated urban centres whose inhabitants were unrelenting in their hostility and antagonism to our advance* . . . Golan rubbed his gritty eyes and adjusted the sheet of plant fibre in the light of his single candle. Unfriendly indigenes, yes. No surprise there. Why should they welcome an invading army? And why should this Bakar, a ragged survivor – a deserter no doubt – claim otherwise?

Golan scanned further down the parchment . . . *of the manifold monstrosities that assaulted us, the man-leopard was the worst. Countless soldiers fell in the river of red that was his rabid hunger. Yet this is not to diminish the daily predations of the snake-women, or the carnivorous bird-women* . . . Bird-women? Golan pinched his eyes. False gods! Please let there be one useful scintilla of information he could sift from this ridiculous fabrication.

Inland from the river, at a distance of some leagues, we did perceive large structures tall above the canopy of forest and we remaining few were cheered for we believed we had at last arrived at the fabled Jakal Viharn itself and would soon walk its golden pavements and claim the gossamer magics that infuse its streets, and capture its ruling deathless great Queen herself. A floating reception of some four thousands of natives met us, occupying some hundreds of war canoes. The inhabitants wore brilliant feather cloaks – or so we thought at first. Only the ferocity of Master Rust's theurgist response allowed us to escape their attack. From the resultant great conflagration I alone did emerge . . .

Golan let the account fall to the table and sat back, sighing. Four thousand warriors? Hundreds of war canoes? This deserter ought to have been more modest in his invention; this strained credulity beyond reason. And Jakal Viharn as a great city in the jungle? Please! It's jungle! Raw primitive nature could in no way support such a large population. Only agriculture is capable of that. These indigenes – if any at all – must certainly number no more than a few scattered hundreds squatting in leaf huts, digging grubs and scratching their flea-bitten bare behinds.

He sipped his wine and stared at the blank canvas wall of the tent. Already mould and damp stained its weave. Beyond, monkeys howled to the risen moon and a roar sounded from the distance, some sort of hunting cat. *The truth behind this man-leopard, perhaps? And yet . . . earlier Masters admit that some few survivors of their first experiments did escape. And of these, some may have made their way to the jungles and there survived. This no doubt is the real truth behind these accounts of bird-headed men and snake-women, and other such monstrosities glimpsed in the night and embellished in the imagination.*

And speaking of monstrosities . . .

Golan tapped his baton to the table and the flap was lifted. 'Yes, Lord Thaumaturg?' U-Pre enquired.

'What news of our Isturé?'

'They say their commander has not yet returned from pursuing one of the night creatures.'

'And how many of them are unaccounted for?'

'Just the four, Master.'

Golan stirred the wine glass. 'Very good. Keep a close eye on our guests. Let me know immediately if any more "disappear".'

'Yes, Master.'

Bowing, the second in command let the flap fall. Golan now frowned at the fibre paper and its handwritten account. *Produced under duress – mustn't forget that. Still, our outlander Skinner and his Isturé seem assured that what they deal with here is known to them – these D'ivers and Soletaken. Perhaps. Perhaps the truth is a mixture of all. In any case, such genealogy is no interest of ours. It suffices only that Skinner deal with them, allowing his forces to subjugate Ardata and her ragged-arse people. Surely that is not asking too much.*

Then Skinner can squat in these woods, if he likes.

For a time.

Golan partook of a modest meal of vegetable stew and bread baked of a coarsely cracked grain. He was about to return to his reading when his rod of office, set within its iron stand, developed a frosty blue glow. He immediately stood, snuffed the candle, then crossed to the tent entrance. Pulling aside the heavy cloth he ordered the yakshaka guard: 'Let none enter.'

The guard bowed wordlessly. Golan let the cloth fall then found to his distaste that he had to wipe his hands of its slimy damp. *Rotting already?*

He arranged his robes and stood at attention before the baton. 'I am here, Masters.'

'There are troubling disturbances among the lines of power, Golan,' came the wavering faint voice of Master Surin.

'Disturbances, Master?'

'How goes the advance? Any . . . complications as yet?'

'None – as yet. We advance as scheduled.'

'Very good, Golan. And the estimate of arrival at Jakal Viharn?'

'No more than one moon.'

'Very good. Continue your advance. We are already moving along your route. It would not do for us to have to step over you, would it?'

Golan bowed, touching his forehead to the ground. 'No, Masters.'

The watery blue light flickered then disappeared as if snatched away. Golan was plunged into utter dark, as no light whatsoever could penetrate the heavy cloth of the tent. He cursed in the tar-like night. After crashing into the table and hearing the candle drop to the ground he was forced to summon a glow in order to locate it. A humiliatingly trivial use of his Thaumaturg training. To make up for the lapse he resolved to use mundane methods to relight the candle.

It was some time before the warm yellow glow of the candle reasserted itself. Golan sat back, snapping shut the tinderbox and flexing his hand, cramped as it was from clutching the flint. *There! Well, success at last. Too bad it is now time to get some sleep . . .* He reached out to snuff the wick.

'Commander!' U-Pre called from without.

Golan let his hand fall. 'Yes!' he snapped impatiently.

'You are needed!'

Normally he would tell the man to wait until the morning but there was an unseemly urgency in his second in command's voice – and Golan also knew he would not dare disturb him unless the matter were truly important. He picked up the candle to guide himself to the entrance then shook it out. 'Coming,' he sighed.

U-Pre guided him through the camp. A light rain fell and the ground was soft with it, oddly yielding, as if at any moment it would slide out from under Golan's sandals. His yakshaka bodyguards had fallen in behind. 'A soldier attacked his fellows,' U-Pre was explaining. 'He was on guard, and when he returned from the pickets he fell upon his phalam. He was killed during the resultant fight.'

One of Golan's servants ran up from the dark. Bowing, the man offered a rolled parasol that Golan took and shook out to raise above his head – not only would it protect him from the unhealthy warm rain, but a parasol was also as much a marker of his rank as the baton itself. 'And why, U-Pre, does such a pedestrian matter demand my immediate and personal attention?'

His second bowed as he led him along between puddles and fields of churned mud. 'True, it may be the mere question of a personal grudge or hatred. But the soldiers are talking . . . already there are rumours . . .'

'Such as?'

'Possession. The work of the Demon-Queen. An insanity carried by the unhealthy vapours of the rains and the land. That the water-terror madness now walks among us. Or that the ghosts of the jungle had driven him amok. The mazes of Himatan. A fate that awaits us all . . .'

'Enough, U-Pre. I believe I see the pattern. All the worst possibilities.' Ahead, a cordon of officers held back a crowd of curious soldiers. Golan waved a hand over his shoulder. 'Disperse these gawkers.'

Two of his yakshaka bodyguards lumbered forward. The soldiers melted before them. The minor field officers bowed, moving aside. Golan moved up to examine the scene of the fight. He stepped

139

daintily over the wet fresh corpses where they lay sprawled. *Grievous injuries! The soldier must have been wielding the largest of weapons – perhaps a two-handed yataghan.* He bent to study the multiple slashes across one man's torso. *Frenzied, these cuts – artless.*

Without raising his head he asked: 'And the attacker?'

U-Pre found the carcass, pointed with his rattan stick of office. The rain pattered lightly on Golan's parasol as he bent to his haunches next to the body. He scanned the man's multiple wounds. 'Many of these are severely debilitating,' he said aloud, musing.

'Yes, lord.'

'Yet he appears to have ignored them all to continue his attack.' Golan found a broken stick, which he used to edge the man's head over; he found bloody pink foam at the lips and chin. 'Ergo the rumours, good U-Pre.' The fellow's face was also frozen in a grotesque mask, as if in a frenzy, or extreme agony.

'Yes, lord.'

'However,' and Golan began examining the corpse's limbs, 'a number of possible causes exist for said foaming, the rictus, and the apparent indifference to pain. Ah – and here we are . . .' He held up the man's right foot.

U-Pre bent closer, frowning. He saw a swollen circular wound, discoloured, a ferocious red lump on the sole of the man's foot. 'And this is?'

'The bite of the yellow recluse. Its venom attacks the nerves inducing a horrific anguish greater than any a mundane torturer could inflict. I've heard it described as an "ecstasy of agony." The man was driven to commit suicide to escape the pain.'

U-Pre's tanned features paled and he swallowed. 'And . . . this yellow recluse . . . it is rare?'

Golan wiped his hands on the already muddy trim of his robes. 'Quite common, actually. Have the troops briefed regarding them – and all the other poisonous spiders. And the scorpions, of course. And the stinging red centipedes.'

U-Pre was nodding. 'Stinging red centipedes, yes. Anything else?'

Golan gave a negligent wave. 'Oh yes, but those are the worst. The rest are just nuisances. It is possible to survive their bites.'

'I am ever so reassured, sir.'

Golan chuckled, straightening. 'The campaign is loosening you up, good U-Pre. Have the bodies buried without witnesses.'

'Yes, lord.'

Golan signed to his yakshaka and headed back to his tent. Along the way he mused: *a lost yakshaka soldier, an early attack from one of the odd sports that infest Ardata's lands, the troops seething with rumours already, our Isturé allies missing . . . It is as I informed the Nine: nothing of any significance as yet.*

*   *   *

Alone in the jungle, Kenjak Ashevajak paused, listening. Drops falling from the high canopy struck the ferns and brush around him in a constant low patter. The humus beneath his feet shifted under his weight as the water saturating it oozed within. Somewhere to his left a short beast nosed the rotting logs and heaped leaves. As he stood frozen, knees bent, shortsword out, the beast snuffled its way around the trunk of a tree to emerge as a hairy anteater. Normally, Kenjak would kill the beast for meat – but he did not want the Thaumaturg and his men to eat. He hissed his imitation of a hunting fire cat and the anteater jumped, startled. Its quills rattled erect and it backed warily away. Kenjak shooed it on.

A new scent brushed his nose and he breathed again, testing for it. He crooked a smile. Thet-mun. The kid's stink was unique. 'I hear you,' he murmured, waving to his left. 'Who is it? Myint? Thet? Loor-San?'

A good distance away a figure straightened from the brush. Thet-mun. 'How could you have heard me?' the skinny youth complained. 'You always hear me.'

Crouching, Kenjak waved him close. 'What news? How are the lads?'

The youth adjusted his undersized leather cap and his ancient discoloured hauberk. His hair hung wet and his lean weasel-like face was a livid flushed crimson from some sort of illness that he could not shake. 'Hungry. Unhappy.'

'What does Myint say?'

'She doesn't like the idea of taking the Thaumaturg. Says it won't play out.'

Kenjak slammed his shortsword into its sheath. 'We don't want the damned Thaumaturg! That's not the plan! What in the name of the Night Spirits did you tell her?'

The lad – perhaps only a year or two junior to Kenjak – flinched, then pouted, shrugging. 'Nothing different from what you told me . . .'

'Never mind. Listen. Forget the Thaumaturg bastard—'

'Easy for you to say,' Thet-mun grumbled. 'We ain't never taken one of them down afore.'

141

Kenjak cuffed him across his tiny leather cap. 'We aren't going to. Okay? Now listen. The bitch – is she still headed into the Fangs?'

Straightening his cap, the lad nodded sulkily. 'Yeah. Plain as day. Them yakshaka leave a trail like an elephant.'

'By the Abyss. Maybe she really is working for the Demon-Queen.'

'If that's the case, me 'n' the lads, we think we should head—'

'I don't care what you and the lads think. Tell Myint and Loor I'm taking them to Chanar Keep.'

The lad gaped, then giggled, covering his uneven rotting teeth as if self-conscious because of them. 'Naw – no way they'd go in there!'

Kenjak knew their deathly fear of Chanar Keep – and the reason behind it. He used that very dread to build his own reputation among them. All they knew was that he and his right-hand man, Loor, could enter the ruins as they pleased, never mind how. He gave the lad an exaggerated wink. 'I told this Thaumaturg I'd introduce him to Khun-Sen.'

The lad's eyes widened in amazement. 'No way! Great gods . . .' He hunched suddenly, pressing down on his cap. 'But then . . . no way I'm going in *there*!'

Kenjak raised a placating hand. 'Fine. Don't. Loor and I will. Tell him to go ahead and clean the place up. It has to look halfway decent.'

'Well – so long as we're nowhere near there come nightfall . . .'

'Yes. That's the plan. Then we collect the bitch and the yakshaka.'

Thet-mun wiped his grimed sleeve across his nose and dropped his gaze. 'Yeah . . . about that . . .'

Kenjak quelled an urge to smack the lad across his head again. 'We'll fucking net him, okay? Tie him up and carry him! All right?'

'I dunno, Jak. Sounds kinda risky. Maybe we should just lead this Thaumaturg to them and let 'em fight it out? Then we step in smooth as honey aft'wards . . . hey?' and he peered up from under his brows, warily.

'Because there's too many of them, okay? Need to level the odds. Because he might blow our prize into little pretty pieces! All sorts of possibilities, all right? Yes?'

The lad was digging at his blackened fingernails. 'Well . . . if you say so.'

'Yes!' Kenjak straightened. 'Go on then.'

'Well – actually – I kinda want that anteater . . .'

Kenjak hung his head. *Ancient Demon-King forgive them!* He waved him off. 'Fine. Go get him.'

Grinning, Thet-mun drew a long curved knife from his belt.

'Thank my old ma and da! Meat tonight!' He ducked into the brush, disappearing.

Kenjak stood still, listening once again, but heard nothing. *The lad really is damned quiet. Too bad he stinks so gods-awful.* He headed back to the column.

Before entering the camp pickets he stashed the shortsword where he could retrieve it tomorrow morning. When he returned to camp the soldiers grabbed his arms and marched him to their commander. Overseer Tun ignored the fact that he returned of his own cognizance and took hold of his neck and drove him to his knees where the Thaumaturg rested in the shade of the wide leaves of a plantain tree, all to impress him with his diligence and ruthlessness.

'Well, Jak,' the young officer demanded, 'you have found the trail?'

'Yes, Magister. They are still headed east. She must be returning to the Demon-Queen!'

The youth fanned his gleaming sweaty face, frowning. 'I did not ask for your opinion.'

Tun cuffed him across the back of his head and tears started from his eyes – the overseer had metal studs on his thick gloves. 'Yes, Magister.'

'How far ahead?'

'A good three days at least, lord. They are moving faster than us. Yakshaka never rest, do they?'

A scowl of distaste from the Thaumaturg brought another strike to Kenjak's head. Stars flashed in his vision. His swimming gaze found a wide concourse of ants winding their way up and down the trunk of the tall plantain. While he watched, a gang of the black insects struggled with the cumbersome load of a captured nectar wasp; they were dragging it down to the nest somewhere among the roots. Kenjak took great satisfaction from that sign offered up by the jungle itself: unimportant, unremarked beings overcoming and winning a far larger prize.

Gritting his teeth against the pain, he began, 'M'lord, if I may . . .'

Still fanning himself, the Thaumaturg youth – *some snotty privileged spoiled noble's son!* – signed that he might continue. 'Seven Peaks Pass, Magister. Chanar Keep. It will cut days from the journey.'

The young man's gaze returned from wherever he had gone in his contemplation then slid to him. His long straight black hair fell forward and he pushed it back, adjusting the jade comb that held it secured at the nape of his neck. A surge of rage coursed through

Kenjak at the sight of his preening. *Pampered rich boy! No servant now to comb that so carefully kept mane. Soon enough I'll have that piece of jewellery and I will use it to yank the knots from my hair!*

'So you insist,' the Thaumaturg sighed, as if tired of the matter. 'If this is so – why hasn't the girl taken it?'

'These locals fear Khun-Sen. He used to raid them.'

The Thaumaturg youth raised one quizzical brow. 'Used to?'

Kenjak hung his head, feeling his cheeks flushing in his panic. *Damn the Old King! What a stupid mistake!*

'Don't pretend you're no raider, Jak,' the youth drily noted.

Kenjak stilled, his gaze on the layers of rotting leaves and branches across the jungle floor. An immense relief eased his shoulders and he went limp in the hands of the guards. *He thinks I lied to protect myself. Thank the goddess.*

'We will take the trail to Seven Peaks Pass. You will lead us, Jak. I would pay my respects to old Khun-Sen.'

Kenjak bowed even lower, his arms held wide to either side. 'As you command, Magister.' *You'll pay your respects to him all right, you damned snotty puke. But not as you imagine!*

CHAPTER IV

The magnificent city of Jakal Viharn lies westward of those lands known as Fist, or Korel, and inland. It lieth under the equinoctial line, and it hath more abundance of gold than any other region of the world. I have been assured as such by accounts from earlier travellers who have witnessed such wonders and have seen with their own eyes the great city. For its richness, and the excellence of its seat, this great city far exceedeth any of the world.

Allar Ralle
The Discovery of the Empire of Jacuruku

THE ADWAMI CAVALRY NOW MADE STEADY PROGRESS ACROSS THE great flat plain that was the Ghetan Plateau. This was Jatal's fifth raid and as before he was very impressed by the land's immensity and fertility. Broad fields stretched one after the other, each cut by a maze of irrigation canals, ditches and spillways. Interspersed between these stood copses of timber, trimmed orchards, and ruled-straight windbreaks. It all seemed to go on for ever, as if continuously unrolling before them. And when the heat of the baking sun left him swimming in his robes and the constant roll of his mount eased him into a sort of undulating daydream of passing leagues, each indistinguishable from the many before, sometimes he fancied he'd never come to see the end of it all.

Of any armed resistance, there had been little so far. This was of no surprise to the Adwami. Generations of raiding had taught them the miserliness of the Thaumaturgs. It seemed they would rather endure the nuisance losses of raids than suffer the painful outlay of maintaining any adequate garrison. A strategy that would serve them ill – now that the Adwami were set upon a sudden near invasion. And

145

yet again it struck Jatal as odd that this Warleader, a foreigner to their lands, could have foreseen this weakness; unless perhaps he had met or interrogated escapees or fugitives from these regions and such information had suggested the idea in the first place. Indeed, why stop there among the sea of possibilities? The man talked and carried himself as one quite educated and cultured. Perhaps he was familiar with that ancient Seven Cities traveller Ular Takeq, and his *Customs of Ancient Jakal-Uku*. Or the castaway mariner Whelhen and his account of ten years among the villagers of the jungles in his *Narrative of a Shipwreck and Captivity within a Mythical Land*. These sources alone could perhaps have served to germinate a strategy.

Perhaps he should be more forceful in his efforts to sit down with the man to get to know him better. So far, however, the Warleader had been quite forceful in his habit of retiring early to his tent. Where, it was rumoured, he inhaled the fumes of various burning substances, thereby smoking himself into stupefaction every night.

Jatal adjusted his headscarf against the glaring sun and eased himself up in his saddle for a moment, stretching his sore thighs. He peered up and down the column as they advanced at a quick walking pace. Speaking of stupefaction – he was drifting into his own reverie. What had he been considering? Oh yes, resistance. It wouldn't remain so thin. For a time they would manage to stay ahead of word of their advance, but eventually the enemy would be ready for them. Probably at Isana Pura.

Until then, encounters would remain merely a matter of entering the small farming hamlets and depots, disarming the bewildered guards, and sorting through the plunder, including captives, who were sent back in gangs under minimum escort.

What in truth concerned Jatal was the state of the knife-thin accord between the Adwami tribes themselves. Only two blood-feud killings so far – a tribute to the new restraint requested by the Warleader, and the anticipation of the size of the future rewards to accrue from such cooperation. This line of musing brought Jatal to the subject of Princess Andanii and her Vehajarwi. So far, the public face of mutual tolerance between their two tribes, the two largest and most intractable traditional enemies, served to anchor this unaccustomed peace. And what of the princess in all her most seductively alluring flesh? What was he to make of her?

Jatal cleared his throat against the kicked-up dust of the road. From the folds of his robes over his armour he drew out his travel copy of Shivanara's *Songs of the Perfumed Lands* and opened it with his thumb.

146

Sing me, my Prince, the Wonders of True Devotion!
As the caress of the cooling Western wind they are,
As Natural as the unfolding of the Azal blossom,
And as enduring.

Jatal shut the tiny booklet and squeezed it in his fist. He rubbed his eyes, dry and gritty from scanning the endless horizons day after day. Yes, what was he to make of her? The heat of lingering sidelong glances from above her veil as she rode by with her guard of lancers. Their brief exchanges at chance encounters, during which she was in turns mocking or mildly provoking. All a pose? And what of his behaviour? Resolutely formal and courtly: the very model of the traditional Adwami aristocrat.

That, too, no more than a pose?

And how much of a provocation was that, given her proposal? And all the oh-so-much-more it implied?

Yet how could he be certain? Was he a coward not to have attempted to sneak into her private tents already? Yet think of the absurd image of himself caught by Vehajarwi guards and paraded about as some honourless prurient seducer. Such humiliation could not be endured. Indeed, there was a summation of the male quandary: so much suppressed by the terror of being humiliated . . .

'My lord Hafinaj . . .' A gravelly voice spoke from nearby and Jatal glanced down, blinking, to see the Warleader's lieutenant, Scarza, walking along in lazy loping strides next to his mount. He eased back Ash's pace and edged aside of the column.

'Yes, Lieutenant?'

The giant's tangled dark brows climbed his lined forehead. 'Lieutenant? Nay. Just Scarza I am and Scarza I remain. I hold to none of these absurd pomposities of rank – my prince.'

Jatal crooked a smile at the man's slanting irreverence and reined Ash in. 'Speaking only for yourself, of course.'

'Of course.'

'What news then? Any further sightings of our damned Agon friends?'

A hand the size of a shovel rose to rub wide unshaven jowls. 'None at all. Keeping as low as the scorpions, them.'

'How appropriate too.'

'I thought so.'

Jatal regarded the man for a time. Of Thelomen blood? Or the ones named Toblakai? 'And where are you from, Scarza?'

'From my mother, m'lord. Bless her bounteous bosom. In the

meantime, sir, the Warleader requests your presence in an insignificant fleabite of a village east of here, if you would. There is something there he believes may be of interest to you, as a scholar and such.'

'I see. Thank you, Scarza-who-eschews-all-rank.'

The man flashed his formidable canines. 'Eschews? Too fancy a word by far for this lowly Scarza. I'll show you the way, m'lord.'

Village was far too generous a description for the wretched cluster of rundown shabby huts. They passed Thaumaturg chattels who merely paused in their field labours, heads bowed and shoulders stooped, before returning to their tasks. The Warleader awaited them amid his honour-guard of twenty Adwami knights selected from the various tribes. Bowing, the bodyguards eased their mounts aside to make room for Jatal. The Warleader sat leaning forward on the horn of his saddle. He directed Jatal's attention to the simple mechanism of a muscle-powered grain mill. Only, this being Thaumaturg land, the mechanism was not so simple. Instead of a mule or an ox providing the muscle powering the arm that turned the stone to grind the seed, it was the massive legs, broad back, and trunk-like arms of a man, who, had he lived in any other land, would no doubt be a champion wrestler or fighter.

The Warleader gestured to the figure as it continued its endless round fettered to the wooden arm of the mill, strangely unconcerned despite the troop of foreign cavalry crowded around. 'The work of the Thaumaturgs,' the Warleader said. 'Know you of their . . . creations?'

The unease coiling in Jatal's stomach tightened. He had in fact grown up hearing the stories brought back by the generations of his forebears' raids into these lands. Tales of humans bred or distorted by the Thaumaturgs to serve certain . . . needs. Most of his brethren, he knew, laughed at such accounts, dismissing them as mere bedtime stories meant to scare children. Jatal, however, had read written narratives penned by travellers from disparate regions and times, all of which mentioned such research – and universally condemned the practice and its products.

The sight of the broad back of the unfortunate as he continued his eternal labouring circle raised a fluttering unease within Jatal. Vague recollections of some of the descriptions he'd read returned as half-glimpsed horrors – many too dreadful to believe. Meanwhile, the human dray animal paced on, his head hanging, his long hair filthy and crawling with vermin – just like any neglected mule or ox. Jatal swallowed his disquiet, murmuring, 'I have read first-hand accounts . . .'

The Warlord grunted his satisfaction and waved Scarza forward. 'Bring him to us.'

The half-Thelomen or Trell sized the man up – fully as massive as he – and his hand went to his shortsword.

'Unnecessary, good Scarza, I assure you. You'll find the fellow fully as gentle as any cow or sheep.'

The giant cocked a sceptical eye to the Warleader then shrugged his compliance. He stepped on to the beaten circular track to stand in the way of the fellow as he came around on yet another pass. The wooden arm swung around and struck him in the stomach, bouncing, then paused as the chattel stopped his pacing. The constant background grumbling of the mortar stones stilled.

'You'll come with me now,' Scarza said gently. 'No one intends you any harm.'

The man didn't answer. Nor did he even raise his head. He was filthy, unwashed, his simple rag loinwrap rotting off him. Scarza looked to the Warleader for guidance.

'Untie him.'

Scarza unwrapped the leather straps that secured the man's hands to the wooden arm. It occurred to Jatal that those straps and that arm, no more than a tree branch, were in no way adequate to imprison such a brute. The lieutenant led him by those straps to the Warleader.

'Lift his head,' the Warleader said.

Even the half-breed betrayed a hesitation born of unease, yet he obeyed, using his hand to push the man's chin up.

Jatal winced and the bodyguards cursed their surprise and disgust. The poor fellow's eyes were no more than empty pits where the ends of tendons and muscles writhed.

'Open his mouth,' the Warleader ordered in a strange sort of calm detachment, as if he were examining some curious insect or piece of artwork and not a man at all. Scarza's great expanse of chest lifted as he took a steadying breath, but he did comply. He squeezed the man's cheeks, forcing his jaws apart.

Jatal glimpsed within the emptiness of the cavity of his mouth then quickly averted his gaze. The poor unfortunate's tongue also had been carved away.

'Now lift his hair from his forehead, Scarza. Push it back.'

'*That is quite enough,*' Jatal breathed shakily.

The Warleader somehow trapped Jatal's averted gaze. His stare was strangely compelling, his dark eyes almost hidden within the tight folds of his tanned features, his mouth bracketed by severe lines. For a moment, the image of a mask occurred to Jatal. He fancied that the flesh of the Warleader's face was itself a mask and that what lay beneath was not human. 'That is certainly not enough, young prince. This is only the beginning. Turn and look upon the handiwork of the Thaumaturgs. This is what they would intend for you.' He nodded curtly to Scarza, who thrust back the slave's hair.

Beginning near the temples lay twin pearly scars. Each traced lines up the sides of the man's forehead to disappear up amid his hairline. Jatal squinted his puzzlement. 'What is this?'

'You have heard, no doubt,' said the Warleader, 'of those who have endured head wounds that have left them behaving oddly? Forgetful? Even mindless?'

His gaze still on the disfigured face of the slave, Jatal nodded. 'Yes. I have read treatises from chirurgeons and mediciners speculating upon the head as the seat of some aspects of personality.'

'Just so, my prince. This man still has a sort of intelligence – he can stand, probably eat what is given him. And no doubt follow simple orders. But his essence, his identity as an individual capable of initiative and self-awareness, has been taken from him. Our Thaumaturgs view flesh as you view clay or wood – to be shaped as required. And what we see here is a mild example of the true depths of their . . . research.'

Something more than disgust churned acid in Jatal's stomach. He knew these things intellectually of course . . . but to be confronted with the reality – in the flesh, as they say – made him feel threatened on a level far more intimate than any mundane enemy. It felt as if what these Thaumaturgs practised somehow endangered his own distinctiveness, his claim to uniqueness as a human being. It made him shiver to his core. *And we are riding into this asylum?*

He pulled his gaze away with a shudder.

'What should we do with him?' the Warleader asked, again his neutral tone suggesting that what they discussed was no more than the fate of a sack of grain or a hog.

Jatal wanted to draw his sword and hack the perverted thing to pieces. He forced himself to take a calming breath. This unfortunate, abhorrent though he might be, was in fact the victim. Destroying him would solve nothing. It was the inhuman authors of his suffering who ought to be eliminated: these Thaumaturgs – but that was not their mission. Jatal shifted his attention to the Warleader to find the man studying him with a steady gaze, as if *he* were the true subject of all this. 'Killing him would be pointless. But we cannot let him be seen.' Jatal paused, searching for the right words. 'It would cause . . . unease . . . within the ranks.'

The Warleader nodded curtly. 'I concur. He should be disposed of – even though such things will become ever more common as we advance. Regardless, better to delay such discoveries for as long as possible.' He waved to Scarza. 'Get rid of it.'

The giant rubbed his wide jaws. 'Perchance we could simply let him go . . .'

'He'd merely sit down somewhere and starve to death. No, it is a mercy.'

Still the lieutenant hesitated, frowning. He tapped a thumb to one curving canine. ''Tis no fault of his own . . .'

The Warleader's voice hardened: 'Then perhaps we should track down his father who sold him into it!' And in a single blur he drew the heavy bastard sword at his side, swung it up, and brought it cleaving down atop the creature's head, chopping the skull clear down past its ears.

Jatal and the surrounding bodyguards flinched in their saddles. The huge carcass twitched, still standing though quite dead. The severed tendons of the eye pits squirmed, the mouth fell open, and as the body tottered to its side, the blade grated its path clear of the skull.

'Now get rid of it, Lieutenant,' the Warleader announced into the silence, his voice low. 'If you would be so good.'

Scarza wiped away the spattering of fresh droplets that dotted his chest, then saluted. 'Aye, Warleader.' He grasped an ankle and dragged the body off.

The Warleader wiped the blade on a scrap of cloth then resheathed it. He crossed his arms on the horn of the saddle and regarded Jatal through half-slit eyes. 'Still . . . these Thaumaturgs and their horrors ought to be wiped from the earth, yes?'

'That is not our goal, Warleader. But yes, if it could be done.'

The man gave a slow thoughtful nod. 'Yes. If it could be done.'

Jatal inclined his head a fraction and then urged his mount aside. 'Until later.'

The Warleader bowed. 'Aye, prince of the Hafinaj.'

As he walked Ash back to the column, something urged Jatal to glance behind; he found the Warleader's gaze yet remained upon him, steady and unblinking. Under that hot stabbing stare he rode on feeling a new foreboding.

~

That evening in his tent, reclining on the unrolled carpets and bedding, Jatal attempted yet again to ease his mind by treating himself to selections from Shivanara. But the magic of the words eluded him – his mind wandered elsewhere, flirting with the stories of the Thaumaturgs he'd heard whispered at wayside inns and round the hearthfires late at night. Of harems of playthings drugged into unending desire, or their bodies altered to heighten their master's ecstasy – the manner of said refinements usually varying with the teller. Privately, he'd scoffed at such heated prurient imaginings. It seemed to him that these theurgists were far too keenly preoccupied with matters of life and death to waste time and resources on such debauchery. Yet the low class labourers, soldiers and servants did enjoy the titillation of such fantasies.

Sighing, he pressed the slim volume to his forehead, murmuring, 'Apologies, O Poet.'

The heavy cloth flap lifted and a female servant entered, bowing, a tray in her arms. 'An evening repast, my prince?'

He waved to the low table and shut his eyes, attempting to steady his thoughts. What awaited them at Isana Pura? How large a garrison? They needed better intelligence. Perhaps he should investigate . . .'

Jatal frowned and opened his eyes: the servant yet remained, head bowed. 'Yes?'

The woman raised her head and Jatal stared, stunned. Princess Andanii regarded him, one expressive brow cocked. He sprang to his feet. 'Princess! By the ancestors—' He clamped his mouth shut, hunching, terrified he'd been overheard.

She covered her mouth to stifle a giggle. 'If only you could have seen your face, Jatal.'

He crossed to her side, hissing, 'What are you doing here?'

Her teasing smile hardened. 'Really, Prince. What sort of question is that?'

Jatal flinched, bowing. 'Apologies, Princess. I mean – what if you are discovered? Your reputation . . .'

'If I am discovered?' She pressed a hand to her chest, 'All will sigh . . . *Ah, young love!*'

Jatal forced himself to a low table to pour himself a tumbler of wine from one of the decanters. He sat, rather heavily, and set down the leather-bound volume. 'Of course, my princess . . .'

She reclined opposite, regarded him, chin in fist. 'Is that why you have not come to me?'

Jatal hurriedly swallowed his drink. 'I'm sorry?'

'My reputation. You feared compromising my reputation.'

'Of course!'

'Ah, yes. Of course . . .'

She lay back, stretching. Her breasts rose beneath the thin servant's shift. Jatal looked away. 'Have you given more thought to our union?' she asked.

Jatal coughed on his drink. He gestured to the glass, which he hurriedly set down. He cleared his throat. 'Yes, my princess. I have. I believe we should keep it secret. Only the master of your horse, and mine, need know. Publicly, our uneasy accord stands. Privately, we have agreed to a – temporary – formal cessation of hostilities.'

Andanii sat up. She affected a frown and tugged at the string tying the front of her plain servant's blouse. 'A cessation of hostilities only . . . my prince? Not an intimate . . . partnership? A union of our . . . resources?'

Prince Jatal found he could not speak. His pulse was now a pounding roar; his throat as parched as the worst quarter of their Quar-el emptiness. He could only watch fascinated as Andanii glided towards him on all fours.

'In some lands,' she began, her voice low, 'a woman who is not afraid of power is denounced as a shameless seductress. A slut and a whore. While a man from that same culture who reaches out and takes what he wants is lauded as justly virile, a daring hero.' She pushed him back upon the bedding and straddled him. 'What think you of that inconsistency, O learned prince?'

Jatal slid his hands over her thighs, up under her skirt, found them hot and slick with sweat. He forced a swallow to wet his throat, almost dizzy with need. 'I think that any man who denounces a woman merely for acting as he would . . .' he hissed as Andanii clenched her thighs, 'is a very small and frightened little man.'

Andanii began untying his belt. 'And you, Jatal? Are you frightened?'

'No, my princess. I am not frightened.' *Not of you. It is your ambition that terrifies me. Are you here with me now because you see a worthy alliance . . . or a weak partner easily dominated? This uncertainty tortures me. That, and the truth that I do not know what I would do . . . if either should prove true.*

A line from Shivanara came to him then:

*And – oh, gods – what does it mean that amid fields of
    rotting corpses
The most fragrant blossoms grow?*

153

The moment the solid canopy of tall trees closed over him, Murk knew he didn't want to be where he was. The column of Malazan regulars, however, plunged on without pause, as if some enraged Ascendant were on their tails – which, frankly, was as close to the truth as Murk wished to tiptoe. He and Sour followed the chest strapped in its litter, bouncing and being knocked about as Dee and Ostler stumbled over exposed roots, banged into trees, and ducked branches. And with each knock and judder of the chest Sour, at his side, would grab his arm, or gasp, or whine, until sick of it Murk shook him off, growling, 'It ain't made of glass, damn it!'

Sour released his arm, hunching like a browbeaten child. Sighing, Murk jerked a thumb to the rear. 'Cover our tracks.'

The crab-like fellow straightened, his brows shooting up. 'Oh! Right.'

Murk watched, sidelong, as his partner's gaze got that absent look and turned inward. He walked now avoiding roots and branches, but without actually looking directly at anything. Behind them Murk knew a distracting maze of misdirection, erasures and blind paths was now uncoiling, all springing from the muddled mind at his side. A frustrating addled mess that would drive any sane person who tried to order it into despair. How Sour did it was a mystery to him: a personal twisted melding of Thyr and Mockra, or simply a path demarking the borderlands between. Either way, it helped immensely that the fellow wasn't quite sane in the conventional sense.

As for himself, it was time for him to do his part. If Sour was deflecting any effort to trace them, then he would see to it they weren't really here at all. He summoned his Warren and with his next step he not only trod the jungle around them but simultaneously walked the paths of Meanas.

He found that he now walked two jungles. One was of Jacuruku; the other was a shadow-forest of dark trees. The discovery almost made him trip over his own feet. He knew this shadow-forest: it was a feature, a hazard, of the Shadow Realm that all avoided. A wide impenetrable wood from which none ever returned. *So this was what it hid. Or mirrored. Jacuruku. Or, perhaps more accurately, a Shadow of Ardata's realm.*

In any case, bad news for him. There was little he could do here. He would have to limit himself to manipulations from outside the Warren proper. *In fact, I've lingered long enough as it is . . .*

He was about to drop his access when he glimpsed a bright light off to one side.

Now, a light in the woods might not be too unusual. But this was Shadow, where a bright glow was as natural as a pool of water in the coals of a blacksmith's forge. He knew it was stupid, and he shouldn't, but he *was* curious – what could possibly be generating such a radiance here in the very home of Shadow? He picked his way onward, threading between the brittle black branches.

It was the glowing image of child, a young girl, perhaps six or so. Yet the image was not really a child as it was sculpted of a pale greenish luminosity. She was peering about as if fascinated, displaying no fear at all, just curiosity – rather like himself.

Murk stepped into the glade. 'Who are you, child?'

She turned to face him and he flinched from eyes of pure jade brilliance. 'Who am I?' she echoed in a high piping voice. 'I do not know. No one here really knows.'

Alarms of all sorts clanged in Murk's awareness, loud enough to drown out the surrounding creaking and complaining of the forest of trees. The hairs on his forearms rose tingling from his skin and he found it difficult to talk. 'Have you a name, child?' he managed, clearing his throat.

Her gaze became distant as she tilted her head. 'For the longest time I did not know I needed one. Why distinguish one's self from the other when there is no other? Then someone spoke to me and I knew the need. I asked for a name and he gave me one.'

'And . . . what name was that, child?'

'Celeste.'

Murk blew out a breath as if gut-punched. *Not without a certain grim sense of humour, whoever that was.* 'And what are you doing here, Celeste?'

'I do not know. I thought you'd know since you brought me here.'

Murk discovered he was sitting. He blinked up at the child who was now uncomfortably close, hands on knees, peering down at him. 'You were dreaming for a time,' she said. 'Is that normal?'

'It is when you've been hit over the head by a mattock,' he grumbled under his breath.

She giggled, a hand covering her mouth. 'I like you.'

'That's just dandy.' Then he froze, listening. The surrounding woods had become quiet, almost breathless. 'How long was I dreaming?'

She shrugged her thin shoulders. 'I do not know your measure of time.'

'Listen, we have to get out of here. It isn't safe for . . . for you.'

'But I rather like it here.'

'That is good,' said a new voice, a deep reverberating one. 'For you will be imprisoned here for ever.'

Murk slowly turned his head. It was a demon – one of the shadowkind, a great hulking Artorallah, all covered in bristly black hair. 'I wouldn't mess with this child if I were you,' he warned. 'I really wouldn't.'

The demon pressed a taloned hand to its broad chest. 'I? It is not I who will act. These woods are here to keep you trespassers out. It is they who will act.'

Celeste was frowning as she regarded the demon. 'I don't know if I like you,' she said.

Murk reached out to her. 'Celeste—' He broke off because he discovered he could not move. Knotted roots had grown up over his legs. Black fresh earth was now climbing his thighs. With enormous effort he managed to contain his panic, and he raised his eyes to the Artorallah. 'You are making a mistake. Edgewalker would not countenance this.'

The demon's fangs grated as it sneered. 'What do you know of He Who Guards The Realm?'

Roots now clenched Murk's waist, crushing the breath from him. 'I know he banishes! He doesn't . . .' he grunted his pain, 'imprison.'

'Stop this,' Celeste demanded of the Artorallah.

'I am sorry, little mage,' the demon answered Murk, sounding genuinely regretful. 'But you have entered the forest of the Azathanai. There will be no escape for you.'

'I told you to stop this!' Celeste repeated, and she stamped her foot.

In answer to that tiny gesture, the ground shook as if wrenched by an earthquake. The nearest trees juddered from root to tip, branches whipping and snapping. The eruption travelled onward through the woods in an ever-widening circle. Murk was thrown free. The Artorallah steadied itself against a trunk. What must have been stunned disbelief played across its alien face. The ground beneath Celeste's feet steamed and glowed as if molten.

'Please, child!' Murk shouted from where he lay. 'Let us just go!'

She tossed her head high, her short hair flicking. 'Well . . . if you wish. Very well.' She waved a hand.

Blinking, Murk now peered up at the looming, concerned, lopsided face of Sour. He flinched from the warm stink of the man's breath.

156

'You was gone a long time there, Murk.'

He rubbed his face with both damp cold hands, let out a long hissed breath. He glanced about: it was evening, a light rain was falling, camp had been made. Someone had sat him down under a tree. Unfortunately in a damp spot and now the seat of his pants was sodden. Unless he was responsible for that damp spot – the moment he realized whom he'd met.

His gaze snapped to the nearby pack where it lay tied to its litter. So, no manifestation here. Was that a good thing or a bad thing? Could it – she – hear, see, what was going on around it? Could he communicate with her? Did he want the responsibility?

Captain Yusen emerged from the mist as Sour wandered off on some errand of his own. He squatted to study Murk through his narrowed slit gaze. 'You find something?'

Murk inclined his head to the litter. 'It's aware, Captain.'

The gaze shifted to the pack, narrowed almost closed amid all the wrinkles and folds from a lifetime of such tightening. *Decades of squinting across fields for the tiniest betraying details of threats or deployments.* 'What do you mean, "aware"?'

'I mean aware. We met. Calls herself Celeste. Might be listening right now.'

Now the mouth pursed tight. The hatchet lines bracketing it deepened and lengthened. *A worrier, this one, always thinking.* 'I see . . .'

'Might be best to let the lads know. Watch their mouths. Act respectfully.'

A brief nod. 'I understand. I'll have a word with them. A way off.' He straightened, cast one lingering glance to the litter, then offered Murk a nod. 'Later.'

Murk fought the urge to salute. 'Cap'n.'

Sour returned carrying a bowl of something steaming. He offered it and a fist of hardbread. 'Reminds me too much of Blackdog.'

Murk winced. 'I don't want to hear about Blackdog.' Gods, that mess! It still made him shiver. Just a lad then, fresh from his 'prenticeship with old blind Eghen. The man never did forgive him for joining the enemy . . .

''Cept it's a lot warmer,' Sour continued, musing. 'An' there's *way* more rain. An' it's a jungle and not a forest or a bog.' He wriggled down into a nook of dry roots close to Murk under the protection of the tall tree. 'What's the difference anyway? 'Tween a jungle and a forest?'

Murk edged away from him. 'Damned if I know. Just words.' He sucked on the bread, held the bowl between his knees, which were drawn up close to his chest. 'I guess they mean places people feel threatened, where they don't feel in charge or in control. Makes 'em want to hack it all down, that fear.'

'What about the people living here?'

'Hunh. Good question. 'Cause we're foreigners to these lands we might think they feel the same fearful way about it, hey? But I don't think they do. I think they call it home.'

Dusk came quickly beneath the cloud cover and the thick canopy. Sour's eyes glistened in the dark and they shifted to the litter, and its burden, under guard of five soldiers. 'And our guest? Somethin' to fear? We don't control it, neither . . .'

Murk chewed on the bread and winced as he bit down on a stone. He felt about for it then spat aside. 'No. Not just now, anyway. It – she's – curious right now. It's as if . . .' He swallowed any further speculation. It seemed premature. His partner's attention swung briefly to him, then away. He tucked his hands up under his armpits and let his chin fall to his chest. Almost immediately the rise and fall of the fellow's chest steadied and to all appearances he was asleep. But Murk knew he wasn't; Sour had cast his awareness outwards and was watching the surroundings for anyone's approach. Halfway into the night it would be his turn and so he wrapped his arms around his knees, set his chin on to his knees and let his eyes close.

What he hadn't said was that this shard, or sliver, or whatever it was, seemed to have acted as if it had never met anyone before. As if it had always been alone, or imprisoned, or lost, or whatever. Innocent of everything. Naïve. An ignorant god. Laughable idea, wasn't it? But there it was.

So, question was – what was he to do about it? Teach the thing the ways of the world? Him? A failed cadre mage and thief? No. Not for him. Way too much responsibility, that. Not in the job description. Still . . . there were others around this region who'd jump at the chance, weren't there, Murk me boy? Would you want these Thaumaturgs teaching it what to believe? Or this Ardata and her menagerie? Who else was there? Maybe this Yusen fellow? Gods – did he want to be the one to offer someone such a dangerous choice? To be responsible for – well, for the disaster that could follow? Dare he do that to the man? Or anyone, for that matter?

A stick poked him and Murk cracked open one eye. Sweetly stood peering down at him; the scout looked to have been dragged through a mud pit. 'Way?' the man asked, hardly moving his lips, his hair plastered down by the rain.

Murk blinked up at him. 'Way? You mean . . . which way? To go?' The scout just stared, his jaws bunching as he chewed on something. 'You mean tomorrow? Which way to go tomorrow?' More silent chewing, the eyes flat and devoid of any emotion. Murk held up his open hands. 'Look, Sweetly . . . this mysterious man of few words act is really getting up my nose. I've seen the act a thousand times and frankly, I'm tired of it. Okay? So . . . what do you say to that, hey?'

The eyes slid aside to squint into the dark for a time then returned to him. The scout chewed, thoughtful, then he ventured, 'South?'

Murk let his head fall until his forehead pressed against his knees. 'Yes. South. For now – south.' He heard nothing but knew the man was gone. *May the gods learn wisdom!* What choice did he have? It would have to be him.

No one else around here seemed sane enough.

*   *   *

It was perhaps the constant unchanging drone of the insects that did it. That insistent buzzing that grated on one's consciousness, sleeping and waking. The only defence was to block it out. To raise walls. If only to protect one's mind. So would Shimmer sometimes come to herself, blinking and twitching, like a sleeper breaching the surface of a deep slumber. During these moments she often found she was standing at the rail staring at the murky river's surface where branches and other wrack drifted past – even the occasional fat and gorgeously bright flower blossom. Sometimes it would be day, the sun blurred as if seen through air like a thick sticky soup; other times it would be night, the Scimitar glowing deep jade behind the cloud cover of the seasonal rains. It did not seem to matter. In any case, the scenery never changed: thick impenetrable jungle choked the shores. Occasionally she glimpsed what might have been the decaying remains of a dugout canoe lying on the muddy shore, or an overgrown clearing of cultivated land, or the rotted woven walls of what might have once been a collection of huts.

But all this was merely the mundane scenery. Bizarre visions also assaulted her. Storms of gaudy multicoloured birds would gyre past the vessel. Immense creatures resembling giant bats – wyverns? – glided through the night. Sometimes it seemed that faces appeared beneath the river, met her gaze, then drifted away. And she would catch glimpses of the oddest silhouettes of creatures she had no name for stalking the shores to either side: creatures half human and half beast. D'ivers? Soletaken? Or something completely unknown to her?

All the while some nagging irksome worry plucked and tugged at her. Something was wrong. *Something* . . . Blinking, she glanced about to see her fellow Avowed standing silent and immobile, as if dead, or enchanted. Broken branches cluttered the deck along with leaves and fallen equipment; the masts and yardarms hung draped in shreds of rotten sailcloth; vines the ship had scraped from trees dragged in the weak wash behind the vessel.

Shimmer blinked again then jerked, wrenching her hands from the rail. *No! K'azz!* Where was he? *Must find him.* In an immense lurch of mental effort she forced herself to turn to her nearest companion: Cole. She prodded the man, but he failed to respond. Drawing back her hand she slapped him across the face.

He rocked, his sandy hair flying. Then he touched at his jaw and frowned. 'Shimmer?'

'Where's K'azz? Find him.'

'Yes . . . right.'

Shimmer moved off, stepping carefully over the litter choking the deck. She found him near the bow, leaning on the railing. Rutana stood with him; she seemed to be studying him. 'K'azz!' He did not respond. She leaned close, trying to catch his gaze. 'K'azz!'

His attention slowly rose to her. His pale hazel eyes focused. 'Yes?'

'We haven't eaten in days. We need to put in. We're all weakening.'

He cocked his head as if trying to recall something, then nodded thoughtfully. 'Ah, yes.' He turned to Rutana. 'We must put in.'

Leaning on the railing, hands clenching her upper arms, the woman crooked her maddening half-smile. 'You can try . . .'

'I demand it,' said K'azz and he moved to the unmanned tiller.

Shimmer glanced ahead and pointed. 'There! A clearing.'

K'azz slewed the tiller arm over. At first nothing happened. Perhaps it was K'azz's will, or a grudging acquiescence on the part of whatever drove the vessel, but gradually the bowsprit, draped in its hanging creepers and branches, edged over towards the shore.

The servant of Ardata pursed her wrinkled lips, as if determined to appear indifferent.

'Wake everyone,' K'azz told Shimmer. She went to obey.

When the vessel neared the shore Cole and Amatt dived in, swam to the root-choked slope and dragged themselves up. The best ropes that could be found were tossed, and they tied them off where they could. A tiny dory was lowered. All this, Rutana and her compatriot Nagal watched from the rail, arms crossed, their expressions set in mild disapproval.

Turgal, Amatt and Cole set off into the dense woods as a hunting party. Shimmer and the two mages walked about the shore, relieved to be free of the river for a time. Like everyone, Shimmer had long since abandoned her metal armour and now wore only her long padded gambeson, metal-studded, and hung with straps and buckles. She carried her long whipsword on her back, a knife belted at her side. Her hair hung loose, sticking to the back of her neck. She knew it stank of old sweat.

Here, between deluges of the rainy season, the ground was dry, the undergrowth long dead. Perhaps new shoots were soon to arise. The humidity in the close confines of the jungle, the rankness of rotting vegetation, all oppressed her. Exploring, she found the remains of an old village, perhaps even the layered remains of many such. Decaying bamboo poles stood from the ground. Stones lay half buried: for grinding? For building? She picked up one worked into a haft or long handle. A pestle? What could they have been grinding here? She'd seen only small gardens.

The snap of branches brought her attention round; her absent-minded wandering had brought her far from the others, and much farther from the riverside than she'd intended. Shapes moved through the woods around her. Hunched forward they were, gangly, with long arms and long heads. They closed now from all sides. Shimmer turned in place, reaching back to draw her whipsword.

'Who are you? What do you want?'

One of the creatures stilled, rising back on its rear legs. 'Impertinence!' it coughed, as if barking. 'That you should demand such of us!'

'We who live here,' said another, from close behind, making Shimmer spin about.

Closer now, they resembled Soletaken, yet not. A great deal of the man-jackal Ryllandaras looked to be in them as they resembled half men, half dogs, with long dark muzzles, and coats of hair striped tawny and black across their backs. She even glimpsed multiple teats on one – females, too?

'What do you want?' she demanded, striking a ready stance. It surprised her that though it was distorted and slurred by their canine mouths, they were speaking an accented Talian.

'You should ask that of us!' the first growled again. 'You who invade our lands!'

'*Your* lands?'

The creature threw its taloned hands wide as if enraged. Grey hair lined its stomach. 'Who else? Stupid trespasser.'

'You speak Talian . . .'

'We speak your Isturé tongue, yes. You brothers and sisters of betrayers and turncoats.'

'You mean Skinner . . .'

Many about her hunched, hissing and growling at the name. 'Yes. Now, get back in your thing that floats and go away. We do not want you here. You are not welcome. Go away.'

'Ardata invited us.'

The creatures snarled anew, hands spasming as if eager to tear at her. Long carmine tongues lolled as they panted. 'Speak not *her* name! You are unworthy. You are betrayers and untrue.'

'Betrayers? So Skinner—'

Enraged, they closed all at once. Shimmer spun, the keen blade of her whipsword flashing in the light. The nearest lurched away clutching at slashed forearms, muzzles, throats. In the pause of surprise that followed, she warned, 'I mean you no harm!'

Something struck her from behind and she fell, twisting, to look up at another. '*Eat the bitch!*' this one howled and threw its maw wide, teeth reaching for her.

Flames lanced over Shimmer, roaring like an opened furnace. The creatures yowled their agony. She clenched her eyes, holding her breath, and turned her face into the hot dry earth. A great rushing wind pulled at her and the heat dissipated. She lifted her face to dare a glance. The dry brush was aflame all about her. Smoking blackened carcasses lay amid the ash, seeping boiling juices. She straightened, gingerly, whipsword ready.

To one side stood a figure as familiar as it was impossible that he should be here: her dead fellow Avowed, Smoky. He appeared just as stunned as she. He studied his hands, obviously quite bewildered.

'How . . .' she began, amazed.

'Got no damned idea,' he said before he dissipated into blown dust that drifted away on the anaemic wind.

Someone approached, steps crackling in the burnt grass. Shimmer turned to see the Jacuruku witch Rutana. She was kneading the many leather straps that encircled her arms as she studied the seared earth. She lifted her chin. 'I told you not to leave the ship.'

'Foreigner . . .' a voice grated, weak and wet.

Shimmer glanced about searching for the source of the faint call. She found that one of the blackened shapes still breathed. 'Yes?'

The dog-creature licked its lips. It breathed in quick short pants. 'Leave,' it grated. 'You do not deserve her. You will never – you will never . . . love her . . .'

'Love her?'

The creature's short breaths slowed. The light in its brown eyes dimmed and they took on a fixed stare. Shimmer turned her puzzled gaze to Rutana. 'Love her? Ardata?'

The witch watched her silently for a time while reaching some sort of decision, then scorn twisted her slash of a lipless mouth. 'We do not want you here. Nor do we need you.'

Shimmer brushed past the woman. 'Funny – that's exactly how I feel.'

On her way back to the vessel, Shimmer shouted a recall. She found Lor and ordered her to spread the word. K'azz she found exactly where he'd been earlier. Something in her anger must have communicated itself through the stamp of her booted feet because he turned at her approach, one brow raised.

'Yes, Shimmer?'

'Why in the Abyss are we here?' she demanded.

He crossed his arms, sighing, and seeing these old familiar mannerisms worn by this old man made Shimmer wince yet again. *What has happened to him? Is the power of the Vow doing this to him? Eating him alive? Should I feel pity? All I feel is revulsion.*

'We are here to deal with Skinner.'

'You have already disavowed him.'

'It seems that is not enough.'

'You mean he is still bound?'

He gave a slow reluctant nod. 'Yes. It appears so.'

'Then we will never be rid of him!'

A sad smile crossed his aged face. 'Like family, Shimmer.'

She slumped against the rail. 'Damn it to Hood!'

Gwynn and Lor joined them. 'What has happened?' Gwynn asked. 'There's a familiar smell in the air . . .'

Shimmer nodded. 'I was attacked. The locals don't want us here.'

'I could have told you that,' Lor murmured, peering down to where Cole, Turgal and Amatt struggled in the mud to push the vessel from the shore.

'I was rescued by an Avowed – but a dead one. Smoky.' She tried to catch K'azz's gaze. 'How could that be?'

The man would not meet her eye. Head lowered, he began, 'The locals call this region *Himatan*. They claim it is half of the real world

163

and half of the spirit realm. Perhaps the Brethren are closer to us here . . .'

Ahh, K'azz! So smooth a liar to others. Yet so poor a liar to us! What are you hiding? She turned her attention to the mages and found them just as uneasy as she. 'Perhaps,' she allowed. Her gaze promised the two words later. 'Yet for now we—'

The vessel's lurching interrupted her. Everyone righted themselves as the ship ground free of the shore. Shimmer glanced down to see the three Avowed all standing in the waist-high waters and staring their bemusement at a grinning Nagal as the big man brushed his hands together, appearing quite self-satisfied.

Shimmer frowned, thinking, *Did that fellow alone just . . . ?*

She broke off as K'azz walked away. 'What about Smoky?' she called after him.

'In time, Shimmer,' he answered without turning. 'We'll see – in time.'

*   *   *

Saeng had never before dared enter the Gangrek Mounts that marked the formal border between Thaumaturg holdings and Ardata's lands. Some named them the Fangs, or the Dragon's Fangs, for their similarity to jutting teeth as they shot so suddenly from the flat jungle to rise sheer for hundreds of feet. They seemed to have grown so swiftly they brought the jungle with them; it hung down their black rock faces in vines, creepers and roots. Verdant greenery topped them like mussed shaggy pelts.

Hanu led, hacking his way through the denser brush and carrying her over the deeper sinks and the mires of choked pools. A troop of monkeys shadowed them, hooting and shaking the leaves amid the high canopy. Brightly coloured birds shot from branches in explosions of flame crimson and sapphire blue. They shrieked and chattered their irritation. Some flew on to roost high in the vegetation hanging from the rearing mountains. Closer now, she knew that mountains was something of a misnomer. Mountains, she understood, could be as big as countries. They took days, sometimes weeks, to climb or cross. These features were in no way as gigantic.

What these mounts did possess that made them potentially just as dangerous, however, were sudden sheer drops into seemingly bottomless sinkholes. Some of these were immense, containing entire lakes that she and Hanu were forced to detour around. The pits and openings dotted the ground, making it impossible to move after dark. And so come the evening, as the clouds thickened for the nightly rain, they would seek shelter amid these caves and sit out the rains, awaiting the dawn.

And it was into one of these pits one dark twilight that Hanu disappeared.

He was there one moment, cutting the brush from their path, and then he was gone. So sudden and silent was his disappearance it was as if the jungle had snatched him away. Saeng froze. 'Hanu?' she called, still not believing he was gone. 'Hanu?'

Silence answered her, but not true silence: the ringing cacophony of the jungle – full of the brushing of broad heavy leaves, the creaking of trunks, the constant keen whirring of an infinity of insects, the piercing songs of unseen birds, and the distant rush of falling water. *'Hanu!'*

She edged forward one step, then another, parted the leafed vines. The path ended at a sheer drop into darkness. Water streamed down in a thin sheen and the hanging vines swung weakly as if slowing from a disturbance. 'Hanu!'

She waited but no answer emerged from the dark. The evening's warm deluge now pattered down, slapping her shoulders and hair.

'Dammit to the Dark King . . .' She took hold of the vines and yanked on them to test their strength. The hand-hold seemed solid enough. 'I'm coming!' She swung out over the abyss, fought to entwine her legs, and began letting herself down.

She descended into darkness. Immediately, her arms began to ache, her hands to numb. Her vision adjusted until she could make out an immense cavern. What little light remained beamed down as a thin glow illuminating the centre of a heaped pile of overgrown debris. The vines she clung to hung as a curtain halfway out over the gulf. Water streamed all about, hissing as it sliced into hidden pools. Suddenly dizzy, she turned her face away from the height to press it to the waxy leaves of the vines and their sweet stink. She descended by alternately easing the grip of each hand. The woody bark cut her palms and sliced the skin of her fingers but she held on for her life.

Eventually, after the pain became more than she believed she could take, she stumbled down on to uneven rocks. She had to force her hands open to free them from the bunched tangled vine she gripped. 'Hanu?' she called, panting. 'Hanu?'

Where could he . . . By the restless dead, girl, are you some sort of mage or not? Saeng willed herself to see. In a swirl of colours the dark took on shades of deep crimson and bright yellow. She could

165

see, but not normally: it seemed to depend upon what areas had been in the light – these glowed the brightest – while the depths of the cavern held a deep, almost black carmine. She set out searching among the jumble of fallen rock.

She splashed through pools of standing water. The sheets of falling rain obscured her vision. A sort of slime of rotting vegetation and mud covered the rocks, making her footing treacherous. While she searched through the grotto the crashing of the many streaming waterfalls swelled into a commingled roar.

It occurred to her that the pool she splashed through was rising. She slogged her way to the cavern's centre, where the last of the light streamed down, and gave one last yell: '*Hanu!*'

Her voice returned to her, echoing. Panic rose choking her as the thought came: *We'll drown!* Somehow the thought of imminent death calmed her, perhaps because it was something she was so very familiar with. *Yes, death. Just two more ghosts, he and I. And thinking of that – aren't you a damned witch?* Saeng pressed the heels of her palms to her eyes. *Gods, girl! Use these damned magics they showed you!*

She took three slow breaths before reaching out with her awareness, trying to sense him. She came up with nothing, which she thought odd. She ought to be able to sense him. Then she remembered all the countless protections and investments she'd layered upon him the many nights he'd accompanied her into the jungle. She reordered her thoughts so that she was reaching out to her brother, Hanu himself, from before he'd been taken from them. And now she sensed him. She sloshed through the rising waters and found him lying insensate, or dead, entangled in a heap of fallen vines.

She tried shaking him. 'Hanu. Wake up!' She felt over his stone-like armoured body, his enclosed helm, found no obvious wound, crack, or blood. Water now thundered down from all sides. A current began to push her as the waters flowed past. She had to raise Hanu's head to keep it out of the rush.

An outlet. There must be some sort of an outlet, an underground stream, or river.

Something bashed into her and she clutched at the vines to support herself: a branch pushed past, carried along by the current. *I'm standing in the bed of an underground stream!*

The flow deepened and strengthened. She fought it, one arm entwined around a handful of the hanging vines, the other under the armoured chin of her brother. But it pulled at his limp heavy body. And he was far more massive than she. As time passed the

166

cold water drained the strength from her. She came to understand that she would have to choose: it would have to be either the vines or him. But not both.

She held on for as long as she could in the swelling current. Her feet were swept out from beneath her. She locked her elbow under her brother's chin, wrapped her other arm around the vines, but the water now sometimes overtopped her, choking her. What could she possibly do? What magery could save them? She couldn't fly! Couldn't breathe water! One thing only occurred to her, one last possibility should she lose her grip in what was now almost utter darkness.

The time finally came when the pull of the current upon her brother's body was simply too much for her chilled bones and flagging strength. Screaming her frustration, she let go of the vines to hug the armoured body, striving to keep it on the surface. At the same instant she summoned her powers to work upon the form to keep it afloat, even buoyant, so that she could cling to it to save herself.

The roaring churning flow swept them out from under the cavern's opening, and glancing ahead, Saeng now realized true blackness awaited them. It sucked them in like a swallowing throat. She took one panicked breath, considered using her magery to give herself some sort of further vision, dismissed the thought as there was nothing she could do, vision or not, and relaxed to allow the swift charging flow to drag her along.

Hanu in his armour crashed into unseen obstacles, scraping in a dragging of his stone armour against rock, and Saeng hoped he wasn't enduring too much damage, while at the same time she was grateful that he was saving her from these same jagged hazards. At times her vision returned as the flow swept them along beneath similar openings. Through the gaps she glimpsed clouds and sheets of falling rain. They passed beneath a waterfall that pounded them, briefly submerging her. Saeng emerged spluttering and hiked up Hanu's helm where she gripped his neck. She thought she felt him spasm then, perhaps coughing, and a new fear assaulted her: what if he should truly awake? Wouldn't his first unthinking reaction be to strike out? To free himself?

'It's me,' she whispered then, next to his helmed head, 'Saeng.'

But he did not answer; nor did he move again.

A much louder roaring was gathering ahead. It sounded exactly like what she feared it would be: the course was nearing a massive waterfall. She could see no options, no way out. They were being swept along, helpless. Yet her power remained. It seemed to be working in keeping Hanu afloat. She would use it again – somehow – to keep them alive.

Still in complete and utter dark, which was perhaps a mercy in that she could not see the true horror that awaited them, they careered along in the grip of the rushing waters until the thundering engulfed them and, falling, they were airborne for a time. In her moment of greatest panic Saeng threw all her remaining strength and energy into one last effort to protect them, holding back nothing for herself.

Whatever it was she summoned pulled everything from her and the darkness of unconsciousness took her before she knew what their fate would be.

Birdsong awoke her. High sharp calls. She opened her eyes, wincing and blinking, into bright daylight. The crash of a waterfall rumbled nearby – the same one? Probably not. This one coursed in open daylight. She was sodden, chilled, aching all over from countless bruises and bumps, but otherwise seemed whole. She lay in the fall's shallow rocky pond, perhaps deposited by the weakening current.

In a sudden panic she pushed herself erect and peered about, her wet hair whipping.

'He's over there,' a child's voice piped.

Saeng jerked, turning: a boy sat on the rocks nearby. He wore only a cotton wrap about his waist and his head was shaved in the manner of only the most backward and traditional villages. He held a stick in both hands, which he brought to his mouth and blew upon, piping the high birdsong that had woken her. He motioned with the crude handmade flute, pointing.

Gritting her teeth against her exhaustion, she struggled to her feet to limp over to where the lad indicated. Some distance off lay Hanu. He was on his side, immobile. She slumped to her knees next to him and shook him, water dripping from her clothes. 'Hanu! Wake up. Can you hear me?'

'So there's someone in there?' the lad said. 'Is that one of those living statues that are the slaves of the mages?'

'It's just fancy armour,' Saeng answered dully. She was so very tired. Was he dead? How could she even tell?

'Is it?' the lad answered in an oddly knowing tone that brought her gaze to him, squinting. 'I've called Moon,' the boy said, and he blew another piercing blast on the flute.

Saeng blinked, studying him. She must be more worn out than she'd thought. 'I'm sorry? Did you say you called the moon?'

The boy made a great show of his scorn. 'Not *the* Moon. Old Man Moon. He's coming. But he's slow. Not what he used to be, is Old Man Moon.' And he blew a jaunty little tune.

Saeng just blinked anew, her brow clenching. What was going on? Something was, she was sure. She pressed a cold hand to her ringing head. 'Where are we?'

'In the jungle.'

'Thank you.' Saeng squinted up to the canopy of high branches where the sun glared through. It looked to her as if . . . 'Are we east of the mountains?'

'East. West. What is that to those who live their lives in the shadows of the jungle?'

She bit down on her exasperation – she suspected that she wasn't really dealing with a young boy. She ventured: 'Does the sun set behind the mountains?'

'Of course it does. Why shouldn't it? For a grown-up you don't seem to know very much.'

'Thank you. I'll keep that in mind.' So, they'd made it. Passed through to the other side. Entered Himatan, where, she'd always heard, one walked half in the realm of spirits. A realm ruled by the most powerful spirit of all, Ardata, its Queen.

The lad blew a quick series of notes. 'Ah! Here's Moon.'

An old man emerged from among the tangled undergrowth. At least, he had the skinny hunched shape of an old man, but he appeared to be covered in black fur.

'What's this?' he called. 'Strangers in the jungle?'

Walking carefully, he edged his way down to the pond, his limbs stiff and stick-thin. Closer, Saeng could make out that what resembled a thick black pelt was in fact a dense matting of inked tattoos that covered him from head to toe. He studied her, peering down with tiny black eyes under greying tangled brows and surrounded by spidery glyphs. A lively humour seemed to dance in those eyes. 'And what is your name, child?'

'Saeng.'

'And who is this unfortunate?'

'My brother Hanu. Is he – can you tell, is he alive?'

The man's brows rose in surprise. '*You*, of anyone, ought to know who is alive and who is not. But . . . he is your brother and so emotion intervenes. Try to see – calm your mind. See through your fears.'

Saeng nodded at the old man's words. Yes, of course she should be able to sense this. It was just . . . she so dreaded the answer . . .

Yet she had to know, and so she closed her eyes, still nodding, and reached out.

She found a slow steady heartbeat.

A half-gasp half-laugh of relief escaped her and she covered her mouth. *Thank the Ancient Cult!*

'There!' the old man announced. 'That wasn't so hard. Yes, he lives. But he dreams – he has taken a blow to the head, perhaps? I will have to examine him.'

'Examine him? How can you? He's – do you know how to remove the armour?'

A wave dismissed the difficulty. 'I could if I had to, I suppose. But I needn't. Now, let's get him back to my house.'

Saeng looked the frail old man up and down. 'You'll send the boy for help, I imagine.'

Another wave of a hand completely covered in a web of hieroglyphs and symbols of power – even down to the fingertips. 'I live alone but for my young offspring.' He clambered down to Hanu's side. 'Now, the sooner we start the better . . . I am not as swift as I used to be.'

Saeng knew two hale men couldn't lift her brother, encased as he was in his stone armour. It would be like attempting to lift an ox. 'You can't possibly . . .' Her objection died away as the old man picked up Hanu's arm and hiked her brother on to his back so that his armoured limbs hung down over the skinny shoulders that jutted no more than bare bone under tattooed skin.

Bent practically double, his head no higher than his waist, the old man pronounced: 'There! Not so bad. Follow me, yes?'

Saeng stared, astounded, then quickly shuffled backwards out of the fellow's way. 'Yes. Yes . . . of course.'

'Ripan! Lead the way.'

'Must I, Moon?' the youth sighed.

'Ripan . . .'

The youth rose, sullen, rolling his eyes. Kicking at the stones and spinning his flute, he wandered into the jungle. The old man followed. His pace seemed no slower than when he emerged. Saeng brought up the rear.

As they went, Saeng heard the youth, Ripan, unseen ahead through the dense leafed underbrush, begin singing: 'Poor Old Man Moon! How he has waned! Forgot his powers and learnin'. Now he is no more than a beast of burden!'

'Ripan . . .' the old man warned once again, his voice quite unstrained beneath his enormous burden. 'We have guests.'

In answer the youth blew a blast upon his flute. Then he started up once more: 'Poor Hanu stone soldier! Banged his head. Now I wonder . . . is their blood red?'

'Ripan! Manners . . .'

A raw piercing blast from the flute answered that. Silent throughout this exchange, Saeng found it oddly reassuring that no matter where you were, or who, or what, it seemed that family relations were the same everywhere. After a time Ripan contented himself with playing quick irreverent tunes upon the flute, as if in sly counterpoint to Moon's ponderous progress.

They came to a small clearing and at its centre a hut on tall poles, its walls and roof built of woven leaves. A rickety ladder of lashed branches led up to the slouched dwelling. It reminded Saeng of the poorest and most wretched huts of any village she'd ever visited. It frankly wasn't at all what she'd been expecting.

To her gathering horror Moon started up the ladder, her brother draped over his back like a great sack of rice far larger than its bearer. She rushed forward. 'Perhaps we could remain outside . . .'

'No, no. No problem at all.' He climbed a rung. The wood creaked and bent, but held. 'You are my guests! You must stay within.'

'What – both of us?'

'Most assuredly. I insist.'

Grunting, he reached the top of the ladder, and in a great heave deposited her brother inside, his arms scraping the sides of the entrance, his legs sticking out. Moon pushed him in further then crawled in behind. A tattooed arm emerged to beckon: 'Come, come!'

Fearing the entire structure would collapse at any moment, Saeng set one tentative foot on the ladder. The lad, Ripan, now leaned with his back to a post. He sighed his boredom while studying his flute. Gritting her teeth, she climbed. Within, there was only enough room for her to sit cross-legged next to the opening. Moon knelt at Hanu's side, studying him. Her brother lay on bedding of grass and rough woven blankets, all tattered and moth-eaten. Other than this, the hut was empty: utterly without any other feature, possession, or item. No bowl, no pots, no utensils or any other personal touch.

This fact made Saeng the most uneasy. After watching Moon hunched over her brother for a time, she opened her mouth to ask how he was but noticed something that stilled the words in her throat. The dense forest of tattooed symbols and glyphs that covered Moon's back in band after band were actually moving. Each pulsed, individually, almost imperceptibly. Waxing and

171

waning, they revolved in their separate bands while the entire panoply appeared to be edging ever so slowly across the curve of his bent back.

Like the arch of the night sky turning came the thought, unbidden. She swallowed and steadied herself against the pole of the opening. 'How is he?' she managed, her voice weak.

'He has suffered a severe blow to the head. His mind has become unmoored and wanders now in a deep fugue.' Grunting, the old man shifted, facing her. 'He may never awaken again.'

'Can you – is it in your power – to heal him?'

The man's gaze flashed again with humour. 'It just so happens that such matters are my particular area of specialty. You are lucky to have met me.'

And what does luck have to do with anything here in Himatan? was Saeng's first thought, but she smiled her gratitude, letting out her breath. 'I am so very relieved. Would you . . . please?'

His tangled salt and pepper brows rose. 'Ah . . . as to that. We must strike a bargain, you and I.'

'I would give anything to have him healed.'

Now those brows lowered in disapproval. 'Do not be so quick to give everything away, child. There are those in these wilds who would take advantage of such an offer.' Then he barked, loudly, 'Ripan!'

The ladder swayed, then the youth's comely head appeared. 'Yes?' he sighed.

'Bring food for our guests.'

Ripan eyed Saeng up and down, almost grimacing his distaste. 'Food?'

'Yes.'

'Such as . . . ?'

'Fowl, I would suggest. Cooked over a fire on a stick.'

Disgust twisted the youth's angelic face. 'That's a vile thing to do to a bird.'

'Do so in any case.' He waved the youth away. 'Go on.'

Ripan rolled his eyes again and heaved a sigh. 'If I must.' He slid out of sight.

Moon faced Saeng. 'Now. As to our bargain. Over many years I have struck countless such. A favour for a favour. And with each bargain I have always asked just one service in particular.'

It was difficult for Saeng to find her voice but eventually she managed to ask, hoarsely, 'And that is . . . ?'

In a silent yet eloquent gesture the old man swept a hand down

172

his bony ribcage and the round pot of his stomach, over the tangled maze of tattoos that covered every exposed wrinkle and bulge of skin.

Saeng drew a shuddering breath. Her palms suddenly pricked with sweat and her heart lurched from beat to beat. 'Ah. I see . . .'

* * *

It was now only in passing that Osserc noted how the gathering glow of daylight outside the House's grimed glazing dimmed into night and the watery green wash of the Visitor rippled across the table and Gothos opposite, only to give way to the bronze of dawn, and again, and once more, until he ignored the count of the changing light.

What does this creature want? More than all else, this troubled him. *Jaghut!* How they troubled everyone. He'd never been satisfied with his understanding of them. He studied the figure, as immobile as if carved from stone. What cast was that he saw in the line of the lips, the crinkle of the lined flesh at the corner of the amber eyes? Sublime amused condescension? More of their typical assumed superiority? Or was that just what *he* saw within them? If only he could know for certain.

Finally, he could no longer fight the rising strength of his resentment and he cleared his dust-dry throat to demand, loudly and harshly, 'And why are *you* here? What do you believe will accrue to you?'

The bright golden eyes slit by their vertical pupils blinked. Gothos stirred, brushed cobwebs from his gnarled hands. 'Nothing, I assure you. In this I am the mere messenger. The disinterested observer. As always.'

'Why am I not assured?'

Gothos plucked another cobweb from his elbow. 'Yes, why are you not? It would seem that otherwise this effort is entirely futile. Yes?'

'Assure me.'

The glowing eyes narrowed almost dangerously. A long hissed breath escaped the Jaghut. Then, his lips drawing down in obvious distaste, he began, 'For how long have I been accused of scheming, conniving, or otherwise plotting dark plots? Ages of machination . . .' He lifted his hands to gesture about the empty room. 'And look where I am . . .'

'I propose you are just where you choose to be.'

'It is true that my choices have brought me to where I am.' Gothos

173

tilted his head, his long grimed hair swinging. 'The same is true for everyone.'

'Events and the agency of others always intervene . . .'

'True. One exists *in* the world. Categorically speaking, things will always happen. The test, then, is the choices one makes in response.'

Osserc noted a cobweb on his own shoulder. He brushed it away. 'Can we set aside the mountain ascetic philosophizing?'

'Yes, can we? I find it tiresome.'

Now Osserc glared. He clenched his teeth until they grated. Through clamped jaws he ground out: 'So . . . why are you here?'

The Jaghut touched his fingertips together. 'I do not know for certain. Nothing was said, of course. I merely found myself here. For a time I wondered – why me? Why of all those the Azath have at their disposal should I find myself here? And of course the obvious answer came that it is something *of* me, a quality or character, that is desired. Therefore, I am merely being me. That is all that is required. I am here to be your goad. Your adversary. A spur.' He bared his scarred yellowed tusks in a mocking grin. 'In short, I am to act as a prick.'

Osserc could not resist throwing his head back to bark a laugh. Even if the Jaghut's expression displayed his awareness of the many layers he commented upon. Osserc's answering smile was just as frosty. 'Well . . . it is as if you were born to the role.'

Nothing more was said, as nothing more need be said. Osserc stared out the opaque window glazing, layered in grime and dirt, that cast a dim limpid glow within, the source of which he could not be certain was day or night. So. What was he to make of the fellow's words? Jaghut. So many lies had they woven over the millennia. Yet false claims had been made on all sides. No one was innocent – they were always the first to die, the first to be trampled in others' ruthless scramble for power and Ascension.

Yet Anomandaris . . . Cursing beneath his breath, Osserc broke off his musing to blink and refocus upon the room. Someone, or thing, had entered. He heard the pad and shush of light footsteps, yet saw nothing. Then the one other chair at the table, empty, scraped backwards as if of its own volition. A head appeared, brown and knobbly, shaped rather like the stone ammunition of an onager. Dark sly eyes slid side to side to regard him and Gothos, then the mouth parted in the wide expanse of a red yawn.

Osserc regarded the monkey-like creature that seemed to have the run of the House. While he watched, the beast arranged its wrinkled features into something resembling fixed concentration.

174

Yet even as Osserc's own gaze narrowed in annoyance, the creature began to nod, its head sinking, jerking, catching itself, glaring about panicked. Only to blink heavily yet again, its eyelids falling once more.

Osserc raised his gaze to the murk disguising the ceiling. *Ancient Primordial Entities.* Why had the Azath chosen to torture him in this fashion? They would have their revenge, wouldn't they? And of course this – *pricking* – stung so much worse than any slap to the face.

CHAPTER V

The natives of this land are difficult and obstinate in the extreme. Those we capture to serve as our bearers are sullen and lazy workers at best. Some deliberately sabotage the columns by dropping their loads into streams or over cliffs. I was forced to kill a great number of them before they learned to cooperate and understand the benefits of friendship with civilized people.

Hemach Stenay
Journey to the City of Gold

GOLAN DID NOT MENTION TO HIS SUPERIORS THAT THE GREAT meandering beast that was the invasion force, with all its supporting trains of baggage pulled by oxen and carried on the backs of groaning labourers, together with the wagons of the field surgeries, the smithies, the various messes, and the well-ordered miscellaneous supplies of tents and shovels and whatnot, was well behind schedule. The landscape they were entering descended away from the broken jagged peaks of rock and caves and deadly sinkholes of the Gangrek Mounts into a soggy maze of dense brush and tangled vines overtopped by a layered canopy that blocked out nearly all light and enclosed everything beneath in a choking miasma of air so thick one could hardly push oneself through it. Nor did it help at all that these conditions were of course faithfully recorded in the memoirs and field diaries from prior expeditions in his possession – those few who returned alive, of course – as it was one thing to read of such an environment and quite another to wake up to it one choking steamy morning after another.

It was, in a word, all so very enervating. And not just physically, though quite sufficiently so. Golan also felt a strange sort of creeping mental and spiritual malaise. Even the most mundane and fundamental of tasks became tiresome, even somehow unnecessary. Some days ago, for example, he had run a hand over his normally cleanly shaven pate and cheeks to find an unseemly stubble. A rather shocking slip of standards that he could not quite recall having allowed.

Yet such outward fleshly betrayals were as nothing compared to the disturbing dreaminess he sometimes found himself slipping into while enduring the mind-numbing monotony of the march, bobbing from side to side in his litter. Odd musings came to him as his mind drifted unmoored, as it were, within this ocean of green. Why all these strivings, he wondered? To what end? Surely his masters could do nothing with so unpromising a wasteland. Even if it were all burned to the ground it would take generations to squeeze even the least profit from it. And even if they succeeded in ousting Ardata and replacing her with a tame figurehead, either drawn from among these foreigners, or another, what then? The character of this land had escaped them for generations. What *were* they trying to accomplish?

Come to think of it, he could not recall one single instance of the Queen of Monsters invading their territory. It was not as if she was an inimical neighbour. It was just that this huge expanse ought to be ruled by someone who would do something productive with it instead of leaving it to run wild, home to sports and oddities that never amounted to anything.

Golan's wandering thoughts latched on to this familiar line of logic out of his days at the Academy. He could even remember the circumstances: he and his fellow apprentices walking the carefully manicured gardens of the school following the lean stick-figure of Master Legem as he held forth. Utility. Order. Service. Following such a rationale one could argue that these jungle leagues were in truth without any prior claim whatsoever. This so-called 'Queen', in her negligence and inattention, hardly counted as in possession in any practical sense at all. These lands lay unspoken for, virgin, open to seizure by responsible conscientious stewards.

'And make no mistake,' ferocious Master Legem announced, turning upon them one crooked accusing finger. 'We are this responsible party. And not through any self-serving myth of divine ordination or selection. We are this party because we alone are conscientious enough to reach out and act in this capacity. We have stemmed countless threats to the wider order. All without recognition or reward! For such frivolities are not our goal. Our goal is order. The ordering of the world. And the taming of the threats to that order. That is our calling.'

Rocking in his litter, Golan pulled his sodden shirt from his sweaty chest and sighed. Yes, all very laudable and noble. Why then these misgivings? His mission was, in a sense, heroic. Bringing order, light and rationalism to where only darkness, ignorance and superstition ruled. Really, if there was any justice in the world he ought to be given a medal when all this was over and done.

Snorting, Golan hawked up a mouthful of phlegm and spat it to the ground. But of course, as Master Legem constantly reminded him and his fellow aspirants, anything so juvenile as honours or rewards were beneath them. The Circle of Masters strove not for personal gain but for the betterment of the human condition. Their work was for the common good. These doubts and odd misgivings that came wafting in this sickly miasma were therefore unworthy; an insult to generations of selfless labour.

He must work harder to find the proper state of right-thinking.

Chief of Staff U-Pre appeared next to his litter, saluted with fingertips pressed to forehead then swept down. Golan nodded in answer to the salute. 'Yes, Second in Command?'

The man's face shone with sweat; it ran in streams from under his stained leather helmet. His face was ghostly pale as well, as if he were struggling against exhaustion, or constant pain. 'Trouble at the van, Master. I've ordered a temporary halt.'

Golan cocked his head to listen but heard nothing beyond the surrounding crash of the march. Shortly, however, the litter swayed as his yakshaka bearers stopped. The noise lessened, but only slightly as bearers coughed and hawked, oxen lowed, and overseers shouted orders. 'What sort of trouble?' he enquired mildly.

U-Pre gestured, inviting him onward. Golan ordered his bearers forward once again. They carried him alongside the main column.

'We have come to a wide clearing, Master,' U-Pre explained as he walked. 'A meadow, I imagine you might call it. Full of rather pretty white flowers. I ordered a party ahead to scout. They did not return. I then ordered a second group . . . they too have not returned.'

Golan nodded his approval. 'I see. Your caution is commendable. However, must I remind you that we are behind schedule?'

U-Pre bowed his head at this rebuke. 'I understand, Master.'

His bearers brought him to the front where soldiers had formed line facing the startlingly bright opening in the canopy. Golan shaded his gaze to squint between the last screen of trees to the expanse of a huge clearing floored, as his second reported, by a seeming ocean of creamy-white blossoms.

'Were they attacked?' he asked U-Pre. 'Did you see anything?'

'We saw nothing. Both parties advanced out of sight. The meadow climbs, as you see. It appears to be higher ground. Excellent position for an encampment.'

'Perhaps.' Golan tapped the blackwood baton to his chin. 'You were right to order the halt, Second in Command. Something is not right. I shall have a look.'

'Master, you mustn't . . .'

'Down!' The yakshaka knelt. Golan stepped out only to wince and knead his numb legs. 'You presume to tell me what I may or may not do, Second?'

U-Pre appeared stricken. 'No, Master! Not at all . . . We merely daren't risk losing you.'

'Ah! I see.' He extended the Rod of Execution to U-Pre, who stared at it in disbelief before reluctantly raising a hand to take it. 'Is it not for such strange manifestations that I was sent? Should I not return, report my failure.'

'Yes, Master. That is, no, Master. You shall return.'

'We shall see. Now, you are keeping up with your journal of the campaign?'

'Yes, Master.'

'Very good. You will see to it that my fall shall be glorious, yes?'

U-Pre struggled to keep his face straight. He appeared torn between anxiety and mirth. 'Yes, Master. Should you fall it shall be most glorious. Yet you will not fall. You shall succeed – gloriously.'

Golan allowed himself a look of bright surprise. 'Well, then. It would appear we can turn round now as I am assured of glory in either case.' He cuffed U-Pre's shoulder. 'Remember this – the truth of what really happens anywhere at any time can never be retrieved or known. All that matters are the reviews.' And he walked off, hands clasped behind his back, leaving behind a rather perplexed U-Pre rubbing a thumb over the smooth night-black wood of the Thaumaturg Rod of Execution.

Forward of the ordered ranks of troops, Golan found a thin skirmish line of their allied Isturé. He approached the nearest, a female in layered leathers, stained crimson, that descended to her muddy armoured feet. Each engraved leather scale was edged in bronze and studded in blackened iron. Her long strikingly red hair was piled high upon her head and pinned there by a series of gleaming opalescent shell clasps. He would have thought her quite beautiful but for the many inevitable scars of a lifetime of campaigning that marred her face. That, her unseemly muscular build, and the two longswords hanging from her belts. 'You are . . . ?' he asked.

179

The woman inclined her head in only the most minimal acknowledgement. 'They call me Jacinth.' And she added, after a long pause, 'M'lord.'

'And where is your commander?'

'Still absent.'

'I see. Dare we expect the privilege of his attendance any time soon?'

The foreign woman blinked her utter disinterest. 'I have no idea.'

'Perhaps he has fallen to one of these creatures.'

An amused half-smile lifted an edge of the woman's lips and she turned her gaze to the field of bobbing white flowers. 'If you think that, then you know nothing of him. There is nothing that walks this world that can defeat him.'

Absurd claim. Yet the reasons behind such a delusion might be mildly interesting. 'So he fears nothing?'

'Oh, he fears plenty. There was one blade he was wary of – but it has since been destroyed.'

Ah, well. All creation feared that sword. Golan tilted his head to the field beyond. 'What think you of this manifestation?'

'I'm . . . suspicious.'

'Commendable. You and your fellow Isturé shall maintain this cordon. I have elected to have a look.'

'Of course you will.'

Golan frowned; he was not used to such a disrespectful tone. 'What do you mean – *of course* I will?'

The woman's smile deepened as if she were actually enjoying his discomfiture. Eyes still studying the field, she explained: 'You are a trained Thaumaturg of the highest rank. Where I am from your title would be High Mage and it would be your job to investigate such things to make certain they are safe for the soldiers to advance.'

Golan cocked a brow. *How curious.* 'Well, Isturé. We are civilized here. And that is completely backwards.' Giving the woman an ironic bow of farewell, he started forward.

'Yet here you are,' she called after him.

He did not pause. 'In case you have not yet noticed – time is pressing.' *Ignorant foreigner.*

The glade, he found, was a welcome change from the dark gloom of the surrounding jungle. It was in fact quite pleasant. As pleasant as it is possible for any unwelcome delay to be. If he was not mistaken, a slight breath of air actually touched him here in the open. The fat carpet of creamy blossoms bobbed and nodded heavily, brushing his shins. A dusting of their golden pollen now coated his sandals and feet. As he climbed the slight rise he saw that what appeared a mere glade was in fact the minor bay of a far larger sea. A veritable pocket prairie, extending in all directions. *Ancient lost gods! It would take days to cross this!* Still he could see no sign of the advance parties. A broad flat-topped hill covered in the white blossoms beckoned from the distance and he made for it, hoping for a view.

The hilltop commanded a vista proving that, if quite large, the meadow was in truth nothing more than a brief interruption in an eternity of surrounding dark verdant jungle. Here a coughing fit struck and he hacked up a wad of phlegm that he spat aside. *Some sort of irritant. The pollen, perhaps.* A tiny smear in the undifferentiated creamy fields caught his eye. *Just one last check, then return. The parties must have continued on.*

Something turned under his foot – the ground had been quite uneven – and he paused to brush aside the obscuring flowers. It took a moment for him to apprehend what he had stood on and when the realization did snap into place Golan flinched backwards as if stabbed. An animal corpse. He stood on the skeletal corpse of some sort of beast. Yet all he could smell was the sickly-sweet scent of the flowers.

And they grew so thick he could see nothing of the ground . . .

A terrible suspicion took hold of Golan's stomach. He kicked at the ground, pushing aside the surface layer to reveal yet more bones. Each dusted in a furry layer of . . . tiny white flowers. Almost frantic now, he knelt, digging. His sweep threw up animal vertebrae and skulls, rotting hides that might have been clothes, a worked stone knife blade, on and on, ever descending.

He sat back, hands on thighs, panting. This entire mound . . . a heap of unsuspecting victims . . . a feast for the white flowers . . .

A phrase came to him then. A mysterious reference from one of the expedition accounts: *the White Plague.*

He jerked to his feet and the move raised a cloud of the golden pollen that watered his eyes and convulsed him in a fit of coughing. Straightening, wiping the streaming tears, he studied his smeared yellowed hands and sleeves with wonder. *And yet I live . . .* His Thaumaturg treatments, of course. Years of small dosings against countless poisons and drugs. His many wards and protections. The surgeries and complete mastery of his metabolism. Somewhere in all that resided the inoculation against these spores or fungus.

Still coughing, he headed down the hillside. Here he found the body of one of the advance scouting parties. The man lay outstretched. Had fallen running, or perhaps staggering. He'd been headed back to the main column. Golan knelt next to the body. The last to fall, perhaps: running to bring the news. Already a dusting of tiny white blossoms covered the corpse, leather armour and all.

Imagine if they'd marched on through. Countless hundreds falling before realization struck. Perhaps a good thousand or more lost here alone. He headed back to the column, rubbing a thumb over the short beard now covering his chin. What were they heading into? This was just the first of who knew how many deadly turns and traps. Was this to be one enormous killing ground?

Short of the jungle's verge he halted. There in the shade awaited U-Pre, his guards, and several of the Isturé. 'Come no further!' he called. He summoned his power. Blue flame burst to life all about him. Golan scorched himself until the pain made him flinch and the mage-fire flickered away. He brushed the burnt stubble from his head and cheeks then slapped the blackened threads and ash from his robes.

This done, he joined U-Pre. The second in command respectfully proffered the baton in both hands. 'What now?' he asked.

Golan negligently took the baton then inclined his head back to the clearing. 'Burn it all . . .'

*   *   *

It might be an island they walked; Mara wasn't certain. In any case, the priest of the Shattered God led them along a coastline of black volcanic rock where young translucent green plants clung to crevasses and depressions. Each appeared suddenly before Mara like an emerald emerging from gritty stone. A rough iron-blue sea pounded the shore in white crests and spray. The sky held drifting tatters of dark clouds, as of the slow angry dispersal of a storm.

Petal brought up the rear. Though distant, she could still hear his wet gasping breaths and wheezing. The man was not one for long hikes. Skinner walked with the priest; or rather, the priest capered alongside their commander. The bent rat-like fellow urged him on, beckoning and waving his arms, hopping and jumping in his unnerving demented gait.

These errands, or missions, or favours, call them what you will, taken up at the behest of the Crippled God, troubled her. What need had her commander for this position, King of the House of Chains? Its benefits, if any, seemed dubious at best. Was it protection he sought? A safeguard against powerful enemies? The time for any such patronage was now past. Surely, it would be *their* enemies who needed protection now. Surely it was time he set aside this unseemly role of errand boy. She could see how it galled him. What was the man waiting for?

If he would not rouse himself to end this relationship then perhaps the onus would fall upon her to act on his behalf. It would be for his own good – and she could imagine that he would most likely not take it well.

As they neared a tall headland of spray-soaked rock, Mara granted that he *had* moved against Ardata . . . eventually. Just as he had moved against K'azz. It seemed his nature not to endure standing next to power – when he himself could hold it. As before, then, she would have to give him more time and hold fast to the proof that, so far at least, he'd always followed his nature.

Musing, she came abreast of Skinner and their antic priest guide where the rock spit ended, offering a view of a lagoon and a distant line of reef. There, hung up on the far coral rocks, a bizarre vision presented itself. Mara had the impression of a mass of shattered ship hulls and broad raft-like platforms all jumbled and smashed together. The entire collection appeared as large as the tumbled remains of a broken fortress.

'What's this?' she asked the priest.

The man licked his lips, twitching and shuddering as if in the grip of an ague. 'You have heard of the Meckros, yes?'

She raised her chin in acknowledgement. 'Ah.'

'A fragment of one of their great floating cities. Washed up here on this desolate shore. Within is what we seek.'

Yes. The Meckros. Seafolk. Worshippers of the ancient sea-god. Mechanicians and artificers of renown. Somewhere on this wreck lay a fragment of the Shattered God? Doubtful. More likely it resided now on the bottom of the sea. She motioned to Skinner. 'This is a waste of time. Let us return.'

'We will investigate.'

Mara let out a heavy breath.

'Can you get us out there?' he asked her.

'No.'

'Petal?'

'I regret not,' he answered, short of breath.

Skinner drew off his blackened full helm, tucked it under an arm, and mussed his great mass of sweaty burnt-blond hair. 'Well, no matter.' He gestured to the rocky shore where bleached logs and other wrack lay in great jumbled heaps. 'There's plenty of wood. We'll build a raft.'

Mara looked to the sky. *Oh, unreliable gods! Must they?*

Skinner did all the work. The priest tried to help; he scampered about fumbling with the logs and generally getting underfoot. Her commander impatiently thrust the man away from time to time, dunking him in the wash once. She and Petal sat among the rocks, watching: she, hunched, arms tucked into her layered robes; he, legs out, back to a rock, pulling on his prominent lower lip.

'I do not like this,' he opined after eyeing the wreckage for the majority of the afternoon.

'Oh? What's possibly not to like?

He shifted his gaze, shaded and guarded beneath the shelf of his deep wide brow, to her. 'You are making unhelpful caustic observations at my expense?'

'At *all* our expense, Petal.'

'This is true. I sense a danger out there amid those ruins.'

'A shard is there.'

'This is also true.'

'What can you do about it?'

'Myself? Not much, I am thinking. Though I shall remain as readied as possible.'

Her gaze found Skinner standing in thigh-high water, still in his armour, lashing the scavenged driftwood together. 'Why are we here, Petal?' she asked, then, remembering the man's obtuse pedantic nature, she added, 'Here, collecting these pieces?'

He clasped his thick fingers across one knee. 'Well, it has occurred to me that with every shard or fragment returned to the Shattered God, he is strengthened. And therefore his enemies, our enemies, are correspondingly hampered.'

Mara nodded thoughtfully to herself. *Well, there is that . . .*

Let us hope that every piece we've retrieved so far translates into many more dead Malazans . . .

She blinked, seeing Skinner watching them; he snapped an impatient wave. Stirring, she muttered aside to Petal: 'I do believe he's done.'

'At last. It certainly took long enough.'

Mara clambered down to examine the lashed logs and timber planks. 'This will just fall to pieces.'

'Then hang on to a piece and kick,' Skinner answered, completely untroubled.

'My robes will get wet.'

'Then take them off.'

'Fine!'

Before stepping into the water she pulled her robes over her head and heaped all but one aside on a dry rock. This left her in nothing more than a loincloth wrap and a thin silk shirt. She folded the one robe to hold above her head. When she climbed aboard the assemblage of logs Petal's wide jowls took on a flush of deep crimson and he turned away. The priest, on the other hand, displayed no shame in looking her up and down. His stained tongue emerged to wet his lips and his loincloth wrap bulged, straining. These two reactions to her Dal Hon beauty she knew well, and so she ignored them both. Skinner, however, acted as if nothing had changed and this irked her more than she'd imagined it would.

Damn you, man! Perhaps it is true, as they say, that only the prospect of power will get you out of that armour. Always, it seemed, there'd been someone else. First Shimmer held his eye – perhaps not incidentally as she was a rival lieutenant of the Guard. Then Ardata. And now . . . plain power itself? She knew how to counter the first two – but this last? How does one compete against a fascination such as that? The truth is one cannot. It seemed long-nurtured hopes were no closer to their realization. Despite her support in the coup against Ardata, her unquestioning loyalty during the attempted usurpation of the Guard, and now her continued faithfulness.

Crouched on the logs, the waves slapping coldly against her bare thighs, the equally chilling suspicion came to her that perhaps it was this very dog-like obedience that brought its only due reward in his eyes: contempt.

Her hands pressed to her thighs clenched into fists.

The sheltered waters of the lagoon allowed them to paddle out to the reef where ocean breakers pounded their spray far into the air. The jagged canted fragments of the Meckros city reared above in cliffs of timber. Wreckage littered the exposed coral rocks: tatters of sun-faded cloth, broken furniture, clothes reduced to rags. Heavier objects cluttered the sands of the lagoon: broken pots, chains, and general household goods such as utensils, plates and candlesticks. Mixed among this corroding metal lay the bones of the Meckros citizens. Mara noted the sleek silhouettes of sharks drifting past beneath them.

'Where do we start?' she called to Skinner over the crash of the waves.

By way of answer he turned to the priest, who pointed up. Mara grunted her understanding. Skinner kicked the raft along while he searched for an easy route up into the wreck. Soon they came to a broken hull that offered entrance. Skinner climbed up. The priest motioned for Mara to go ahead of him, his gaze fixed on her naked flank. She cuffed him forward. Petal came last. This vessel appeared to have been used as a granary. Shattered amphorae had spilled their cargo of precious grain in great heaps. Damp and rotting, it was now a banquet for insects and mice. A ladder led up to a deck of living quarters where hammocks hung empty. Chests of personal goods lay overturned, their contents of clothes and knives and cheap trinkets everywhere. Whatever it had been had happened quickly: no time to pack at all. A storm? Perhaps a typhoon? Certainly not pirates, anyway. Above decks rigging hung from broken spars and masts in a nearly impenetrable maze.

Skinner turned to the priest who scanned the wreckage, then pointed to one side. Mara took the opportunity to throw on her one robe and tie it off at a shoulder. She pushed back her mass of hair. Petal cleared his throat in a signal for attention. She and Skinner turned quickly; the mage indicated a heap at the gunwale. It was a desiccated corpse. Some ferocious blow had slain the Meckros citizen. The wound had shattered the bones of the forearm and swung on, cleaving ribs to sever the spine. Few men could have delivered such a blow. The viscera were gone now, a feast for seabirds, but the sinew and dried muscle of the carcass remained, heaving with maggots.

Mara straightened from her examination of the corpse. So, not *just* a natural disaster . . .

She and Petal shared a significant look and both readied their Warrens. Skinner rested a hand on his sword grip. The priest scampered out on to the broken slats of some sort of platform that crossed to the next vessel. Here gnawed human bones and the stains of spilled fluids offered further testimony to the violence that had taken the city. Skinner knelt to pick up a bone that he examined before holding it out to Mara: it was the upper portion of a femur, still bearing a mess of sinew. Something had crushed the bone, splitting it. Something possessing extraordinarily strong jaws. It reminded her of a large predator or scavenger such as a Dal Hon plains hyena or a Fenn mountain bear. Yet out here away from the shore?

The priest led them on, scampering over fallen rigging and splintered timber. The light of the day waned, but slowly, lingering in a long twilight tinged by green from the arc of the lurid glowing Banner, the Visitor, foretelling whatever apocalypse one preferred. Considering the nature of their own errands, it was now hard for her to continue to dismiss these dire predictions as nonsense.

As she climbed over the ruins of the Meckros city – just the first of many calamities to come? – she wondered whether it was their own actions that were in fact calling the Banner down upon them. After all, it was said that the Shattered God had fallen from the sky ages ago, drawn down by humanity's hubris and blindness. Could they not be somehow contributing to a second Great Destruction and the annihilation that was said to have followed?

She paused on a canted platform of decking. *In fact, why should I believe I would even survive such a world-shattering impact and conflagration? Disavowed or no?*

Petal arrived at her side, panting, his shirt stained dark with sweat. 'You are troubled?' he asked, studying her.

'Yes. I am quite troubled . . .'

'I feel it too. Many eyes upon us. But I cannot get a grip upon them – their minds are strange.'

'Tell Skinner.'

'Very good.' The big fellow moved on awkwardly, using handholds to steady himself.

Mara watched him go without really seeing him. Could their actions be ensuring this Banner's impact? Could she be complicit in a second Great Fall?

And why by all the gods had she not considered this before?

She realized she'd fallen behind and hurried to catch up.

She found Skinner confronting a cringing anxious priest: the man was wringing his hands and peering about for escape like a cornered dog. 'What's going on?' she asked Petal.

Skinner raised an armoured finger. 'This man has been leading us in circles for hours.'

'It's moved, I tell you!' the priest shrieked. 'It's moving.' He thrust out a hand. 'It's behind us now!'

'Moving . . .' Skinner mused within his helm. He swung a gauntleted hand, smashing the priest to the decking. 'You fool! You've allowed it to lead us exactly where it wants us!' The priest lay mewling, wiping at the blood streaming from his squashed nose. Skinner's blade slid soundlessly from its wood sheath.

Mara and Petal put their backs to his, forming a rough triangle.

'How many?' Skinner asked Petal.

'Many.'

'Mara?'

'What can I do on this unsure footing? Everything's split already!'

Their commander growled his displeasure. 'Well . . . let us see what we've walked into.'

Mara eyed the surrounding canted huts, heaps of fallen equipment, and platforms and decks all of differing levels and angles. From among this maze shapes emerged. The deepening purple of twilight lent them an even greater horror. Malformed humans they were; shambling, so distorted as to be near caricatures of the human form. Many possessed huge curving crab-like claws as long as swords and now she understood the many cracked bones scattered across the wreckage. 'What *are* they . . . ?' she breathed, speaking her thoughts aloud.

'The influence of the shard, no doubt,' Petal answered, as literal-minded as ever.

'Can you affect them?'

'Barely, I suspect.'

Damn. I dare not let loose myself – this wreckage would fly apart beneath us.

The creatures shambled forward and she saw now that she was wrong in her first suspicion that these were the poor unfortunates of the Meckros city now transformed by the Crippled God's contamination into monstrosities of claw and shell carapace. No human form could endure such fundamental deformities. Six limbs? Backward-bending joints? Gaping mouths full of worm-like appendages? Surely these must be local denizens of the reef, crab, lobster, prawn and other crustaceans, warped now into mockeries of the human form. Such a conceit must have amused the Shattered God – what mattered the shape of the flesh when all was alien and strange?

It also explained why Petal's Mockra-based magics would have so little effect: these minds were not human to be clouded, confused or broken.

The creatures were however still flesh and blood, and Mara gestured, drawing as lightly as she could upon D'riss. A bare few of them staggered backwards. The priest, she noted peripherally, was nowhere to be seen.

Skinner stepped up. His mottled black and magenta blade blurred. Limbs fell away in gushes of clear fluids. Carapaces sheared off, cut through entirely. The mob of anatomical impossibilities swerved before him and she and Petal ducked away to give him room to lay about himself fully. She climbed up what might have once been a deckhouse while Petal heaved himself into the rigging of a tilted mast.

Skinner wrought havoc among the creatures but more and more came dragging themselves up, many still wet from the lagoon. Enormous crab claws grated across his glistening scaled coat, unable to catch any purchase or penetrate its invested metal. A great pincer as hefty as a bastard sword closed on the man's thigh and he snarled his agony, slicing through the shell exoskeleton. The jagged-toothed pincer fell away as it too was not powerful enough to break through Ardata's sorceries. Yet Skinner limped now, the leg perhaps numb.

A sharp whistle sounded, cracking like a whip across the decking. It was followed by a strange series of poppings and cracklings. The creatures all backed away. Some new figure came pushing its way through the monstrosities. So strange was this thing that it took some time for Mara to understand just what she was looking at. It was a jerking, walking mechanism of rusted metal bands and wire. Its creaking and whirring reached her like the sounds water clocks and other such automata make as they run and turn. Yet this was not the most eerie thing about this manifestation: what was ghastly was the fact that it wore over its metal torso, like a cape or a robe, the flayed skin of a human being. And stuck on a metal rod jutting above the body lolled a rotting severed head.

'Greetings!' boomed a hollow metallic voice.

Now Mara knew they faced magery as well, for the creature seemed to have spoken in Dal Hon, which she knew was a virtual impossibility. *So, not* just *an automaton wearing a cloak of flayed human skin . . .*

'I sense the one I name Kasminod has sent you. I believe I saw one of his rats!'

'Who are you?' Skinner called. He still held his blade ready – though Mara wondered what the weapon could possibly do to a creature without flesh.

Iron and bronze screeched and grated as the thing described a shallow bow. Through gaps in the tattered skin Mara glimpsed within its torso coils of rusted metal tightening then expanding like the workings of a showpiece clock she saw once in Tali. 'I am Veng. King Veng. Welcome to my kingdom.'

Skinner made a show of peering about. 'Your kingdom, Veng, is sinking.'

More high-pitched scraping of metal as Veng shrugged the rods and wire and bent straps that made up its arms – arms that ended in jagged rusted iron blades. 'What of it? A mere change in the weather. One must make the best of change.'

'What are you?' Petal shouted from the rigging, and Mara almost smiled, thinking how the man would let no circumstance interfere with his curiosity.

'Excellent question!' the thing boomed once more. 'What am I indeed . . . I have been hailed as a masterpiece of the venerated

Meckros mechanicians. For generations I guarded this floating city – Ambajenad, it was called.' Veng bowed again, yet jerkily, as if miming a marionette. 'Ahh . . . but then the Meckros smiths sought to perfect their creation. Their deep sea nets brought up an item from the ocean's floor. A unique item of inexhaustible power. This they placed within me and – by the gods! – I lived! No more winding or moments of darkness during which I sensed nothing. I lived . . . no differently from you creatures of flesh. Yet I will not die. Being of metal I am immortal and am thus far superior to you.'

Skinner motioned with his blade. 'Why then the skin and the head?'

'Ah, yes. Well, since I live among you I thought I ought to look the part. Convincing, yes?'

'Extraordinarily.' This from Petal.

Skinner nodded his helmed head as if in understanding and then he shouted, pointing: 'I order you to stand down! Your job is finished.'

A spine-grating screech of metal scraping sounded then from the creature and Mara realized this was its laughter. The head rocked obscenely as Veng edged closer. 'Too late for orders – but a worthy gambit. No. No more orders for Veng now. Veng is king and King Veng gives the orders now. And Veng's order is . . .' it raised its two jagged blades, 'death.'

The creature charged. Yet so too did Skinner. They met in a blacksmith's ring of clashing metal. The automaton's blades of toothed and notched iron caught and snagged at Skinner's weapon. The guardian swung with inhuman power, his blows like battering rams that Skinner slipped or barely edged aside. Their commander thrust through the creature's guard easily. His blade pierced the workings of the torso and Mara heard wires pinging like plucked instruments and metal bands grating. None of these strikes appeared to trouble the automaton.

One thrust from the monster, as deadly quick as a released crossbow, struck her commander only to rebound from the black scales of the man's coat. Such a blow would have penetrated any other armour but this unique scale seemed true to its reputation: utterly impenetrable.

Yet the power of the thrust had been immense – like the release of a siege engine – and Skinner now clutched his side, parrying one-handed. Ribs broken, probably.

Veng pressed its advantage. Its weirdly articulated limbs spun and lashed with even greater speed. It appeared to Mara that no swordsman could hope to continue to deflect such a storm of blows. No doubt Skinner understood this too as at that instant he closed, dropping his blade, to hug the creature.

The two slid and scraped together in a grating of iron as the creature's metalwork scoured Skinner's coat of scale. Veng's blades slashed his back in blows like the hammering of mattocks.

Skinner thrust a gauntleted hand into the innards of Veng's torso. Wire popped and rang, metal screeched. The creature let out a shriek like iron pushed past its endurance. Skinner twisted bands and wires and cylinders of wound metal strips. What sounded like a panicked shriek of tearing bronze escaped Veng. It lurched as if attempting to escape, dragging Skinner with it. The two fell in a tangle of limbs and rolled to a break in the fractured decking to slip from sight. Mara heard a great splash as they struck the surf below.

At first she could not believe what she'd just witnessed. Never had Skinner been bested. The surrounding monstrosities, however, did not take heart from what they saw; they squealed and chattered and clicked in what appeared to be a wave of panic. It seemed that Veng – or the thing within it – might have held some sort of compelling control over them. Summoning her Warren, Mara cast a wave of pressure in a swath across the decking, sending them and all the wrack of loose abandoned equipment tumbling backwards. This broke the creatures and they scattered in a lurching rush for the sides. In moments the deck was clear of them. Mara climbed down to cross to the break in the timbers.

Waves surged below, crashing among the black rocks of the reef. It seemed to her that the force of those breakers might simply dash Skinner to pieces.

Petal joined her. 'I do not see him,' he murmured. 'What should we do? Lower a rope?'

She peered around. 'Where's the damned priest?'

'Fled. Perhaps eaten.'

'Let's hope he poisons them.'

Petal heaved a sigh. 'So? What now? Shall we search?'

'No. If he's alive he'll make for shore. If he's dead – he's dead.'

'And the fragment?'

Rising, she brushed off her robe. 'I really do not give a damn.'

Petal released his lower lip. 'Very good. We return to shore then.'

They found the raft unmolested where they'd left it. Veng seemed to have been quite certain of itself. Heaving off they made little progress towards shore until Mara tapped her Warren to provide a force that allowed the raft to push through the breakers and advance to the distant line of surf that marked the strand.

On the beach they found the priest awaiting them, bouncing and twitching, his hair a dripping greasy mass of tangles. 'Well?' the man demanded. 'Do you have it? Give it to me.'

Mara brushed him aside but he would not be put off. He hopped from foot to foot before her. 'Ha! You do not fool me. You would keep it. Use it. Fool! Go ahead – it will consume you!'

'Shut up.'

'I will start a fire,' Petal said.

'And find us something to eat.'

The big man nodded ponderously. 'Yes, yes. Always it is me sent to lure in a hare or two. Or . . .' he raised a thick sausage-like finger, 'lobster, perhaps?'

Mara stared at the man. 'Enchantress forgive us, Petal. Did you just try a joke?'

'I judged it potentially amusing – given the recent unappetizing display of—'

'Yes, yes,' Mara interrupted before he could go on and describe the entire spectacle. She waved him off. 'And a fire.'

All this time the priest's fevered gaze had been flicking between them. Now the bloodshot orbs narrowed and the man pointed. 'I surmise you do not have it. You have failed! Return and retrieve it!'

Mara waved him to the wreck. 'Be our guest.'

'That is not the agreement. You do the retrieving. Otherwise our master will be displeased.'

Mara had been searching for her robes and she found them now and pulled them on. 'What of it?'

The priest jerked as if slapped. '*What of it?* You should ask such a question given what we have just witnessed?'

Mara sat heavily in the sand. 'We would not be of much use to your master twisted in such a fashion.'

'That would be your problem,' the man returned so smugly that Mara considered killing him on the spot. But, exhausted, she could only be bothered to again wave vaguely to the wreck.

'We shall see.'

Stymied for the moment, the priest edged from foot to foot, all the while mouthing complaints under his breath. Petal arrived carrying an armload of driftwood, then set to lighting a handful of dry grass with flint and steel. This drove the priest to snipe: 'Some magi you two are. Can't you even start a fire?'

'Certainly I can,' Petal answered, then continued striking, tongue clenched between his lips as he concentrated.

'I favour taking a lit stick from one fire and touching it to another,' said Mara.

Petal sat back with a satisfied sigh to fan a thin plume of white smoke. 'That can be known to work also,' he allowed, squinting.

The priest stormed off, hopping and twitching as if the sands were white-hot embers beneath his feet.

Mara brushed the grit from her hands. 'Well, at least we're rid of him. So, what do you think now?'

Petal tossed twigs on the gathering fire. 'By morning, I should think.'

'Agreed.'

'And for the meantime,' he sighed, 'I should like some privacy to dry my clothes. If you do not mind.'

'Shouldn't I remain in case a lovesick whale should lunge on to the beach . . .'

Pausing at his shirt-ties Petal let his head hang. 'Again the caustic humour. I have warned you it hurts my feelings.'

Mara rolled her eyes to the darkening sky. 'My apologies. I'll go have a look around.'

'Very good.'

It was full night when Mara returned to the fire. Petal sat in his undershirt. His wide pantaloons and outer robes hung over sticks next to the fire. The priest had returned as well and now sat glum and quiet, staring out to the glowing surf. 'Anything?' she asked.

Petal shook his head. 'I'll take first watch,' he added.

Mara grunted her acknowledgement and promptly rolled up in her robes to sleep. This she found difficult as not only was the Banner high as usual, so too was the moon. The light was almost bright enough to read by. She threw a fold of cloth over her head.

It seemed as if immediately someone tapped her shoulder and she jerked, yanking down the cloth. 'What?'

'Something,' Petal said.

She sat up. The priest was already down amid the surf frantically waving his arms and jumping. Further out, in the lagoon, a dark shape was making its slow laborious way towards them. 'Go help him,' she told Petal.

'Only now have I just dried . . .'

'Go on!'

The man winced as if hurt. 'Well . . . if it so be that I must . . .' and he lumbered down to push awkwardly into the surf, leaning forward to advance through the waves out to the figure, which was

193

now plainly Skinner, still in his black armour, but missing his full helm, his blond hair and beard sodden and streaming with water.

He was dragging what looked like some sort of box or chest but Mara knew it must be the remains of Veng's body. Just up from the surf he dropped it one-handed to the sands. Petal dragged it the rest of the way while the priest tore at it as if worrying a corpse – *just like a dog*, she thought.

She went to Skinner who stood weaving unsteadily, looking far more pale than usual, his helm in his other hand. 'Sit at the fire,' she told him. 'The leg?'

'The ribs,' he ground out. She helped him to the fire where he slumped like a sack of grain and hissed his pain.

'Your armour . . .' She ran a hand down the back, searching for catches or ties. Strangely, the individual scales of the coat seemed to shift beneath her fingers.

He shrugged her away. 'No! Just . . . just get me to Gwynn— Red.'

Red was their best bonesetter and surgeon now that Gwynn had deserted them to rejoin K'azz. Mara looked to the priest. 'We have to leave! Now!'

The man had literally thrust his head into Veng's torso. He was tearing at the wreck, which, horrifically, still jerked and writhed like the crippled wind-up automaton that it was. The metal bands of its arms still flexed and the remains of its torn legs twitched. The priest flinched away, yelping, 'Aya!' He studied a hand that he then thrust into his mouth. He kicked the shuddering beetle-like body and yelped again, hopping on one foot.

'I cannot get it out!' he wailed. 'All is lost! I will be refused my lord's reward!'

Skinner lifted his chin to the wreck. 'Mara . . .'

She let out a snarled breath. *Stupid useless fool* . . . She shoved the priest aside and studied the mangled torso. Something did reside there wrapped in bands of bronze in the middle of the chest. *The heart. How . . . poetic.*

She focused her Warren and envisioned those bands parting. Metal stretched and deformed. The thrashing of the creature became frantic, as if it sensed the end. Reports of metal parting sounded like the popping of small munitions. The torso spasmed the way anyone might, were you in the process of tearing out their heart.

Bronze parted shrieking and something fell to the sands. The body slumped, suddenly quiescent. The priest dived upon the object, cackling and chuckling, and wrapped it round and round with rags.

Mara released her Warren, suddenly exhausted. Petal stepped up next to her. Pulling on his lower lip he asked, 'Did you see it?'

'Just a glimpse. It looked like a black rock.'

The man grunted thoughtfully, still plucking at his lip.

Mara blinked, remembering Skinner. 'We must go now!'

The priest was hugging his prize to his chest. He seemed to be crooning to it. 'Yes, yes,' he answered without even glancing up.

'Return us to the column.'

'Of course! Just four more to go.'

'Four? There's four pieces left?'

'That we know of!' the priest snapped, and he slid the object behind his back as if Mara had made a lunge for it.

She raised a finger to his face. 'Now.'

The priest backed away. His bloodshot eyes darted about as if seeking escape. 'Get your commander then! We must all be together.'

'Fine.' She marched off. The fine sands squeaked and slid under her boots. Back at the fire Skinner had somehow managed to lever himself to his feet. She saw that his sheath hung empty at his side and she remembered that when he emerged from the waters he carried only the automaton and his helm.

Skinner, it seemed, had lost his sword.

*   *   *

The sky might be partially overcast, but there was no respite from the heat. Their local guide led them past intermittent jungle now. They climbed a rising slope bringing them to the first of the naked stone cliffs of the Gangrek Mounts, known to some as the Fangs, or the Dragon's Fangs.

They had lost a man yesterday. He'd disappeared down a crack hardly large enough for anyone to slip through. Pon-lor sent a fellow after him on a rope. The man reported that no one answered his calls and that the torch he dropped fell a great distance before it dashed itself out on rocks. Pressed for time, Pon-lor was forced to call off the search and they'd continued on.

That concern for time also forced them to march on into the night. Their captured bandit guide, Jak, led carrying a torch while two of Pon-lor's soldiers followed. Even the sun sliding down behind the steaming ocean of jungle behind them to the west did little for the heat. Though Pon-lor had grown up knowing such heat it felt different here – perhaps because the air was so humid that streamers of water seemed to hang within it. In the middle of the column he pulled his sweat-soaked shirt from his chest and paused for a moment to catch his breath. His guards halted about him.

He'd known such claustrophobic heat before, and the memory did not sit well with him – his childhood quarters in the Academy at the capital, Anditi Pura. They were taken as children. They were always taken as children. All would-be Aspirants. He did not know what supposedly guided that choice: some demonstrated predilection or talent? In his case he remembered being taken into a hot overcrowded room and led to a low cloth-covered table. There lay an assemblage of trinkets, some bright and rich-looking, others plain and worn: rings, cups, necklaces of beads or of gems (fake no doubt), combs, knives, and assorted other mundane possessions. He remembered his confusion, not knowing what was expected of him, facing these gathered fierce-looking old men and women in that hot smelly room. He'd searched their gazes hoping for some sign, some hint, of what he must do. And thankfully he found it. While a number of them kept their eyes on him, a few kept darting their gazes to the table and those glances kept returning to one area in particular among the proffered bits and pieces. Experimentally, he extended his hand in that direction and was rewarded by an almost imperceptible tension gathering within the tiny room. He moved his hand closer, passing over several of the offerings, a silver wristlet among them: one of the most attractive trinkets, gleaming brightly in the lamplight. The breathing of all those gathered slowed in expectation. A few breaths even caught. Emboldened, he edged his hand further across the table towards the edge. The atmosphere subtly changed. It was as if the room had suddenly expanded, the ancients now distant and withdrawn.

By then he'd identified it. The object, the thing they seemed to want him to pick but wouldn't, or couldn't, say. A silly game. All to get him to pick a plain wooden stick – the least interesting item laid out on the table.

And so he chose it. And they chose him.

And now, standing in the dark and the rain, the sweet cloying scent that permeated the jungle slipping from his nostrils, Pon-lor wondered, had it been just that all along: a test of awareness, of a kind of native intelligence? Or were those old Thaumaturgs of the testing board blithely unaware of their own subverting of the entire selection process? If so, so much for the organization's conviction of its privileged superiority – held by virtue of having passed the test!

A tautology affirming only the most appalling self-delusion . . .

But no. Those of the selection board must be briefed in how to

196

run the test. Acuity of mind, awareness and perception must be the desired traits, and the test designed appropriately. And yet – what of certain youths from certain influential families selected despite any demonstrated virtues or abilities that he could see? What of that? And their quick promotions to positions far above his – one and all! Again, no. He was simply of too low a rank to know the reasons behind such choices. He mustn't question the sagacity or plans of his superiors.

His sodden robes now sucked out his warmth and he shivered. He focused upon warming himself and was rewarded by the sensation of heat flowing outwards from his core. Mist began to rise from his clinging robes.

Torches approached from the van and their youthful guide appeared, though not that much younger than he, Pon-lor had to remind himself. His guards flanked the fellow. Some sort of worry rode the youth's brows and in his eyes Pon-lor read open hatred and, oddly enough, a kind of prideful contempt for all he viewed.

'You have stopped?' the youth asked, delivering the question more as a challenge. As if to imply: had enough walking? Too weak? Frightened?

And now Pon-lor had to come up with a justifiable reason for why he'd stopped. 'Our destination is close?' he asked, his tone one of lofty scepticism.

Insulted, Jak drew himself up tall. 'Not far. We can camp at the Gates of Chanar.'

Pon-lor arched a brow. 'The Gates of Chanar . . . ?'

The local hunched slightly, lowering his chin. 'A stone arch. It marks the beginning of the path to the fortress, and the pass.'

'I see. Very good.' Pon-lor waved him onward. The youth sketched a perfunctory bow. The burning pitch of his torch hissed and spluttered, dripping now and then. He headed back to the van. Soon all that could be seen of him was the floating yellow globe bobbing between the black tree trunks and obscuring leaves. Pon-lor followed, walking slowly. The rain intensified, slashing down to erase all distances and all other noises of the jungle. As Pon-lor was not of sufficient rank to be allowed to hold a parasol – it was the symbol of a master of the order – he gestured to a nearby guard and this man unfurled one to hold above him while he walked.

And so do we find our ways around rules and prohibitions, he mused, stepping over moss-covered fallen logs, loose talus sliding sometimes beneath his sandals. Was this not the case even among the Thaumaturgs? The thought left him uncomfortable. Though he wished he could forget, he remembered his days – and nights – in the dormitory of the Aspirants. Certain teachers arriving in the dark to take boys off alone for *special attention*. Including himself. He remembered the fate of the boys who complained to the masters of their treatment. How they were assured steps would be taken – though none ever were. And later, how it was these boys, among the entire class, who failed to advance in the courses, and they who fell behind and came to be relegated to menial positions. Yet the Thaumaturgs prided themselves on an organization based on skill and merit alone. Perhaps it is the case that no organization or hierarchy can withstand the closest of scrutiny. Not even a smugly self-touted meritocracy. The success and persistence of utter fools everywhere is sad testament to that.

The roar of falling water soon overcame all other sounds and they came abreast of a stream of water splashing down a sheer black cliff. Vines hung like groping limbs sent down by the great rearing prominence itself. Bright dashes of white, pink and orange dotted the wall where flowers clung: parasitic orchids whose flesh, curves and coloration he found . . . disturbing.

I hear they bear more than a slight similarity to the sex of women – though fortunately, or unfortunately, I would not know.

His guards showed him the way around slick rocks and over rushing narrow channels, all the while scanning the surrounding jungle, hands on sword grips.

Jak stood ahead, awaiting him, his torch extinguished. Behind him rose a natural stone arch, an uneven vault eroded from the rock of the prominence itself. Beneath, steps hacked from the rock led upwards. In places streams of run-off writhed across the wide black ledges. 'The Gates of Chanar,' Jak announced with the smallest of bows.

Pon-lor gave no response to the impudent sketch of a bow. He studied the lad while his eyes were downcast. Black hair plastered flat, a widow's peak, sharp nose and sharp chin. A mouth always tight as if it must hold back so much. *The lad hates us. Why? Some past injustice? Or simply that we represent the fist of rulership? Probably that. The Circle rules through fear, and that does not cultivate devotion among those ruled.*

Then he noted the discoloration of the arch to the left and right. Chalk markings ran dissolving in the rain. A dense overlay of new glyphs over old. He recognized the old magic in their appeals: calls for blessings, calls to turn away, curses and damning. And laid out on the stones before the arch, a litter of offerings: clay cups that probably once held rice or plum wine for propitiations; shallow dishes that no doubt would have held blood for curses; prayer flags faded to grey; twists of rotting fibre paper that once held appeals; clay lamps, candle stubs; chips of broken pottery inscribed with names – death wishes, those.

He turned a raised brow on Jak.

The young man waved his contempt. 'Peasants. You know them. Ignorant and superstitious.'

Superstitious of what? But he did not challenge him. He gestured to his guards. 'We'll camp here.'

Overseer Tun bowed. 'As you order.'

'Oh, and Overseer,' Pon-lor added. 'Tie up our friend here.'

The man's fat lips pulled back over greying rotten teeth. 'Yes, Magister.'

Their guide said nothing; if anything, his mouth hardened to flint against all that he could have said.

He is enraged yet he voices no complaint? Interesting . . .

Wrapping his soaked robes more tightly about himself, Pon-lor moved to where a rock overhang offered shelter. Here bone-dry leaves crackled beneath his sandals and swirled about him. He crossed his legs, rested his hands palms upward on his knees, and turned inward.

Up until now his pitiful lack of results had caused him to neglect his obligations. But he could put it off no longer. It was long past time to contact Master Golan.

It took longer than usual to achieve the necessary centring and no-mind inner calm before he found himself looking down upon himself seated cross-legged, his long black hair draped like an unruly mane down the back of his robes. Having separated his *self* from that which was the mere flesh, this accidental temporary *vessel*, he turned away and sought the strong glowing vitality that would be Master Golan.

So strong in fact was his master's essence that he found himself drawn as inexorably as a stone down a steep slope. He followed the man's trail with ease until he reached a point where it suddenly thinned. Here the normally crystal-clear plane of the élan vital, that which inhabits and thus animates the corporal and profane flesh, clouded. Entities swirled ahead. Creatures of energy and essence that could feed upon him. All moved within a larger influence, a permeating misty radiance that appeared to pulse outwards from some central hidden presence.

Ardata herself. The Queen of the Ancient Kind.

He was too late. Master Golan had already entered her demesnes.

He turned about and willed his return to his vessel.

Under the rock shelf Pon-lor's chest rose in a shuddering intake of breath and his eyelids fluttered. As always came the agony of ghost-knife jabbings and pricklings tormenting him as he returned to his body. The flesh was chilled in the damp as well, dangerously so. He began the meditative course that would raise his body temperature. Soon tendrils of steam began wafting into the chill night air.

Overseer Tun knelt awkwardly before him. 'Orders, Magister?'

'We continue on, Overseer.'

'Very good, lord.'

Pon-lor eased his effort of focusing his energy and began on a course of muscle relaxation. Dimly, he became aware of the heat of a steady hard stare. Without shifting his gaze he identified the narrowed glittering eyes of their guide out amid the darkness. The usual expected hostility filled them. Yet he was also surprised – and amused – to detect a ferocious pride coupled with an equally ferocious contempt held for him. *It seems our village raider all-in-patches harbours a very high opinion of himself. Well, who doesn't? Yet it is obvious that it has brought him nothing but torment.* Pon-lor closed his eyes. *No matter. Tomorrow we will be rid of him.*

In the morning he broke his fast on a pinch of rice, some smoked fish, and tea. Even as he squatted to take care of the needs of his body, his robes hiked up, two guardsmen kept watch, as it was the philosophy of the Thaumaturgs that such values as modesty and squeamishness no longer pertain once all ties to the profane flesh have been cast aside.

Overseer Tun determined the order of march. Their guide led, followed immediately by the overseer and two guards. A second unit of four guards followed this group, then Pon-lor and the rest of the detachment. The cliffs of the prominence steamed in the early morning sun. As they climbed, more and more of the jungle expanse to the west came into view. Great streamers of mist clung to the canopy and it seemed to Pon-lor as if suspended rivers were meandering through the treetops.

The stone ledges also steamed, and were slick with the last of the run-off that came crashing down out of the unseen heights. His guards hacked at the fat hanging leaves and the tangles of roots and vines, or held the worst aside for his passage. Birds startled everyone as they burst screeching and shrieking from the foliage in explosions of brilliant colour. Each time, Pon-lor's hands clenched. It was the suddenness of it that always shocked him.

Monkeys scampering through the hanging forest scolded them with their chatter. And once, from far above, came the roar of a jungle cat. That, Pon-lor noted, gave his men pause. While all were armed with swords, shields and knives, they carried very few spears or bows.

A regrettable oversight, that. Have to let Principal Scribe Thorn know of it when I return.

What would he do, should such a beast attack the column? Not that any living Thaumaturg had any personal experience in the matter: all such wild animals, the great fanged cat, the lesser fire cat, the man-hunting leopard, the tusk-boar, the titanic cave bear, the two-horned rhinoceros, and all the great river beasts, had all been eradicated from their lands generations ago. Still, a hunting cat shouldn't attack any large body of men, armed or not. At least that was his learning on the subject. Unless of course the old folk tales were true and all the many fanged and toothed denizens of the jungle obeyed the commands of the Ancient Queen herself; to say nothing of every spirit, demon, shape-changer, ghost, elemental, and all such supernatural entities.

He wiped his sleeve across his sweaty face. *Not a thought to dwell upon as we approach her demesnes . . .*

The path continued up the side of the rock outcropping, or mount. At times it was no wider than a goat trail. In many places rockslides had ploughed across the trail and only the most rudimentary track had been cleared. He scrambled with his hands over the sharp broken rock.

This path has not seen much commerce! There must be other ways up.

On his right, empty sky gaped as the route wound round the vertical cliff. The sun was near its highest – and these days the arching glow of the Banner, or Fallen God's Chariot, as some cults would have it, still marred the sky – when a scream froze them all where they edged along.

It had come from the rear. Pon-lor began shuffling backwards to investigate. Voices called from the van but the wind rendered them unintelligible. His guards gathered behind him, hands on sword grips. A lone guard came round the nearest curve of the overhanging cliff. He set his hands to his mouth to yell: 'The last man fell!'

'What happened?' Pon-lor called.

'I did not see it!'

Damn. 'Was there blood? Sign?'

'No, m'lord!'

He tightened his robes about himself against the rising wind. 'Very well!' To his men, 'Close up. No one walks alone.'

'Aye, m'lord.'

Past a rockfall Tun waited with the van guards, together with their guide. 'What happened, Magister?' the overseer asked, his slit gaze on Jak.

'A man fell. The last.'

Tun's eyes almost disappeared in their pockets of fat. His hands tightened in their studded leather wraps. 'Odd that it should be the very last.'

'No one saw what happened. I do not want to lose anyone else so we will tighten up the order of march.'

Tun bowed. 'Very good, Magister.'

Progress slowed to a hesitant crawl. Now the greatest danger came from each other as rocks turned underfoot and tumbled down the path, threatening those behind. *Who are these people?* Pon-lor found himself wondering. *Mountain goats?*

Late in the day the ground levelled. They had reached the top, or at least a level portion of the heights. He was exhausted. His shirting beneath his robes stuck to him and his calves felt as if they had seized. Here, they re-entered dense jungle of tall fat kapok trees draped in vines. Pink and gold orchids hung in the vines as if snared in the act of climbing. A layer of rotting leaves and other fallen litter carpeted the rocky ground. It was as if they had climbed nothing at all. Except, that was, for the wind; strong gusts now brushed the branches overhead and stirred the hanging parasitical creepers, sending them rustling and whispering.

Still their guide led them on, though no trail or path was visible through the underbrush.

No one has come this way in some time. Yet we are heading east, and the Pass of Seven Peaks is supposed to be an easy descent. Perhaps we are coming up behind the fortress.

Yet something troubled him and he pushed ahead, his guards keeping pace, to reach their guide. The young man bowed his head – slightly. 'It must be difficult bringing up supplies . . .' Pon-lor offered as they walked along.

Jak glanced back the way they had come. 'There are other paths,' he answered off-handedly. 'M'lord.'

'And are we close?'

The lad frowned, thinking. 'We won't make it before nightfall.'

'No?' Pon-lor felt a touch of irritation. 'Then we should camp for the night. We've just come off a hard climb.' It seemed to him that the raider youth actually sneered before quickly turning away.

'That?' He waved aside the suggestion. 'That was nothing – I used to run up and down that path all day as a child.'

'Nevertheless,' Pon-lor answered, icily. 'Find us a suitable site.'

Jak stopped and bowed. 'Pardon . . . m'lord. But the rains are gathering. Wouldn't you rather sleep in warm quarters tonight?'

The suggestion did have its attractions. Yet what of this fellow's insolence? He seemed to suggest that Pon-lor was not up to such exertion. Obviously he knew nothing of Thaumaturg training and arts and what they could extract from the human body . . . He pinched the bridge of his nose, sighing. Whatever should he care regarding the opinions of such a wretched specimen? He waved the ever-hovering overseer closer. 'A break in the march, Tun. For a rest and a short meal.'

'Very good, Magister.'

The guide merely bowed as well.

Pon-lor sat at the base of a huge bo tree. Its limbs arched all around, creating something of a natural temple. He allowed himself a pinch of rice, water and fresh fruit gathered during the day. The men took turns resting, eating and standing guard. Tun called an end to the break, and the men were forming up when a second scream – this one of agony – froze them all.

The men's wide eyes scanned the bobbing leaves and shadowed aisles between the trees. Then Tun grunted an order and they jumped to encircle Pon-lor while two went with the overseer to investigate. As an afterthought, Tun waved Jak to accompany them.

Waiting, Pon-lor also eyed the impenetrable tangle of vines and draping leaves. Another fall? Surely not. What, then? Had a servant of the Demon-Queen found them already? He wished it would show itself. Thaumaturg training did not lend itself to such real-time scrying, sensing or detection. The leaves shook and Overseer Tun emerged. He walked straight up to Pon-lor and bowed to one knee.

'We have lost another, m'lord.'

'What was it?'

'There was no sign of the man. But there was plenty of blood. And a trail. We did not follow.'

'No? Why not?'

'The guide says it was a hunting cat. One of the great fanged ones.'

Pon-lor could not suppress a shiver of atavistic fear. A fanged cat! Nearly a horse's weight of muscle, tooth and claw. As tall as nine hands at the shoulder, some claimed. Long eradicated from Thaumaturg lands. No wonder they did not pursue.

Their guide was the last to emerge, and he came walking backwards, his gaze fixed on the undergrowth. 'Jak,' Pon-lor called. 'You will take us to the fortress – now.'

The young man bowed. 'Of course . . . m'lord.'

Tun clapped his wrapped hands and the column formed immediately and they set out at once.

The evening's rain began soon after. A guard offered Pon-lor his parasol but he waved it off; the undergrowth was too pressing. Often he had to duck under thick creepers, or swing a leg over the fat roots that writhed all over the hard stony ground. With the rains arrived the evening: a darkness even greater than a densely overcast night as they struggled beneath an impenetrable canopy. He could make out shafts from the Visitor lancing down here and there through breaks in the tangled branches. A strong wind tossed those branches, making the green radiance dance and flicker. Ahead, the men of the column would appear and disappear in the wavering light as if shifting from one Realm to another.

After a long sodden march the column halted and Tun emerged from the drifting mist of rain to invite Pon-lor forward. He was led to where their guide waited and when he arrived Jak gestured in the dark.

'Fortress Chanar.'

Pon-lor squinted into the gloom. Eventually a much denser black emerged from the murk to resolve into a rearing heap of stone. A golden glow shone here and there from what he presumed to be windows. At ground level a whipping flame revealed where a torch might be set at a doorway.

'Very good, Jak.' He urged the guide onward.

Overgrown stone heaps lay to either side. They appeared to be walking an ancient road, or ceremonial way. The heaps proved to be squat plinths supporting equally squat monolithic heads as big as huts. Roots gripped these enormous heads and most sported tall trees like fanciful hats, but all were identical. Portraits, they were, of a man in an armoured helm. Savage hard staring eyes, a long straight nose, and a slit mouth that looked as if not one word of mercy had ever passed its lips.

And Pon-lor knew that face, that man. And his breath left him in one gust. A cold slither of something gouged a nail up his spine.

That face. Always the same face. He'd seen it before on the coins and funerary statues that littered the tables in Master Varman's study – his hobby of collecting pre-catastrophe artefacts – where, spurred by curiosity, half knowing the answer already, he'd asked: this ancient likeness, is it a man or a god?

And Master Varman had studied him for some time in silence, his head lowered, eyeing him from under his thick brows, until finally he cleared his throat to say, 'Strange that you should put it that way, Pon-lor. As you no doubt suspect, that is the face of the greatest evil of his day, the self-proclaimed God-King, the High King. These days the ignorant name him the Fallen One or the Demon-King, the infernal Kell-Vor. But that in truth is not his real name – *that* I shall never speak aloud. For it carries with it a curse. A terrible ageless curse.'

Pon-lor blinked now in the rain, suddenly more chilled than he had been in days. Was Chanar merely built on these ancient pre-Fall ruins? Or was this building one of the few surviving structures from that age? In any case, the scholar within Pon-lor was roused. What an unlooked-for opportunity! Here in the wilds of the border region. Yet, where else? Was he not approaching the lands of the Ancient Queen? And were there not legends that claimed King and Queen ruled together and that the catastrophe of the long ago Fall slew the King while the Queen survived? A twisted shadow-play of the truth, no doubt. But still, both figures could be traced back to those hoary dawn ages of humanity.

'Magister . . . ?' a voice called from the dark. Their guide.

He'd been standing in the rain for some time, his guards encircling him. He nodded. 'Yes, coming.'

A single guard in plain leathers awaited them at the gate. A young man of his age, spear in hand, a bow at his side. 'Welcome,' this one murmured. 'The lord will see you in the Great Hall.'

Jak invited Pon-lor forward. 'I know the way.'

Overseer Tun blocked the narrow stone entranceway. 'I will walk with you, little guide.' He waved for two guards to remain at the gaping stone portal, then signed for the rest to attend on Pon-lor.

Jak shrugged, and lit a torch. 'This way.'

The halls were dark. Pon-lor's wet sandalled feet kicked through a wind-blown litter of leaves. In side corridors tiny animals scampered from the light, and cobwebs choked the ceilings and corners.

'These halls are abandoned?' Pon-lor asked Jak.

'Khun-Sen is an old man. He has few remaining servants or followers. And each year they are fewer.'

'Ah. I see.' So, soon this great brooding edifice overlooking the Pass of Seven Peaks would once more lie empty. As it had for thousands of years. For with its cyclopean stone construction, its dark sandstone blocks, its flat squared lintels and mottling of lichen growth, Pon-lor recognized it for what it was – the colossal and overbearing architecture of the self-glorying God-King.

They exited on to a narrow inner bailey that was nothing more than a miniature jungle of tall trees. Across the way, stairs climbed to a higher inner structure and faint light glowed from high windows. Pon-lor had no training in military readiness but even he was appalled by the neglect and dilapidation. 'Was no effort made to clear the overgrowth?' he asked Jak.

The young man gave an unconcerned shrug. 'No. It was no priority of Khun-Sen's.'

'I see.' When he returned he would have much to report regarding the activities, or rather the lack of activities, of this self-styled general on their borders.

Within, the overall neglect continued with trash and wind-blown litter hastily brushed aside, and a minimum of torches and lamps lit. Chambers to either side lay dark and empty. In one, a long low table held the remains of a meal, plates and goblets in place. In the unlit gloom Pon-lor thought he glimpsed cobwebs on the table. 'Where is everyone?' he asked.

'Readying themselves to greet you, perhaps,' Jak answered, his voice tight with some emotion. Fear, was it? Was he also unnerved? Somehow Pon-lor found this reassuring.

They entered a large room. A bonfire burned in a central fire-pit. A second-storey viewing terrace encircled the walls. Pon-lor assumed this was the main hall. He turned to Jak. 'A rather subdued reception . . .'

The young man wet his lips, his dark eyes glittering as he scanned the viewing terrace. 'There must be some problem,' he murmured. 'Perhaps the lord is ill. I will go and see.' He turned to leave.

'Halt!' Tun snapped. He signed to two guards. 'Accompany our guide. We would not want him to get lost.'

One of the guards gathered up a handful of cloth at Jak's shoulder and the three marched up a passageway. The glow of their torch slowly faded. Tun edged close to Pon-lor to whisper: 'I do not like this, Magister. This is an ill-omened place at best. We should go.'

'Ill-omened?'

'Yes. Tales of travellers disappearing. Of a midnight court of the dead.'

Pon-lor arched a brow. 'Really? I'm not familiar with such folk tales. However, I agree. Perhaps we were better off with the fanged cat after all. Call the men. We will withdraw.'

'Very good, Magister.' Tun paced to the passage entrance and bellowed: 'Harun! Vayach! Recall!'

Something like a weak shout echoed down the corridor.

'Did you hear that?' Pon-lor asked.

'Yes, Magister. A cry. But distant. Should we advance?'

'No. I'm beginning to believe we have come much further than we should have. We will withdraw. We know the way.'

Tun snapped a sign and the men surrounded Pon-lor. *My remaining men! By the ancient false gods, I've already lost a quarter of my command. If this is an ambush then it has been masterfully played.*

Tun led the withdrawal. At a sign from him the men drew their blades and raised their shields. From his place at the centre of the column Pon-lor spied a figure ahead in the darkness blocking the exit to the inner court. Shifting moonlight behind revealed it to be someone new. One of Khun-Sen's men? 'What is going on here?' he called. 'I am a representative of the Circle of Rulership.'

The armoured figure did not answer. Tun waved him aside, bellowing, 'Make way for a magister of the Thaumaturgs!'

In answer the newcomer thrust forward and a spearhead burst from the back of Tun's studded leather hauberk. The overseer dropped his torch, which snuffed out in the damp. The lead men loosed yells of shock and rage and hacked at the figure. Despite taking a number of solid blows it calmly yanked its spear free.

Those strikes sounded strange to Pon-lor. It was as if his men were hacking stone. And that reminded him of something. Something alarming. 'Retreat!' he yelled. 'Back up, now!'

Even as he shouted one of the lead men fell to the spear. 'Damn you!' he roared. 'Do as I say!' The troops began edging backwards. The figure advanced with them, but slowly, a black silhouette against the night beyond. It was too dark to see much, so Pon-lor could not be sure of his guess, but the man's slow shuffling walk fitted in with what he suspected. Back in the main hall, he ordered men to scout the other exits. In moments all reported back that the ways were blocked by other figures. He ordered a defensive circle close to the hearth bonfire. At least now they did not lack for light, anyway!

Then a laugh of scorn echoed through the chamber. It came from the second-storey terrace. Pon-lor raised his gaze, knowing just whom he would see. It was their raider-in-tatters, Jak. The young man held a bow. 'How does it feel to be the hunted one now?' the lad shouted down.

'What is this?' Pon-lor asked, his voice mild.

'What is this? What does it look like? Revenge, fool! Justice.'

Dragging steps sounded from all around. His guards shifted, fearful, hunched with swords ready. 'Revenge?' Pon-lor asked. 'Justice? Whatever for? What have I done to you?'

The question seemed to enrage the youth. 'Done? What have you done!' He snapped a quick shot, which Pon-lor sidestepped. 'Rich pampered bastard! Look at you! Your family probably bought you your rank!'

'I have no memory of my parents. I was taken from them when I was very young.'

Jak fired another shot that a guard caught on his shield. The former guide appeared almost maniacal in rage and coiled eagerness. He lifted his gaze across the hall and gave a fierce nod.

Pon-lor felt his shoulders fall. *Damn. Allowed myself to be distracted.* 'Ware!' a guard shouted the instant something hammered into Pon-lor's back, punching out all his breath. Only his years of Thaumaturg training allowed him to stop the shock from dominating his mind.

Isolate the pain. Breathe. Constrict the vessels.

His diaphragm expanded and breath rushed into him once again. *Too low for a lung. Thank the ancestors!*

'Protect the magister!' a guard yelled, his voice oddly distant. Men crowded, shields raised.

A part of Pon-lor calmly studied the many side portals. Figures now emerged all around. Their gait was unnaturally stiff. They were a mix of male and female, armoured soldiers and clothed civilians. They held spears and tarnished swords in awkward, unswerving grips. There was something familiar in their rigidity; it plucked at a thread from his training. He just could not be certain . . . yet.

A number of his men bellowed war cries and charged, either battle-maddened or unable to endure the wait. Pon-lor clutched at one fellow to keep himself erect. 'No,' he snarled through teeth clenched against the pain. 'Disengage!'

'Aye,' the man answered. He yelled: 'Fall back, dogs! Withdraw!'

The majority could not hear – or chose not to. Iron rang from iron or bit into wood and armour. The encircling figures hardly defended themselves. They moved in a sort of dreamy slow motion, but with deadly power. Leather armour hung in rotting strips. A few wore chain or banded coats half fallen away or flapping uselessly in rusting sections. Some wore plain clothes now in rags. Immobile faces held a strange grey pallor, the eyes empty pits. That, and the ring of metal on stone when a guard smashed the face of one, confirmed what Pon-lor had suspected.

Oh, poor fool! Stupid fool! He lures us here to die at the hands of these cursed souls, little knowing just where their curse came from! 'Jak!' he called, having now mastered the agony of the wound. 'Why do they not attack you?'

The young man was squinting down the length of a nocked arrow, searching for an opening through the guards' raised shields. 'I did not lie, you bastard! I *am* from here. They attack no one of their blood.'

Yes. They retain at least that much sense of their past lives, imprisoned as they are in flesh that has betrayed them. Thank you, Jak.

These pathetic shuffling figures were the cursed soldiers, civilians and court of Chanar Keep.

Still advancing, they clutched at the limbs and armour of Pon-lor's guards to grapple with unbreakable grips or thrust or choke with fingers as strong as stone – for stone they were, flesh accursed to harden into petrification.

The dismissal, man! Think! How does it begin? Pon-lor fell to his knees and covered his eyes to blot out the sight of his men falling before him, screaming and gagging, throats torn. Then he had it, the opening invocation, and it all flowed from there with ease, the sequence hammered into his mind through countless repetitions sitting legs crossed in the ritual centre, chanting from sunrise to sunset, sometimes all through the night until he slumped forward unconscious.

'Magister . . .' a guard breathed above him, awed.

He dared open his eyes, his lips moving soundlessly.

Stone hands were reaching for him not an arm's length away. Frozen now in the act of stretching. And as he watched an invisible wind gnawed at those fingers and the expressionless mask-like faces behind. Grain by grain the petrified flesh fell away like dust in a sandstorm. The clouds of dust swirled, wind-driven, obscuring the chamber. Even the bones of the hands disappeared, scoured away into blunt stubs, the arms following.

'*What?*' he heard Jak yell through the churning ashen clouds. 'What is this?'

'Who did you think lowered this curse upon Khun-Sen?' Pon-lor shouted.

'All know this as the work of the Demon-Queen!'

Pon-lor straightened to his feet. The invocation had centred him fully. Pain could not touch him now, nor could hunger nor fatigue, until he should ease out of the state, or eventually fall unconscious, or dead. He had closed off the bleeding. Clenched muscles and flesh against the wound. As he could now suppress any or all physical damage unless instantly fatal. 'No, Jak,' he began, his voice calm and strong. 'An understandable assumption, but no. The Ruling Circle sent this curse against Khun-Sen – why I do not know. But it is our curse . . . and I am dismissing it now.'

'I will see you dead!' the young man howled.

'He has run, Magister,' a guard said, his gaze shaded against the swirling dust.

Metal clattered to the stone flagging as limbs cracked or hissed away into nothing. Faces had been gouged away into flat discs, bone and all. A head snapped off as the thinned neck gave way with a crack. Which of these, if any, was cursed Khun-Sen himself Pon-lor could not bring himself to care. One cursed figure, an elderly soldier, perhaps Khun-Sen, toppled over to burst into fragments.

'Shall we pursue, m'lord?' a guard asked, his tone now far more respectful.

'No. They know this labyrinth. We'll never track them. Let's find the eastern path.'

'Yes, m'lord.'

The dense iron-grey cloud of dust was dissipating. Pon-lor could now see across the chamber. A good finger's thickness covered every surface. He tilted his head to brush the fine powdered stone from his hair. Armour and weapons littered the floor, along with the corpses of his dead. As the last of the grit sifted away Pon-lor faced a mere four standing guards, all wrapped in shrouds of grey, like the ghosts of Chanar Keep themselves. The four stood blinking at one another through the smeared masks of pulverized stone as if shocked to find themselves alive.

'Magister . . .' murmured one, gesturing to his side.

Pon-lor peered down to see the bloodied, now dust-caked arrow-head and a good hand's width of haft standing from his torso. He'd almost forgotten about it. 'Break it off and pull it out,' he told the guards.

They exchanged uneasy glances but nodded their acquiescence.

'This will hurt, Magister . . .' one told him, reaching for the haft.

Pon-lor took hold of the man's sash to steady himself. 'No, Melesh – it is Melesh? Yes? I quite assure you it will not.'

If any ships witnessed the storm that arose upon the great empty tract of ocean between Quon Tali and the shores of Jacuruku, none survived to tell the wonders of the sight. No natural tempest was this. The sea clashed as if driven to war against itself. Mountainous waves swelled as current surged against current. Deep troughs the size of valleys opened as if to reveal the infinite depths. The winds battled and slashed each other into shreds of cloud and sleet.

Through these howling squalls a single vessel did push south by southwest. Long and low it was, of black wood lacquered in countless layers. It possessed no masts. Its deck was fully enclosed but for a single small hatch. Single banks of twenty oars to a side fought the contrary winds and slam of waves in a steady inhumanly powerful stroke.

As if in defiance of the storm a woman stood open to the elements upon the deck. Her clothes hung from her, utterly soaked. Water ran in rivulets from her hacked short hair and slid wind-driven across her face. She stood with arms crossed beneath her outer robes, her gaze slit against the cutting sleet. Twice a day another woman emerged from the small hatch. This one wore light leather armour, belted and studded. A pale mask hid half her face. Though the deck was featureless polished wood and the wind raged in gusting contrary blows her footing was sure as she crossed to the first woman. Here she offered a meagre ball of food or a skin of water that the first always refused, and then she would withdraw, bowing.

Who would it be? T'riss, the Enchantress, Queen of Dreams, and one-time companion to Anomandaris, wondered. *Which of them shall be first?* She sensed them all far to the west, all gathered for the potential transfiguration. *And who shall it be, and into which state? And will they be pleased with the results?* Too many futures now beckoned for any to see the clear path. Even she.

And it is the mortals who will choose.

There it was. The unwelcome truth – her forte. As ash-dry in her mouth as in anyone's.

After all these ages . . . the choice was no longer hers. Indeed, she saw now that it never was. That what she had taken as control, the subtle manipulation, all the light plucking of such diverse threads, had been no more than the kicking of stones down a hill. They do end up at the bottom where you want them, but how they got there . . . well . . . one can hardly take the credit.

And speaking of tumbling stones . . . she sensed them, then, her first visitors.

Get of the Errant. The vindictive two-faced Twins.

It was the Lad who faced her. The rain slashed through his wavering translucent image. His pointed ferret face twitched in something resembling a wink.

'What do you want?' she said and he heard her though the raging winds annihilated her words.

He took on an expression of anxious concern. 'I have come to warn you.'

'Warn me of what?'

He wavered closer as if to impart some secret news. 'Have you not seen there is a strong chance that this gambit of yours will bring you to your end?'

I have seen that and infinitely more than you can conceive of, you capering fool. 'Yes.'

The Lady swung round from her rear. The wind did not touch her long brushed hair. Her pale face pulled down in a sad moue. She sighed: 'How desperately you must have loved him from afar . . .'

For a moment T'riss lost her footing and stumbled backwards. She righted herself, her brows crimped in puzzlement. 'What nonsense is this?'

The Lady sighed once more, as if in empathy. But malice glittered in her black eyes. 'Unrequited love is the cruellest, they say. And now he is gone.'

The Queen of Dreams' brows rose as understanding came. 'No . . .'

The Twins circled her now. 'Do not throw your life away in some mad plan,' the Lad urged.

'You were as nothing to him, in any case,' the Lady said with a flick of her hand.

Why do they seek to dissuade me? I wonder which of all the possible outcomes it is that they fear. And how could I ever know for certain? She offered an easy shrug. 'You presume too much.'

The Lady stopped before her. Her mouth tightened into a cruel knowing slash. '*She* will destroy you.'

'Perhaps.'

'She has barred you from her lands,' said the Lad.

'So she has.'

'She's tried to kill you already,' the Lady added.

T'riss stood deathly still for a time. When she spoke her voice was frigid: 'You presume *far* too much . . . That is enough from you.'

The Twins bowed – yet mockingly. 'No,' said the Lady, 'that is enough from you . . .'

'. . . as there shall be no more from you,' finished the Lad.

212

And the two faded from sight leaving the glistening black deck empty, rain-slashed and awash in spray.

T'riss sensed the approach of her Seguleh bodyguard, Ina. The woman stopped next to her. She was crouched, her bent legs leaning with the drunken yaw and pitch of the deck. In the tilt of her masked head T'riss read a question.

'It was nothing, Ina. Just a chance encounter.'

CHAPTER VI

I am amused by the attitude of these people of Jakal Uku towards antiques and the possessions of any deceased person generally. Childishly, they absolutely do not wish to possess such objects and have no desire for them. I once noted a wonderful pugal (a carved low sitting table) left in an abandoned hut. 'What a fine piece of the woodcarver's art!' I exclaimed to my local friend. 'Why is it thrown aside?'

'I would not touch it,' he answered. 'I would think of the persons who sat at it before me and whether their lives were happy and if they are happy now watching me sit where they once did.'

Whelhen Mariner
Narrative of a Shipwreck and Captivity
within a Mythical Land

OLD MAN MOON MADE ALL THE PREPARATIONS. THROUGH THE heat of the day Saeng sat in the hut on its tall poles. She fanned Hanu, all the while feeling rather like a bird in a cage. She watched Moon coming and going from the surrounding jungle. In the clear light of day he appeared no more than a tattooed old man. A village elder, priest, or monk. He laid up a great pile of firewood, set the fire, then set to grinding various ingredients in a mortar: charcoal, some kind of red dirt or clay, and plant roots. The mortar was no more than a slab of basalt bearing a depression in its top that he pushed a stone across. He then set a number of pointed sticks on a slab of wood together with a row of grey earthenware pots. Last, he unrolled a long sheet of woven rattan matting.

The boy Ripan, meanwhile, had been tasked with watching the fire. This he pursued only in the most negligent manner, heaving loud aggrieved sighs, and raising a palm leaf fan over the fire in a desultory wave.

One time when Moon had gone off into the woods, the lad drew out his flute. He blew a series of descending hauntingly sad notes, and sang: 'Woe to whoever would reach for the Moon . . . they fail to see the cliff before their feet . . .' and he sent her a sharp-toothed grin.

Towards evening Old Man Moon's wrinkled tattooed face appeared at the hut's entrance. 'Things are nearly ready.'

'Perhaps,' called Ripan from the fire, 'you should wait for the Night of our Ancestors, or the Festival of Cleansing. Those would be far more propitious . . .'

'You forget whom you speak to,' the old man snapped in his first betrayal of any temper in front of Saeng. He smiled up reassuringly. 'I am Old Man Moon! I decide what times are propitious, and which are not. Now come, we will begin.'

'And my brother?'

He raised a placating hand. 'Later. After your payment.'

Saeng did not move. 'Payment usually follows services.'

'I always receive my due first. But, if it makes you feel any better, I assure you that what you provide for me will not be binding or efficacious unless I pay for it. It's all part of the exchange.'

Saeng was not completely convinced, but there appeared to be nothing she could hold the man to. Her mouth tight with misgiving, she climbed down the ladder, assisted by Moon.

'Very good!' he exclaimed. 'Play for us, Ripan.'

The youth rolled his eyes to the purpling, half-overcast sky.

'There, now.' Moon stood next to the rattan matting. He set to rolling up his waistcloth wrap and exposed a loincloth that was no more than a strip running vertically between his flat wrinkled flanks.

Not only was Saeng horrified to be presented with the old man's withered buttocks, but she saw that each was entirely pristine.

Oh, my ancestors, no! Not this.

He lay on his stomach and rested his head on his folded arms. He sighed contentedly. 'Very good.'

Saeng cleared her throat. 'So. I'm to tattoo your . . .' She couldn't think of any way to say it.

'As you can see, I'm running out of options. I could turn over. Would you prefer that?'

'*No!* No thank you. This is fine.'

'I thought as much. Ripan – you're not playing.'

'It's not time yet,' the lad answered resentfully.

Moon raised his head to peer up at the trees and the gathering evening. 'Ah! You are right. I've got ahead of myself, I am so eager.' He looked over his shoulder. 'I apologize. I haven't been myself since I had something of an accident recently. But tonight should go a long way to remedying that.'

Saeng frowned down at the old man. *A recent accident?* She remembered a night not so long ago. Her neighbours screaming, pointing up at the black sky. And on the moon: had she glimpsed a flash of light? Then darkness swirling across the scarred round face obscuring it for nights on end.

'Are you the moon?' she asked, unable to withhold all wonder from her voice.

He chuckled indulgently. 'No, child. Not itself, of course. But I live its life and it mine. Long ago I chose to tie myself to it as intimately as if it were my twin. I can still remember when the vision of it first revealed itself to me all those ages ago.' He laid his head back down on his folded arms. 'At that time I moved through darkness without being aware what darkness was – it was all I knew. But then, unbidden, the vision came to me of the moon floating among the stars. Glorious, it seemed to me. A hanging pool of quicksilver. Its light was silvery cool. Magical. I swore then that I had found my essence and I took the moon as my patron. My inspiration. My source.' He glanced back to her once again. 'Do you know what I mean by that?'

'I believe so,' she answered, slowly. She recalled a few of the more ancient shades from her childhood speaking of the greatest of the entities that emerged from the vastness of the past. And how each had their Aspect, their province, or facet. Earth, Dark, Water, Light, and more. Why not the moon?

'Of course you know what happened then, yes?'

She shook her head then realized he couldn't see and so murmured, 'No.' Before her eyes the spinning glyphs and symbols continued their shimmering graceful arc across the old man's back, as if mirroring the turning of the infinite night above.

'The moon fades.' Ripan spoke up, and he blew a long sad note that trailed down into silence.

'Yes. The sun rose. The moon was but stealing its glow from the sun. For the first time I beheld the sun and it terrified me. It seemed my wanderings had brought me into Tiste lands. I paid my respects to Mother Dark but kept to myself mostly. Now I live here and I pay my respects to Lady Ardata.'

'You serve the Demon-Queen?'

'Demons?' He cocked his head. 'Well, there are a *few*, I suppose. But there are one or two of *everything* here. Long ago Ardata offered sanctuary to all the creatures and spirits you humans cared to name monsters. Which, it seems, conveniently includes everything other than *you*. Here you will find many things that have elsewhere disappeared from the face of the earth. Even some things that have been forgotten all together.'

'Himatan . . .' Saeng breathed.

'Indeed. Some few humans live in the jungles as well. But they are just one kind among many. And they tread lightly for it.' He closed his eyes and sighed once more. 'Ah, child. You should have seen it then. The moon, I mean. Wondrous! It used to be much larger in the sky, you know. Very much larger. These late days it is but a shrunken grey shadow of its former glory. And it had brothers and sisters, then. Other moons.'

'All gone now,' murmured Ripan, pointedly.

'Yes. Some lost their way and wandered off. Others fell to break up in great fiery cascades.' He shook his head in sad reminiscence.

Saeng studied the assemblage of tattooing instruments and what she assumed to be powdered pigments or tints in the coarsely fired earthenware pots. She picked up one long stick to find it tipped in an iron point that glimmered blue-grey in the fading twilight.

Struck by a thought, she said, 'I always assumed you'd be female, you know. Where I come from, the moon is always portrayed as female.'

The old man nodded where he lay, his head on his folded arms. 'Yes. I understand that is how it is now – among you humans. And the Tiste as well, I believe. But in the eldest cults, the ones that date back to when awareness first raised its eyes to the sky in wonder, among these, where people move in unison with the seasons, the moon is always male and the sun female. Such is the irrefutable logic of fertility. The sun gives life. The sun provides. What does the moon do? It has no light of its own – it can only steal some small glow from the sun. It is but a pale modest attendant to the infinitely flowing and infinitely giving life abundance that is the sun.'

She found him gazing at her over his shoulder. 'As part of me is to Light.'

Saeng frowned and opened her mouth to ask what he meant by that but he raised his head, announcing, 'Ah! Now we can begin.' Saeng peered about, wondering why suddenly it was time. Then she saw it. The moon had risen. Its pallid magical light streamed through the trees. A few narrow beams of wavering liquid silver now fell across Old Man Moon's elbow and one shoulder. The tattoos within this light blazed to life like distant stars.

Saeng raised the instrument in her hand. 'But . . . what do I do?'

'Ah! Simplicity itself!' Moon shifted an arm and smoothed a patch of earth. He scratched a symbol in the dirt. 'Start with that one.'

Swallowing her distaste, she examined his right buttock. 'Where?'

'The outside top. Work inward.'

Wonderful. Work inward! But what do I do when I reach . . . well, maybe I should cross that bridge when I come to it.

'And what do I use, you know, for ink?'

'Ah. Take up the nearest pot . . .'

Saeng lifted it and peered inside: the dust scintillated like powdered silver.

'. . . and spit into it.'

Spit? 'What? Spit? Really?'

'Yes. Quite so. It is required.'

Gods look away! This was getting worse and worse. Hanu better damn well appreciate it! She spat, but as she did so a great gust of the powder blew up into her face and she coughed, nearly dropping the pot. She wiped her watering eyes. 'I'm so sorry!'

Ripan laughed, and it was not a friendly laugh.

'It is fine,' Moon assured her. To Ripan, a curt, 'Play!'

The youth took up his flute and blew a squalling note. He winked over the instrument.

'Try not to exhale next time,' Moon explained.

'I'll try,' she answered tightly, rather annoyed that he hadn't mentioned it before.

She crouched next to him, tucked her legs beneath her, and bent down over his withered flanks. She dabbed the tip of the instrument into the globe of liquid silver her spit had become, then studied the symbol the old man had drawn.

Taking a deep breath, she set to work.

Old Man Moon talked the entire time. Concentrating on her task, Saeng hardly heard half of what he said. Occasionally he would raise a hand, saying, 'good enough' or 'extend that line'. But other than these simple instructions he seemed content to leave her to it. Each new glyph or arcane symbol he traced in the dirt for her. As the work progressed Saeng was disconcerted to see some of her handiwork join the orderly march of signs spinning across the old man's flank and back. Ripan kept up a low tuneless accompaniment that seemed to wander drearily, and frankly was no help to her concentration.

It might have been her imagination, but it seemed as if the moon shone brighter for her as she worked.

After one particularly screeching note Old Man Moon caught her glaring in the youth's direction. He smiled indulgently. 'Never you mind Ripan, child. He and my other offspring, they have no sympathy for me. That is just how it is. Not as among you humans, I know. So long as I remain strong and whole they will remain in my shadow – so to speak. They are merely waiting. Waiting for my destruction or dissolution. Then all my power will devolve upon them. Then they will rule all that is the province of the sublunary. Is that not so, Ripan?'

The youth blew a long eerie note, and winked. 'I can hardly wait.'

Saeng sat back from her work, appalled. 'That is awful.' She shook the long-handled needle at Ripan. 'You should honour your father. Wish him long life, health, prosperity.'

Old Man Moon chuckled. 'Yet is this not how it is among you living kind? When you strip away all the sentiment and affection – real or not – the old must make way for the young. The new generation replaces the prior. Is this not so?'

Saeng bit at her lip 'Well. In the harshest possible light, yes.'

'That light is the cold radiance of the moon, child. That is one aspect of the sublunary. I call to that most basic of drives. The un-said half of procreation. A drive that supersedes even the urge to survival.'

Moon reached down to scratch his buttock and Saeng had to comment silently: *I'm feeling no such urge right now, old man.*

'Did you know,' Moon went on, oblivious, 'that on one certain moon every year animals of the depths heave themselves up on to beaches on many lands to lay their eggs, to procreate, even though it means their death? This is what I speak of.'

Saeng spat into another roughly formed earthenware cup. 'It's different for people.'

He sighed. 'So they tell themselves.'

She forced herself to examine the man's flank. She'd been given a rag to wipe away the blood and excess dye from the tattooing and this she balled up once more to wipe the skin. Yet in the pale watery moonlight the stain looked more like melted silver than dark like blood. 'How much more am I to do? The moon will set, surely.'

The old man chuckled again. 'Do not worry. We will have as long as is necessary. You are almost done, in any case. Just the one side.'

Well, thank the ancestors for that mercy! 'Very good. What's next?'

'Ah! This one is tricky.' He scratched in the dirt. 'A circle with a line through it and an undulating line beneath. The line beneath must be marked in the fifth cup's ink, if you please.'

'Fine.' Saeng clamped that needle between her teeth and asked through it, 'Why me? Why not Ripan, or anyone else?'

The old man now had his chin on his flat hands. 'Ripan? Tiam's blood, no. He is not suited for such service. You, however, are perfect.'

'Oh? How?'

'Thyrllan moves through your heart and your hands, child. I feel it like a surge, a tidal pull, when you touch me.'

'Thyrllan? Whatever do you mean, Thyrllan?'

'Light, child.'

Saeng jerked, stabbing, and the old man hissed. Mercury drops ran down his tattooed flesh. Saeng wiped them away. 'Sorry.'

'Quite all right. Unfortunately, there is no narcotic in creation powerful enough to dull my senses.'

Light again, dammit. But what was she to *do*? She took the second needle from her mouth and began working on the undulating line. 'I'm looking for a temple to Light. The Great Temple.'

'It lies within Ardata's demesnes.'

'Where?'

The old man shrugged. 'I do not know. You must simply look for it. You will meet the multiform denizens of Ardata's protection. Some will be of no help. Others will help you.'

How very helpful. 'I was warned that something was coming. Something terrible.'

He straightened an arm to point to the west. There the unearthly jade light of the Visitor played through the trees. 'Perhaps it has something to do with that.'

'Don't you know? I mean, the moon. The stars. Divination! Foretelling the future and all that?'

An indulgent chuckle from the man. 'Oh, yes. All *that*. My child – the moon rises, the moon sets. Every day is the same to me. I cannot see the future any more than I can revisit the past. I see only what I am looking down upon.'

'But people . . .'

'People will always believe what they want to believe. Grant things as much power as they choose to give them.' He shrugged again. 'Such is how it is.'

'But you know what I'm talking about, don't you? The prophecies. The Visitor. Some name it the Sword of the Gods. An evil curse. It would be a cataclysm.'

The old man rubbed a shoulder and grimaced as if at an old wound. 'Yes. As it happens, I know exactly what you mean . . . but child, what is that to me? The world revolves on. The moon rises. The moon sets. It matters not who walks upon the face of the land.'

Saeng sat back once more, the needle forgotten in her hand. Such indifference! It almost took her breath away. Didn't he care? And he'd seemed so *kind*. Then she remembered the angry snarled words of the leopard-man: *those who would stand aside* . . .

'So you won't help me.'

'I *am* helping you, child. A service for a service. And you are almost done. Just a few last symbols and we are finished.'

She *was* tired. Bleary with exhaustion, in fact. To see clearly for the work she had to squint her eyes until they hurt and her back felt as if daggers were stabbing it. 'Then you will heal Hanu,' she said, blinking heavily.

'Yes. Surely. For if I do not all that you have given me will drain away into nothing. Like moonbeams cupped in your hands.'

'Fine. What's next?'

He sketched once more in the dirt.

In the end she could not remember whether she finished or not. All she knew was that she found herself jerking her eyes open again and again. The needle wavering in her hand. She remembered a sea of beautiful arcane symbols dancing and gyring before her as if in a sea of stormy night-black ink. Then the old man's voice rang as if from afar, deep and profound. 'That is enough. You have given me so very much, Priestess of Light. Sleep now, safe and warded, under the light of the moon.'

And she remembered no more.

The heat of the sun upon her face woke her. She sat up, blinking and wincing, and covered her gaze. Morning mist hovered over the clearing and among the trees. Thick clouds half obscured the sky. The humidity was choking. Already beads of sweat pricked her arms and face.

Hanu! She leaped to her feet only to stagger, almost falling, hands to her head. Gods! What happened? She was hardly able to walk. *Of course, fool! You expect to walk away from an all-night ritual? You've just done the most demanding work of your life!*

She peered around for Moon's hut but couldn't see it. What she did spot was Hanu lying in the glade among the tall grass. She stumbled over to fall to her knees next to him. She shook him.

221

'Hanu! Can you hear me? Hanu?'

He groaned and rolled on to his back.

She covered her mouth to smother a yell of triumph.

He fumbled at his great full helm, drew it off, then blinked in the bright light just as she had. His mild brown eyes found her, sent a look of wonder.

'You fell.'

He cocked his head, thinking. Then he nodded.

'I came down for you, then an underground stream took us.'

He nodded again, holding his head. An inarticulate groan of pain escaped his lips.

'You hit your head.'

He gave the sign for emphatic agreement – three times.

'Can you walk?'

By way of answer he slowly began heaving himself up. She tried to help but didn't think she made much difference. He stood weaving, as unsure on his feet as she felt. He signed, *'Where?'*

'We're in Himatan now. The stream brought us.' He peered around, confused, obviously searching for the stream. 'I dragged you as far as I could.'

He grunted, signed, *'Heavy.'*

Smiling indulgently, Saeng reached out in her thoughts: *'Don't you remember I opened the path between our thoughts?'*

He rubbed his forehead, grimacing at himself. *'Oh, yes.'*

'I couldn't bring you too far. Can you walk?'

He nodded, picked up the helm and tucked it under an arm, checked his weapons. Saeng started east. 'This way.'

But Hanu did not follow. She peered back to see him near the centre of the sunlit glade staring down at something. As she returned he gestured to his feet.

Hidden among the tall grass was a tiny house no taller than her knees. It stood on short poles and had a doll's ladder that led up to its front opening. Peering down at it Saeng felt as if she would faint. Her vision darkened and a roaring gathered in her ears. Hanu's strong grip on her shoulder steadied her. 'A spirit house,' she breathed. A symbol above the opening proclaimed who it was made for. And Saeng knew who that was, of course.

The moon spirit. Am I the one who has lost her mind?

'Careful,' Hanu sent.

'Yes,' she murmured. 'I know. Bad luck to disturb them . . . Let's go.'

She never made it to the edge of the open glade. Her knees gave

way and she collapsed. *Utterly spent. Gods! No strength left at all
. . . Can barely think.*

The next thing she became aware of was the sensation of floating. The tree canopy of arching branches passing overhead. Firm
arms under her knees and shoulders. *Hanu's turn*, she thought, and
tucked her head into his shoulder to sleep.

*　　*　　*

The scene outside the hanging cloth of Golan's litter remained
depressingly repetitive. *Jungle and more jungle. Ancient Elders, will
it ever end?* And their pace was slowing. Each day's march crossed
less ground. Ground! As if it could be called that! A morass of rotting
vegetation, tangled creepers, and hidden swamp. At times the land
seemed indistinguishable from the water.

He opened the loose yellowed and brittle pages that were his copy
of Brother Fel-esh's *Travels in the Most Ancient of Lands*:

*And so it was less than twelve days' journey after the village of
Payam Tani, that we beheld floating above the wide jungle canopy
the golden edifices that were the assembled temples and palaces of
Jakal Viharn . . .*

Golan carefully closed the pages and bound them up once more.
*So, some fifteen days to the village . . . less than one moon's travel,
all told. Yet Bakar wrote that it took them nearly twice that time to
reach the Gangrek Mounts after fleeing the capital . . . None of these
travel times match up!*

It was most frustrating.

Someone cleared their throat outside the litter and Golan said,
'Yes, U-Pre?' He moved the cloth a fraction aside to see the man.
The second in command walked bent with hands clasped behind his
back. He seemed reluctant to meet Golan's gaze. His leathers bore
dark stains and the white dusting of dried salts. He was unshaven, his
face glistening with sweat, and he appeared to have lost weight. The
thought struck Golan that perhaps the man was sick. *He is pushing
himself hard; I mustn't blame him.* 'More bad news, Second?'

The man nodded. 'The train is bogged down, Master. We won't
be able to get them moving again any time soon. We may as well
hold here.'

We've hardly moved today! Golan bit back his outburst. He took
a long calming breath as he had been trained a lifetime to do. 'I see,
Second. This is unwelcome news. We are behind schedule. What is
it this time?'

'The wagons, Master. The ground is too soft and the obstacles too thick.'

'Yet we need those stores, Second. We are travelling in a hostile land.'

'Yes, Master.'

'Very well, Second. It would not do to get too far ahead, would it?'

'No, Master.'

Golan gave a small wave to dismiss the man and let the cloth fall back. He noted how tattered the gauze had become. *These voracious jungle insects are eating it. Soon there will be nothing left . . . Oh dear . . .*

U-Pre's scrawny shadow, Principal Scribe Thorn, was not far behind. Golan lay back yet kept the fellow in the edge of his vision until the man's awkward gait brought him close enough for him to pronounce: 'Welcome, Principal Scribe! What news?'

The man gaped up, his prominent Adam's apple bobbing like a swallowed ball. 'Master! How did you know? Astounding!'

Every day it was so – and by now Golan was beginning to wonder if perhaps the man had been making fun of *him* all this time. 'Your report?'

The man's unusually long neck bent as he peered down at his woven fibre sheets. 'Twelve wagons, Master.'

'Total?'

'Today.'

Golan glared at the man. 'Today? Twelve wagons lost all in one day?'

The Principal Scribe was consulting his notes and so unaware of his angry stare. 'Broken axles, rotted beds. Disassembled for spare parts, Master.'

'And their stores?'

'Abandoned, Master.'

'*Abandoned*, Principal Scribe? What stores would they be?'

The man noted that tone, hunching. He consulted the thick sheaves of manifests in the bulging shoulder bag at his side. 'Firewood, mostly, Master,' he announced, obviously pleased to have so quickly located the requested information.

Golan straightened so abruptly he had to grasp the side of the litter to steady himself. '*Firewood*?' he said, disbelieving. 'We are dragging wood into a *forest*?' He waved the blackwood baton in a wide circle. 'False gods, man! Have a look around. We're surrounded by trees.'

The scribe nervously fingered the globular jade inkwell hanging from his neck. 'With the greatest of respect, Master – none of these trees are suitable. They are too green and damp to burn.'

Golan was almost at a loss for words. 'Well . . . then . . . dead trees. Fallen trees!'

'Again, Master. I am most sorry, but they rot immediately, never truly drying out.'

'I see.' Golan studied the man. His uneven eyes, one higher than the other, and gawking cross-eyed bird-like stare. His lips ink-stained from his habit of holding his writing instrument in his mouth. *Was he truly mocking him all this time?* 'So, you are trying to tell me that nothing ever burns in this jungle?'

'Oh, no, m'lord. Fires rage through here regularly during the dry season. But only the leaves and bracken and such on the forest floor are consumed. The trees endure.'

'Thank you for that lesson in natural philosophy, Principal Scribe. I am most illuminated.'

'Ever glad to be of service, Master.'

Golan eyed the fellow closely for a time. 'Anything else?'

'Yes.' Thorn retrieved a new set of sheets. 'The rate of troop disappearances is growing. We believe it is a combination of desertions and unfortunate attacks.'

'*Unfortunate* attacks?'

'Yes, m'lord. For example, four soldiers spotted something that resembled a pig and despite your orders against entering the jungle they chased after it. None was seen again. It is presumed they were victims of wild animals, or some other jungle denizen.'

'*Jungle denizen.* A delicate euphemism, Thorn.'

'So it is entered in the official campaign history.'

I am beginning to fear that that official record is all that will be left of us. 'My thanks, Principal Scribe. Until tomorrow's report.'

The scribe bowed then scuttled off in quick small steps.

Golan tapped the Rod of Execution to his chin. He reflected that Brother Fel-esh wrote in his account of *his* discoveries, and *his* groundbreaking exploration, all the while conveniently failing to mention the full army of attendants, guards and servants, some three hundred strong in total, who supported him in his 'adventure'.

And he barely made it out alive.

Whereas I lead five thousand troops and two hundred yakshaka, supported by fifteen thousand slaves, labourers, bearers and assorted camp followers.

225

I hope to do slightly better. He tapped the baton to his litter. 'Set me down and have my tent erected.'

The yakshaka bowed.

That night there came an attack that Golan knew even the most creative record-keeping could not cover up as *unfortunate*. He was in his tent reporting to the Circle of Nine when the first of the shouts and calls reached him through the layered cloth walls. Standing before the glowing silver chasing on his baton of office, Golan groaned inwardly at what the alarms announced. He cleared his throat and interjected: 'That is all for now, then. Am continuing to press forward.'

'*See that you do,*' came the stern whisper of Master Surin. '*We are counting on your advance to divert all attention from us. This is your purpose and role—*'

'Understood, Masters. Thank you. Goodnight.'

'*You are encountering difficulties?*' Master Surin enquired, his voice becoming silky soft, as it always did when he sensed prevarication or, worse, failure.

Golan switched to vague honesty. 'Of course, Masters. We all knew this would be difficult.'

The yells had turned to screams and a general tumult outside the tent.

'*Well,*' Surin answered, grudgingly appeased, '*see to it.*'

'Of course. My thanks, Masters.'

The frosty blue glow faded leaving Golan in the dark. Arms extended, he felt about for the opening, heaved aside the thick cloth. And stepped into chaos.

A storm of some sort appeared to have engulfed the camp. Labourers and workers, male and female, all ran pell-mell, waving their arms over their heads, even covering their faces. Clouds of insects choked the air like a sandstorm. They swooped over the ground in great swarms. U-Pre stood next to the opening, batting at his face and arms and hopping from foot to foot. 'What are we to do, sir?' he shouted.

'What of the Isturé mages?' Golan called back. A warm rush spread over his feet and he peered down to see a thick crimson carpet of swarming ants. He hopped and kicked at the tide.

'I've heard nothing from them,' U-Pre shouted, batting at his arms and hissing his pain at the red welts revealed.

A fat yellow centipede now rode atop U-Pre's helmet as if it were some sort of whimsical crest. Golan recognized it as one of the fatally poisonous kind. Summoning his power he flicked it aside without saying anything. He bent closer to shout: 'I will see to them. Start fires, Second. Many fires.'

U-Pre saluted and jogged off. Golan went in search of an Isturé. His yakshaka bodyguard immediately surrounded him; they appeared either impervious to the plague of insects or merely hardened against their bites and stings, and the unnerving sensation of things crawling where they shouldn't. For his part, Golan summoned his power to maintain a flickering blue aura about his person that turned aside the swarms. The encampment was a riot of screaming and writhing men and women batting at their ears and faces. Any fires were almost smothered beneath the thousands of winged bodies drawn to their heat. Golan lent power to each he passed, allowing them to flare up once more, hungry and all-consuming. He hoped their smoke would also contribute to dispersing the hordes.

Close to the border of the camp he found an Isturé. The man wore heavy armour of plates at chest and shoulders over a mail coat, and a full helm. All had once been blackened, but was now scraped and worn through heavy use to an iron-grey shine. He was leaning on a tall rectangular shield and waving a gauntleted hand before the visor of his helm as if the attack were nothing more than a show put on for his amusement.

'Where are your mages, Isturé?' Golan demanded.

'The name is Black the Lesser,' came a sullen rumble from within the helm.

'Mages, Black. Where are your vaunted Isturé mages?'

'Not our battle.'

'Not your— Why else are you here, ancients take you?'

'We watch for these monsters you're so fearful of. Lizard-cats, lion-men and other bugaboos.'

'I demand you take action! At once! Or I will leave you behind as useless!'

Heaving a loud sigh, the big man threw his shield on to his back and waved for Golan to follow. He led him to an old man sitting cross-legged on the ground. His greying hair stood in all directions and a great baggy set of robes enveloped him like a tattered shapeless bag. Black stopped in front of him and tilted his helm to indicate Golan. The old man cocked a sallow rheumy eye to Golan. 'What is it?'

'What is it? *What is it?*'

Golan thrust out his hand only to realize that he'd left the Rod of Execution in the tent. He waved around instead. 'Can't you do something about this!'

The old man gave a shrug that was smothered within the bag. 'I could. Why don't you?'

Golan drew himself up straight, offended, then was forced to wave a hand before his face where scores of alarmingly huge flying cockroaches now fluttered their stiff brown wings and bumped at every one of his orifices. 'The time has not yet come for me to announce myself,' he said between clenched teeth.

'She knows you're here.'

'She does not know a master of the Inner Circle has been sent!'

The old man snorted a loud laugh as if what Golan had said was immensely amusing. His arched brow climbed even higher. 'Do you really think that matters one damned bit?'

Golan decided to dismiss the man's words as empty bluster. *What would this foreigner know anyway?* Then he noted how of the swarms of insects seething over the ground not one touched the man's robes and this settled the matter for him. 'Do something about this plague or I shall reconsider our agreement, Isturé. What would your Skinner think of that? He would not take it well, I think.'

The old man's gimlet eye shifted to Black. The two appeared to share some sort of unspoken communication and then it was the old man's turn to heave a sigh. He climbed awkwardly to his feet, began rooting through what appeared to be innumerable pockets lining his loose robes.

Meanwhile the swarming continued. Solid flights of tiny midges or flies completely enmeshed their victims, who quickly fell, becoming nothing more than twitching heaps of glittering black multitudes. 'Do something,' Golan snarled, his hands impotent fists at his sides.

The old man produced a feather from his robes. It was grimed and plain, perhaps taken from some seabird. Golan sensed the blossoming of the man's power – a far different flavour from the foreign 'Warrens'. More chthonic, seething wild and feral. The old man blew upon the feather and it shot straight up into the fat scudding clouds above. Then he sat once more and pulled his robes higher about his pale neck.

'That's it?' Golan demanded.

'Done.' He sniffed, coughed, then hawked something up that he spat aside. 'All this damp,' he complained to Black. 'Bad for the lungs.'

'Wouldn't know,' Black rumbled. 'I'm still a young shoot.' And he laughed while the old man cackled harshly.

What strange people, these foreigners. Was that a reference to this Vow of theirs?

Something was coming. Golan could feel it in the air now brushing past him. In the distance, the dark canopy of the jungle writhed as if in the fists of giants. A great boom crashed overhead like a burst of thunder. Black, he noted, had braced himself, hunching and digging in his rear foot. Golan had opened his mouth to ask what was happening when a wall of air punched into him and sent him flying backwards, his feet swinging up violently. He landed on the back of his neck, stunned; fortunately the muddy ground was soft beneath him.

After the stars cleared from his vision the Thaumaturg found himself peering upwards at shattered branches whipping overhead, along with great wads of detritus dug up by the hurricane winds that now scoured the encampment like a rough sweeping hand. The noise was tremendous, deafening, a thundering storm howl that eliminated any possibility of communication. Not that he could move in any case.

The front, or blast-wave, now diminished, roiling onwards. Golan could push himself up on to his elbows. Of the thick black swarms of insects there remained no sign. He stood, his yakshaka bodyguards rising with him, and headed for the main staging area. Here the troops and labourers were slowly straightening, stunned amazement clear upon their features. He found that the plague of insects was not the only thing missing: the tents had been swept clean from the field. Wagons lay overturned, their contents scattered across the mud and mire. His own tent was completely absent; his servants crawled through his strewn possessions lying in a trail of wreckage that disappeared among the trees.

A yakshaka soldier approached and respectfully proffered the Rod of Execution in both armoured hands. Golan took it absently while he continued to scan the wide field of scattered stores and tossed debris. The baton was muddy and he used the edge of his robes to wipe it clean.

A second boom crashed down upon them, making the troops flinch, and it was as if the clouds were overturned as a great downpour struck, hammering everything further into the muck. Golan stood quite still in the torrent, drops falling from his chin and his fingertips, watching reams of pressed plant fibre papers dissolving in the rain and filth.

Funny. The bastard probably thinks this is all so very funny.

*   *   *

229

They established their headquarters in the valley just before the one occupied by the southern capital of the Thaumaturgs, Isana Pura. Dismounting from an inspection of the pickets and the deployment of his lancers, Prince Jatal straightened the white cotton robes he wore over his armour and tucked his gauntlets into his belt. That he was not looking forward to this strategy council was something of an understatement. The head of every family would have a place at the table and there would be as many opinions as mouths flapping. Yet attend he must. It was required. As the head of one of the two largest factions his was a position of leadership among this temporary coalition. Not that said position carried any attendant authority whatsoever.

He drew off his helmet and tucked it under an arm. Its bright chain camail rattled and hissed as he walked. The Warleader's guards at the entrance nodded their acknowledgement – the deepest gesture of respect any of the Adwami could expect from these foreign mercenaries, who reserved their salutes for the Warleader himself.

He pushed aside the cloth hangings and entered into a yelling match. His fellow representatives lay on pillows and carpets about the tent shouting and cursing one another. Across the way, the Warleader sat accoutred as was his habit in his long mail coat, cross-legged, chin in one fist, his face flushed and rigid with control. The ligaments of his neck stood out as taut as bowstrings. Jatal found Princess Andanii sitting back on a pillow, idly stroking a jewelled dagger at her hip. She offered him a quick veiled glance.

Now aware of Jatal's entrance, several of the minor families most closely allied with the Hafinaj sought to enlist him in support of their cause. He raised his hands, helpless. 'Please! Jher-ef, Waress! Not all at once, if you would be so kind.' He sat, sweeping out his robes, and extended a hand to the Warleader. 'Let us hear the opinion of our hired expert.'

'Bah!' scoffed Ganell from where he sat. 'That one is only interested in seizing all the best spoils for himself.'

Jatal arched a brow, inviting the Warleader to respond.

The man drew a heavy grating breath. 'It only makes sense, my prince,' he began, his voice almost fracturing in the effort to remain civil. 'My troops should storm the Thaumaturgs' precincts while your lancers patrol the streets to control the city and outlying grounds.'

Jatal swung his gaze to Ganell. 'Sounds reasonable to me.'

The big man waved his arms. 'The real treasure will be with the damned Thaumaturgs!'

Jatal made a show of considering this. 'Yet . . . are we not agreed to share all spoils?'

'What little will be left of it,' Ganell grumbled darkly, shifting uncomfortably.

Jatal pursed his lips. He turned to the Warleader. 'Perhaps a force of Adwami men-at-arms may accompany you, Warleader? Some thousand soldiers, perhaps? Drawn from a number of the families?'

The Warleader's severe lined face, held as immobile as a stone mask, gave no hint of what he thought of the suggestion, but he did finally incline his head in assent. His ropy iron-grey hair fell forward, hanging as long as his wiry beard. 'I have no objection, my lords.'

'And who is to command this force?' Sher' Tal, Horsemaster of the Saar, called out. He thrust a finger at Ganell. 'Not *him*!'

'Buffalo . . .' Ganell murmured, baring his teeth at the man.

Jatal raised a hand to quiet the rising tension. 'I admit to some curiosity regarding the practices of these infernal Thaumaturgs. Perhaps I may command this force – with the permission of the council.'

'I too wish to witness the evils of these magi!' Princess Andanii announced quickly. 'Perhaps command should be shared.'

Jher-ef, elderly head of the Fal'esh, waved a curt dismissal. 'Such distasteful sights should not be for your eyes, my princess.'

Her mouth hardening, Andanii eased herself upright. 'Perhaps we should face one another at a hundred paces armed with bows – then we shall see who comes away with eyes to see.'

The old man's jowls reddened behind his grey beard. He glared about, puffing. 'Unheard-of insolence . . . it was agreed . . . no challenges during the concord!'

'And be thankful for it, Jher-ef,' Jatal murmured to his old family ally, aside. Then, to the room as a whole, he said: 'I propose we now vote upon it . . .'

But Jatal's motion for a vote had to wait. Further counter-proposals were introduced. Alternative strategies were thrown up at the last moment and the entire process of whittling down had to begin again. It was close to dawn before consensus was reached; and that, Jatal imagined, only out of pure exhaustion.

So it was reluctantly granted that the Warleader would rush straight for the Thaumaturgs' main ritual centre and residences to secure them, while the lancers and other Adwami mounted troops would control and pacify the city proper. Accompanying the Warleader would be an Adwami force co-commanded by Prince Jatal and

Princess Andanii. The impatient Warleader was loudly reminded that as a mere hireling, he, too, would be under their joint command.

This the Warleader took with his long lined face held as rigid as a stone sculpture close to fracturing. His lieutenant however, reclining at his side, chuckled silently at the man's mortification, all the while wolfing down a giant's share of the roast goat and lamb. As it was already dawn, the attack was scheduled for that night.

After the council was formally dismissed most of the family heads mumbled their bleary farewells and headed to their own tents to sleep. Jatal remained. He had a few questions for the Warleader. As the man rose, rather stiff-legged, he asked, 'What of intelligence? You seem remarkably unconcerned regarding troop numbers and such.'

The Warleader adjusted the old leather belt about his mail coat and peered down at Jatal with his flinty grey eyes. *Dead flat eyes – the most dismissive eyes I have ever encountered.*

'I have sent agents ahead into the city. They have long been reporting back.'

Jatal nodded his agreement with such precautions. 'I even considered slipping into the city myself, disguised as a pilgrim or a penitent.'

'My prince – had you attempted such a thing I would have ordered Scarza here to knock you on the head and drag you back.'

The sting of such audacious disrespect was muted by the broad comical wink sent from the man in question, who was still reclining at the Warleader's feet. Jatal bit back his outrage and shook his head instead, either in admiration or astonishment, he wasn't sure which. 'Well . . . you sent him after me already, didn't you?'

'Indeed I did, Prince. Such heroic adventures may be standard fare among bards and storytellers, but a prince should hardly be sent straight into an enemy stronghold. That is what expendable personnel are for – yes?'

Expendable personnel. The man had an unsettling ability to cut through all the mush and romanticism that surrounded raiding and warfare. Yes, expendable. That was what it all came down to, wasn't it? No matter how distasteful the sentiment may be.

Jatal motioned to a servant for tea. His discomfort – had he just been slapped down? – drove him to ask, 'Yet you agreed to myself and the princess commanding the force that would strike for the Thaumaturg premises.'

The old man lifted his shoulders in an indifferent shrug. 'I knew some noble would be foisted upon me. Better you than some others.'

232

Again, Jatal gathered the distinct impression of being handed an insult wrapped in a compliment. Still dissatisfied, he pressed on: 'You have an estimate, then, of the number of yakshaka soldiers we may expect to meet?'

The man's thin cracked lips pursed. The lines bracketing his mouth deepened like fissures in granite. 'No more than fifty, certainly.'

Jatal was quite startled. 'Fifty? That is as good as an army. How can we overcome fifty yakshaka?'

The Warleader waved a gnarled, age-spotted hand, the nails yellowed and jagged like talons. 'They will not emerge to meet us in battle. Their duty is to protect the Thaumaturgs. And we are not here to kill them. Rather, we will be there to stop them from interfering in the sacking and pillaging of the city. Besides, they are formidable, but not indestructible.' He cleared his throat. 'Now, if you will excuse me. At my age it is important to take the time to rest and recuperate . . .'

Jatal bowed as his tea arrived steaming on a silver platter. 'Of course. Later, then.'

The Warleader bowed shallowly and departed.

Gone to his tent, no doubt, where, Jatal heard reported by servants, he applied himself assiduously to the goal of stupefying himself with mind-numbing smoke. Well, so far it didn't seem to have interfered with his performance. Perhaps he dosed himself in order to tolerate the fractious Adwami. In any case, it was none of his business.

Their forces began marshalling just before dusk. Princess Andanii arrived surrounded by a personal bodyguard of twenty Vehajarwi knights. She wore heavy leathers and a silk-wrapped conical iron helmet, a curved sword at her side, her bow on her back. Jatal bowed to her. 'Princess. We leave at once. Before we go, however, I must ask again whether you think it is prudent that both of us accompany this force.'

Her glance was sharp at first, but softened as she nodded her understanding. She leaned close in her saddle, her voice low. 'This cohort drawn from all the families was a masterstroke, my prince. Do you not see they must accept both of us as commanders? We will have need of a force that we alone control. One free of family obligations. Will we not?'

Jatal was quite flustered and adjusted his seating on Ash's back to cover his reaction. He brushed at the long hanging sides of his mail coat, his robes and sword. By the Demon-King Kell-Vor! He hadn't thought of that! He'd merely proposed this ad-hoc force to quell internecine bickering and to shuffle everything along. But now that she had mentioned it; yes, such a body could be extremely useful should they declare themselves . . .

And if Andanii wishes to believe it was all part of a deliberate long-term plan on my part, well, so much the better for my standing in her eyes.

He cleared his throat and twisted a hand in Ash's reins. 'Well, the Warleader is of the opinion that we will probably see no action, in any case.'

Andanii frowned her scepticism. 'Why should that be?'

'He claims the yakshakas' first duty is to guard the Thaumaturgs. So long as we do not threaten them they should stay out of the fight.'

'And where does a foreigner come by such intimate knowledge of our neighbours?'

Jatal gazed at the young woman in stunned admiration. *Shades of my ancestors!* Again, such a question hadn't even occurred! *What an impressive leader this one will be. Beautiful, cunning . . . and that night . . . Gods, the memory of her reaching down to grasp my manhood even as I . . .*

She leaned to him, her dark eyes concerned. 'You are all right?'

Jatal nodded, taking a shaky breath. He rubbed the sleeve of his light cotton robe across his slick face. 'Yes. I am fine. I was just thinking . . . that is a very good question, my princess. Perhaps I should strive to learn more of this man. Where he is from. Why he knows so much.'

A curt nod. 'Yes. Do so. For the time will come when we will no longer need him.'

Jatal now eyed the woman sidelong in suspicion. Did she plan on not honouring their agreement with the mercenary? Perhaps she was merely considering all the possible alternatives. *So . . . beautiful, cunning, passionate . . . and ruthless.*

Their force of picked Adwami mounted men-at-arms formed column as the first element. The Warleader's mercenary troops would follow. While the troops ordered themselves, the Warleader rode up on his dappled pale stallion. He saluted Jatal and Andanii. 'As commanders, you shall lead. I will ride with my troops. We make for the central administrative compound.' For an instant it seemed a mocking half-smile cracked the man's severe features. He turned his mount aside and trotted back along the column.

Jatal was more than irritated; the Warleader possessed the best intelligence regarding the city, its environs and defences. That they should lead was, well . . . was worse than ridiculous. It was inviting disaster. He waved over Gorot, his master-at-arms. The squat veteran urged his horse closer. 'Send out your swiftest riders. Scout the damned city.' Gorot saluted and fell back. Jatal watched him go, thinking himself wise not to have gone to the lancer knights, where, usually, such an 'honour' would be bestowed. Better now to find an actual scout who could ride rather than some young minor noble's scion out to make a name for him or her self.

It was halfway into the night when they reached the valley floor to knee their mounts up on to a wide cobbled road that would take them to the city. Visibility remained excellent as the moon was high and waxing, while the great arc of the Scimitar very nearly over-powered it. Again Jatal admired the Thaumaturgs' engineering works: not only the road, but the canals and reservoirs they passed – all interlocking elements of a complex system of irrigation.

A stream of mounted scouts came and went reporting on the way ahead. No roadblocks, no fielded army. Hamlets and farmers' cottages all remained dark and quiet as the column clattered past. The glow of the city swelled ahead, though it was not as bright as Jatal imagined it ought to have been, given that Isana Pura was the southern capital.

Further scouts reported no barricades or columns massed in the streets to challenge them. Many of the surrounding bodyguard lancers grinned at the news but Jatal was not encouraged. What did they imagine was going on? That these mages had surrendered already? Fled? No. These reports only troubled him. If the magi and their soldiers and yakshaka guardians were not in the streets – then where were they?

Across the front of the column he caught Andanii's eye and in her pale moonlit features, framed by her tall helmet, her lips held as a hardened slash, he thought he read similar misgivings. Regardless, onward they swept, passing field after farmed field, the alien sprawl of Isana Pura, population perhaps a million souls, spreading out before them.

After a series of outlying collections of farmers' huts, wayside travellers' compounds, and what appeared to be merchants' staging areas, they rode on to the city proper. Here, the streets narrowed to a point where only three could ride abreast. The houses and shops lined the ways as solid walls of sun-dried brick relieved only by small barred windows and shut doors. Each street lay before them eerily empty and the jangle and clatter of their advance echoed loudly until Jatal believed that the entire city must be wincing with the racket of it. Yet no door cracked open and no gawping residents came pouring forth to crowd the way – which itself would have been an effective enough deterrent to stop their advance.

He expected imminent ambush or counter-attack and couldn't suppress a flinch at each intersection. He and his flanking guards, and Princess Andanii ahead with her guards, all rode now with reins in one hand and naked blade in the other. Each turn brought them to a street nearly identical to the one before. It was a grim and unadorned urban conglomeration that Jatal knew from travellers' accounts to be typical of Thaumaturg architecture and planning. Yet it remained a city of ghosts – for where was everyone? From what he knew of these mages' firm hand of rule, he suspected the inhabitants were all cringing in root cellars and back larders: helpless and unarmed, forbidden weapons by their imperious masters.

By now he was utterly without a sense of which way to turn either to advance or to retreat. He could see no further than the looming two-storey walls surrounding him in this puzzle-box of a city. Yet hovering over these brick walls floated the pointed bell-like towers of what he imagined must be the Thaumaturgs' quarters. In their twistings and turnings at every intersection, Andanii and her bodyguards appeared to be attempting to reach it. At one meeting of five crooked narrow ways they came roaring to a halt, drawing reins, the hooves of their mounts loud on the cobbles as they stamped and reared.

'Where are our damned scouts!' Andanii called to him.

'I do not know!' This apparent disappearance of their forward riders troubled him greatly, but he wasn't about to say that aloud. He worked to settle Ash – who champed and twisted his neck as he had been trained for fighting – and noted to the rear of their column that the Warleader and his troops no longer followed. Damn the man! Had they lost him? Or had this been his intent all along?

He'd been desperately trying to dredge up a traveller's brief description of the city that he'd read some time ago and it came to him then and he gestured with his bared sword. 'Keep inward. I'm fairly sure—'

'Very good!' Andanii sawed her mount's head about and kicked its sides to send it leaping onward. Jatal followed, hoping to all the foreign gods that he had the right of it.

They charged through a series of long, relatively straight roads each no wider than two arm-spans. Jatal had spent every night of his life in his family gathering of tents where the wind brushed freely, and wide uninterrupted vistas spread on all sides. If these cramped ways and grim squat dwellings were typical of city life then he knew he wanted none of it. Also, his stomach clenched and churned, anticipating at any moment ambush or raking arrow-fire. The curious bell-shaped domed towers of the Thaumaturgs, however, reared steadily ever closer.

A turn brought Andanii into a near collision with a mounted Adwami scout – a youth of the Manahir. The column crowded to a stamping, clattering, sudden halt.

'What news?' the princess demanded of the young unblooded boy as each struggled to settle their mounts.

'The streets are deserted, my lady,' he answered, stammering, quite flustered to be directly addressing so prominent a noble.

'I can see that,' she snapped. 'Where are your fellows? Were you attacked?'

'No, m'lady. I believe they have, ah, lost their way.'

'Lost their way . . .' she echoed in disbelief. '*Lost!*'

The youth winced, ducking his head. He waved to the surroundings. 'These strange twisting ways . . . I have never seen the like.'

Andanii rubbed and patted her mount's neck to soothe it. 'Well . . . true enough,' she allowed.

Separated by the guards, Jatal reared high in his saddle to point to the blunt towers. 'Know you the way?'

The scout jerked a nod. 'Aye, noble born. A large walled compound. But its doors are shut.'

'Take us immediately, damn you!' Andanii snapped and the young man gaped, not knowing what to say. In Jatal's opinion he made the right choice by merely hauling his mount around and stamping off without delay. The column followed.

After more twistings and turnings – the horses trampling abandoned baskets of goods and wares along the way – the alley ended abruptly at an even narrower path that ran along an unadorned wall of dark stone blocks. The wall of the compound. Andanii followed at the heels of the scout, sheering to the right, slowing in her headlong dash. The extraordinary narrowness of the channel forced them to ride single file. Jatal's boots nearly scraped the walls to either side as he went.

The constricted path continued ruler-straight along the border of the Thaumaturgs' quarters, but the scout halted at a set of slim stone stairs that led up to a portal in the wall. The opening was just large enough for a person to duck within. A door of plain wooden planks barred it. Andanii dismounted and threw herself against it.

'Locked – or barred!' she announced.

The door did not look too strong to Jatal. He dismounted and shook it: ironmongery rattled thinly. He raised a booted foot and slammed the aged planks. The door swung inward with a snap of metal. One of Andanii's bodyguards laughed his scorn at this, but Jatal did not share the man's confidence. Rather, this apparent lack of preparedness or concern for any direct assault only added to his unease. Something was wrong here. Profoundly wrong. He felt it in the acid filling his stomach, his sand-dry mouth, and a cruel iron band that was tightening about his skull.

Yet he dared speak none of this out loud. He knew that among these Vehajarwi, and the larger circle of Adwami nobles, his reputation was that of scholar and philosopher, not a warrior such as his brothers. And so he knew how any disquiet voiced by him would be received. Better, then, not to give this one guard any chance for further scorn.

And there was always Andanii, as well.

Spurred by the heat of her standing now so close, her quick panting breath in his ears, her face flushed and sweaty with anticipation, he stepped through first. The way led down into an inner open court, also quite narrow, rather like an encircling flagged path that allowed access to the many enclosed buildings. This too was deserted. The air here was much hotter and drier than the narrow shaded alleyways still cool with the night air. The sun's heat now penetrating to the surrounding walls of dressed blue-black stone. From his readings, Jatal knew the rock to be of volcanic origin, even to the point of containing tiny shards of black glass. The guards crowded protectively about him and Andanii.

'Now what?' she asked him in the profound quiet. At first Jatal could not answer, such was the clash of emotions and thoughts the question elicited: elation that perhaps she truly did rely upon his judgement, versus anger and resentment that perhaps she thought him so weak as to be in need of such bolstering. 'We should leave a quarter of the lancers with the horses,' he managed coolly. 'The rest should secure this court.'

Andanii nodded to the captain of her guard, who went to relay the orders. The quiet of the surroundings made Jatal suppress his breath as he listened. He caught distant yells over the brush and jangle of the troops' armour as they spread out. Perhaps the Warleader and his men had reached the compound before them. Oddly enough, though no plants or flowers were in evidence, a cloyingly sweet perfume choked the air making him faintly nauseous.

'M'lady,' a lancer called from one of the neighbouring buildings. Andanii crossed in response and Jatal followed. They passed through the crowd of troops to an airy stone hall, perhaps a meditation space, or classroom. Within, a field of corpses lay sprawled across the flagged stone floor. All dead Thaumaturg magi. Or, since most were quite young, a class of their acolytes, students or postulants. The nearest was a girl. Her dark hair was cropped close to her skull, almost like fur, and her flesh was snowy pale where her legs and arms showed beyond her plain robes. The seeming reason her flesh was so unnaturally ashen was that her blood was now all pooled across the stones. The same was true of all the others.

A grisly assemblage of some thirty freshly dead.

'Those fool mercenaries!' Andanii snarled, and she pressed the back of a hand to her mouth. 'They will bring the yakshaka down upon us!'

Jatal was not so certain of this; the mercenaries seemed to be across the compound. And the students lay toppled forward from cross-legged positions – a pose of meditation. Their features were still serene, though smeared in drying gore. The Warleader's men were mercenaries, true, but they did not strike him as so coldblooded. Besides, if one of the mercenaries had come across such a pretty girl as this, Jatal had no doubt he would have done more than merely strike her down.

He turned to his second, Gorot. 'Take charge of the main body – secure that courtyard.'

The old campaigner saluted and jogged off.

'M'lady,' Andanii's guard captain called. He'd been examining the bodies and he peered up now, wonderment and a touch of unease in his gaze. 'I see no wounds among them.'

A set of prints crossed the pooled gore. A calm unhurried set of bare splay-toed feet that walked on across the next court leaving behind a trail of drying blood. The killer? None of the mercenaries went barefoot. A fellow Thaumaturg? Yet the acolytes' slippers lay in a jumbled heap next to the entrance – these people did not go barefoot.

Someone did. The detail nagged at Jatal. It was familiar but he could not quite place it. The prints somehow mesmerized him; he could not help but follow them. They climbed on to a raised colonnaded walk of a series of stone arches, where Andanii joined him. 'We have to stop these fools from spilling any more blood.'

Jatal peered up from the path of blood. 'We should not move on until we've secured this area.'

The princess slammed her sword home. 'We have to link up with the Warleader and his troops in any case. And where in the name of the holy sun is everyone?'

'The cowards have fled,' Andanii's captain put in, coming abreast of them.

Jatal studied the man. *Did he really think it would be this easy?* He raised a hand for patience. 'We mustn't wander willy-nilly like a lost wind searching. We'll send out small scouting parties to locate them.'

Andanii's clenched brows rose and for an instant Jatal thought he saw something like admiration touch her eyes. She gave a fierce nod. 'Very good, Prince of the Hafinaj. Sound strategy.' She waved to her captain, who bowed and jogged off.

'This Warleader had better have an excellent excuse,' she growled, hands on her armoured hips.

'He will no doubt claim to have lost us in that maze.'

'Yes. He shows a strong head,' she said, grinning. 'We'll have to keep him on a shorter rope.'

Jatal answered the grin. Yes, the language of horse-breaking for their hired Warleader. The man seemed to have forgotten that he worked for them.

The sudden crash of metal and a man's scream of agony made Jatal flinch. Andanii spun, sword drawn instantly. Their guards converged on a tall stone altar-like plinth where one figure towered over all – one of the Thaumaturgs' armoured bodyguards, the yakshaka.

Even as the princess moved to close two guards blocked her way. From his raised position on the steps Jatal could see that this yakshaka had been in a fight: it wielded its great yataghan one-handed. Its other arm hung useless, its bright inset stones now smeared in dark wetness. Yet in just a few blows two of their men-at-arms had already fallen.

Yells of alarm now sounded to their rear. Jatal turned a slow circle: on every side the fearsome yakshaka had stepped ponderously from the cover of walls and open portals. They had been encircled. 'Make for the exit!' he bellowed. He urged one of Andanii's guards to shuffle her onward.

And where was Gorot now when he needed him most? Organizing the main body!

'This way, my nobles,' the guard captain called, waving aside. Their party made for an open-sided building and onward to another alleyway. Andanii's guards hurried them along between a series of cell-like stone buildings.

Here the noise and shouts of fighting echoed and re-echoed in a dull directionless roar. Jatal suspected that this captain had no idea where he was taking them – just that he was fleeing a potential slaughter. They stumbled into a tiny flagged yard enclosed on three sides.

'Now which way?' Andanii demanded.

The man did not respond. Instead, he directed one of the twelve guards to the way they had come. 'Watch the entrance.'

'You have no idea, have you?'

He turned to regard her. A small smile raised the edge of his mouth. 'We will, ah, circle round, my princess.'

'Captain!' a guard called from a wall. This enclosure appeared to be a dormitory, open to the central shared space, complete with a fire-pit and a few pots. Jatal thought it perhaps servant's quarters. Andanii and he crossed to the guard. Under the narrow stone roof lay scattered straw, covered here and there by thin blankets. The guard waved to a tiny opening where a stone staircase led down into darkness. The moist air emerging carried a repellent stink of rot.

'Perhaps this is where everyone has gone,' Jatal mused.

'The serpents' den,' the captain snarled. A shouted alarm snapped everyone's attention to their rear, where yakshaka now closed with their ponderous loud steps. Iron clashed as the guards blocked and slipped the first massive swings. 'Nothing for it,' the captain said, and waved down four men. Two of these were Jatal's, and he gave his own assent to their questioning glances.

The captain invited Andanii onward. 'My princess . . .'

Andanii shot him a glare as if determined not to betray any hint of disgust or dread. She drew her slim sabre and started down – even she had to turn sideways to manage the pit-like opening. The captain turned next to Jatal. 'My lord?'

'After you.'

'I must organize the retreat.'

'Then do so.'

The captain inclined his helmeted head just a touch, and Jatal was reminded that this man had spent his entire career skirmishing and raiding against him and his allies. 'Wait here then, if you would . . . my lord.'

From the pit's opening Jatal watched while the captain jogged to the line of defence. Four of their guards had fallen to the lumbering monstrosities and now the captain waved the rest into a retreating rearguard action, yielding ground towards the stairs.

Jatal waited until they had nearly reached him then hurried down into the dark and near solid stomach-gagging stink. Beneath, it was not so murky as it had seemed from above. Slim corridors lined with dressed stone led off in three directions. It seemed that slits and chutes cunningly hidden among the stonework allowed shafts of light from the Fallen One's Chariot to play down among them. Andanii waited here with her two guards. Of the other two, Jatal's, he saw no sign.

'What now?' she asked him again, her voice low and quite choked by the stench.

This time Jatal did not wonder about the motive behind her asking. He heard the clenched panic behind the words and felt it himself. With each choice, they'd been driven, or been foolish enough, to advance ever further into the Thaumaturgs' embrace. Inwardly he was already of the conviction that none of them would escape here alive.

Andanii's captain and the rest of the guards came crashing down the near-vertical stone stairs. Armour scraped the walls and bared swords rang and clashed. Heavy steps sounded above, but that was all. Jatal was certain there was no way such behemoths could manage what seemed a mere servants' entrance.

'We should move,' Jatal answered Andanii at last. 'They'll know another way down.'

'Yes,' the captain added. He had seized a torch from a wall sconce, and now motioned aside with it. 'This way looks to head back.'

Jatal did not dispute that, but he was sceptical that they would so easily negotiate this maze. He caught Andanii's attention. 'Where are the other two guards?'

She pointed. 'They went to scout.'

'We can't leave them.'

The captain urged them on. 'Come, Princess.'

Andanii had sheathed her sabre. 'They will follow,' she hissed, and set off to follow her guards.

For a moment Jatal stood motionless, alone, listening. What had been that fellow's name? Oroth? Something like that. 'Oroth!' he called. 'Myin-el? Can you hear me? We're moving! Come back!' He listened again but heard nothing distinct, only the breath of the damp air moving through the tunnels, and once again something like distant muted screams and yells.

Do not become separated from them! his dread howled. Cursing himself and Andanii, he set off to follow.

He found them soon enough, all jammed up together in a tunnel. He pushed his way to the fore. 'What is it? Why aren't you moving?'

Andanii and her captain did not answer; they did not have to. At their feet lay the corpse of a yakshaka guardian. Jatal's first thought was that they had bested it, though he'd heard nothing of any struggle. Then, in the flickering golden light of the captain's torch, he made out what held their attention: some sort of black fluid, thick and oozing, dripped from every joint of the armoured giant: at hips, elbows, shoulders and neck. The stench of putrefaction was overpowering. It physically drove Jatal to retreat a step. '*Gods!*' He gagged, a hand at his mouth.

'Not the work of our friends the mercenaries,' the captain observed from behind a fold of cloth pressed to his face.

'Then who?'

'We'll see,' Andanii answered, and she strung her great bow, as tall as she. 'I will go first. Captain, hold the light behind me.'

Jatal disagreed with this order of march but the captain bowed, murmuring, 'Yes, Princess.' It seemed that the members of her entourage were used, or trained, to defer to her. Stepping over the obscene corpse of the Thaumaturg guardian, Jatal followed the captain.

The tunnel complex wound on. All openings were corbelled arches, an ancient architecture Jatal recognized from the written narratives of travellers through the region, even those of thousands of years ago. He glimpsed in passing what looked like dormitories, study halls, and small meditation or prayer cells.

He thought he'd gained something of an insight into these Thaumaturgs from this hidden maze of structures – presumably their true habitation. It was as if the surface was of no interest to them, or was used merely as sleight of hand to deceive and mislead. Their true vocation and interests lay beneath, hidden or shielded. And from what he'd seen so far, these practices struck him as detestable and obscene.

They passed more sprawled corpses, these of older men and women, all Thaumaturgs, or their servants. None of the bodies bore any obvious wounds. All lay disfigured, bloated, or, in some cases, with their flesh traumatized and torn as if having burst from within. The stink of sickness and rotting flesh was unrelenting but by now Jatal was able to endure it without his gorge constantly licking at the back of his throat.

They entered a larger chamber, its flagged floor crowded with bodies. At first he thought it some sort of infirmary or training centre for physicians. Corpses in various stages of dissection lay on stone plinths, while the weak torchlight hinted at mummified bodies along the walls. The ones hung on the walls appeared to be aids in instruction: each displayed a differing system within the human body. On one, the musculature lay exposed and preserved in all its ropes and cable-like twinings over the bones. On another, the circulatory system of veins and arteries lay highlighted and tinted like so many streams, channels and rivulets upon a map.

In an instant it struck Jatal that what he observed was not a ward for the healing and reknitting of the flesh, but rather its opposite: a theatre for the systematic disassembling and deconstruction of the human body. The insight left him dizzy with revulsion. For an instant his only thought was to flee. He felt as if his very breath carried into his body some sort of contagion or contamination that could poison it.

One of the guards leaned over to heave up the contents of his stomach and the captain cursed the man. In the quiet following the ragged gagging and gasping, slow shuffled steps sounded from the darkness of a tunnel opening. Jatal gradually shifted his blade in that direction as did everyone else, all in complete silence. Andanii's bow creaked next to Jatal's ear as she drew it fully back, the bright needle point of the arrow steady upon the opening. He knew that from this distance it could punch through solid iron plate.

Instead of the expected giant yakshaka, however, a dark-robed stick-figure of a man tottered unsteadily out of the dark. A Thaumaturg mage. One pale hand groped the air blindly before him while the other clutched at the wall. As the theurgist stepped further into the torchlight Jatal grunted his shock upon seeing that the man's eyes gaped as empty pits while his face was smeared in gore, as if the orbs had melted, to dribble like melted wax down his cheeks. Burst sores at his neck oozed a clear fluid down his robes.

Swallowing his dread, his visceral revulsion, and the acid pressure from his stomach, Jatal managed to speak. 'What has happened here?'

The blind Thaumaturg cocked his head. A smile that might have been contemptuous, or one of self-mockery, climbed his lips. 'It has been said,' he began, 'that flesh is stronger than iron. Yet this is not so. For are we not all heir to the countless failings of the flesh? Are we not in life only one step from its corruption and decay?'

Snarled loathing from Andanii announced the bow's thrumming and the figure jerked back a step.

Yet he remained standing. From a mere few paces the arrow had passed completely through him.

The smile broadened and blackened blood welled up through his lips as the man spoke again: 'Tell me, children . . . what would you sacrifice to live for ever?'

Bellowing his rage and horror the captain leaped forward, sword swinging, and the Thaumaturg's head flew from his shoulders.

The body slumped to the floor. The captain turned to them, his chest heaving, his eyes white all around. 'By the ancestors, what is happening here?'

'I think I may know,' Jatal answered. He gestured to the opening. 'We should go that way.'

The guards scrounged lamps from the classroom, or theatre, or whatever the chamber was, and lit them.

Andanii readied another arrow. 'I will lead. Jatal – will you accompany me?'

'Of course.'

Two guards held lamps close as he and Andanii edged their way down the damp chill tunnel. 'So what is it you think?' she whispered. 'I am not so dense as to imagine this has anything to do with our mercenaries.'

'You are right,' he answered, low. 'I am beginning to suspect we did not come alone, my princess.'

She frowned at this, uncertain of his meaning. But he remembered the bare footprints. He knew a group who spurned all such trappings of so-called civilization: sandals to protect their feet, clothing to warm themselves, even fires to cook their food. And add to this all the talk of flesh and corruption.

He wondered now which of the two he dreaded the more: the Thaumaturg magi, or these mad Shaduwam priests of Agon.

They next entered a nest of smaller chambers with numerous side tunnels and portals. The stench of decomposition was so thick here that Jatal felt as if he had to blink it away. Everyone breathed now in short quick gasps, barely allowing the fetid air to pass their lips.

The crash of iron on stone and a scream brought Jatal about. Their rearguard had been cut down by a yakshaka that must have stepped out from a side portal. In the narrow tunnel only the next guard in line could reach the giant and he chopped frantically, chipping the bright reflective stones from the creature's chest. But the two-handed yataghan the monster wielded next appeared in an eruption of blood from the leather armour of the man's back. The corpse slid backwards off the broad wet blade.

The captain was next and he adjusted his stance, sword ready in both hands.

Andanii's great bow creaked like a bending tree trunk just next to Jatal's ear. '*Down!*' he bellowed.

The captain ducked just as the yakshaka reared up for a two-handed descending cut and Jatal marvelled once more, for the blade came to within a finger's breadth of the tall corbelled arch of the tunnel and he realized that this entire complex had been designed precisely to accommodate these guardians.

The bow released in a punishing snap.

The creature's helm shattered in a flurry of shards as the arrow took it through the vision slit to burst out the rear of its skull. The giant tottered stiffly backwards, rocked like an unbalanced obelisk, and fell in a crash of stone.

Jatal, the captain, and the two remaining guards all turned their wondering gazes upon Andanii. The captain bowed, sheathing his sword. 'Magnificent, my princess.'

She inclined her chin a fraction, pleased, then drew another yard-long arrow from the bag at her side.

As they renewed their careful advance, Jatal asked aside, 'How did you know . . . ?'

'I didn't. I just tried it.'

'I see.' There, it seemed, lay the profound difference between them. He needed to *know* before he would act. She, it seemed, required no such assurance and would simply act, unhesitating, decisive. While he admired such supreme confidence, he could not shake the suspicion that it would also lead to disaster.

They entered into the largest chamber yet of the subterranean complex. The flickering lamplight suggested it was a great circle, the distances lost in the gloom. Glassware, tools and instruments glinted from the middle of the broad chamber, while serried about the circumference of the room lay countless stone sarcophagi. The rotting flesh stench seemed to be emanating from these stone beds.

Edging up to one, a guard peered in only to immediately flinch away, gagging, the back of a gloved hand to his mouth. Jatal glanced to Andanii: she was covering the chamber with her bow while her captain guarded her, so he steeled himself to take a look.

The stone-flagged floor was slick and sticky beneath his boots with some sort of tacky dark ooze that had slopped over the sides of many of the sarcophagi. The fetid reek was exactly that of corpses left to decompose after battle.

A hand pressed to his face, Jatal bent to glance in the nearest and though intellectually he had already deduced what awaited there, he could not suppress the atavistic human wrenching of his gut. He stood for a time, frozen. He'd been driven beyond horror, beyond any connection to the pathetic thing that lay within.

'What is it?' Andanii called.

Gods, yes, what was it? The stew of a human body amid hardened crusted fluids, flesh fallen away from bones and floating amid the stone plates of armour peeled away . . . or perhaps unable to adhere? The process interrupted . . . contaminated . . . corrupted. *The clutching clawed hands of bare tendon and bone. The skull fleshless where the bath had eaten all soft tissue but for a cap of scalp and hair. This poor creature had been alive!*

Then beyond Jatal's comprehension the skull turned towards him and a skeletal hand rose, beseeching.

The next thing Jatal knew he was clenched in the arms of the captain, Andanii facing him, demanding something.

'Speak, damn you! What was it? What happened?'

Jatal blinked at her. He felt his heart hammering as if he'd fought the duel of his life. A cold sweat chilled him from his brows to his feet. Andanii appeared to see the awareness in his eyes for she nodded over his shoulder and the captain released him. His sword, he noted, lay now amid the muck of the floor.

'What happened?' he asked.

The princess shifted uneasily, rubbing an arm, her bow still in her hand. 'That's what we want to know.'

'What did you see?'

She frowned, eyeing him as if uncertain of his sanity. *And she would not be so wrong. Merciless gods! It lived! What a terrifying curse.*

'What did you see?' he asked again, calmer, straightening his hauberk and shirts.

She shrugged. 'You screamed and stabbed the corpse. And you kept stabbing . . .'

'That is – was – no corpse.'

Andanii waved that aside as absurd. 'Impossible. I saw it. It wasn't even a body any more – just a tub of . . .' She trailed off, unable to find the words.

'Pus? Haemorrhaging? Diseased secretions?'

She winced, nodding. Now he noted how pale she was, how dark her lips in contrast. *Yes. You did see it, didn't you?*

'We must move on . . .' the captain murmured.

Jatal collected his sword and searched about for something to wipe away the foul green and black emissions that smeared it. He found a bit of rag amid the wreckage on the floor. 'No, Captain. No more need to stumble blindly about all these tunnels, dormitories and classrooms. Not when we are not alone.'

He faced the dark, sheathed his sword. 'So if you are listening –

come out! I know you are there and I know who you are. You've followed us all the way, haven't you? Come to wage war upon your old enemy . . .'

He felt the heat of Andanii near his side. 'Jatal,' she began, gently, as if soothing a skittish horse. 'Listen to yourself. You must calm down.' He turned to find her face close, her dark eyes searching his, yet veiled, evaluative.

'You think me mad?'

She bit at her lip. 'Please, Jatal. Listen to yourself. There is no one out there.'

Jatal felt his every muscle quivering. His shirting clung to him soaked in his cold sweat. Was he unhinged? Certainly such sights would drive anyone beyond reason. Into delusion. Yet it all made such clear sense! He rubbed his gritty burning eyes. Perhaps he was wrong – he always suspected he was wrong. In everything. Every choice. Wrong. Such a poor leader he was . . .

'*The darkness is never empty,*' a man called from the writhing shadows beyond the lamplight.

Jatal heard the stamp of feet and shush of drawn blades as the captain and remaining guards readied themselves. Andanii's bow creaked once more from just behind his ear. Yet he rested his hands on his weapon belt, thumbs tucked in, and cocked his head, waiting, while a figure came gliding silently from the murk.

He was not the one who had come uninvited to accost them during their meeting. But he could have been his brother, or father. Hair a matted nest of filth upon his head. His limbs and torso smeared in dirt, or perhaps the corrupt muck from the sarcophagi, now cracked and flaking. Eyes glared white all around from behind a near-mask of soot or dirt caked on by some fluid, perhaps blood.

One of the shaduwam of Agon.

Jatal sensed Andanii flinching away from the priest's advance. Soft curses of recognition and dread sounded from the guards.

'With these acts you have plunged us into irrevocable war, damn you all,' Jatal ground out.

The man's gaze seemed to be fixed upon Andanii. He appeared unperturbed. 'We have been at war for centuries,' he answered indifferently.

'With your brothers, the Thaumaturgs.'

The bright orbs of the man's eyes shifted to Jatal and his teeth gleamed bright as he smiled. For a moment Jatal thought the man was about to bite him. 'Best not to reveal *all* one knows, or suspects, my prince. But you are correct. There is no antipathy so ferocious as between those closest in their philosophies or tenets, yes? The narrower the disagreement of dogma, the wider the ocean of blood spilled. So it has always been.' He shrugged his lean bare shoulders. 'It would be different if we were far more alien to one another in our beliefs. Then there would be only mutual contempt, or disinterest.'

Andanii stepped up to Jatal's side. She now carried her bow hugged to her chest. 'You are all lunatics. The Thaumaturgs will fall upon us with all their might.'

The man smiled even more broadly. 'Then we must strike first – expunge them.'

Jatal wanted to strike that smug knowing smirk from the man's face, but he was right. And such no doubt had been their intent. To instigate war. And they had succeeded. All talk was vain now. He pressed the back of a gloved hand to his slick hot forehead, and sighed his utter, sickened exhaustion. 'Take us to the Warleader.'

The shaduwam bowed mockingly. 'At once, O my prince.'

*

'When I arrived I found just the same slaughter you describe,' the Warleader explained. They stood in one of the squat towers that studded the Thaumaturgs' compound. His armoured back to Jatal, the Warleader overlooked the boxy sprawl of the city where, in the golden early morning light, plumes of black smoke rose here and there – the inevitable byproduct of any sacking. Jatal and Andanii remained close to the slit of a stairway that their priest guide had shown them, as if unwilling to approach the man.

The Warleader glanced over his shoulder. 'We were separated almost immediately from your column.' He offered a slight shrug. 'My troops are not such great riders as yours.'

'So you knew nothing of their plans?' Andanii demanded. 'These Agons did not contact you?'

The foreigner glanced back once more, his gaze flat and dead – lizard eyes, Jatal decided. The man had an unnervingly alien gaze. Like that of the grey opalescent eeriness of the great river crocodiles that were occasionally found on the borders of their lands.

'No,' the man answered in his ashes-dry voice. Turning, he faced them. He rested his hands on his worn belt where his thick yellowed nails grated against the metal rings of his mail coat. His mouth behind his grizzled iron wire beard turned down. For a moment Jatal felt as if he faced some hoary stern elder god out of legend. 'Now we must consider the future,' he said. 'You can be certain that through

249

their arts the Thaumaturgs are aware of this massacre. They will not let it go unanswered . . .'

Andanii thrust out her chin and cut a hand through the air. 'We must press our advantage!'

The Warleader nodded. 'Indeed.'

Jatal swung his stunned gaze between the two. 'What? Are you fools? Press onward? No – we must return home. Warn all the clans. Prepare our defences.'

Andanii turned upon him, grasping his shoulder. 'Do you not see, Jatal? We have the advantage! We must strike again – and quickly.'

The Warleader nodded his agreement. 'Exactly, my prince. Like it or not, war has been declared. For the moment initiative and momentum are ours. We must not let them slip from our fingers.'

Jatal felt cornered and outflanked. As if he faced an opponent who'd anticipated all his options and had systematically eliminated them. Yet – what could they hope to achieve? The path the Warleader appeared to be offering was merely the same old beaten road so depressingly familiar from all the histories. Escalation answering escalation until the only remaining option is annihilation. It was so pathetic and short-sighted. Couldn't these two see the repeated insanity of it?

'And what do you suggest?' he asked, openly scornful.

'Anditi Pura. If we can crush them there then we will break their grip on the country.'

'Their capital? At the centre of their lands? A few thousand riders against all the might of their nation?' Jatal shook his head. 'You counsel suicide.'

'Not at all,' Andanii interjected, affronted, as if he'd insulted her. 'It will take them time to muster their forces. If we do not delay we will have a chance.'

The Warleader raised a hand to silence her. 'And – if I may – these Agon priests have questioned captives and what they have discovered may change your mind, my prince.'

'If they are not lying.'

For an instant anger sparked in the man's dead reptilian eyes, only to be quickly hidden. He spoke through clenched teeth. 'Of course all intelligence must be verified. However, if it *is* confirmed then it is good news for us. Apparently the Thaumaturgs are already at war and this is the reason why they are so thin upon the ground. They have already marched east against Ardata.'

'The gods are with us!' Andanii enthused. Her eyes glowed with an ambition that Jatal now knew to be a perhaps insatiable hunger with her. 'All the more reason not to delay.'

'Indeed . . . Princess.'

'What of the council?' Jatal asked.

'The two of you can continue to herd them along, I am sure.' And the Warleader allowed them his abbreviated bow. 'If you will permit – I will see to securing the compound.'

Andanii waved him off. 'Of course. Begin planning contingencies for a march on the capital. We will gather the council.'

'Very good.' And the foreigner swept out. The ragged length of his mail coat scraped along the stone flagging as he went and his ropy iron-grey hair brushed his armoured shoulders. A gnarled age-spotted hand rested on the pommel of his bastard sword.

Andanii waited until the man was gone then turned to Jatal, who raised a hand to forestall her. 'I know what you will say and I say it is madness. We could not succeed.'

'And why not?' She waved contemptuously to the maze of flat roofs beyond the compound walls. 'You have seen them. These sheep care not who holds the rod. Us or the Thaumaturgs. It is all the same to them.'

'And what of the Agons and their outrages? Already word is spreading, no doubt.'

She shrugged her indifference. 'We make little of it. A feud between priesthoods, nothing more.'

'You do not think we will be next once they have finished with the magi?'

Andanii closed the distance between them. Her dark eyes peered up into his, avid and consuming. 'No, I do not believe we will be. They are fanatics. Once they have hunted down the Thaumaturgs they will retreat once more to their hermit caves, their boneyards, their desert dunes. They care nothing for rulership.' Her gaze searched his, narrowing. 'What then troubles you?'

What could he answer? Mere wisps of hints and impressions. An eerie familiarity about this Warleader. That odd worshipful glance from the Agon priest to the man. And just now his casual warning that he was aware of the alliance between the two of them.

And how did he get to the compound before us?

And – oh, my dear – what happened to my two men down in the tunnels?

He mutely shook his head, half turning away. 'I . . . I cannot say for certain. Fear, I suppose. Fear for our chances.'

She grasped hold of his arm. Her hands were hot, even through his

251

armour. 'I understand. Nothing is certain. But if we stand together I know of nothing that can oppose us.'

Yes. If we stand together.

He offered her a smile and though he knew it to be a poor effort, she raised herself to press her lips to his. She whispered huskily. 'Tonight, my prince. While the Adwami celebrate their victory, look for your humble serving girl – come to offer whatever your heart may desire.'

And though he hated himself for it he felt his own hunger rising and he answered the kiss. *Am I the fool? I may be. Yet even this does not stop me.* He realized that nothing would stop him. The possession of her body meant that much to him. *Ancestors forgive me. I risk everything for the perfume that is her sweat. The honey that is her wetness. The music that is her pleasure.*

I am damned.

CHAPTER VII

At nightfall we arrived close to an inhabited place. We heard the dull blows of axes resounding from the depths of the jungle. It was a new village under construction. Suddenly, piercing cries rang in our ears and in front of me, barely a few rods away, a monstrous half-man, half-animal appeared leaping on all fours. It was dragging a child off. Crying out, my porters and I gave chase, shouting, in pursuit of the ferocious beast. A few moments later we found the child, which the monster had dropped in its flight. Taking it into my arms, I was astounded to see that it bore not one scratch from its ordeal.

Francal Garner
Travels in Jacuruku,
Jacal River Exploration Report, Vol. 1

IT ANNOYED MURK NO END THAT SOUR KEPT WALKING DIRECTLY ahead of him. The man had the infuriating habit of pushing his way through the jungle fronds only to let them whip back to slap him in the face. For the twentieth time that day he had to restrain himself from throttling the squat bow-legged mage. Now he almost ran into him as Sour stopped abruptly, bringing the entire following column to an unexpected halt.

Sour thrust his hands in their tattered leather gauntlets up at Murk who couldn't help flinching away – mostly from the ripe pong that surrounded his grimed and sweaty companion. He was aware that he himself certainly didn't smell of cloves after the days of slogging through the dense jungle and sleeping in the warm rain, but some people just had a nasty stink to them. Maybe it was the man's diet. They were pretty much out of food and Murk had no idea what his partner was eating these days.

'Lookit this,' Sour announced, and, taking off a gauntlet, he pinched at his left thumb, pulling, and the entire outer layer of white skin slid off the digit. Like a snake shedding. The Shadow mage waved the empty sac of flesh. 'It's like a pouch, or somethin'.'

Murk slapped the man's hands aside. 'Did you have to show me that? That's disgusting. Why in the Abyss would I want to see that?'

Offended, Sour blinked his bulging mismatched eyes and turned away. 'Think that's disgusting . . . you should see my feet.'

Murk didn't want to see the man's feet. In fact, he didn't want to see his own feet. Just the thought of what might be going on in his rotting leather boots made him shiver in revulsion. Each step was a squishy slide of wetness. He could imagine the soft flesh all mushed together . . .

With a shudder, he straight-armed Sour onward.

The plan was to find a settlement. Some sort of civilization. Acquire guides to a capital, or whatever would pass for a major trading settlement, and arrange passage out.

That was the plan. Problem was, when their hired vessel had deserted them it took away all their stores and spare equipment. They'd been left with only the few supplies they'd brought ashore and now those were gone. They marched with just the clothes, weapons, and armour on their back. And now even this was rotting away. All the leather armour and fittings stretched and weakened in the constant warmth and damp until Murk could tear it with his bare hands. And all the metal, be it iron, bronze or copper – studs, clasps and buckles, even the swords – was rusting and corroding. Some of the mercenaries had thrown it all off entirely and now marched only in the long under-padding from their armour, such as plain quilted gambesons that hung to their knees.

Murk had almost immediately thrown away his helmet. He marched now in a laced leather jerkin over a silk undershirt. His jerkin fared better than most as his sweat kept it well oiled, and his pantaloons were really no more than cloth wrappings that ran from his calves to his thighs. He'd considered carrying his knife inside his shirt where the body oils would help protect the iron blade, but he'd seen too many die in agony from cuts poisoned by rust – the locked jaw, the convulsions, the muscles constricting savagely enough to snap bones. One of the most ghastly ways to go. And so he wrapped the knife in rags and carried it tucked into his belt.

Sour, on the other hand, looked to have made no concessions whatsoever to the deathly heat and damp. He still wore his stained leather cap, which had now grown a layer of mould. His leather hauberk, with all its jangling rusted iron clasps and studs, hung from him like a rotting ill-fitting sack. His leather riding trousers flapped in tatters as he walked. The crossbow on his back was so corroded it surely must be seized. All in all, the fellow looked like an escapee from a lich yard.

But we're none of us much better off, Murk had to admit. The real worry – aside from disease and infection – was food. They'd lost two soldiers already to some kind of bloody stomach and intestine illness. Both had been supplementing their meagre rations with gods knew what things they'd found growing in the jungle. Meanwhile, he was suffering from gut-twisting cramps together with what the veterans so colourfully named 'the trots'. Diarrhoea, the runs, Seven Cities' Revenge, the flux, trooper's stomach, the two-step. Whatever you wanted to call it, it wasn't pretty. Especially with all that blood in it.

Behind them in the column, Dee and Ostler still carried the tiny jewellery box on its stretcher. An honour-guard, of sorts, surrounded the two and their light cargo: at least five mercenaries at all times. He wondered what their guest, Celeste, thought of that. Would she be flattered . . . or threatened? There was no knowing how her mind worked. He'd seen nothing of her of late. Off exploring perhaps. Fine with him. Dealing with her was like trying to juggle Moranth munitions: no knowing when she might go off in your face.

A halt was called towards noon. Or at least what Murk thought was near noon. The sun remained hidden behind layer after layer of overlapping leaves and canopy. The heat was at its most crushing while a choking humidity from the night's rain misted about them, coiling into the high canopy and the sky above. Presumably only to rain down upon them once more in the cool of the eve.

Murk slumped down on to a ridged snaking root of one of the gigantic trees that reared taller than any tower, temple or palace that he'd ever seen. Fat vines hung from its high branches and they stirred feebly, rubbing in the almost non-existent breeze. A veritable chorus of noise surrounded their party. Birds unfamiliar to him let loose their sharp piercing calls, insects chirruped and whirred incessantly, especially at night, nearly driving him crazy. Now that he wasn't moving the bugs clouded about him. They crawled like a contagion over his face, scalp and arms while they stung and bit his skin and sucked his blood. He swiped at them lazily, already tired of having to brush them away every minute of the day and night. He'd heard of animals and people being driven mad by their constant nipping harassment and he could believe it now.

He'd seen little of all the wildlife that must crowd this jungle; the noise the column made crashing through the underbrush must send them all fleeing. Even so, Yusen had scouts out hunting. Murk prayed to Togg and Fanderay that one of them would get lucky.

Not all the animals had run off, though. He wiped the sweat from his eyes and squinted up at the surrounding canopy. After a short search he spotted a few of the troop of long-tailed monkeys who wouldn't leave them alone. Trailed their line of march they did, hooting, grimacing and lip smacking. They were gawking just as openly as any peasant farmers at a passing cavalcade of foreigners. It seemed the Oponn-damned carnival had arrived. He bared his own teeth back at them; things must be slow in the jungle if they were the best show in town.

Without thinking about it he automatically reached to his side for his skin of water only to find nothing there. Empty and gone these last three days now. He figured they'd be dried corpses by now if it weren't for everyone's licking raindrops from the leaves. Instead of the missing waterskin, he searched for and found the leather pouch containing the last of his dried rations. Reaching inside, his fingers found not hard strips but a soft yielding mush. He snatched out his hand to find a smear of rotting meat dotted by writhing maggots. His shoulders slumped even further and he gritted his teeth against his revulsion. He tossed aside the pouch then wiped his hand on the rough surface of the root.

Blinking heavily he peered around at the rest of the troop. Men and women sat slumped at the bases of trees, hoarding their energy, motionless but for batting at the dancing insects. Everyone seemed to feel the drain of the heat. Everyone, that was, except . . .

Sour thumped down next to him on the root. 'What'cha doing, pard?'

'Melting.'

'Ha!' Leaning aside, Sour blocked one nostril and blew a great stream of mucus on to the dead leaves. "T'aint that bad.'

'Not that bad? Where were you born? The fiery floor of that after-world some Seven Cities cults go on about?'

'Naw.' He squinted about with his mismatched goggling eyes, then admitted, his voice low, 'The Horn. I grew up on the Horn.'

'The desert horn? South of Dal Hon?'

Sour waved his hands, his rotted leather gauntlets flapping. 'Keep it quiet! Not something to brag about.'

Murk was intrigued. His partner had never hinted at such. In fact, he'd always gone to great pains to emphasize his city upbringing. 'But there's nothing there . . .'

'Not true. Was a trading port. Ships always laid over. Came from everywhere, they did. I ain't no hick!'

'All right, all right. So that's why you can take the heat . . .'

Looking away Sour remarked, 'Ain't the heat – it's the humidity.'

Once more Murk wanted to throttle his partner. What stayed his hands was what Sour had already noted: the approach of the Seven Cities officer, Burastan, or whatever her name really was. The long-legged, broad-shouldered woman was still an easy place to rest the eyes, even amid all this stink and decay. She wore wide cotton pantaloons tucked into tall leather moccasins, well oiled. A loose white robe over a thin silk chemise and sash completed her garb. She had arranged her long black hair in coils atop her head, away from her neck. *Seven Cities*, Murk thought resentfully. No wonder she was up and about in the heat. Still, sweat glistened on her lovely upper lip even as that mouth twisted its contempt as it always did whenever she caught sight of them.

'Cap'n wants you. Forward.'

Murk took a moment to gather his energy to rise. At his side, Sour saluted his flapping gauntlet. 'Yes, ma'am, Banshur.'

'That's Burastan to you, monkeyface.'

'Yes, ma'am.'

She led the way. Sour whispered aside to Murk, 'What did she mean, monkeyface?'

Murk waved to the surrounding walls of foliage. 'She was noting a likeness to your brothers and sisters.'

The man's wizened whiskered face scrunched up in puzzlement. 'Who?'

'Never mind.'

The captain, Yusen, awaited them amid a great thicket of hanging serrated-edged fronds, each the size of a shield. With him was the wiry taciturn scout, Sweetly. A twig, as always, rode at the edge of the scout's mouth. The twig seemed to be the man's sole method of communication in an otherwise emotionless cipher of a face. An upward position indicated an approachable mood. During such times Murk dared venture a joke or two. A downward position indicated a nasty mood; at such times no one spoke to him. Currently the twig registered a straight outward position; neutral.

The chattering and whistling of bird calls was a deafening clamour here. Murk imagined a large flock must roost nearby. 'What is it?' he asked while Sour saluted.

The captain ignored the salute. He gestured ahead. 'This way.'

Sweetly pushed aside the wide leaves, causing a torrent of droplets to fall from their frills of dagger-like edges. Sour cursed the man and lunged to cup his hands beneath the drops. Rather than responding to Sour the scout shifted his blank gaze to Yusen.

'Water's not our worry now,' the captain said, and he gestured Sweetly onward. The scout advanced very carefully. He edged aside another handful of the thick underbrush and as he did so a great blast of noise erupted from all around of countless birds launching from the canopy. Bright glaring sunlight struck Murk who winced and turned aside, shading his gaze. Sour cursed the scout again.

Blinking, Murk saw that they stood at the crowded edge of a river. A near impenetrable wall of bright green verdancy lined both shores. The water was a slow-moving rust-red course that carried clumps of fallen branches and leaves along with it. Above, the sky was a clear bright blue except where a wall of dark clouds lurked in the east – the night's rain. The wave of disturbed birdlife washed onward along the shore, brilliant shapes darting and swooping in gleaming emerald and sapphire. Like an explosion in a jewellery bourse, it seemed to Murk.

Yusen crouched at the descent to the muddy edge. 'Should we swim it?' he asked Murk.

Murk turned to Sour. 'Want to take a peek?'

'She won't like it,' he warned while adjusting his mouldering cap.

'Who won't?' Yusen asked sharply.

'Ardata,' Murk half-mouthed.

'Ah. I thought perhaps he meant . . .'

Murk shook his head. 'No, not *her*. I don't think she cares what we do.'

The captain's thoughtful expression said that he didn't know whether to be reassured by that. Murk nodded the go-ahead to Sour, who took a deep breath. 'All right,' he sighed. 'But there's gonna be trouble . . .' He edged down the slope.

Murk, the captain and Sweetly watched while the crab-legged mage sniffed about the shore. He poked at the mud and picked up bits and pieces of flotsam that he examined so close to his goggle eyes that Murk could see them cross. Satisfied at last, he sat with his back to them and tossed the collected litter on to a piece of leather spread on the mud. He peered down at the mess for some time.

The blanket of heat and humidity caused Murk's eyelids to droop and his shoulders to sag. His attention wandered to find Sweetly staring off upriver. The scout's fixed interest stirred his unease. 'What is it?' he whispered.

The scout's flat gaze flicked to him and the twig clamped tightly between his slit lips fell almost straight down.

Shit. He nodded, then shut his eyes against the painful, unfamiliar glare of open sky. Raising his Warren was the last thing he wanted to do, but it was his responsibility. If he and Sour expected the troops to fight in their defence then they, in turn, were expected to utilize their talents to defend the column. That was the Malazan way: always an even exchange. And frankly, he wouldn't be able to face them if they saw he was coasting on their backs. He didn't know if Sour felt the same way about it all. He suspected not; the man was a far worse match to the rules and strictures of military life. And anyway, the troopers treated him more like a stray dog – one that had been kicked in the head once too often.

When he opened his eyes once more he found that he was still within the murky tangle of the Shadow woods. What that demon had named the forest of the Azathanai. How absurd it was that the one feature of all Shadow he dared not enter should be the place jammed right over where he was stuck. He decided to minimize his exposure by using the Warren merely to shift from place to place.

He caught Yusen's attention, murmured, 'Be right back,' and stepped into the nearest shadow. From here he shifted to another, then another, and in this manner he moved southward. He scanned the jungle from the cover of a number of different shadows and once he was reasonably sure no one was about, he stepped out. He saw no sign of what might've interested the scout. It may just have been the nervous birds. *One more trick.* He felt through the shadow-stuff, the ephemeral Emurlahn ether, the shades of Rashan. He was searching for something specific among the flickering shapes and eventually he found it cast against the broad trunk of a tree: the silhouette of a nearly naked man, crouched, armed with spear and bow.

He returned to Yusen.

Down on the shore, Sour slipped and slid through the sticky mud flats. He poked at the clutter that accumulated along any river edge, the silvery tree branches, the layers of rotting leaves, and the thick cake-like pats of clay. Satisfied at last, he flicked his hands to clean them of the clinging mud, his gauntlet tatters flapping madly, then struggled up the naked dirt slope.

Reaching the top, he took a moment to catch his breath. Everyone waited silently for his judgement. He wiped a hand across his brow to brush away the beaded sweat but only succeeded in smearing a thick swipe of ochre-hued mud across his face.

Murk hissed out an impatient breath. 'So? Should we cross?'

'What's that? Cross? No. Not a good idea.'

'So we don't cross.'

'No. I didn't say that.'

'Yes, you did – just now.'

'No. That's not what I said.'

Murk took a quick breath to yell his frustration but Yusen raised a hand for silence. Murk clenched his teeth until they hurt. 'So . . .' the captain said to Sour, slowly, as if speaking to a child, 'what should we do?'

'We shouldn't cross . . .' A pained grunt of suppressed wrath escaped Murk '. . . least not right now.'

Yusen's brows rose. 'I see. Or I believe I do. Very good.' He lifted his attention to Sweetly. 'South – for now.'

The lanky scout's jaws bunched and he turned away. The twig was held so straight down in his mouth it was pressing against his chin.

When the captain turned his back, Murk threw a cuff at Sour who ducked away, mouthing, 'What?'

South. Wonderful. Towards our watching friends.

As they returned to the column, Murk asked, 'So . . . what's the problem? Why can't we cross? What does Miss Nibs say?'

Sour was brushing the drying mud and clay from himself. 'I don't ask *her*. Don't you know nothing? Does crazy Ammanas answer your every question?' He raised his voice mockingly. 'Dear Murk – you lent your knife to Lengen. That's why you can't find it.'

Murk did cuff him this time. '*Quiet.*'

'Why?'

Murk tilted his head to the south and answered low. ''Cause we're not alone.'

'Who? Them?' He flapped a tattered leather gauntlet. 'Bah! They been watchin' us for some time now.'

Murk gaped at his partner. 'Then why didn't you . . .' Almost beyond words, he managed, resentfully, 'And how would you know?'

Sour jerked a thumb to his chest. 'Hey, I follow the Enchantress. Believe me – I know when I'm bein' watched.'

Murk jumped on that. 'There! You see! That's exactly what I was getting at. She come and whisper in your ear?'

'No, no. I keep tellin' ya. Nothing like that.' The squat fellow dug at one ear, smearing it in clay, while he tried to find the right words. 'It's more like a school of thought. Or a set a disciplines. Her way allows a deep access that kinda borders on Mockra, y'know? It's a path she's shaped that we follow. Get it?' He peered up expectantly, brows raised.

Murk shook his head. 'No. I don't get it. That's just a bunch of twaddle. Look, either she's mistress of the Warren, or she's a nobody.'

'No! This ain't Shadow. It ain't a Realm – or a shadow of a real one.' Murk flicked a gauntlet. 'Houses, Holds, Realms. All that hoary old stuff. That's the past. It's all about paths now. No pledges or pacts or none o' that stuff. It's a new world, my friend.'

Murk was still shaking his head. 'Can't be that easy. Has to be a price . . .'

Sour just shrugged his humped shoulders.

'Well – why didn't we cross, then?'

'That? Oh . . . I didn't like the water. Gave me a bad feeling.'

Back at the column Burastan was waiting for them. She saluted Yusen then crooked a finger to call over Murk and Sour.

'You two . . . maybe you could keep it down. I can't hear the volcanoes or the stampeding elephants.'

'Sorry, Bannister, ma'am,' Sour mumbled.

The woman shook her head in disgust and stalked off. She threw over her shoulder: 'And don't wander so far from our guest.'

Sour threw up his dirty hands. 'You called us . . .' But she was gone. He turned his hurt gaze to Murk. 'That gal. What'd we ever do to her?'

'Don't know. Why don't you ask her one of these days?'

'Yeah. Maybe.'

Murk just rubbed his gritty aching eyes. *Ye gods . . .*

That night was his worst yet. There was no food to be had at all. The scouts reported that something had scared off all the game. Murk sat with his arms wrapped around his knees. He sucked morosely on a knuckle of leather cut from a belt. At least when the rain started up they'd have some water to drink. Problem was all that fluid just went straight through him like a sieve. It came out looking exactly the same it did going in.

He and Sour traded off watches through the night. It was his turn when Yusen emerged from the sheeting rain to crouch down where they'd curled under the cover of a great towering tree.

'We're missing a patrol,' he said, peering from beneath the dripping rim of his helmet.

Murk unclasped his knees. 'I didn't sense anything. How many?'

261

'I'm not blaming you. Five. Scouts say the trail just up and disappears.'

'What do you want me to do?'

The ex-officer looked offended. 'What do I want you to do? I want you to find them, that's what.' He waved to the rain and Burastan emerged from the gloom. 'Take a squad.' The lieutenant nodded. Yusen jabbed a finger to him then jerked a thumb.

Murk took a deep breath to gather his strength then pushed himself awkwardly to his feet. He spat out the piece of leather he'd tucked into his cheek. Burastan waved him onward. He held up a hand for a pause. He stepped over a root as tall as his knees to find Sour nestled in where the root joined its fellow. If he hadn't known the man was there he'd have passed right over him; mud-smeared, he resembled just another fat knot of wood. He poked Sour's shoulder and the fellow jerked as if stung.

Eyes opened to glisten among the caked mud, leaves and twigs. 'What d'ya want?'

'Mind the store. I gotta go.' And he gestured to where Burastan stood waiting in the rain. Sour goggled at the woman, his eyes growing huge. 'Right . . .'

Murk wondered at his partner's reaction until he got closer to the Seven Cities woman; her robes and top were near transparent in the rain. Against the pale milky skin of her jutting breasts her dark areolae stood out quite plainly. The woman impatiently gestured him onward again.

Burastan collected a squad. The men and women lumbered heavily to their feet and checked their weapons and shields. Then she curtly waved Murk into the jungle. 'That way.'

Murk headed off, all the while wondering what this woman had against him and Sour. He walked slowly, and soon the lieutenant was level with him. 'I'm not really the right fellow for this, you know,' he told her, his voice held low.

Her answering snort told him she knew this damned well.

Huge drops pattered down from the canopy far above, slapping his head and shoulders. 'You have any experience with large predators?' he asked as he pushed aside broad leaves the size of himself.

'Just men.'

Fair enough. Was this her problem? One of those man-haters? Yet she appeared to get along with the rest of the mercs well enough. And she followed Yusen's orders without any resentment. She seemed to reserve her scorn for him and his partner.

Once he was far enough from the camp Murk halted. The squad

spread out behind him and he felt Burastan's warm disapproving presence just to his rear. He raised his Warren the slightest touch and felt it shimmering there near his fingertips.

'What are you doing?' Burastan whispered. 'We're supposed to be looking.'

'I am.'

'Really?' The remark carried a wealth of contempt.

'I am searching among the shadows.'

'What for?'

Murk felt his patience finally slipping away. 'For one that doesn't belong. Now, if you don't mind . . . ?'

Her snort conveyed how little she minded.

Thanks to his Shadow talents the night was as clear as day for him. He sifted through the shadows nearby, finding nothing. Glancing back to Burastan, he saw in the woman's clenched brows that she was a touch nervous out here in the dark so far from camp. *Good. Let's see how she likes stumbling about in the night.* 'This way, you say?'

She nodded, her jaws clenched. 'Yes. The scouts found a blood-spoor but lost it in the rain.'

'Let's move on then.' And he started forward.

After a brief hesitation, she followed, and the squad brought up the rear.

'You don't seem to have much time for me or Sour . . .' he said as he pushed his way through stands of thick razor-sharp grasses.

'Shouldn't we be quiet?' she answered, exasperated.

He stopped again to search among the shadows. 'We're making so much noise crashing through the underbrush that whatever it was is long gone by now. So . . . ?'

Close to his side she scowled, a hand going to the grip of her curved sword. After a time she ground out, 'I fought in the Insurrection. I have seen Malazan High Mages raise their might. I felt the Whirlwind and saw it brought low. I grew up hearing stories of Aren's fall.' Her gaze shifted from scanning the jungle and she made a show of looking him up and down. 'You two. You're a pathetic joke. That's what you are. The might of Malaz . . .' She snorted her contempt once again.

Ah. A touch bitter, are we? Well, we all have our stories. Fought in the Insurrection, did you? Which side, I wonder . . .

He gestured ahead. 'A bit further.'

'Wait.' She waved up two of the escort. 'Take point.' The men nodded, hefted their large shields and drew their swords.

Here, the undergrowth was thin; the canopy so dense as to cut off all hint of the overcast sky. The ground was a slick morass of reddish clay. Murk was no farmer but so far the soil, if you could call it that, didn't strike him as particularly fertile. Rich soil, so he understood, had to have rotting plant matter mixed up in it. This soil – or dirt – possessed none. The insects, fungus, mould and such seemed to immediately eat up most of the fallen vegetation, leaving the soil as desiccated and lifeless as any desert.

Their crawling progress slowed even further as the two guards, practically blind in the dense gloom, edged their way forward. 'This is absurd,' he whispered to the lieutenant. 'Let me go ahead. I'm the only one who can see.'

'Can't have you wandering off.'

'So you *do* care . . .'

The tall woman glared down at him. 'Yusen would have my head.'

'And this Yusen . . . ex-Sixth Army?'

She gestured impatiently ahead. 'Stay focused.'

They had arrived at the base of a particularly ancient tree. As broad as any peasant's hut, its fat trunk supported its own forest of hanging creepers. Here Murk sensed something and he raised a hand for a pause. Then he cursed, realizing no one could see. 'Wait,' he murmured to Burastan. The woman gave a low whistle and the guards all stilled. 'Spread out,' he mouthed low. Another whistle and the patrol shifted to establish a perimeter.

Murk eased his awareness just the merest touch into Shadow. He began to search among the shapes cast recently. Fat drops pummelled him here beneath this giant tree, slapping his shoulders and head. After a time he found something; or rather, something flitted past him so fast he almost missed it. A strange Shadow. Humanoid, it was. Yet as he watched it move it bent down, hunched, then leaped, springing, to fly away in a great bound, clearly outlined as an immense cat.

Murk grunted his dread as if punched. *Bad news. A kind of Soletaken or D'ivers. Just like Trake, Rikkter or Ryllandaras. Call it what you will. Way out of our class.*

'Murk,' Burastan whispered from nearby.

Normally, enmeshed as he was within his Warren, he would have ignored such an interruption, but there was something in the woman's voice. Something he'd never heard before. Blinking, he opened his eyes on to the jungle and hissed impatiently, 'What?'

The lieutenant appeared to have lost some of her colour and she raised a hand to indicate his shoulder. He glanced and grunted once again. The fat drops that had been punishing him here amid the thick vines were not rainwater. He slowly raised his gaze and it took him a moment to understand what he was seeing. Above him, upside down and gutted like butcher's carcasses, their arms slowly swinging, dripping blood from their fingertips, hung the missing patrol.

Murk lowered his stunned gaze to Burastan. She now had her blade out though he'd not heard her draw it. Carved glyphs ran down its length and red enamel or paint gleamed in the delicate script. Red, Murk realized. She'd been of the Seven Cities Red Swords.

'Locals?' the woman breathed, peering about, her eyes bright.

Murk swallowed to talk past the acid choking his throat. 'You could say that.'

That morning Yusen ended all patrols. He kept everyone except the scouts close to the column. Murk kept a wary eye on his partner after the man's claim that he could sense the locals. They all knew they were there – question was, how close and how many.

He noticed the crab-legged fellow peering about at the jungle far more anxiously than before. He was pulling repeatedly on his helmet and rubbing his dirty hands on his flapping trousers, all the while sneaking sidelong glances into the leaves. Murk sidled closer to murmur, 'Who is it?'

'Our friends. All around us now.'

'All around? Then why haven't you—' At that moment the order came back for a halt. Troopers waved the pair forward.

They arrived to find Yusen in the cover of a copse of trees. 'Reception committee ahead,' he told them. 'You're with me.'

'They're all around,' Sour warned.

The captain grimaced his displeasure. 'Yeah. Our scouts and theirs been playing tag all day. Let's see if we can come to an understanding before someone gets hurt.'

Murk emphatically agreed, as it was his thinking that that someone would most likely be them.

Yusen started forward through the dense hanging leaves. A short march later Sweetly emerged from cover to join them. The man's twig stood straight out from his lips: neutral, or undecided. Murk took this as an encouraging sign.

It seemed to Murk that the four men waiting ahead amid the tree trunks appeared as if by their own brand of magery. But he knew this for an illusion. They had merely been standing so still and so calm that his eye could not separate them from their surroundings. No magic, no animism or Elder sorcery. Still, it made him profoundly uneasy the way they just seemed to flicker in and out of the jungle background like that. They wore loincloths only, with bands of leather, or fibre ropes, tied round their arms and legs. Some sort of jewellery flashed at ears and noses, and hung from necks and arms. Looking at them carefully now he realized that half their camouflage was swirls of tattooing that splashed across upper thighs, stomachs, arms, necks, and even half-obscured faces.

They were a wary lot. Two held spears ready while the other two had arrows nocked. The bows were slim but as tall as they. The arrow points were tiny – better suited to bringing down birds, but they gleamed darkly and he realized with a jolt that they were poisoned. His stomach clenched even tighter at the discovery and his hand strayed to the knife at his side.

The two with the bows straightened taller, the gut strings of the bows creaking.

Sour suddenly threw his hands out wide, pulling all eyes to him. The squat fellow made an exaggerated pantomime show of untying his weapon-belt and dropping it to the ground. Murk knew this as an empty gesture as the sword was rusted in its sheath. But their friends knew no better.

The two with the spears eased them up a touch. Murk followed along by throwing down his knife. The spears straightened upright even more. Murk murmured aside to Yusen, 'Drop your sword.'

A hissed breath communicated their commander's unease.

'Has to be done . . .'

The man swore under his breath but unbuckled the belt and let it fall.

Murk glanced sideways to Sweetly. The scout's twig now rested downward. 'Slowly and sweetly now . . .' he whispered. The man's slit gaze remained bland but the twig edged straight down. He slowly reached behind his back to draw out two oiled gleaming long-knives that he let fall.

The two bowmen relaxed their gut strings and lowered the bows to point downward. Murk eased out his clenched breath. Sour started forward with his bandy-legged awkward stride then thumped down, sitting halfway between the two parties. Grumbling inwardly, Murk followed.

One of the spearmen, perhaps the eldest of the party, handed his weapon to the other and came forward. Closer now, Murk could see that he was quite sun-darkened, and very lean. His hair was straight and black, touched very slightly with grey. Bands of bluish tattooing

266

encircled most of his muscular legs and arms, and his neck. He sat smoothly and Murk was again impressed by the man's strength – life here in the jungle was obviously very demanding. The man's dark eyes moved between him and Sour. They were guarded and wary, but also touched by curiosity.

Murk pointed to himself. 'Murk.'

'Sour.'

The leader inclined his lean aristocratic head then nodded to himself. 'Oroth-en.'

Murk frowned at an eerie suspicion. 'You understand Talian?'

'Tal-ian? Is this the speech of the demons? A few of us Elders remember it, and them, too well.'

A sudden dread took hold of Murk. 'Demons? We know of no demons. We are lost. We want to find a city. A city? You know city?' He held his arms out wide. 'Many people.'

Unease clouded the man's features and his brows drew down. 'You seek the Ritual Centres? Why seek them? There is nothing there. Only death.'

Murk struggled to make sense of what he was hearing. 'So . . . no people?'

'No. No longer. All gone. Fled into the jungle.'

Murk glanced aside to Yusen.

The captain looked as if he'd just tasted something exceedingly sour. He cleared his throat. 'Oroth-en . . . we are lost and we wish to return home. Can you help us?'

The local pointed back up their path. 'Turn round, strangers. Return from where you came. Flee Himatan.'

Yusen rubbed his neck as if to ease a tightening knot and let out a long troubled breath. 'I understand. Today, however, my people hunger. Can you spare some food?'

Oroth-en gave a firm nod. 'Come with us.'

*   *   *

Ina awoke and surged to her feet, blade ready all in one swift movement. The tiny cell she occupied in the foreign vessel was night-dark but it was not something here that had roused her from her sleep. Rather, it was the lack of something: a lack of movement or noise. No longer did the vessel pitch or roll as if tossed by giants' hands. No longer did the timbers shudder beneath the crash of great waves washing over them.

She charged for the ladder and was up in an instant.

On deck she took in that the storm still dominated the seas encircling them but that some sort of eye or pall of calm currently kept it at bay. Further up the long deck two shadowy figures confronted her mistress. All this she took in even as a great plank-juddering growl sounded near her shoulder. She spun slashing to find only swirling smoke, or shadows, from which pale frosty eyes glared eager hunger.

'Call them off,' came her mistress's clear voice.

A weak flick from one of the obscured figures and the rumbling presence sank as if to haunches, backing away. Ina padded along the wet planks to her mistress's side. 'Call *these* two off,' she murmured to the Queen of Dreams. 'I beg of you. We know them' – she flicked her blade to the near-translucent one who wavered hardly more than a hanging scrap of shadow – 'the Deceiver, and,' she motioned to the other far more substantial presence, 'the patron of killers. They have no honour, m'lady.'

The Queen of Dreams stood with one thick arm crossed over her heavy bosom, supporting the other, chin in hand while she studied the two. 'My dealings have been few, Ina. Do not worry yourself.' She heaved a great sigh as if preparing herself for a distasteful task and let her arms fall. 'What is it you wish, Usurper? No, wait, let me tell you what it is you wish. In brief, you hope to turn every unfolding, every meeting or event, all to your eventual benefit, yes?'

Ina could plainly see through to the rolling dark waves behind the hunched figure as it gave what might have been a shrug. 'You have the truth. I confess that I am no different from you, Enchantress.'

'You may congratulate yourself on some few superficial resemblances. But we differ profoundly, Usurper. You are young while I am old. This persists as an unbridgeable gulf between us that you yet may cross. Eventually . . . a century at a time.'

The wavering scarves of shadow that outlined the Deceiver shifted then, as if affronted. 'That title. You persist in that title. One throne is as good as any other. Are you trying to provoke me?'

The Enchantress squinted southwards as if tired of the conversation. 'Shadow has a throne, Usurper.'

'That again. Shadow is . . . broken. And the throne with it.'

A tired, almost sad smile came and went from the Queen.

The slit eyes of the other figure, the Rope, had not left Ina the entire time and he leaned to his cohort to murmur, 'Time.'

The Deceiver waved a limp hand once again. 'Yes, yes. We are currently enmeshed in said unfoldings to the west. Suggestively close to the west, in fact. Many wonder at the peculiar timing of your journey . . .'

'All will shy away once they are certain of whom I am going to meet. You can be sure of that.'

The tatters of shadow wavered as if the figure were shifting from foot to foot. 'Ah, yes. Well . . . you have our warning! Have a care! Now, we must go. Charming though you may be in your disarming coquetry, we can hardly be expected to idle about here all the day and night. Much to do.'

The two faded away like passing scraps of shade.

'Warning?' Ina asked. 'What does he mean?'

The Queen of Dreams hugged herself, crossing her arms as if chilled. 'Not even he knows. But I would not have him change. Shadow finds him . . . amusing. At least for now. And that is a good thing.'

Ina studied the muted seas. She self-consciously touched a finger to her mask as she did so – it was hopelessly smeared blue now from the constant damp. 'Have we stopped?'

'No, this calm will pass.'

'And our destination?'

The Queen of Dreams studied her for a time. 'Jacuruku. You have heard of it?'

'We have heard the travellers' tales. City of riches. City of magic. Where any wish may be granted by the one who awaits within. Ardata the Perilous.'

The Queen of Dreams hugged herself even tighter. 'Yes, Ina. Perilous. Very perilous.'

*

Within the plains of Shadow, Ammanas and his cohort, Dancer, kicked their way through the worn stones of an ancient nameless ruin.

'What was that all about?' Dancer asked, rather irritated. 'A warning? A warning about what?'

Shadowthrone gave another negligent flick of his hand. 'That? Oh, I just throw those out. It confuses them.'

'That it does,' Dancer breathed aside. Then he stopped as his partner had come to a halt, facing away. Ammanas now peered to where a dark brooding forest dominated the landscape. The hounds surrounding them paced restlessly, uneasy this close to these woods. *The forest of the Azathanai.*

Ammanas gave a shudder. His hands tightened on the silver hound's head of his walking stick. He raised his hooded eyes to

Dancer. 'The Azathanai.' And he shivered again. 'Inhuman and thus incomprehensible.' He raised the walking stick in emphasis. 'Oh, I try. I do try. But there—' and he pointed to the woods. 'But there. There lies true impenetrability. Their goals – if they can even be said to possess such – what are they? They vex me. They truly do.'

'You're not the first.'

Ammanas gave a faint laugh. 'No. Certainly not. Yet . . .' and he raised a crooked finger. 'Perhaps I shall be the last, no?'

'We can only hope – and plan.'

'Indeed.'

Ammanas set off again. His slippered feet shuffled through the dust. After a time he cleared his throat. 'So, what do you think that damned Azathanai meant – the throne? What sort of nonsense is that?' His tiny eyes darted about from one shadow to another. 'You don't think it's true . . . do you?'

Dancer smiled as if somehow secretly pleased by his cohort's unease. He gave a mimicked negligent wave. 'That? Oh, I think she just tossed that off to confuse you.'

*　　*　　*

For Pon-lor, descending out of the Gangrek Mounts and entering the green abyss that stretched before them to the eastern horizon was like slowly submerging himself into warm poisoned water. The dense high canopy closed over his head like the surface of the sea and beneath he found the atmosphere so humid as to be almost unbreathable. Sweat started from his brow, back and limbs. His robes hung from him as smothering weights.

Two of the guards he had led from the slaughter within Chanar Keep had not survived their wounds. Of the two remaining, one was already ill beyond his skill to heal. Many, he knew, blamed the air itself; unhealthy, bearer of sicknesses in its heavy wafting miasmas. But Thaumaturg teachings insisted that it was in fact the countless insects. They were a maddening curse. Bites left smears of blood across faces and necks. Some of these wounds refused to heal, becoming swollen livid welts that wept a clear humour that only attracted even greater clouds of the midges, mites and flies of all types. He said nothing, but he knew that many of these creatures carried parasites and fevers, and that some were even laying eggs within the wounds, which would eventually hatch to feast upon the host's flesh. As for his own bites, he could purify himself through his Thaumaturg arts.

270

This morning the sick guard, Lo-sen, would not waken. He lay gripped in a burning fever, delirious, hardly even aware of his surroundings. The remaining guard, Toru, stood aside, scanning the surrounding jungle while Pon-lor studied his companion. He set a hand to the man's sweaty brow and found it searing hot to the touch. *I can heal flesh and break flesh . . . but I cannot cure a fever.*

He raised his eyes to Toru. 'There is nothing I can do.'

Looking away, the man flexed his grip upon his sword. After a time he grated: 'There is one thing.'

Pon-lor dropped his gaze. *Yes. One last thing. The onus is upon me.* He summoned his powers and drew a hand down across the blank staring eyes. He felt the heart racing like a terrified colt trapped in the man's chest and he soothed it. He eased the mad beating then slowed it even more to a calm easy rest. The man's clenched frame relaxed and a long breath eased from him. When Pon-lor removed his hand the man's heart beat no more. Pon-lor stood, straightened his robes.

'Thank you, Magister,' Toru said.

Thank me? No – you should curse me. I have led you poorly. Lost my command. My only hope to redeem myself is to return with the damned yakshaka, or this witch herself. Collecting that bastard Jak's head along the way wouldn't hurt either.

He gestured into the jungle. 'This way.'

After the sun had passed its zenith – from what he could glimpse of it through the layers of canopy – he chanced upon a plant he recognized. It was a thick crimson-hued vine dotted by large cup-shaped flowers, pale and veined, like flesh. *Alistophalia. The Pitcher. Also known as Ardata's Cup.*

He broke off one blossom and examined it while he pushed aside leaves and grasses. Within, trapped by the clear sticky ichors, lay corpses of insects all in varying degrees of decomposition.

It feeds upon those it attracts.

He remembered the words of an ancient writer: *Beware the Queen's gifts, for poison and death lie hidden within.*

Yet their Thaumaturg lore had found many uses for poison. This one's could deaden nerves and mask pain. In larger doses it induced a trance-like sleep that to all outward appearances mimicked death. In just a slightly stronger dose it brought the eternal sleep itself. It was Master Surin's serum of choice for his dissections. Under its influence a subject lived even as Surin exposed the heart and vital organs. The diaphragm continued to expand, the lungs to operate.

271

Surin's slick hands slid amid the glistening organs as he indicated this feature and that. Pon-lor and his classmates had crowded close round the table.

Surin had turned his attention to the head. He'd raised his keen scalpel blade to the immobilized face. 'And now, gentlemen,' he'd said, 'the miracle of adaptation that is the eye.' And the blade had descended to slide into the exposed clear orb. Pon-lor remembered thinking, appalled: *This man is still alive, still aware trapped within.*

Did he watch as the knife-edge penetrated his eye?

'My lord?' Toru asked.

Pon-lor halted, blinking. He peered up. 'Yes?'

The guard gestured to a gap through the fronds, where the earth was bare and beaten. He squatted to examine the spoor. 'Some sort of animal track. Heading east for now.' He raised his helmeted head to look at Pon-lor, cocked a brow.

'If you think it safe . . .'

Toru straightened. 'I believe so, Magister.'

Pon-lor started forward but Toru stepped in front. 'With your permission – I will lead.' He drew his blade.

'Very well.' Following, Pon-lor returned his attention to the cup-shaped blossom in his hand. *Beautiful . . . but deadly.*

He cast it aside.

The track veered to the north and then to the south but tended to return to the east. He was grateful; along its relatively clear way they made good time. As the shafts of sunlight that managed to penetrate the canopy slanted ever more and took on a deep rich gold, he began to consider where to stop for the night. A wide tree would offer cover against the rain. However, after a few more hours of walking they came to the perfect cover against the gathering dusk and its inevitable downpour, but Pon-lor did not know if he dared enter.

It was a long-abandoned heap of stones that might have at one time been a temple or shrine, perhaps even a sort of border marker. Roots choked it now, and trees grew tall from its slanted sides. The questing roots had heaved aside the huge blocks of dressed limestone. Some had fallen away from the building. None of this gave Pon-lor pause. What troubled him were the heaped goat skulls. They lay in a great pile before the entrance: bleached white bone beneath black curved horns. Many had been set into the crotches of nearby trees. Some of these had since been overgrown and incorporated into the flesh of the tree. *Trees with grinning dead animal faces. Why did this disturb him so?*

An old practice, he realized. *All long ago.*

He waved Toru forward to examine the structure. After studying the ground and the interior, the guard returned. By now it was quite dark beneath the trees. 'No one,' Toru reported. 'Only animal tracks.'

'Very well. We'll spend the night.' His remaining guard was obviously reluctant but said nothing. 'What is it?' he invited.

'An ill-omened place, Magister.'

'This entire jungle is ill-omened, I fear, Toru. We'll just have to make do, yes?'

'Yes, Magister.'

They climbed the stone stairs to the enclosure. Geckos scampered from Pon-lor's path in bright olive streaks. Spiders the size of outstretched hands hung in thick webs about the abandoned shrine. Pon-lor brushed dirt and leaf litter from the stones, wrapped his robes about himself, and sat.

Toru took first watch. 'Magister . . .' he asked after watching the darkening forest for a time. 'Was this – do you think this was dedicated to . . . *her*?'

Pon-lor raised his chin from his fists. 'For a time, perhaps. However, originally, no. This dates back far before her. And what need has she for temples or shrines? The entire jungle of Himatan seems to be dedicated to her.'

Toru grunted his understanding and was quiet after that. Thunder echoed and rumbled above. Then the rains began again. A spider that had been hunting among the stones padded up to Pon-lor's side. As if curious it gently stroked his robes with its long hairy forelimbs. It was larger than Pon-lor's hand. He edged it aside. Perhaps it was merely hoping to escape the rain.

When Toru woke him for his watch the rains had long ceased. Fat drops now pattered down from the canopy as heavy as slingstones. He lowered himself to the stone lip of the small shrine's entrance and wrapped his robes about himself for warmth. He sat hunched, watching the glittering wet wall of foliage. The cry of a hunting cat sounded through the night. Then the ghosts came.

They arrived as a file of youths escorted by a priest in rags. They chivvied along a goat with them. The priest and many of the youths, male and female, carried suppurating sores on their limbs, faces and necks. Pon-lor recognized the symptoms of the Weeping Pestilence as recorded in Thaumaturg histories. It had struck centuries before. Named 'Weeping', it was thought, for the obvious reference to the constant drainage of the sores that erupted everywhere, and for the pain and misery it inflicted upon the entire society. *Weeping indeed.*

Yet these ghastly wounds and scars were not the only marks they carried. The youths were emaciated, little more than walking skeletons. The priest's ragged feathered robe hung from him loose and soiled. Pon-lor recognized the starvation – and desperation – that accompanied plague and the breakdown of social order.

'Great Queen,' the priest announced, falling to his knees, 'we beg for your pity.' He gestured curtly to the children, who knelt as well. The youngest held a crude twine rope tied about the goat's neck. 'Spare our village. Turn your hand of condemnation from us and our devotion will be without end.' He waved the goat forward and the child, a boy of no more than perhaps five years, pulled it to the fore. It bleated, nervous and unhappy.

'Please accept this offering and smile upon us, great Queen! Protect us. Turn aside your Avenger.'

The priest drew a curved blade and rested a hand upon the goat's side.

Pon-lor jerked then, muffling a cry, as the blade flashed and sank into the chest of the boy.

Toru leaped up drawing his sword at once. 'What?' he demanded, bleary, half-awake.

Pon-lor could not take his eyes from the horrifying tableau. He swallowed the acid in his throat and managed to answer, his voice thick, 'Nothing. A shadow. Just a shadow.'

Toru grunted, a touch irritated, and lay down once more.

The boy had clasped the priest's wrist. His expression was one of startled surprise and hurt. The priest now hugged the child and, weeping silently, gently lowered him to the ground.

The eldest youth present, a girl, held out a bowl to the priest. The children all gathered round, eager, their lean faces full of hunger.

Pon-lor found himself slowly rising, a formless revulsion choking him, backing away. His gorge rose in his throat, his heart clenched so tight it could not beat, yet he could not pull his gaze away. *Ancient Demon-King forgive them . . . not even you . . .*

To his relief, the priest yanked the blade free to slash the goat's throat. The girl held the bowl to the neck while blood pumped and jetted, darkening her hands. The children pressed close, cupping their hands and hungrily licking. Meanwhile, the corpse of the boy lay unremarked as if forgotten.

Pon-lor forced his eyes aside and wiped a cold wetness from his cheeks.

Chopping sounded and Pon-lor glanced back to see the priest using a stone hatchet to cut the goat's head free. This he set among the stones exactly where a bleached fleshless skull now rested. The youths picked up the goat carcass and hurried off with it. The priest reverently gathered up the boy. Turning, he gave one last bow to the shrine, and backed away into a screen of shimmering trees that no longer existed, a sort of orchard, well tended and maintained.

Pon-lor watched the phantoms slip away then sat without moving, hugging himself, hands inside his robes for warmth. Never, even in the most rabid denunciations of the Queen of Monsters, was there any hint of human sacrifice. Could his forebears have been so ignorant of the degenerate practices hidden away here within this green abyss? Yet the priest had been weeping, a man close to breaking. All of them sick and starving. Histories told of plague sweeping though the jungles generations ago. Could it have been this appalling? Blind desperation. He had witnessed a people driven to the edge and it felt as if a hot knife had carved out his heart.

He hugged himself tighter and leaned forward to rest his sweaty brow against his knees.

The next thing he knew stirrings from behind woke him and he turned to see Toru searching among their meagre supplies. He cleared his throat. 'Have we anything?'

'Little enough,' the man grunted. He lowered a pouch. 'Magister, for a time I kept an eye on you. You . . . saw something in the night?'

Pon-lor struggled to rise on legs numb and stiff. 'A tragedy, Toru. I was allowed – or cursed with – a vision of tragedy.'

The guard said nothing, merely handed over a few scraps of dried meat and a knot of stale rice wrapped in leaves. After this brief meal, Pon-lor taking tiny bites and chewing as long as possible, they took sips from the one remaining skin of water and resumed their march.

Toru led. He returned to the animal path. It was so well-trodden that it curved along as naked red-tinted dirt weaving between the thick hard-barked roots. Yet they met no animals. Pon-lor imagined their clumsy tramping must be driving them away.

Towards midmorning, the unseen sun's heat driving straight down upon their heads, Toru, a good few paces ahead, disappeared amid a great crashing of dry branches followed by a gasped cry of agony. Pon-lor charged forward to find a shallow pit. Toru had managed to turn slightly as he fell and he lay on sharpened stakes impaled through his side along his torso and legs. Pon-lor threw himself flat and reached out to the man. 'Take my hand!'

The guard struggled to speak but only coughed up a great gout of blood that exploded across his face and chest. He pointed, his lips

275

working. A scuff sounded next to Pon-lor and something cracked on his skull. Flashes of light exploded in his vision and all went to dark.

*

Stinging awoke him. Sharp stinging impacts across his face. He opened his eyes just in time to see a woman slap him once more. He sat propped up against a tree, his hands tied behind his back, a gag across his mouth. The woman who peered down at him with open hate and a touch of fear was the ugliest he had ever seen. Pox scars from a savage encounter with that illness gouged her cheeks and brow, and a cleft lip, a harelip, pulled her mouth into a permanent open twist. That she was quite young only made the disfigurements all the more painful to see. Straightening, she kicked him in the crotch, doubling him over, hardly able to breathe.

'He's awake!' she yelled.

Pon-lor merely thanked the gods he hadn't vomited from the pain. He would have asphyxiated behind the gag. Blinking the tears from his eyes he saw someone new crouched on his haunches beside him. Looking up, his eyes met the grinning familiar features of their erstwhile guide, Jak.

The youth was squatting with his hands hanging loose before his knees. He cocked his head, making a show of looking Pon-lor up and down. 'You don't look so good right now, mister rich pretty brat. You know, you should be more careful wandering around the woods when you got no idea what you're doing.'

He leaned forward to push a stiffened finger into Pon-lor's side. The mage yelled behind his gag.

'Yeah. I knew Loor tagged you good there. Damned Thaumaturgs. What in the Abyss does it take to kill you?'

Another youth came shambling up, skinny and awkward. This one wore oversized blood-spattered armour of banded hauberk, helm, and greaves that Pon-lor recognized: Toru's. 'We *should* just kill 'im,' he whined. 'They're dangerous—'

'Course he's dangerous,' Jak sneered. 'He'd be worthless otherwise, wouldn't he? Just like you,' and he slapped the youth's side. Unnoticed by the crouching Jak, anger suffused the lad's narrow face but was quickly hidden behind a morose dejection. The lad shuffled away. 'Find the damned witch's trail, Thet!' Jak shouted after him.

Pon-lor relaxed his tight shoulders, unclenched his fisted hands and eased back against the trunk. He was suddenly glad he'd delayed unleashing his own outrage against these ragtag castoffs – for that was what he recognized them as: squatters, runaways, or outright criminal exiles from the eastern villages. So far he'd counted eleven in the group.

Then it struck him and he laughed as loud as he could behind the lashings of cloth tied across his mouth. *Of course! Too rich! Oh, so very rich!*

Jak rose, uneasy. 'What's so funny?'

Pon-lor snorted. *Kenjak Ashevajak – the Bandit Lord! Ha!*

'What!' Jak demanded, kicking him.

'Hanthet Hord,' Pon-lor mouthed behind his gag. And he laughed anew, more at himself than at this skinny young man quivering in rage before him.

Jak's face darkened as understanding came and he lashed out again, connecting with the side of Pon-lor's head and sending him down. Po-lor, however, continued to laugh even with his face pressed into the dirt. 'Watch him, Myint,' the youth snarled and marched off.

Hands none too gently yanked Pon-lor upright. The woman regarded him closely. This near, her scarred battleground face was even more of a horror. *Could have had that cured at the capital*, Pon-lor thought. Not something to mention, though. Her sharp deep eyes studied him and he saw a keen intelligence behind them. *Dangerous, this one.*

'I don't think we need you,' she murmured, intimate and low. 'And I know one way to kill you.' She drew a wide scimitar blade from her side and pressed its finely honed edge to his neck. 'Stories are this is one sure way. Want to find out?'

He edged his head in a sideways negative. She nodded. 'For now. Remember, I'll be behind you all the way . . .' She pushed him with the point to start him walking. 'Let's go.'

Pon-lor cooperated, falling into line among the 'bandits' as they started off. At first he'd been astounded that Jak had let him live, but now he thought he had an idea of the Bandit Lord's plans. No doubt he intended to collect a rich ransom for handing over a living Thaumaturg to the Queen of the Witches. This on top of the reward he expected for the yakshaka, should he manage to intercept the witch escorting it now, and present it as his own prize.

Good, then, that the cretin should lead him to his own goal. He'd thought little of his own chances of tracking her down; all his hopes had rested on Toru and Lo-sen. Many would perhaps not believe that a powerful theurgist mage should find himself lost in the jungle. But this was far from their training and expertise, as the ease of his capture had shown. The common villagers would never have dared the attempt, such was the dread of the Thaumaturg name. Yet Pon-lor did not think that these dregs and misfits – bandits! – understood this at all. They'd merely acted out of an assured confidence in their own mastery of this environment – an obviously justified assumption. And in his own concomitant helplessness – an unjustified assumption. Just as misguided as their quaint belief that merely by binding his hands and gagging him they'd rendered him powerless.

For the moment he saw no reason to demonstrate the error of their thinking. Especially when they were leading him to the suborned yakshaka and its captor. Once they had accomplished that unintended service he would regain control of the yakshaka, or, failing that, destroy it, and deal with this Night-Queen's spy. Then he would allow himself the indulgence of meting out punishment for the loss of his command. In that strict order.

Until then, he would endure these indignities and petty insults. But later these *bandits* would all writhe in indescribable agony. He would see to it.

∗   ∗   ∗

Osserc did not sleep. But he did dream. Waking dreams they were. Almost indistinguishable from mundane seated reality. They came and went like flitting scraps of shadow or idle thoughts passing before his gaze to disappear as if mere blurs against the rippled glazing of this murky window here in the Azath construct on Malaz Isle, which the locals named the Dead House.

Across the table of rough-hewn wooden slats covered in wax dribbles and cluttered by bottles and dusty glasses of all styles and fashions, the Jaghut Gothos was, in contrast, solid and unrelentingly permanent. The soft glow of his golden irises varied faintly as the entity blinked, occasionally. His head was sunk leaving his long iron-grey hair to hang as a ragged curtain. Gnarled hands, all swollen joints and misaligned fingers ending in yellowed talon-like nails, rested motionless upon the table's slats. Even his breathing barely registered as the slightest rise and fall of his solid wide shoulders. Osserc vaguely wondered if breathing were even necessary for such a one as this.

Clamping his jaws tighter, he now reluctantly slid his gaze to the third party at their table. Its head was of roughly the same size and hairiness as a coconut. A Nacht it was, a strange monkey-like creature said to have once been native to this island. It sat so short its chin barely cleared the height of the table. It was asleep,

278

or pretending to be, its coconut head nested in its arms. Yet this was only its appearance; the thing was far from any sort of natural animal. He suspected it to be a demon, though of what sort he had no idea. Clearly, it served this house – that is, was a chosen servant of the Azath. Similar to the guardians who sometimes manifested to defend the houses.

The creature's knobby head popped up as if it were preternaturally aware of his quiet regard. Its tiny black eyes blinked sleepily then sharpened. It raised a hand to brush the hairs over its wide mouth as if in profound thoughtfulness.

Osserc let out a loud grating exhalation.

The creature nodded as if in agreement and then switched to pulling on the scraggly hairs of its chin as if stroking a goatee.

He dragged his gaze away to rest upon the grimed and leaded window glazing. Why did the Azath always torment him so? Was this merely a symptom of its alien character? But all that was mere distraction – and perhaps that was all it was in truth. Distraction.

Through the filthy rippled glazing it was impossible to tell if it were day or night over the modest port city of Malaz.

Was this perhaps a comment on how the Azath saw the world? Through a distorting lens?

Osserc sensed beyond the isle, to the south, the potent wintry heartbeat of power that was the brooding presence of the entities known as the Stormriders. Entities of utter frigid ice and rime. His gaze shifted to study anew the Jaghut opposite. A connection? Many postulated as much.

And truly alien. Not unlike the Azath as well. Anastomotic? Perhaps.

Yet none of these lines of inquiry tugged at him. Distraction. It was all mere distraction from the path he ought to be pursuing. He shut his eyes to rest them for a moment and when he opened them once more he found his gaze had returned to the warped opaque glass of the window.

So. Eyes looking outward are blind.

'What are you thinking?' came the dry croaked voice of Gothos. It startled Osserc, so long had it been since either of them had spoken. Steeling himself, he turned to meet the bright amber churning of the Jaghut's eyes. He could not help but flinch slightly from the unyielding demands of that gaze.

'I am thinking that you are irrelevant. That this creature is irrelevant. Even this construct. All are mere irrelevancies and distraction from where I ought to be looking.'

279

Gothos raised a jagged fragment of blue glass from the table and held it to one eye. 'Memories are not the truth of the past. We sculpt them to suit our images of our present selves. And, in any case, the truth of then is not the truth of now.'

Osserc snorted his scorn, but within he felt something he had not known for ages untold – a profound unnerving, as if something he'd thought utterly unshakable had just revealed an empty gulf beneath. 'You surprise me, Gothos. I thought you of all beings would argue for timeless enduring truths. Bedrock absolutes.'

'Exactly. You thought.'

He made a conscious effort to move his gaze away as if disinterested. 'You will hear no admissions from me. No confessions.'

The Jaghut scowled his profound distaste. 'Of course not. I would be the last to want such mush and mawkishness. Which is perhaps precisely why I am here. As you say – I am irrelevant.'

As none other possibly could be.

So be it. Osserc closed his eyes. The memory of a flash of an indescribable brilliance seemed to blind him then. *Ancient ones, such power! Such astounding potency.* A young man's voice echoed in his thoughts. A scream of anguish. *Father!*

His eyes fluttered open and for an instant his heart and limbs trembled in memory of that fright. He clenched his jaws and shifted in his seat. 'I have guarded the wellspring of Thyrllan from all who sought to exploit it. Kept it apart. Walled it off at costs few could imagine.'

He turned his gaze on Gothos as if accusing, attempting to lance into those pits of argent. 'Who would dare ask more of me?' Yet he found within those pits no opponent, no challenge or quarrel. The flat steady gaze seemed to deflect his accusation upon himself.

'Who indeed,' the Jaghut said, a lip curling from one thrusting tusk.

Or so Osserc thought he said. Perhaps he imagined it. He was, after all, still within the Azath House. It, or they, set the rules here.

Irrelevant. Once more I shy away from the gulf. I am like prey caught fascinated by the predator's gaze. Terrified and circling, yet unable to break away. I could if I wish merely walk out that door – yet what of all that I have struggled to understand, to achieve? Final answers ungrasped? If there are any to grasp. Perhaps there are none.

Then at least I would possess that knowledge.

So be it. He sat at the table as if relaxed, his legs crossed, hands one over the other upon one knee. Yet he felt those hands tighten to clamps on his leg. 'I have asked nothing of others that I have not demanded of myself,' he began, then immediately wished he hadn't and clenched his lips. *Too much of a damned justification. Why the urge to explain to this one?* Especially when this entity had nothing but contempt for explanations or justifications. To this one they were all no better than self-serving pleas and apologies.

As they are to me as well . . .

Yet Gothos refrained from heaping scorn on that statement. Instead, he edged his head to peer through his ragged curtain of hair and his cracked lips drew back even further from his tusks in a merciless smile as if reading those very thoughts. 'Exactly, Osserc. You have asked nothing of others. And so . . . by your own admission . . .' Osserc's hands clenched painfully upon his leg '. . . you have asked nothing of yourself.'

He came as close then to walking away as he ever did. Despite all the risks he had taken. All the costs and cunning it took to gain entry to the Azath. He nearly slammed back the chair and walked out. *How* dare *he! The audacity! No one would dare! Not even . . . well, perhaps he. And Caladan. And T'riss. Azathanai those two. Yet Gothos is not.*

Odd then that Gothos should bother himself. He does not serve the Azath, surely.

Osserc crossed his arms. 'Odd to hear such a charge from one who has spent ages hiding himself away.'

The grimace of bared yellowed teeth that was Gothos' smile flashed again. 'Is that what you call what *we* are doing here?' Before Osserc could answer that a gnarled hand rose to brush the murky air. 'But no matter. As I am – what was it we both agreed upon . . . irrelevant?'

Again the deflection. Yet again the prey survives to circle the predator in the night. And if I am the prey and Gothos is not the trap nor the jaws awaiting me – then who? Or what? The Azath themselves?

'The charge that I have asked nothing of myself is so absurd in the extreme that I would have slain anyone else for suggesting it. I closed Kurald Thyrllan! I have maintained the peace! I have done nothing but watch and ward the boundaries of that realm. I cannot even begin to tell you of the countless efforts to breach Thyrllan that I have crushed. Even my—' He bit his tongue, so sharply did he cut himself off.

It seemed to him that the Jaghut's smile took on an even more hungry and satisfied curl. 'Yes?' he prompted, though the knowledge lay in his eyes of liquid gold.

No! I will not simper here. Not before this one. Osserc leaned back to clasp his knee once more. 'Even those of my own blood have had to be . . . dissuaded . . . now and then.'

'How sad for you. But I was speaking of demands placed upon yourself, not others. Warding Thyrllan is all very well. It has kept you busy, I suppose. I'm sure that it has been most . . . distracting.'

Distracting? The word infuriated him – as did everything out of the damned Jaghut's mouth – but then it began to take on a terrifying weight. *Distracting?* Distracting from what? Was there something . . .

He pulled his gaze away to find himself once more staring at their audience, the Nacht. Its head lay nestled in its skinny folded arms. Its mouth was open showing tiny sharp teeth. It was snoring quietly. Drool wet the table before it.

Another none-too-veiled comment? Am I trying the patience even of immortal otherworldly entities such as these? Is this a stunning victory or an abject failure? The answer to that question would go far to solving this impasse.

*   *   *

Shimmer dreamed of the day the Crimson Guard swore the Vow. They'd been on the run for weeks. Hunted by imperial columns. Fleeing a disastrous direct challenge of Kellanved's forces. K'azz led them ever northward – or was being driven ever northward. They'd been part of a proud field army of fifty thousand, an alliance of contingents from across the continent. But with failure came fragmentation, desertion, and an utter melting away of any hope of alliance. Now they were reduced to little more than a ragged band of some six hundred. The hard unbowed annealed core. The true believers – such as herself. Oh, certainly, some remained because they lusted for battle, or could never admit defeat – Skinner and his followers among their numbers. But most remained for only one overriding motive. For *him*. For K'azz.

Of all the battles K'azz had personally led or marshalled, or the flanks he commanded, he had lost not one. It was an old story: winning the battles but losing the war. Time and again they had been let down, abandoned, or outright betrayed by those they fought beside or for. The Bloorian league of nobles. Cawn switching sides on the day of battle. Tali's lukewarm support, as if resenting K'azz's growing lustre as a potential political rival. The number of times the man had succeeded in extracting them from seemingly hopeless disasters under the patronage of petty princes and barons across Quon were too many to count.

But now rumours were circulating that the self-styled Emperor of Quon had lost his patience with them. That he had turned his most dreaded weapon upon them. The army of undead that he had raised through his monstrous and unhallowed black arts. The T'lan Imass.

For her part, Shimmer did not believe that only now had Kellanved taken note of them. Rather, it seemed to her that he had probably come to the conclusion that in K'azz lay a figurehead who could possibly unite resistance to his growing hegemony and here was a chance to be rid of him.

That day as they filed through the narrow ravines and passes of the foothills of the Fenn Range it came to her that they were no longer making for what she naturally assumed had been K'azz's objective all along: the northernmost mountain fastness of his homeland, D'Avore.

Curious, she had kneed her mount forward to draw up beside him. 'My prince—'

An easy laugh from him had stopped her. 'Prince?' he said, still chuckling. As always it was an infectious gently chiding laughter that made her flush, self-conscious. 'Honorary at best, Shimmer. Those Bloorians do love their titles.' The smile fell away. 'At least they used to. I hear Kellanved has ordered all nobles executed. Every family in Bloor must be in the woods now burying their ridiculous fancy coats of arms.'

And he shook his head at the absurdity of it. How sad he looked, it occurred to her. Even this trivial episode had touched his heart. She lowered her attention to one of her mail-backed gloves, adjusted it. 'We do not make for the Red Keep?'

'No, Shimmer. Not yet, at least. A side venture first. A visit to an old locale . . .' He appeared about to say more but shook his head instead. 'Indulge me in this, yes?'

'Of course, my—' She caught herself.

'Captain?' he suggested, his mouth quirking up.

The expression made him appear even more youthful – his un- shaven chin hardly dusted in light reddish-blond hairs. Shimmer cleared her throat, feeling her face heating once more. 'Duke, at least, I should think.'

He inclined his head in acceptance. 'Very good, Shimmer. Yes. Duke. At the least – and the most.'

Shimmer tilted her helmeted head to excuse herself and fell back. K'azz bent to talk with his old teacher and adviser mounted at his side: Stoop, siegemaster to the D'Avore family for nearly half a century.

She found herself between Blues and Smoky. Blues rode easily with a leg negligently curled up around his pommel, Seti-style. His hands free, he practised with two sticks, twisting and flicking them in blurred mesmerizing patterns. Smoky, on the other hand, rode with both hands in a death-grip on his pommel, legs clamped tight. He appeared terrified, as if his mount, desperate to murder him, was about to throw itself off the ledge they walked.

'What word?' Blues asked.

'He wouldn't say.'

Smoky let out an angry snort. 'Why am I not surprised?'

Blues eyed the surrounding rocky slopes and the distant peaks. 'There's power in these mountains,' he murmured.

'I feel it too,' Smoky growled and he hunched even lower on his mount. It seemed to Shimmer that the horse almost sighed its exasperation. 'Nothing familiar though. Can't place it.'

The sticks clacked together in one of Blues' hands. He eyed the ridge ahead. 'Gettin' closer.'

Shimmer glanced back down the column where it twisted along the narrow trail. She spied Skinner in his long coat of armour riding close to the rear. Cowl was next to him, wrapped as usual in his shroud-like dirty ash-grey cloak. Together again, those two. That damned sneering assassin disturbed her like none other she'd met over a lifetime's career of war and conflict. But even she, grudgingly, had to give the man his due: he did his job and kept Dancer's Talons at bay.

Still, it saddened her to see Skinner drifting more and more into that one's company. Once he'd been inseparable from K'azz. Always at his side. Their champion, many had even thought him – then. Their answer to Dassem Ultor. But each defeat and setback in their campaigning seemed to drive the man ever further from K'azz's side. There was an element, she knew, among the guard who were of the opinion that a company's lack of success was the fault of its commander. And this was especially true of any mercenary company.

Riding the trail, the cool wind brushing at her hair where it escaped her helmet, Shimmer tightened the reins round her fist and pulled on her mail coat where it caught at her thigh. She'd been against that from the start – the idea of their turning mercenary. She'd never quite fully understood K'azz's rationale. Something about ease of movement across Quon Tali, and not being a threat to local suzerainty.

At least so it was on the face of the papers and treaties they signed with the various princes, kings, chieftains, councillors and nobles with whom they'd taken 'employment'. Papers these representatives were quick to throw to the wind the moment Kellanved and his motley army appeared on their borders.

In any case, turning mercenary did swell their numbers. The lustre of K'azz's family name drew many, together with those associated with him: Skinner, Blues, Lazar, Cal-Brinn and Bars. Even the name Cowl drew recruits who wished to work with him – and learn his trade. The sort of men and women she thought they could do without. Such as Isha, Lacy and the Wickan renegade, Tarkhan.

Now, though, those who fought for money alone had long since drifted away. Now, only those who'd always regarded themselves as part of the personal guard of the Red Duke remained.

Or so she'd thought at the time.

K'azz led them up on to a narrow natural plateau hidden away among the climbing ridges of the Fenn Range. It was thickly grassed, the air cold. Nearby, a herd of wild horses startled Shimmer as they thundered off, wary of their advance.

Here K'azz had them dismount and gather in a circle. Pushing her way through the thigh-high grasses, Shimmer noted dark fisted knots of stone poking up here and there. Standing stones. But hardly cyclopean. Small and eroded. No more than headstones.

'Feel it sizzle?' she heard Blues murmur to the skinny young mage now at his side, Fingers.

'It's like ten stones pressing down on my skull,' the kid groaned, and he held a hand to his forehead.

'Gather round!' K'azz called from the dusk.

'Have a care, K'azz. This is no ordinary field,' Smoky answered, warning.

'I know. Gather round.'

Shimmer pressed forward into the tightening ring of the remaining guard encircling K'azz. The faces of some, she noted, held an anxious worry. And then it came to her like a sudden panic: was this it? All their battles and struggle to come to an end here in this isolated, inauspicious place? Had he brought them here to disband? Here, this very night? The suspicion clenched her heart and made it hard to breathe.

Yet across the small clear circle Stoop was not concerned. To the contrary, the old saboteur looked positively pleased. He held a crooked smile behind his grizzled beard while he scratched at his chin with the stump of his elbow.

K'azz raised his arms for silence. Yet even as he did so Skinner pressed forward, frowning, as if sharing Shimmer's fears. Shimmer felt a brief echo of the attraction she once held for him as his blond hair blew about his still handsome features. 'Why have we ventured so far north, K'azz?' he demanded. 'Are we yielding the fight?' He turned to address the crowded company. 'I have always maintained we should head to Tali. The city would rise to our banner. We could lead a liberating force eastward.'

The audacity! The man had just announced his plans should K'azz dissolve the company. Shimmer drew breath to shout him down, but K'azz merely raised a hand for silence and she reluctantly subsided. 'Are you vowing that you will never abandon the fight?' he asked in a manner remarkably composed, given this implied challenge to his authority.

Skinner now frowned in earnest. He peered about, gauging the mood of the company, and Shimmer was relieved to see hardly any support for him in the hard, disapproving expressions around the circle. 'Of course,' he answered easily, as if to shrug off the ridiculous question. 'That is my very point. I counsel that we return to the struggle.'

K'azz merely gave a small nod of assent, and in this guarded reaction – giving away nothing – Shimmer recognized the commander at his most dangerous. He had somehow manoeuvred Skinner exactly where he wanted him, she realized. *Yet of course he reveals nothing of it.* 'Very good. For that is my intent. That is why I have brought us here.' He raised his chin to address the entire gathered company. 'We are here to swear a vow!' he began, loudly, catching everyone's attention. 'As many of you have already noticed, this is no random field. It is an ancient site. A place of power. Holy to our family, to our ancestors, and, some say, even to those ancient ones who preceded us upon these lands.

'We gather here on this day in the sight of one another to swear a binding oath. What we here swear is unrelenting and unending opposition to the Malazan Empire for so long as it shall endure. To never abandon or turn away from such opposition. To this cause all gathered here must give their individual agreement and binding commitment. Those of you who know doubt, or who feel unable to pledge yourselves utterly to this cause, are free to go. Nay, are encouraged to go. And all without rancour or ill-feelings.'

While talking K'azz turned full circle to peer at every face, to fix a hard gauging eye upon every member of his remaining guard. 'So . . . this is my Vow. This is what I here pledge and what I, in turn, ask of anyone who would choose to follow me. Now . . . what say you, Stoop?'

The wiry old siegemaster gave an easy shrug. 'I so swear, a course.'

'Blues?'

Their unofficial weaponmaster nodded solemnly. 'I so swear.'

K'azz then faced Skinner. 'Skinner? What of you?'

He was still frowning, as if sensing a trap but unable to pin it down. Finally he shrugged as well. 'Of course. I also swear. Fighting on has been my intent all along.'

K'azz's hard gaze now fell upon Shimmer and a cold finger seemed to press itself upon her spine. She felt a sudden weight, as if she were being sucked down into the earth beneath her feet, or the earth itself were rising up to swallow her. The pounding of hooves returned to her ears and she thought perhaps the herd of wild horses had returned. But the thunder was too deep for mere horses. *Something immense moving across the land. Or is it simply my heart?* She tried to speak but could make no sound. After what seemed an eternity the words escaped her numb lips.

'I so swear.'

The punishing weight of that gaze moved on and she could breathe again. All that must have been as an instant. Blinking to clear inexplicable tears from her gaze she peered out across the tall stands of grasses weaving in the evening winds and there she spied a lone dark figure, watching. It was a woman; that much was clear. But broad, powerful and dark-skinned, her long kinky black hair wind-tossed.

Strangely panicked by the appearance of one woman – some sort of displaced tribal, Seti or Wickan – Shimmer glanced to K'azz, now asking Lean to swear. Dare she interrupt? She returned her gaze to the grasses but the woman was gone. Moved on. A refugee, perhaps, from the fighting in the south. Odd that she should be alone.

The swearing continued, K'azz demanding a personal pledge from all gathered. For some reason the ritual awakened another memory in Shimmer and she found herself drifting back even further in time to when she was a child.

'*Shimmer* . . .'

Had that been the wind? A distant voice calling her name?

If she tried very hard she could remember a little of her youth. A farm in one of the more rural Kan provinces. She could recall feeding chickens and pigs. Harvesting rice. Playing with an army of brothers and sisters in the dry dusty ground before their family hut.

287

A hard upbringing. But for the most part a happy one. Until all came to an end.

Until *he* came. A man so old as to be nothing more than dried flesh and wisps of white hair. Or so it appeared to the child she was at the time.

She remembered her father bending down before her. He took her shoulders in his big hard farmer's hands. 'You will go with this man, Iko. It is a great merit to your family that he has chosen you. Be studious. Learn his teachings. But above all – be obedient! For it is by honouring him that you honour us. Your parents and all your ancestors before you. Do you understand?'

And she looking up at him, blinking through tears, hardly understanding. 'Yes, Father. I swear.'

'Very good, Iko. Do not cry. You go now to the capital. To a great school. Dance well. Bring us merit.'

'Yes, Father.'

Then a cruel dry grip upon her wrist tugging her along and a rasping mutter. 'I do not know why I bother. Too short you are. Too short by far. But,' and the hand swung her up on to a cart, 'one must do the best one can with what the gods provide.'

And if her childhood had been deprived but benign, the school proved a hundred times as harsh and in no way benign. For the discipline of the dance of the whipsword was unforgiving.

'*Shimmer.*'

There it was again. That voice. Calling. More insistent this time.

The school's lessons had been brutal but she'd survived. She wondered if she was the last of the whipsword dancers, now that the Kan court had been obliterated. Thinking back, she couldn't exactly remember how or why she'd survived the Malazan encirclement and siege. She, the last of the Kan king's bodyguards.

'*Shimmer!*'

The voice had a presence now. An image coalesced to impose itself upon her. It was the ghostly figure of Stoop, their old siegemaster. He was peering at her closely, anxiety on his crimped brows. 'You've drifted far, lass. Any further and you'll not make it back, I think. Best to return, yes?'

She peered at him, confused. 'You're not supposed to be here . . .'

'No less than you, lass. Now stop your daydreaming. We're in a dangerous place. Most dangerous the Guard's ever been, I'm thinking.'

'Dreaming?' She frowned, glanced about at the drifting and wavering images that surrounded her. They appeared to her like the rippling reflections from a lake.

Or a river.

Her gaze snapped back to Stoop. 'Where am I?'

'Lost among your memories.'

'How do I . . .'

He raised a brow. 'Get back?' He started off, but paused when she did not move. He beckoned her onward. 'Just you follow me, lass. Any way'll do.' And he set off once more.

She stalked after him, full of wonder, but touched by anger as well. She now knew she was not physically present wherever this place was – her own mind, no doubt – yet she took a great deal of reassurance from the hiss and shift of her long mail coat as she moved.

She came to herself once more at the railing of the *Serpent*. Only now the river was hardly wider than a stream. Its dense jungle verges reached out to one another almost closing out the sun and blue sky overhead. And the vessel was not moving. They appeared to have run aground on a sand bar, or shallows. She now wore only thin linen trousers, a shirt and leather sandals. The heat and close humidity was unbearable. She could barely breathe the thick miasma. And who knew for how long they had been marooned here, the ship rotting beneath them?

Yet could this not be another dream?

'This isn't a dream,' said the voice of Stoop.

She glanced aside to see him standing with her at the railing. The macabre humour of such a claim coming from him, a dead man, raised a smile to her lips. 'It is if you're here,' she answered.

'I'm close now, aye. We all are. All the Brethren. We're frightened, Shimmer.'

The half-amused smile fell away. 'Frightened?'

'Aye. Of where we're headed. Of who is awaiting us there. She's like nothing else here in the world – 'cept maybe the Shattered God.' He raised dead eyes to peer at her directly. 'She has the power to steal us away, Shimmer. You won't let that happen, yes?'

'I promise, Stoop. I won't let that happen to you.'

'To me? I'm talking about all of us, lass. Now close your eyes.'

She could not help but shut them for an instant. When she opened them he was gone. She peered about the ship's side. The rest of her companions sat about, or sprawled as if asleep. She pulled her hands from their clawed grip of the dried and splitting wood. The nails were blackened and broken. Insect bites dotted the flesh of her arms, livid and swollen, most unhealed. The noise from the surrounding jungle was now deafening: a cacophony of bird shrieks and whistles, insect whirrings, and the warning calls of unseen large animals. She went to find K'azz.

He was at the stern, sitting hunched, his head bowed. Everyone, it seemed, was bewitched. 'K'azz,' she urged. 'Wake up. K'azz? What has happened to you?'

'He dreams.'

Shimmer spun to find the Jacuruku witch, Rutana, uncomfortably close behind. This near, she could see that the whites of the woman's eyes were not white at all, but a sickly yellow. And the pupils now appeared different, as if slit vertically. 'What have you done?' she breathed, and she slid back a step, a hand going to the knife at her belt.

'I? Nothing. I do not have such power. My mistress, now. Well . . . that is a different matter.' Her familiar sneering smile twitched her lips. 'What you experience now is merely a side effect of her presence. Imagine, then, if she were to actively raise her might . . .' She lifted her bony shoulders. 'Well, there are none who could withstand her.'

'Not even Skinner?'

Hate raged in those sallow eyes and things seemed to writhe beneath the flesh of the woman's neck and arms. Grimacing, she clamped a hand to the amulets and charms tied to her arm and squeezed there, the hand whitening with effort. She lurched away a short distance and then stopped, turning to glare. '*Him* she permitted to leave. Permitted! Remember that, Avowed.' She stormed off.

'Must you bait the woman?'

Shimmer looked to see that K'azz was now gazing up at her. 'She insists upon baiting me.' She extended a hand to him and pulled him upright.

'I dreamed,' he murmured, his gaze narrowed on the glimmering waters of the river.

'So do we all.'

'I have read philosophers who posit that life itself is a dream.'

'Life bleeds,' Shimmer answered, full of contempt for such a claim.

The man's slit gaze shifted to her and she felt its weight. 'You may just have something there, Shimmer. Though even the basest animals bleed.'

Sighing, she leaned her weight on the cracked, sun-faded wood of the ship's side. 'Then we are animals, K'azz. And we are base.'

He joined her, peering at her while she steadfastly regarded the light glimmering from the murky blood-red waters. 'Well done,' he said. 'You have come to the preferred response in the philosophical dialogue. And so I ask – what sets us apart then, if anything, from the animal?'

She felt so tired. It seemed as if she'd slept all these last weeks, yet she felt unaccountably exhausted. Worn out, or ground down. As if her will was under some sort of relentless crushing pressure. She rubbed her eyes, bruised as they were by the stabbing scintillating reflections. What was he going on about? Surely he must have some point – he was no fool. Perhaps it merely eluded her. She was not tutored in philosophy as he was. 'I don't know, K'azz,' she whispered – or believed she did. 'We have each other.'

'Yes. Exactly, Shimmer. Each other. Society. That is what sets us apart.'

She'd heard this argument before, in many shapes and versions. The critique came to her at once. 'The herd. The group. So – we are sheep.' Still she refused to meet his gaze.

He snorted as if mildly amused by the rebuttal. 'That old line. Sheep and wolves. People who push that analogy haven't spent much time with either animal. Truth is, the wolves' society is *more* sophisticated. Wolves have a hierarchy. And the worst fate for any wolf is to be cast out of the pack. If a sheep becomes lost it just wanders around until something eats it. If a wolf is cast out, it dies of loneliness. Human society shares much more with the wolf than the sheep. So that comparison isn't valid.'

Frustrated now, Shimmer turned on her commander. This close, his sickness, or condition, made her almost wince. Parchment-like skin stretched taut over high cheekbones, the skull's orbits of the eyes clearly visible. His hair was a thin white mat flattened now by sweat and grime. Reading her reaction, he turned his face away.

That in her thoughtlessness she had hurt him stabbed her and she cursed her stupidity. *I am not the one who is ill. Or dying.* Yet she had to believe he still spoke with a purpose. 'What are you trying to say, K'azz?'

Head turned away, he said, his voice now rough, 'Where we are going there is neither sheep nor wolf, Shimmer. I believe the entity awaiting us does not even know what society is. Has never been part of a group, or even a family, such as we know or understand it. She, or it, is unfathomably alien to us. Remember that, Shimmer. In the days to come.'

'Yes, K'azz. I will.'

Straightening, he cleared his throat. 'Very good. Shall we go wake the others, then?'

'Yes.'

CHAPTER VIII

Fortunately for us, our impressed bearers and scouts, of the
village we currently occupied, then assured us that the neighbouring village, with whom they had warred for years, were
in fact cannibals of the worst sort. Forewarned, we fell upon
the village with fire and sword and utterly exterminated the
nest of vile monsters.

Infantryman Bakar
Testimony to the Circle of Masters

IN THE END, JATAL FOUND THAT THE COUNCIL TOOK VERY LITTLE CON-
vincing. The various Adwami family heads were easily steered
towards considering further advance into Thaumaturg territory –
half-drunk as they were with the heady ease of their victory in crushing and pillaging Isana Pura. He and Andanii took turns guiding the
debate, at times staging confrontations and disagreements over this
or that minor point in the order of march, or the division of spoils.
Such quarrels the minor houses eagerly fixed upon and fanned,
pleased to think they were driving a wedge between the Hafinaj and
the Vehajarwi. A perception he and Andanii were pleased to allow
them.

Eventually each family secured its division of the loot, including
slaves, and sent them rearward in one long straggling caravan of
guarded wagons and carts. Watching the various men-at-arms
securing the accumulated boxes and crates of silver and gold
jewellery, fine cloths and the best furniture, Jatal almost laughed
aloud at the ridiculousness of it. Somehow, it now struck him as
absurd, this squirrel-like fixation upon the accumulation of goods
and objects, even though just a short time ago he too would have
been among those evaluating the merits of this silver fork versus that.

What had changed, he wondered, as he sat watching, his hands crossed over the pommel of his saddle, his helmet pushed back high upon his head. Was it he? Or perhaps the object that he fought for had changed. Gold, rubies, jewelled daggers, fine robes or engraved leatherwork: none held the appeal they once commanded when compared to a certain bright smile and eager, challenging gaze.

It struck him that the heat of his desire could perhaps be no more than this substitution of one object of possession for another. And perhaps it was. He pressed a sleeve of his robe to his face to wipe away the sweat and the dust. He found that the question troubled him not, although he knew that it should. No matter. They had cast their lots together. Their fates would rise or fall upon the success or failure of this throw. Having up until now lived the careful and considered life of a student and scholar, he found this new audaciousness and daring quite, well, delicious.

Jatal pulled his helmet down and turned Ash to face the column. *Yet could this be nothing more than the oh-so-clichéd exhilaration and allure of the illicit affair?*

He gave Ash a sharp knee to urge him on, and, for the first time he could remember, found that he wished he could just turn off his damned mind. Suddenly he saw all his second-guessing, quibbling and differing analyses of any given situation as the weakness his brothers had always mocked him for.

Is this because only now have I found the passion and ambition they were born with?

Oh, shut up.

He returned to the van of the column. Here, at the very head of the troops, because no family of the concord would now allow any other family the honour, if only symbolic, of leading, rode the Warleader, with a small troop of guards and staff. Then came Jatal and Andanii as co-leaders of the Adwami Elite – the name Andanii had seemingly invented at the first council gathering after the sack of Isana Pura.

And what a stroke that was. Jatal had since found himself besieged by requests to place this son or that within the ranks of the 'Elite'.

It was a wonder to him that no one else saw how hollow and absurd it all was. Other than Andanii, of course. And perhaps this foreigner warrior. How he had arched one bristling brow at that word, *elite*. He saw it for the shabby vacant trick that it was. He had merely pursed his wrinkled lips and pinned Jatal with that knowing glance.

Yet we all have our secrets, do we not?

Jatal nodded to Andanii who rode surrounded by her honour-guard. She blew out a frustrated breath and waved a hand to call attention to the column's crawling advance. He nodded his commiseration.

I see that no ragged shaduwam march with us.

And which army, I wonder, is the real one?

Andanii, he knew, was emphatic that they discover more about this foreign mercenary commander. And so that is what he would pursue during this march north. The evening meals were far too public for any meaningful discussion. The gathered family heads watched each other like a clutch of baby birds jealously measuring the attention and feeding each one received. Certainly not the place to probe the foreigner regarding the shaduwam and the seeming pact, or understanding, he had somehow managed to strike with them.

Until then, he would maintain his public face and play the game of alliance-building among the various jostling families, together with his outward frostiness towards Princess Andanii and her family allies, however stupid and unnecessary the entire puppet show seemed to him.

That evening, during the interminable dinner in the massive main tent, he waited and watched until the Warleader excused himself early, as was his habit. Shortly afterwards he too begged off listening – yet again – to another of Ganell's stories, and exited the tent.

The night was quiet and dark, half overcast by high thin clouds. The eerie arc of the Visitor waxed now brighter than ever. It lanced across the sky like a tossed torch. Would it smash upon them in the flame and destruction so many dreaded? Perhaps their unparalleled foray into northern territory was merely the realization of this heavenly portent of apocalypse – for the Thaumaturgs, that was. Jatal wrapped his robes tighter about himself against the chill evening air and made for the Warleader's tent.

Guards called for him to halt at the entrance and he waited while one enquired as to the Warleader's disposition. To one side, the hulking Scarza sat against a saddle, his rather stubby legs stretched out before him while he ate. Jatal offered him a brief bow of acknowledgement, to which the half-giant raised the haunch he gnawed upon. Shortly thereafter, Jatal was waved in. A mercenary guard used the haft of his spear to hold aside the heavy cloth flap. Jatal ducked within.

The interior was much darker than the general encampment, with its torches planted between the tents and the Visitor glaring down upon them all. Here, a single lamp on a side table cast a small globe of amber light that hardly touched the canvas ceiling and walls. His first impression was that the sparsely furnished tent was empty, and then movement from the shadows revealed the Warleader crossing into the light. He wore now only a long linen shirt over trousers bound by leather swathing, and faded hide moccasins. It might have been a trick of the uncertain light, but it appeared as if the thick canvas of the tent was moving where the Warleader had been. He went to the table and poured himself wine from a tall cut crystal decanter. Peering over his shoulder at Jatal, he hefted the heavy vessel. 'Spoils of war,' he observed.

'A very beautiful prize.'

The Warleader gestured to a leather saddle seat against one wall. 'Thank you,' Jatal said.

'Drink?'

'Yes, thank you.'

The old man selected another glass. The tent was ripe with the lingering spicy smoke that the man doused himself with, but Jatal thought he could detect another scent amid the heady melange. A familiar one he could not quite place.

The Warleader crossed the tent to hand him a tumbler filled with red wine. 'You have changed,' he said as he seated himself. He stretched out his long thin legs and held his glass in his fingertips on his lap.

'Oh? How so?'

'When I first saw you, you were an innocent soul.'

Jatal decided it was his turn to arch a brow. 'And what am I now, pray tell?'

The man cocked his head on one side and studied him anew. Jatal felt as if the inhumanly cold and lazy eyes were dissecting him, laying exposed his every self-doubt, ambition and lie. 'You are now a political soul. May the gods forgive you.'

Jatal took a sip of the wine while he considered that and grimaced his distaste: the red was as thick and sweet as blood. The Warleader raised a hand. 'My apologies. I should have warned you. This is a strong fortified wine. It is like the truth . . . not to everyone's taste.'

Jatal forced the sip down yet kept hold of the tumbler, if only so as not to offend his host. 'When I arrived I was nothing more than the youngest of my father's sons, the least of the brood, with no hopes or prospects. Then I was happy buried in my books and studies.'

'And now . . . ?' the foreigner prompted. Yet Jatal heard no interest in his voice; if anything, the man sounded bored, or disappointed.

'Now I find myself swept up in a gamble more insane and

foolhardy than any I could have ever imagined. Even the ancient lays and stories of the old heroes cannot compare to this audacious throw. Sometimes I fear the very gods have caught their breath.'

The old soldier's gaze had drifted down to his glass, which he lifted and finished in one last gulp. Then he gave a heavy sigh. It seemed to Jatal that the man must have heard such last-minute qualms a thousand times before. 'You have doubts and worries,' he said, sounding utterly wearied by Jatal's doubts and worries. 'That is only normal for any man or woman cursed with intelligence, such as yourself. As to this gamble, or throw of the dice, as you put it . . . every battle is a risk. That is why sane men prefer to avoid them.' He held out his open hands, the empty glass loose in one. 'However, I have spent an entire lifetime – that is, my entire life – pursuing such risks and ventures and I can assure you that this is a sound one. If we can keep these Thaumaturgs on the run there is a good chance that within a month they will no longer be in charge of their own country.' He leaned forward to rest his elbows on his knees and dangled his large hands. 'And so, my prince of the Hafinaj. You came here to speak to me . . . what is it you wish to say?'

Fascinated by the fish-like dead eyes Jatal could not find his voice. Was this what passed as the man's candour, or his mockery? Was he not taking any of this seriously? Jatal could not shake the feeling that he was being played with. The suspicion stoked his anger and he found the resolve to blurt out, 'What are the shaduwam to you?'

The Warleader tilted his head. His dusk-grey eyes slit in thought. He sighed, then pushed on his knees to stand up and crossed to the side table. He poured another glass of the thick treacle-like wine. Turning, he tossed the drink down and sucked his teeth in a hiss. 'What are the shaduwam to me?' he repeated, musing. He leaned back against the table, crossing his arms. 'They are as nothing to me. I would not care one whit should they all be swept from the face of the earth tomorrow. Is that enough of an answer for you, my prince?'

Jatal studied the man as he turned to light one of several tall yellow candles that cluttered the table. He gathered the impression that this man wouldn't care a whit should just about any or every thing be swept from the face of the earth, very probably including Jatal himself. A detached part of him wondered whether this was calculated to intimidate or impress. In any other man he would assume so; yet this one struck him as different from any other he had ever met. One who did not give a damn what he or anyone else thought. And so he decided that in fact, no, this foreign Warleader was not trying to impress or intimidate or overawe him in any way at all. That would presume that he cared, when he very clearly did not. So he opted to pursue the issue, if only to shake the bushes, as they say, to see how the man would respond. 'You have formed no agreement with them, then? No sort of alliance?'

'I did not say that,' the man answered flatly. He waved a hand to direct the fumes of the candle to his face and inhaled.

Ye gods, this man is difficult! Jatal set his glass aside. 'Care to provide the particulars?'

The man shrugged his shoulders, still wide and powerful despite his age. 'Certainly. They approached me and explained that while you noble Adwami might have foolishly and shortsightedly rejected the offer of their support, they would advance in any case. And would strike to achieve their goals.'

'So, an alliance.'

'Not at all. Convenience. When the lion strikes, the jackals and vultures also get their share.'

'I'm sure the shaduwam do not see themselves as jackals or vultures.'

'I am certain as well. Yet that is irrelevant.'

Jatal sensed more here than was being admitted, but he could not press further at this time. And in any case, this explanation *could* adequately serve should the relationship ever become known. He studied his hands clasped on his lap. 'I see. Thank you, Warleader, for the intelligence. However, may I suggest that in the future you convey to the council *all* information regarding the campaign?'

The Warleader regarded him from heavy-lidded eyes. Like something inhuman – a creature of legend or myth. 'And just who would you suggest I report to?' he asked, rather drily.

Beneath the coldly evaluating stare, Jatal cleared his throat. 'Why, myself, of course. As the council's representative.'

A smile that was more like a death's grin came and went from the man and he looked almost saddened. 'You see, my prince, I *was* right about you.'

More uncomfortable than ever, Jatal rose, collected his glass, and crossed to replace it on the side table. 'Good evening, Warleader. Perhaps we could retire together again, to discuss other, more pleasant matters. Philosophy, possibly? Or history?'

The man suddenly appeared wary. As if Jatal had just somehow challenged him. He retreated from the table, waving vaguely. 'Of course. It would be my pleasure.'

Jatal accepted the dismissal – this was, after all, the Warleader's tent – and turned to go. Pushing aside the heavy cloth it occurred to him that he had glimpsed not two used glasses upon the side table, but three.

That night he waited long after the mid-hour but Andanii did not appear.

* * *

The native chief, or warlord, Oroth-en, had sent one of his warriors ahead to give notice – and no doubt warn – of their advance. He then guided their column through the forest. Between the thick tree trunks, Murk caught occasional glimpses of the local warriors. They moved with as much ease and familiarity as any of the wild inhabitants of the woods, which, he reflected, in fact they were.

They came to a natural meadow of stiff knife-edged grasses taller than Murk's head and here Oroth-en had them halt. He indicated that the majority of the company should wait there while Yusen and a few chosen attendants should accompany him. The captain signed to Burastan to remain, then gestured Murk and Sour forward.

'I don't like it,' the Seven Cities woman muttered aside to Murk.

'Our friend can't very well lead a pocket army into his village. As far as he knows we might just up and take over the place.'

She wrinkled her nose in annoyance. 'Why would we want his wretched village?'

'Well, for one thing they have food in their wretched village. Which is a lot more than we have. And second, they're probably always fighting their neighbours for territory and resources and such. It's a way of life.'

The tall woman wasn't convinced and she snorted her derision. 'Resources? What resources?' She waved to the tangled trees. 'This is a wasteland. It's like one of our Seven Netherworlds, only here on earth.'

'Burastan, Lieutenant, *they're* here and that means this ain't no wasteland. Get it?'

Then Yusen urged Murk on again, but he flicked his gaze to the travois and its wrapped burden. The captain frowned, uneasy, then let out a breath. He signed to Burastan: *guard it.* The lieutenant nodded her understanding.

Murk peered around for Sour but couldn't find the man anywhere. Finally he spotted him bent down all the way to his stomach studying a fat blossom growing out of a notch in the roots of one of the trees. To Murk, the sky-blue flower appeared almost obscene the way its swollen petals seemed to burst from the tree. He pulled his partner up by the collar of his rotting leather hauberk. 'What in the name of D'rek are you doing? Let's go.'

'Ain't never seen one like that afore,' Sour explained as he dragged him along.

'This ain't no natural philosophy hike, Hood take you!' Murk growled. 'Stay focused.'

They caught up with Yusen and Oroth-en, and the village elder led them on.

Through the afternoon he began to see more and more signs of human occupation. The seemingly meandering way they walked met a narrow path and this in turn merged with a definite trail travelled enough to expose naked beaten dirt. As they went, Sour kept pointing out more and more of the fat, vaguely hand-shaped, dusty blue blossoms. Some clung to the trunks of trees or hung from branches overhead. He kept grinning and winking at Murk, as if he'd put them there himself.

Murk just rolled his eyes. *Fine, so they grow around here. Big deal.*

'Climbing Blue!' Sour suddenly announced as he walked along, all hunched and side to side in his bow-legged gait.

Murk scowled his annoyance. 'What're you going on about?'

The mage waved a hand, flapping his tattered leather and mail gauntlet. 'Them flowers. I'm gonna name them Climbing Blues.'

'Climbing—' Murk caught himself almost taking a swipe at his partner. 'You can't just up and name some plant! What makes you think you can do that?'

''Cause I discovered it. That's why.'

'Discovered it? You didn't—' The astounding claim stole Murk's breath. 'Idiots tripping over things is no way to hand out names. And anyway, what about these local folks? Don't you think they know it? Or have a name for 'em?'

Sour scrunched up his already wrinkled face, thinking. 'Well . . . we don't know any of that, do we?'

'Oh, so because of *your* ignorance *their* hundreds of years old names for everything get tossed aside. Well, that's just great.'

'Well, maybe I'll ask then!'

'Well, fine! Go ahead.'

'I will.'

'G'wan.'

Sour opened his mouth but he and Murk noted Yusen glaring back at them and both hunched guiltily. They passed another of the blue flowers and Murk quelled an urge to kick the damned thing.

Later Sour bumped him then flicked his eyes aside. Murk followed his gaze to catch a fleeting glimpse of one of the locals watching from the dense cover. After this he spotted a number of them. They carried bows and braces of javelins, or short spears, on their backs. Murk had yet to see any signs of metal on any of them – weapons or armour.

Then, with startling suddenness, they emerged into a village. It was arranged in a great oval hacked out of the surrounding jungle. Its centre was an open clearing dotted by fire-pits. The circle of huts all faced the clearing. Most of the huts stood upon short poles and most were no more than walls woven through with branches of broad leaves. The roofs were thick layers of thatched grass.

The villagers stilled, watching them, silent. Some tended low fires, or beat gathered branches. Some were sitting hunched over making implements, weaving plant fibre twine, or carving sticks – making arrows or darts, perhaps. Many lay in hammocks within the airy huts. An old woman pounded a mortar with a pestle, both made of wood. All wore little more than simple loincloths together with numerous ornaments, amulets or charms, tied to legs and arms. Bright stones glimmered from the ears and noses of some. Naked children watched from the open doorways of the huts. Some sort of welcoming committee waited in the clearing.

Murk cocked an eye to his partner, who nodded, but then shut his eyes, his hands twitching at his sides, and abruptly fell to the ground. Murk froze, surprised, then rushed to help him up. The little man fought for a moment, flailing his arms. After this he calmed to peer about, surprised. Blood ran in a crimson torrent from his nose and he wiped it away with the back of his grimed gauntlet. 'Gods! That ain't never happened afore!' he told Murk, stunned wonder in his voice.

Yusen peered down at them, his gaze narrow with worry. 'You okay?'

'Yeah.' Sour straightened up. 'Okay.' He sent Murk a significant look, signed, '*Her.*' 'Was just surprised by somethin', is all.'

Murk said nothing, but he was quite alarmed. *Her!* So it must be true, this antipathy between Ardata and the Queen of Dreams. 'Did you get it?' he asked, trying to keep his voice casual.

While Oroth-en watched, Sour straightened his torn hauberk. 'Yeah. I got it . . . Barely.'

'Okay then.' Murk gestured, inviting Yusen to keep going. The captain flicked his gaze between the two mages then nodded his cooperation. He continued on.

The warriors, both male and female, crowded round Oroth-en. None looked happy. One young fellow spoke, and thanks to Sour's efforts Murk could now understand their language: 'Why have you brought these Isturé demons?' this one challenged. 'They will murder us!'

'I do not believe these are of the Isturé,' Oroth-en answered, calmly enough.

'They are like,' another observed. 'They carry iron.'

'True. They are foreigners. Most foreigners carry such things. That is their way.'

'If they are not of the Isturé, then we should kill them and take their iron,' one of the female warriors declared.

'Their numbers are too many,' Oroth-en explained.

'Numbers? How many are there?' another demanded.

'Many hands.'

This quietened the warriors for a time. Then the female warrior who had spoken before, hefty and scarred, eyed Yusen and scowled bitterly. 'I see. So . . . what are their demands?'

Sour's brows shot up and he looked to Murk, who raised his gaze to the open sky. *Why does it always have to be me?* He stepped forward, his hands open. 'Do you understand me?'

All gathered went quiet once more. Oroth-en turned to regard him, and even his gaze was now suspicious. 'Why did you not reveal this before?' he asked, quite coldly.

'Because only now can I do so.' He gestured to Sour. 'My partner and I are what we call mages. You understand mages? Yes?'

Oroth-en edged backwards, eyed him and Sour anew. 'You are shaduwam?'

Shaduwam? Ah – shaman. 'Yes . . . of a kind. You have your own shaduwam, yes?'

The warriors exchanged uneasy glances, but none said anything.

So. Something here. Something they won't reveal. Fine. None of my business. He addressed Oroth-en. 'We are lost and hungry here in this jungle. We ask your aid. Aid in returning home. And food – whatever you can spare.'

Oroth-en turned to his warriors. 'You see? They come as guests asking our help. Are we so heartless as to turn them away?'

The large female warrior scowled her displeasure. Her hair was a great mass of locks about her head and shoulders, and her cured leather shirt, her armour, strained to contain her chest. She planted the butt of her spear and tossed her heavy mane. 'So might the snake beg entry to the hut.'

'Then keep an eye upon them, Ursa.'

'I shall!' and she fixed her critical gaze on Murk.

It seemed to him that Oroth-en hid a quirk of a smile as he half turned away. 'Very good. Come, guests, sit and eat with us,' and he gestured to the largest of the huts, the main house, perhaps.

The meal was the oddest one Murk had ever had, or failed to have, as he actually ate almost none of it. They sat in a great circle on a raised floor of woven mats over slim wooden poles. He and Sour translated for Yusen, as Sour wasn't about to attempt to raise his Warren again. Food was carried in and served round on broad leaves that went from hand to hand. One ate with the right hand and received the leaf with the left. Children tottered about in between, begging titbits from everyone, but only peering fascinated at the strangers.

He wondered how to get any of this food to their companions now squatting in the jungle, waiting. From the lean figures of these natives he could guess that there was hardly enough to go round as it was. How could they possibly take on fifty additional mouths? They'd probably have to completely despoil the surrounding acres to manage it. And then there'd be nothing left.

Yet he was reluctant even to name what came across his lap as 'food', let alone try it. Some leaves arrived heaped with what looked like inoffensive mashed plant matter, pulped roots perhaps, yet smelled vile, or crawled with ants. He thought the ants nothing more than an unavoidable nuisance until a leaf arrived with a great steaming heap of them cooked in some sort of a sticky sauce. Much worse was to come. Leaves covered in beetles and fat white grubs, still writhing, that the locals popped down like candies. Then more of the vegetable mush which they gathered up in their fingers like porridge. Murk didn't know what was more disgusting: the idea of eating these dishes, or the sight of Sour eagerly sampling each and every one that came by.

Eventually, he could stand it no longer and he sent a dark scowl of disgust Sour's way. 'Gods, man,' he hissed, 'do you really have to?'

The skinny fellow cocked one walleye, half a black beetle pinched in his fingers, chewing. 'Wha'?'

He leaned closer, lowering his voice. 'Eat, man. This . . . *stuff.*'

Sour popped in the last of the huge beetle. 'Stuff?' he said around his mouthful. 'It's food. This is what they eat!'

Murk flinched away, wincing his distaste. 'Yeah . . . but how *can* you?'

302

'Food's food, friend.' He tapped a dirty finger to his temple. 'It's all in the mind.'

From where he sat down the circle Yusen raised a hand in the sign for *manners*, then turned to Oroth-en who sat next to him. 'Thank you for the meal,' he said, loudly. 'It is greatly appreciated.'

Oroth-en translated for everyone and they all smiled and nodded, then proceeded to push more of the heaped leaves on them. Sour sat up and spoke to Oroth-en: 'May I go to thank those cooking?'

The elder appeared quite bemused by the request but waved his agreement. 'Of course.'

Sour ambled off. Watching him go, Murk frowned his confusion. *What in the name of all the gods is he doing?*

Movement on his other side distracted him and he turned. He almost jumped to see that now sitting next to him was the considerable bulk of the woman warrior, Ursa. Gone was the thick leather shirt, the skirting and the weapons. The woman now wore a simple cloth wrap tied at her immense breast. She glowered down at him.

He decided that he ought to take Yusen's warning to heart and so nodded a polite greeting. 'Yes?'

'You are not eating,' she accused him.

Smiling and giggling, women round him held out the leaves of insects and pulped plant matter.

He struggled for a time, desperate to find a reason, only to finish, lamely, 'I am not hungry.'

'You will need your strength for the trial ahead, little man.'

Murk felt his brows climb. 'Oh? Why?'

'Why? Have you not guessed?' The women nearby hid smiles behind their hands. He eyed them all. A terrifying possibility began to form in his mind.

'You are the first foreigner sorcerer male I have met,' the woman continued, undeterred. 'I have heard all sorts of rumours about your kind. That your members are so tiny you can only bugger boys. That those sorcerers to the west have sworn off all mating whatsoever. And that the shaduwam to the south slice them off entirely!' She made a cutting motion with her fingers across Murk's lap. He flinched away, almost slapping his hands down to cover his crotch. The women, young and old, giggled anew.

'So which is it?' she demanded.

'Which what?'

'Which are you?'

'Me?' He peered round and caught Yusen's amused gaze. He

glared in response then turned to Ursa. 'I'm quite healthy in that –
area, thank you. No need to wonder.'

She looked him up and down, as one might a horse at auction. 'I
will decide that, foreigner. Now, come with me.'

'Come with . . . you?'

She stood to peer down at him from over the wide shelf of her
bosom. 'Yes! Come. Let us see how much of a man you are.'

Well – how could he let such a challenge go unanswered? He
stood also, and bowed his farewell to Oroth-en who answered with
a nod, the same small smile at his lips as had been there before. *He'd
known all evening.* Next to the elder, Yusen used the marine sign-
language to send: *onward!*

Murk gave his own emphatic sign to the captain then followed the
big woman out.

Much later he was thoroughly exhausted, content and dreaming
when the very floor of the hut seemed to rise up and throw him
aside. He sat up, dazed, to see Ursa tying on her wrap.

'I heard something,' she whispered, snatching her spear. 'Something I've never heard before.'

'What?'

'Quiet,' she hissed.

Then he heard it, a bright sharp blare; and knew what it was.
He fumbled for his linen trousers and stumbled down from the hut
into the starlit central clearing. Here the villagers gathered, peering
about, quite terrified. Hopping to slip on his boots, Murk found
Yusen and Sour. 'The rally horn!' he called.

Yusen nodded, grim. 'They're under attack.'

Oroth-en came pushing his way through the clamouring crowd.
'What is this noise?' he demanded.

'Our friends are being attacked.'

'Attacked?' the elder repeated, quite surprised.

'Will you guide us back, please?'

Oroth-en instantly set aside his confusion to nod his agreement.
'Of course. Collect your weapons.'

Yusen gave a quick bow of thanks. He turned to Sour and Murk.
'Get your gear then return here.' Both turned and ran. At the hut
Murk found Ursa pulling on her thick leather skirting and shirt.
'What are you doing?' he demanded as he sorted through their
commingled gear, all tossed down together in the heat of their first
round of lovemaking.

'I am going.'

Murk pulled on his laced shirt. 'No, you're not. Stay here. It'll be dangerous.'

'Dangerous?' The woman let out a great braying laugh and slapped him on the shoulder so hard he almost fell over. 'You have no idea how dangerous it is out there, foreigner.' She hefted her spear. 'Come!' and she leaped from the hut.

Oroth-en and a portion of the village's warriors guided them through the woods. The moment Murk slipped under the surrounding jungle edge he entered a deep shadowed darkness. He gestured, summoning Meanas, and cast a Shadow-derived mage vision over Sour and Yusen, who signed back indicating that they had it. He then hurried to Oroth-en's side.

'As a mage, a shaduwam, I can help you see in the night—' he began, but the elder waved the offer aside.

'No need. We have no difficulty.'

Indeed, now that Oroth-en said this, Murk realized that his warriors and scouts had all dodged ahead, slipping into the dark with ease. The fact of this now troubled him as he jogged along, struggling to keep up. Soon his breath came short – he was in poor shape after so many days of privation.

Blasts of munitions now echoed from the jungle far ahead. The shockwaves raised howls, cries and shrieks of protest from the many night-creatures. Swarms of bats churned overhead, disturbed from the highest reaches of the canopy. *Damn. Gettin' serious. Who's attacking? Another village?*

Ursa emerged from the brush to come to his side. 'What is this new noise like thunder, lover?' she demanded.

'Munitions – ah, powerful blasts, like magery.' She grunted her half-understanding. 'Watch out—' but she was gone again, dodging into the thick fronds of the undergrowth.

Gods damn them! No one's listening!

It began to rain. The advance was a nightmare of flashing bodies dodging between trees, slapping branches and dripping leaves. He turned his ankle on a fallen log and limped along as best he could. All around him the locals sent up war whoops and yipping challenges to the night. They clashed the hafts of their spears against the shells and lattices of sticks they wore woven over leather as armour.

Why are they making so damned much noise? Then it came to him – *putting up a scare.* They were hoping drive off the attackers. He lent his own voice to the shouts.

Far too long later, long after the distant clash and eruptions of munitions had died away, Murk emerged into the meadow and stepped on to the torn mud of the aftermath of battle. Members of the company knelt with those fallen, wrapping wounds or comforting ones too far gone. He sought out Burastan. He found her with Yusen, her face slashed and the cloth and armour of her arm ragged and torn as if some sort of animal had been raging at it.

'Who was it?' he demanded, barging into their conversation.

'Creatures,' she answered, exhausted. 'Half-human, half-monster.'

'D'ivers? Soletaken?'

Her answer was an unknowing, utterly spent shrug.

Nearby, Oroth-en listened to reports from his scouts who slipped into the clearing, whispered to him, then sped off once more. His warriors helped guard the clearing's perimeter.

'You have a count?' Yusen asked Burastan.

She nodded, wiped a bloodied sleeve across her face. 'Some fifteen seriously wounded. Eight dead.'

Murk peered about for Sour and spotted him already tending to a wounded trooper. Good. The man wasn't much of a bonesetter, but he was the best they had – gods help them. Strangely, two of the locals were kneeling there helping with the binding and treatment and they appeared to be debating techniques with him.

He then began hunting through the tall grass for the litter and its perilous burden. The troopers had obviously hidden it away, but the power of the object glowed like a dazzling ember in his mage-vision, guiding him. He found Dee and Ostler standing guard.

He asked Dee: 'Did it . . . do . . . anything?'

The big swordsman eyed him as if he were an idiot. 'Whaddya mean?'

He turned away. 'Never mind.'

While he was walking off the swordsman called, 'I will tell ya this, cadre. They wanted it. Them beasties wanted it.'

Murk offered a nod for the information – accurate or not. A thought came to him and he paused, considering. There was some-one else he could question here regarding the attack. It – she – had been gone lately, and he was frankly quite happy to leave things at that. But perhaps . . .

'Celeste . . .' he called through Meanas. 'Celeste . . . are you—'

He broke off because in his mage-vision he could see the faint jade glow of something approaching through the grasses. The image of a young girl. Nearby, Dee and Ostler acted as if nothing were happen-ing; they were obviously completely unaware of its – her – presence. He moved off into the dense grasses for more privacy.

He was terrified to have to talk to this thing. Who knew what she might do? She might get annoyed by something he said and blast him from the face of the earth with the flick of a finger. Yet out of everyone here he was the one who ought to be doing this, and so he remembered his mage training and struggled to relax his mind into the state of 'forced calm'.

The diminutive flickering image stopped before him. She peered about curiously with her big child-like eyes as if fascinated, yet completely mystified, by the mercenary soldiers coming and going. Closer now, he was struck by something familiar in the simple straight style of her hair and plain peasant clothes. She looked like a farm girl from northern Quon Tali. Had it taken this image from his mind? But then he remembered that she'd mentioned another.

'I am here,' she said. 'I have always been here. Whether you were aware of me or not.'

'I see. So, did you see the attack?'

She frowned prettily. 'Attack?'

Queen give me strength! How can I put this? 'Others came. Creatures different from us, and there was fighting. Many were hurt.'

She peered up at him with a directness of gaze that made him want to flee. 'You are all alike to me.'

Murk felt the strength leaving his knees. *Ye gods! Try another tack!* 'So, what have you been doing – if I may ask?'

'There *is* another here. A different sort of entity. I have been trying to understand it.'

Ah. Ardata. 'Yes?'

She shook her head with an awed expression oddly appropriate to a child's face. 'Its awareness exists on a level incalculably far beyond you or me.'

Murk flinched as if struck. *What? Is this what we are facing?*

He asked, his voice faint, 'Any . . . progress?'

'I am wary. I wonder – how might the process of becoming able to understand this awareness, this entity, cause a change in me? And do I wish to be changed?' She peered up at him suddenly then, as if pleading, appearing so very vulnerable. 'What would you do?'

If Murk had been terrified and appalled before, all was as nothing compared to what now overwhelmed him. *Gods above and below! What to say? And will it be the right choice? Perhaps they had something here that could counter this goddess's power . . . Use her? How could I even consider such a thing? Am I no better than what I've heard of these Thaumaturgs?*

And yet . . . gods, the temptation! Imagine. The right word here or there and who knew how much power might be his . . .

He drew a shuddering dizzying breath. 'I, too, would be wary. As you are.' He swallowed to ease the tension banded about his chest. 'I would wait. Watch. Until I knew more about – well, about everything.'

She'd been nodding solemnly with his words and brushing a hand through the grasses. 'Yes. That was what I was thinking.' She smiled shyly up at him. 'Thank you. Your words are a relief.' She waved her hands as if to encompass all their surroundings. 'This is all so very new and strange.'

'I'm sure it is.'

Still nodding distractedly, she wandered off, and Murk watched her go until the glow faded away into nothing and he knew she was gone. He rocked then, almost tottering as his knees wobbled. He doubled over, hands on thighs, and breathed deeply. *K'rul guide me!* Had that been the right choice? Had he let an unmatched opportunity slip through his fingers? Time would tell. Still weak-kneed, he went to find Yusen.

The captain was standing with Oroth-en. Both were silent, watching the woods. They seemed much alike these two, both guarded and stingy with their words.

'They have fled far,' Oroth-en told Murk and he nodded, having already surmised this. He addressed the elder. 'What are they?'

'They are the children of the Great Goddess. Queen of the Forest.'

'Why did they attack?'

The man frowned his uncertainty. The lines and swirls tattooed in blue around his mouth exaggerated the expression. 'I am not sure. You are foreigners, invaders. They are perhaps defending their lands.'

'Do they attack you?'

'They are a danger to anyone in the woods.'

'But do they attack your villages?'

The suggestion surprised him. 'Goddess, no. Why should they do that?'

Exactly, Murk thought. *Something utterly outside your experience. Why should they? And we possess far more fighting men than you, my friend.* He faced Yusen. 'While it's dark I want to try to contact one of them. Feel them out.'

The captain's expressive brows shot up, but he nodded. 'If you think you can handle it.'

'Yes – well, I *think* so.'

'All right.'

Oroth-en's gaze had been moving between them, narrowed. 'What is this?'

'I'm going to go out for a chat.'

The elder jerked a curt negative. 'I cannot countenance that. It would be very foolish. They are angry. Something has disturbed them.'

I think I know what that is. 'Don't worry. I can take care of myself. I am shaduwam, remember?'

The warlord was unconvinced. He shook his head, very worried. 'Do you know the fate of all the shaduwam, your *mages*, Thaumaturg or otherwise, who dare enter Himatan?'

Murk knew he was about to find out – and that he wouldn't like it.

'The forest consumes all, foreigner.' He raised his arms to the surroundings. 'Everyone and everything is consumed. No matter how powerful they may think themselves. The only way to survive here is to accept this. As we have.'

Murk cocked an eyebrow, but that was all. He was too aware of the precariousness of their position to openly argue with the man. He knew his environment, after all. And they were his guests. 'Well . . .' he said, offering a considered nod. 'I'll keep it in mind.' He saluted Yusen. 'Cap'n . . .'

Yusen just waved him on.

Before he reached the jungle verge a spear haft suddenly snapped across his path and the broad bulk of Ursa blocked his way. 'What is this I hear of you going alone to the children of the Great Queen?' she rumbled.

'I can speak to them.'

'And they can eat you, lover.'

'Do not forget I am a shaduwam. I will be safe.'

She shook her head stubbornly, refusing to move from his path. 'No others have been. Not Thaumaturg or otherwise.'

Murk sighed. *Just what I need – a protective mothering lover. Nothing else for it.*

He raised his Warren and entered Meanas. To Ursa's eyes it was as if he simply disappeared. 'Great Mother!' he heard her exclaim as he hurried on round her. He hadn't really disappeared in truth, merely used a weaving of shadows to hide his presence. He no longer dared enter the Shadow realm of Emurlahn proper.

Enmeshed in his shifting slithering cloak of shadows he jogged past scouts watching the dense jungle. He spotted Sweetly up against the wide trunk of a tree. The scout's gaze seemed to follow him and he raised a hand to tap one ear while shaking his head. Murk just grimaced. *Making too much damned noise. Fine. Fucking show-off.*

He continued on for nearly the rest of the night. By this time, the nightly rains had long since moved on to the southwest. The bright waxing moon had set. Yet the stars remained sharp and the great hanging arc of the portent hung luminous enough to send shafts of jade light down through the canopy. Murk followed the tuggings of his Warren until he sensed the presence of one of the creatures. Here he stopped and crouched among dense broad fronds to weave a sort of sending of Shadows that would speak for him. He worked to weave the slippery half-light until a shifting presence of dusk hovered before him. It rippled as if in some sort of unearthly breeze, perhaps crossing from Emurlahn. This he sent off towards the D'ivers, or Soletaken, or whatever it was, while drops of cold rain fell on his neck and shoulders from the leaves.

His Warren poised, Murk peered through the Shadow-weaving, searching until he found the creature, sprawled, wounded, panting among twisting roots of a dense grove of golden shower trees. It was human, vaguely, but barely so. A sort of half-bird thing, his upper torso feathered and his head that of some species of bird of prey with a savage curved beak and blood-red eyes. Those eyes followed the slow drifting advance of Murk's weaving.

'Compared to the Thaumaturg army of peasants and farmers,' it said, its voice harsh but weak, 'you foreigners fight well.'

A Thaumaturg army? Now? 'Why did you attack us?'

'Why?' A stuttering that Murk supposed was laughter shook it, followed by a convulsion of pain as it huddled into a tighter ball. 'Why? You ask such a stupid question? You invade our lands. You trespass without our leave. And then you have the nerve to think yourselves the victims?'

'We are trying to get home.'

'Home? This is not your home. You do not belong here. And you bring this *thing* with you! We do not want it. Take it away! Go away. Leave us in peace.'

Peace? Gods and demons! 'I'm sorry. We didn't know. We do not think of this – a jungle, a wild land – as peaceful.'

'You are foreigners. Yet we all live the same lives. We are born, we strive, we die. The difference is we do not make war upon our land. We accept it. We are at peace with it.' The creature's gaze shifted from Murk, as if peering above him. 'And here comes peace for me now.'

Struggling to see through the obscuring sending, Murk flinched as something fell upon the thing. A much larger beast, this one scaled mud-grey and olive-green. It raised its bloodied fanged snout from the carcass now clenched in its taloned feet. Nictitating opalescent eyes stabbed at Murk through the sending.

'You are near, mage,' it hissed. 'I can smell you.'

Uh-oh. Time to go.

Sliding from shadow to shadow, Murk succeeded in returning to the clearing where the troop had re-formed a cordon of guards. He slipped through to appear next to Sour – who made a show of casual recognition of his presence without looking up from his work cleaning a ragged savage gash down a merc's leg.

A touch miffed – *how did the man always know?* – Murk crouched beside him. 'Need any help?'

'No. These local boys and girls really know their stuff.'

Murk poked a finger at the leaves and moss gathered on peeled strips of bark. 'What's this?'

'Local medicines. From what I understand they get all they need from the plants 'n' such around.'

Murk grunted as an idea struck. 'No shaduwam.'

'Exactly. Don't need 'em. Everyone knows their stuff and can collect it free of charge.'

He eyed the ugly ragged tear of parted flesh across the woman's lower thigh. 'Nasty wound. Nails and talons. Not like a clean sword cut.'

Sour nodded as was his wont: sourly. He whispered, low, 'Anywhere else I'd say goodbye to the leg. But these locals claim this stuff will hold off any fever and rot.'

'Let's hope.' Murk gave the merc a reassuring nod. She was a swordswoman named Cryseth, hailing from the island of Strike in Falar. 'Have this bound up and good in no time.'

She gave a taut answering jerk of her head and mouthed through clenched teeth, 'An even exchange, mage.'

Murk continued his nod. *Yes, an even exchange. I'll do my damned best.* 'Where's the cap'n?'

Sour tilted his head aside. 'Chattin' with Oroth-en. Something 'bout boats.'

'Right.' He rose but Sour grabbed hold of his jerkin.

'You get through?' he asked, low, now pointing his bearded chin towards the litter.

'Yeah.'

'And?'

'Neutral. So far.'

The little man let out a thankful breath. 'Good. Later.'

Murk grunted an assent and headed off through the tall grasses.

His jerkin, he noted, was now smeared in clotted blood where his partner had clenched a handhold. *Not a goddamned sign, please, Enchantress.*

If Oroth-en and the captain had been talking they weren't now. Yusen looked stymied, rubbing his neck. The elder appeared wary and watchful. Catching sight of Murk the captain nodded a greeting while Oroth-en's surprise was softened by a crooked smile.

Yusen cleared his throat. He appeared to have come to some sort of decision as he crossed his arms and gave Murk his full attention. 'Your report, cadre?'

Murk couldn't help raising a brow, but declined to comment – for now. *Cadre now, is it?* 'They want us gone, sir. Was a warning more than anything else.'

The man did not appear impressed. The long lines that framed his mouth, now partially hidden behind a salt and pepper beard, lengthened as he frowned. 'So I gather.'

'I mean it wasn't random, or hunting, or feeding. Was defensive.'

Now Yusen's brows wrinkled in disbelief. '*Defensive*? They attacked us.'

'In defence of their lands. They call us invaders. Trespassers.'

The man peered about as if searching for something. He waved a hand to the surroundings. 'Trespassers? It's a jungle. An empty blasted wilderness. There's nothing here.' Murk flicked his eyes aside to Oroth-en. 'Other than a few locals, of course,' Yusen added, quickly.

If the elder understood he did not show it. He did incline his head, however, as if granting the point. 'Yes,' he said, 'we are here. I agree with the shaduwam. The children of the forest hope to turn you back. You *are* invaders. Only those countenanced by the Queen may enter here. As for us, we too are children of these lands. Our blood and bones come from it. And in time, we all shall return to it. This is how it should be.'

'But not us . . .' Murk prompted.

The warlord gave an amused half-smile. 'Do not be deceived, Shaduwam. The jungle will eat you just as readily. Even if you are invaders.'

'Eat?' Murk answered. 'You make it sound as if it were some sort of a huge beast . . .'

'It is.'

'Oroth-en and I were discussing boats,' Yusen cut in, impatient.

'Yes?'

'They don't have enough.' Yusen held Murk's gaze, his expression flat, as he added, 'And it would take a very long time to make more. Many days.'

Murk understood the man's meaning and gave a small answering nod. *And in the meantime feeding us would consume everything these people have.*

'What is your advice, cadre?' Yusen asked, his words very slow and solemn.

Sheeit. We are in formal crisis-of-command mode now. He rubbed his slick greasy forehead and winced as the night chittering of the insects suddenly grated on his nerves. They were returning to full blasting force now that the clearing was quiet. *Gods, I'm tired. Only a few hours of the night left. What to do? Every option has its problems. Best to cut our losses, I say.* 'I advise heading back to the coast. We build our own craft then skirt around the shore to the west.'

Oroth-en held out his open hands. 'You may stay with us, of course – but it would be difficult.'

Yusen shook his head. 'Our thanks, but we are too many for you to take in. You hardly have enough as it is.'

'The land will provide. We will forage more widely.'

'I am sure you are capable. But we would not trouble you so.' The ex-officer squinted aside. 'No. We'll head southwest. I understand there's a borderland there. A cordillera. We'll trace it south. Stay under cover.'

Murk nodded curtly. *There we have it. The man's done his job – made a command decision. Glad I'm not the one to have to.* He saluted. 'Seventh Army, yes?'

Yusen's answering salute was more of a dismissal. 'We'll head out tomorrow.'

Murk gave a grin. 'Aye, aye,' and headed off in search of Sour. He looked all over through the trampled stands of grasses of the meadow but found him nowhere. He came across mercenaries lying asleep here and there, wounded men and women sitting up in pain, and their guards plus the local warriors keeping watch on the jungle verge. Where had the fool got to, he wondered, when a spear haft across his chest halted him once more and a great tall familiar figure smothered him in a hug and lifted him from his feet.

'Ha! Returned from the depths of the jungle, I see. Alone you treated with our wild kin, hey? Who else could do such a brave thing!'

Murk pushed himself free of the embrace. 'Yes. Hello, Ursa.'

She stamped the butt of the spear to the ground. 'Hello? Is that all

Ursa gets from her man? You will give me much more later, yes?' and she cuffed him, almost knocking him from his feet.

'Absolutely. Looking forward to it,' he murmured, then, louder, 'I'm searching for my partner, Sour. Seen him?'

She wrinkled her broad nose. 'The smelly fellow? Yes. Headed off with the scouts.'

Murk was surprised. 'What's he doing?'

She waved her irritation. 'Asking a lot of foolish questions.'

'Ah. Well. I will see you later then.' He began backing away.

'Yes! Till then!'

'Right.'

As he walked away he heard her shouting to her comrades: 'All alone he went! What a man! Who else would dare such a thing? Did I not choose well?' He hung his head and felt his shoulders falling. Mercenaries nearby offered merciless grins. Some blew noisy kisses.

Then he ran into Burastan. The Seven Cities woman wore only her loose silk shirt and linen trousers. Her long dark hair hung dishevelled down over her shoulders and her arm was tightly wrapped. She seemed to glower at him, frowning. Annoyed, he snapped, 'What are you looking at?'

'Just trying to figure out what she sees.'

He pushed past her. 'Thanks a lot.' He happened to glance back and saw her still watching after him. *What in the Abyss? Maybe it's as they say: there's nothing that interests a woman more than another woman's interest.*

He sat down in a nook of two roots of a tall wide tree. What the locals called a strangler fig. Here he sat, unable to sleep, and dawn was just a few hours away in any case.

It was after dawn that Sour emerged from the jungle verge accompanied by a gaggle of Oroth-en's scouts. The mercenaries were already up building cookfires, readying equipment and changing bindings on wounds. Murk pushed himself up on to his numb tingling legs, stamped them, and headed over.

'Where were you, dammit?' he demanded, storming up. Then he paused, startled, as his partner turned to him. Gone was his rotting corroded helmet. His greasy curly mop of hair was pulled back and tied. And his face was painted in an approximation of the locals' tattooing. Murk looked him up and down, unable to contain a sneer. 'What's all this? You're no local.'

The man blinked his bulging mismatched eyes. 'No. But these folks know what they're doin' so I figure—'

314

'Well don't. Everyone's going to laugh at you and you'll make us look like idiots. Now wash all that off.'

Sour's pleased expression dropped and he kicked at the dirt. 'I think it's kinda like camouflage, their tattooing 'n' all,' he said, his head lowered. 'I think it could help us, you know.'

'You just look like a play-acting fool.'

Now Sour twisted his mud-caked fingers together, picking at the dried dirt. 'I was just thinking that since they get by maybe we should look at how they do things, you know. Like their medicines!' He shot a quick glance up. 'You should see what they got out here. It's amazing! They say there's this one flower, and if you . . .'

He trailed off. Murk was shaking his head in obvious disapproval. 'What's got into you, Sour? You don't sound like the man I used to know.' He raised his hands. 'Okay. Fine. So they're new and different and interesting. That doesn't mean you have to go all gushing puppy-eyed on them.'

'I wasn't . . .'

But Murk wasn't looking at him any longer. Another figure had emerged from the verdant ocean-green of the hanging leaves. A smeared mixture of the ochre-red soil merged with the thick grey-green of clay covered the man from head to foot. Beneath this layer he wore only a light leather hauberk and a hanging skirt of loose cloth that fell to his knees. Leather swathing wound round his calves down to leather sandals. Twinned long-knives hung on two belts round his waist, and he carried a spear that was nothing more than a stripped branch. This he stamped into the ground as he halted before them. The twig clenched between his teeth slowly lowered.

'What?' the man grunted, and moved on past.

Sour was fairly hugging himself in suppressed glee. 'You was sayin'?' he prompted.

'Nothing,' Murk snapped, and he walked away.

*   *   *

A river stopped their eastward advance. They came upon it suddenly – as one comes across everything suddenly in the deep jungle. Pushing aside wide leaves, Hanu nearly pitched forward down the steep cliff of its shore in a repeat of his plunge into the sinkhole. As it was, he pulled himself back by grasping handholds of the thick leaves and wrenching the brush and nearby trunks. This set off an explosion of startled birds that spread their squawking and squalling alarm in all directions.

Among the dispersing storm Saeng glimpsed crimson longtailed parrots that glided across the river, a gyring flock of brilliant emerald parakeets, and many sunbirds with their bright gold breasts. A shower of flower petals followed the birds' sudden flight. They floated down to cover Hanu's glittering armour in a layer of even more intense sapphire blue and creamy gold.

'*Sunbirds!*' Hanu sent to her, pointing. Saeng nodded and covered a smile at the image of a yakshaka warrior decked out like a giddy child during the spring festival of Light. '*Didn't Mother say those birds were sacred to the old Sun worship?*'

Saeng lost her smile. She shrugged her impatience. 'They're everywhere. Anyway,' she gestured angrily to the sluggish course of the river, 'how're we going to get across *that*?'

'*I don't know.*'

Saeng agreed with the wariness she heard in her brother's thoughts. She knew that others were not afraid of water, but her people were taught to avoid it as treacherous and the carrier of disease and sickness. She didn't know anyone who could swim. As to boats or canoes – she'd never even seen one. And Hanu, well, he'd sink like a stone.

'*I suppose,*' Hanu continued, '*we trace the shore and hope to find a village. They might have canoes.*'

'You can't cross that! You'd sink . . . wouldn't you?'

He edged back from the shore and started pushing his way south, clearing her a path. '*Can't be helped.*'

Saeng followed, picking her way through the serrated knife-sharp edges of the broad leaves. 'Hanu,' she asked after a while, 'in all that time,' *cruel gods – twelve years! Has it truly been that long?* 'was there anyone for you? A girlfriend? Perhaps even . . . a wife?'

He paused in his heaving aside of the thick brush. In his broad armoured back, hunched now, she read an aching sadness. Ancestors knew what emotions might have overcome her should she have dared to touch upon his thoughts. As it was, an image flashed across her mind of searing hot metal and, bewildering to her, an even more painful sense of burning shame. He turned to her, sap running in thick clots down his armoured arms, his helmed head lowered.

'*We are not allowed such things,*' he finally communicated, allowing only a tight sliver of a channel from his thoughts. '*Our loyalty is to be absolute.*'

'Yet you . . . deserted.'

'*They were too late. I had already pledged my loyalty.*'

Something in that frank declaration disturbed Saeng and she backed away. 'To . . . me?'

Perhaps it was the closeness of their linked thoughts, but he seemed to understand her unease and he swept an armoured hand between them as if to diffuse her disquiet. *'As your guardian, Saeng. You yourself conspired in this, yes?'*

Yes, poor Hanu, I did. What choice did you ever have? There, you have found it. My true distress. You have spoken it. My guilt in your bindings. If not for them you never would have . . .

But she could not continue. Could not say it even to herself. And so she turned away to fiercely wipe her eyes, her lips clenched against sobs that tore at her throat. *Oh, Hanu! What have I done to you . . .*

Yet her brother continued, unaware. *'All those nights, Saeng. Watching. Guarding you. After a time I saw hints of the passing spirits as they came to you. So many! The Nak-ta all pledging their service and loyalty . . . to you. I knew then that you were special. That the most important thing for me would be to somehow serve as well. And I know now what you were, are, to them. And to me.'*

Terrible gods, give me the strength! Saeng forced herself round to face her brother – she owed him that. She pulled the back of her hand across her eyes to clear them and stammered, her voice almost strangled with emotion, 'And that is?'

'Our priestess, Saeng. The Priestess of Light come again.'

'No.'

'What else?' He swept his heavy arms wide. *'Is all this for naught? This upheaval? A great change is pending – I heard it whispered among the Thaumaturgs. They fear some rising power. Could this not be you?'*

She backed away in earnest now, shaking her head. 'I do not seek power.'

'Whether you seek it or not, it is on its way. Best be prepared then, yes?'

'Best listen to the lad,' a new voice snarled down upon them and they started, peering about. Hanu's broad yataghan whispered from its oiled wood sheath. Then Saeng spotted the source among a dense tangle of hanging lianas: some sort of long-limbed golden-haired creature peering down with its glittering tiny black eyes. 'Who are you?' she demanded, lifting her chin.

With startling speed the creature descended hand over hand to settle with a heavy thump. It straightened its hunched shaggy back to stand fully as tall as the towering Hanu, then stretched extraordinarily long hairy arms and exposed yellow fangs in a grin. It reminded her of a monstrous gibbon.

'Listen to the freak,' it said and jerked a thumb at Hanu.

317

Caught utterly surprised, Saeng almost choked out a laugh. This *thing* calls Hanu a freak?

Remembering her prior encounter with these children of the Queen of Witches, Saeng found her courage and kept her gaze steady. 'What do you want?'

'I have come all the way down to the profane earth to give you warning.'

'Warning? About what?'

'This.' And the creature thrust out one impossibly long arm to slam Hanu in the chest, sending him flying backwards into the brush. With his other arm he reached out to wrap a long-fingered hand round Saeng's arm and dragged her close. A flip and he now had her leg and he dangled her in the air before his grinning face. 'What would you do, child, were I to do this to you?'

From the brush a groan sounded. The creature's bright black eyes slid aside. 'Shall I twist his head off?'

'No! Please. Don't. I beg you—'

It shook her. 'Beg?' it snarled, offended. 'You're in the jungle, child. Begging won't serve. Did Citravaghra teach you nothing?'

'Citravaghra?'

The creature brought its hand to its mouth to mimic long bared fangs. 'The Night Hunter.'

Ah. So that is his name. 'He spoke to me. He said I – that I had power.'

'Exactly!' The beast tossed her high then caught her leg once more, jerking her neck fiercely. 'Do not move,' he suddenly warned, pointing aside.

Craning her aching neck she spotted Hanu, weapon readied, facing the monster.

'So,' it continued, eyeing her now. 'Have power, do you?' It drew her closer to sniff at her face. Its breath was repulsive. 'Let's see it. Come on.' It shook her anew.

Knives of pain slit into Saeng's neck. 'Please don't do that.'

'What? This?' It dangled her even more savagely.

Blasted insulting creature. Fine! I'll give you power. Saeng reached within herself, remembering the guiding words of her countless tutors to form and concentrate her inner wellspring. Then she gathered all the energy she envisaged dwelling within and sent it lancing at the beast.

A great clap of displaced air boomed before her and the ground leaped up to smack her in the back. She lay for a time, dazed, then slowly straightened, groaning and dizzy.

'Saeng . . .' Hanu murmured, awed.

Before her a great swath had been cut from the ground. It gouged a path through the brush to end at the base of a towering tualang where the broad bulwark of its arched roots had absorbed the blast. But not without damage as a bright fresh crack now curved up its tower-thick trunk. Branches and leaves pelted down from on high. On all sides roars and shrieks and squalls of protest sounded into the waning afternoon light.

Movement and a scrabbling of nails on bark and the gibbon-like creature emerged from among the buttressing roots. It slapped a hand to its head. 'That's . . . a start,' it gasped, breathless.

'A start to what?' Saeng demanded. 'Speak!'

The beast began edging up the trunk by feeling behind itself with its elongated hands and feet. 'To what is to come.' It grinned, baring its teeth.

Saeng closed on the giant of a tree. 'And that is?' she shouted up at the creature.

Now close to the mid-canopy heights it called down, mockingly: 'Something for which you must prepare.'

'Not good enough,' she snarled to herself. Hanu had come to her side but she pushed him back. 'Prepare for *this*, you insolent ape!'

She pooled all her resentment, rage and frustration into one concentrated searing spark and threw it against the base of the tualang.

The release tossed her flying backwards. The next thing she was aware of was Hanu pulling her upright and steadying her. She stood with his aid, blinking, dazed. '*Look!*' he urged, sounding almost fearful.

The immense straight length of the tall emergent tree was swaying and bending like a whipped sapling. Hanu's strong arm urged her back now as bursting explosions shook its base and, one after another, each of the broad arching supporting roots snapped.

Slowly, the great sky-tall stretch of its trunk came tilting down through the canopy, which it crushed and parted with ease. The trunk, far broader round than any hut, slid off its fresh stump, shaking the ground, and seemed to simply lie down across the jungle like a giant taking its ease. Reverberations of the series of crashes echoed from all about. Yet this time the surrounding leagues of forest were utterly silent, as if shocked, or disbelieving.

Strangely, the only thought that came to her was: *I hope I fall as gracefully.*

At her side, Hanu raised his yataghan blade to examine it, shook

319

his helmed head, and sheathed it. *'You hardly need my protection, Saeng.'*

'But I want it.'

He grunted something that might have been a shy sort of gratitude. *'Well.'* He invited her forward. *'Let's see how our friend fared.'*

He helped her up the great tilted base with its torn roots like severed arms reaching to the sky. Together they walked the length of the trunk. It lay as a clear easy path through the crushed tangle. Close to where the crown had snapped away they found the beast. It lay next to the slim bole, one arm beneath it, blinking up at them. 'Shouldn't go throwing trees at people,' it croaked.

'What do you know?' Saeng demanded.

It tugged on its arm. 'Ah, well. Nothing, really. Serves me right. Just what the seers among us sense. A terrifying thing is coming. And you may play a part.'

She knelt to better peer down at it. 'What is your name?'

'My name? Varakapi.'

'And what is this terrifying thing?'

'*Saeng* . . .' Hanu murmured, calling her attention.

'This thing?' the creature answered. A fresh grin grew, pulling its black lips away from its prominent fangs. 'Why, that most terrifying thing of all. Change, of course.'

'*Saeng* . . .' Hanu urged anew.

She straightened. 'What?' He lifted his armoured chin ahead. She turned to squint into the deepening honey gloom of dusk. The fall of the giant tualang had parted a swath of the jungle and now she could glimpse a section of the river. There, in the far distance, a bizarre feature seemed to overtop its flat course. It took some time for her to understand what she was looking at as she'd never before seen one of its type. It appeared to be an enormous bridge.

She glanced down to ask Varakapi of it but snapped her mouth shut. He was gone. She snorted her grudging half-admiration. *Cunning beast.* Yet not truly a beast. A man-ape, child of the jungle, ward of the Queen of Witches, Ardata.

It was long after dusk when they reached the structure. Saeng was in an awful mood. The last stretch had been the worst she'd experienced yet: low-lying swampy ground plagued by biting insects. She was filthy with sweat and reeking mud. And the evening downpour was gathering in rumblings and distant flashes of lightning. The wide causeway that led to the bridge emerged from the muck as if from the sea. Saeng imagined the river must have flooded countless times, or shifted its course, since the edifice was built. Indeed, huge jungle emergents crowned the causeway. They had pushed aside its cyclopean blocks the way a child might knock over toys. The river coursed ahead, silent and dark.

'*We may just make it . . .*' Hanu murmured.

'Not tonight. Not in the dark.'

He glittered now in the night. The rain had cleaned the dust and mud from his inlay mosaic of semi-precious stones. Sapphire, emerald and gold flashed keenly as he moved. He gestured aside. '*Perhaps there is cover from the rain below.*'

'And beasts.'

'*Nothing you cannot handle, Saeng.*'

She followed, wishing she shared his confidence in her abilities. There was cover where the wide arch of the stone bridge cleared the shore, but there was also thick clammy mud that weighted her sandals. Hanu led her to a modest hump where the mud had dried to a hardened cracked surface. She spread her thick sleeping blanket and sat, tucking her legs beneath her.

'*I will try to find dry wood,*' Hanu said and pushed off through the tall stands of grass and cattails.

Once Hanu had been gone for a time the dead came.

Saeng turned her face away; she did not want to deal with them now. Their endless demands and neediness. Who would have imagined that the dead should be so needy? But they were. They did not know the meaning of the word surcease. Which was probably why they wandered, ever searching – searching for something they would not even recognize should they find it.

They watched her silently from among the brush. On all sides their sad liquid eyes implored her. Girls mostly here. Young women. 'What do you want?' she hissed, keeping her gaze lowered.

'*Help us,*' they whispered in her thoughts, pleading.

'How?'

'*Help us.*'

The barest hint of their longing and profound grief touched her then and she felt tears mark their hot descent down her cheeks. 'Go away. I cannot help you.'

'*Help us.*' Something disturbed them then and they retreated into the gloom. Their fading was like a heartbreaking sigh in the night. Hanu emerged from the dry brush to set down an armload of driftwood. He started preparing a fire.

After the blaze came alight, he sat back to regard the surroundings. '*This is a sad place,*' he said.

'Yes. The misery here is so strong even you can sense it, Hanu.' She edged closer to the fire to dry her skirts. 'It seems that for many centuries this bridge has been a favourite site for suicides. Both voluntary and involuntary. Young girls mostly.'

'*Involuntary?*'

'Yes. Pregnant, or lovesick, or just plain despairing, they drowned themselves here. Or were drowned.' She rubbed at her neck. 'I can feel them, Hanu,' she said, her voice growing ever more faint. 'Hundreds of hands at my throat, choking. I am peering up through the water at the faces of brothers and fathers, some rapists, some not. I know that later I will be blamed for my own death. But the most tragic thing is, Hanu, that even now, I still love my family. Even as they—'

'*Saeng!*' Hanu exclaimed, horrorstruck. '*Do not torture yourself. There is nothing you can do.*'

'They seem to think there is.'

'*Well . . . they are mistaken.*'

Saeng didn't know if they were or not – no doubt they pleaded for help from everyone who could sense them. She lay on her side and pulled her legs up close to her chest, tucking in her skirts around them, and stared into the dancing flames of the fire. Something ought to be done. She just had no idea what.

Hanu straightened and turned to face away from the fire.

'You still will not sleep?'

'*No. I will keep watch. The . . . treatments . . . and conditioning leave me able to answer that need while remaining awake.*'

'I see.' She wanted to say she was sorry, but worried that perhaps she shouldn't. After all, this was how he was now and nothing could be done.

With the dawn they ate a very meagre meal of a few remaining scraps of dried fish, the last of their rice and foraged overripe fruit. Then they walked round to climb up on to the broad course of the stone bridge. Saeng had no idea how old it was but was certain her people could never have raised such an immense edifice. It was ancient, then, and cyclopean. Like a mountain of stone laid across the river. Yet some sort of equally vast trauma appeared to have assaulted it. Wide columns and plinths to either side lay fallen or sheared, broken ages ago. The arches no longer ran true, but had been pushed to the side as if a giant had heaved against them. From the silts of the flood plain a massive stone face stared at the sky, its eyes now clumps of grasses, its lips buried in the mud. Cruel, that face appeared to her. Or perhaps merely unfathomable. Saeng brushed at the eternal clouds of insects that surrounded her, while shimmering dragonflies darted about partaking of the massed offering.

Hanu stilled. A man stood awaiting them in the middle of the bridge. With a hand at his back, Saeng urged him onward.

'Greetings,' the man welcomed them, bowing. He was old, dressed in rags that might have once been robes of some kind. His wild hair was a halo about his sun- and wind-darkened wrinkled features and his eyes and grin had a touched, manic look to them. 'Please, accompany me. We get so few visitors. It is an honour! Please,' and he gestured, inviting.

In answer Hanu drew his yataghan and pressed its honed point to the man's bony chest. 'Hanu!' Saeng cried.

'*He is one of them.*'

'Thaumaturg?'

The old man nodded jerkily, grinning his antic manic grin. 'Yes, yes. Such things cannot be hidden from our very own servants, yes? Yes, once. Now I am not. I fled them – but I could not escape them. Yes? You know what I mean. Follow me!' And he turned abruptly, heading off with a quick shuffling gait.

'*He is mad,*' Hanu whispered.

Saeng merely arched a brow. 'What makes you say that?'

'*No – I am certain. It is one of the curses the Thaumaturgs level against any among their number who disagree, foment trouble, or desert the common orthodoxy.*'

Following along, Saeng answered, 'Wouldn't it be easier just to kill them?'

Hanu's armoured boots scraped over the huge paving stones. He walked with his hands clasped at his back. '*No. You miss the point entirely – which is to your credit. You do not understand cruelty. The Thaumaturgs value their thinking minds above all else. To have that torn from you is punishment indeed. Also, keeping such unfortunates about is most instructional to the rest of the rank and file, yes?*'

Saeng shuddered. 'You are right. I do not understand the regimen of cruelty.'

'*For that I am glad.*'

The madman waved them on, grinning like a child on his birthday. 'Come, come. Follow my lead.' He sidled up close to Saeng and lowered his voice as if conferring a secret: 'Though in truth you cannot, as I think differently now and see things which my blinkered brethren are incapable of.'

Saeng nodded her guarded agreement. 'Of that I have no doubt.'

323

'Exactly! And so I must thank them. The method of instruction may be vindictive and inexcusable but in this case it *has* led to enlightenment.' He opened his hands as if to express the obviousness of it. 'You see?

'Yes. I . . . see.'

'Excellent! It is a shame, really. I am suffused with pity for my brothers and sisters who can only writhe like blind worms in the mud while I now soar among boundless vistas.'

'Where are you taking us?' Ahead winds shivered the massed emerald jungle canopy. A storm of crimson and gold flower petals came showering down in the gusts like swirling flocks of birds. Hanu brushed them from his shoulders. The priest held out his cupped hands to gather a few stray petals.

'Tears of Himatan,' he said, offering them to Saeng.

'Pardon?'

'Flower petals. This is what they are. Tears of Himatan.'

Saeng hadn't heard that old superstition since she sat listening to ghost stories as a child. A stray thought – a touch mocking – moved her to ask, 'And what does Himatan weep for?'

'For her children.'

That answer made her shiver and the small hairs of her arms and neck actually stirred. *Mad*, she told herself. *The man is mad.*

Once they were clear of the far end of the cyclopean bridge the forest engulfed them once more and Saeng felt chilled to be among the gloom and dappled shadows. She missed the clean heat of the sun and the woods that had seemed so full of life next to the river – so many new bird calls. One possessed a piercing rising and falling whistle that made her jump each time it let loose.

Carefully, Hanu gestured aside. Two children, a boy and a girl, had emerged from the dense brush. Seeing them just after the madman's odd pronouncement unnerved Saeng even further. They wore only the very traditional, even outmoded now, loin wrap. Their hair also had been prepared in the old style that one only hears of in the folk tales: the head shaved but for a single small tightly braided queue hanging on one side. Each held out a circlet woven of pink and orange flower blossoms.

'Please, take them,' the Thaumaturg said.

Saeng felt positively alarmed now, but offered the children a smile then bent low. The girl slipped her lei over her head. Hanu merely peered down at the boy. Saeng gestured for him to comply. His stance betraying a sigh, her brother took the lei and slipped it over his helm.

'Now you are our honoured guests,' the mage announced. 'Come.

A banquet is being prepared. A momentous event is to come. Sit, rest, enjoy.'

The children led them off the raised causeway into the dense jungle. If there was a path here Saeng could see no sign of it. Then she smelled the familiar homey scent of wood smoke and cooking – or thought she did. Perhaps it was merely the memory of such things that had come to mind. Ahead rose the peaks of some ten or twelve huts standing tall on their poles, as in the traditional construction. The children ran ahead, scattering chickens. Pigs, captured wild ones, rooted under the huts. Each was secured by a rope of woven twine.

'Come, come,' the mage urged and he motioned to a hut where the villagers were gathering. The men and women all looked as if they had been taken straight from some old story from her childhood: hair brush-cut severely short, both men and women, and all in plain blue-dyed shirts. Each bowed to Saeng and Hanu, who answered. They motioned to the main hut's short set of stairs, inviting them in.

Here Saeng paused. So far she had been willing to go along with whatever emerged from the jungle. Some encounters seemed more or less random – such as their meeting with Varakapi – which could have occurred at any day or time. But other meetings seemed fated, or unavoidable. As if they'd been arranged by someone or something. What, or who, that might be Saeng had no idea, though she had her suspicions. The encounter with the man-leopard Citravaghra had possessed that flavour. And she felt it here again, as well. She was inclined to cooperate in that she sensed nothing malign in the attention. Yet it was of course disturbing that she could not yet understand – nor yet know even whether she was capable of understanding.

And as the demented Thaumaturg was a demonstration: some lessons can be most harrowing indeed.

And so she mounted the stairs and took her place on the mats arranged in a broad oval. The mage sat on her right while Hanu took her left. Children came bearing banana leaves, which they laid before each person at the banquet. Then came rice steaming in wide clay pots. Saeng sampled the rice and the stewed meats and spiced vegetable dishes before her but tasted none of it. Flowers adorned every selection. Indeed, a few of the dishes mainly comprised edible flowers. And blossoms adorned every child and adult present.

Outside night fell quickly and torches on poles were lit against the dark. The bright jade glow of the Omen had been haunting the west and now with the darkness it came to dominate the night far more brightly than any full moon. Saeng squinted at one of the open windows, troubled. The Banner, or Scimitar, seemed unaccountably intense this evening. She raised a hand to the west. 'What do you call that light?'

The Thaumaturg's manic features turned down and he sighed heavily, as if suddenly overcome by an unbearable sadness. 'That is the coming judgement of the High King, Kallor. This night it shall fall.'

Saeng dropped the ball of rice she had gathered in her hand. The room darkened as her vision closed to a tight tunnel and a roaring swelled in her hearing as if the descending Omen itself were crashing in upon her. She lowered her head, blinking, and forced the air deep within her chest.

'*Saeng?*' Hanu enquired from her side. She raised a hand to re-assure him. Now she knew why the food tasted of nothing and why the smells seemed only remembered. All were ghosts. The people. The children. Even the village itself. Gone, long gone. Wiped from the earth.

She took a long slow breath to calm the fluttering in her chest then shot a glance to the mage. 'When?'

He raised his head to the west. 'Soon,' he sighed. 'Any moment now.'

Saeng was appalled. She swept a hand over the banquet. 'Then why this? Why not flee now?'

'There is no time. And nowhere to go. What I argued against has come to pass.'

'Then . . . why . . .' Again she gestured helplessly to the gathered bounty.

The madman smiled his understanding. 'We celebrate the High King. Under him we have known centuries of peace and we honour him now. It is our way of saying farewell.'

Saeng could only blink at the mage. 'You . . . *honour* Kallor?'

Now he studied her as if she were the touched one. 'Of course.'

She turned from the madman. 'Hanu,' she began, uncertain how to convey this.

'*Yes?*'

'This insane Thaumaturg says—'

A blazing emerald light pierced the hut and Saeng broke off to cover her gaze. All stood to face the west, hands and arms shading their gazes. A pillar of green light now dominated the western horizon only to fade to nothing even as Saeng glimpsed it. All was complete silence, for the jungle had stilled in every direction. Eerie it was, the unnatural quiet. Saeng blinked, blinded, as after staring at the fire at night.

'Now it comes,' the Thaumaturg breathed into the silence.

Saeng turned on the man. 'Tell me what to do! What must I do to avert this?'

'I do not know what you must do, High Priestess. I can only say that you must not despair. What rises must fall only to rise again. What has gone shall come again. It is the way of the world.'

The surrounding treetops now stirred and groaned in a rising wind and Saeng knew that what was on its way was far more than a strong wind. She took hold of the man's tattered shirt front. 'What does this mean? Platitudes? I asked you to help me, damn you!'

'Saeng?' Hanu asked again. *'What is going on?'*

The man's gaze was fixed far beyond her. 'Yea,' he murmured, 'those who reach for fire shall be destroyed by fire. For she is the Destroyer and the Creator and in her dance are we revealed.'

'What? Babbling . . .' Saeng's attention shifted to the west where a moaning now climbed to a roar as of continuous thunder. Around her parents held children, faces pressed to faces; loved ones hugged, crying and rocking. Then a wall of churning and billowing darkness hammered through the jungle verge, obliterating it, and Saeng screamed.

*   *   *

Mara fell into thin ochre-red muddy soil and rotting leaf matter. Convulsing, she dry-heaved, her body attempting to rid itself of any possible ingested toxins, yet her stomach was empty and so only sticky acid bile burned on her tongue. She spat and gagged.

Birdsong assaulted her ears, along with the whirring and buzzing of countless insects, including the startlingly loud cicadas, which she found particularly maddening. Lurching to her feet she staggered, hands mimicking strangulation. 'Where is he!' she slurred and spat, wiping her mouth. 'I'll fucking kill him.' In the distance, through the fronds and tree trunks, she glimpsed Thaumaturg soldiery marching single file. Labourers passed, bent almost horizontal beneath the tump-lines of enormous loads.

'He's run off,' Petal groaned from nearby.

She searched for and found the man lying like a beached whale. For a moment she entertained the idea of attempting to help him up, reconsidered. There was no way she could budge that great bulk.

Skinner arrived then, and clasping the man by the robes at his shoulder, hauled him to his feet. 'We are returned,' Petal announced, peering about.

'Indeed,' Mara murmured, but only half scathingly. She'd learned more of the man during this mission than she'd ever known before – or in truth had bothered to know before. While he might be awkward, plodding and pedantic in his mannerisms, he was also no fool. She might have been wrong to be so dismissive of him all these years. He was loyal, and conveniently apolitical. Perhaps she should dedicate some time to finding the lever that would bind him to her. If she could then cajole Red to her side . . . then . . . then she would have real clout and could consider intervening in command decisions. If necessary. For Skinner's own good, of course.

A Thaumaturg officer approached, pushing aside the ferns and hanging vines. He saluted Skinner. 'Master Golan has a standing order that you report at once, sir.'

Skinner did not answer the salute. 'Fine,' he growled. The officer inclined his head and marched stiffly away. Skinner indicated the column. 'They are making even less time than I'd imagined.'

'None will see daylight again,' Petal affirmed.

'Well then,' Mara said, and she invited Skinner onward. 'Things are proceeding nicely.'

Master Golan's covered palanquin was now no more than a sagging chair on poles. He sat in it glowering down at them and slapping a horsehair switch about his head and shoulders to ward off the hanging clouds of insects. 'And where have you been?' he demanded. 'Perhaps it is an amusing idiosyncrasy of mine, but I prefer my allies to be present at my battles.'

Skinner gave a vague gesture. 'We were pursuing leads. There have been many attacks, then?'

The Thaumaturg's wide frog mouth clamped shut and he frowned, seemingly uncomfortable.

A scrawny clerk nearby cleared his throat. 'Attacks from the Witch-Queen's creatures have in fact fallen off sharply.'

Master Golan glared at the man.

Skinner gave a slow nod of agreement. 'Excellent. Our approach is working, then. Anything else?'

'No,' the Thaumaturg allowed, almost choking on the word. 'That is all. You will notify me when you next plan on wandering off pursuing these, ah, *leads*. Yes?'

Skinner half bowed. 'Yes.'

'Very good.' Master Golan waved the switch. 'You may go.'

Walking away, Skinner ordered Mara, 'Find me Jacinth and Shijel.'

They met together in conclave around a fire that, like all those kindled here in Himatan, generated far more smoke than any appreciable heat or flame. Skinner stood, helm under an arm, his thick dirty-blond hair flattened with sweat. He was growing a full ruddy-blond beard as well. No scabbard hung from his weapon belt; he'd thrown it away as useless. While everyone else's armour and fittings betrayed the green, black and ochre-rust of corrosion from the constant damp, the glittering black mail that swept down to his ankles revealed no such deterioration. It occurred to Mara that perhaps it was enamelled, or consisted of some sort of non-metal layering. A hardened resin, perhaps.

Shijel had discarded any pretence to armour and wore now only a hauberk of banded layers of leather, and a scarlet silk sash over wide black trousers pulled tight at the ankles by tall sandals. His twinned Untan duelling swords were thrust through the sash. The man had always dressed his black hair straight and long. But now because of the lack of water for washing and the crabs and lice that infested everyone, he had hacked it all off and now stood with a stubbled scalp, scraped raw and clotted by dried scabs of blood. His lean wolfish features held a barely suppressed impatience.

Red, the company's third surviving mage, stood wrapped in his tattered old camp blanket. The grey stubble of a beard, as no one was shaving any more, lined his sunken aged cheeks. The patches of iron-grey hair on his mostly bald pate stood unkempt in all directions. His rheumy eyes, however, still held their usual humour. As if this were all one big joke – on them. Petal stood next to him, appearing even greater in bulk for it. He nibbled on a yellow star-shaped fruit taken from the jungle.

Jacinth came to stand next to Mara and she nodded her greeting. The lieutenant's thick auburn hair was piled up high off her neck and held there by long metal pins. Her armour of leather scales, enamelled bright crimson and engraved in intaglio swirls, appeared no worse for wear. She must oil the damned suit every night. So far Mara had always got along with her, or at least Jacinth was no more dismissive and scornful of her than of anyone else. Everyone knew there was only one reason why she stood now with Skinner – because Shimmer had not.

'Casualties?' Skinner asked her.

She frowned a negative, to which Skinner grunted his acceptance.

This was as much cooperation as the swordswoman ever allowed; she'd probably tell the god of death to piss off.

'We're wasting our time here,' Shijel growled.

Skinner scratched his chin beneath his beard. His gaze remained on the smouldering fire, thoughtful.

Petal cleared his throat, cautiously. 'I am of a mind with our weaponmaster,' he put in.

Shijel appeared quite surprised. 'You are?'

'How so?' Skinner asked, not looking up.

All other eyes turned to the big man and his cheeks flushed. He picked at the fruit. 'Well, clearly Ardata's attention is not here – yes?'

Jacinth rolled her eyes to the branches of the jungle canopy arching above. Mara took it upon herself to prompt, 'Yes?'

'Just so.' Petal nodded, his fat neck wobbling. 'So. The question implied by this is – just what *is* commanding her attention?'

Skinner's gaze rose, slit now almost closed. 'I see your point, Petal.'

The fat man was nodding even more vigorously, his chin doubling and tripling. 'Yes. We were perhaps wrong to so casually allow a certain thing to wander willy-nilly through the jungle. What if it should fall into *her* hands? Would this not complicate things?'

Mara started, surprised. *Ye gods! Why didn't I think of that?*

Skinner was stroking his chin, his gaze on the shadowed recesses of the jungle. 'Thank you, Petal. Perhaps I was too hasty earlier.' The big mage hunched his rounded shoulders, keenly embarrassed by the praise. 'Now we just have to find that damned priest.'

'I believe he travels with the labourers,' Mara supplied.

Skinner gave a curt nod and a wave, indicating the end of the meeting. Everyone went their own way.

＊　　＊　　＊

Many generations ago the fisherfolk of Tien learned not to fool with the field of towering dolmens that lay on this spit of land. It was not for them. Foreigners, however, appeared to never learn better. Every few years or so ships would come and these foreigners would unload their cargo of weapons and metal equipage. Then they would troop inland.

Mostly they returned much diminished in treasure and in blood. Sometimes they never returned. Often these visitations were accompanied by unnatural lights and sounds, or low clouds in which shadowy shapes moved. Sometimes even the earth itself shook. When this happened the fisherfolk hid in their huts, clutched their idols, and prayed to every god and demon in existence that they be passed over.

And so it was even stranger than usual that the low churning clouds should return so long after the latest batch of foreigners had fled. Flickering aurora-like flares cast their glow against the night sky and muted roars and cries terrorized everyone. The earth even shuddered now and then. The clustered households, hardly a village, gathered to decide what to do. Mostly they yelled and wept and struck one another but out of the free-for-all emerged the sound consensus that most societies reach: that the weakest and least important of them should go have a look.

So useless Gall, mostly just called Lackwit, was kicked from the hut and told to go or never be fed again. He cried and clutched the doorpost, but a well-placed bare foot to his face sent their brave scout on his way.

He blubbered and wiped the snot from his face as he staggered up the dunes into the storm of winds and dark roiling clouds. Fiercely blowing sands struck him, as would be the case in any normal windstorm. But this one raged only over the dolmens and not further up the spit in either direction. He tied a scrap of rag over his mouth and nose and leaned into the wind. It was dark now. Churned sand and dust mixed with the clouds to paint everything a dirty yellow. The inconsistent winds gusted fiercely only to suddenly die out to nothing. Gall was reduced to crawling on all fours.

He banged his head into a stone and lay with his arms wrapped around his throbbing skull. After a time he opened his eyes to see that he'd found a dolmen. He could make out other noises now over the booming winds: what sounded like great snarling roars of rage such as those from some enormous animal. Like a bear, was all that he could think of. Except much larger. Large enough to shake the earth.

Yet occasionally other sounds emerged from the dark. What sounded like a woman's cries of pain and grunts of effort. Or dark cursing in words he could not understand. This confused him as he lay behind the cover of the dolmen, until he hit upon the image of a woman cornered by a bear. Another image briefly came to mind, of a bear and a woman mating, and even though the idea aroused him he set it aside because he wanted to be the one mating with the woman. This happy idea emboldened him to crawl closer.

Ahead, the storm of dust and thrown sand thickened to a near soup of darkness. Yet he could still make out something thrashing within: rearing, reaching, writhing. Unfortunately, it didn't resemble either a bear or a woman. The only thing it reminded him of was either a monstrous bat – as he thought he'd glimpsed something like a webbed wing – or a snake, given all the flailing and twisting.

Then a limb emerged above the thickest roiling clouds of dust. It kept on rising, uncoiling, and at its end was an immense dagger-like head. All thoughts of bears and women and bats and snakes slid from Gall. It was something he'd heard told of and described in the stories he loved to listen to at night. A naga. A lizard-snake of the sort who served the Night-Queen, ruler of all the jungle. Caught here in the dolmens. Was that what this field of dolmens was? A huge trap for these creatures? Was this why they'd never seen one before?

The head and long neck thrashed, straining from side to side. Unseen wings pumped, churning up a massive billowing dirty yellow mass of sand and dust that stung his slit eyes. An unnerving groan of grinding stone rose then. A shearing sound, like rock in pain. A great tall silhouette in the darkness shifted. One of the dolmens fell inward, sliding into its separate piled sections. Something struck the ground nearby, in a meaty thump and shush of dry sliding sand and gravel, followed by silence.

The dark cloud slowly dispersed as the sands and dust came drifting down. The inner central ring of gravel appeared to have returned to its normal smooth calm. Heat radiated from it, though, like a stone taken from a fire. To Gall it felt as if he were pressing his face right up against a hearth.

A groan and a cough sounded from somewhere among the standing dolmens. He was encouraged once again, for it sounded like a woman. He searched among the forest of pillars. First he found the missing one. Or rather, where it had once stood at the very edge of the central ring. Now nothing of it remained. Gall wondered where it had gone. Had the naga flown off with it?

Then he found her. The woman. And she was naked! Despite his recent terror Gall's member stirred to urgent life. Now they would mate. He would tell her he rescued her from the naga – just as in the old stories! He, Gall, naga-slayer!

The woman pushed herself upright and peered about. Gall's member wilted as he saw how her eyes sizzled like the sun touching the horizon and how the sands smoked beneath her. Those eyes found him and their hooded gaze seemed to lacerate him like knives. He fell flat to his stomach, cringing and whimpering.

With his hands over his head he could only see the ground nearby. Here bare feet stopped and the goddess – perhaps the Night-Queen herself – spoke: 'I would take your pitiful rags but I see that you've peed in them. And worse.' The feet moved on.

After a time he worked up the courage to raise his head. She was gone. Perhaps the naga had come and taken her too. Or perhaps she rode it like a horse. There were stories of that too. But no, her footprints were clear. She was headed south. Of course! Back to Himatan! Where else would such a one go? Or come from, for that matter.

Gall headed back to the shore. He was frowning and distracted as he tried to work through what he'd seen. It was a labour he was unaccustomed to and it made his head hurt. At the hut the others confronted him.

'What did you see?'

'Were there foreigners there?'

'We heard a yell in the winds – was that you crying for your mother?'

It was a strange sensation for Gall to suddenly discover that everyone was depending upon him. He realized that he didn't want to let them down. And so he clenched his hands and brows and began, slowly, choosing his words with great care: 'I believe a powerful spirit wandered out of Himatan and was trapped by the dolmens. It escaped and returned to the jungle.'

The others stared, stunned and amazed by the most eloquent and cogent speech they'd ever heard from him. Then as a group they fell upon him, beating his back and head with their fists and kicking him.

'Fool!'

'Liar!'

'Expect us to believe that?'

'You never even went, did you!'

Crouched beneath the flurry of blows, Gall wished then that he'd stayed with the whole naga-slaying and mating story instead.

CHAPTER IX

Of the semi-mythical lands some know as 'Jacuruku', accounts from returned shipwrecked sailors tell of great earthworks and large reservoirs within the boundless tracts of deadly jungle. Such claims, if true, lead one to wonder just who may have constructed such large edifices. Very probably they are the remnants of relatives of our own ancestors who themselves, according to legend, once migrated by ship across the waters in search of other lands. For who else could possess the intelligence, the drive and the determination to conquer such unmitigated wilds?

Authors Various
A History of Mare Shipwrecks and Wanderings

FROM GOLAN'S SIDE, PRINCIPAL SCRIBE THORN ANNOUNCED LOUDLY: 'So, a great river blocks our advance, Magister.' Golan's fists, clasping the Rod of Execution behind his back, tightened until they tingled. He noted that he and the scribe stood not a pace from the mud shore of said great river that extended on and on before them as a gently rippling rust-red span many chains across. From the corner of his vision he studied the man for any sign of sarcasm or smirking mockery. Finding no such overt hints on the sallow features, he let go a heavy wondering sigh. 'Indeed, Principal Scribe. Anything else new to report?'

Undeterred, the man consulted a rolled sheet of fibre paper. 'Yes, Magister. Losses continue. Losses among the draught and food animals from sickness, wild animal attacks and desertions. Losses among the—' He broke off as Golan had raised a hand to signal a query.

'Excuse me, Principal Scribe. But did you say "desertions"?'

'Yes, lord.'

'Our draught oxen and mules and our feed cows are deserting us?'

'Yes, lord.'

'Our cause is hopeless indeed,' Golan murmured aside.

Principal Scribe Thorn bowed, his prominent Adam's apple bobbing. 'Magister, each animal is a member of this Righteous Army of Chastisement. Duly entered and so registered. Should they abandon the column for the wilds without permission or orders then we are required to record them as deserters.'

Golan tapped the blackwood rod in one palm. He raised his brows. 'Do go on.'

Thorn returned to the scroll. He tapped his feather quill to his chin. 'The last of the wagons and carts and other such means of transport have been abandoned as undesirable.'

'Meaning there are not enough men and animals to continue to drag the useless things through the jungle.'

'Quite so.'

Golan frowned in slight confusion. 'Yet you say draught animals remain with us – the few who have not fallen to the foaming at the mouth, the walking in circles, these horrifying worm infestations, or this hoof-rot illness.'

'All remaining animals are being transferred to feed stock.'

'Ah, ergo the desertions,' Golan muttered, enlightened.

'I'm sorry, Magister. Was that new orders?' Thorn enquired.

'No. Please do continue.'

Thorn consulted the scroll. 'Ah! Happily, stores and supplies have been reduced to such a point that all can easily be carried by the remaining bearers.'

'Encouraging news indeed.'

'I knew it would please you.'

'And casualties?'

'No casualties from enemy actions or resistance reported, Magister.'

'No casualties? Excellent news.'

The scribe touched the point of his quill to his tongue, which was blackened by the habit. He scribbled on the sheet. 'I did not say that, lord,' he murmured into the limp dissolving papers.

'No? You did not? Go on.'

'Magister, should present rates of deaths from illness and infections continue, then I am saddened to report that we would all be dead within the month.'

'Such a report would show admirable dedication given that we would all be dead.'

Principal Scribe Thorn did not raise his eyes from the sheet as he observed mildly, 'My lord's sophisticated banter is far beyond his humble servant.'

Damn. Thought I had him there. Point to him. Golan returned to tapping the Rod of Execution behind his back. 'And no enemy actions whatsoever? Any reports?'

Thorn rummaged through the misshapen bulging bag at his side, withdrew a roll of parchment. 'No enemy troops, scouts, personnel or forces sighted so far, Magister.'

'Other than those monsters, who, I am given to understand, are known as her children.'

Thorn peered lower down the sheet. 'I have them listed under free agents. Would you have me reassign them?'

'I would not presume to be such a burden.'

The Principal Scribe blinked up at him innocently. 'We all have our burdens to bear, Magister.'

By the ancients, I walked into that one. Today's exchange to him. Golan pursed his lips as he studied the river's sluggish course. 'Your entry, then, for today?'

Principal Scribe Thorn thrust the scroll into the bag and slipped free another sheet. 'The glorious Army of Righteous Chastisement continues its advance, crushing all enemies within its path,' he read.

Golan's brows rose even higher. 'Indeed. Crushing them. Beneath the wheels of our immobilized wagons perhaps. Thorn, we have yet to meet *any* of the enemy.'

'And are crushing them all the more easily for it.'

Golan tilted his head, considering. 'True. Their oversight, then. This not showing up business.'

'Quite.'

Golan slapped his hands together, the rod between. 'Good. Glad to be informed of our glorious advance. Almost all our stores are rotted or abandoned. Our labour force is more than halved. The sick troops outnumber the hale and we have yet to even meet the enemy. All the while our useless Isturé allies merely wander alongside us. Our fate is obviously assured, Thorn.'

The Principal Scribe beamed. 'Your unflagging resoluteness is an inspiration, Magister.'

'An obligation of command, Scribe. Now, if you will excuse me, I really should go and order people about.'

'The troops breathlessly await, I am sure.'

Golan half turned back, almost meaning to call the scribe on that last observation, but in the face of the man's bowing and servile smiling he could only nod as if to agree with the sentiment – however it might have been intended. He headed back to the column. *Must try another tack. Inscrutable obtuseness, perhaps. No, that would allow him full rein. Deliberate contrary misunderstanding then. Yes. That might gain me some ground.*

He waved to waiting officers. 'Start the labourers building rafts.'

The officers bowed. One dropped to a knee before him. 'And the troops, Lord Thaumaturg?'

Golan paused, frowned his uncertainty. 'Yes, what of them?'

Head still bowed, the officer continued, 'Shall they lend a hand with the preparation of the rafts? It would speed construction greatly.'

'By the Wise Ancients, no! They're soldiers, not labourers. Really – ah . . .' To his great discomfort Golan realized he had no idea whom he addressed.

'Sub-commander Waris,' the man supplied, intuiting Golan's predicament.

'Yes, Waris. Really, man. Simply because we are hard pressed here in this barbaric wasteland we mustn't set aside the distinctions of civilized life.'

'Of course, Master.'

Golan tapped the Rod of Execution while peering about. 'Good. Now, set me on my way to the infirmary tents.' The sub-commander urged forward a trooper.

The ranking surgeon was reluctant to direct Golan onward to where awnings hung over shapes laid side by side on the jungle floor. 'There is not much time left him,' the man observed as he wiped the excess blood and gore from his hands and shook them to spatter the trampled grasses and ferns. His apron hung wet with the fluids from his sawing and cutting and this too dripped to the ground. The instruments of his crude trade hung clanking from a belt over his leather apron and were likewise smeared in gore: knives, probes, awls, chisels, and saws of various sizes.

Golan understood that in other cultures these men and women, chirurgeons, doctors, mediciners, call them what you will, were often held in high regard for their knowledge and, presumably, concomitant wisdom. But among the Thaumaturgs they were simply considered skilled labourers, no more important than accomplished seamstresses or glaziers. They merely cut and sewed the flesh. They were no better than carpenters of muscle and bone.

'All I could do was have him choke down a dose of the poppy and leave him to dream his last hours away in peace.' The man took up a file that hung from a leather cord looped at his belt and began sharpening the teeth of one of the saws. He frowned at the short instrument, spat upon it, then rubbed it on his apron leaving it – in Golan's estimation – no cleaner than before. His motions were tired and slow and his eyes were sunk in dark circles. He was clearly exhausted and buried in work.

'Thank you, surgeon. That is all.' The man bowed and turned away to return to the operating table where his assistants held the limbs of his current patient. 'What was it, may I ask?' Golan added.

'Infection, blood-poisoning, gangrene,' the surgeon said, and he gestured to the soldier on the table to indicate that it was all too common. Then he raised the saw and nodded to his assistants. They tensed and the soldier between them sent up a gurgling howl from behind the wide leather gag buckled over his mouth.

Golan headed off, tapping the Rod of Execution behind his back as he walked. Infection. How sad. That one aspect of the flesh that had so far eluded Thaumaturg control. Some theorized that contaminants transferred to the blood whenever it was exposed to the air, as from a wound or puncture. Others insisted that it was an imbalance within the fluids and humours of the body itself. And the human body was a bag of so many such various fluids sloshing and oozing about. *Just look at the pancreas and the gall bladder: no one's even certain what it is they do. The liver flushes the blood; that much has been established with reasonable certitude. But the pancreas? And why in the name of all ancients are there two kidneys? They really must be quite vital.*

Yes, Golan reflected, in agreement with the main course of Thaumaturg thinking: the human body was a truly disorganized organism. A monkey assembled by a committee, as one of his instructors once put it in the Academy. Best to attempt to perfect it – as had been the driving purpose of their inquiry through all the ages.

He reached the most isolated of the awnings tied between the trees and knew then viscerally what he'd known intellectually: here was where the dying were sent. The stench of rotting flesh was indescribable. That and the reek of dressings heavy and sodden with pus, and of course the inevitable sewer stink of voided bowels. Fortunately for Golan, his training and conditioning rendered the fetid atmosphere completely irrelevant: one smell was as any other to him. And strikingly, thinking of scents, flower blossoms did lie tucked in here and there among the stricken in luminous splashes of orange and pink. The infirmary workers must be picking them and laying them here and Golan wondered: was it a gesture for the benefit of the dying, or the benefit of the workers?

The dying lay in well-organized files. Officers, troopers and camp followers, male and female, crammed side by side. Golan was disconcerted to find among their numbers here and there common labourers in their plain dirty loincloths, and he frowned, displeased. The surgeons and their assistants appeared to be taking far too egalitarian an approach to their work. He would have to have a word with them – even if he agreed intellectually with the gesture: in the end all men and women were mere bags of blood and bile no different from one another. It was the principle of rank and class that mattered here. Not the underlying truth of commonality, demonstrated so very, well . . . messily.

Walking the long files of dead and dying he found his man at last and knelt on his haunches next to him: U-Pre, Second in Command. He was pleased to see that the man still lived.

'U-Pre?' he urged, peering closer. The wet reek of gangrene hung as thick as cloth here but Golan was untroubled. 'You are awake?'

The eyelids fluttered open. The head turned and the eyes searched blankly then found his face. Golan noted the pupil dilation of d'bayang poppy. 'Magister,' U-Pre breathed, confused. He suddenly appeared stricken and moved an arm weakly as if to rouse himself. 'My pardon . . .'

Golan waved a hand. 'Do not trouble yourself.' He gave a heavy sigh, nodding at what he saw before him. 'So . . . you are dying. I am saddened. I find I relied upon you a great deal.'

'My apologies, lord,' U-Pre responded, rather dreamily. 'For the inconvenience.'

Golan continued his slow thoughtful nod. 'Yes. This necessity of actually having to give my orders irks me no end. What shall I do?'

U-Pre whispered something too faint for Golan to decipher. 'I'm sorry? What was that?'

The man's brows clenched in concentration and he murmured, 'Sub . . . commander . . . Waris . . .'

'Of course! Yes. The man has already addressed me. Shows subtlety and anticipation. Excellent choice. My thanks, Second in Command. I knew I could rely upon you.'

U-Pre nodded, easing back in relaxation. Golan crouched, quite patient. He was no stranger to death and its stages. The man's pulse at his neck and the strength of his inhalations indicated that he possessed some time yet. Ever the scholar of the body, Golan dispassionately noted movement among the far too old crusted dressings round the man's thigh where one by one pale maggots wiggled free to drop to the ground. *And so too shall we all go. Death is the true great leveller. We humans are perhaps no more than ambulant fertilizer due to deposit ourselves at some future unknown time and place.*

Chilling thoughts for anyone but a Thaumaturg whose eyes have been opened to the deepest wisdom of the underlying truths of existence. Human so-called dignity, individual identity, achievements and accomplishments, all are as nothing. The present is no more than a sweeping eternal fall into a futurity that none can know. To grasp this is to know profound humility. And profound indifference to one's fate.

Golan raised the blackwood Rod of Execution and pressed it to his brow. *I salute you, good servant. The lesson of your life is . . . duty and equanimity.*

He stood to go. At his feet U-Pre stirred as if alarmed. He plucked at his side with a hand. Golan frowned his puzzlement and crouched once more. 'Yes? What is it?'

A corner of tattered parchment peeped out from beneath the man. Golan drew it free and recognized the expedition's journal. He patted U-Pre's shoulder, noted the searing fevered flesh. 'Of course. Evidence. Without this it would be as if we never existed, yes? Very good.' He tucked it under an arm. He touched the rod to his brow once more. 'Farewell, friend.'

At the shore his yakshaka attendants surrounded him once again. Officers came running up, bowing on one knee. 'Where is Sub-commander Waris?' Golan called.

An officer straightened and approached. Golan recognized him as indeed the one who had addressed him earlier. He studied the man's teakwood-dark face, his narrow eyes, now downturned in respect, the thin dusting of a moustache at his lips, and a mouth that appeared to never give anything away. He wore the standard officer's leather banded armour, its fittings staining it in rust now. His dark green Thaumaturg surcoat hung in salt-crusted tatters – as did everyone's.

'You are now second in command, Waris. Congratulations.' The man bowed, saying nothing, and thus confirming Golan's impression of him. He extended the water-stained pages of the journal. 'The Official Expeditionary Annals. For you to keep now.' The man raised both hands to receive the string-bound sheets. 'You spoke to me of the troops lending a hand with the labour. These are dangerous revolutionary ideas you have, Waris. Have a care.

340

However, considering the unusual extremity of our plight, I will allow them to lend a hand. We *are* behind schedule, as you conscientiously point out.' He nodded to his second in command. 'Your proposal carries.'

The man bowed again and backed away, still bent. Five paces off he turned and walked quickly, beckoning the other officers to attend him.

A man of few words. Too few, perhaps.

Glancing about for his litter, Golan glimpsed Principal Scribe Thorn scribbling furiously on his curled sheets, his neck bent like a vulture's, back hunched, blackened tongue clamped firmly between his crooked grey teeth.

Or perhaps not.

*   *   *

Every day's ride brought Prince Jatal and the rag-tag army of the Adwami thrusting ever deeper into Thaumaturg lands, and sank the prince ever further into an uneasy dread. Surely they were fools to believe they could dominate an entire nation with their few thousand horse. Yet the Warleader's arguments were compelling. Somehow the man swept every debate, seemed to have anticipated every objection. Jatal felt as he had as a youth when facing a master across the troughs table. The man was an extraordinarily gifted tactician. These Thaumaturgs were utterly centralized, he constantly assured the council. Control that centre, he told them, and you controlled the provinces.

Such political and strategic doubts were as nothing, however, compared to the searing agony he inflicted upon himself day and night when his thoughts turned to Andanii. Not since the sack of Isana Pura had she come to his tent and he wondered: was she done with him now that victory beckoned so close? Oh, once perhaps she had needed his cooperation to attain her goals. But now that he was no longer necessary, he was as nothing to her. With such jagged thoughts did he slash himself all through the day and on into the awful unbearable evenings while he thrashed and moaned amid his beddings.

And yet . . . what of her whispered words of love and devotion when they had lain wrapped in one another's arms, slick with sweat and deliciously breathless? What of those? How could anyone be that false?

Fool! he berated himself. Look to your brothers! *They* rejected her. And rightly so. You are the weakling to have succumbed to her seductions. How she must have laughed at you. The eager puppy so easy to train!

Nearly blind to his surroundings, Jatal reeled in the saddle, and was almost unhorsed as his mount jumped to avoid a rut in the stone road. Ganell came abreast and peered closely from under the rim of his scarf-wrapped helmet. 'You are unwell, Jatal?' he enquired. 'Perhaps it is the heat – this interminable ride?'

Sudden fury darkened Jatal's vision. *Does this fat oaf think me too soft? Scholar, he considers me? Philosopher? Unable to keep up?*

'I can ride as hard and long as anyone!' he snapped.

The chief of the Awamir pulled his fingers through his thick curled beard, his brows rising.

Jatal pressed the sleeve of his robe to his sweaty heated brow. 'No – my apologies, Ganell. Perhaps it is this quiet. I like it not.'

The big man nodded thoughtfully. 'Aye. Yet our Warleader says we are moving faster than their armies – for now. If we seize Anditi Pura then they will not know what to do, shorn of their Thaumaturg masters.'

'So he assures us.'

'Everything he has predicted, so has it fallen out. Yet he is an out-lander. I understand your doubts. And we far outnumber his men.'

Jatal gave his ally a reassuring nod. 'Yes. Have you seen the princess?'

'She rides with him now at the van. They are together much these days.' He pulled at his beard. 'You do not suspect connivance, do you?' And he added, musing, 'Yet with what would she bribe him?'

Ganell missed the sharp narrowed look Jatal shot him. 'Indeed,' the prince answered tartly.

'Three days to Anditi Pura,' Ganell continued, oblivious of his comrade's mood. 'So says our all too imperious Warleader. Then we—' The big man squinted ahead, raising himself high in his stirrups. 'What in the name of the Hearth-Goddess . . .'

Jatal broke off his musings to shade his gaze. Riders returning from far up the road – scouts by the look of them. He heeled Ash to surge ahead. When he arrived at the van the Warleader had already raised his hand for a halt. He joined the older man and the princess as the scouts babbled their reports, breathless and pointing ahead.

Frowning his disgust, the Warleader raised a gauntleted hand. 'Silence!' He pointed to one. 'You. Report.'

This one drew a deep breath. 'Many men, sir. Across a narrowed way ahead. Ordered for battle.'

Jatal tried to catch Andanii's eyes but she kept her gaze fixed upon the foreign commander. His silvered brows rose. 'Indeed. I am quite surprised. Someone in the capital has shown initiative.'

'What do we do?' Andanii breathed, sounding uncharacteristically nervous.

The Warleader shrugged his broad shoulders and signed the advance. 'We take a look.'

They cantered down a gentle valley slope, Jatal and Andanii at the head of the Elites, together with the Warleader. A dark mass stirred on the slope opposite. It lay athwart the road, while to the south a dense wood extended between the two forces. To the north, dark fields lay glistening in the mid-afternoon sun. Again the foreigner raised his hand for a halt then eased forward on the creaking leather of his saddle, studying the vista. He gestured to the north. 'They have flooded the fields.'

'I thought you said they would marshal no army,' Jatal accused, sounding far more petulant than he'd intended.

If the Warleader was offended, he showed none of it. 'That is no army,' he answered darkly.

'What is it then?' Andanii demanded, not to be put off.

'A mob. Civilians. Farmers. City-dwellers. This only displays their desperation.'

'Or determination?' Jatal suggested. The Warleader turned a ferocious glare on him and for an instant Jatal experienced a startling sense of dislocation. He suddenly knew he'd seen the harsh graven lines of that disapproving face before. Exactly where, though, he could not place.

The Warleader waved for the advance.

'We charge?' Andanii gasped, shocked.

'Of course. Are you not lancers? Ride the filth down!' And the Warleader kneed his mount to gallop ahead.

Andanii urged her mount after him and Jatal, disbelieving, could only do the same. The two thousand Elites surged as well, followed by another five thousand mixed Adwami nobles, knights and lesser mounted retainers. The Warleader's mercenaries, far poorer riders, brought up the rear.

As they closed upon the defenders, Jatal saw that the Warleader was correct. It was a rag-tag mob of men and women, mostly unarmoured, bearing a mismatched forest of weaponry varying from spears to rusted billhooks to farming implements and axes. They had been formed in tight ranks across the road and massed to each side. Clearly they hoped to dull the impetus of the Adwami charge then surround them and drag them down from all sides.

Even though their mounts were far from fresh, Jatal did not doubt that they would win through. There was no way these farmers could hold against a charge. They would break and scatter and the mounted ranks would simply continue on, leaving the trampled obstruction in their dust. All this, it seemed, the foreign Warleader had intuited in an instant. He had come to a decision and enacted his strategy while they still gaped, uncomprehending. A Lord of War indeed. Who was this man? And what would such a one truly want if not riches?

As he tucked the haft of his lance under his right arm, it occurred to him that the answer had lain before him all this time: power, dominion, rulership. A position they were in the process of winning for him.

And has Andanii grasped this already?

Luckily for Jatal they did not face experienced soldiers, for with his flinch at that agonizing thought his lance went wide. Yet Ash knew his work even though his master fumbled. The trained warhorse trampled and pushed aside all who faced him, rearing and kicking on all sides. Jatal threw the lance, as it was useless in such close quarters, and spurred Ash forward, for he knew that further waves were pushing in behind. He slashed with his sabre, a short dirk in his off hand. With no shield in this press he was at a fatal disadvantage and so he kept urging Ash onward. Incredibly, the horde had not broken. It had not given even a reflexive shudder as the long column of horseflesh ploughed into it and now Jatal saw the reason. It sickened him, but there was nothing he could do except continue slashing to either side.

These farmers, or labourers, or city-dwellers, poor men and women alike, were each shackled to their position, fettered to bronze pins hammered between the stones or into the dirt. Most, it was obvious now, cringed from him, shrieking not in battle rage but in abject terror. They waved and thrust their makeshift weapons uselessly and Jatal contemptuously brushed them aside.

What could be the purpose of such a hopeless demonstration?

Rear ranks, including the Warleader's men, now charged ahead, pushing forward, trampling the fettered wretches who could not dodge aside. Jatal rose in his stirrups searching for any sign of Andanii. Then everything changed. The front coursers of the Adwami broke through the massed ranks only to suddenly fall as if scythed down by invisible blades taking their legs out from under them. Jatal heard the rattling and clanking of chain over stone as something quivered, spanning the road and stretching out across the dirt to either side.

Some sort of chain barrier! We are trapped!

Then screams from the forest edge behind him where the flanks of the mass now quivered, surging inward like some animal roused to flight. Jatal glimpsed there towering armoured figures bullying and thrusting, urging the horde inward. Yakshaka. A trap. A Sky-King damned trap! The urge overtook him to find that damned arrogant outlander and cut his head off. *And where was Andanii!*

He did not need to search far for the Warleader for he emerged from the wailing fettered infantry, hacking his way clear with great swings of his two-handed bastard sword. Blood webbed his mail coat and he pushed back his hooded coif to catch Jatal's gaze. His iron-grey hair plastered his head, sweat-soaked. At that moment he appeared to Jatal as the very god of war.

'Take your Elites and bring down those yakshaka scum!' the Warleader commanded.

'*What?*' Jatal shouted, steadying Ash who fought and reared smelling so much blood.

'Thaumaturgs must be here. Commanding. Leave them to me! Go!' and he slapped Ash's flank.

Jatal reared in his saddle raising the *rally* sign and shouting for the Elites, then hauled Ash round and headed for the rear. Line after line of the lancers curved off to follow. For a moment Jatal had despaired. He'd thought the day lost. But this was just their first brush with resistance – it would be absurd to think their goal of dominion could be accomplished without a fight. The Warleader, damn him, was right.

Jatal's lance was gone but he had his sabre and this he waved high, encouraging the Elites. He swung Ash over, rounding the border of the infantry mass, and headed for the nearest giant yakshaka soldier. They could hardly be missed, rearing so tall above the horde, and glittering gold and pink in the late afternoon light.

Charging, he leaned as far forward over his saddle as he dared. He extended the sabre out before him, bearing down upon a giant who only now became aware of the threat. Its armoured helm turned slowly to track him. A huge two-handed yataghan rose like an executioner's axe.

Jatal stormed abreast and swung his sabre, which rebounded ringing as if he'd hammered a stone pillar. Then he was past, his arm hanging utterly numb. His sabre swung dangling from its leather wrist-strap. He yanked one-handed on Ash's reins to curve outward and away, meaning to come round for another pass. Behind came the smash of lances impacting. Wood snapped and burst as charges hit home on the armoured giants. Jatal straightened in his saddle to scan the jammed press of humanity that was the roadway. Some few lancers remained trapped within, but far fewer than before. Even as he watched, a number fell, dragged from their saddles by countless grasping hands to disappear screaming and flailing into the horde.

He glimpsed a Saar lancer charging a yakshaka and the giant's broad yataghan striking the mount's neck to nearly sever it in one massive blow. Rider and mount fell in a tangle of snapping bones and thrown dirt. Elsewhere the giants actually shouldered aside horses that came too close, or reached out and grasped legs or tack to tear riders from their mounts as they passed. But for all that, many now reeled impaled on hafts of wood that stood from them like bizarre decorations.

Yet are any down? I see none. But they are too few. Less than a hundred all told, I should guess. We will grind them down.

He circled his tingling and aching right arm above his head to encourage the column and continued on round to complete the flying circle. Ahead, a lance stood from the ground next to a fallen knight. Jatal leaned far over on his left and reached for it. He snatched it in passing and tucked it under his arm. The crash of hooves announced a rider closing with him: it was Ganell on a massive black stallion. The big man sported a shattered lance that, laughing his battle glee, he raised to salute Jatal.

'They are impossible to miss!' he bellowed, grinning.

Jatal waved him on. Ganell saluted again and charged off, his immense mount pounding the earth.

A great chorus of horrifying screams sounded then and Jatal peered round. It came from the throats of that surging mass of compressed humanity and so full of despair and terror was it that it turned his flesh cold. Even as he watched, a swath of the mass fell, mowed down by some unseen contagion that rolled on to strike a section of the Adwami column. These riders and their mounts fell as well: the horses threw back their heads and tumbled as if mattocked. Their riders rocked backwards as if struck, their robes and armour immediately stained red, and they fell limp.

A portion of the field had now been wiped empty of any standing living being but for one. This single figure sent an atavistic shiver down Jatal's spine: he stood alone in his long blood-spattered mail, his bastard sword red to the hilts. The Warleader. He extended a mail-clad hand, pointing to some hidden foe. Then he charged.

Now Jatal *had* to know. Had to find out. Who was this man that the Thaumaturgs' witchery should not affect him? And why was it that their curse should fall just where *he* was standing? Jatal urged Ash round the clamouring press to follow.

At the swath of fallen corpses Ash suddenly reared as if terrified. He snorted and shook his head, his eyes rolling whitely. He refused to advance despite Jatal's commands. Not wanting to waste any more time fighting his mount, Jatal slid off the saddle and left him there, his reins hanging free. As a trained warhorse he could defend himself.

Some feeling had returned to his hand and he clenched it and shook it as he went. The fallen rabble infantry lay thick here, so thick it was hard to avoid them. The ground was wet and slick with fluids. When he did step on a corpse it gave sickeningly, like a yielding half-full sack of water. It was as if the flesh had been pulverized, reduced to spongy fat. From this cleared swath he had a good view of the battlefield. Ahead, a knot of resistance revealed an inner cordon of yakshaka guarding a circle of Thaumaturg mages at the centre of the formation. Some few Adwami lancers who had forged to the middle assaulted the yakshaka there. As did the Warleader. Somehow he had won through to the Thaumaturgs themselves and there he wreaked bloody slaughter. Jatal ran for him.

On his way he stepped over two fallen yakshaka warriors. Both had suffered astonishing wounds: an arm severed, a torso slashed through from collarbone to ribs revealing its layers of stone armour, bone and fibrous flesh oozing clear fluid. Who was this Warleader to deliver such blows?

He reached the knot of hacked and slaughtered Thaumaturgs even as the Warleader cleaved the last in a great sweep of his two-handed bastard sword. One wounded mage the man grasped by the throat in an armoured fist to raise up close to his face.

'So perished your forebears,' the Warleader snarled, his voice hoarse and quivering, almost inhuman.

The Thaumaturg's eyes widened to huge circles of white all round and he gaped, choking. He raised a bloody shaking hand to point. '*You* . . .' he half-gasped, half-mouthed. Then the fist closed with a popping of cartilage and tearing flesh and the mage spasmed, his body falling limp.

The Warleader's gaze swung round straight into Jatal's staring eyes. What Jatal caught for an instant in those unguarded depths froze him to the spot. Hot rapine and bloodshed blazed there, yes, but beneath this howled a hurricane of rage and a soul-destroying bottomless black despair. This mere glimpse sent him to his knees, almost faint. The Warleader closed over him, raising his gore-slick bastard sword as if he would strike – but hooves shook the ground announcing the arrival of lancers and the Warleader stepped away. His blazing eyes still lingered on Jatal, slit now in suspicion. Their weight seemed to rob him of the ability to speak.

'The yakshaka fight on,' announced Sher' Tal, glowering down, his thick black beard braided now, and tied by leather lacing that hung like ribbons.

'Destroy them,' commanded the Warleader.

But Sher' Tal ignored the order and the Warleader himself; he remained unmoving, his eyes on Jatal. Straightening, Jatal nodded. He drew a shuddering breath. 'Yes. They must be destroyed.'

Sher' Tal scowled but jerked a nod of assent. 'Very well.' He yanked his mount round, favoured the Warleader with one disapproving glare, then charged away.

The Warleader paced off a distance. He stooped to clean his blade on the robes of a dead Thaumaturg. 'As you have no doubt guessed,' he began, gesturing to the corpse, 'they and I have had dealings in the past.'

'Why conceal this?'

The Warleader straightened, turning, but would not meet his eye. 'It was long ago – and I deem it my business.'

'I should think it bears upon our contract.'

The foreigner – and now Jatal wondered, truly a foreigner? – waved a bloodied gauntleted hand in dismissal. 'What care you? You shall have your conquered territory, while I shall have—'

'Your revenge?' Jatal suggested.

The Warleader was quiet for a time. Behind the iron-grey grizzled beard his mouth turned down as if in consideration. Sheathing his sword, he grunted his reluctant agreement. 'Aye . . . my vengeance.'

It seemed to Jatal that he had just learned a fair bit about their mysterious Warleader. He would have to talk all this over—

He spun, searching the corpse-strewn battlefield. 'Andanii!'

To his surprise, and deep annoyance, the Warleader also jerked as if stung. 'This way,' he said, and strode away. He led Jatal off the roadway. They stepped over the trampled fallen, some yet alive and cringing, towards the forest edge. Across the field two or three knots of remaining yakshaka still resisted the circling Adwami. All sported multiple shafts of shattered lances impaling torsos or limbs. Jatal could only wonder at their astounding vitality.

Ahead, a troop of Vehajarwi lancers stood guard in a tight group.

Jatal recognized members of Andanii's personal bodyguard. At their approach they parted, though a touch resentfully, at what they obviously judged an intrusion. Within, Andanii stood steadying herself with a hand tight on a horse's tack. Ar-doard, an old family retainer and her general, knelt at her side busy wrapping her leg over her torn bloodied leathers.

Jatal almost lunged forward but managed to check himself. 'Princess!' he burst out, overly loud. 'You are injured?'

Andanii laughed the comment aside and pushed the sweat-damp hair from her face, dragging a smear of blood across her cheek. 'It is nothing.'

'A fine charge,' the Warleader announced, easing forward. 'Bravely done.'

She inclined her head in pleased acknowledgement of the Warleader's compliment. The man gestured to the saddle. 'May I?'

'Of course you may,' she answered, her lips quirking up.

The Warleader took her into his arms and lifted her into the saddle with familiar ease. Something like an acid fist squeezed Jatal's heart and his vision darkened for a moment; he took a step to steady himself.

'I have studied alchemy and healing for many years, Princess,' the Warleader said. 'Perhaps I may be of assistance?'

Andanii slowly curled the leather reins round one fist. She inclined her head in agreement. 'You may come to my tent.' She gave Jatal a curt nod, 'Prince,' then urged her mount on.

Jatal watched her go. Around him the bodyguard scrambled to their mounts. It seemed to him that the Warleader might have cast him a sidelong glance but Jatal spared the man no attention. His eyes followed Andanii as she rode away. *Look back*, he urged her. *You must. Send me a sign. A hint. Anything to grasp for I am a man drowning.*

But she did not glance back and something broke in Jatal. Something that once broken can never be replaced.

So be it. The lines of an ancient Adwami poet came to him.

> *Love does blossom like the flower*
> *and petals fall like tears.*

*

That night the Adwami celebrated their victory. Jatal thought it would be a subdued affair yet it proved far from it. The cheering and laughter among the gathered hetmen, chieftains and their picked lieutenants in the main tent was as heady as the wine. This had been their first real confrontation with the Thaumaturg forces and they had emerged victorious. Triumph in a few days' time at the capital now seemed certain. Jatal joined in with the toasts but not the cheering and certainly not the laughter. A rigid polite smile was fixed at his lips and his eyes kept returning to two empty positions: neither Andanii nor the Warleader was in attendance. *And who is this Warleader? An old vassal of the Thaumaturgs, obviously. Perhaps decades ago he led one of their countless expeditions into Ardata's jungle abyss. Or perhaps as a dissatisfied general he rose in revolt against them. In any case, that mage certainly recognized him. Shouldn't he share what he now knew with Andanii?*

As the evening lengthened, Jatal could stand it no longer. He rose to his feet, waved off Ganell's entreaties to remain, bowed to his closest allies among the Lesser families, and pushed aside the hanging flap to step out into the cool air of the night. A light rain now fell. A storm rumbled and muttered far off to the east. The tents cast shadows through the fading emerald glow of the Stranger as it arced, now frighteningly dragging its long tail after it.

He headed for Andanii's tent. Long before he reached it, a massive fist took hold of his arm and pulled him aside. Jatal went for his sword. Another large hand pushed the blade back down into its sheath.

'Cool your blood now, Prince,' a low voice rumbled, muted.

Jatal squinted up at the concerned face of the Warleader's second, Scarza. He dropped his gaze to the man's hand at his arm. The hand was removed. 'What is the meaning of this?' he demanded.

'I was thinking we could share a skin of wine and you could tell me all about the glorious victory which I was so negligent as to miss.'

Jatal peered past him to the alley between the tents leading off to the Vehajarwi encampment. Blinking, he squinted up at the half-Trell. 'Where were you?'

'Running and puffing along on my own two feet. I arrived after the battle. Convenient, wouldn't you say?'

Jatal fought a smile, compressed his lips. 'Another time, Scarza.' He moved to pass but the big man interposed himself.

'I did escort the Warleader to the princess's tent,' he said. 'He brought his chest of phials and powders and exotic dusts. I've no doubt she's dreaming pleasant dreams right now.'

'And the Warleader?'

Scarza's round face drew down. 'Well, returned to his tent. Or watching over the progress of the patient.'

Jatal motioned up the lane. 'Let me pass.'

'Now, lad . . .'

'Lad?' Jatal sent his harshest glare.

Scarza scratched his unkempt mess of hair, sighing. 'Ah, Prince,' he sighed. 'There's no need . . .'

Jatal pushed past the man, who made no further effort to intervene. Jatal left him standing there, frowning down at the wineskin in his knotted hands, his thick brows crushed together and his lips pressed tight over his prominent tusks.

A picket of Vehajarwi knights stopped him before he reached the tent. Jatal recognized the captain of Andanii's bodyguard. 'What do you want, Hafinaj?' this one demanded.

Jatal chose to overlook the failure to offer his full title. 'I wish to offer my regards to the princess. And we have matters of command to discuss.'

The captain shook his head. 'She left orders she wasn't to be disturbed.'

'She will receive me. Send word.'

'No. Her orders were clear. No one.'

No one save the damned Warleader! Jatal gritted his teeth. 'You cannot forestall me. As commander—'

The captain looked to the men and women of his contingent. His lips drew back in scorn. 'You command none here among us Vehajarwi.'

Jatal had no idea what to do next. Such an insult demanded a challenge yet that would destroy the alliance. Here, on the very doorstep of their victory. The slap of the man's disrespect was like ice down his back and he felt a strange calm descend upon him. He nodded thoughtfully. 'I see. You are a loyal dog following your mistress's command. I understand such devotion.' He gave the faintest of bows. 'Another time, then.'

The captain watched him narrowly now, uncertain. He glanced to his fellows as if searching for guidance. Jatal turned and walked away. After he had gone a few paces laughter rang through the night – mockery following some insulting murmured comment, no doubt. The iciness gave way to a burning furnace heat that started somewhere in Jatal's belly and rose all the way to sear his face and brow. He continued on stiff legs, a strange blurriness to his vision.

They think I will swallow these insults because I am a weakling – scholar, philosopher and poet. Well, we shall see. There will come a time and I will show them who is weak.

It seemed to Shimmer that the strange creatures of the jungle had lost interest in them. Perhaps she and her companions had lost their novelty; or they had travelled beyond the creatures' territory; or perhaps they were at last drawing near to Ardata and the hidden city of Jakal Viharn. In any case, when she studied the passing vine-hung jungle she glimpsed only mundane animals among the trees and stands of grasses at the shore.

One afternoon her breath caught as they glided noiselessly past a stand of dense brown grasses and there in the midst a great cat crouched at the shore lapping up a drink. It was fully the size of a pony, coloured tawny brown, with enormous fangs that curved down alongside its muzzle. The fanged cat Rutana had mentioned, she imagined. Such beauty and murderous grace bound together. It galled her, but she had to admit that it reminded her of Skinner.

For a time a troop of bearded monkeys shadowed their progress. They employed all their limbs – tails included – to hang from branches far out over the water to investigate the ship as it drifted by. The vessel's ghostly silence must have emboldened them. She, K'azz, Amatt, and Cole watched without speaking or moving as the troop clambered down bent limbs to study them with their large liquid brown eyes.

When one reached out a delicate hand to touch the vessel's side Rutana finally snarled and waved her arms, sending them scattering in a burst of howling shrieking panic. Blazingly bright parakeets and macaws erupted from the nearby cover. They swooped over the river as streaks of snow-white, flaming red and iridescent blue.

'Damned animals,' the woman grumbled. 'I hate them.'

'Animals in general, or monkeys in particular?' Shimmer asked.

Rutana just turned away, muttering beneath her breath.

'We almost had a new crew,' K'azz commented to Shimmer, startling her: it had been so long since he spoke.

She nodded her agreement. 'I've heard stories of vessels crewed by monkeys. A traveller told of how he'd met someone who swore seeing such a ship arrive in Darujhistan.'

K'azz leaned on the railing. 'Seeing that would make me wonder more . . . wherever would such a ship set sail *from?*'

Shimmer crooked a smile. 'Why, from the Land of the Monkey-King, of course.'

K'azz inclined his head to the jungle. 'Something tells me we're not so far from such a land.'

Shimmer lost her smile. 'Perhaps not. Monkey-Queen, then?'

'Queen, yes. Monkeys, no.'

The *Serpent* rocked then, quite gently, as if brushing over a sand-bar, and Shimmer and K'azz shared alarmed glances. They peered over the edge to study the passing murky-ochre waters. Gwynn and Lor-sinn appeared from below. Shimmer noted how the old mage's white hair had grown to a remarkable extent, hanging about his head and shoulders like a great mane, while Lor-sinn appeared to have lost almost all her plumpness and now stood lean and bony in her oversized robes.

A scouring and grating sounded from below and everyone was jerked forward as the bows jumped upwards and the *Serpent* came to a sudden halt in midriver. A rotted spar fell from the shard of the forward mast to crash to the deck. Turgal, Cole and Amatt did not even flinch though the wreckage missed them by a bare arm's length.

'We are run aground?' Lor-sinn wondered aloud.

'In the middle of the channel?' Rutana answered, derisive.

Shimmer noticed that the jungle surrounding them was very quiet. The birds were silent, and no animal hooted or roared. It was as if everything that lived among the trees and shore was suddenly tensed, listening.

In the spell of suspended motion – Shimmer somehow feeling as if they were still moving – K'azz stepped quietly to Cole's side. 'Check the hull,' he murmured.

The short barrel-shaped swordsman flashed a smile of assent and headed for the companionway. Rutana snapped her fingers for Nagal's attention then waved to the bow. The unnaturally large man – perhaps, Shimmer speculated, carrying a touch of the ancient Thelomen blood – actually crouched and edged forward as if wary of attack. The sight of that wariness sent a thrill of fear down Shimmer's spine. *What is it they dread?*

Cole emerged from below and Shimmer glanced to him then could not look away. The swordsman, almost always ready with a smile or a joke, now stood as if bewildered, confusion and unease wrinkling his face.

'Yes?' K'azz urged the man.

'Hull's gone in the bottom,' he murmured, and he rubbed his brow. 'Looks like it rotted away long ago.'

'How then—' Shimmer began but a hiss from Nagal silenced her. He then cast a scathing glare to Rutana who winced and clamped a hand on the amulets tied round her arm and squeezed there, as if massaging a wound. Shimmer dared a step towards the bow and

Rutana let out a low snarl of warning: she ignored it and took one more. Closer to the pointed bow she could see that the *Serpent* had fetched up on some sort of sandbar or bank. Though what such a feature was doing here near the middle of the river she had no idea.

She blew out her breath in disgust. *Gods! What are these two on about?* She turned to K'azz. 'It's just a—' she was silenced again, this time by Nagal snapping up a hand. He eased the hand down to the water as if inviting her to peer closer. Shimmer leaned out over the side. She squinted to see past the dazzling glimmer of the light on the waves and it seemed to her that the sandbar curved downward, disappearing into the darkness of the river rather than shallowing at its edges. In fact, the obstruction now struck her as the shape of a submerged cylinder, like an immense log of titanic scale, fully as large around as their ship itself. Yet pale as if carved of marble. More detail reached her and she backed away, her hand going to her throat. She turned a mute stare of awe on Rutana.

A smile of savage satisfaction crept up the woman's lips and she nodded. *Oh yes, fool!* she seemed to gloat.

For the log or cylinder was not smooth. It was scaled in serried rows and those plate-sized scales pulsed opalescent. It was alive and it was easily of great enough girth to swallow the entire ship.

Slowly, step by step, she eased her way to K'azz's side. They had all gathered around him. Gwynn's white hair now stood up as if in utter fright and he carried his staff readied in both hands. Lorsinn had thrown off her robes and now stood in a thin white silk blouse, the sleeves pushed up her arms. Her Warren was raised, for Shimmer could make out the aura of cobalt mage-fire dancing about her hands and in her eyes. Cole, Turgal and Amatt had ranged themselves before K'azz. Turgal had readied his broad infantryman's shield. Amatt held his two-handed blade, sheathed, in one hand.

'What is it?' Shimmer asked of Gwynn.

'It is a Worm of the Earth,' he answered grimly. 'A scion of D'rek.'

'Older than D'rek,' K'azz answered as if distracted, gazing over the river.

Gwynn frowned at this and eyed his commander as if troubled. Shimmer resolved to question the mage later as to why – should there be a later for any of them. For here was a foe before which even they, Avowed of the Crimson Guard, were helpless.

Nagal urged Rutana forward. Clutching at the mass of amulets that clacked and swung from her neck, she gingerly crossed the littered deck. The *Serpent*'s foredeck couldn't really be called a forecastle in that it was quite low, rising less than Shimmer's height.

It narrowed to a long steeply raked bowsprit. Past this, Shimmer caught movement far upriver: a swelling bulge sweeping the waters as of something immense beneath shifting sluggishly. A sudden bizarre thought struck her then and she almost laughed aloud at its insanity. *How long was this beast and did it follow the entire course of the river – or did the course of the river follow it?*

Nagal, his long hair hanging free down nearly to his waist, grasped Rutana's wrist and lowered her out over the side of the *Serpent*. The Avowed crowded the side as he did so. Shimmer could not speak for her fellow Guards, but she felt a sort of shamefaced embarrassment that this woman should be the one to have to act on their behalf. That, and enormous relief.

Leaning far out and showing almost inhuman strength, Nagal gingerly lowered the sinewy woman into the water until she came to rest upon the back of the colossal beast. Up to her waist in the waters she bent over, hands extended. She murmured and whispered as she rubbed the beast's back.

Shimmer shared an awed glance with Lor-sinn who blew out a breath, suitably impressed. K'azz's angular, bony face revealed only a calm detachment, as if he were merely a disinterested observer and none of this had any bearing upon them.

After a time Shimmer noted another of the unaccountably large waves disturb the surface of the river. It wove up and down towards them until it reached their position and Shimmer caught her breath as the monstrous girth shifted, rolling, and taking Rutana with it. She disappeared into the murky rust-hued waves. Shimmer looked to Nagal, but the man did not appear dismayed; rather, he scanned the waters as if confident of her reappearance.

A grating and scraping shook the decking beneath their feet. The *Serpent* shuddered. Shimmer imagined shield-sized scales gouging wood as they shifted. The bow fell, rocking, and it was apparent to her that the ship had sunk far lower in the water than before. They now had no more freeboard above the waves than the length of her arm.

A splash sounded followed by a gasp and there was Rutana. She threw back her head, her thick mane of kinky hair tossing spray. She swam for the *Serpent*. Nagal reached out again and they clasped wrists and he lifted her up on to the deck. She stood in her sodden layered dresses, water pouring from her. She lifted her chin to them as if in defiance. Her lips were tightly clenched, utterly colourless.

K'azz inclined his head as if to say, well done.

She tossed her hair again, her eyes flashing, and Shimmer's disquiet grew. For the witch's eyes had shone a golden yellow at that instant, and it seemed to her that the pupils were slit like those of a serpent as well.

'And what was that?' Shimmer asked, her voice hoarse with disuse.

The wiry woman shrugged her thin shoulders. 'You could call it a guardian, I suppose. Some say they are drawn here by our mistress. Or perhaps they have merely been driven out of all other regions.'

Like you, Shimmer suddenly realized. *Like these creatures, you and Nagal are worshippers of Ardata and no more human than they. You don't want us, you said. Why do you resent K'azz? Is it because he is human? Are you afraid of losing your goddess, Rutana?*

The woman clamped her lips tight once again, as if regretting even these few words. A shudder took her bony frame, perhaps from the cold, and she lifted her pointed chin upriver. 'We are close now.' She turned away.

Shimmer looked to her Avowed brethren. Cole blew out a breath as if to say, thank the gods! Amatt drew off his great helm revealing his scarred cheeks and ragged beard. He sent a scowl to the waters. Turgal likewise began unbuckling his rusted armour. The cerulean flickerings of Lor-sinn's Warren energies died away and the woman sat heavily on a hatch-cover as if her legs could no longer support her weight. K'azz had already turned away and now stood facing the waters once more, his sinewy hands clasped behind his back. Gwynn met Shimmer's gaze; somehow the man appeared even more unfriendly and gloomy than usual. She gestured him to her. He raised a snowy brow then came to her side.

'Yes?'

She turned away to face the passing waters and reaching jungle branches. Shapes undulated just below the murky waves alongside the vessel. From their spiked back-ridges she knew them as giant sturgeon. 'Good eating, those,' she said, motioning to the fish.

The mage pursed his lips, his eyes questioning. 'So I have heard.'

Shimmer tried to recall her last meal, failed. She spoke as if distracted. 'You say you never came to the interior?'

He straightened, nodding. 'Yes.'

'You heard no rumours? No hints of what we might be facing?'

The older mage's lips drew up as if the questioning amused him. 'I heard many rumours.'

'What were your duties, then, during the time you were here?'

'As I said. We were in the south. Skinner ordered a port city built.'

'So it was his plan to open the country to trade and travel?'

'Yes . . . Eventually.'

'Eventually?'

He shrugged his rounded shoulders. 'The coast is a treacherous swamp. There are no suitable quarries. The fever of chilling-sweats is rampant – people died in droves. These beast Soletaken raided us, dragging men and women into the jungle. We lost many workers and constantly had to raid the villages to procure more.'

Shimmer stared despite herself. She had no idea Skinner's rule had been *that* terrible. 'I didn't know,' she breathed.

The old mage winced, hunching even more. 'I'm not proud of it.'

'You refused to return.'

'Yes. I couldn't go back.'

She then asked, swiftly, in an effort to catch an unguarded re-action, 'What is it about K'azz that makes you uneasy?' The man blinked, surprised. His gaze skittered aside. *Too guarded, this one. Serves me right for trying to get the drop on a mage.*

'You have known him for longer than I,' he began tentatively. 'Did he ever show any, er, *talent*? Any access to the Warrens?'

'No. None that I know of. Why?'

He frowned in thought. 'I cannot place it. But I feel a dim aura around him. It is as if he were connected to a Warren, or a source of some sort. It is like a faint scent in the air. One I cannot identify. And he knows things. Things he shouldn't know.'

'Oh? Things you do not know, so how could he? Is that what you mean?'

A crooked twitch of a smile from the man. 'You are too direct, Shimmer.' He tilted his head as if reconsidering. 'Still – a blustering reaction could have betrayed the truth. But no. Things he ought not to know.'

'Such as?'

Again a shrug. 'Many such instances. Just now, when he remarked that these Worms are far older than D'rek. As soon as he said it I recognized the truth of it. Yet it had never before occurred to me.'

Shimmer grunted, disappointed. She'd hoped for something more. Something pointing to an answer to the mystery that the man had become. 'He has . . . changed,' she remarked, her voice low.

'Yes. He is now closed to me.'

Closed. Yes. He has walled himself off from the rest of us. Why? What is he afraid of? Or hiding? Or protecting us from?

'Look there!' Rutana called, pointing, her voice shrill.

Stone humps stood from the river ahead. As the *Serpent* drew closer they resolved into statues and architectural features – a bell-shaped stupa, a cyclopean lintel over a submerged entranceway. All were gripped in the fists of trees and hung with flowering lianas. All were eroded to shapeless forms. The statues might have once carried human, or even beast, characteristics. All elements of faces or forms had been scoured away. Time and the relentless probing tendrils and roots of the flowers had ground the rock away as if it were mere sand.

'We are close,' Rutana reaffirmed. 'Very close now.'

Close to what? Shimmer wondered. *All I see is a gulf of time. An immensity I cannot even begin to comprehend. Yet is it so? Perhaps it has been only a few brief centuries or decades and that is all that is required to wipe away all remnants and signs of human existence.*

Perhaps this is the true lesson Himatan presents here.

*   *   *

The first hint Pon-lor had that something was going on was when the weasel-thin Thet-mun rushed to Jak's side and whispered excitedly to him. The column had halted and Pon-lor stood breathing heavily, his legs leaden and aching – he wasn't used to so much walking. His arms were tied tightly behind his back. His robes now hung from him sodden and torn, no better than rags. At night he was left lying in the rain. For food, scraps were thrown in the dirt before him; so far he'd refused them all.

It was, he decided, the harshest test yet of his Thaumaturg training in the denial and mastering of the demands of the flesh. Should he survive he might even suggest instituting it as a sort of final examination. Any normal man, he knew, would have succumbed long ago: to starvation, exposure, or any one of a number of sicknesses.

Jak snapped out a series of low orders then swaggered over to stand before him. As he always did, he reached up and made a show of running Pon-lor's jade comb through his long hair. Finishing his ministrations, he knotted the hair through itself then looked him up and down and sniffed his disapproval. 'You're a mess, spoiled noble boy,' he said. 'Want a drink?'

Pon-lor knew a drink wouldn't be forthcoming but his ferocious thirst demanded he nod the affirmative. Jak signed for a skin of water. He took a long drink then stoppered it and handed it off, all the while holding his laughing gaze on Pon-lor's eyes. He edged a half-step closer.

358

'I'm going to break you, noble brat,' he purred, his voice silky with pleasure. 'In a few days you'll beg to drink my piss.'

'I've had worse,' Pon-lor managed to grate, barely.

The youth's arrogant twist of the lips pulled back into rage and his right arm came up. His fist exploded against the side of Pon-lor's head and sent him to the ground. Darkness and bursts of light warred in his vision. Myint's hysterical hyena laugh sounded over him. Her knee pressed into his stomach, cutting off his breath. A gag was wrestled over his mouth. He was dragged through the mud and slammed against a tree. More ropes secured him to it.

When his vision cleared and he shook his loosened hair from before his face the troop had disappeared into the jungle. One guard remained. The least of them, a kid named Heng-lon whose appearance had so far evoked only sympathy from Pon-lor: beneath his bristling brush-cut hair the left side of his skull was flattened and pushed in, the eye on that side stared off permanently to the left, he breathed through his mouth, and he had the mental age of a five-year-old.

The youth clutched his spear in both hands, scanning the jungle, obviously terrified to be alone. Seeing Pon-lor awake he wet his lips and sidled over. Grinning, he set his spear against the tree then fumbled at the ties of his short trousers.

Pon-lor quickly lowered his head. A warm stream hissed against his crown then splashed over his shoulder and down into his lap. The kid giggled. 'Always wanted to do that,' he said. 'No one c'n top this story!'

This is proving quite the test indeed . . .

I could give you a story no one could top. 'How my head got to be on this shelf' perhaps. Or 'How I lost all my limbs'. But that would be too easy.

Pon-lor struggled instead with keeping his hands, tied behind him, in the meditative position of forefingers touching thumbs.

'What'cha doin'?' Heng-lon asked.

Pon-lor looked up, raising his chin and the gag tied there. The youth reached for the gag then stopped, thinking better of it. He took up his spear and backed away. While Pon-lor meditated, the youth set to starting a fire.

It took a great deal of effort to force himself to slow his breathing, but Pon-lor finally managed to isolate all the tension, locate the suppressed rage, and mentally uncoil it to ease his flesh into the requisite degree of relaxation. From this point he was able to concentrate upon separating his spirit – the Nak – from its fleshly housing.

What are they up to out there? Well, we shall soon see.

But he'd forgotten the psychic storm that was Ardata's aura. The punishing stream snatched him and cast him spinning. He knew he was an instant from wandering lost forever when he remembered his lessons and forced himself to re-imagine his presence not as a solid entity but as downy fluff, as dust, as a handful of drifting motes. Now the storm raged on but passed through him, like wind through a tree.

He searched for Jak and his band of pathetic cast-off bandits.

Before he could track down their auras a blazing presence in the psychic landscape screamed for his attention. For an instant he felt himself shrinking in fear: was this *her*? The Queen of Monsters herself?

But the essence was entirely different. In fact, it was so entirely different it appeared almost alien. What was this thing? Was it a denizen of this jungle? Yet such awesome power. If he were a candle flame of presence flickering in the half-spirit realm then this thing's projection here towered as a coruscating sky-high pillar. He dared to drift closer to the presence and cast a greeting.

'*Who are you?*'

'*Who are you?*' a voice answered in his consciousness – a child's voice, unbelievably.

'*What are you?*'

'*I do not know. What are you?*'

'*A mage. A traveller here.*'

'*A mage? Ah – a manipulator of interdimensional leakage.*'

A what? Pon-lor wondered.

'*The flavour of your art is oddly familiar to me. Why should this be? I must examine you.*'

A bulge swelled the side of the towering white-argent pillar. A mountain of puissance descended towards him – enough to scatter his atoms.

Pon-lor snapped away. His chest swelled reflexively, drawing in a panicked breath. He opened his eyes expecting a firestorm about him, the trees drifting away in motes of soot. His palms tingled with sweat and his heart was pounding as if he'd just completed a full course of muscle isolation.

All was quiet. Heng-lon glanced back to him from where he sat poking at the fire, his spear across his lap. It was night. A light rain had begun. They were not alone; someone was approaching.

A large party. He sensed them but the kid hadn't yet. Presently, the lad sprang to his feet, spear levelled in both hands. He jerked the iron point left and right. It trembled in the firelight. The youth backed up until he stood level with Pon-lor. He drew a short-bladed knife from his sash.

Not so stupid after all, then, if his plan is to release me to help in any possible fight to come.

But it was a grinning Thet-mun who emerged from the dark. The firelight glimmered from his teeth and eyes. He looked immensely pleased and went straight to their heaped gear. 'Where's the palm wine?' he demanded. 'Ha! Here's my beauty.' He lifted a skin and took a long pull, wiped his mouth.

'We have them, turtle-boy! Got them both. You should've seen it. It was laughable. They walked right in. Ha!' He raised the skin and poured another stream into his mouth.

Heng-lon – turtle-boy, apparently – laughed as well, though he obviously had no idea why.

The rest of the bandit crew now came tumbling in from the dark. All were grinning and snorting laughs. Two carried a roped body between them that they threw down next to Pon-lor. A girl, or rather a young woman. She was unconscious.

By the Founders! Was this the witch? Could they have really . . .

Jak arrived to snatch the skin of palm wine from Thet-mun's hand. He leaned over Pon-lor, took a sip, then stood staring down at him for some time. Finally, he pulled an exaggerated moue of disappointment. 'You high and mighties. Look at you. Useless.' He straightened to peer about, spread his arms wide. 'I beat you! Me! A lowly cast-out nobody you *sneered* at! Well . . . look at you now!'

'Coming!' one of the bandits shouted from the jungle.

Coming? What could they . . .

Heavy measured steps sounded over the pattering of raindrops. They came from beyond the cover of thick wide leaves. Pon-lor straightened where he sat. *They've done it! Brought it to me! Time to end this ridiculous charade.*

A heavy curved blade flashed before his vision to press against his neck. Myint's head rested on his shoulder from behind. 'Don't try anything, sweetie.' And she blew a kiss into his ear.

Pon-lor let his shoulders drop. *Why do I keep underestimating these wretches?*

Jak snapped his fingers, gesturing. A spear was thrown to him and he spun it to rest its keen bright iron point against the unconscious woman's side. The stand of tall ferns shook, tossing raindrops everywhere, then was thrust aside and an armoured giant strode through, a wide bright yataghan blade outstretched before it.

'Hold!' Jak called. 'Or I thrust through your mistress.'

To Pon-lor's utter astonishment the yakshaka froze.

'Sheathe your weapon.'

The soldier complied.

Pon-lor stared, dumbfounded. How was this possible? How was its conditioning overcome? He had to discover how. This simply had to be reported to the ruling Circle of Masters.

Jak was nodding to himself and he shot Pon-lor a quick triumphant glance to make certain he was taking this in. 'Your mistress will be under guard constantly. Someone will always be within sword's reach. So behave.' He pointed to a tree on the far side of the encampment. 'Sit.'

The armoured giant's helm turned aside as it regarded the tree. Then it lumbered heavily to the spot and put its back to the trunk to stand glittering in the shadows, arms crossed.

Jak shrugged. 'Good enough.' He looked to Pon-lor, jerked his head to the yakshaka. 'I couldn't believe it understood me.' He frowned, lowered his voice. 'Is there a man in there?' Then, realizing, he waved the question aside.

'What about you, sweetmeat?' Myint breathed into his ear. 'You gonna behave?'

Pon-lor gave a long slow nod. Yes, he would. At least until he had questioned this witch.

'Aw.' Myint pouted her disappointment. It was an awful twisting of her features, given her disfigured lip. She slit the gag, managing to slice his cheek and ear at the same time. 'Sorry,' she dropped, not sorry at all, as she walked away.

Pon-lor felt the warm blood drip down his neck while he sat crosslegged, staring straight ahead at the shadowed figure across the camp where the firelight winked and flashed from its mosaic inlay. Perhaps it was only his impression, but it seemed the creature dropped its helmed head as if unable to meet his gaze.

The next day Pon-lor was awake before everyone, as usual. He waited for the woman to rouse. Through the night the bandits had been trading off watches, keeping someone always close. Now it was Myint's turn and she hauled the woman up and marched her off – perhaps to see to her morning toilet.

Pon-lor was disappointed by what he saw. She was just a local girl; a peasant from any one of their villages. For a time he'd played with the possibility that she was some sort of agent for Ardata and that by capturing her he could learn secrets of the Witch-Queen's court in fabled Jakal Viharn. Now, however, he had to wrestle with the mystery of how this peasant could possibly have suborned a yakshaka soldier. The most likely answer was that she had not; that this soldier was flawed and had somehow fixated upon her. She probably had no idea why this thing was following her around, and had become terrified and run off.

Or had been run off by her terrified fellow villagers.

As the bandits broke camp Pon-lor sat, still tied up, and wondered why Jak had brought her back. If she really was an agent of Ardata then he ought to have killed her right away. That would have been the safest course. Like him, then, Jak must have realized that she was no servant of the Witch-Queen. She was merely his convenient guarantor of the yakshaka's cooperation. Clearly, then, once Jak had delivered his prize, he would still have her for his revenge.

Very greedy is this Kenjak Ashevajak, the Bandit Lord.

And clearly it was about time to end this investigation. A word or two with the girl should settle things one way or the other and then he would be free to collect their wayward property for examination and dissection back in Anditi Pura. This particular soldier must possess some flaw that had allowed it to shake off its immediate orders. But there was no way it would be able to resist the deep-conditioned key command words that lay at the foundation of its reconstructed consciousness.

Pon-lor broke off his musing as he became aware of someone's steady regard. He turned to see the villager, the young woman, frozen at the edge of camp, staring at him with ferocious intensity. He gave her a small nod that said: yes indeed, I am a Thaumaturg. Then he raised his brows to say: don't you think we ought to have a chat?

Her reaction surprised him. Instead of deflating, terrified, she raised her chin and waved him off with the back of a hand as if to answer: I will accept no aid from a filthy wretch such as yourself.

Whence came such regal poise? Then he glanced to the silent waiting yakshaka and shook his head in sad regret. *Ah, child, just because you may command such a thing for the moment does not mean you have conquered the world.*

Myint jabbed with her spear none too gently, urging the young woman onward. Jak, wolfing down the last of his morning meal of rice and boiled plants, came to meet her. He was brushing his hands free of the sticky grains. 'You surprised me once before, witch,' he

363

said. 'But not again. Try anything and you'll get run through before you can raise your spells. Understand?'

Though her hair was a dirty nest of twigs, her face smudged with dirt, and her skirts sodden and muddy, the young woman still managed to maintain her poise. The answering nod she bestowed upon the bandit was a sneer.

Pon-lor winced, for he knew this was precisely the wrong approach to take with Kenjak Ashevajak. The young man raised his hand to strike her across the face but the grating of stone and the hiss of steel on wood halted him. All eyes turned to the yakshaka; it had taken a step and half drawn its sword.

Jak slowly lowered his hand. 'For now, bitch,' he murmured, low. 'For now.'

Throughout, the young woman hadn't flinched, and Pon-lor felt a grudging admiration. He also saw now that the woman had adopted this attitude of scornful superiority precisely because it so enraged the bandit – just as he wielded it as well.

Jak turned to the camp where everyone stood or crouched, motionless, watching. 'Well?' he demanded. 'What are you all standing around for? You lazy useless idiots!' He swung a kick at Thet-mun. 'Let's get going!'

Through the last preparations of breaking camp, Pon-lor wondered which course he ought to pursue. Should he slay the lot of them? They were now leading him in entirely the wrong direction. Yet without their guidance he would be utterly lost in this dense green abyss. Coercion or bribery then. He would leave one alive and promise him or her a rich reward for guiding him back – or he would torture the outlaw into cooperation. So, which one?

A point jabbed him in the back and he flinched into motion while glaring over his shoulder. It was a grinning Thet-mun, his livid facial pocks and pimples even worse now, and his hair a matted glistening ropy cascade.

Pon-lor realized that he had his man. They marched through the thick undergrowth, shouldering aside hanging lianas dense with clinging blossoms and pushing through stands of razor-edged grasses. After the line of march had strung everyone out, Pon-lor cleared his throat and murmured, low, 'That fool Jak treats you like a dog.'

The point jabbed him. 'Quiet, you.'

'You deserve better – you're the best scout here. Where would they be without you?'

He was jabbed again. ''Strue,' the youth snarled. 'But Jak . . . He has the plans.'

'You could too—'

'Don't listen to that one,' a girl cut in from behind.

Pon-lor peered back over his shoulder. The witch paced behind Thet-mun. Myint walked behind her, laughing silently, spear in hand. 'You should kill him right now,' the witch continued. 'His kind mean to bring the Visitor down upon us and wipe all of us from the face of the earth.'

Pon-lor stared back at the young peasant woman. Her answering gaze remained steady and defiant. 'That's nonsense. The ruling Circle of Masters would never do such a thing.'

'How do you know this?'

Pon-lor drew breath to answer, clamped his mouth shut. *Because . . . there are rumours . . . they'd tried it before. And it had been a disaster.*

In the face of his silence Myint laughed her hyena scorn. She set her spearhead alongside the woman's neck. 'Speak again and it'll be gags for both of you.'

Pon-lor turned away. *Damn the witch. By the teachings of the ancients, I am now tired of this. I have quite demonstrated my denial of the flesh, my indifferent endurance of arduous conditions. The Masters cannot fault my assiduousness here! At the next stop, when everyone's gathered together, I'll put an end to it.*

Towards midday the troop gathered for a break in the march. The sun stabbed down in a punishing blinding glare through gaps in the high canopy. The bird whistles and distant animal hoots and roars had died down with the heat of noon. The ground here was covered by an overlay of twisting knotted roots that supported the surrounding massive trunks, which were bulwarked by enormously wide bases, as large as buildings. Pon-lor made a show of throwing himself down to sit hunched. He drew in great shuddering breaths as if he were utterly spent.

Another of the troop guarded him now, a quiet oldster with a hard cold gaze. Probably a runaway petty criminal. Or maybe not. He mustn't make the mistake of underestimating these outcasts again. Perhaps the man was a multiple murderer. Or a violent rapist. There was no way to know. He wasn't certain of his name – not that it mattered. Weenas, perhaps. Something like that.

He turned his head to glance sideways up at the man. 'Hey . . . you.'

The eyes snapped to his, then narrowed, calculating. Without a change of his indifferent expression he jabbed the glinting point of his spearhead into Pon-lor's shoulder. The point withdrew smeared a bright crimson. Pon-lor clamped down on the pain and kept his face flat, determined to match the man's impassiveness. The oldster, Weeras, studied the wound and licked his lips, smiling.

Sadist. Even worse than I'd imagined. The throat for this one, I think. So vital, that one slim locale. So much going on in such a narrow passage.

Pon-lor pitched his voice low: 'How can you breathe with . . .' then he trailed off as he realized something.

The old man's face wrinkled up in annoyance. 'What?'

Pon-lor searched the surrounding jungle. It was silent. The constant hum and susurration of insects had fallen away. No birds called from the canopy. Casting his awareness wide he now detected why: they were surrounded. The yakshaka, he noted, had turned its helmed head to stare off into the dense leaves as if at nothing. He stood, called out, 'Jak!'

'Shut the abyss up!' Weeras snarled, and thrust at him.

He easily sidestepped the point and kicked the old man down. 'Where are your scouts?' he called to Jak who now stared, frozen, a handful of rice at his mouth.

Thet-mun, next to the bandit leader, was not so slow to understand. He threw himself flat, disappearing immediately between the thick snaking roots everyone sat upon.

I chose well in that one, Pon-lor congratulated himself.

A hissing like bees sounded all round. Leaves were flicked, then a storm of arrows punished the gathered bandits. Complete chaos engulfed the troop. Everyone scattered. Some even dropped their weapons to run, terrified.

'Cannibals!' someone screeched.

Cannibals? Pon-lor wondered, quite astonished. He shifted to put his back to one of the immense tree trunks. He edged his head aside as something darted towards him. A slim arrow slammed into the thick spongy bark next to his head. Paint and feathers decorated the deadly graceful object and he understood. *Ah, these villagers are from the border region. They grew up hearing the stories of the natives of Himatan. Ardata's Children, call them what you will. Cannibals, head-hunters. Of course such a reputation for ferocity serves these locals well – it keeps everyone away, doesn't it?*

A sudden wash of enormous power, like a huge wave, thrust him back into the tree. The witch was raising her aura. And what strength! He stared, stunned by the depth of it. How came she by such might? She screamed however, then, and her aura flickered, snapping away just as it burgeoned to life. She clutched her leg where an arrow now pierced her thigh.

Jak and Myint had pulled together a group and this knot now charged the jungle, probably meaning to break through the encirclement. Showing surprising speed, the yakshaka scooped up the witch and stormed off in the opposite direction, crashing through the undergrowth like an enraged elephant.

Pon-lor searched for, and found, Thet-mun's frantic gaze where he peered out over the top of a root. Pon-lor motioned aside, after the fleeing yakshaka, and after scanning his fallen cohorts around him the lad gave a curt nod.

His arms still tied behind his back, Pon-lor ran after the yakshaka. Arrows hissed past him. One plucked his arm. As he ran he sensed a growing numbness in that arm – a toxin. He suppressed the blood flow to that limb and hoped to live long enough to deal with it later.

Lying among the dead leaves ahead was one of these Himatan locals. The warrior was painted head to foot and wore a kind of armour over his chest of bent bamboo and rattan strips lashed together. His head was crushed as from some terrific blow. The yakshaka. At least he was still on the right trail. Soon, however, he knew he would lose his way. He believed he could now sense this witch should he put his mind to it; but the question was how best to get from here to there, what to eat, and what not to step on.

He ran on then, not certain of his direction, but wanting to put some distance between himself and the ambush behind. After some time, pushing through hanging vines and tracing round the fallen rotting logs of these forest giants, he paused for breath, panting. This time he was not faking it; Thaumaturg training, it seemed, was perhaps negligent of raw physical endurance.

He flinched, then, jumping, as someone emerged from the thick dripping fronds next to him: Thet-mun. 'You're too loud,' the youth growled, peering warily about.

'Cut my bonds.'

'What for? What will you do for me?'

'Get me back and I'll see to it that you're richly rewarded.'

The youth grinned. 'That's more like it.' He pulled out a large, wicked-looking curved knife.

After which I'll see you executed as a criminal.

He sawed through Pon-lor's bonds. 'You're wounded,' he yelped, indicating his arm.

'Yes.'

The youth stared, confused. 'But . . . there's poison on them arrows.'

'Yes, there is.'

The youth's face revealed unguarded wonder. He drew a small packet from within his shirt. He offered it to Pon-lor. 'Well . . . try this.'

Pon-lor unwrapped it to reveal a whitish paste. 'What is this?'

'Should kill that poison.'

Kill it? Ah, an antidote of some kind. Perhaps an alkaline agent. I am impressed. He smeared some on the cut. Thet-mun tore a strip of cloth and bound it. 'How did you learn this?' Pon-lor asked.

'My ol' aunt taught me the recipe. Come to think of it, some called her a witch, too.'

'Ah. So, which way now?'

The youth pointed the blade. 'That way's west.'

'No. Which way to the yakshaka?'

The scout flinched, hunching. 'Wha'? No one said anything about trackin' *him* down.'

'I have to return with it. That's the only way I – we – can get our reward.'

Sheathing his blade, the pock-marked youth glanced away, frowning, sullen.

Pon-lor could see his mind working: how he was thinking that maybe he would have a better chance alone after all, and so he murmured, 'What will you do when you run into those cannibals again?' A shudder of terror rewarded him. 'Or the Night Children? They say the man-leopard, that legendary killer, still haunts these forests. Tell me, Thet. What will you do if he comes for you in the night?'

The youth ground his teeth, almost whining in his frustration and fear. 'You made yer damned point.'

'Very good. Now, which way?'

He gestured onward. 'Couldn't miss it if you was blind.'

Pon-lor invited him to lead the way.

*   *   *

Alone in the jungle a woman knelt drinking water she cupped in a hand from a thin stream. She wore only a cloth wrapped about her loins. Her breasts were high and firm, the areolae a dark nut-brown. Sweat-caked dust and dirt smeared her limbs, face and torso. Her hair stood in all directions as a wet black nest. Hand at her mouth she paused. Her bright hazel eyes shifted aside and she smiled, humourlessly.

Straightening, Spite kept her arms loose at her sides. She cocked her head, scanning the bamboo thicket surrounding her. She called in a sing-song voice: 'Come out, come out, wherever you are . . .'

The amber light of dawn fought the lingering emerald glow of the Visitor, which now bruised the sky all the night and the day. Mist coiled among bamboo shafts and through the vapours low hunched shapes slunk forward. Spite turned, scanning the grove; she was surrounded.

The nearest creature reared up on its hind legs, squat and wide, yet far taller than she. It was vaguely humanoid with thick muscular limbs bristling with hair, and a wide deep chest. It stood hunched as if unable to straighten fully. Its wide blunt head, likewise thick with bristling hair, boasting thrusting tusks and black glittering eyes, resembled more that of a giant wild boar than anything human.

Spite sneered her distaste. 'Soletaken degenerates. Gone feral, I see. What would you have of me?'

The creature waved a wide, black-taloned hand. 'Begone.'

'Begone? How dare you? Do you know who I am? My *lineage*?'

'Aye,' the boar-beast growled deep in its throat. 'We know you. Thus – we wish you gone.'

'Well . . . no. I will not. I seek something stolen from me. This has nothing to do with you.'

'We do not care. We want you gone.'

'Sorry to disappoint.'

The boar-beast raised its gaze to indicate the way she had come. 'There is a pit in the north that awaits you, Spite. Perhaps we shall shove you back in.'

Spite's bright amber eyes hardened and her lips compressed. 'Do not tempt my anger, you pathetic night-beasts. Slink away before I tire of you.'

The boar-beast drew itself up even taller. 'We tire of *you*!' And it leaped.

A blast of argent power met it in mid-leap. The creature spun away, crashing through the bamboo. Another beast slammed into Spite, sending her tumbling. Wide and far more burly than any human, it shambled off on all fours, its thick black hair all grey down its back.

Snarling her rage Spite climbed to her feet and wiped the mud from her face. 'I'll have all your heads for this!'

'But the muck and mire is a fitting place for you, Spite,' commented a new voice, one much more smooth and cultured. A man emerged from the mist. Lean and muscled, this one's hair was a short tawny yellow, like a pelt, and his eyes glowed as brightly amber as Spite's. The fangs of a hunting cat dominated his mouth.

Spite hunched, now wary. '*You* I know.'

The man inclined his head, acknowledging the compliment. 'We have warned you, Spite. We ask that you go. Just leave and you will live.'

A scoffing laugh burst from her. 'None of you are a threat to *me*.'

'Not now, no. But who knows when – on some day or night to come – you will suddenly feel my teeth upon your neck.' He raised a hand and snapped it shut into a fist. 'Then, well . . . it will be too late and I will break your spine.'

'Well. In that case. The prudent course for me would be . . . to kill you now.' Her power flickered to life about her, licking in crimson and argent flames.

The man-leopard raised his eyes to the tops of the bamboo forest lost in the mist above her. 'It is not I you must worry about today, Spite.'

Her mouth curled her annoyance and she turned, raising her gaze. 'Oh, what now? Surely not your fabled bird-women.' Seeing a hint of movement she squinted. The mist swirled, disturbed by the descent of a something massive. Darkness blossomed immediately above her; an immense yawning mouth, close to three fathoms across, set in a slim featureless albino head resembling that of a salamander.

Spite's shoulders slumped. 'Oh, shit.'

The titanic Worm of Autumn lunged, smashing into the muddy ground, snapping the rearing bamboo. The man-leopard leaped aside, running half on all fours. Of Spite, no sign remained. The monstrous beast writhed, flailing, its jaws working. Its length could not be guessed as its segmented mass disappeared into the murky distance.

The Worm's thrashing reduced the grove to a wreckage of smashed and broken bamboo. It writhed and twisted, gouging great swaths of mud. Thumping blows shook the ground until it boomed and echoed. The battering raged on even as the sun broke the horizon to begin burning off the mist from the night's rain.

An eruption of power shone blazing argent, for an instant brighter than the rising sun. A thunderclap followed, shuddering the distant standing trees. It blasted leaves from branches in all directions, sending them flying.

The Worm lay still. The gigantic body ended at a tattered stump of blackened smoking flesh. Gobbets of muscle and fat and skin littered the expanse of the flattened bamboo grove. A fresh mist rose from the steaming gore. Among the fat and segments of torn organs the size of a man, something shifted. A shape lurched erect: Spite, sheathed in mucus and pulped flesh.

She wiped the smeared gore from her. She retched and staggered upright. Her frenzied gaze raked the surroundings. 'You see!' she shrieked, transported in an ecstasy of rage. '*You see!* Nothing here is a match for me! I will destroy you *all*!'

A disembodied voice answered from the jungle depths: 'Foolish girl . . . we could only lure here . . . the *smallest* of them.'

CHAPTER X

The Moon, in his first quarter, was only a fine inlay of silver against a sky of lapis lazuli, which fused into the dreamy serenity of the stream by which I gradually felt impregnated . . . I would have liked to have communicated with the wild nature surrounding us, to listen to her dark language and to understand her, to become like the simple people of this country. And so I lost myself in dreams that floated from one bank to the other, until a far away voice tore me from my solitude.

Matha Banness
In Jacuruku

SAENG AWOKE TO A JOLT THAT SPASMED HER AND SENT FRESH KNIFE-edges of agony shooting through her thigh. She sat up and clutched at the leg, finding fresh clean bindings encircling it. *What has happened?* She remembered the crashing flight through the jungle in Hanu's arms. The burgeoning searing pain of the stab. Then the terrible slow numbness spreading from the wound until she could no longer feel the leg. Then, horrifyingly, the other. All the while the hardest thing for her to endure had been Hanu's helpless panic and sorrow – for they both knew what the killing numbness presaged.

She lay now in a small cave, a shrine or jungle temple. Rain pattered down in fat heavy drops beyond its stone lip. A small fire of dried moss, leaf litter and twigs smouldered, offering a dim orange glow. In the darkness next to her someone moved. 'Hanu,' she said, relieved.

But it was not Hanu. It was that damned captured Thaumaturg. So stunned was she that he had the time to put a hand high on her bared thigh to test the dressings. 'Careful of them,' he murmured.

She slapped his hand away. 'Where is my brother?'

The young man's thick black brows rose. 'Your brother?' Then he nodded to himself. 'I see . . . how very interesting.'

Ignoring him, she yelled, or tried to: 'Hanu!' The effort brought black spots to her vision and left her dizzy.

'I am here,' came the answer.

'Where are you?' she sent in kind.

'Guarding.'

'What happened?'

'The Thaumaturg saved your life.'

'Really? In truth? Why would he do that?'

'I believe he means to use you to control me.'

Ah. She studied the young acolyte more closely. *I see.* One of their officers, plainly. She pushed herself up on her elbows then slid backwards to lean against the cold stone wall. He was pale, like all of them – never working under the sun like everyone else. Unusually, his hair was long and it now hung as an unkempt mess. Facial hair dusted his lip and chin. 'What is your rank?' she demanded.

Again the man arched a brow. 'Not the thanks I was expecting, but I will answer regardless. I have the black, if that is what you mean.'

So, trained to the highest level. But she knew that beyond that threshold lay a near-infinity of subtle gradations of rank leading all the way up to the highest achievement: the ruling Inner Circle of Masters. 'What do you want?'

Now the lips crooked in a mocking half-smile. 'Still no thanks?'

Saeng adjusted her skirts over her legs, crossed her arms, took a deep breath and levelled her gaze. 'My thanks.'

He tilted his head in acceptance. Leaning forward, he warmed his hands at the anaemic fire. 'So, your brother, you say? I am very surprised. Well, in any case, by now you no doubt understand that he has developed . . . how shall I put it? *Flaws* . . . problems that must be treated.' He raised his eyes to meet her gaze. 'So will you not help me by returning him to Anditi Pura so that he may be healed?'

'Healed?' she sent to Hanu.

'They will no doubt try to erase my mind,' he answered, radiating amusement at this idea of 'healing'.

She felt her mouth draw down in a hard scowl. 'Never mind Hanu. You have far larger problems.'

'Oh?'

'Your masters are intent upon bringing the Visitor down upon us.

The firestorm will annihilate everyone alive in these lands. Including you.'

The officer threw himself from the fire to lean back against the chamber's stone wall. She noted how mould and lichen mottled the wall in black, green and white. 'That again,' he snorted, derisive. 'How came you to this insanity? Is this what has driven you here into Himatan? Are you—' He stopped himself, and she could read him forcing himself to relax. 'What is your name, anyway, girl?'

'Girl? I'm no younger than you, I should think. What of you? What is your name?'

He eyed her, his gaze superior, and then she saw him remember that he wanted her cooperation. The natural arrogance of his class was quickly tucked away and a carefully constructed expression of neutrality replaced it. 'Pon-lor,' he allowed.

'Saeng.'

He eased himself into a more comfortable position – though she understood that this was all show as the Thaumaturgs scorned all allowances for the flesh. 'Well . . . Saeng. It would appear that we are in disagreement regarding this impending catastrophe. Perhaps after it fails to materialize we could return to Anditi Pura?'

'Perhaps I could have Han— my brother throttle you in your sleep?' she suggested with a smile.

He smiled back just as winningly. 'I believe I could *severely* wound Hanu, if not kill him, before he succeeded.'

He probably could, at that, she had to admit. *Damn him. And I did mention Hanu's name. Still, he seems to have no hold over him. He can tag along then. So long as he keeps that superior smirk off his face.*

A new figure came scuttling in from the rain and Saeng jerked upright – a damned bandit!

The Thaumaturg actually rested a hand on her shoulder, which she immediately struck aside. 'It is all right,' he said, lowering his arm. 'He's with me.'

The sopping wet lad made a show of avoiding Saeng to bend close to Pon-lor's ear and murmur something. He then hurried off, but not before shooting Saeng a look of sullen resentment and fear.

'What's his story?' she asked.

'He works for me now.'

To Saeng's surprise she couldn't detect a single hint of self-satisfaction in that pronouncement. 'Well, tell him to keep his distance.'

He laughed then, but not mockingly. Through the wind-brushed canopy high above silver moonlight flickered upon them and it struck her that not only was the man a member of her nation's ruling aristocracy – he was an unfairly handsome bastard too. 'Pray tell what is so amusing?' she enquired, overly sweetly.

The Thaumaturg gestured to the cave mouth. 'Keeping his distance is not his problem, Saeng. It was all I could do to convince him to have anything to do with you. The lad's terrified of you. He's convinced you're a servant of Ardata. He believes you bewitched the yakshaka. That you even summoned the locals that attacked us.'

'Well,' she enquired, 'how do you know I didn't?'

He merely smiled indulgently, as if to say: come now child, we both know how.

The conceit that he could somehow see through her troubled her more than she thought it would. She was suddenly conscious of her dirty torn skirts and shirt, the awful state of her hair. It occurred to her that she must certainly look the part of a witch. 'No? What am I then?' she asked, smoothing her skirts further then hugging herself, feeling very cold in the dampness of the cave.

He studied her in the darkness across the sputtering fire. 'You are a village girl who has come into power but has no idea what to do with it. You are scared and lost and terrified of what you possess.' He cocked his head as if struck by a new thought. 'Come to Anditi Pura with me. We could train you. Teach you how to harness that power.'

She snorted a laugh and shivered. 'I have had more teachers than you could imagine. Most older than your vaunted Thaumaturg Academy. Have you not considered that perhaps that is why power terrifies me?' She adjusted her seating on the litter on the floor of the cave, peered out into the dark where Hanu's broad armoured back was just visible in the shifting glow of the Visitor. 'In any case, I know what to do. I must find the Great Temple – the old temple to Light.'

The Thaumaturg was quiet for a time. She glanced over to see him eyeing the fire, his mouth gently pursed. 'And should you find this temple,' he murmured, 'and find there is no impending calamity . . . what then? What will you do? Where would you go?'

Saeng felt her eyes drooping. Gods of the Abyss, she was tired. Her leg ached abominably, her back was stiff, her buttocks numb. 'I do not know. Hanu cannot have a life here – hunted by you and Ardata's creatures as well. Perhaps we will leave this cursed land. Sail away. I have heard many stories of all the continents across the seas. Of beautiful fields of ice. Rich empires. Huge cities.'

'You are cold,' the Thaumaturg said. 'May I strengthen the fire?'
'Go ahead.'

The man did something, she wasn't sure what, and the fire bright-ened, leaping to life. A wave of warmth enveloped her. Yet sleep would not come – not immediately – not with an enemy across from her. Through slit eyes she watched him in the flickering glow. He was staring out of the cave mouth, looking very thoughtful, show-ing no sign of exhaustion. She knew these Thaumaturgs could go for days without sleep and she knew that he intended to keep watch through the night.

As her eyes blinked heavier and heavier the thought came to her – just like Hanu.

In the morning the bandit lad, Thet-mun, produced root bulbs he'd collected from various plants in the jungle. He showed them how to prepare them and cook them over the fire on sticks. The entire time not once did he directly look at or address Saeng. Though, furtively, he did make warding gestures her way against hexing and evil. Pon-lor spoke for her, asking what the plants looked like, whether the time of year mattered, and such questions. It seemed the lad had learned all this esoteric natural history from his aunt.

Pon-lor then explained that Saeng was looking for a great temple, a major structure of some sort, and asked whether Thet-mun had heard of any such thing. He hadn't. But he did admit that his aunt had told him stories of such things here in the forest of Himatan. He said he'd climb a tree and have a look around. Which he promptly ran off to do – perhaps merely to get away from Saeng.

As she sat there nibbling the hot bulb on its stick, it occurred to Saeng that they all owed this lad's aunt a great deal.

After she finished eating, Saeng limped a short distance off to relieve herself. She found fresh rainwater trapped in broad leaves and tipped it into her mouth. She even wet a corner of her skirt to clean her face as best she could. When she returned Thet-mun was back. Spotting her, he quickly turned away, slouching, and hurried off. Pon-lor came to her.

'The lad says he saw no tall hillock or structure standing above the canopy in any direction.' He offered a small apologetic rise of his shoulders. 'I'm sorry. But there's nothing here.'

'Well. We'll just keep going then.'

His brows crimped in frustration. 'Saeng . . .' he began, but she brushed past him, gingerly, holding her leg. She motioned to Hanu.

'*We do not need him,*' she sent to Hanu.

'We could use the lad.'

Saeng paused. *'True. But we'll just have to go without.'*

'Saeng,' the Thaumaturg repeated, a note of warning in his voice. She turned, crossed her arms. 'Yes?'

'I cannot let you wander further into the jungle. We must return.' He took a deep breath, as though saddened. 'I'm sorry.'

She looked to Hanu. 'We've been through all this already . . .'

'I thought you would listen to reason.'

'Reason?' she snorted. *'Your* thinking is reason? Then pray tell, what is mine? Blind wilful childishness?'

He gave her that indulgent look again – the one that seemed to say: oh, come now.

She waved him away, dismissing him to the jungle and his own fate. 'We're going, Hanu.'

'Hanu . . .' the young master called, low but firmly. Saeng glanced back, for some reason alarmed. What was this? Some sort of new trick? The Thaumaturg continued in slow and clear command: *'Yeosh than'al. Azgreth sethul.'*

Her gaze snapped to her brother. He had stilled, seeming immobile. *'Hanu!'* she sent, pleading. He did not respond. Then he moved in slow heavy steps towards Pon-lor. *'Hanu!'* she fairly wailed.

The damned Thaumaturg awaited him, arms crossed, nodding his satisfaction.

Saeng's power erupted about her, sending the litter of the jungle floor flying in a rising gyre.

'Hold!' Pon-lor yelled, raising an arm. 'I control your brother now. Shall I command him to kill himself?'

Saeng held herself quivering in tensed suppressed energies. She felt as if she should explode. That she should throw herself upon the man in an ecstasy of ripping and destruction. But before she could act Hanu snapped out an arm to grab the man by his throat.

Saeng's power dropped from her in a rush. Her shoulders slumped, her hair falling.

Pon-lor's hands scrabbled at Hanu's armoured gauntlet. He gurgled, his face reddening. Her brother lifted him from his feet. The man was gasping now, frantic, his face purpling.

'Hanu . . .' she called, warning.

The man's eyes found hers. They glistened in panic.

'Drop him,' she urged. When her brother did not respond she sent, *'Please do not kill him, Hanu.'*

The man crashed limply to the ground. She came to stand where he lay wheezing and flailing groggily.

'You owe me your life,' she told him. 'Now kindly leave us alone.'
She motioned to Hanu, and, taking his arm, limped away.

*

When Pon-lor's vision cleared he found Thet-mun, crouched, peering down at him. He was moodily chewing on some sort of stick or stalk.

The lad was shaking his head. 'Man. I really can pick 'em, can't I? First Jak, now you. Fuckin' losers.' He shook his head again.

Pon-lor sat up and rubbed his neck. He experimentally edged his head from side to side. 'We will follow them at a discreet distance.'

'No we fucking won't. You can. I won't. I'm goin'. I've had it.'

Massaging his neck, Pon-lor squinted up at him. 'No? I could compel you, you know.'

The lad straightened. He took the stick from his mouth, picked at his teeth. 'And there's a thousand ways I could get you killed in this jungle. I could feed you something that would eat you from the inside out. I could direct you into poisonous leaves. Lead you over a pit.'

Pon-lor flexed his neck, felt the vertebrae pop. 'I get the idea.'

The lad was nodding vigorously. 'Yeah. So . . . there you go. I'm leavin'.'

'Would you like my advice? Before you go?'

Thet-mun scowled down at him, uncertain. 'What? Advice? Whaddya mean?'

Pon-lor waved him off. 'Go home, Thet. Go back to your village. Claim your quarter section of land. Take a wife. Raise some kids.'

The lad chuffed a laugh. 'Yeah, right. That's for losers. Farming! Ha!' And he walked away, laughing and shaking his head. He disappeared almost immediately as if swallowed whole.

Pon-lor sat for a time. He massaged his neck. In the silence, the jungle noise of birds calling and insects whirring swelled to fill the air. The sun shafted down through the canopy raising steaming tendrils of mist where it touched. Ants swarmed over the disturbed rotting vegetation that littered the floor.

Sighing, he rose, dusted himself off. He tore a strip of cloth from the edge of his robe and used it to tie back his hair. He cast his awareness out upon the leagues surrounding him. Almost instantly he sensed her there. The signature of her aura was unmistakable. Suppressed for now, but present all the same.

Clasping his hands behind his back, he set off. Here and there amid the root-tangled dirt he discerned the hardened depression of the yakshaka's heavy tread. Broken stems and brushed aside branches betrayed his lumbering progress. He nodded his satisfaction to himself. Yes, very good. All those days observing the bandits finding their way through the jungle. Following spoor. Identifying sign.

He reclasped his hands and rocked back and forth on his sandals in meditation. *Yes. I do believe I'm getting the hang of it.*

*　　*　　*

The priest had promised to drop them some way from the target so that they would have time to recover from the Crippled God's magics. As it was, Mara found that her reaction was nowhere near as violent as before. She was shaken, dizzy and nauseous, yes, but far from her earlier experience of nearly blacking out. She wondered whether she should be relieved or alarmed by the development.

She staggered to a nearby tree to lean, panting, bent over, hands on knees. She caught her breath, swallowed stinging bile. Her vision had cleared and now she could see her fellows picking themselves up off the leaf-littered jungle floor. Some had vomited – the new ones: Shijel and Black. They straightened now, recovering. Shijel drew his longswords and Black spat to clear his mouth then dropped his visor and readied his wide shield.

This was a piece of work long delayed. The priest had been missing for a good week. Mara had been of the hopeful opinion that he'd died – succumbed to one of the many diseases he obviously carried. And good riddance. Yet eventually he'd surfaced again, accosting them last night, even more emaciated and insanely obsessed than before. And Skinner had surprised him, promising to go after the shard lost in Himatan. He said he'd return the next night to run the errand. And so he had. And here they were.

Skinner now looked to Petal, who motioned aside. 'We're close. It's a large party – too large. We'll have to try to snatch it.'

'Very well. Get us as close as you can and we'll make a lunge for it.'

The big man's neck bulged as he gave a curt answering nod. Skinner pointed to the priest. 'You. Be quiet or I'll run you through.'

The priest's response was a long low inarticulate snarl.

Petal gestured, raising his Warren, then motioned them on. The party advanced, Petal and Skinner leading, Shijel and Black with the priest, while Mara brought up the rear. Petal's magics would obscure them – at least momentarily – perhaps enough to allow them to grab the prize then escape by way of the priest. Mara glimpsed the raiders through the trees and was surprised. At first she thought them locals who'd taken up arms and armour, dressed and painted as they were. But the stock differed, heavier, and darker or lighter of skin. The equipage troubled her; too familiar. A mercenary force out of Quon Tali? Perhaps.

Petal led them in a roundabout way towards their goal. It blazed unmistakable, like a lodestone of power in Mara's vision. It lay wrapped on a makeshift litter of poles and cloth. They were almost at the shard when one of the painted raiders, a squat frog-like fellow with bulging mismatched eyes, stood up right before them and kicked Petal in his ample stomach.

Everything went to the Abyss after that. She instantly raised her Warren to blast away all those nearby. She unfortunately tossed aside Shijel and Black as well. Battle commands sounded amid the kicked-up dust and dead leaves and a thrill of recognition blazed through her. *Malazans!* Damned Malazans making their own play for the shard! It seemed this new emperor differed from his predecessors regarding the Shattered God. The others had been far too timid, to her mind.

The damned priest was right – this could not be allowed.

She turned for the litter but it wasn't there. It had been spirited away somehow when she'd been distracted. Petal rose nearby, grasping his gut in both hands. He murmured, wincing, 'The Enchantress herself works against us.'

Blast it! They'd been so close!

Skinner appeared, his bared Thaumaturg officer's sword bloodied. He dragged the priest along by his shirt. 'We startled them but they're regrouping,' he said, grimly. To Petal, 'Where is it?'

The fat mage was rubbing his wide middle. 'Hidden away.'

'Well – find it!'

'It will take time. This one is an inspired practitioner . . . his mind is particularly atypical.'

'We don't have time.' Skinner restrained the priest like an uncooperative dog.

'They will attack!' the priest wailed.

'Of course,' Skinner answered, studying the surrounding jungle. 'They're Malazans.'

Black and Shijel came running up. 'On their way,' Black announced.

Skinner shook the gangly priest savagely, demanding, '*Can you track it?*'

The man yanked his rag shirt free and smoothed it down in a sad effort to regain his dignity. His gaze became sly as he peered past Mara. 'Of course. Yes. No one can hide my master from *me*.' He brushed past her closely, taking the opportunity to run a hand up her trousers over her buttock. He sped onward, her backhanded slap just missing his head.

Starting off, Skinner ordered, 'Petal. Take these two and run these Malazans off our track. Mara, you're with me.' He chased after the priest.

Mara followed. As she left she heard a despairing Petal murmur, 'Ah, running . . . Oh, dear.'

The chase was a confusing dash through a maze of immensely tall and wide tree trunks that almost touched one another. Thick roots writhed over the ground like ridged snakes, some nearly as tall as she. Ahead, Skinner jumped the roots, pushed through tall fronds of undergrowth and parted stands of stiff spear-like grasses. The nightly rain started falling from the canopy in fat drops. In his glittering black armour the man moved like a patch of deeper night amid the streamers of starlight and the Jade Banner's glow. Unencumbered by heavy armour or weapons, Mara kept up.

She almost slammed into the priest who was standing stock still, poised as if listening to the night. Skinner stood nearby. 'What is it?' she asked him, her voice low. The big man's shrug of contempt seemed to call a curse down on all this damned mummery.

'Something new,' the priest answered. He pointed to the darkness. 'Another mage. Follower of that pathetic usurper, Shadowthrone.'

'Can you still track it?' Skinner demanded, unimpressed.

The man jerked, insulted. 'Of course! Yes. It calls to me. Offspring of my master.'

Skinner waved him onward. 'Well . . .'

'Fine!' He adjusted the rags that passed as his long shirting, hanging down past his loin wrap, then ran on. Skinner chuffed his scorn and followed. Mara fell in behind. They went slower now, tracing a winding route. The dense woods and stands of bamboo appeared far more dark this night than Mara remembered. *Meanas, closing in upon us.* To either side routes beckoned, appearing to be the way Skinner had taken, but she ignored them, keeping her eye upon the trail the priest had broken; somehow his passage erased or overlay the puzzling twisting of ways and paths that wove all about her. Tatters of shadows even seemed to hang here and there like torn spiderweb.

Then she burst in upon a standoff, almost tumbling forward. The priest struggled in the grip of a soldier while another faced Skinner. Two others, the mages, stood at the litter.

'Back off or he's dead,' the Malazan holding the priest warned.

Skinner gave an off-hand wave. 'A good plan, soldier. But there's a flaw. You see – I don't give a damn.' And he attacked, clashing swords with the soldier who faced him.

'Gotta do it, Murk . . .' one of the mages warned the other.

The second winced. 'Oh man, I really don't want to . . .'

Do what? Mara summoned energies for a strike. Then the two mages and the litter between them disappeared as if smothered by darkness. *Hood take it!* The soldier holding the priest threw him into Skinner then the two Malazans fled in opposite directions.

Skinner snatched the priest by his throat. '*Where did they go?*'

'I do not know!' he wailed. 'It is gone! My torment will be unending!'

'Oh, shut up.' He turned his helmed head to Mara.

She studied the dissipating lines of manipulation: a distraction? Were they in truth still there? Merely disguised? Yet she detected a betraying blurring and melting away. 'Shadow,' she judged.

'*Him!*' the priest snarled. 'Upstart. Poseur. He is nothing!'

Skinner shook the priest again, making his teeth clack. 'Can you follow?'

The priest batted at Skinner's armoured forearm. 'Yes, I shall! My master's reach knows no boundaries. Ready yourselves.'

Mara clenched her gut and throat in queasy anticipation.

The surroundings blurred darkly, as if enmeshed in thickening shifting murk. Then the nauseating inner twist seemed to yank her inside out and she fell to her knees and one hand, gagging. This could not be good for her, she decided.

'*Sacred Queen!*' someone yelped.

'Do not move,' Skinner barked.

Blinking to clear her vision, Mara peered up. They'd found them. Two mages sitting with the litter. She glanced around: they were still within woods, but this one was very different. Far more dark and crowded, the trees and brush all black, bare and brittle, seemingly dead. The sky churned above them like a cauldron of lead. Shadow. How it unnerved her. People shouldn't be here. *This is not our realm.*

The priest was pawing at the wrapped package, chuckling and whispering to it. One of the mages slapped him away and he hissed at the man.

'You led us on a good chase, Malazan,' Skinner said. 'But it's done now. Stand aside.'

The taller, slimmer mage in the tattered shirt and vest sent something through his Warren. *He's the one!* Mara sent a thrust of power against him, slapping him backwards to smack his skull against a tree trunk. Broken branches rained down. The man wrapped his arms around his head and curled into a ball. He groaned his pain.

'What was that?' Skinner demanded.

'He sent something. A summoning.'

'Take it!' Skinner ordered. 'We must go.'

'Yes, yes.' The priest tore at the strapping securing the pack to the litter.

Snarling under his breath, Skinner started forward, impatient. 'Just—' He stopped, as the priest had frozen, staring off into the woods. Something was approaching, pushing its way stiffly through the dense brush. Mara experienced a momentary thrill of terror when, for an instant, she thought it an Imass.

But it was not – though the resemblance was strong. It was a desiccated corpse in ancient tattered armour of leather and mail, a tall sword at its back. Patches of hair still clung to cured tea-brown scraps of flesh over a round skull. Empty dark sockets regarded them. The dried lips had pulled back from yellowed teeth. The animated corpse pointed a finger – all sinew and knobby joints – to the litter.

'Who brought this here?' it asked. Its voice was a breathless stirring of dead things.

The other Malazan mage's eyes had grown huge at the appearance of this ghoul and he spluttered, 'Er, we did, sir. But we didn't mean no insult. We was just fleeing this one!' He pointed to Skinner, who merely crossed his arms in a slither of armoured scales.

'I know of you, skulker of borders,' the priest sneered from where he crouched hugging the pack. 'I know your strictures. You cannot interfere!'

Mara started, shocked. *Skulker of borders? Edgewalker?* She raised her Warren to its greatest intensity. All mages are warned of this one – the most potent haunt of Shadow.

'True,' it breathed, its voice so soft. 'However, you are within Emurlahn.'

'Then we shall go,' Skinner announced, and he reached for the pack.

In a leathery creaking of dried muscle and ligament, the legendary creature edged its head to one side, as if it were listening to some voice none other could hear. 'I cannot foresee the outcome,' it said, in warning.

Skinner paused. 'What was that?'

'Is this your wish?' the haunt asked, facing away once more, as if addressing nothing.

Ignoring the creature, Skinner closed a gauntleted fist on the pack and pointed furiously to the priest. Howling his terror, the servant of the Chained God gestured and threw himself aside. The wrenching inner yanking snatched Mara, pulling her backwards, and she almost fainted from the clawing sense of violation. Her vision blackened and stars dazzled her eyes. She fell upon dirt, groaning, her stomach heaving. Still groggy, she pushed herself upright.

Skinner was there, the bag in his hand. But it hung limp, in tatters. He raised the torn canvas and leather strapping to his visor, studied it, then threw it down with a curse. The priest lay kicking and pounding the ground. It was as if he'd been taken by some sort of fit: shrieking curses, babbling in strange languages, even chewing and biting at the dirt in the extremity of his rage.

'They cannot remain in Shadow,' Skinner said. 'They will return.'

This seemed to work upon the priest and he calmed, his convulsions easing. He pushed himself to his knees yet still appeared stricken, weaving, his eyes sleepy, not focusing upon anything at all. 'Yes,' he whispered. 'We must await them. Our master requires as many disparate parts as possible. He is much assailed. All his children he must gather to himself. Greater power is needed . . .'

Curious, Mara asked, 'For what?'

Slowly the priest raised his head. His eyes lost their emptiness to focus upon her, and flooded with hate almost insane in its intensity. 'Why, to win free of course, you useless fool!'

*

It was a blessing and a curse that Murk had been off squatting in the woods when the attack came. A blessing because he was out of sight in a stand of brittle grasses, but a curse in that he wasn't done.

Shouts of astonishment and surprise sounded from the camp, followed by an explosion of power that knocked him over even though he was squatting down, his feet wide splayed. Uprooted plants and broken branches slapped across him, followed by a haze of suspended dust and dirt. '*What the fuck?*' he exclaimed before clamping his mouth shut and cursing himself for a fool. He allowed one wipe to his bare arse with a handful of leaves then pulled up his trousers and fumbled at the lacing.

He pushed his way out of the dense stand. All was quiet now, the camp deserted but for new figures whom he merely glimpsed before ducking back into cover. He pushed through to the other side of the stand and ran, raising Meanas to cloak him as he went. A drifting haze of Mockra-laid mental confusion, distraction and a profusion of false trails lay revealed before him. It would have completely defeated him had not he and Sour worked together so long that they automatically allowed paths for each other through their defences and traps. He raced on, sensing their direction already.

They had gone to ground in a clearing at the centre of a ring of thick trunks that the locals called raintrees. He dropped his disguise of shadows, making Ostler and Dee jump – even though Sour had no doubt warned them he was on his way.

'They're comin',' Sour announced.

'All right.' He waved to Ostler and Dee. 'You two, take off. We'll cover you.'

The two sheathed their swords, picked up the litter, and ran.

He and Sour started after, more slowly, interweaving a mesh of Meanas and Mockra with hidden snares of Thyr from Sour.

'I think they're good,' Sour panted. 'What a punch that gal has! My ears are still ringing.'

'Focus on the job,' Murk growled.

'Right. Still, great legs on her.'

Together they spread such a maze of confusion, distortion and misdirection that Murk was certain no one could possibly win through. Yet whenever he cast his awareness to their rear he found them, and closing.

'Can't shake 'em,' Sour gasped, near exhaustion. 'How're they doin' it?' He sounded close to weeping his fear and frustration.

'Must have a tag on us somehow. Somethin' . . .' Murk hit a fist to his forehead. 'The damned shard! They're tracking it. Must stand out like Burn's own tits. Gotta change the plan.'

Sour halted, hands on a broad leaf cut by deep serrations as long as a murderer's blade. 'How's that?' he asked.

Murk gestured ahead. 'Tell Dee to turn the game.'

'On it. Just like that time in Mott.'

Murk snapped his fingers to urge his partner on. 'I told you never to mention that Hood-damned place!'

Sour hurried away, muttering, 'Okay, okay. Just 'cause the apes caught ya! Sheesh.'

Dee and Ostler took charge of the ambush. They impatiently waved Murk and Sour to the litter. Moments later a skinny gangly fellow came crashing through the brush to run right into Dee, who wrapped a forearm round his neck. The fellow squawked but quietened down when Dee pressed the blade of his heavy parrying gauche to his bulbous Adam's apple.

Two more figures emerged and the first punched Murk's breath away because he recognized him from stories he'd heard. Skinner. Fucking Crimson Guard renegade. What was he doing here? He'd heard they'd left Jacuruku. *This could be it for us. We're outclassed.*

So struck was he that he missed something and now Skinner charged Ostler.

'Gotta do it, Murk,' Sour whimpered, revealing that he also knew whom they faced.

He said some stupid last words and took them into Shadow.

They emerged still within the confines of the forest of the Azathanai. The image of Celeste shimmered here as if awaiting them. 'Hello,' she greeted them, smiling, pleased to see them. 'Who are those others?'

'They've come to take you away. Bring you to your . . . ah, parent.'

The girl-shade giggled. 'Parent! How quaint. I'm sorry, Murk, but that comes nowhere near our relationship.'

Distracted, he murmured, 'Well. Have to start somewhere.' *Can't stay here – gonna be entombed for ever by these damned trees.* 'We have to move,' he told Sour who answered with a *you're damned right* nod.

A patch of the woods nearby roiled and blurred as if melting. Murk stared, stunned. *I don't fucking believe it!* The Crippled God priest appeared and lunged for the litter. He and Sour eyed the rearing dark figure of Skinner who emerged looking like the ghost of Hood himself. The Crimson Guard Dal Hon gal followed but the transition was hard on her: she fell to her knees, gagging. Still, her D'riss Warren sizzled about her as an aurora of blue flames.

'*Sacred Queen,*' Sour squawked, a hand going to his mouth.

Murk shifted to kick the damned priest away.

'Do not move,' Skinner warned.

The priest was untying the straps. Murk couldn't help trying to smack him aside. He saw the surrounding branches and roots stirring, but slowly. Far too slowly. To one side, the flickering image of Celeste watched the newcomers as if they were rare exotic animals while none of them even spared her a glance – not even the priest. *They can't see her either. Only I can. Her choice, I suppose. And this filthy priest is about to get his hands on her! Have to do something.*

That they had physically brought the shard through into Shadow gave him an idea. It ought to bring someone who could stand down even Skinner. Abyss, from the stories and rumours he'd heard among those who knew Shadow he could stand down *anyone*.

The Crimson Guardsman said something but Murk wasn't listening; he was concentrating his power. Because he had nothing to lose, he sent a summoning. The instant he did the D'riss mage was on him. She hit like an avalanche and all he knew was a hammer slamming into his stomach knocking him backwards, then a spike driving into his head. Everything was lost in a burning sea of pain.

He came to holding his head. He unclenched his arms and peered up, blinking. They were still in Shadow. Celeste stood over him, studying him with her big green eyes. 'You are in pain?' she asked.

His head felt like it had cracked open. He swallowed the pasty coating in his mouth and ventured a weak, 'Yeah . . .'

'It appears quite incommoding. Not a good adaptation.'

'What was that?' Sour asked. 'You okay?'

He shifted to sit up – carefully. 'She's here. You can't see her?'

Sour peered around. 'No. I guess only you can.'

'Ah. So . . . give it to me. What happened.'

The fellow rubbed his bulbous nose, smearing his green and grey face paint. 'Well. The scariest guy I've ever seen showed up and kicked them out of Shadow.'

'He was here? He came!' *And I missed it! I can't believe it! How could I— A thousand unanswered questions. What an opportunity . . .* He shook his head and winced.

'Yeah,' Sour answered, then he frowned, confused. 'Who?'

'Edgewalker.'

Sour's brows, one higher than the other, rose. 'Oh! I heard a him. I hear he's the worst reason you should never trespass in Shadow.'

'That is how you know this being, then?' Celeste asked. 'A menace?'

Murk blew out a breath while probing the back of his head. 'Yeah. Why?'

'He is not threatening. He only makes me sad.'

Murk gave her a hard glance, but, seeing that she would say nothing more, turned his attention to the surrounding forest. 'The trees aren't moving against us,' he murmured, surprised.

Sour nodded, eager. 'Yeah. Your Edgewalker guy told them to leave us alone.'

Murk jerked, amazed, then held his head to contain the blazing pain that spiked there. *He told the forest of the Azathanai to leave us alone? Who is this guy?* He'd heard stories, of course. Garbled versions that circulated among the apprentices and equally absurd speculations in written legends. How it had been he who had slain the first king of Kurald Emurlahn, Elder Shadow, and how he was now cursed to wander it for ever. Or that he had shattered Emurlahn in the first place, damning himself in the process. *And now Celeste says he makes her sad.* No one knew the truth of all those events lost so far in the mists of the ancient past. And Edgewalker himself certainly wasn't talking.

Sour wiggled a finger in his ear, studied it then flicked it. 'But he only did that 'cause I promised we'd go soon.'

Yes. They couldn't hide here for ever. Edgewalker might be able to restrain the forest, but Murk had his doubts about the Hounds, should they come sniffing. 'Can you disguise her presence? Hide her?'

His partner cocked a brow. 'It, you mean. Don't ya?'

He waved a hand impatiently. 'Whatever.'

Sour took a deep breath, his scrawny shoulders rising and falling. 'Nope. Too powerful.'

'No? Just like that? Think of it as a professional challenge.'

'I just ain't got the pull, Murk. Sorry. Maybe it – she – can help.'

Murk managed not to slap his hand to his head. What a fool he'd been! Somehow he'd fallen into treating her, it, as some kind of helpless ward he'd picked up. He shifted on his knees to regard her more directly. Seeing him turning to her she sat on a log and clasped her hands on her knees, regarding him intently. Murk felt his mouth go dry. 'Celeste,' he began gently, 'we need you to hide your presence. It would be a great help to us.'

A frown creased her pretty features. 'I do not think I understand you. Hide myself? However does one do that?'

Right. How to explain? Throw a blanket over oneself? Abyss, she don't even know what a blanket is! He cleared his throat. 'These people searching for you. They want to take you away. We need to make it hard for them to find you . . .'

She was picking at the rotting bark of the log, her head lowered, seemingly embarrassed. 'Well,' she said, 'I *have* been thinking. I'd like to explore more of that entity, that awareness I spoke of, and that would mean seeking it out. I would be hard to locate, exactly, then.' She dared a glance to Murk, almost coy. 'Do you think I could?'

Gods above, help me. What to say? Should she? Would I just be serving my own interests to say yes? But how should I know? Dammit! I've had no training in raising a damned child god! 'Well,' he began. 'I guess that if you would like to then perhaps you ought to have a try at it . . .'

She beamed a smile and clasped her hands exactly like a child delighted. 'Oh, thank you, Murk. I shall.' The ghostly transparent casting that was her presence thinned then, dimming until it faded away entirely into nothing.

Murk sat back on his haunches. He felt saddened. Would he never see her again? He assumed it was just was well – who knew what awful future blunders this sidestepped. And yet he felt a strange sort of disappointment. *Was that it? Just like that?*

'What happened?' Sour asked. 'You look all lost.'

He peered about the woods. 'She's gone.'

His partner frowned. 'What? Gone gone? Where?'

'Waiting for us to call her back. I think.'

'I'm all for goin' too. Don't want to meet those damned Hounds.' He added, eyeing him critically, 'And if she *is* gone then that's all for the best, man. Playin' with fire, I say.'

Murk shook his head; he couldn't muster the resentment for a fight. 'I know, I know. We'll go back. Yusen must be getting worried.'

Sour let blow a long breath. 'Any chase you walk away from is a good chase. That's what I say.'

The scouts found them and brought them to Yusen who had relocated camp to another clearing. A doubled picket let them through and the commander met them fully armoured, helmet under an arm. A small grin of vindication plucked at his lips but the worry remained in the many deep wrinkles around his always tightened eyes. 'You made it,' he said. 'Good.' Only gripping the poles of the litter stopped Murk from saluting. 'But, ah . . .' He eyed the litter and the blanket-wrapped object tied down with bits of rope and strips of torn cloth.

They set the litter down. 'We think they won't be able to spot it again. Not easily, anyway.'

Yusen grunted his acceptance of this. 'And the *they*? There's wild talk of the Crimson Guard.'

'Ex-Guard. Skinner and his command were disavowed by K'azz. Stories were they'd left Jacuruku. I guess they've come back.'

'All the more reason for us to leave,' Yusen said, scratching his unshaven chin.

'With permission, sir,' Murk ventured, 'they can probably guess we're headed west. They'll keep an eye out.'

Their commander frowned his displeasure, but Murk knew it wasn't directed at him; it was at their situation. 'Looks like we have the proverbial tiger by the tail,' he murmured.

'Aye, and we can't let go.'

'So? What's your answer?' And I hope to Fanderay you've got one.'

Murk shared a look with Sour, who urged him on. 'Well . . . rumours are that there was some kinda falling out between Skinner and Ardata. It looks to me like he's hunting this to maybe use against her . . .'

Yusen pulled his hand down his chin, nodding. 'So. The enemy of my enemy . . .'

'Yeah.' Murk shrugged apologetically. 'Best I can do.'

'It's a plan.' The ex-officer gave a curt nod of acceptance. 'Always good to have one of those.' He raised a hand and signalled. Burastan, Sweetly and others jogged up. 'We're headed east, double-time.'

Sweetly's gaze swung to Murk and Sour and the twig that had been standing straight out from his clenched lips slowly fell. The expression that compressed the man's face was far from sweet.

Murk raised his open hands as if to deny all responsibility. The scout didn't buy it. He went off, shaking his head in disgust.

'East,' Burastan repeated in disbelief. 'Further into Himatan . . .'

'Yes.'

'You're certain?'

'Quite, Lieutenant.'

Her disapproving gaze raked Murk and Sour. 'Very good, sir.'

Murk offered another apologetic shrug. *Man, we're not winnin' any popularity contests round here, that's for sure. Nothin' new in that. Soldiers are a notoriously superstitious lot. Bad luck and setbacks always get laid at the feet of the mages. Just how it is.*

* * *

Rough seas kept Ina below for days on end. The Seguleh were an island people and she was used to sea-travel, but a deep ocean crossing was new to her. And she could freely admit it was a terrifying experience. Here was an enemy no matchless skill with any blade, or exceptional mental focus, could defeat.

She regretted yet again not apportioning slightly more time to her sea-going practice and experience as she leaned over a bucket sloshing with her own vomit and coughed-up bile, her mask pushed up high on her brow. *Well, one cannot know the future. Nor prepare for every eventuality.*

The unnatural ensorcelled vessel rode the waves high and buoyant like a cork. And these deep-ocean waves rolled like prairie hills beneath its keel. Ina felt as if she were riding an impossibly fast horse up and down mountain ridges. The incessant rocking made her dizzy.

During one of these moments, when she sat back wiping her mouth after dry-heaving yet again, her stomach long empty, she sensed her mistress was no longer alone. *Who is it this time?* she wondered, straightening her mask. *Hood? The Sky King? Legendary Mother Dark?*

It occurred to her that given who *had* visited perhaps she ought not be quite so offhand. She climbed the ladder and determined to be utterly resolute no matter who or what appeared.

Legs braced, one hand on the wet cord-wrapped grip of her sword and the other shielding her vision from the dashing spray that surged over the sides, she made her way down the long featureless deck. Her mistress stood as usual near the flat pointed bow, her clothes soaked and clinging to her, well, rather plump and matronly form. Yet she stood with arms crossed, legs shoulder-width apart, as firm as if she'd been built into the carpentry of the vessel.

Standing opposite her was the oddly contrasting, yet strangely complementary, figure of a squat man. He was mostly bald, with a bulbous nose and a sack of a face, barefoot, in an old stained vest and tattered pants held up by a rope belt. Had she not known otherwise she might have mistaken the two for an impoverished old married couple. Yet imposing strength communicated itself from the man's broad humped shoulders and wide gnarled stonemason's hands.

He nodded her a greeting, and what might have been warmth softened eyes the colour of ocean depths. 'Ina of the Jistarii. Welcome,' he said, his voice somehow carrying easily over the groans of the vessel, the crashing spray, and the bow hissing through the mountainous waves.

The Enchantress spoke without turning: 'You may go.'

As an answer Ina planted her feet more widely and crossed her arms. Her mistress gave an exasperated wave. 'You see?' she told the man. 'They never do what you want them to.'

'Our problem in a walnut, T'riss,' answered the man. 'Always has been.'

'You know my answer.'

The fellow wiped a blunt paw across his unshaven jowls. 'It's not for everyone,' he said, 'especially coming from you.'

'It's time.'

'But can you convince her of that?'

The Enchantress shook her head. '*I* cannot convince her of anything.'

'At least we are in agreement on that,' the man muttered darkly. 'Once you land and enter that jungle you'll be beyond my help. Beyond all our help.'

'I know. Rather convincing, that . . . wouldn't you say?'

A wince of pain crossed the man's ugly features and he half turned away. 'I do not like it,' he said, as if confessing to the waters. 'Yet I will not try to stop you. We're cowards, all of us. In the end we're just damned cowards.'

'Not at all, Bugg,' the Enchantress answered. And she embraced the man, who did not raise his arms. '*You* have changed though change is terrifying.'

He edged his face away even further but not before Ina glimpsed tears in his eyes – though it might have been the spray. Those tears shook her more than anything she heard or half understood here. What she gathered was that her mistress was journeying into great danger.

Reaching round, the man grasped her mistress's hands and held them between his. After a time he peered up into her face, his gaze searching, and said, 'Come to me afterwards . . . yes? We have much to speak of.'

Ina heard beneath the request the unspoken: you must survive . . .

Her mistress answered, 'Yes. I shall.' But what Ina heard was, I will try . . .

This ugly lumpish fellow, Bugg, pressed the Enchantress's hands to his lips, then walked off the edge of the deck to disappear into the waves.

Only a quick sign from her mistress stopped Ina from throwing herself after him. 'He'll drown! Will he . . . not?'

Hugging herself, the Enchantress shook her head. 'No. That, Ina, was the one some name the god of the seas.'

'*That* fellow?' She wiped droplets of spray from her chin. 'His real name is Bugg?'

The Enchantress smiled. 'Really, Ina. Don't you know he is worshipped as the god of a thousand names?'

Oh yes. She'd heard that. God of a thousand names and faces. *Well, there you are. And not all are going to be handsome, are they?* Then it struck her that in such a manner – a thousand different experiences – might one come to know humanity far more richly. The life experience of a crippled poor child would, after all, be far different from that of a pampered merchant prince. 'He has empathy for us,' she murmured. 'For what it means to be human.'

'Yes. *He* does,' the Enchantress answered, her voice low, as if she were thinking of other things.

Ina slid her gaze aside to her mistress. It occurred to her that while Mael might have empathy for people, her mistress, the Queen of Dreams, had plans.

The next day the seas quietened and on the southern horizon a dark line of land appeared. It resolved into a swampy shore of mangroves standing on their tangled nests of roots. Ina could see no way past to the firm land beyond. Yet the bow of the vessel continued onward. It sliced the calm turquoise waters of the shallows, heading straight for the dense line of trees. She found herself bracing for an impact, one leg sliding back behind her, turning sideways to the direction of movement.

At the last moment the Enchantress raised an arm and edged it across her front as if brushing something away. The mass of mangrove trees ahead flinched, branches creaking and snapping, as something unseen edged them aside. The waters clouded with great clots of reddish silts that churned with the torn roots. It was as if the entire stretch of coast bled. The long thin vessel slid into the cut like a dagger entering the flesh of the land.

They continued onward for a good league until the bow struck firm soil, grating and groaning. Ina was thrown forward, hopping to keep her footing. The bow rose a few feet then stopped, settling slightly. The noise of grating broken branches scratching the sides of the ship abated and for a moment silence bloomed. Then the surrounding jungle asserted itself and a loud susurrance of insects set up a droning hum. Monkeys hooted and called from distant treetops. Birds shocked her with piercing whistles.

The Enchantress brushed her hands together. 'There. That wasn't so bad.'

Ina inclined her masked head in agreement.

'Let us go.' Her mistress started down the sloped decking towards the vessel's edge.

'A moment,' Ina called, and she went to collect a shoulder bag of gear and skins of water that she'd scavenged from the cabin. 'I will go first.'

The Enchantress shrugged. 'If you must.'

Ina let the bag fall to the sands then jumped down. She reached up for her mistress. 'You will have to let yourself down.'

Awkwardly, the Enchantress let her legs dangle over the side. She then slid – in a very unbecoming manner – to fall into Ina's arms. The Seguleh grunted at the load, but managed to remain standing. *Why is it the world's most potent sorceress should be such a solid washerwoman?* she wondered to herself.

The Queen of Dreams set off through the dense woods. 'This way.'

Ina scrambled after, stepping over roots and low tangles of vines. Branches snagged at her leather hauberk and scratched her scalp. So impenetrable was the press of trees and brush that even the immense hulk of the abandoned ship disappeared from view almost immediately. She wondered how many years it would last, resting there. If it was half as ensorcelled as she suspected then quite some time. She imagined explorers or adventurers crossing this desolate shore some time in the future and coming across its overgrown hull stranded so far inland. What a puzzle it would pose for them.

Then it came to her, and the realization rooted her to the spot. A mysterious destination. An uninhabited jungle shore. A region the very god of the seas considered perilous.

Jacuruku. They had arrived.

It seemed they had just left behind yet another legend for fabled Jacuruku.

That thought put her in mind of that other most famous mythic thread of this land: the legendary city of Jakal Viharn. Even in the streets of Cant such stories were told. Stories of a lost city. Of riches, magic, and the perilous Queen of all Witches who inhabited it. One with the power, so the stories went, to grant any wish to whoever should succeed in reaching her there in the heart of the enchanted jungle . . . Her thoughts tumbled to a halt as it came to her: *By the lost First! Could this be my mistress's intent?*

She rushed closer to the Enchantress's side, moved out of the way a thick hanging liana strung with clinging pink and white blossoms. 'Mistress,' she began, haltingly, 'it is not my place, but I must ask . . .'

The Enchantress halted, one thick brow cocked. 'Yes?'

Ina shivered beneath that arched look. 'I have heard stories of this Ardata . . .'

Both dark brows rose. 'Ah. The stories. Of course.'

Ina gave a quick bow. 'Yes. That all who reach her die. That her blessing is a curse. That she is a witch—'

'I have been damned as a witch,' her mistress calmly observed.

Ina bowed to one knee, stricken. 'Please do not be angered. It is your safety that concerns me. I must know. Do you intend to confront this demon goddess?'

The Enchantress tilted her head in a thoughtful expression. 'Confront . . .' she murmured. 'Such a harsh word. Perhaps,' she added, gesturing to the jungle, 'we had better turn our concerns to closer threats.'

Ina spun, sword hissing free of its wooden sheath. Shapes moved through the thick brush all about them. She bowed her head to her mistress. 'I am a fool!'

The Enchantress pushed back her wet tangled hair. 'Later.'

Ina snapped a curt nod then stood, sword out. The lumbering heavy figures surrounded them. They pushed their way awkwardly through the undergrowth with slow cumbersome steps. As they came nearer she could see them more clearly and an atavistic loathing clamped itself at her throat. Naked they were, shambling forward on thick trunk-like legs – but there any direct resemblance to human stock ceased. The flesh of their stomachs and chests rippled like pale corrugated armour. Their arms were short yet powerful, ending in massive claws. Their heads were reptilian travesties, all jutting bent teeth, slit eyes and plated skin.

Yet she faced them relaxed and confident. None displayed any weapon other than their own teeth and claws. She would cut them to pieces. Her mistress's hand, however, rested upon her shoulder.

'Wait,' the Enchantress murmured, then, louder, 'What do you wish?'

The closest tilted its thick head, as if puzzled. It blinked slowly and coughed. 'We thought . . . we sensed our Queen. But you are not she.'

Ina dared a quick glance to her mistress. The Enchantress was shaking her head. A small amused smile played about her mouth. 'No,' she answered. 'I am not.'

'And yet . . .' the creature continued in a growl, 'there is much of her in you.'

The Enchantress's eyes narrowed, no longer amused. 'Well. You see that I am not. You may go.'

The beast-men – Ina thought them perhaps Soletaken – grumbled and chuffed among themselves. Their leader pulled back its lips to bare its blunt yellowed teeth even further, perhaps displaying disgust or anger. 'We do not answer to you. Why are you here? What is it you wish?'

'I am come to see your mistress,' the Enchantress announced readily enough. She added, 'So do not interfere.'

The creature thumped a clawed hand to its chest. 'We decide who sees the goddess. We are her guardians.'

The beasts all coughed and roared at this pronouncement, sending up a great cacophony of noise that impacted Ina's chest. She eased into a ready stance once again, both hands on her longsword.

'Tell me,' the Enchantress began, her voice thoughtful, 'should your mistress choose to walk through the jungle here, would you bar her way? Because if you wouldn't,' and her voice hardened, 'then you mustn't bar mine.'

The creature's dark eyes widened and it ducked its head as if chastened. It waved a trunk-thick arm to its fellows. Awkwardly, stiffly, all the surrounding beast-men fell to one knee and bowed to the Enchantress.

Quite calmly, the Queen of Dreams gestured Ina onward. As they passed the group's leader, it growled, its head lowered, 'So very much alike . . .'

Ina shot a glance to the Enchantress who continued walking as if nothing had been said. She led the way into the denser brush and Ina had to dodge ahead, sword still ready, brushing aside branches and fronds. She turned the flat of the blade to do so, as it would be an insult to the years put into its cutting edge to use it on mere plants. Not long into the trek she found that she could contain her curiosity no longer. The creature's suggestions of likenesses kept going round and round her mind. Among Ardata's titles was Queen of Witches, and it came to her now that the Enchantress was also known as the Queen of Dreams. These beasts referred to Ardata as their 'goddess' – as the Enchantress was also regarded by her worshippers. They even seemed to think of her as their mistress – just as she so regarded the Enchantress.

As the canopy thickened and layered, the undergrowth thinned, starved of light. Ina fell back to the Enchantress's side. 'Mistress,' she began tentatively. 'Those creatures . . . they are Soletaken?'

The Queen of Dreams walked with her hands clasped at her back. She peered about at the jungle as if interested in every plant and tree. Her skirts hung mud-spattered, torn already. Her hair, drying without any attention from her, was an unkempt matted mess. Ina restrained herself from suggesting that the Enchantress ought to attend to it. Perhaps later, when they stopped for the night, she could simply offer her her comb. At her question the Enchantress had raised her brows, 'Hmm? These inhabitants of Himatan?'

'Yes. They are shapechangers?'

'Shapechangers,' her mistress repeated thoughtfully. 'No. They are as you saw them. They do not change their shape. Few things are capable of changing shape – unless they be of the Eleint. Their blood partakes of chaos, you know.' Ina did not know that. However, she remained silent as her goal was to get her mistress talking. After saying nothing for a time the Enchantress continued, 'Once – long ago – there lived a species, a kind, who could change shape from beast to human. Or perhaps they occupied a place between. It was natural to them. This was not magic as you would understand it.' Ina did not understand magic at all, but she maintained her silence. 'This ability bred true with them. Over thousands of years they spread, parted into clans and tribes. Some lost the ability through interbreeding with other stock – or at least it became very diminished. Others held true to it. And so, over the centuries, that base stock gave rise to many differing forms and kinds of populations – even some indistinguishable from you.'

'I believe I see,' Ina said at last, genuinely grateful for the lesson. Any knowledge offered from a source such as the Queen of Dreams should be honoured.

'Here in Himatan,' the Enchantress continued, musing, 'they have lived undisturbed for a very long time. They have obviously penetrated into differing areas of it. Humankind walk these paths very lightly, Ina. You do not rule here . . . unlike almost everywhere else.'

Ina said nothing but she was rather intrigued by that *almost* – she'd thought otherwise. 'So they are a race, then. Yet they are not of the four founding races.'

The Queen of Dreams gave a very unqueen-like braying laugh. 'The four founding races is a self-justifying myth. Just like all of your origin myths.'

Ina noted the *your* and merely nodded her masked head. Now for the real thrust, she decided. 'And the likeness they spoke of? The similarities between you and . . . Ardata?'

The Enchantress's gaze shifted to rest upon her while they walked. The Seguleh Jistarii, taught since infancy to search for the subtlest of hints in any opponent's eyes, found it impossible to hold the woman's gaze. They did not *look* like any other's eyes. They seemed to lead on to an infinity of depth; she feared she would lose herself within them and never recover.

'Well,' the Enchantress said after a time. 'As to that. The explanation is simple. You could say that she and I are sisters.'

Ina was struck immobile. It was as if she'd forgotten her legs. The Enchantress continued on apparently unconcerned by what she had just divulged. *Sisters! By the First! She and this Queen of Monsters?*

And so what did that make her? Another sort of monster?

Ina examined her thoughts. She was not a worshipper. To her the woman was powerful, yes, and thus indistinguishable from the multitude of gods and goddesses and other powerful spirits and phantoms that crowded the world. That was how it had always been. There were cults in the world that put their number in the countless millions. And as such, then, did that not make the woman's position almost pedestrian? Why should she be surprised? There are gods and goddesses everywhere. One cannot turn over a rock without finding one. She'd heard stories that here in Himatan was preserved the ancient manner of seeing the world; that every tree, every stream and stone possessed a spirit.

And some are far more powerful than others. Like beads on a necklace they form a continuum of existence. A continuum that serves to connect the human with the infinite. That is comforting. Finding a place in an incomprehensible universe is a comforting thing.

Some distance off the Enchantress stopped and turned. 'You are coming?' she called.

Ina blinked, rousing herself, and ducked her head in apology. 'Yes, Mistress.'

*   *   *

'And so begins the great assault upon the water barrier thrown up against the Army of Righteous Chastisement's . . . ah, righteous . . . advance,' Principal Scribe Thorn pronounced, scratching at a parchment sheet on a wooden backing held in his off hand.

Beneath his parasol, one arm upraised holding the Rod of Execution, Master Golan forced a steadying breath through his gritted teeth. 'Not *quite* yet,' he murmured testily. He lowered the arm and officers shouted orders and the first of the troops marched down to the waters to ford out to the awaiting rafts. '*Now* it begins.'

Principal Scribe Thorn raised his gaze from the parchment to blink myopically at the river. 'Ah . . . I see.' He returned to scratching at the parchment.

'Second in Command!' Golan called out. Down below the short earthen cliff that Golan held, overseeing the assault, Second in Command Waris turned from the circle of officers and messengers gathered on the mud shore to bow. 'Remember,' Golan reminded the man, 'they mustn't drink the water. Water is quite unhealthy.'

Waris bowed his head in acknowledgement and returned to his staff.

What will it take to tear a word from that man? Golan wondered.

'Commander Golan assures everyone that water is very unhealthy,' Thorn murmured while writing, his black tongue protruding.

Unlike this one. 'Perhaps the opposite shore would provide a better vantage,' Golan suggested to Thorn.

Without raising his head the scribe read aloud, scribbling, 'The illustrious commander Master Golan offers to lead the assault.'

Golan discovered his jaws clenched tight once more. 'I believe the shovels require re-counting,' he grated.

The Principal Scribe murmured as he wrote: 'No detail is too small to escape Master Golan's eagle eye.'

Golan let hiss another long steadying breath. *Is this the revenge of these outland gods?* Below, new figures emerged from the thick jungle verge to come walking down to the shore just below him: the damned Isturé commander and his pet mages. Golan motioned to the river where the first of the rafts was about to set out, guided on their way across the wide muddy course by ropes dragged and secured, at great loss of life, across the river. 'The advance begins,' he announced, then damned himself as he suspected that sounded far too smug.

The Isturé commander wore his tall full helm. He crossed his arms, the sun glinting from the enamelled black scales of his long coat of armour. 'Indeed. Impressive.'

It was hard to tell since the man's face was obscured, but Golan wondered if he detected mockery from this fellow as well. Was he to be surrounded by detractors? He tucked the Rod of Execution into the sash of his robes, tilted the parasol at a more rakish angle. Yet perhaps not. Perhaps he was merely feeling a touch . . . sensitive . . . and under assault, given the rather, well, troubled character of the campaign's performance to date.

It will unfortunately be held as a personal reflection, after all.

Therefore, it was all the more vital that this operation unfold without hindrance. Yes, quite vital. He watched the soldiers steadying the broad lead raft as they clambered on. A number of the troops took hold of the fixed rope and heaved, pulling hand over hand, drawing the raft along and across the river. They also carried a second length of rope – what remaining stout cords could be found that had yet to succumb to the damp and rot. This would be used to establish a second ferry crossing slightly further downstream. With both operating continuously, Golan calculated they would complete the exercise in two days.

As the morning waned the sun hove directly overhead. It glared down with a punishing heat. The immediately surrounding forest tracts now fell uncharacteristically silent. The army's presence had already naturally quietened the birds and wildlife. Golan wondered if it was the heat of noon that drove all the animals to ground.

Both rafts were now steadily crossing and recrossing the wide ochre-brown rippling flow of the river. Now the possibility of a counter-attack came to haunt Golan. A sufficient portion of the force would be stranded on the opposite side to make it strategically worthwhile. He called down to his second in command: 'Send the Isturé across.'

His second turned to the Isturé commander still standing where he had planted himself. Like a statue, Golan thought. Very like a yakshaka. Waris bowed and gestured, inviting the man down to the line of troops awaiting their turn. The Isturé commander, Skinner, raised his helmed head – still wearing the helm in this heat! – to Golan, who also extended an inviting arm towards the river.

The foreigner said nothing – perhaps aping Golan's impressively taciturn second. He merely flicked a gauntleted hand to the jungle's edge and from the line of nodding broad leaves and brush emerged the full force of his command: some forty of the Disavowed.

They marched down to the shore; an impressive force. All far better armed and armoured than the Thaumaturg regulars, who wore leather hauberks and skirtings and carried spears and wide-bladed iron shortswords at their sides. They commandeered one of the rafts, filling it entire, then pulled their way across.

'Master Golan,' said Thorn, scribbling again, 'gallantly allows his foreign allies the honour of leading the charge.'

Golan ignored the man. New suspicions now nibbled at his mind. There they had been. All gathered together. Waiting. It was as if the foreign dog had anticipated his mind. Knew that he would be sent across early to endure the worst of any counter-attack. An unsettling thought. And pursuing that thought brought Golan to another, even more disturbing suspicion: what if the dog *wanted* to be sent over early? What if it served his black-hearted purpose?

After all, given that the vast majority of the Thaumaturg forces still resided here on the near bank, it would now be easy for the man to simply walk away. Golan took hold of the Rod of Execution in his sash – almost raised it to order that they return – when a more cynical turn of mind suggested: *Come now, man, they could have walked away at any time of their choosing.*

Golan relaxed his hand. And he had to admit, grudgingly, that he could not possibly have recalled them in any case.

At that moment the raft carrying the Isturé reached the middle of the broad rippling breadth of the river and the surface seemed to explode.

The gathered army reflexively shrank away from the shore in a collective gasp of wonder and horror as some huge thing emerged, writhing, from within the river to send the raft flying skyward as it shattered into individual logs, men and women flying like dolls. The ropes snapped in exploding reports. Golan could not be certain, but the thing resembled the descriptions he had read in travel accounts of an immense snake, or worm. He had dismissed such writings as nonsense, of course. A girth as great as any sea-going vessel! Ridiculous. Purported eyewitness accounts had such creatures pulling ships beneath the surface, even sweeping up entire armies into their great maws.

Tall combers now crashed into the river's edge, sending the troops scrambling from the shore. Up on his mud cliff Golan watched while the foam and flotsam washed close to the pointed silken tips of his slippers. Once the waves subsided, the river's surface smoothed once more, flexing slightly, as if the beast yet shifted in the shallow muddy waters.

Of the raft and its Isturé cargo, only a few isolated logs bobbing downriver remained to mark that they had ever existed.

'The foreign dogs,' Principal Scribe Thorn announced from his side, scribbling, 'proved no match for Master Golan's cunning stratagems.'

Golan shifted his tired gaze to the gangly, thatch-haired old scribe. 'Perhaps you would do better to note that the river itself has risen to challenge our advance.'

The scribe's head shot up, his tangled brows rising like twin hedges. 'You are a wonder, Master. You anticipate my very thoughts!' He jabbed the quill to his tongue to resume scribbling.

Below, the second in command could actually be heard yelling orders. *It is a day of wonders*, Golan decided, rubbing his gritty eyes. 'Resecure the ropes, Second!' he ordered, his eyes pinched shut.

While the troops waited, watching, squatting in the mud, labourers were pushed out into the shallows and encouraged through stiff beatings to grasp hold of poles or other pieces of floating detritus to kick their way across the river. Many set out clutching lengths of wood under their chins. Golan followed their bobbing black heads while the current swept them downstream. Eventually he lost sight of them.

The afternoon waned; Golan tapped the Rod of Execution into a palm behind his back. The shadow of the western jungle verge crept out over the river. All manner of speculations – each more alarming than the one before – assailed him. Had a force been waiting there across the river? Was the foothold crushed? What of the damned Isturé? Had they reappeared? Had they perhaps taken this opportunity to turn upon him? Attacked the stranded force in an effort to weaken the army? Would this water beast return?

Black-haired heads now appeared among the rippling waves. They came bobbing down from further up-current. Troopers waded out to pull them ashore where they knelt on all fours in the mud, naked and exhausted. Two had come kicking a long pole from which a rope now trailed leading back across the river in a long bow-shaped curve. The troopers reported to overseers, who, in turn, reported to cohort commanders, who then bowed to Second-in-Command Waris to offer the findings.

Master Golan fidgeted throughout, clasping and reclasping the rod in his sweaty slick hands. Waris dismissed the officers then jogged up the mud cliff to bow before Golan. 'You have news?' Golan enquired, struggling to keep his voice mild, seemingly disinterested.

On one knee, head down, Waris answered, 'No hostilities. The Isturé emerged unhurt and marched away into the jungle. A new raft is being constructed. We are delayed one day, Master.'

Golan took in this intelligence while nodding to himself. *Not so bad as I had imagined. And the Isturé unhurt – a pity that. Abandoning us? Just as well, perhaps.* 'Thank you, Second. You are to be commended for your, ah, brevity.'

The man merely bowed his head even lower, backed away, then jogged down to the shore. Golan cocked an eye to Principal Scribe Thorn. The scribe tapped the quill to his tongue in thought, then wrote, speaking aloud: 'All the many disastrous setbacks are met with redoubled effort.'

Master Golan winced.

Two days later saw the majority of the army on the eastern shore. To the great relief of the army's rank and file, the monstrous water beast had not returned to destroy any further rafts. For an idle moment Golan wondered how it had chanced that the raft carrying the Isturé should be the only one to suffer attack, but more pressing matters chased the speculation from his mind.

Leading elements of the army had already set out to select and mark the best route through the dense growth. It was late on this second day that Golan's new aide – whose name he could not

402

remember since they now came and went so very quickly as illness took them – announced that the ranking army surgeon requested a hearing.

Searching among his chests and boxes, Golan nodded a distracted affirmative. He was in his personal tent that was no longer a tent, not possessing sufficient cloth to merit the name. More of an awning. A personal awning. One that merely served to keep the sun off his head in the day and the rain in the night.

He might be misremembering, but it seemed to him that he was missing one or two pieces of baggage. He was aware that there was always the chance of losses during river crossings, but still, it was quite irking. It would seem that he was without a camp stool.

Turning, he found the tall lean figure of the ranking army surgeon – whose name he could not recall – awaiting him. He waved the man forward. 'Yes? You have a report?' The man bowed, stiff with exhaustion. He was without his stained leather apron of office. He appeared as worn as always, yet a new expression tightened the bruised flesh round his eyes. Golan thought he read suppressed despair. 'What is it?' he asked.

'A new . . . illness . . . has come to my attention, Master. I believe it to be connected to the crossing.'

'Yes? What of it? Sickness is rampant throughout the ranks, as you well know. There is the foot rot, the crotch rot, infections of all kinds, suppurating sores, debilitating heatstroke, poisoning from a multitude of stings and bites, general dehydration, the tremors, loss of teeth, loss of appetite, the runs, vomiting, lassitude and weakness from the thinning of the blood. Need I go on? Yes, no?'

'I am well aware of the health of the army,' the ranking surgeon answered in a slow dull tone. He was pale and swaying himself, appearing hardly able to stand. 'This is a . . . parasitical . . . infestation.'

Golan's brows lifted in interest. 'Oh?' Parasites were a particular hobby of his. He'd quite enjoyed the classes on them at the Academy. 'Which? Is it that awful fly that has been laying its eggs in everyone's eyes? Does it have a water-borne stage?'

'No, sir . . .'

'This type of chigger whose larvae are gnawing everyone's flesh? I understand they can be asphyxiated through the application of a compress.'

'Yes, sir . . .'

'The hookworm is worse now? The ringworm numbers? Surely not the tapeworms! Bad for morale, those. Especially when they're vomited up during communal meals. Or is it that worm that you have to pull out of the flesh of the leg? One specimen was as long as the fellow carrying it was tall, if I remember correctly.'

'Fascinating, I'm sure. If I may, sir . . .'

'Yes? What is it?'

'I suggest very strongly that you come and see for yourself . . .'

Golan turned to the crowd of officers and staff waiting outside the awning. He gestured to them with both arms. 'Seeing as I have nothing more pressing to attend to?'

The ranking surgeon's tongue emerged to lick his cracked lips. He swayed, something even more desperate, yet firmly suppressed, pinching his gaze. 'Please . . . sir. It is really . . . quite . . . pressing.'

Golan clasped his hands at his back. 'Oh, very well!' He glowered at the importuning surgeon. 'Only out of scholarly interest, mind you.'

The patient was a young lad on a table alone in a private tent. He was perhaps in his teens – it was hard for Golan to tell exactly, as early illnesses or starvation can blunt an individual's development. Skinny, emaciated even, he was one of the labourers. A grimed rag wrapped his loins, but other than that he was naked. He appeared to be drugged into unconsciousness. Leather straps held his ankles and wrists. A leather gag covered his mouth. Golan raised his brows at the restraints.

'He would have killed himself from the pain,' the surgeon explained.

'Pain?'

By way of answer, the surgeon indicated that Golan should more closely examine the lad's body. Frowning, Golan leaned closer. After a moment, what he discerned all over the lad's limbs and torso made even him, a trained Thaumaturg, flinch away.

Things writhed just beneath the lad's skin. Long worm-like lengths twisted and squirmed all up and down his legs, arms, stomach and chest.

'What is this?' Golan breathed, impressed. Even a touch fearful.

The ranking surgeon's expression was flat and dull, as if the man had been driven beyond all feeling, all empathy. 'They are as you suggested. A form of worm infestation. Similar, I believe, to the infamous Ganari-worm that has been eradicated from our lands, only a far more virulent offshoot. Unlike its cousins, this one does not spare its hosts. These worms are consuming the lad from the inside out.'

At that moment Golan wanted nothing more than to flee the tent.

He even felt his stomach tightening in nausea – a feeling he'd thought squeezed from him long ago. Pride in his position, however, demanded that he display nothing. Thus he simply nodded in what he hoped resembled scholarly appreciation of an interesting phenomenon. He clasped his hands at his back. 'They were in the water, then?' he asked, his voice a touch hoarse and faint.

'I believe so. As far as I can establish, this lad was among those who assembled the rafts. He and his coworkers spent a great deal of time standing in the water.'

Golan's throat choked almost closed, and he grasped the table edge behind him to keep from falling. *All the labourers. And the soldiers. Had they not all taken it in turns to wade in to help?*

The surgeon was studying Golan closely, a bloodied hand raised to help. He appeared to understand that his commander now grasped the severity of the situation and nodded, grimly. 'Indeed.'

'We must find the infected. Isolate them.'

The surgeon's face remained bleak. 'I would think it more of a mercy if you would order the yakshaka to—' The man gaped, his gaze fixed beyond Golan, his eyes growing huge.

Golan heard wet things slipping and slithering to the ground behind him. The tiny hairs of his arms stood up straight and icy fingers traced their nails up his spine. His training took hold immediately and he turned, steadily, having withdrawn into Thaumaturg calmness of mind.

The youth's body was a horror of thousands of wriggling worms, all writhing free of his flesh from every inch of skin. They even emerged squirming and questing blindly from his eyes, ears, mouth and nostrils. They slithered free to tumble and fall and snake off under the lips of the tent.

Golan heard the surgeon fall insensate behind him. Coolly, he raised a hand and the sagging shape of bones and limp skin amid its forest of twisting parasites burst into sizzling blue and white flames. It was the least he could do for the lad, though, in truth, it was more like housecleaning.

He turned to the prone form of the surgeon, used his toe to flick aside a few of the worms nosing his body. 'Get up, man,' he urged. 'We've work to do. We must segregate the infected. Come.'

The surgeon groaned, flailing. Golan nudged him with his toe. 'Come, man. We—'

Golan broke off, for distantly, across the encampment, here and there, rose shrill screams of agony and uncomprehending terror – the shrieks of those being eaten alive from within.

In the quiet of the gloomy chamber Osserc blinked rapidly, coming to himself. He peered about quickly, a touch panicked. All was as before: the monkey creature lay asleep at the table, its head down, snoring contentedly, drool dripping from its open mouth. Across the gouged slats of the tabletop, Gothos still sat immobile. His knotted hands lay flat before him. His roped iron-grey hair hung like moss to his shoulders. It was as if the Jaghut was carved from granite.

He'd been thinking of his youth among the Tiste and the halls of his father's hold. All so different from now. So much lost. It was all he could do to hold on to even a fraction of it. He'd always been of the mind that one must look back to know how to proceed. Yet now this creature sitting opposite seemed to be suggesting that holding on to the past – being guided by the past – was wrong. A self-limiting trap.

Odd to hear such things coming from a Jaghut, of all creatures. Though they always did have a pragmatic streak. For his part he never truly understood them. Perhaps there can be no true understanding between the races. A downturned smile pulled at his lips. The historical record attests that such relations hold little promise for understanding.

Very well. The lesson is to be guided by the past without being trapped by it. A pithy homily. Why be guided by lessons of the past? For wisdom, of course. Ah. Here we approach the meat of the matter. Wisdom.

Not something usually associated with his name.

Anomander, now, that was another thing. Wise beyond his years, everyone thought him. The wisdom of Anomander. Whereas Osserc . . . well, few mentioned wisdom and Osserc in the same breath.

What, then, had he gathered? Knowledge. A great deal of knowledge. He had wandered the very shores of creation. Tasted the blood of the Eleint. Plumbed the depths of the Abyss itself. Studied the verges of the Realms. He had questioned the Azathanai repeatedly – though he came away with little to show for it. And now he had even investigated the Azath. Few could boast of as thorough an interrogation of the underlying truths of existence.

Yet what had all this study and probing and ruthless examination taught him? He considered his hands on the table before him. He turned them over to inspect the lined palms.

Only his appalling ignorance.

He might have assembled a truly impressive archive of facts, yet one area remained a dark chasm before him. Self-knowledge. The sort of exploration that inflicted true pain. Was this why he'd so . . . studiously . . . avoided it? And how then could he be puzzled as to why he did not understand anyone else when he did not know himself? Some would argue that was plainly obvious.

He remembered, then, the time L'oric had been trapped within the shrinking fragment of a shattered realm. He'd had to rescue the fool. Then, he'd felt only anger at the lad's stupidity, resentment at the intrusion and embarrassment that one of his should have been so careless. Of course he'd communicated none of this to L'oric.

Now, reflecting back, it struck him that what the lad had been doing was in fact emulating him. That, if anyone was to blame, it was he for bringing into being such exploratory recklessness and pushing of boundaries. For his utter neglect and lack of guidance.

Osserc felt a hot sharp stabbing in his chest and his breath came short and tight. He clutched the wooden slats as if he would fall. Across the table Gothos' gaze, hidden deep within his curtain of hair, shifted, glittering like sunken wells.

If this be the price of self-knowledge I want none of it. It is just too much . . . Not the errors of the forefathers revisited. Not that. Too painful by far.

So – is the judgement that I have learned nothing? That I stand now as an even poorer example than my own poor father? Perhaps so. Perhaps so.

The eternal question then, that we return to once again, is how to proceed from this datum . . .

The head of the monkey creature, the Nacht, popped up from the table. Blinking, it peered about suspiciously. Across the table Gothos' hands drew in closer to his body. The talon-like nails raked lines in the wood.

'What is it?' Osserc asked. His voice sounded shockingly loud in the silence.

The Jaghut turned his head to the hall leading to the front door. 'Something . . .'

Osserc then heard a sound. It appeared to be coming from the front – a scratching and tearing noise. It was oddly dim, or muted. He stood away from the table and headed up the hall. The sound, whatever it might be, was coming from outside. Osserc regarded the barrier of the thick planks of the front door, the beaten iron handle. He turned back to peer up the hall; Gothos had stood as well and now regarded him, his arms crossed.

Osserc gestured to the door. 'Shall I?'

The Jaghut shrugged eloquently. 'It is not up to me.'

Very well. He tried the door: it opened, creaking loudly. Outside it was an overcast night. It had been raining. The glow of the moon and the Visitor behind the massed clouds gleamed from the wet slates of the walkway. Mist obscured the surrounding stone buildings. The sea broke surging against the nearby shore.

A ragged human figure lay on the ground. A trail of churned-up dirt lay behind it. The trail ended at the steaming heap of a disturbed burial barrow.

Osserc called up the hall: 'Something's escaping. Or tried.'

Gothos approached. He peered out past Osserc's shoulder. 'Indeed?'

While they stood watching, the figure thrust out an arm ahead of itself to grasp a fistful of grass and dirt to pull, heaving itself one agonizing hand's-breadth along. It looked like a man, but stick-thin, in rags and caked in dirt.

'Know you it, or him?'

Gothos scratched his chin with a thick yellowed nail. His upthrusting Jaghut tusk-like teeth, so close now, appeared to bear the scars of once having been capped. 'One of the more recently interred.'

'How is it he's got this far? Is the House weakening?'

Gothos shook his head. 'No . . . Not in this case.'

The jangle of metal announced someone jogging down the street. He appeared from the mist as an iron-grey shape in heavy banded armour. A battered helmet boasting wide cheek-guards completely obscured his face. He looked quite formidable, barrel-chested, with a confident rolling bear-like gait. Osserc was mildly surprised to see such a martial figure here on this small backwater island. The soldier, or guard, took up a post near the low wall surrounding the House's grounds – the point that the crawling escapee appeared to be making for.

Osserc and Gothos continued to watch while the escapee made his agonizingly slow way towards the wall. Osserc noted that although the many roots writhing like mats across the yard grasped at him they seemed unable to retain their grip as he slipped onward through their hold.

'I admire his . . . persistence,' Gothos murmured. 'But he is called . . .'

'Called?' Osserc asked, but the Jaghut did not respond.

The wretched figure made the wall and, by scrabbling at the piled fieldstones, pulled himself upright. He was wearing tattered dirt-caked rich silks that might have once been black. Thin baldrics that might once have held weapons criss-crossed his back. His hair was black, touched by grey. He was a slim, aristocratic-looking fellow.

The moment he straightened the soldier ran him through. The broad heavy blade of the soldier's longsword emerged from the man's back then was withdrawn, scraping on bone.

The escapee did not so much as flinch. He remained standing. Shaking his head, he gave a long low chuckle that sounded quite crazed.

'Let him go,' Gothos called. 'The House has no hold over him.'

'How in the name o' Togg could that be?' the soldier answered in a rough, parade-ground bark.

The figure had thrown a leg over the wall; the soldier shield-bashed him to tumble back on to the ground where he lay laughing a high giggle as if the situation was hilarious.

'Let him go, Temper,' Gothos called once more, sounding bored. 'You cannot stop him.'

'Wait a damned minute,' the soldier, Temper, growled. He pointed an armoured finger. 'I know this bastard. It's Cowl! There's no way I'm lettin' this ghoul free in *my* town!'

The figure, perhaps Cowl, grew quite still at that. Then he was up on his feet in an instant, crouched, a knife in each dirt-smeared hand. '*Your* town!' he hissed. '*Yours!* You don't actually think I want to spend more than one second in this pathetic shithole?' He lifted his chin as if to gather his dignity, and brushed at his tattered shirt as if to smooth it. 'Business elsewhere calls me. I have a message to deliver to my commander.' Then he pressed a hand to his mouth to stifle a laugh that almost doubled him over.

Temper set his fists on his waist. 'Well – seems I can't kill you, seeing as you're already dead.' He lifted his armoured head to Osserc and Gothos at the door. 'What guarantee can you offer?'

Gothos snorted his disgust and walked away up the hall. Osserc remained. Crossing his arms, he called to Cowl, 'You intend to leave?'

The figure offered a mocking courtier's bow. Osserc had placed that name now: Cowl, chief assassin and High Mage of the mercenary army, the Crimson Guard. A powerful and dangerous entity to be allowed his freedom on any continent. Yet how could this one possess the strength to shrug off entombment by the Azath? He personally knew of several far more potent beings currently inhumed on these very grounds – some he had battled and was quite glad were now writhing, constrained, beneath his feet. Some who possessed the very blood of the Azathanai themselves. Why, even one of his own daughters had once been taken by a House . . . Well, that was between them.

And he *had* warned them.

'The House cannot, or chooses not to, hold him,' he called. 'Let him go. I've no doubt he'll flee.'

'*Flee!*' Cowl echoed, outraged.

Temper laughed his scorn – as Osserc hoped he would. 'Yeah,' the soldier scoffed, 'run away, you pissant knifer. No-good backstabber.' He backed up a step, inviting Cowl forward.

The assassin was hunched, as if suspicious. But he drew a hand across his mouth, the knife's blued blade shimmering in the moonlight. In one quick fluid motion he was over the low wall. He tilted his head then, to the soldier, and disappeared in a flicker of shadows.

'You take a lot upon yourself, soldier,' Osserc called.

'That?' the soldier sneered. He hawked up a mouthful of phlegm and spat where the assassin had been standing. 'That was nothin'. Come down here and take one step outside and I'll run *you* through. 'Bout time some someone took you down to size.'

Osserc raised a brow. He was half tempted to accept the challenge. But right now he had no intention of gaining D'rek's ire. For he recognized her touch upon the man. And so he merely saluted the fellow and pulled the door shut.

He found Gothos reseated, as if nothing had happened, hands flat once more upon the slats of the table. He sat opposite. After a time he found that he could no longer contain his curiosity and so he said: 'Very well. I must ask – why doesn't the House have a hold on this man? Surely he is no more powerful than others of the interred.'

Gothos sighed his world-weariness. 'Because,' he murmured, completely disinterested, 'he has already been claimed.'

Osserc grunted his understanding, or rather his complete lack of understanding. That was an answer – but at the same time it answered nothing. Claimed? Whatever did he mean? His thoughts, however, were interrupted by a loud scraping noise of metal over stone echoing from the hallway.

The Nacht creature appeared. It was muttering under its breath, perhaps even mouthing curses. It came dragging a long-handled shovel after it, up the hallway towards the front.

After a moment Osserc heard the front door open then slam shut.

CHAPTER XI

Ancient legend has it that within the central tower of the
ceremonial complex dwells a goddess, or genie, formed in
the shape of a giant serpent with nine heads. During certain
propitious nights of the year this genie appears in the shape
of a woman, with whom the god-king must couple. Should
the king fail to keep his tryst, disaster is sure to follow.

Ular Takeq
Customs of Ancient Jakal-Uku

THE STRATEGY MEETING TO CONSIDER THE ATTACK UPON THE
Thaumaturg capital, Anditi Pura, was a much less contentious
affair than the earlier one for Isana Pura. From his seat among
the scattered cushions, Prince Jatal studied the reclining figures of the
various family heads and could not believe what he was witnessing.
In their ease and laughter, their self-assurance and certainty of the
victory ahead, he read ignorance, over-confidence – even childish
recklessness.

To his sustained astonishment, they merely accepted every assurance the foreign Warleader offered. All would be as at Isana Pura,
the ancient promised them. The populace constituted no threat. The
Thaumaturgs would be contained within their walled precincts,
their Inner City, and the shaduwam, whom they had been waiting
for, would deal with them. Throughout the man's explanations
the various chiefs had nodded their acceptance, including Princess
Andanii.

'What of the organized resistance we met upon the road?' Jatal
demanded. 'Someone is obviously mustering their opposition.'

The Warleader turned his dead grey gaze upon him. He made a

vague gesture of dismissal. 'Yes, my prince. And it has been crushed. So much for it.'

The circle of family heads laughed at that, toasting the victory. It was all Jatal could do to stop himself from damning them as a carnival of fools – but that would win him no allies. Steadying himself with a deep breath, he tried again: 'And these reports of barricades and roadblocks throughout the city?'

Another impatient flick of a veined hand from the old commander. 'Yes. By now they understand that they face a mounted threat and some few efforts are being made to block the roads. However, they cannot stop up every entrance. The Adwami will win through, yes?'

The various chiefs and family heads cheered at that and pledged to win through no matter what.

It was precisely this 'no matter what' that worried Jatal. Who knew what faced them? Perhaps things would go as at Isana Pura. Perhaps not. To his mind it was too great a risk to blindly thrust one's head into the leopard's mouth trusting it to work a second time.

Yet, a voice whispered in the back of his mind, *do not great gains demand great risks? Is this meekness speaking? Cowardice?*

And so, seeing that the Warleader had won round Princess Andanii and all her Vehajarwi allies, Jatal said no more. Better not to alienate or sideline himself from the general council. 'The Elites plus your mercenaries will secure the inner precincts then?' he asked.

The Warleader inclined his head in agreement. 'Of course. As before.' The mercenary commander then swept the circle of reclining chiefs. 'If there are no more questions – then we are decided. We ride before dawn.'

More cheering and toasting – completely idiotic in Jatal's opinion – followed this pronouncement. Throughout, his gaze held upon Princess Andanii, who sat close to the Warleader. The entire time she refused to meet his eyes. How he wished to send her a yearning glance, a silent plea for a sign – any sign at all. But that would be weakness and so he kept his gaze hard and flat. He would not abase himself before anyone. He excused himself at the first opportunity.

In his tent, he dismissed his Horsemaster and aides and servants then threw himself down on his bedding of piled blankets and cushions. But sleep would not come. Instead he tossed and turned, sweating in the warm humid night. Finally, he sat up and pulled a night table close for a glass of cold tea. He considered his sleeplessness. He should be resting before the attack. Was this the base writhing of a coward before battle? *No, let us say not.* What, then? Reasonable and understandable nerves in the face of such profound unknowns?

Perhaps. Yet it felt so much stronger, so much more visceral. He had it then. Dread. A presaging of doom. An absolute certainty of failure.

He peered round the murky tent walls. What to do? Flee? No. He knew he was without options. There was only one course available – to go through with it. He felt like a man on his way to his execution, his feet bringing him steadily closer to the headsman's sword. The longing thought brushed through him then: would she come?

No. No more weakness. No more mewling or cringing. He must resign himself to his coming destruction. He remembered, then, what he as a prince of the Hafinaj ought to be doing in preparation for impending death.

He dug out his personal satchel of books and writing materials. He opened the wooden case holding the inkstone, spread a sheet of clean vellum.

He paused, holding himself still, sensing the moment, his mood, his churning spinning thoughts. Then he composed:

> *The wind blows across the sands*
> *My steps ahead lie as unknown*
> *As those behind*

He set down the sharpened quill. There. Last duty done. He dusted the ink then folded up the sheet and tucked it into his shirt over his heart.

Now perhaps sleep would come.

Woken before dawn, Jatal found himself in a rare fey mood. His aides dressed and armoured him. He consumed a light breakfast of hot tea and fruit. Readying to go, he thrust two daggers through his belt, tested the weight of his sword, then tucked his helmet under an arm. At the tent flap he turned to the aides and tilted his head in salute. 'Good hunting today, gentlemen.'

They bowed. 'Victory, Prince.' Jatal accepted this with a nod, let the flap fall. Yes, victory. But whose? He went in search of Pinal.

The Horsemaster found him first. Ash was ready, accoutred in his light armour bardings. Jatal stroked his neck and fed him an apple he'd kept from breakfast. 'Good hunting today, friend,' he murmured to the stallion who shook his head in answer, jesses jangling.

'The Elites are mustering,' Pinal said as he mounted.

'You will ride with the regulars today, Pinal,' he told the Horsemaster, whose brows rose in surprise. 'Command in my name. And . . . take good care of them. Yes? That is your first duty.'

413

His old companion bowed silently, though wonder and hurt warred upon his face. Jatal kneed Ash onward.

The Elites were indeed gathering. Princess Andanii was already in attendance. An even stronger bodyguard of Vehajarwi captains surrounded her. Jatal bowed a greeting. 'Princess.'

She too eyed him uncertainly, as if detecting something odd in his tone or manner. Jatal thought she looked flushed and wary. For an instant hope flared in his chest as he imagined that it was shame that brought such colour to her cheeks. Shame and regret. Then another voice sneered upon such hopes: *She only now is touched by a true awareness of the enormity of what she attempts.*

Yet to his admiring gaze she appeared an inspiringly warlike figure in her white robes, with her wind-whipped headscarf hanging dazzlingly bright over her bands of enamelled green and silver armour. Her great longbow stood tall at her back. Her peaked helmet sported its Vehajarwi crest of a stylized leaping horse.

'Prince,' she responded. 'This day we may realize our ambitions.'

'Indeed.' *But which ambitions might those be?*

She reared tall in her saddle to peer back over the assembled Elites. A new fervour glowed in her brown eyes and she thrust up an arm, shouting: 'Glory to the Adwami!'

A great roar answered her as two thousand throats echoed the shout. Jatal bowed his answer. *Indeed, may this day bring glory to the Adwami. If only that.* Andanii brought her arm down chopping forward and they surged ahead, charging for the road to the capital.

It was not yet dawn. A golden pink light suffused the flat eastern horizon. Behind, the night was purple and dark ocean-green with the clinging sullen glow of the Visitor. The air was crisp and cool. It dried Jatal's sweaty face and neck. His hands upon the reins became numb. The road was empty – either word of their presence had spread, or traffic was always rather light. From what Jatal had seen so far of the lack of commerce for such a large population, he suspected the latter.

They did pass field after field, some fallow, most crowded with tall stands of rice. The food production at least was impressive. One could give the Thaumaturgs that: they were organized. What was lacking, however, was anything beyond a mere agrarian society. They rode past clutches of farmers' hamlets, granaries, even corrals for livestock, but where were the merchant houses, the inns, the manufacturers or traders? These magus-scholar overlords seemed to encourage none of those. They were no doubt quite happy to keep their populace chained to the countryside.

414

As they drew nearer the capital, this populace revealed itself in greater numbers. Figures worked hunched in the fields, bent wretches in rags bowed to them from the sides of the road as they stormed past. No doubt they were required by law to move aside for anyone riding by – under the logic that anyone not busy working the land must be an official.

This lack of reliance on mechanisms and domesticated animals struck Jatal as further serving to subjugate the populace. The work they must do was simply all that much greater. They passed more of those Thaumaturg-altered oxen-like labourers: some toiled in the fields pulling simple wooden implements; others were strapped to irrigation water-wheels or pulling carts.

So far the Warleader's predictions appeared borne out: this populace constituted no threat. So beaten down were they that anything beyond the limited horizons of their daily grinding round was as alien as travel to another land. Yet this very seeming lack of humanity profoundly disturbed Jatal. They seemed incapable of anything, yet at the same time chillingly capable of everything imaginable.

The outskirts of the capital hove into view. Like Isana Pura in the south, this urban centre lay as a huge rambling conglomeration of low, single- or double-storey brick and clay box-like buildings. Laundry hung drying from flat ceilings or on stands. Striped awnings stretched out over the narrow streets.

Crowds of pedestrians fled from them down side streets or into doorways. They encountered a few pathetic efforts to raise barricades. At their approach the city-dwellers manning these simply ran, abandoning the overturned carts and heaped barrels and wooden chests. These the Adwami jumped or quickly demolished. Their mounted scouts kept reappearing to urge the main column onward.

They reached the Inner City complex. A massive wall of rust-hued brick surrounded it and its main gate, a good two rods in height and sheathed in iron-studded bronze, remained sealed. A broad open marshalling field – or killing ground – surrounded the walls, complete with narrow stone ditches.

The scouts milled here, far back from the main gate. A scattering of dead men and horses littered the paved ground. Tall spears, or javelins, stood from their bodies. 'What is this?' Jatal demanded of the nearest rider. 'Who is defending?'

'Yakshaka on the walls,' the Awamir rider answered.

'Why is the way yet sealed?'

'We are to await the Warleader's mercenaries,' Andanii called. 'They will open the way.'

What was this? More secrets between them? Here was further evidence of their intimacy. And of his irrelevance. He did not know which writhed in his chest the worse. What more details might they have arranged behind his back? Perhaps this attack was intended to rid her and the Warleader of more than one obstacle to their supremacy. Perhaps he was riding to his death.

Well . . . she has slain me already. This flesh is but a hollow shell. But my people, what of them? Pinal will protect them. He will withdraw.

The clatter of hooves marked the arrival of the Warleader's van. He rode at the fore. The giant Scarza loped alongside his horse, a monstrous two-bladed axe over one shoulder. *His warhound,* Jatal sneered. And yet the man had seemed quite friendly earlier – *all the more to quell your suspicions!*

Jatal acknowledged the Warleader's arrival with an impatient wave. 'Our advance is halted already!'

'A small matter,' the Warleader answered. 'My men will take it.' Dismounting, he motioned to the half-Trell. 'Scarza, you will lead the assault.'

The giant grinned, further revealing his great yellowed tusks. 'We will be within in moments.' He passed Jatal and gave a conspiratorial wink. 'Now you will see the professionals at work, yes?'

Jatal found he could no longer answer the man's jesting banter in kind. The Trell turned away, frowning as if uneasy, and clapped his enormous hands together. 'Come, lads! Form up!'

From his vantage point mounted on Ash's back, it appeared to Jatal like an all-out assault. Troops formed to a wide front. He saw teams of shieldmen and crossbowmen gathering, and what one might call sappers, or siegeworkers, who carried coiled rope and large iron grapnels. Behind this attack force rallied ranks of archers who would presumably provide covering fire.

Still mounted on his heavy warhorse, the Warleader walked it to the fore. Turning, he regarded the ranks. More than ever he now struck Jatal as a figure of war and rapine. His battered and ragged mail coat hung iron-grey down the sides of his mount. His equally ashen beard seemed to meld with the neck of his camail. His flat smoky eyes seemed forged from iron. The Grey Man, he sometimes overheard the mercenaries calling him. Or the Grey Ghost.

Behind him, tall gleaming figures now moved slowly at the crenellations of the walls – the yakshaka forming into position.

'Soldiers,' the Warleader began, his voice strong, 'you follow me as a proven war leader. Today you will have your reward! Take this position and this city and all it contains will be yours to choose from. Enough riches to buy estates in any country of your choice. Or you may choose to remain here and share in the rulership of these lands. Victory here could win you everything. Defeat will bring you nothing. From this point onward, the choice is yours.' And he bowed his head to them, briefly, as if to reinforce: this day is yours.

The mercenaries howled their answer like bloodthirsty wolves. They shook their weapons. Scarza goaded them on, bellowing and roaring. The sound froze Jatal's blood. He'd never heard the like. *This must be how they conduct war in other lands.* It struck him as barbaric.

The trained scholar within, however, coolly observed, *They are working themselves into a frenzy to do what they must: a direct assault on the gate. Many will die and only chance will decide which.*

Desperate men and women making an all or nothing throw against long odds. It was a wager Jatal wouldn't take.

His gaze found Andanii's pale and sweat-sheathed face. She watched the mercenaries and their preparations as if mesmerized. The realization came to him then: *You fool! You are in the midst of such a throw now. And you may very well have already lost . . .*

Still roaring, the mercenaries charged. Teams spread out to tackle as wide a front as possible. They clambered down the sloping sides of the slit ditches then scrabbled up the far sides. The ranks of archers followed more slowly, stopping to fire salvos that arched for the walls.

And where are these vaunted Thaumaturgs? Duelling the shaduwam within, I hope.

At the walls yakshaka appeared with what looked like javelins. These they heaved in mighty throws far outstripping anything a common man might manage. The missiles landed with earsplitting clanging and ringing. They slammed into the stone-flagged grounds to stand erect. Where they stuck mercenaries, shieldmen or no, they passed straight through, pinning the unfortunate to the spot.

Those are solid bronze rods, Jatal realized, awed. Now he knew why the horses had fallen: they had been completely run through as well.

The assault wave reached the walls. Grapnels flew, trailing knotted ropes. The yakshaka moved to respond. Men and women climbed with desperate speed. Here and there yakshaka took hold of the grapnels, and, despite the astounding weight of several attackers, heaved the line free to send them falling in a screaming heap.

Arrows stood from the armoured giants like forests of quills; they seemed to pay them no attention. They dropped their bronze spears straight down. The missiles wrought a horrific price among the clumped besiegers. Yet it looked to Jatal as though there were far more lines than defenders. Mercenaries now made the battlements atop the walls. Here they met the yakshaka, who cut them down as they came.

With attackers on the walls, the archers eased off. The Warleader barked a command and they roared their own growling throaty answer. They charged, adding their numbers to the assault.

Had this been an attack on any other wall in any other place with the attackers so outnumbering the defenders, Jatal imagined that the outcome would not have been in doubt. But these were armoured yakshaka guards. They swept the mercenaries from the walls. Cut them down with great blows of their two-handed blades. The attack appeared to be stalling.

Jatal spotted Scarza climbing a rope at one of the uncontrolled sections of wall. He rose hand over hand, his axe swinging at his back. Making the battlements, he charged for the front line. Jatal glimpsed him between crenellations, dodging and ducking as he made his way closer to the line of defenders. Then a yakshaka came tottering from the battlement, overbalanced, then fell in utter silence. It crashed to the ground, shattering upon the stone flags in an explosion like an enormous pot breaking.

An answering cheer arose from the mercenaries waiting their turn on the ropes.

Jatal again glimpsed the broad form of the Trell as he shouldered aside another of the defenders and straight-armed it over a low section of the crenellations. This one also fell in complete silence to burst like a dropped pot.

Do those things not even know fear? Jatal wondered. Why no scream or roar of protest?

Scarza charged the gatehouse tower. 'He might just make it,' Jatal murmured to the Warleader.

The mercenary was stroking his grizzled beard. 'Scarza has never failed me,' he answered, in the smug tone one might use when discussing a prized dog or horse.

That tone drove Jatal to flinch in distaste, only to realize: *I am no better.* He returned to studying the battle. *Have I wronged you, foreigner?*

The Warleader nodded to Andanii, who pulled her rapt gaze from the wall and jerked a curt answer. She turned on her mount to the marshalled Elites, yelled: 'Ready to advance!'

Jatal thought her voice a touch too choked and shrill. Perhaps she had lost her taste for adventure and daring, now that the price to pay was so bitter. It occurred to him that their positions had seemingly reversed: he, once reluctant and fearful, was now completely open to whatever the day might bring.

They waited. Horses nickered their tension. Fittings jangled and rang. Jatal was surprised to find his breathing even. He glanced to Andanii and found her eyes on him; she quickly looked away. *Checking my resolve? Searching for signs of fear? Today you'll find none. Today we shall see who is truly weak.*

I swear to that.

The foreign mercenaries kept climbing; by now most of the archers had gained the wall. Sounds of fighting echoed from within. Then the crash of cavalry reached them: it was distant, from elsewhere about the city. The Adwami tribes invading from all quarters. Jatal glimpsed pillars of smoke climbing into the sky over the low roofs.

The tall twin leaves of the gate shook as if from a great blow. Dust sifted down their iron-studded faces. They creaked and groaned, moving. Then slowly swung apart revealing Scarza and the cheering mercenaries.

The Warleader raised his arm. Andanii too thrust her arm high. He brought his swinging down like a scythe. She echoed the gesture. Jatal bellowed a war cry and heeled Ash into a gallop. He drew his sword and bent forward over Ash's neck aiming the curved blade ahead.

The crash and reverberation of a storm of hooves marked the column following. He passed the narrow ditches, the litter of fallen men and horses. Ash jumped one dead Saar mount. Ahead, Scarza beckoned from the wide gate. Jatal's heart hammered even louder than Ash's hooves. What awaited them? The Warleader had said to make for the central complex.

A wide main approach faced Jatal. It was flanked by long buildings looking like dormitories or housing of some sort. As before at Isana Pura, the architecture offered almost no hint as to which buildings were more important than any other: all were low and uniform. A glimpse into the Thaumaturg mind and philosophy, of course. Following plain logic, Jatal urged Ash onward, making for the centre.

The approach ended at a wide set of stone stairs leading up to a broad columned building – a reception hall perhaps. Jatal yanked

Ash to a halt and dismounted. Here, the first sign of violence within the gates offered itself. Corpses in dark robes lay sprawled on the stairs, black fluids dribbling like treacle. Ash flinched away, rearing and sounding his unease. The horrific stench raised Jatal's gorge, yet despite this, or because of it, he climbed the stairs. His boots slipped and slid on the thick flowing mush. The corpses consisted of dead Thaumaturgs plus a few attacking shaduwam – the first he'd seen since Isana Pura. Like their brethren, these were mostly naked, filthy and unwashed. By their bent shattered bones and burst flesh, it looked as if their deaths had been as grotesque as they seemed to hope for. The Thaumaturgs, on the other hand, appeared to have succumbed to some sort of rotting curse: their bones lay still articulated by ligaments and sinew within their robes, yet mostly sloughed of all soft flesh. That flesh – skin, fat, muscle and organs – ran as a melted slush to spread from under the lips of their robes and sleeves and come seeping down the stairs in a broad red carpet.

Jatal pressed the back of his hand to his mouth and turned away. *By all the gods of the world!* He was leading Andanii into *this*? He glimpsed his bared sword and nearly laughed at the ridiculousness of the gesture. The Warleader had come up behind him. He surveyed the ghastly scene without a flicker of expression, though he did nod as if satisfied. 'Good,' he murmured. Then, advancing, gestured, *this way.*

The column fell in behind the Warleader. Jatal peered sidelong to Andanii. The Vehajarwi princess had paled to snow. She swallowed nervously and wiped her gleaming sweaty brow, her gaze darting everywhere.

Good, Jatal thought. *Her conscience plagues her. She knows doubts – yet it is too late. Far too late.*

More corpses littered the hall in smeared fluids. The warm humid air stank of excrement. Jatal stepped over the sprawled, obscenely flattened bodies. 'The shaduwam appear to have won through,' the Warleader observed.

Ahead, stairs descended into an interior sunken court surrounded by smaller, separate buildings. Statues bordered the court on all sides. These were the first depictions of the human form Jatal had seen from the Thaumaturgs: they were uniform, a figure bent in reflection, hands clasped, yet mouth open as if about to speak. The Warleader led the way down the stairs and across the court. Here were the bodies of several shaduwam. They lay contorted, hands at throats, their faces sculptures of agony. They had actually gouged bloody wounds at their necks with their own dirty broken nails. The

420

sight made Jatal unbearably uneasy. Was this some sort of Thauma-turg curse?

As the leading element of the column reached the top of the opposite stairs, stones shifted behind in a loud grinding and Jatal spun. A mist gusted from the mouths of the surrounding statues in one long loud exhalation. The troopers caught in the sunken court, some thirty of them, clutched at their throats. Weapons clattered to the stones. Andanii lurched down the stairs as if she would rescue the nearest, but Jatal thrust an arm across her chest, stopping her. 'They are dead already,' he told her.

Across the court the rest of the column halted, glaring left and right, their eyes wide. 'Go round!' Jatal called. The leading ranks acknowledged this, saluting. They led the way to the sides, searching for a way through. Somehow, Jatal did not think this would be easy; they had entered a labyrinth of traps or dead ends. All prepared by the Thaumaturgs for unwary invaders long ago.

'What now?' Andanii asked the Warleader.

The man's perpetual expression of impatient disapproval twisted even further as he peered ahead. He motioned aside. 'This way, I believe.' He strode on without waiting.

Jatal moved to follow but Andanii stilled him with a hand on his arm. 'We need to talk,' she whispered, low.

Her voice, so husky and close, raised an answering thrill in his blood. Yet he clamped down on the sensation and kept his expres-sion indifferent. *A final confession, my princess?*

'Regarding what?' he asked, and applauded himself for the casual steadiness of his voice.

Her brows wrinkled prettily as she eyed him sidelong. *How beau-tiful you appear, my princess – even here surrounded by death.*

'I've had no time. He has been watching me. I have suspicions . . .' she shook her head and dabbed her sleeve to her sweaty lips, 'but you will think me mad . . .'

I, too, have my suspicions, my princess of death. Their remain-ing troops waited for orders a respectful distance away. Jatal noted that every one of them was a member of her picked Vehajarwi body-guard. *Ahh, my princess . . . So this is how it is to be?*

Up the hall, the iron-grey figure of the Warleader paused. He glanced back over his shoulder. 'You are coming?' Andanii flinched, her mouth clamping shut. She motioned her bodyguard to fall in line.

How meekly she follows this man! His merest gesture is her command!

Andanii . . . I do not understand you at all.

He searched her face as if he could read some hint of the workings of her mind there; she answered with a discouraging curt jerk of her head as if to demand silence.

So be it, my princess. Silence it shall be.

Their route brought them up a hall lined by narrow cells. Most held the slumped figure of a Thaumaturg, in robes that were once white but now bore the broad stains of spilled blood. They appeared to have been felled while in meditation. When the Warleader reached the end of the hall a metallic note rang out, clear and throbbing. It sounded like a struck bell. Its reverberations hung in the air as if suspended. The tone strengthened with each pulse. It stabbed at Jatal's ears. The Warleader paused. He cocked his head as if puzzled.

Andanii said something but Jatal heard nothing of it over the throbbing of the bell. A hand took hold of Jatal's arm. He glanced round and was horrified to see a female Thaumaturg in her blood-stained robes. Whether she was dead or yet alive it was impossible to tell. One-handed, he ran the woman through. Despite the sword thrust through her stomach she held on. Her face betrayed nothing; just an inhuman curiosity, as if everything was a surprise to her.

From every cell up and down the hall the fallen bodies now emerged and closed upon them. The Warleader contemptuously batted one down. It slowly climbed to its feet again. The bodyguard strove to cut them down, but the narrow confines of the hall limited their swordplay. Most switched to their heavy fighting dirks and thrust at faces and chests.

It became obvious that even the worst slashing or head wound did nothing to slow the creatures. Jatal saw one of Andanii's bodyguards push a dirk blade through one eye and into the brain behind yet the creature continued to grip the man's arm. It carried the hilted weapon in its eye as no more than some sort of grisly decoration.

Yet he sheathed his own sword and also frantically drew a fighting knife. Next to him, one of the things had hold of both arms of a bodyguard. It drew the man close while at the same time throwing open its mouth to an unnatural degree. Out poured a vomited torrent of ghastly steaming fluids straight on to the guard's face and neck to run down his front over and beneath his armour. The man howled and writhed in the creature's grip.

Jatal stared, gagging and sickened, yet also mesmerized by the appalling sight. The man's flesh smoked where the greenish-black muck had sprayed. It dripped and ran as if melting, falling away. White bone appeared beneath the mess at jaw and collarbone. The man threw back his head in a shriek of utter insane agony. His neck burst in a spray of blood as the flesh of the throat was eaten through, collapsing. The head fell backwards at an impossible angle, half decapitated. The corpse would have fallen but for the support of the creature's grip. It bent forward now, mouth open, and took a great bite from the tangle of wet ligaments and sinew at the angle of shoulder and ruined neck.

All this Jatal witnessed in a frantic instant while fending off the swipes and searching hands of the creatures surrounding him. Now he turned to the one that had hold of his arm. It was all he could do to resist screaming his own mindless panic at the thought of what awaited him. His gorge rose in unspeakable terror and anticipation. An idea came to him and he threw down his knife to take hold of the grip of his sword once more and yank it free. Up and down the hall the men of the bodyguard were falling beneath the grasping hands of the Thaumaturg-warped creatures. Ahead, the Warleader appeared to be hacking his way free. Andanii, he saw, was close behind.

Desperate with disgust and terror, he swung at the creature's wrist. It parted from the arm – though the hand yet maintained its grip on his bicep. Jatal pressed forward. Every hand that reached for him he swung at, leaving blunt waving stumps behind.

Ahead, the Warleader had hacked his way clear to reach a set of stairs leading down. He spared one brief glance backwards; his dead ashen-hued eyes seemed to grant his followers nothing – not even a common humanity. He turned his back and continued on, abandoning them. Close behind, dodging and ducking, leaving scraps of her robes in clenched waving hands, Andanii also made the stairs. She too paused to glance back, all the while bending and stringing her longbow. Her gaze briefly brushed Jatal's only to flick down to where the Warleader had disappeared. She followed the man at a run.

In that brief contact, Jatal thought he read a desperate agony mixed with a ferocious ruthless resolve. *So it was done. The coward! Relying on others to do what she couldn't face herself. She would discard him to follow the foreigner!*

Her actions so shocked Jatal that he fell backwards into the arms of one of the creatures. It moved to wrap its limbs around him but he managed to bring his blade up inside the hug and hack through the wrists to duck free.

I will have her head!

His rage saw him through: kicking the creatures down, decapitating in wild swings, not caring who was near, stepping and slipping on the fallen. His onslaught opened up a route that five of Andanii's bodyguards followed to reach the stairs. Here he paused, his chest heaving in his ecstasy of near blind rage and terror, until he saw that the surviving fiends were still following.

He pointed his sword and gasped, his voice almost completely gone, 'This way . . .'

They entered a maze of subterranean tunnels, just as at Isana Pura, yet even more terrifying and grotesque. They passed what were perhaps a series of operating chambers. On stone slabs lay the current victims of experimentation: a female cleanly flensed of all skin; the twined ropy muscles and gleaming bone of her frame perfectly revealed as if she were an anatomical sculpture. Here, one of the bodyguards came close, a lantern held high, and they all jerked as her bared lidless eyes shifted towards the light. Her throat moved, her naked jaws working. But as she had no cheeks, her words came out as gurglings and hissings.

Snarling his horror and disgust, the guard swung his blade to decapitate her. Yet he failed. His sword jammed in her neck – perhaps her ligaments and bones had been hardened for preservation – in any case, he yanked but could not free the blade. She rose then, swiftly, and her fingers, all sinew, bone and long, curved, yellowed nails, found his face to gouge and dig in.

He howled, abandoning the sword to grasp her hands. Everyone hacked at the thing. They finally managed to dismember it but not before the guard had fallen, his face and throat a bloody torn ruin. Jatal picked up the lantern where it had rolled aside, luckily not extinguishing. 'Do not touch anything!' he snarled, and limped onward.

They passed a chamber where rank after rank of small short figures, children in Thaumaturg robes, sat as if in meditation. They faced away towards the far wall. Jatal stepped into the room, raising the lantern high. 'Flee, all of you,' he called. 'The shaduwam are here.'

Heads turned. Some forty pale faces regarded him silently. Jatal's vision darkened in abhorrence; the eyes and mouth of each child had been sewn shut.

Behind him, the guards cursed softly and gagged. Jatal pushed them back as he retreated from the room. He lowered the lantern and the heads calmly turned away as the children – children! Was that what they were? – returned to their meditation. Jatal stood in the hall, unsteady on his feet. His heart hammered and his throat was as dry as kiln-heated sand yet it burned with suppressed acid bile.

A madhouse! Inhuman!

All Jatal wanted now was escape. He urged the men onward. Was this why the Thaumaturgs offered no resistance? They no longer thought like humans, no longer shared common human values and fears? Were no longer even human? Perhaps they considered them no more a threat than an ant or a lizard? Who could know? None of this seemed remotely sane.

Unfortunately, the path led downward. They descended narrow slick stone stairs. At the bottom they found a heavy iron gate that had been smashed aside. Beyond lay a large chamber with halls leading off into utter darkness. Jatal raised the lantern; the stairs descended into dark water that covered the floor. It stank like a sewer and gnawed, half-skeletal corpses floated about, both Thaumaturg and shaduwam. He had no idea of the water's depth, or what it might contain. The lantern's weak light just brushed a distant figure somehow raised above the surface of the pool – a figure that wore the remains of tattered white robes over gleaming armour.

The guards surged forward. They descended the stairs into the water up to their waists. Jatal followed, holding the lantern high. They pushed their way through the water. The sloshing and splashing echoed about the chamber and halls to return loud and distorted.

It was Andanii; she had pulled herself on to, or been laid upon, a stone slab similar to the other operating platforms they'd seen everywhere. She bled from numerous wounds – what looked like vicious bites that had gouged rounded chunks from her flesh.

'Princess!' the men called, outraged, choked with tears. Their voices seemed to rouse her; she stirred, her limbs shifting. Jatal pressed forward. *She has earned this! Why then am I terrified for her?*

'Andanii,' he whispered, his face almost pressed to hers. Blood smeared her mouth and chin.

She shook her head, mumbled something.

'What? What is it?' *Say it*, something in him urged her. *Say it was all a mistake!*

'. . . no . . . trap . . .' she gurgled in a mouthful of blood.

Jatal set down the lantern to scoop her up in his arms. 'Ware! Trap!'

The remaining four of Andanii's bodyguard spread out, surrounding them. One picked up the lantern to hold it high. 'There!' he called, pointing his sword. Hunched shapes came lurching their way up the halls. They appeared naked, hairless, with long ropy arms ending in great taloned hands.

The group retreated to the stairs. Water surged, rising and splashing as a number of the creatures straightened from the murky waves to block their path. Closer now, Jatal could see that they were of basic human stock. *No real monsters here – the true monsters are the Thaumaturgs.*

Yet things had been done to them. Thaumaturg experimentation. Their heads were narrower than any skull ought to be, the flat eyes devoid of emotion or intelligence; Jatal read in their opalescent depths hunger only – no recognition of a common humanity. Their mouths hung open to make room for teeth that stood out as sharpened and serrated weapons. Jatal did not think that they could close their mouths even should they try. They raised their clawed hands and made blood-chilling noises all the more horrific for sounding almost like words.

'Keep going!' Jatal urged. 'Make for the stairs!'

The group charged. Swords slashed and the creatures fell. Yet more of them surged from behind, falling upon the guards and dragging them down below the water to disappear. Jatal rushed for the stairs. He shouldered his way through the melee. The man holding the lantern fell, his scream ending in a mouthful of the foul water. The light snuffed out, hissing.

Jatal blundered on, reaching the stairs and finding the opening by slamming an elbow into its stone lip. He charged up without pause. He leaned against a wall to support himself and when that wall ended in an opening he tumbled into a side chamber, crashing into furniture that broke beneath him. Yet he managed to keep Andanii out of the way, cushioning her with his own body. He laid her down and bent over her. In the absolute dark he remembered his waist pouch and a nub of candle that he kept there. He found it and the small tinderbox. He set the box on the cold stone floor, opened it, and set to striking into it. The flashing sparks each revealed the room for an instant, leaving lingering after-images of a broken frail desk, of walls dark with painted frescoes.

The tinder lit and he gently blew. He used it to light the thin wick. The candle caught, filling the room with a light that was incredibly bright to his starved eyes. He took Andanii's head on to his lap. 'Andanii – my princess . . . can you hear me?'

The eyelids fluttered. A smile came to the lips – followed by a wash of blood that spilled down her chin. As awareness rose within

426

her, the smile twisted into a panicked grimace and her hands fought him then clenched his arms. '*Flee . . .*' she breathed.

All anger was gone from him now. All resentment. He thought he understood her at last. She'd had ambition and the ruthlessness to chase it. In short . . . he'd cursed her for doing nothing more than acting like a man. Acting as any of his brothers would have done. For acting as he could not bring himself to do.

'I understand,' he whispered to her tenderly. 'You made your choices. Why should I be resentful? You acted in the best interests of your people.'

She smiled now, almost wistfully. 'You understand . . . do you?' She gripped him tighter, convulsing. 'Jatal – my prince . . . promise me this . . . Promise!'

He ducked his head. Tears fell from his eyes to wash the blood from her cheek. 'I promise.'

She nodded, easing her arms. 'Good . . . Go. Flee. Return to the tents of the Adwami. Read your books. Write your poetry. And try . . . try to forgive me . . .'

'Forgive! Andanii . . . You are my life!' But she did not answer. Her head eased to one side.

Jatal pressed his own hot face to her cooling cheek and wept.

How long he crouched there, trembling and weeping, he knew not. At length, he gently set her head down on the cold stone and rose. He picked up the tiny stub of candle. Its weak light barely illuminated the room yet he could make out a painting of a dark throne and a seated figure. Its face had been chiselled from the stone – deliberately disfigured. He was hardly conscious of his surroundings as he staggered into the hall.

What followed struck him as a carnival of horrors. Nightmare images came and went as he stumbled through room after room. Which were real, and which he imagined, he did not know. At one point he lurched into a horde of the black-robed children all gathered around a corpse, feeding. As one they raised their pale faces to him, their mouths bright crimson.

But no . . . their mouths had been sewn closed . . .

At some point later he faced a lone Thaumaturg in an empty hallway. Half the man's head was gone, smashed in by a brutal blow. Yet awareness and intelligence filled the remaining eye. This wandering eye found him, and winked. 'Where does life end?' the man asked, his voice listless and dull. 'With the mind or with the heart?'

Then the mage stiffened. The single eye widened; awareness of some secret known only to him dilated the pupil. The mouth opened

427

as if he would speak but only fouled fluids poured out in a thick dark red sheen. He toppled – but not before the ghost of a sad smile touched those painted lips. Behind stood the begrimed and blood-smeared figure of a shaduwam. He held out his hand to show something to Jatal. It was a lump of muscle; a heart still quivering.

The shaduwam raised it to his mouth and took a great bite. Swallowing, he licked his lips. All the while his eyes gripped Jatal's numbed gaze, eyes like black subterranean pools. 'That is where we differed,' he explained. 'They say the mind. We say the heart.'

Everything came crashing down upon Jatal at that moment and he staggered against a wall. His stomach heaved and he vomited up what little remained. He felt as if he were sinking into that abyssal underground pool of icy water, drowning. He tried to speak but nothing came. The darkness swallowed him.

Roaring woke him. A distant constant roar as of a storm, or a herd of horses running. He raised his head, blinking. He sat beneath a smoke-filled night sky. The moon, which had been waxing, shone a watery silver light that was occluded by the burgeoning Visitor whose jade glare nearly flickered, so near did it loom. He was among a crowd of men and women: a mix of Adwami troopers, Thaumaturg acolytes and civilian peasants. Even one or two of the foreign mercenaries sat with them, their heads hanging. Everyone bore wounds, from sword strikes to beatings. All were disarmed.

They were crowded together in one of the stone courtyards of the Thaumaturgs' Inner City. Shaduwam priests carrying clubs and staves guarded them. Now and then, two of the Agon priests came to collect one of the captives and drag him or her up the stairs and into what Jatal presumed was a temple or cloister. What went on within, he did not have to imagine.

Dully, he noticed that the roaring came from without – from beyond the tall walls of the Inner City where plumes of smoke coiled all about. The noise resolved into the sound of a city that has roused itself like a kicked beast. It struck him that even an anthill would rally to defend itself when disturbed. He hoped that Pinal had had the sense to pull the Hafinaj from the engagement. Yet he registered the concern distantly, and hazily.

Nothing, it seemed, troubled him at all at this moment. Not even his impending death at the hands of these betraying defilers. The only thing able to raise a slight crease in his brows was the utter stupid waste of it all. What could the damned Warleader hope to gain from all this? He could not possibly hope to rule here. Nor among the Adwami. What was his purpose – beyond the sowing of chaos and destruction? No doubt such was the goal of the shaduwam: the eradication of their rivals. But what of this old traitor general – if that was what he was. Mere vengeance? All this blood merely to wipe out the sting of some thwarted or blocked ambition? The idea that this was all his own life – and the lives of all those who had fallen around him – was worth just made him tired. In fact, everything made him tired now. Every breath. The idea of continuing to live through the next moment utterly exhausted him.

The group of captives dwindled as the night wore on. Eventually, as he knew they would, two Agon priests came for him. They had to lift him by the arms as he made no effort to put strength into his legs – he saw no reason to cooperate. Oddly, he felt as if he was watching the proceedings as from a great distance, looking down on a play, or a dance of meaningless shadow figures.

They dragged him up the stairs and into the darkened hall. Pools and streaks of messy deaths marred the polished set flags of the floor, as did bloody handprints and smears on the walls. Tapestries lay torn and wet with fluids. The heat of many fires struck him as a furnace exhalation and made him drowsy. He hardly registered a thick greasy miasma of roasting flesh.

A shout halted the two dragging him along. Another priest stood before him; Jatal raised his gaze up the man's completely naked form, caked in drying gore, to the grimed shining face and wild, mud-hardened nest of kinked hair. The man smiled a mouthful of small white teeth filed to sharp points. He looked vaguely familiar.

'Greetings, Prince Jatal of the Hafinaj,' the Agon priest announced. He motioned and the two holding Jatal released his arms. Jatal straightened, swaying slightly. 'I am told you are an educated man. A philosopher.' He gestured for Jatal to join him. 'Come. You may appreciate this.'

'If you would take my heart – go ahead,' he told the priest. 'You are welcome to it. I have no more use for it.'

The priest gave a small deprecatory wave. Jatal now recognized him as the one who had confronted their council what seemed now so long ago. 'If that is truly the case then we do not want it. We are only interested in what others value.'

Jatal frowned, puzzled. 'You mean gold?'

'Oh no. Not wealth. I mean what people *really* value about themselves.' He leaned close to whisper and Jatal smelled the stink of rotting flesh. 'The delusions people hold about themselves.' The priest took his arm to usher him into a side chamber. Here a figure writhed, gagged and bound, on one of the ubiquitous stone operating platforms. It was a Thaumaturg captive. Shaduwam priests appeared to be in the process of burning the flesh from him piece by piece. They pressed white-hot irons to him then lifted them away taking the melted flesh with them. The figure flinched and squirmed with the hiss and smoke of every application.

'So much for their vaunted negation of the flesh,' the priest murmured, sounding greatly satisfied.

Jatal understood now; it came to him as an epiphany that somehow lightened the load upon his shoulders. 'For you there is only the flesh.'

The priest smiled, pleased. 'Exactly, my prince. I knew you would see through to the truth of it. For us there is only the flesh. No good or bad. Only the flesh and its demands. We are all nothing more than that. Why deny it? It follows, then, that there are no opposites. Nothing can be said to be negative, or positive.' He waved his hand dismissing all such figments as he urged Jatal along. 'That is all illusion. Constructs of epistemologies that are at their root flawed, deluded, or self-serving.'

Jatal felt dizzy once more. 'You are saying that morality is an arbitrary construct?'

The priest steadied him as they came to a large chamber. He brightened even more. 'Exactly!' He squeezed Jatal's arm. 'You *are* a philosopher. You begin to see the absurdity of it all, yes?'

Jatal knew he ought to argue, but a strange numbing fog smothered his mind. He strove to rally his thoughts, but all that fell away when he saw that the room ahead was an assembly hall. Corpses littered it; the Thaumaturgs appeared to have put up quite a resistance here. But what he'd seen so far of the shaduwam suggested they were even more fanatical. At the end of the hall, slouched in a high-backed chair carved from black stone, was the Warleader. Shaduwam attended him. They were attempting to treat a wound in his side – though he still wore his mail armour. The priest marched Jatal straight up to him.

Something about this man seated in a tall chair, his mail hood thrown back, his long iron-grey hair sweaty, his gaze utterly dismissive, sent a chill up Jatal's back that was so strong it penetrated the strange numbing haze that blanketed his thoughts.

'Why is this one here?' the Warleader demanded of the priest. 'You are done with him?'

'Yes.'

Jatal hardly understood that they were discussing him. All he

430

knew was that he faced his rival. He swallowed to clear his throat. 'She's dead,' he murmured – or tried to.

The Warleader eyed him, frowning. 'What's that?'

'She is dead. Andanii is dead.'

Pain twisted the man's features. He gestured impatiently to the priests who were busy lighting candles and preparing some sort of draught. 'Do not despair,' he told Jatal, his voice tight. 'Soon you will be as well.'

Puzzlement and outrage wormed their way through the fog of Jatal's thoughts. He stood weaving, suddenly exhausted beyond all effort. 'That is all you have to say? After all she chose to give you?'

The Warleader's thick brows rose. 'Ahh,' he breathed. 'I understand. All she gave me, you say. She gave me a great deal of her time, that is true.' He pointed to the tall tankard of fluids the priests were mixing. 'Now!' he ordered. 'We will do this now.'

'But . . . my lord . . .' one objected. 'You must prepare further.'

'Do you question me?'

The priest fell to his knees. 'Forgive me, lord.'

The Warleader gestured impatiently for the drink. Another of the shaduwam handed it to him. He drank it in a long series of swallows, wiped the spilled thick dark fluids from his beard. He regarded Jatal once again with his dead flat eyes. 'She encouraged me to talk – to tell stories. And I did. More than I ought to have. I was perhaps pleased by her attentions though I certainly knew better. And from listening to me all those evenings your princess came closest of anyone to grasping a certain secret. One not even she could believe. One she dared not pass on to anyone – not even to you. Especially not to you.'

He pointed to a lit candle and a priest brought it to him. The Warleader passed a hand through its smoke, wafting it to his face and inhaling deeply. This he did several times. Jatal assumed he was deadening the pain of the wound in his side, from which a great deal of blood had spilled to smear his armour.

'And so, my prince,' the man said, straightening, 'I choose to give you something in her honour. Something which you do not want. Because, you see, I understand you now. You are just like me. You are a jealous man.' He reached out and pulled a gripping tool from the table nearby. It was an instrument Jatal had seen physicians using in field infirmaries. 'Now,' he said through gritted teeth.

'But, lord, who . . . ?'

The Warleader cuffed the priest aside. '*I* shall. Now.' He pressed the instrument into the wound at his side, turning it and gouging. He gasped at the agony of it, even mitigated by the drink and the fumes he'd inhaled.

He withdrew a blood-smeared object and extended it to Jatal who took it, wonderingly, in both hands. The arrow must have passed almost completely through the Warleader's body, for the point and most of the shaft had been broken off, leaving perhaps two hand's-breadths of wood, and the fletching, embedded in the wound. Jatal turned it over, wiped the blood from its slick surface. All the while, the Warleader watched, his eyes glittering with something that might have been cruel satisfaction.

Jatal pinched the wet feathers to let their colour come through – though he suspected he knew already what to expect.

'She did choose to follow me, Prince Jatal,' the Warleader said, his voice now relaxed, even content. 'She had something to give me, you see.'

The colours of the fletching showed through as Vehajarwi.

'She gave me that. Because, you see, she had given everything else she had to you.'

Rising, the man closed his hard hand over Jatal's on the shaft. 'And now I give it to you. The gift of pain. True soul-destroying anguish. It is yours now. Carry it in your heart.' He waved Jatal off. Turning aside, he addressed the priest: 'Let him live. Let him live long.' The man's words seemed to come from a great distance. A hand pushed Jatal away. 'Go,' the Warleader called. 'Go with my blessing and with my curse.'

Aware of nothing, Jatal stumbled away. He found himself under open golden sky, on a set of stairs; it was late afternoon. He looked down: he still held the bloody shaft in both hands. His cheeks were cold and wet. Shaduwam priests shouldered him aside, ignoring him. They led prisoners up the stairs: some were from among the mercenaries who had followed the Warleader, others were of the Adwami. None he saw were of the Hafinaj.

Blinking, Jatal started forward once more, his eyes on the arrow shaft. When he looked up again, strangely dizzy, he found he walked a narrow alley that opened on to a broad main thoroughfare. This he entered. A party of shaduwam brushed past him; they paid him no more attention than if he'd been a shade.

The wide approach ended at tall double gates in the walls of the Inner City. Jatal passed through the open gates to enter the narrow ways of the city proper. Its peasant citizens stared from open doorways as he passed. He stepped over corpses, through the ashen remains of burned-down barriers, past the bodies of horses, the still-wet remains of Adwami troopers, torn into fragments.

Oh Andanii . . . I betrayed you even while you held true. I am not worthy of your sacrifice.

A few of the peasant inhabitants followed him now, at a distance, as he stumbled along. Some, he noted, stooped now and then to pick up rocks. Something struck his shoulder, hard. He blinked, confused. The words of the poet came to him: *Blood is brightest / Against the purest snow . . .*

A blow to his head spun him into a wall. He leaned against it, dazed. Stones smacked into the brick wall about him. The crowd of inhabitants closed now, emboldened. Frenzied enraged eyes glared their murder at him. Clawed hands reached for him. They tore the bloodied robes from him; their ragged nails gouged his flesh; they yanked his hair as if meaning to tear the top of his head off. Hands fought to unbuckle the straps of his armour. Men and women spat and screamed their rage at him. Thumbs jammed into his eyes. Fingers pulled and tore at his lips. Their press squeezed the breath from his lungs.

My love . . . I come to you . . . Please do not turn from me.

A petrifying bellowed roar shook the stones beneath him. Light reached his eyes as the piled-on bodies scattered. An immense figure was there, straddling him, throwing the peasants like children to smash into the walls. His armour hung from him in tattered links and hanging straps. He swung the broken haft of his axe, pulverizing heads with each blow: Scarza, bloodied yet whole.

The half-giant lifted Jatal to his feet. 'You'll live?' he growled.

'Yes – no.'

The lieutenant eyed him with a strange expression. 'Well, this way. The bastard betrayed all of us but we can still get away.'

'No.'

'What?'

'No.' He peered down: he still held the shaft in both hands. The blood had dried, sticking his fingers closed.

'Ah. I see.' The fellow peered up and down the street, empty now that the mob had fled. 'She's gone then?'

'Yes.'

'I'm sorry, lad.'

'Sorry?'

'For this.'

Jatal frowned, blinking. The axe handle blurred for him and he knew nothing more.

Pain brought him to consciousness. He brought his hands to his head and held it; a great bump had swelled up on the side of his skull just behind the temple.

'Not broken, is it?' Scarza's low voice enquired from the dark.

'I wish it were.'

'I understand.'

'No, you don't.' They were in a copse next to fields. A distant yellow glow marked what Jatal imagined must be the fires of Anditi Pura.

'I wouldn't be too sure of that,' Scarza answered from where he sat up against a tree.

Jatal simply waved to grant the man the point. He shifted over to lean against another trunk. 'You shouldn't have intervened.'

'I was just happening by. Spur of the moment thing.'

Jatal eyed the dark hulking figure, half obscured by a shadow cast by the shafts of the Visitor. 'Why are you here?'

'Those were my men. Bastards, half of them. Murderers, rapists. But still, mine. Can't let some jumped-up Warleader sell them out. Or me, to be honest.'

'Do you know who he is?'

'Him?' The wide dark shoulders shrugged. 'Does it matter? Some renegade general. Maybe years ago he tried to take over from these Thaumaturgs – fails. Flees abroad. Gathers himself a mercenary army. Makes a deal with the neighbouring country. Comes back and makes them pay. It's an old story. Seen it a thousand times.'

'I think there's more to it than that.'

'Think what you will. You can question him all you want after we catch him.'

Jatal studied the shaded figure. His eyes gleamed hungrily in the dark. A spark of humour actually animated the man's expression. *Is he as mad as I should be? Am I mad? Am I imagining this?* 'What do you mean? He's surrounded by his shaduwam pets.'

'No, he isn't. He rode off alone like the very fiends of the Abyss were after his spirit. Which they are, I'm sure.'

Jatal half rose, then fell back, slumping. 'Then he's gone. We've missed him. And . . .' He stopped himself from going any further.

The half-Trell was silent for a time in the dark. At length he spoke, his voice gentle: 'She was something, Prince of the Hafinaj. She truly was. I am sorry.'

Yes. Sorry. I am sorry. He is. Yet nothing will bring her back. And nothing can redeem me. Unless. Unless I finish her task for her. Then finish myself. Only that might serve to redress so great an injustice.

'When did he leave?'

'Half the night ago.'

Jatal gaped. '*What?* Then why . . . you are cruel. Is this your revenge? Tormenting me so?'

'Not at all. You needed to recover. We will track him and ride even harder.'

Jatal snorted. 'Ride? You?'

'For this I will run.' The half-Trell's voice held an unfamiliar chilling resolve.

'And me? Am I to run as well?'

Scarza tapped a finger to the side of his wide flattened nose. 'There are horses nearby. I smell them.'

'Then why aren't we on our way?'

The dark glittering eyes regarded Jatal closely. 'You are ready? You are resolved?'

'To the end.'

The giant was on his feet in an instant. 'Good. Let us collect as many horses as we can. I may even ride one for an hour or so! Just to catch my breath.'

Jatal stood as well. He felt rested; he was bruised and battered, but that was a minor matter. He hungered also but he would deal with that when he could stand it no longer. After all, what were such demands of the flesh compared to the task he had vowed to see through to the finish.

CHAPTER XII

After the storm passed we were in unfamiliar waters, irrevoca-
bly driven off course. We found ourselves within sight of an unknown coast. We put in for water but lost men to bizarre wild
animals, poisonous plants, and other hazards of its inhospitable
jungle and so we quit the coast in haste. Raising sails, we espied
a simple dugout paddled by one occupant. We allowed the man
to come aboard. He was painted and mostly naked after the
barbarous fashion. He studied the vessel, its equipage, our dress
and accoutrements, all in the most childlike curious wonder.
Then, turning to me, tears welling from his eyes, he said in
slanted Talian: 'Thank the gods for my deliverance. For I am
Whelhen Mariner, shipwrecked these last twelve years.'

Resenal D'Ord,
Master of the *Lance*
Excerpt from ship's journal

T
HE LAND IS SINKING. THIS WAS SHIMMER'S CONCLUSION AFTER
staring for interminable days and nights at a shore that hardly
deserved the name. *Or the waters are rising.* Where the river
ended and the land began appeared to be a debate this jungle was
unable to resolve. Their route twisted and turned. Countless channels
and streams led off from the main way only to reappear round the
next tight bend.

To further muddy the situation the water itself was taking on the
characteristics of the surrounding land. No current could be seen
pulling on the thick layer of lilies and wide flat pads that utterly
choked the surface. The rotting prow of the *Serpent* actually seemed
to catch on the tough plants, tugging and ripping. Tall water birds
flapped from their path looking like disgruntled priests wrapped in

brown robes with long disapproving faces. They walked atop the pads on stilt-like legs and made better progress than the ship. It puzzled her that the channel could really be so shallow. Countless water snakes likewise slithered among the massed floating plants, fleeing the disturbance. Thick clouds of insects hovered above the fat pink and white blossoms of the lilies. Dragonflies the size of her fist stooped these dense clouds while birds chased them all, snapping everything up in their pointed beaks.

The scent of all those blossoms melded into an overpowering stink of corrupted sweetness, which combined with the rot of dead plant matter and the miasma of the standing water. She could almost see the fumes hanging like scarves in the dead air. Or perhaps it was the dust and pollen.

The sun beat down with a drowsy heat made far worse by the unbearable humidity. Merely bending her arm raised drops of sweat. She wore only a long undershirt now, over trousers and open sandals. Her long hair she tied up high with the aid of thin sticks. Her thoughts seemed to coil as turgid as the water itself. Where was this capital Rutana promised? She claimed they were close yet no towers or walls reared above the canopy.

Ruined foundations, stone stelae and tumbled carved blocks did stand here and there, vine-choked and eroded. But no sign of current occupation showed itself. They had better be close, because beneath her hands the wood railing felt spongy with rot. She couldn't imagine what was keeping the vessel together. It ought to have disintegrated long ago.

The troop of longtail monkeys had returned – or another of the tribe. In any case, they travelled alongside their course, swinging from limb to limb. They had no trouble in keeping up with the ship's sluggish progress. Their moustached, wise faces peered from among the boughs, eyes bright and black.

As the vessel pushed beneath overhanging branches, leaves and the luminous petals of countless blossoms rained down upon everyone. Shimmer brushed the gold and purple showers from her shoulders. The littered deck appeared as festive as if decorated for the parades of Fanderay's revival.

They moved through an eerie half-light now. Neither day nor night. It seemed as if she was dreaming. A strange jade glow pervaded all the space beneath the thick canopy that extended above them from all sides. The light reminded her of that unearthly greenish luminosity that comes just before the clouds of a massive storm. Here, however, it never went away.

Then the *Serpent* rounded a bend in what now seemed nothing more than a stagnant swamp. Rutana, near the vine-draped bow, stiffened and pointed ahead. Her breath left her in a loud hiss. Something jutted out among the bobbing lilies and fat table-like leaves. It was just submerged, a stone ledge of some sort, algae-green, canted as if it had sunk into its foundation. The *Serpent* glided up to the ledge and came to a gentle halt.

'We are arrived,' the woman announced.

Shimmer scanned the jungle shore. She saw nothing but interminable trees, low brush and grass. Insects sent up a constant low buzz. 'Arrived? There is nothing here!'

The woman's harsh gaze sharpened even more and her lips pulled back from her teeth in her perpetual sneer. 'Yes, there is.'

'We are here,' whispered a faint voice from beside her and she spun, jerking; K'azz had come up next to her. 'I sense her. She is close.'

'Where?' Shimmer demanded of Rutana.

The woman shrugged, unconcerned. She waved a hand, all sinew and bone, to indicate the jungle. 'About.'

Shimmer clenched her jaws until her teeth ached. Turgal, Cole and Amatt had joined them, as had Lor-sinn and Gwynn. They carried their gear, their armour and weapons, all rolled under their arms. Cole handed Shimmer's over.

K'azz studied them. He motioned to the shore. 'Disembark.'

Shimmer nodded her assent; how glad she was to finally be rid of this rotting hulk! And yet, at the same time, it had come to feel safe. As if all the potential dangers surrounding them couldn't touch them while they occupied it. A kind of floating sanctuary where they were held inviolate. But held by whom?

The vessel was now so low she could let herself down over the side to touch the sunken wharf. Her sandals slipped and slid on the thick algae. The stone appeared to be granite. She carefully edged her way ashore. And what unusual land: ochre-stained sandy soil, soft and loamy to her feet. It felt strange to be off the vessel. Turgal, Cole and Amatt followed. On shore, they undid the belts binding up their gear and armoured themselves. Shimmer followed suit. Gwynn leaned upon his tall staff while Lor studied the surrounding jungle. She blew her hair from her face; catching Shimmer's eye, she shook her head in obvious dismay. After private words with Rutana and Nagal, K'azz came ashore. He wore a plain thin shirt and trousers. A longsword hung from a belt slung over one shoulder. His emaciated form, all bones and ligaments, appalled Shimmer; had he been sick?

438

With his long greying hair and beard the man resembled more a castaway than a mercenary commander. What would Ardata think of him?

And what will Skinner think? He won't come quietly. Yet K'azz is not concerned.

Turgal pulled on his rusted helmet. He hefted his wide infantryman's shield and a loud tearing noise pulled everyone's attention to him. The shield fell from his arm, its leather straps rotted through. He drew his hand-and-a-half sword, brought it overhead, then smashed it down on the shield, which shattered as if it were made of paper. He picked up the remains and with a yell of fury tossed them into the channel. He yanked off his helmet and squeezed it in his gauntleted hands: its visor broke off and the shell creaked and deformed as he pressed upon it. Furious, his face flushed, the man tossed this too into the channel. Next went his gauntlets, the leather straps holding the various plates together also obviously rotten. He was in a quivering rage, gazing down at his hauberk of banded iron. He took hold of his weapon belt and yanked. It too ripped from him. 'Dammit all to the Abyss!' he yelled to everyone. 'Are we to run around bare-arsed?'

'Not me, thank you,' answered Lor.

Cole laughed, as usual the one to find humour in the situation. 'Too bad,' he offered Lor, winking.

'Skinner will laugh,' Amatt observed darkly.

K'azz raised a hand for quiet. 'We're not here to fight,' he said.

Amatt was unbuckling his armour. 'Then why are we here?' he demanded.

It struck Shimmer as no coincidence that now that they had left the river behind, together with the otherworldly glamour that suffused it, all the questions and fears that had somehow been suppressed were boiling over. She fingered her own suit of fine mail. The links were stiff and rusty. It was more of a danger to her than any weapon thrust: it would poison her blood. She began untying her belt. 'Well?' she added, eyeing K'azz.

Their commander scanned the nearby woods. What he saw there, or failed to see, made him wince. He scratched his scalp. 'We're here to try to bring as many as we can back into the fold. Remember that.'

'What of Skinner?' Gwynn asked.

'We'll see.'

Cole threw down his ruined gear and took up his two sheathed swords, which he swung together over a shoulder. 'Fine. Now what?' he asked.

K'azz scratched a cheek. 'We're on our own. Rutana made that plain. I suggest we find some shelter, or make it.'

Gwynn nodded, stroking his beard. 'Very good. Let's have a look round.'

Their commander started walking and they fell in behind. Shimmer chose to take the rear. She'd had no idea what awaited them of course, but this certainly was not what she'd expected. Where was the great sprawling urban centre? The great structures? Not even truncated ruins poked up here or there through the trees. What of the towers of gold? The pavement of gems? All figments of the imagination of the few survivors who managed to escape Ardata's green abyss?

At least the jungle floor was clear. Trees stood as isolated emergents towering far into the sky. Their bases were as large round as huts, while their root systems sprawled across the surface like veins and arteries. They came to a broad open field bordered by tall trees. K'azz led them out on to it. The ground was beaten hard here, tufted by grass. It appeared to be a long concourse of some sort, extending further than many marshalling fields laid end to end. At its far edge lay a heap of dressed granite blocks that might have once formed a raised course but were now heaved and jumbled. K'azz paused before these. Among them lay tarnished bronze bowls and the remains of countless clay pots and cups, so many they formed heaps of their own. Faded flags and scarves draped the stones while drawings were scrawled over every open surface: the squares and circles of ritual protections. Over everything lay a dusting of flower petals all in iridescent blues, pinks and crimsons. Forests of incense sticks stood jammed into cracks and in the dirt. Smoke still curled from some.

Shimmer exchanged a look with everyone at that.

Turgal had salvaged one belt to wear over his padded, sweat-stained gambeson. His sword in its mildewed rotting sheath hung from it. He eased the blade free with his thumb. Shimmer wore her whipsword at her back.

After silently regarding the offerings for a time, K'azz led them aside and they re-entered the cathedral-like aisles of the trees. At length they came to a cluster of abandoned collapsed huts consisting of nothing more than bamboo poles and dried palm fronds.

So much for the legendary Jakal Viharn, shining city in the jungle, Shimmer reflected. Hovels where worshippers squatted in the dirt. Travellers who had survived such privation to reach here must have been driven mad by the discovery. All that suffering for naught! No wonder the exaggerations and reported marvels.

K'azz took hold of a pole and straightened it. He picked up a length of root used as lashing and began retying it. Amatt and Cole exchanged a look then went off into the woods, perhaps seeking fresh leaves or bamboo stalks. Gwynn and Lor-sinn followed. Turgal remained, a hand at his weapon.

Shimmer let out a long even breath, set her hands on her hips. The sun now glared down hot on the top of her head. Sweat ran down her neck and arms. 'And what do we eat?' she wearily asked K'azz while he rebuilt the hut.

'There is much to eat here in Viharn,' answered a voice from behind her.

Turgal cursed, spinning, his sword scraping free. Shimmer merely turned, one brow rising. She flinched at what she saw: it was a woman, but her shape was grotesque. Illness or disease had twisted and deformed half her body. One side of her face and skull was covered in coarse knobbled flesh. One arm hung swollen to three or four times the girth of the other. Its flesh was coarse and rough, as were her legs. As clothes she wore a plain pale wrap of some sort of woven plant fibre. 'One merely has to know where to look,' she continued, unabashed by their reactions.

K'azz lowered Turgal's raised blade. 'We are grateful for your advice,' he said.

'You are welcome.' She seemed to study Shimmer very closely with her one good eye – the other was clouded white. Then she turned her attention to K'azz. 'Why are you here?'

'We are here to see Ardata.'

'All seekers are welcome.'

'Thank you. Where is she? We do not see her.'

'She is here. Just because you do not see her does not mean she is not here.'

'Wonderful,' Turgal muttered and slammed his sword home.

'We would like to meet her,' K'azz continued.

'That is entirely up to you.'

Shimmer blew out a breath and turned a quizzical look on K'azz. He raised his brows. 'I . . . see. My thanks.'

The woman bowed and walked off. Her gait was agonizingly slow and awkward as she swung her deformed legs. Her swollen club feet dragged through the dirt.

'How did she sneak up on us?' Turgal wondered aloud, watching her go.

Shimmer moved to bring her head close to K'azz. She found she was unable to take her gaze from the retreating form. 'Is that the disease that kills all feeling in the flesh?' she asked, her voice low.

441

K'azz's eyes also followed the woman as she went. It seemed to Shimmer that the figure projected a quiet dignity. 'No,' he said. 'That is no disease. She was born that way. Caught halfway into a transformation from human into something else.'

'Something else?'

He shrugged to say he knew not what. 'She must have in her heritage the touch of a shapechanger. This is how it manifested itself.'

A shudder of horror took Shimmer. *Gods! No wonder the old dread of shapechangers.* Yet what an awful fate. And not of her choosing! Sympathy for the woman touched her. She'd probably been driven out of her community. Denounced as evil or corrupting simply because of her appearance. Cruelty and ignorance, it seemed, lay everywhere.

Turgal stood quietly for a time, arms crossed, watching K'azz struggle with assembling the bamboo poles. Finally, letting go an impatient curse, he joined him. 'Start with the short pieces.'

'I was thinking more of a lean-to.'

'And when it rains? You'll want a platform.'

'Ah! No wonder. I see.'

Shaking her head, Shimmer left them to argue the niceties of hut construction. She walked among the immense grey-barked trees. She went without fear; after going to such trouble to bring them here, it seemed to her that Ardata would hardly allow them to be torn to pieces. Her wandering took her deep into the jungle. Something of the manicured nature of the land struck her. It was so flat – cultivated at one time, probably. Perhaps rice paddies. Yet these trees . . . so evenly spaced. Cultivated as well? A food source? Or some other resource?

Circling one giant emergent trunk, its base a series of arches taller than her, she suddenly came face to face with Rutana. The woman held her habitual scowl. She peered past Shimmer to make certain they were alone.

'As you can see – there's nothing here,' she said.

Shimmer held her arms loose, ready to act. 'There was. Once. I think.'

'Perhaps. Long ago. But not now. You should go.'

'I know. You don't want us here.'

'You mock but you have come for nothing. There is nothing here.'

'I was just assured that there is.'

The woman advanced upon her. The forest of amulets about her neck rattled and swayed as she swung a leg over a root. An inhuman intensity shone in her eyes. 'Do you think you are special?' she hissed.

442

'No.'

'She won't come to you.'

'I was told that was up to me.'

Rutana snorted her scorn. 'They wait. They pray. But she does not come. She cares nothing for their desires. Their demands.'

Shimmer was slowly backing away. 'What does she care for?'

The woman pressed a fist to her bony chest. 'Strength! Power!'

'Was that why she came to Skinner?'

A cruel smile now crept up the witch's lips and she chuffed a harsh laugh. 'No, fool. Your Vow.'

'What of the Vow?'

'Ask your commander. You are all of you doomed. I would almost pity you if I did not loathe you so.'

'Doomed? How?'

Rutana waved an arm as if casting her away. 'Ask K'azz. Not me.' She turned her back and walked off.

Shimmer stood still for some time. Leaves fell from on high. Birds whistled and shrieked far above. Distantly, like an echo of thunder, the roar of a hunting cat reverberated through the clearing. In that suspended moment she thought she'd come close to an answer – a hint of what the woman meant. But then it was gone in the wind brushing through the canopy and the rasping of the dead leaves as they swirled about her sandals.

She walked on, distracted. She hardly noticed her surroundings as she grasped after the hint that had touched her thoughts. After a time something blocked her way. Blinking, she became aware that she stood at the lip of a broad sheet of water. It was a reservoir wider than a city block. It ran north as long as a city's main concourse. Lily pads dotted its glass-smooth surface. The sun was almost set now, the day having passed unnoticed. The shadows had gathered a deep mauve and edged closer. As she watched, entranced, the sun's slanting amber rays lit upon the perfectly still surface of the artificial lake and the sheet seemed to erupt into molten gold that rippled and blazed with its own internal fires.

It suddenly struck her vision as an immense causeway paved in sheets of gold. And sparks flashed here and there as tiny waves from insects alighting, or fish feeding, gently rippled the surface. The gems, perhaps, glimmering and beckoning.

She stood utterly still for the time it took the setting sun's rays to edge their way across the surface. When they slipped away, they disappeared all at once as if snuffed out. The reservoir's west border was perfectly aligned for the effect.

She took a deep breath – had she even breathed the entire time? She felt so calm. All her worries struck her as trivial, completely unimportant. What mattered any of it in the face of such an immensity of time and space? She felt as if she could remain here for an eternity contemplating such questions. Perhaps, she reflected, the sensation derived from the satisfaction of having solved at least one of the mysteries of Jakal Viharn, city of gold.

*　　*　　*

It took some time, but eventually Pon-lor had to admit that he'd lost the trail of the yakshaka, Hanu. He'd backtracked a number of times searching for sign. Now the light was fading and the marks of his own passage helped obscure any certainty he might have felt regarding the trail. As night gathered he gave it up as worthless. He'd try again in the morning. The question, then, was what to do for the night.

Night in Himatan. Alone. Not a promising prospect. He'd got through last night by climbing a tree and tying himself in. Even so, he'd hardly slept. Large night hunters prowled all through the hours, chasing other things. Sudden bursts of calls or screeching announced close escapes, or panicked last struggles. His training might allow him to forgo sleep for some time, but there was no dire need to delve into that yet.

Off to one side the ground rose. He headed in that direction. Here he found a hillock of sloping talus and broken stone topped by a steeper rising cliff riddled in caves, now mostly choked by the accumulated detritus of centuries. Mature trees crowned the rise, gripping it in gnarled fists of roots. Underfoot hard talus shifted, grating, and he bent down to select one of the fragments. He brushed it off: it was flat and slightly curved. It was not stone. It was earthen pottery.

Startled by this he staggered slightly, backwards, to peer up and down along the slope, a good two man-heights above the surrounding plain. *Great ancients! A garbage heap the size of a village!* No, the remains of a village. Generation after generation squatting in the same spot, dropping their litter and tamping it into the ground. Simply astounding. And now, the slow work of the ages conspired to wipe from the surface even these last vestiges of humanity's presence.

He crouched down before the largest cave. It actually had the look of an animal burrow but he could not be sure. He brought out a cloth bag containing the bulbs and fruit he'd collected through the day. One by one he inspected his finds. Some he rejected, not certain they conformed to Thet-mun's descriptions of safe foods. The rest he replaced in the bag then brushed the dirt from his hands. Now for a fire. Humanity's best defence against the chills and the horrors of the night. Yet was it not also humanity's challenge, as well? The unmistakable brazen shout to the night: come and get me? Something to consider into the long hours.

He went to collect firewood. Once he'd assembled a pile great enough to last the night he set to priming the fire. Not a skill high on the Thaumaturg curriculum. Dry tinder he clumped together, along with a strip of cloth torn from the edge of his robes. Now for the application of his true training: the focusing of power on to one tiny point, thereby agitating the particles of the field of Aether that pervaded all creation. This in turn should bring into being . . . he turned all his mental energy upon the task, easing out his breath in a long soft hiss, his hands hovering just above the tinder . . . a spark.

A tendril of smoke climbed into the air. He blew, lightly, teasing the tiny ember to life. It caught and soon he had a proper fire blazing. And just in time, as thunder crashed overhead and the night's rain came pattering down upon him. He used larger branches to push the fire in towards the shallow cave's mouth. Here he sat under the cover of the curved wall of pressed litter, cross-legged, his back to the dirt, the fire just before him. Vines hung about him, running now with the rain. The petals of a clinging orchid brushed his hair like the lightest of kisses.

He pushed a bulb on to a stick and extended it over the fire.

Tomorrow. He mustn't lose the trail. She must come to see reason tomorrow. How many days did she think she could just wander blindly about? It was ridiculous. Worse, it was the petulance of a child who would not admit she was wrong.

After he ate, he eased himself into the position of recuperation, hands on his lap, fingertips touching to channel his energy, and closed his eyes.

Late in the night, a huge hunting cat approached. It lay on its stomach hidden among the cover at the bottom of the hillock. Through slit eyes Pon-lor watched the flames reflected in its luminous pupils. After a time a noise sounded from the night: a crash as of wood breaking. The cat chuffed a cough and eased itself to its feet. Long curved fangs caught the light as it turned and glided away.

The crash was followed by another, and another, each closer. Soon an even more massive beast came lumbering up on to the slope of the hillock. It walked on two legs but was barely humanoid. Colossal, it was, with tough plated skin the hue of ash. Its legs were thick trunks ending in great splayed feet. Its head was a hairless stump. Two tiny eyes no larger than pinheads regarded him from atop a mouth that sported broken and misaligned jutting teeth.

'Who are you,' it boomed, 'to light a fire here in the depths of Himatan?'

Wisdom of the ancients, what was this thing? One of the Night-Queen's monstrosities, of course. But beast, man, or other? Was it, as his teachers insisted in the Thaumaturg Academy, the degenerate offspring of centuries of indiscriminate miscegenation – or, perhaps, as he was beginning to suspect, the product of a lineage of survivors adapted and attuned to this region's peculiar demands?

'Someone who would dare to do so,' Pon-lor shouted down. 'Think you on that.'

In what Pon-lor took as a hideous attempt at a grin, the creature's lips drew back even further from its forest of jutting teeth. It waved him down with a trunk-like arm. 'I believe you are a poor lost fellow. Come here and let us discuss this. You can even bring your bright licking friend.'

'The rules of the jungle dictate that I decline your kind invitation. Especially when we have not been introduced.'

The thick ledge of brow above its eyes rose in surprise. 'You do not know who I am? Easily put to rest.' It thumped its chest. 'I am Anmathana. Earth-shaker!'

'Good for you. I am Pon-lor, master of flesh.'

The monster frowned as if bemused. 'Master of flesh? Ah, I see you are one of those invaders. Come down and I will show you the way, little lost magus.'

'Thank you but I am quite comfortable here. Do not trouble yourself.'

'No? You will not descend? This is not a difficulty. I will come up.' He raised a sledge-like foot and jammed it into the slope. He grabbed hold of a nearby tree but in a groaning crash the entire thing tore out of the ground. He angrily threw aside the trunk, began kicking his next foothold.

Unease took hold of Pon-lor's chest but he strove to keep his voice level. He focused his concentration upon the creature. 'How can you climb when you are so short of breath?' he called.

Anmathana paused, reared his bullet-head. 'What's that? Short of breath? I am not—' He pressed a spatulate hand to his chest, frowned.

'Your lungs are full of tiny globes, my friend,' Pon-lor said. 'These distil the life-essence from the air when you inhale. But they cannot do so when they are full of fluid.'

The giant coughed, his eyes rolling wildly. 'What—' he managed, gurgling and choking. He clutched at his throat.

'Retreat and you will breathe again!'

Glaring impotent rage, Anmathana took one step backwards.

'Very good. Keep going.'

He took another step, fell to one knee, his chest working. Pon-lor eased his concentration. The creature drew a ragged hoarse breath. He raised his blunt head. 'I will crush you for this,' he gasped.

'It is foolish to be angry with some one or thing for merely defending itself.'

Anmathana waved a snarling dismissal, turned and stamped off into the jungle. Pon-lor heard the diminishing reports of fists smashing like battering rams into trees as it went.

After a time the jungle was quiet again – as quiet as it ever was as the calls of night hunters rose once more to the moon, insects hissed and chirped, and bats flitted overhead.

'Well done!' another voice called, this one from above. Pon-lor scanned the darkened treetops. 'Can't have the fellow dragging us all down, can we?' Pon-lor spotted the source: a blob of night, all shaggy round the edge, at the notch of a thick branch.

'And you are?'

'Varakapi is the name.'

'Brother to our friend?'

'Only very distantly,' the creature answered, not at all amused. 'I have been watching you.'

'To what end?'

'To pose a question.'

'Oh?' Pon-lor heightened his concentration once more, though he sensed nothing inimical for the moment. 'And that is?'

'What is Himatan?'

Pon-lor blinked, rather startled by such simplicity. 'That's it?'

'Yes. That is all. You could say the question is nothing – yet everything.'

'How very . . . philosophical,' Pon-lor answered drily.

'As a trained Thaumaturg, I thought you would appreciate that.'

Pon-lor narrowed his gaze upon the shaggy blotch. Long pointed elbows stuck out. The shape reminded him of a huge ape or monkey. 'And the purpose behind this question?'

'It is for you to muse upon. I hope you will find in it fertile ground for speculation.'

Frowning now, Pon-lor turned his attention to the dying fire. He pushed more of the dry brush in upon it. Speculation? What speculation could such a question evoke? When he looked up once more the beast was gone. *Well. That is one thing Himatan is: very odd. One might find oneself nearly pushed into a monster's mouth at one moment, then challenged to philosophical debate at the next!* He hoped this was the last of his visitors; he'd been planning to get some rest. Leaning back, he shut his eyes. He tried to calm his mind, but the simple plain question kept circling there round and round.

What is Himatan?

*   *   *

Okay, Murken Warrow, it's time to get a grip on the situation. Everyone's countin' on us to get their puckered sphincters out of here. And who am I lookin' at to pull that off? Fuckin' useless Sour! We're sunk. Absolutely had it. Might as well slit our own throats.

'So, Mage – what now?'

Murk flinched, almost tottering over from where he crouched studying the jungle. He peered up, squinting in the blinding sunlight, to Burastan glowering down. He straightened and as he did so darkness gathered in his vision. *Gotta get some food in me.* 'What do you mean?' His answer sounded defensive even to his ears.

The tall Seven Cities woman rolled her eyes. 'Which way now?'

'East.'

Burastan leaned forward to bring her sweaty grimed face closer to his. Speaking very slowly, she asked: 'Which way east?'

Murk looked away. He swallowed though no spit would come. 'Have to talk that over with the scouts.'

'You do that.'

'If you're all done . . .'

She waved him away. He went to find the scouts – and Sour.

These days the Thyr mage was spending all his time with the scouts. Murk had come across him actually teaching them how to pick flowers! Could you believe it? And these hardened veterans of Seven Cities and the Quon Insurgency campaigns. Murk couldn't credit it. When did this happen?

It all started going haywire after they spent time with Oroth-en and his people. *Sour took to it like a fish to water an' now he's runnin' around wearing leaves and preachin' all this living off the land crap*. Well, as far as Murk was concerned it was all going to end badly for them. A pig can't be a tiger no matter how hard it tries, as his old pa used to say.

He found his goggle-eyed partner showing a plant to four scouts. He was explaining something about the roots being edible at one time of year, the leaves at another, and the berries fine so long as you boiled them.

'Boil them in what?' Murk asked.

His partner blinked up at him, one bulging eye higher than the other. 'Well . . . you could use a helmet, I s'pose. If you had to. Fill it with water and drop in heated stones.'

'An' who's going to do that?'

The fellow shrugged. 'Better than starvin'.'

Was it really, though? Eating grasshoppers and beetles and such? There was no way he'd do that.

Sour nodded to the scouts and they melted away among the broad drooping leaves. Droplets of rainwater pelted down in loud explosions all round them.

'Which way?' Murk asked.

'I'm thinkin' on it.'

'Thinking,' Murk repeated sceptically. 'You're thinking. Well . . . time's passing, you know.'

'I know.'

Murk studied him. There was something new about the man – beyond the natural colouring and dirt powders he'd painted himself in. He wore leather sandals that appeared to have been cut from someone's cast-off armour. His only other covering was a loin wrap of ratty old cloth. The paints had smeared and faded and become mixed with sweat to a smooth layer over his limbs, chest and face. His hair was a greasy mat that was so muddy he looked as if he'd stuck his head into a hole in the ground.

Murk gestured helplessly to the man's head. 'What's with all this . . . ?'

Sour blinked at him, innocently. 'This?'

Murk flapped his hands. 'The hair – the mud!'

The mage's brows shot up. 'Ah! Keeps away the crabs and lice an' scalp-rot 'n' such.'

'An' all this crap you've smeared yourself in? Can't be healthy.'

The man shrank, examined his hands. 'Well . . . the dirt keeps the bugs off. No bites from the chiggers or flies or midges or mites. The layer keeps the sun off too, so no sunburn. An' it helps keep you cool so that keeps down on the sweating too.' He tapped a dirty finger to

449

his chin. His nails were blackened and broken from all the digging he'd been doing. 'That's about it.'

Murk kept his scowl. 'Well . . . you smell like a damned privy.'

Sour snapped his fingers. 'That's right! Yeah, an' the animals can't smell you so it's easer to hunt. You smell just like the jungle . . . you see?'

Murk glared his hardest. 'You smell all right. I can attest to that!' He waved his hand in front of his nose.

Sour's face fell. He kicked at the ground, his shoulders hunching. 'Sorry. But . . . you know . . . you could maybe . . . it keeps the bugs off.'

Murk just glared. 'Which way?'

Sour rubbed a hand on his head, smearing his hair all about. He winced as if contemplating something painful. 'Don't know. Can't choose! There're so many choices – so many ways things could go south round here. Don'cha sense it all?'

'No, I don't. Shadow's no help.' Murk glared now at the gloom of the thick brush. 'It's like all its attention's elsewhere, you know? It's like the shadows are all standing still, afraid to move.'

Sour was nodding eagerly. 'Yeah! I know what you mean.' He pointed to the lurid jade star that was the Visitor clearly visible in the full daylight. 'It's that. It's so close now. I feel like it's hangin' right over my head. Like it was gonna fall right—' He covered his mouth and staggered as if punched, his eyes huge above his hand. 'Burn forgive us!' he murmured into his fingers.

Murk had seen his partner like this before and each time it had saved a lot of lives during the campaign in north Genabackis. 'What is it?' he asked, reaching out to steady him, then pulling his hand away as he remembered he had no shirt. 'What'd you see?'

Sour was gazing off into the distance. 'It could happen,' he breathed, awed by what he'd glimpsed.

'What?'

Sour's gaze snapped to him as if just noticing he was there. He edged close and lowered his voice. 'There's a chance it could fall right here on us,' he whispered. 'I *saw* it.'

Murk immediately glanced about to see if anyone was within hearing. 'Don't start talk like that.'

'I *know*,' Sour answered, fierce. 'But it's real.'

'We have to run this by the captain.'

Sour blinked, quite startled. 'Really? I thought you was just gonna tell me to shut the Abyss up.'

Murk glanced back towards camp and froze. 'Naw,' he murmured, 'if there's a chance . . .' He tilted his head in that direction and Sour glanced over, grunted.

Burastan was headed their way. She halted, set her fists on her hips – wide and muscular ones beneath her tattered and frayed trousers that Murk didn't mind resting his eyes on. She gave them a withering glare up and down. 'What're you two whispering on about like a couple of kids?'

'Oh, nothing,' Murk replied, all airily. The woman's presence quite tied Sour's tongue.

She rolled her eyes. 'Don't try that mysterious mage act on me. I know you're nothing but a village wart-healer.'

'Got any?'

She frowned warily. 'What?'

'Warts.'

Her lips tightened to colourless and her hand went to the wire-wrapped grip of her curved Seven Cities blade. 'You're wanted,' she hissed through rigid jaws.

'Okay,' Murk answered.

'Not you,' she snarled, dismissing him. She raised her chin to Sour. 'You.'

Sour pointed to his own chest in disbelief. 'Me?'

She rolled her eyes once more. 'Yeah you – gods help us. C'mon.'

Burastan led them to a trooper leaning up against a tree, one unshod foot crossed over the other. 'He can't walk,' she told them.

Sour knelt before the man. He unceremoniously took hold of an ankle to study one foot. The man tensed in pain. Sour waved Murk in for a closer look. He indicated the sole. 'See?'

The skin of the sole was an angry engorged red. The skin was covered in blisters and was peeling in thick layers as if it had been boiled. 'What happened?' Murk asked.

'Poisonous plant.' He regarded the man, shook his head. 'Walked round in your bare feet, didn't you?'

'Just to take a piss,' the man answered, his voice whip tight.

'Well don't – walk round in bare feet, I mean. Ever. Until you know what plants to touch and which to stay away from.'

'How am I to know that? We're surrounded by damned plants everywhere!'

'Then keep your sandals on.'

The trooper gestured helplessly. 'The damned things is all rotted away and won't stay on, will they!'

'Watch your tone, Manat,' Burastan growled.

Murk looked to the scowling woman, rather bemused by this

451

defence of Sour. Order among the ranks, he supposed. Sour just bobbed his head. 'Fair enough.' He tapped a knuckle to the trooper's hauberk of layered leather bands. 'Cut that up for sandals and tie them on.'

The infantryman, Manat, stared at Sour as if he'd gone mad. 'Cut up good armour to make sandals?' he repeated in wonder, too stunned by the idea to be scornful. He sent an entreating look to Burastan. 'I'll keep my armour, thank you very much.'

'Oh yeah.' Sour rummaged in the large shoulder bag at his side. He drew out a flattened and bruised blossom of large sky-blue petals. The blue orchid that he had been going on about for days now. He took the trooper's hand and pressed the flower into it. 'There you go. You won't be attacked now. Not unless you stick your finger into a leopard's eye, or somethin' dumb like that.'

Manat shot another look of disbelief to Burastan. He pointed to Sour. 'What fucking mumbo-jumbo is this?'

The lieutenant lunged forward to lean over the man. 'You'll fucking do what you're told,' she hissed, 'or I'll cut the skin from your damned feet and make you walk point! Am I understood?'

Manat shrank under the lieutenant's fury. 'Okay – sir. If you say so. But . . . I'm not walkin' anywhere right now.'

'I'll go get something for that,' Sour said. 'Don't you worry. There's an easy cure for that – you just have ta know where to look, that's all.'

Manat's brows rose. 'Really? You c'n cure this? Man – you do that and I'll eat your Burn-damned flowers.'

Sour straightened, laughing. 'Don't eat that one. Wear it next to your skin. In your shirt, maybe. And when you see a fresh one, pick it and replace the old one. Yes?'

The trooper studied the flattened blossom, still dubious. 'If you say so . . . sir.'

'Okay. I'll have a look. You rest here.' Sour looked to Murk as if seeking his permission, or approval. Murk waved him towards the woods; Sour grinned and headed off. Murk followed. Burastan also came along.

Some distance into the dense undergrowth of a grove of young bamboo, Burastan cleared her throat to call a halt. Sour turned to her; Murk found himself standing aligned with the lieutenant, facing his partner, arms crossed.

'All right. What was that all about?' the Seven Cities woman demanded.

'What?'

The woman reached out as if she would snatch hold of the man's shirtfront, if he had one to grab. 'The Hood-damned flower nonsense. I don't approve of lying to the troops. Even if it's to a good end.'

Confusion wrinkled the man's brow and around his eyes and from long association Murk recognized honest puzzlement. 'She means that fairy tale about the stupid magic flower. Things aren't that bad yet.'

The puzzlement remained in the mage's lined brow and his bulging misaligned dark brown eyes as they flicked from Murk to Burastan. The woman kicked the ground with one rotting boot. 'Look,' she began, exhaling, 'I understand. The men and women are starting to wonder whether any of them are going to make it out. But you should've cleared it with the captain before you started some damned fool story like that.' She raised a warning finger. 'I know this crew. They'll give you the chance. But when you're proved wrong – you're out. Like a pariah dog, you'll be out.'

The little man's brows now climbed his lined and seamed forehead in growing comprehension. 'But it's true! I think I've got a handle on this place. It's got its own rules. You just have to hunt them out.'

Murk exchanged a frustrated glance with Burastan. 'So, the flower?'

The crab-like fellow gave a sharp nod. 'Right. I think I've figured somethin' out. Here, in this jungle, it doesn't matter what you look like or how you crash about making noise or whatnot. What really matters,' and he took a deep breath before plunging on any further, 'what really matters . . . is what you smell like.'

'What? *Smell*?' Murk blurted out.

Sour flinched, but nodded firmly.

Burastan let out a long breath, obviously disappointed. 'I'm sorry, but I have to talk to the captain about this.'

Sour raised his chin, defiant. 'Fine! 'Cause I want to too. I just decided which way we should go.'

Murk wouldn't meet Burastan's searching gaze; it was a hard thing to witness. *The poor guy. Just has to dig a hole for hisself.*

They found Yusen with group of resting troops, talking. Burastan approached and cleared her throat. Yusen gave her a nod then exchanged a few last words with the soldiers. Straightening, he signed for them to move off.

He stopped next to a fat tree Oroth-en had told them was called a Golden Shower. It was not as broad about at the base as many others, but carried a very wide spread of hanging branches. Murk realized they must be near another village as this giant's trunk was festooned with faded garlands of flowers, lengths of woven hair, ribbons, and other bits and pieces such as stones and shapes moulded of clay set here and there as votive offerings. What were they worshipping here, he wondered. This particular tree itself? Or was it merely the altar, or representative, of the forest at large?

Yusen, he noted, now wore merely a long gambeson shirt, belted, with trousers tucked into tall moccasins. He was without a helmet over his brush-cut, retreating greying hair. His scalp showed through red and raw beneath, but his eyes glowed just as bright and sharp as ever. Like sapphires, Murk thought them. Cut gemstones.

'What is it?' the captain said, crossing his arms. His gaze was steady on Burastan.

She indicated Sour. 'This one's laying a line of shit on the troops. He's taking advantage of their trust of the cadre mages. Handing out flowers and claiming they're safe if they wear them. Claims he can't keep.'

The steady gaze shifted to Sour. 'Is that true, soldier?'

Murk felt for the poor guy but he couldn't step in. This was a hole his naivety had spilled him into. His partner squirmed and rubbed a hand over his head, his odd eyes seeming to look in two directions at once, but he was nodding firmly. 'Yes, sir, Cap'n sir. It's true. You wear that flower and you're safe from the jungle. I believe that completely.'

Yusen returned his piercing gaze to Burastan. 'There you are, Lieutenant. The man stands behind his claim. Has it been disproved?'

The woman almost gaped but caught herself. 'Well. No – that is, no, sir.' She waved at Sour. 'But he's not even cadre! Spite told us she pulled them out of prison! Why should we—'

'Hey now!' Sour cut in. He motioned to Murk. 'We're cadre! We even served with—'

Murk loudly cleared his throat and Sour clamped his mouth shut, hunching.

Yusen's glittering gaze shifted between the two of them, settled on Murk. 'You have something to add, soldier?'

Murk raised his open hands. 'No sir. Nothing at all.'

The mercenary captain looked as if he was about to press for more, but something stopped him and he drew a heavy breath instead. His sharp gaze moved to the tree and roved among its clutter of offerings. Murk studied the man. *Why won't you press? Ah, because then we'd push back asking about your past, yes? And just what is that past, Captain Yusen? Seven Cities, wasn't it?*

Were you a green lieutenant then? Did you side with the damned Insurgency?

Burastan recovered enough to shake her head. 'Talk. All talk.' She turned to Yusen. 'Sir, the men and women don't deserve this. Order these two to keep to their place.'

'Lieutenant,' Yusen said, his eyes still on the many garlands and lengths of string woven from human hair. 'Might I remind you that we've crossed nearly half of Himatan. Been chased by damned Disavowed of the Crimson Guard. Are escorting a fragment of the Crippled God. And we're still alive?' He drew a heavy breath. 'I suggest we listen to our hired mages on these matters. If I don't miss my guess is they saw action in Genabackis. Fifth or Sixth Army.' The blue eyes swung to Murk and Sour, and Murk thought them as bright as the deep ice he'd seen in the Northern Range.

'Genabackis?' Burastan repeated wonderingly. 'But that was One Arm . . .' She peered at them more closely now, her gaze sceptical. 'You served with Fist Dujek?'

Murk didn't answer at first; he thought it irrelevant, but Sour knuckled his brow, saying, 'Yes, ma'am.' Murk could almost see the speculations now circulating through the woman's mind: just who else might these two have served beside?

For some reason the old empire carried a lot of weight with this woman for she nodded then, and saluted Yusen, murmuring, 'Very good, Captain.'

But Murk wasn't happy: here he'd wanted to learn more about Yusen's history yet the man had managed to wring theirs out of them instead. Neatly done, that, he had to admit.

Yusen now eyed Sour. Murk thought he read a strange sort of affection in the man's expression. 'So, cadre. You have a recommendation?'

Sour straightened, pushed out his chest. 'Yessir. Scouts report a stream to the southeast. I suggest we march in its bed. That'll keep the troops out of all these poisonous plants and it'll disguise our trail.'

'What about them swarming biting fish?' Murk objected. 'They nearly took that trooper's hand right off! What was his name, anyway?'

'His name's Bait now,' Sour answered. 'Anyways, they only like the shallows and the shores. We keep to the middle and we'll be fine.'

Yusen was frowning his consideration, thinking it through. 'Yet you didn't like the river . . .'

Sour nodded eagerly. 'Yeah. That was cloudy water. Clear water's fine. You keep away from cloudy water. Ain't healthy.'

The captain studied Sour for a time longer, his lips pursed. Then he nodded, slowly and thoughtfully. 'Very good. Lieutenant?'

'Sir?'

'We have our marching orders. See to it.'

To her credit, the woman saluted quickly and smartly. 'Sir.' Seemed an order was an order, no matter what. She waved for Murk and Sour to follow her. They walked away together.

Yusen watched them go. Then, once he was alone, he reached into his gambeson, where the loops and horn catches tied the front, and gently drew a small object from under the shirt. It was a flattened and bruised blue blossom. He held it cradled in the palm of one hand. His gaze went to where the mages and the lieutenant had disappeared among the thick stands of drooping fronds.

He shook his head, snorting lightly. 'Wondered why he gave me the silly thing . . .'

*   *   *

They came to a river and so abrupt was its appearance, so silently did it course, that Ina thought it some sort of a conjuration. She let fall the frayed switch she'd been using to beat a path through the leaves and fronds – some as tall as she – and wiped her hands over the bark of a thick curving root to remove the worst of the sticky sap.

The Enchantress had asked only once why she did not employ her sword to hack her way through the undergrowth. That day she'd been particularly vexed by the hanging lianas, while the dry scimitar-like grasses had cut the back of her hand to bloody ribbons and she had snapped, 'Why don't you use your powers to blast us a route?'

T'riss had been quiet after that. Ina mentally castigated herself for her failure of patience and composure – not to mention any possible blasphemy.

Now she faced a river. A wide ribbon of muddy reddish water moving so smoothly it was almost impossible to detect any flow. Her first thought was to throw herself in and luxuriate in the washing away of the layer of sweat-adhered dust and dirt that she could scrape from her arms with a fingernail. In fact, it appeared as if she could jump right in from the undercut slope she stood on overlooking the river's edge.

A hand took her arm from behind and so startled was she that she reacted automatically: instead of yanking forwards to free herself –

as any untrained person would do – she shot her elbow backwards and up, straight towards the throat or face of the attacker.

A meaty crack rewarded her, and the hand slipped from her arm. She spun, blade emerging at the same instant ready to thrust or block, only for it to fall from her hand as she saw the Enchantress lying sprawled unconscious behind her.

'Good gods!' she cried. She fell to her knees to scoop the woman up, intending to take her to the river's edge to resuscitate her. Grunting with the effort – for T'riss was a solid woman – she rose. Then she remembered her blade. How could she abandon her blade?

But the Enchantress was a more pressing matter so she carried her to where she could bull her way through the brush down the slope to the shore. Here she laid her burden in the grass then padded out into the river to wet her robes. She returned to squeeze the cloth over the woman's face.

T'riss coughed and spluttered, then turned her head aside.

Ina found she could breathe deeply once more as a great pressure eased itself within her chest. *Thank the First! To think I'd almost concussed the Queen of Dreams! Yet . . . how could I have done so?*

She watched the woman sit up and press both hands to her head as if testing its soundness, then she went to retrieve her sword. When she returned T'riss was still sitting, but had a wet fold of cloth pressed to her forehead. When Ina went to her knees before her she raised a hand to forestall any protestations.

'I should have known better than to lay hands on a Seguleh,' she said.

'M'lady – I am stricken. Name your punishment.'

T'riss held the cloth to her brow while nodding thoughtfully. 'Your punishment is to continue to accompany me.'

'M'lady mocks.'

'I hope that I do.'

Ina was quiet for a time. *Has she foreseen my death?*

The Enchantress attempted to rise, unsteadily. Ina offered an arm. The woman straightened carefully. Close now she peered up at Ina's masked face. 'You are wondering how it was you could strike me?'

Ina gave a curt answering nod. 'Yes. I was . . . startled.'

'*You* were startled,' the woman muttered, rubbing her forehead. 'Well. I come to Ardata completely unguarded and open. It is the only way. She would not have accepted me otherwise.'

Ina frowned behind her mask. 'Unguarded?'

'Ah. I speak of my own powers, of course. I do not know what you would name it. My aspect. My manifestation. My territory. An area of concern that, through general neglect and laziness, has become my responsibility.'

'I am sorry, m'lady . . . but you have lost me.'

The Enchantress smiled. 'Of course. I am thinking aloud – to the jungle. Now,' and she let go of Ina's arm, 'a river. Good. We are moving far too slowly while events elsewhere overtake us. Clearly the best way to move through this region is by water. Let us do so.'

She gestured. Off through the surrounding bush there came a noise as of branches snapping, or dragging, brushing against one another in a rising storm of noise. Bits and pieces of driftwood and fallen branches cast up along the shore came sliding towards them. They ranged in size from sticks and branches all the way up to medium-sized logs. They came grating and slithering together into a heap. They twined, moulded and flattened, and before Ina's amazed vision there took form a long slim open hull of woven wood.

'I thought you said you had abandoned your powers,' Ina said, without thinking.

'I did not say I had abandoned them,' the Enchantress objected, a touch impatient. 'I only said that I was unguarded.'

She waved to invite Ina to go first. Still rather dazed by the demonstration, Ina awkwardly stepped on to the slim craft and edged forward towards the bow. Her patron took the stern. Then the Queen of Dreams gently pushed her hands forward, as if parting a cloth, and the vessel slid off the mud into the current. She directed it downstream. The craft sliced through the water at what to Ina was a rather alarming rate. But the Enchantress had said they'd been making slow progress and that events were moving ahead of them; the Queen of Dreams, it seemed, was in a hurry.

They raced for days and nights continuously along the river. Ina slept through the nights while the Enchantress appeared to need no rest. This amused Ina – the Queen of Dreams never slept. It seemed somehow appropriate. When she hungered, Ina had a small nibble from the bag of dried stores that remained. Her lifelong training in privation and restraint served her well here. Water was their sole problem. The Enchantress forbade her to touch the river. Occasionally they passed small clear rivulets draining into the main channel. The Enchantress would direct the craft to the shore here and Ina would collect what she could in the one waterskin that had yet to rot away.

Now that they were without the constant shade from the jungle's canopy the new problem Ina had to deal with was sunstroke. During the day no cloud cover softened the sun's driving rays. She draped her robes over her like a blanket but to begin with neglected her head, and now peeling burnt skin came off in her nails when she probed her scalp.

So great was their speed that when they swept round a river bend they sometimes startled flocks of tall wading birds that swept skyward in great swaths of white and brilliant yellow. The gangly birds cawed their raucous complaints and found temporary perches in the trees along the shore until the branches bowed down almost to the murky surface of the water, festooned with what resembled tall slim flowers.

Ina spent much of her time treating her blade against the constant bite of the humidity. Long ago the Seguleh smiths had found that adding charcoal to their furnaces yielded an iron that was superior in flexibility, while also being particularly resistant to corrosion. Yet it remained an uncertain process and no blade was perfectly impervious. She had run out of the plant oils she usually carried and was now reduced to smearing her own skin's sweat and secretions on to the blade, which, though harmful, were better than nothing.

They raced on, careering round the twisting bends. The river appeared to be widening as they went, gathering tributaries and creeks at every snaking curve.

Then one day Ina was adjusting the cloth of the robe draped over her head when something came screaming down from the sky above. She had one stunning glimpse of a great draconic shape, golden-red, claws extended, stooping, snarling teeth agape, before those claws clamped on to the craft and she was plunged beneath the clouded ochre-hued water.

She came up, gasping and thrashing, yet gripping the hilt of her sheathed sword to make certain it was safe. She swam one-handed for shore. Here she found a woman in nothing more than a ragged loincloth standing over her mistress. She drew immediately.

'Stand aside.'

The woman turned on her and Ina was shaken to see that her eyes churned like twin furnaces of molten gold. 'And what is this?' she asked. 'A Seguleh?' She pointed to Ina's face. 'Your mask is sorely in need of repainting.'

'Please let us go,' the Enchantress said from where she lay sodden and muddy on the shore. 'We are no threat to you.'

'I will be the judge of that,' the woman answered, though she did seem to relax somewhat, lowering her arms. 'Just what are you then?'

The Enchantress shrugged. She wiped her mouth, leaving a smear of blood-red mud across her face. 'I am a sorceress,' she said. 'Out of Tali. Quon Tali.'

'I know Tali,' the woman snarled impatiently. 'More to the point – what are you doing here?'

Again an easy shrug from the Enchantress. 'The power and wisdom of the Queen of Witches is legendary. I would seek her out.'

The woman actually laughed aloud at that. It was a very cruel and scornful laugh. 'For a sorceress, your foresight is remarkably poor.'

'And you?' the Enchantress challenged, quite unintimidated. 'Why attack us?'

The woman snarled anew. Her hands worked as if eager to tear and rend. 'That is my business.'

'It would seem you have made it our business as well. Spite, daughter of Draconus, sister to—'

The woman threw a hand up. 'Not that name! If you wish to live.'

The Enchantress inclined her head, acquiescing.

Spite seemed to think on the Enchantress's words, for she waved a hand dismissively. 'If you must know . . . I am seeking something. Something stolen. You must have a presence, sorceress, for I sensed you and I thought I glimpsed . . . well, I was mistaken.' She turned and walked off, then stopped, facing them once more. 'Take my advice, sorceress. Go back home. Do not seek out Ardata. Only death resides in Jakal Viharn.'

'I hear that Ardata kills no one.'

'That is true. For that she has Himatan.'

Spite then leaped into the air and before falling she transformed into the great terrifying shape Ina had glimpsed. Wide massive wings elongated above them to blot out the sun's rays. They flapped once, heavily and powerfully, propelling Spite skyward and casting up a storm of dust, leaves and twigs that drove Ina to turn her face away. When she looked back, blinking, her gaze shaded, she glimpsed a russet writhing shape disappearing into the distance over the treetops.

Ina turned to the Enchantress. She extended an arm to grasp the woman's hand and pull her up. Red and grey mud smeared the woman's robes. 'She did not know who you are?' Ina asked.

'No. As I said, I have lowered my, ah, manifestation. It would appear that without it I am nothing more than an ageing sorceress.'

Sighing, the Enchantress eyed the wreckage of their vessel.

Her own uselessness in the encounter drove Ina to murmur, 'And I am hardly a bodyguard.'

The Enchantress raised a finger. 'Oh, but you are, my dear. You are vitally important. You have no idea what pause that mask of yours gives people. That you are here accompanying me is quite necessary. Spite would never have believed a sorceress alone. While you, a Seguleh, are the perfect guard.'

So – I am nothing more than the perfect accessory. So much for my vaunted ambitions. Rightly is she named the Queen of Dreams. One further question plagued her, yet she did not know whether it mattered now at all. In the end, her role as bodyguard – if humiliatingly illusory – demanded that she broach the subject.

'Is she your enemy?'

'My enemy?' The woman's thick brows rose. She nodded thoughtfully for a time. 'Well . . . let us just say that she has grounds for resentment.' She gestured. 'This way. One good thing has come of this interruption, Ina.'

'Yes?'

'I do believe that we are close now. Very close.'

*   *   *

They pursued for four days, Jatal stopping only to throw himself down to attempt to catch a few hours of sleep before the dawn – though what he experienced could hardly be called sleep: his haze of exhaustion was more a delirium of nightmare images that flayed him worse than the agony of his lingering wounds. He often awoke feeling more tortured than when he threw himself to the ground.

Two days before, they had passed the corpse of a horse beside the jungle trail; it had been scavenged by predators but the majority of the carcass remained. The locals, it seemed, were unwilling to touch it. It was an Adwami mount. If the men and women they'd questioned along the way were accurate, the Warleader now had only two mounts remaining. Jatal led a string of four; he was confident they would overtake the man soon.

Scarza, of course, did not ride. Instead, he loped next to a mount, a hand on its cantle to help pull himself along. The half-Trell's iron endurance was a wonder to Jatal.

They did not talk. Jatal had nothing more to talk about. Occasionally, as they rested their few hours in the predawn light, he thought he caught Scarza watching him with a worried look.

But he would shut his eyes. It was too late for talk. It was too late for everything. He was already a dead man. Through his weakness, his envy, childishness and petulance, he'd killed himself. He was dead inside.

The next dawn, when the light streamed down through the canopy in a dappled greenish glow, they were off once more. This day they passed close to a village, a small collection of bamboo, grass and palm frond huts standing on tall legs. Here, Jatal dismounted stiffly and waved the nearest villager to him. The old woman, almost black from her decades beneath the sun, all bones and sinew in a cloth wrap, approached and bowed.

'Yes, noble born?' she asked in a quavering voice, her head lowered.

In the Thaumaturg tongue, a dialect not too dissimilar to the Adwami, Jatal said: 'We seek word of a man who may have ridden through here ahead of us. Has anyone seen such?'

The old woman shook her head. 'No, noble born. No one has ridden past us here.'

Jatal cursed his luck. Had the Warleader turned off somewhere? Yet this was the most direct track east.

'That is, no man, noble born,' the woman added; then she paused as if thinking better of continuing.

'Yes? Go on.'

The old woman bowed even lower. 'Forgive us our ignorant superstitions, great one, but some nights ago one of our children claimed to have seen on this very trail a . . . a portent of death. Perhaps even – so the child claimed – death itself.'

'Riding east?'

'Yes, m'lord. A ghost, she thought it. A vision of her own death. A shade riding a horse that steamed like smoke in the night.'

'Thank you, woman.' Jatal tossed a coin into the dirt before her.

By this time Scarza had caught up. He ambled over, rubbing his legs and breathing heavily.

'Still has a good lead on us,' Jatal said. 'Can't understand it. He may be down to only one mount.'

Puffing, Scarza straightened to his full inhuman height, stretching his back. He blew out a great breath. 'The man has strange elixirs and potions. Perhaps he is doping the animals so that they run on past their exhaustion and know no pain.'

'Perhaps,' Jatal grudgingly allowed. He gestured ahead. 'See there, through the trees? The mountains?'

Still drawing in great lungfuls of air, the giant squinted. 'Call those mountains? Those would be regarded as no more than pimples back where I come from. Boils, perhaps, those taller ones.'

Jatal almost ventured a smile, but did not. He frowned instead, and his jaws clenched. 'Well, that is his destination for certain. The Gangrek Mounts. He is fleeing to Himatan. He cannot know we are after him.'

'He would not care,' the giant said. 'No, he must be in a rush to get somewhere – or reach someone. Remember what these villagers are saying. After the army of the Thaumaturgs passed there came a train of wagons. Huge wagons. Each pulled by eight oxen. The train guarded by fifty yakshaka. That is what he pursues. That I swear by my mother's remaining teeth.'

'Alone? What could he hope to accomplish?'

The half-Trell gave an indifferent shrug. 'Perhaps he thinks himself their match? Who knows. It matters not if we catch him first.'

Jatal nodded. 'Indeed. It matters not, as you say.' And he added, more to himself, 'Nothing matters any more.' He threw himself back up on his mount though foaming sweat streaked its sides and its muscles still quivered and jumped. He slapped his blade to its wet flank to set onward once again.

Scarza watched him gallop off and shook his head, frowning. 'Ah, lad. It hurts now, I know it. But don't go throwing yourself away.' He drew in a great breath and hacked up a mouthful of phlegm, spat, then took hold of the cantle of his horse and set off in the prince's wake.

After the foreigners had gone the rest of the nearby villagers gathered round the old woman.

'What were they?' one asked.

'What did they want of us?' another demanded.

'The first was a noble,' she answered. 'From the south, I believe, if tales be true. The other was his monster servant. Summoned perhaps by the shamans of the south.'

The villagers were silent in wonder at this news. They knew it must be so, for Rhyu was their birthing-woman, their healer and fortune-teller.

'They pursue death,' she continued, peering after them with her milky half-blind gaze. 'And will meet him soon.'

*　　*　　*

Scarves of mist coiled among the trees and stands of ferns and brush and for this Golan was grateful. Unfortunately, the day's gathering heat would soon burn it all off. Then little would be left to disguise the shattered and trampled wreckage that used to be the encampment of the Thaumaturg Army of Righteous Chastisement.

Golan stood beneath his canted awning surrounded by his guard of yakshaka. It had been a night of complete and utter terror and chaos – terror for his troops and labourers, gut-twisting shame for himself. What would he tell the Circle of Masters now? How could he continue the march? And yet . . . what other option was there? Turn round? The river was behind them now. Not at sword-point did he think he could force the troops back over that river.

No. They were trapped. They—

The truth of what he'd just realized struck him with the clarity of a mathematical solution and he was stunned by its simplicity and its beauty. Elegant. So very elegant. It was a trap. The entire jungle, all Himatan, was a trap for all those who would seek to invade. *The jungle naturally defends itself.*

There was more to this as well – he was certain of it. A deeper truth. Yet he could not quite reach it. His mind was dulled by his fatigue. His thoughts tramped heavy and laboured. He refocused his attention outwards, rubbed his gritty aching eyes, and took a deep breath of the warm close air.

The last of the rain was drifting down as the clouds moved off to the southwest. Shafts of gold sunlight stabbed through the canopy. The cries of the wounded had diminished through the night. Now, only a low constant moaning sounded over the field that had been a scene of insane slaughter, suicide, horror and sick revulsion. Strangely enough, though they had been rained on all through the night, the surviving wounded now called for water. Low slinking shapes still haunted the verges of the surrounding jungle. The screams and the stink of blood had drawn every night hunter for leagues around. They had gorged themselves on choice viscera – sometimes while the victims still lived. What few cohorts and phalams could be organized had done their best to chase them off. The wreckage of the encampment was emerging now through the dissolving mist and Golan looked away.

He awaited the awful news. The butcher's bill. He steeled himself to expect the worst – all the while suspecting that even that would come nowhere near the truth of it. First to dare approach was Second-in-Command Waris. The man came dragging himself up the

slight rise, quite obviously exhausted and no doubt rather traumatized by all they had gone through.

The yakshaka allowed him entrance – over the course of the last
day and night they'd had to cut down several soldiers who, in their
agony, panic, or plain rage, had thrown themselves at Golan. Waris
knelt to one knee.

'I offer my head, Master,' he began.

Golan cleared his throat of the thick sticky coating of catarrh that
had gathered there. He spat aside. 'No need for that as yet, Second.
This is not of your making. I take full responsibility. Your report,
please.'

Waris bowed even further. 'A portion of those troops that fled into
the woods are returning even as we speak – though much diminished. Creatures attacked them there. Yet ranks are being reordered.
Surviving labourers are being put to work salvaging equipment. I
estimate that we will be ready to march by noon.'

Golan found himself breathing more easily. 'Well done, Second.
Well done. You have my compliments. So enter it into the records.'

'Yes, Master.' He remained bowed, silent.

Golan felt his chest tightening once again. 'Yes? What else?'

'The bodies, Master. It would take a great deal of time to bury
them all. And . . . well, the men may refuse to touch them.'

'Ah. I see. Well?'

'Might I suggest we dispose of them in the river?'

Relieved that the matter was so trivial, Golan waved his switch.
'Yes, of course. Proceed, Second.' Waris backed away, still bowed,
until clear of the circle of yakshaka, when he turned and jogged off.
Good, Golan congratulated himself. The army reconstitutes itself.
Shaken and much diminished, yes. But not shattered. We march on.
We must. There is no alternative.

Golan's improved mood was short-lived. Another figure approached, this one gangly and stick-thin, with a long curved neck
that somehow managed to support an improbably oversized head.
Golan drew a deep steadying breath and awaited the arrival of
Principal Scribe Thorn.

'You live still, Master!' Thorn announced as he closed, a quill
tucked behind one ear, the heavy bag of papers swinging at his side.
'I rejoice. Here so many you lead have passed on yet still you remain!
Thank the fates.'

'Your joy is noted, Principal Scribe. Have you an accounting?'

The scribe drew a sheet from his shoulder bag, squinted low over
it. 'I am hardly done, of course. It will take a long time to count all

those fallen. So many! Such a catastrophe. Yet you have emerged unhurt, I see. That alone makes a victory of the night, yes?'

False gods! This man does not spare me. Golan pinched the bridge of his nose and rested his gritty eyes. 'You do have an estimate?'

'Yes, Master.'

'Well?'

As he studied the sheet, the man's black tongue poked out as if it too was curious. 'I estimate a force of some three thousand remaining serviceable labourers. Of the troops, eighteen hundred are able to march.'

Golan's breath fled him. Their remaining labour force had been halved again. Who would carry all the stores? Cook and break camp? How could they advance?

'Sobering numbers indeed,' Thorn continued, peering further down the sheet. 'Yet encouraging news exists.'

Golan could hardly credit his ears. *Encouraging news?* 'What possible good news could emerge from this disaster?'

'There are now more than enough stores for those surviving!'

'Yet none to carry them.'

Thorn did not miss a beat: 'You anticipate me.'

'I believe I am beginning to, Principal Scribe. You have a report?'

'Quite.' Thorn replaced the sheet and withdrew another. He peered at it myopically, pronounced: 'Once again the Army of Righteous Chastisement emerges victorious.'

Golan found that he had to turn away, his fists clenched rigidly round the Rod of Execution. A long low breath summoned the proper Thaumaturg-taught calm. 'At the rate of these victories we shall soon have the entire jungle conquered,' he remarked aloud, acidly.

He heard the scraping of the quill on paper and he spun. Thorn peered up from the sheet, quill poised, mild innocence upon his narrow pinched features. 'You have more to add, Glorious Leader?'

Through clenched teeth Golan ground out, 'That is more than enough, I am sure.'

Thorn shrugged indifferently. 'We are all at your mercy, Master. What are your orders?'

That you throw yourself into the river. But no, that is unfair. The fault is mine. The responsibility mine and mine alone. He drew another steadying breath, peered down at the blackwood rod with its silver chasing. He tapped it into one palm. 'Record this, Scribe – Master Golan orders that what surplus stores and gear the bearers

466

cannot manage be divided up among the troopers and that the army advance onward into the jungle of Himatan. So it is ordered, so it shall be.'

Thorn's shaggy brows rose while he wrote. He finished with a firm tap to end the entry, and bowed. 'So it shall be, Master.'

CHAPTER XIII

It was almost impossible to compel the locals to enter any ruins or abandoned villages. 'Do you not fear the ghosts?' they would ask. 'There are no ghosts,' I told them. But they disagreed. 'Ghosts live in all dark places in Jacuruku,' they all assured me. 'They are under bridges, in corners, under fallen trees, in all the old villages. They are afoot and very much alive.'

Infantryman Bakar
Testimony to the Circle of Masters

MARA HEAVED HERSELF UP A MUDDY SHORE TO LIE PANTING, pressed into the muck, searching the surrounding dense fronds and hanging creepers. At her feet lay the carcass of a bizarre hybrid creature. A fine dusting of metallic blue and green feathers covered its naked torso down to scaled legs ending in feet bearing claws as large as daggers. Instead of hair, long brown feathers covered its head and back like a mane while its eyes, rolled dead white now, had shone green speckled with gold. The mouth held needle teeth still red with Mara's own blood.

Shuddering, she kicked it further away. A bird-woman! Who would have thought the legends of Jakal Viharn true! Unlike the subjects of all those fantastic stories, however, this one had no wings and could not fly. She could run like a fiend, though. Probably chase down a hound.

The jungle rang all round with the cries and screams of a running battle that had continued through the night and into the day. Feet kicked the ground nearby and Mara spun, her Warren crackling about her, sending the litter of leaves and detritus flying. A guardsman appeared, hands raised. Leuthan.

'Are you wounded?'

She waved him away. 'No.'

He slid down to her. 'You can stand?'

'I am fine!'

'Don't get separated like that.'

She lurched to her feet, shook out her sodden dirt-smeared robes. 'Do not lecture me. Everyone is separated, if you haven't noticed.'

He laughed. 'Well – we're gathering at a rise to the southeast. No more running from these sports.'

'Very good. Take me there.'

He gestured. 'This way.'

Mara followed the Bloorian swordsman. Like everyone she'd met out of Bloor or Gris, he claimed to be the offspring of some noble family. Gods, how they'd fought each other in those petty kingdoms! Family against family, village versus village. Each valley an armed stronghold held against its neighbours. A war of all against all. She shook her head: sometimes she was convinced that the old emperor had done them all a favour when he'd swept them into his pocket one by one.

Shapes darted through the dense underbrush. Shouts sounded: Crimson Guard battle codes. Yet no grating clash of steel against steel rang out; these monstrosities used only tooth and claw. They passed the sprawled gutted corpse of a half . . . something or other. Half-lizard, perhaps. Grey-backed with a white belly. Mara didn't really care. It was enough that it was dead. They were strong and fierce, these things, but no match for armed Disavowed – even if most of everyone's armour had rotted off.

Next they came to the body of Hesta, an Untan swordswoman. One of the tiniest of all the Guard. Her neck had been broken and crushed as if she'd been taken by a predatory cat. Her face was up-turned to the sky, pale now, with a look of complete surprise in her dead staring eyes. Mara exchanged a wary look with Leuthan.

So, *he* was here. One of Ardata's favourites. Citravaghra.

Leuthan urged Mara onward. 'This way.' A moment later he stiffened, cursing. Something huge was crashing directly towards them through the underbrush. A humped grey shape emerged, wide arms brushing aside thickets of saplings. At the sight of them it bellowed a bull-like war call and charged. Though utterly wrung, Mara summoned what remaining energy she possessed. She tapped into her own vitality and felt it almost flicker out. She channelled the force outwards before her. The ground erupted, soil and earth peeling. The thicket curled up and amid the storm of dirt and flung trees the beast fell backwards, roaring his rage, and was sent tumbling, hammered and pummelled by the wreckage. Mara's vision blackened and she felt Leuthan supporting her at the waist.

'He'll be back,' he said, his words strangely distant and echoing.

Mara felt a warm wetness at her face and wiped at it to find a smear of blood across her sleeve. 'What . . . ?'

Then they were running, she half stumbling. They pushed through a bamboo grove. The stalks seemed to multiply and waver in Mara's blurred vision. *Things* moved among them, inhuman eyes bright with intelligence and menace. After this, Leuthan half carrying her, the ground rose up to almost meet her.

In fact, the ground *was* rising. Leuthan was labouring up a steep slope, pulling her along by her waist, scrambling on all fours.

Large hands took her and she found herself squinting up at the tall wide figure of Petal. 'I am spent,' she gasped, blinking to clear her vision.

'You look it,' he murmured.

'We're gathered?'

'Most of us, yes.' He directed her attention to the left. Halfway down the dirt slope of the butte-like rise they occupied stood Skinner. He alone still wore his armour: the ankle-length coat of mail still glittered night-black. He carried his helm under one arm. His long blond hair hung loose, blown in the weak wind. He faced the jungle verge.

Mara's gaze followed his out to the league beyond league of verdant green that was Himatan. Here and there treetops shook and shuddered as more of these creatures converged upon them. So many – who would have guessed the jungle would support such numbers? They must be gathering from all over the region. Everyone knew that a few haunted the groves of Himatan here and there, but she had thought them isolated D'ivers or Soletaken. Individual monstrosities. What she'd glimpsed here put her in mind of an actual *race*.

A people.

Ardata's children. How different, then, from the title given to the Andii: the Children of the Night?

A great din of rising shrieks and calls and roars now rose all about and the tops of the bamboo stalks shook like blades of grass. Skinner raised his arms for silence while the ranks of the Disavowed assembled behind. What could these half-beasts want? Mara wished they'd just go away. She peered behind her to where stone blocks topped the rise, time-gnawed, heaved and awry. A structure of some sort. Perhaps a fort, or cyclopean statue. Towering emergents now topped it. Their fist-like roots gripped the ruins as if feeding upon the tumbled blocks. From the overarching branches a great forest of hanging lianas draped down among them. Their thick woody lengths supported fat blossoms in pink, blood red, orange and creamy white.

'We do not want to spill any more of your blood,' Skinner called down to the jungle.

Challenges and hooted mocking laughter answered him.

He raised his arms once more. 'Let us talk. Know you that for a time I ruled as Ardata's chosen mate. You bowed before me then. Do so again or retreat into your haunts and bother us no more. This is your choice. I give you until sundown.'

Fury answered the ultimatum. Trees shuddered. Torn branches flew to crash upon the rise. Yells and shrieks sent a burst of multicoloured birds to darken the sky. The cloud gyred about the top of the rise before moving on in a weaving dance of flashing iridescence.

Shijel edged down the slope to Skinner and the two conferred. Mara looked to Petal, who was rubbing his wide jowls. 'What do you think?' she whispered.

'I do not know. I believe that we and they know they have us trapped. Skinner probably wishes to goad them into a rush.'

'And if not?'

He frowned, his cheeks and many chins bulging. 'Then I do not know how we shall escape from here.'

The jungle verge was quiet for a time. The sun continued its descent to the west. Clouds gathered in the north. She glimpsed dark shapes moving through the trees. She brushed dried blood from her nose and cheeks, adjusted the knot of her robes at her shoulder.

'What are they doing?' she whispered once more.

'Talking things over, I presume,' he answered, quite seriously. 'I believe we have some time. Perhaps you should sit . . .'

She drew a shuddering breath. 'Thank you. Yes.' She meant to ease herself down but fell quite heavily. She drew her knees up close to her chest and rested her chin upon them.

The wind brushing through the dense leaf cover brought wave after wave of shimmering reflections. The rich shades of jade were almost seductive. It was a shame, really. The land was beautiful after its own fashion; desirable. Were it not for its backward recalcitrant inhabitants. Still, correctly handled campaigns of neglect, discouragement and stifling might get rid of most of them after a generation or two. It would be very much easier to do something with the land after that.

As the afternoon waned she became aware of a tingling pulling at her and she clambered to her feet. Petal, she noted, was headed in this direction. He lumbered heavily in his swinging gait as he worked his way round to her along the line of guardsmen.

'You sense it as well?' he said as he drew near.

She nodded.

He scanned the forest. 'Some sort of manipulation.'

'What kind? I do not recognize it.'

'Elder. Animistic. Yet there is power there.' He stroked his jowls. 'They are preparing something.'

'An attack?' She scanned the edge of the trees; no shapes moved that she could see.

'I do not think so.'

Skinner climbed the slope to join them. 'What is it?' he asked. He still had his helm tucked under one arm. Only now did she notice that he carried no sword. 'You sense something as well?' she asked, surprised.

'Aye.'

She couldn't understand how he, a plain swordsman, could have developed such sensitivity, but she set that aside for later consideration.

Petal was tapping a finger to his thick lips. 'It may be a ritual,' he offered. 'Has that feel.'

'What sort?' Skinner asked.

'There's no—' He cut himself off, his gaze snapping to Mara as they both felt the tearing that the opening of a portal sends rippling through the surrounding mundane matter and all Warrens. Skinner spun as well.

'A gate!' Petal warned. 'Someone or something has come through.'

Mara threw up her Warren. The loose detritus of the slope vibrated beneath her feet as pulses of D'riss leaked from her in waves. Petal and Skinner were both physically pushed away from her; Skinner retreated down the slope.

They waited. Mara noted the warm wet air smelled particularly strongly of the flower blossoms here; a cloying sweet stink that hardly disguised how they hung rotting on the creepers. The day threatened to slip into the twilight of evening that she found came so startlingly suddenly in this land.

Two figures emerged from the shadows of the darkening jungle verge. Skinner turned and waved to Mara. She took a moment to ease her Warren and compose herself, then she carefully edged down the uneven dirt slope.

She knew them both. One by description and reputation, his lean muscular build leading up to a head of loose tawny hair, a feline black nose, bright golden eyes, and the fangs of a hunting-cat: Citravaghra. The other she'd met more than once: Rutana, favoured of Ardata, greatest of her aberrant menagerie of followers and adherents. And an enemy from the very first days of their arrival in this land decades ago.

'What is it you wish?' Skinner asked, grasping the initiative as always.

'Your death,' Rutana answered, readily enough.

Skinner shrugged, indifferent. 'If you wish death, we will happily accommodate all of you.'

Rutana just laughed her harsh cawing hack. 'It is your bones that will add to this pile, Betrayer. All of you. We need only wait.'

Mara studied her more closely. There was something different about her. She was perhaps even more dried and wiry than before – if it were possible for a human being to be nothing more than sinew and stretched ligament – but that was not it. There was an emotion playing about her slit mouth and narrow eyes while she stood grasping and kneading the many amulets hanging about her neck. It took Mara some time to identify it, for she had never seen it on the woman before: an almost bubbling humour. She actually appeared to be working hard to suppress a smile that kept her mouth quirking and twitching.

Mara wondered whether the emotion was contagious, for at her side Citravaghra shared it. His flecked golden eyes held triumph and he seemed to almost purr.

Skinner sensed the strangeness as well; he frowned as if disappointed. 'You know we can wait until the jungle eventually succeeds in grinding this rise flat.'

The twitching smile threatened to burst forth. 'Normally, yes.'

'Normally?'

'You do not know, do you?' Her laughing gaze shifted to Citravaghra. 'He does not know.'

Now Skinner checked an obvious rising anger. 'Know what?'

'They sense nothing of it,' she continued to Citravaghra. 'Isn't that disappointing? Perhaps they truly are Disavowed.'

'Perhaps it is Himatan itself. Or Ardata's doing,' he answered.

Rutana nodded exaggerated thoughtfulness. 'Ah. She has blocked him out. How does it feel,' she asked Skinner, 'being cast aside? Deliberately kept ignorant. Being treated as if you do not matter – at all?'

Skinner crossed his arms. The mail of his armour slid and grated across itself. 'That you are here belies that claim,' he answered, sounding bored.

Yes, Mara silently encouraged him. *How Rutana would hate such a tone.*

'Should we tell him?' the witch fairly growled.

'He really ought to know . . .' Citravaghra answered, and he smiled, revealing the rest of his jagged teeth.

'You have been cast aside, Skinner,' Rutana declared, triumphant. 'She has found another to take your place. You have no hope of returning now.'

Replaced? Return? Mara wondered. *Has this been his plan all along?*

But Skinner laughed. He threw his head back and roared as if their situation, this discussion, everything, was a great joke upon them all. After he caught his breath he shook his head. 'Rutana – you love your mistress too much. You cannot even conceive of someone not wanting to lie down before her, can you? Well, in any case, you do not know her mind. She has declared there is no one else who could possibly stand beside her.'

Yet the woman's taut smile broadened, satisfied, as if her own trap had been sprung. 'But . . . there is *one* who might.'

All the while Mara glimpsed more and more of the creatures gathering, crowding the verge. Their eyes gleamed with eager hunger. *We are trapped. And their numbers seem inexhaustible. Do they plan to overrun us? Soon there may be enough. What is Skinner counting on? Does he not see the danger?*

Skinner waved a gauntleted hand. 'Rutana – it does not matter.'

'You do not care?'

'Difficult as it obviously is for you to believe, I do not. However,' and he gestured to the surrounding jungle, 'as you have in us a captive audience, it would seem that I have no choice but to hear more of this.'

'That is true. You do not. But I believe you will thank me.'

'I will thank you to end the game.'

The smile fell to a straight knife-thin slit. 'That is why I am here, Betrayer. To end it.'

'Rutana . . .' Citravaghra murmured, warning. 'We have them . . .'

She snapped him a curt dismissive wave. 'That is not good enough.'

Mara glanced between Skinner and the woman. *He's baiting her – why? How will this help? Except to satisfy his personal feud? And she has waved off Citravaghra! The man-leopard. The Night Hunter. The most feared of them all. Who – what – is she?*

474

'Very well, Betrayer,' Rutana continued. 'I will give you this news and then I will slay you and then your failure will be utter and complete. Perhaps you would care about that?'

'You have nothing to say that I could possibly care about.'

She grasped hold of the many amulets and charms hung about her neck like a swimmer grasping at a rope and snarled: 'K'azz has come! Ardata sent for him and he has come. He will stand in your place! What say you to that?'

Mara stared, stunned and shaken. *K'azz here? In truth? Why . . .* She looked to Skinner: he was silent, immobile. His stillness shouted of danger to Mara. His blunt features had pulled down in a puzzled frown. 'We would—' he began, only to cut himself off.

Yet we wouldn't know, would we? We are Disavowed. The ghosts of our dead Crimson Guard brethren no longer serve us. And Himatan might disguise K'azz's presence. Or Ardata . . .

He gave an exaggerated shrug. 'What of it? This is your news? You ought not to have bothered. But, now that you have delivered it, you may go.' And he waved her off.

The woman's face paled to a sickly pallid ivory, as if all the blood had utterly drained from her flesh. She shifted a foot backwards, bracing herself.

'Rutana . . .' Citravaghra warned her once more.

'Now I will slay you, Betrayer,' she panted, her voice almost choked in passion. 'As I should have done when you first arrived.'

'Rutana – no!' The man-leopard reached for her but she swatted his arm aside. She snatched at the countless leather loops hanging about her neck, snapping the cords. The amulets and charms fell to the ground, tinkling and bursting. Next she tore at the series of bands at her arms, each knotted in its own amulet. Citravaghra took her waist and steered her back down the slope. She weaved, drunkenly, hardly able to walk. They disappeared among the thick brush bordering the woods.

Skinner motioned Mara back up the steep rise. 'We do not have much time,' he murmured.

'Until what?'

'I do not know what is to come. All I know are rumours. Some say that she emerged from the caves deep underground ages ago. Some say she once sat at the feet of D'rek herself.' They reached the line of guardsmen where Petal awaited. 'All I know is that she will come for me. When this happens you must all run. Head for Jakal Viharn.'

'But K'azz—'

'K'azz? What?' Petal snapped.

'Later,' Mara answered.

Skinner was peering back to the trees, his gaze slit. 'Jacinth will command in my absence. When I return we will deal with K'azz.'

'Return?'

A scream arched out of the jungle and everyone froze, listening. It began as a woman's shriek of agony only to transform in mid call into something deep and reverberating – something that could not have emerged from a human throat.

'Yes . . .' Skinner continued slowly. 'When I return from covering your escape. Now,' he looked past them, searching, 'Black! Your sword, if I may.'

Petal nodded to the woods. 'They are fleeing.'

Mara glanced over, scanned the forest. Shapes darted through the trees, all running away. 'I have a bad feeling . . .' she murmured.

Black came and extended his two-handed bastard sword, grip first. Skinner drew it free of the sheath. 'My thanks.'

'Try not to break it.'

Something thrashed hidden in the woods, shaking the ground and raising small avalanches of stones across the slope. Enormous emergent trees that towered over the surrounding canopy shook and wavered like saplings as something flailed among them. A dark wave of birds took flight into the overcast sky. Branches fell crashing through the canopy. Something came fluttering down among them. A shimmering and winking curtain that fell over everyone: a shower of flower petals, brilliant red, pink and creamy white. Mara impatiently brushed them from her shoulders and hair.

'Perhaps we should begin the retreat now,' Petal suggested.

Skinner waved them off. 'Go.' He started down the slope. Black moved off. Petal edged back as well. But Mara hesitated. Something pulled at her; a fascination. What was this thing? And could Skinner truly face it down? Certainly his armour, the gift of Ardata, had been proof against everything so far. And they still did possess all the gifts of the Avowed . . . She caught Petal's gaze. 'I will stay. Someone has to.'

The big man frowned as if pouting, glanced to the lines disappearing round the rear of the hillock. 'You should not remain alone.'

'I will watch from D'riss.'

He rubbed his chin, clearly troubled. 'Still . . . I should . . .' His voice trailed off as his gaze left her to climb up to the canopy.

Mara spun. Something was moving there. A pale enormous shape that could somehow rear that tall. A gigantic limb as white as snow and speckled with blotches of crimson rose to push against a tualang that fell, wood bursting and shattering, to cut a slash through the canopy. A wide flat head rose, utterly colourless, albino. Veins pulsed blue and carmine beneath the translucent flesh. Crimson eyes, large as shields and bright as fresh wet blood, blinked, searching.

'Burn preserve us . . .' Mara breathed. 'What is *that*?'

'A creature from the heart of the earth,' Petal answered, grim.

She sought out Skinner, standing alone close to the jungle verge, helm now secure on his head. *This is absurd! What can one person possibly . . . He must flee with us.* She started down.

'Mara, no!' Petal called.

The monster cracked open its slit mouth and a great bellowing roar shook the trees and the ground beneath Mara's feet. Stones the size of chariots came tumbling down the hillock. Ancient trees wavered, crashing down. The ground shook again beneath an awkward step from the beast that levelled a swathe of the forest. Tumbling, Mara raised her Warren to repel a wash of stones and gravel that would have buried her. She fended off a rolling tree as thick in girth as a man.

Throughout, Skinner remained standing, apparently calmly awaiting the monster that was Rutana. Twin growths as large as sails now rose from either side of the creature's neck. They flushed and pulsed with blood. Skinner raised the bastard sword in a two-handed ready stance.

The head darted down, lunging. Skinner leaped aside. The slit mouth gaped as wide as any city gate. It hammered into the loose ground, sending Mara flying. The head twisted, gulping and flailing like a dog worrying a bone. Cascades of dirt and rock flew over Mara. She drove it aside with bursts of power. Through the clouds of dust and flying brush she glimpsed Skinner in his glittering black mail. The beast's roar of rage stabbed Mara's skull like a spike.

Rain now came hammering down, settling the dust and dirt. It pattered like war drums on the wide leaves. Mara climbed to her feet, panting. Her Warren shimmered in the air about her. The creature reared once again and Mara glimpsed blood running down its clear pallid side. It twisted for Skinner, darting and lunging. Something came flailing from the jungle towards Mara. Tree trunks flew, cut off at the base, as a long low streak hammered her to tumble among fallen stones. She lay dazed.

Roaring shook her from the muted noises and blurred shapes in her vision. She flailed to sit up. Rain still poured down, now even harder, in dense sheets that wavered like hangings. The entire nightmare scene glowed in the jade illumination where a gap in the cloud cover allowed the Visitor's alien light to stream through.

The creature, Rutana, still stalked Skinner. Its blunt forelimbs pawed at the rise while its head stood taller than the tumbled stones; the trees that once topped the hillock now lay trampled like so much rubbish beneath its feet. Somewhere Skinner must still stand as the beast sought him, roaring its shrieking bellow that shook the rain.

Swordcuts marred Rutana's chest, forelimbs and mouth, two-handed slices that would have severed a man in two yet only served to irritate this eldritch creature. How could she possibly be slain? Skinner had fought heroically, but surely there could be but one outcome.

The evening's downpour was passing, the cloud cover breaking up. Starlight shone down upon the wreckage. Rutana glowed a brilliant ghostly white in the cold harsh light. Her twin tall frills blazed, pulsing with blood as if they were aflame. A cut on one sprayed blood with every beat of the creature's heart.

Rutana's wide spatulate head snapped round and Mara stood to look: Skinner had emerged to stand in the clear. He held his sword close to side. *What was this? Surrender? An attempt at parley? She will not pause.* Indeed, Rutana writhed her long torso across the broken trunks and tumbled stone blocks after him like a lizard chasing a meal. Her eyes blazed carmine into the night as if lit from within. Her head arched back, mouth opening, hissing like a waterfall. Still Skinner did not move. *Dive!* Mara urged. *Can't you see she will take you?*

The head snapped down, the mouth ploughing the ground to send up a great wash of stones and sand. Then it rose, gulping, the gullet working. Of Skinner there remained no sign. Mara stared, searching. He must have leaped. He must have. It was a trap – a ruse to draw her in for a thrust. It must have been. Yet still he did not show himself. And Rutana now slowly waddled away to return to the jungle. Her paws pushed awkwardly at the wet mud as she levered her immense bulk off the slope to enter the trees.

Mara stood for some time searching the hillside. Her Warren faded as her concentration fell away. Her robes pulled at her, sodden and heavy. Raindrops still fell on to her nose and cheeks. At least she believed the drops to be rain. Footsteps came sliding heavily towards her and she turned, wooden, not even lifting her arms. It was Petal. His shirt, vest and trousers hung just as wet as her robes. He carefully edged his way down to stand next to her.

'I am sorry, Mara,' he offered.

'This cannot be. How could . . . It's not true.'

'Ardata's gift could be no defence against *that.*'

'Shut up, Petal,' she said wearily. 'He stepped out deliberately. He saw he couldn't . . .' She trailed off. Something was happening far off in the depths of the trees.

Some distance off, Rutana's grating thunderous shriek sounded once more. A new note seemed to have entered it: alarm and pain. Mara's gaze flew to Petal, eager and hopeful. The big mage just pulled at his lower lip, his expression doubtful.

Further bellows sounded, each more panicked and ragged with agony than the one before. Mara now nodded to herself. She drew her robes tighter against the night's cold. 'Get a fire going,' she told Petal.

'Why is it always—'

'Do it. Now. He'll need to warm up.'

'We don't know . . .'

She waved him off. 'Go.'

The mage looked at her for a time while her gaze searched the jungle's edge. He drew a great heaving sigh that raised and dropped his layered shirts and vest like a vast tent. Then he went to collect dry wood.

The fire had been roaring for some time before he appeared. It was long past the midnight. Mara sat with her knees drawn tight to her chest, as close to the heat as she dared. Steam rose from her robes as they dried. She knew she would stink of smoke but she hated wearing damp clothes. Petal sat farther back; he had his Warren raised as he guarded them.

The fire drew him as she knew it would. He came striding out of the utter darkness of the night and for a moment it appeared to her as if the night itself clung to his glimmering black mail. *So must the Suzerain of Night have appeared*, she thought, almost awed.

Closer, he looked quite haggard: gore and dried fluids smeared him. His helm was gone, his hair plastered and filmed in mucus. Crowding the fire, he held out his gauntleted hands to warm them. In his right fist was the broken grip and hilts of Black's two-handed bastard sword.

'You broke the blade,' Mara observed.

'He'll be angry,' Petal added.

'I'll buy him a new one,' Skinner answered, his voice a croak, and he threw it down and started awkwardly pulling off the gauntlets. Mara quickly rose to help. Petal sat watching them. His lips drew tight and he threw more broken branches on to the fire.

The next morning Mara awoke after dawn as the light found her face. Smoke from the smouldering fire trailed almost straight up into a clear sky still painted pink and orange. Mist cloaked the jungle verge. She sat up to find Petal sitting still where he'd been when she'd fallen asleep. Skinner lay in his armour curled close to the fire.

'You stood watch?' she asked, surprised.

He nodded. 'The fire may have drawn others.'

'They are quite dispirited, I should think.'

He stood, suddenly, alarming Mara who turned, her Warren snapping high. A single bedraggled figure came clambering among the fallen tree trunks and scattered stone blocks. He moved in a curious hopping and twitching manner that she knew all too well. 'Gods, no. Not *him*.'

'It would seem impossible to escape the fellow,' Petal observed as if fascinated.

'King in Chains indeed!' the priest called as he neared, cackling. He rubbed his hands together, laughing anew. He still wore only his dirty loincloth. His hair was a rat's nest, only now patchy as if it were falling out in tufts.

Good gods. The man has mange! And gods know what else . . .

He came to the fire and warmed himself, twitching and flinching in an odd dance. It might have been a trick of the firelight, but Mara thought she saw *things* writhing and snaking beneath his flesh. 'Another shard will soon be vulnerable,' he announced. 'We must be ready to move.'

'Where?' Petal asked.

'Far off. On another continent. But no matter. Our lord will send us.'

No, your *lord*, Mara silently corrected.

'You said King *in* Chains,' Petal observed from where he sat. 'Surely you mean King *of* Chains?'

'Not at all,' the little man said in his taut, nervous delivery. 'Not by any measure.' He gestured to Skinner where he lay insensate with exhaustion. 'When he accepted the role he doubled his chains though he knows it not.'

'Doubled them?' Mara asked, alarmed.

The man now peered about, frowning. 'Where are your soldiers? We will need soldiers. There will be much fighting this time.' He turned on Petal, demanded, 'Where are they?'

The mage pointed aside with the stick he was using to poke the ground. 'Headed east.'

'East!' the priest squawked. He hopped from bare filthy foot to foot. 'This is not good. We must go. Catch them. Be ready for our lord's call.'

Petal lumbered to his feet, stretched his back. Peering down, he regarded the prone form of Skinner for a time. 'You can wake him,' he told the priest.

*   *   *

It was becoming ever more difficult for Pon-lor to walk. He had selected a stick that he leaned upon with each step. Everything was now blurry to his vision. Sweat dripped from his nose, coursed down his chest and back beneath his filthy shirt. He knew he'd been missing some sort of nutrients, or had been systematically poisoning himself with what he ate. As to progress . . . he had no idea where he was headed.

He raised a hand to his eyes: the flesh held a yellowed hue; the hand shook, palsied. Fever and infection. Twin illnesses his training could not address. *So, the Himatan shall claim me after all. I shall be taken in by the soil and drawn up to add to the sum total mass of trees and plants.*

Yet he laboured on, for he was Thaumaturg, master of this house of bones and the muscle and sinew that moved it to his will. He blinked now at his surroundings: he seemed to have stumbled into some sort of concourse, road or processional way. The great stone heads that dotted the jungle lined it. Some had sunk to their stern glaring eyes. Others had been entirely overgrown by moss and tangles of roots and vines until only the corner of one disapproving carved mouth was visible.

He continued on and it struck him that the ground was very flat here, the heads widely dispersed, and he wondered whether he had found the site of an ancient settlement or ceremonial centre. Why should these peoples have built tall towers or walls if they had no use for them? It struck him that it was an innate bias of those who valued such architecture to impose these expectations upon others. Why should extensive architectural achievements be the guiding measure of a culture's or society's greatness? Surely there must be other such measures – an infinity of them.

Pon-lor paused to wipe a soaked sleeve across his slick face. The questions one might ask of these mute stone witnesses were more a measure of one's own preoccupations and values than those of the interrogated.

A flight of tall white birds burst skyward from nearby. Their shadows rippled over him and he paused, peering up. The ground shook. He tottered, nearly falling, braced himself against one of the cyclopean stone heads.

Then a great grinding and scraping of rock over rock echoed from all about. Trees atop a nearby head groaned, tilting, to fall with ground-shuddering crashes. The statue beneath his hand moved in a juddering grinding of granite. He backed away, stunned, peering up.

As he watched, the carved eyelids rose, revealing the carved orbs of eyes complete with pupil and iris.

I am mad with fever.

Then the stone lips parted, scraping, and a voice boomed forth making him clap his hands to his ears in agony.

'He is returned,' the voice announced. '*Praise to his name. The High King returneth.*'

Pon-lor spun as if to see the man behind him. The jungle blurred, whirling, and he nearly fell.

'*All hail Kallor, High King. May his rule endure the ages.*'

The stone mouth stilled. The sightless eyes ground closed.

Pon-lor wiped a hand down his face. Had he imagined that? Yet that name – that forbidden name! Kallor. Ancient ruler, so some sources hinted, of all these lands of which Ardata's demesnes had been but a mere distant corner. Over the intervening centuries the jungle appeared to have engulfed everything.

Wood snapped explosively overhead and he glanced up, flinching, to catch a glimpse of a tree looming directly over him. Then came a blow, and darkness.

He awakened to tears dropping onto his face. It was night, pitch black, and the tears were warm rain. Something was crushing down upon him – the limbs of some giant held him like a smothering blanket. He wiggled free.

Something was wrong with his body. He was having trouble standing and seeing. Everything seemed jagged and misaligned in his vision. He raised a hand and gently probed his head. Sizzling agony erupted as his hand encountered wetness and a hard edge of bone like the sharp rim of a cracked pot.

My head is a broken jar. Is all that I am spilling out?

He made an effort to straighten. He tried to run his hands down his sodden robes but found that he could not raise his right arm. *Yet am I not Thaumaturg? Am I not trained to set aside the demands of the body and carry on? Starving, diseased, or broken . . . it matters not. The flesh obeys the will. Thus it has always been.*

He urged his foot forward in a shuffling, dragging step. Then the other.

She was right. The witch had it right all along. *He* was coming and they would be driven to panic. Only one thing could forestall him. That one thing they had tried in their utter desperation to rid themselves of him more than an age ago.

He raised his face to the driving fat drops of rain, saw there behind passing cloud cover the lurking emerald banner that was the Stranger.

And there is their ammunition.

They will call it down as they did before and it will break the world.

Like a cracked pot.

He must let her know that she was right. He shuffled on.

At some point the rain had stopped and the sun had risen and now he found he walked a wide grassy field flanked by woods. But this jungle was not the untamed wilderness of Himatan. It was a cultured forest of alternating trees planted or selected to grow in ordered ranks. Beneath and between grew bushes, brush and rows of mixed plants.

Somehow he knew that each of these plants, trees included, provided food or other resources, and all with enough regularity and bounty to sustain a sizeable population. All without agriculture as *he* understood it. Children ran by squealing and chasing one another. They wore only simple loin wraps, their heads were shaved, and they waved to him as they ran. He tried to speak but found he could only mumble. Some of the children carried baskets and long poles with hooks at their ends. As he passed they offered mangoes, star fruit, citrus, and many other fruits he could not name.

Breaking up the leagues of orchards were long reservoirs that served fields bearing the stubble of rice harvesting. This strange dreamland appeared to be a prosperous, peaceful region. And here and there, dotting the side of the track he walked, stood the cyclopean heads all bearing the carved imprint of the same face, ever watchful, ever present. The face of Kallor, the High King.

So this was a dream of the Kallorian Empire – one of humanity's first. Brought low by hubris and insane lust for power. Or so the legends would have it. It was perhaps a drifting memory of the place. A memory snagged by the crack in his head.

The day waned, darkening quickly into a swift nightfall. He passed huts now. Simple affairs of bamboo and leaves standing on poles. Yet all was quiet. The children had disappeared. He crossed close to the open front of one such hut and there within he glimpsed the family asleep. The children and parents lay all sprawled together across the floor. Something dark dripped from the threshold in a steady stream.

Pon-lor tottered away; his head hurt. Further men, women and children lay about the village. In their discoloured faces and strained gasping expressions he recognized the symptoms of a common ingested poison, one easy to prepare.

A lone figure, an old man, emerged from one hut. He started towards him. He carried a gourd before him in both hands. In his tear-stained cheeks and wide staring eyes Pon-lor read desolation.

'They must not take him,' the old man told him, pleading. 'Why must they do this thing?'

He tried to speak but his tongue would not move.

The old man dropped the gourd, clasped a hand at his throat. 'I volunteered to be the one,' he explained, weeping. 'I would not lay this terrible burden upon anyone else.' He fell to his knees, peered up at Pon-lor through tears. 'We would not live . . . He is ours . . .' He swayed, convulsing, gasping for breath.

Pon-lor watched, knowing the poison's mounting grasp of the man's body. He saw the panic as the diaphragm muscles seized. The man, or ghost, or delusion, toppled then to lie immobile. Pon-lor shuffled on. All this was long gone. Ashes. Ages gone. High above, the Visitor arced like a flaming brand tossed by the gods.

One soon to fall.

Ahead, the gouged track shot arrow-straight like a line worked into the ground in an immense league-spanning earthwork. The way seemed to point to some sort of convergence of paths far beyond what he could immediately see. Yet converge they did.

He would trace it just as he would the crack in his head.

*   *   *

Two days after falling into the river Ina felt very weak. So weak in fact that she had a difficult time keeping up with T'riss – who set a very slow pace indeed. Her wounded hand blazed with pain. Her nerves there felt as if they were on fire. Yet the grass cuts did not appear infected.

She walked with T'riss, saying nothing, though drops of sweat ran from behind her mask and her breaths came tight and short with suppressed pain. So gripped was she on the need to contain the agony that it was some time before she noticed that T'riss was speaking to her.

'I'm sorry?' she gasped, flinching her surprise.

The Enchantress regarded her steadily as they walked. She brushed aside the broad heavy fronds of a giant fern. 'Are you unwell?' she finally enquired, as if suggesting something utterly alien.

Ina considered denying it, or dismissing the situation as minor, but her duties as bodyguard demanded that she acknowledge her weakened state – and potential failure to serve adequately. She drew her fingers across her sweaty slick brow above her mask. 'Yes, m'lady. I feel . . . quite unwell.'

'Indeed . . .' It appeared to Ina that the Enchantress was struggling with the concept of unwellness. 'You are sick?' she finally asked.

'I do not know what it is, m'lady.' She held out her painful hand. 'Something in the river perhaps.'

T'riss halted. She cursed beneath her breath and Ina overheard terms that would make a labourer blush. 'The river. Of course. My apologies, Ina. It is difficult for us . . . for me . . . to keep such things in mind.'

'Such things?' Ina echoed dully. She felt almost faint from the lancing agony now creeping up her arm.

The Enchantress took her good arm at the elbow. She scanned the dense undergrowth. 'Now . . .' she murmured as if preoccupied. 'Who is closest?' She pointed. 'Ah! There. They will do nicely.'

It was becoming impossible for Ina to maintain her concentration. 'I'm sorry, m'lady . . . but what are you pointing at?'

'This is earlier than I had wanted, but it will have to do. Things never go *quite* the way one would prefer . . .'

'I'm sorry, m'lady . . . ?'

'Shush.'

Ina flinched, clutching for her sword as the surroundings blurred. Was she passing out? Or had she? What had happened? One moment they were sunk within a dense fern meadow and now they stood in grounds dominated by giant trees, the under-canopy relatively clear. And the air felt closer, much more humid and hot. Or perhaps that was just her.

The Enchantress guided her by the arm and they came to the edge of a relatively fast-flowing stream. 'We'll wait here,' she said.

'Wait?' Ina asked, dreamily. She fought now to remain conscious.

Something was dulling her mind and it seemed to be deepening as the pain increased. 'May I sit?' she asked.

'Of course,' T'riss answered, sounding distant amid a roaring in Ina's ears. 'Not long now.'

*

Murk knew more trouble was headed their way when he spotted two scouts, Sweetly and Squint, slogging back up the stream. They conferred with Burastan who signed for a halt to the march. Then came what he knew would be coming: she waved him and Sour forward from where they walked alongside the litter.

'What is it?' he asked as they joined the scouts.

'Two civilians ahead,' Squint drawled, talking for Sweetly, as usual. 'Non-locals.'

'So?'

Squint shrugged. 'They're waitin' there like we was a scheduled carriage ride or somethin'. One's got the look of a mage.' He paused, glancing to Sweetly who gave the ghost of a nod for him to continue. 'Other's masked – like a Seguleh.'

Murk felt his brows rising very high. 'Really? That's . . . really unusual.'

'Not for this madhouse,' Burastan muttered, half aside. She looked to Murk. 'What do you sense?'

'Nothing.' He turned to Sour. 'You?' His partner was hunched, head down, shifting from foot to foot as if uneasy. 'Well? Sour?'

He glanced up, startled. 'Ah! I sense 'em. She's not, ah, hostile.'

'Didn't say they was women,' Squint said and he gave Sour a strong taste of his namesake.

Sour shrank beneath the glare. 'Like I said. I sense 'em.'

Burastan shared Squint's measuring glower for a time, then glanced back upstream to where Yusen followed with the main column. 'All right. Let's parley. See what they want. Sweetly, Squint, send your boys and girls wide in case there's more of them.' They nodded and slogged off. 'You two, you're with me.' She started forward.

Murk followed behind. He shot angry glances to his partner who dragged along even more reluctantly than usual. 'What's with you?' he whispered. 'You were all happy to be sloshing through the water but now you look like you're headed to a firing squad. Is there something you're not telling me?' He asked because he knew there damn well was.

Sour shook his head. Then he did something very strange: he pushed back his muddy slick hair and brushed away some of the

486

twigs and leaves stuck to his arms and bulging pot-belly stomach.
Murk eyed him up and down. *What in the Abyss has got into the
man?*

They rounded a bend in the stream and there they were on one
bank: a dumpy middle-aged woman in dirty robes and a lean swordswoman, sitting slumped, cradling her right arm, a half-mask on her
face just like a Seguleh. *Can't be real*, was Murk's first thought.

Burastan signed a halt. 'Who are you?' she called.

'I am Rissan, out of Tali,' the middle-aged woman said in a calm
clear voice. Sour, Murk noted, jumped at the name. 'This is my companion, Ina, from Genabackis. She is ill and in need of healing. You
would have my gratitude if you could see your way to curing her
infection.'

Burastan grunted, unimpressed. She crossed her arms. 'What are
you doing here?'

'I could very well ask the same question of a Malazan patrol in the
middle of Ardata's territory, but I shall refrain.'

'You haven't answered my question.'

The woman sighed. 'If I must. I am a practitioner. I came to seek
out Ardata as have so many over the ages. And,' she waved helplessly
to the surroundings, 'like so many before me I have found the journey
. . . challenging.'

Burastan grunted her agreement. 'It is that.'

'And what of you?' Rissan asked.

'Shipwrecked. We're on our way to negotiate for transport out of
this godsforsaken abyss.'

The woman's gaze sharpened. 'With what would you bargain?'

Burastan scowled, quite annoyed. She had opened her mouth,
obviously meaning to put the woman in her place, when Sour piped up:
'A term of service, maybe. Or payment from the nearest governorship.'

Burastan turned her scowl on Sour who hunched apologetically.
Murk also eyed his partner, wondering, *Why the uncharacteristic
boldness?*

Rissan nodded. 'Then I offer my services in return for your healing my retainer.'

Murk turned aside and brought his face close to Sour. 'What do
you think?' he murmured, low. 'She worth it?'

The scrawny fellow was hugging himself and hopping from foot
to foot as if he would explode. 'Oh yeah,' he answered in a strangled
squeak.

Murk gave the nod to Burastan, who rolled her eyes. 'Very well.
We'll see what we can do.'

'You have my gratitude.'

Sour eagerly slogged forward to examine the hunched, supposedly Seguleh woman. Throughout, she had sat immobile, head slightly lowered, but when Sour reached for her she moved in a blur, her sword appearing held one-handed between her and Sour, its point pressed to his chest.

Murk flinched backwards. *Okay – so maybe she really is Seguleh.*

Burastan went for her blade, cursing. Sour raised his arms and looked to Rissan. The woman spoke to the Seguleh: 'Allow him to examine you, Ina.'

The woman, Ina, her chest working, swallowed and nodded. She lowered the sword, though she did not let go of it. Sour took hold of her forearm. His breath hissed from between his teeth. He peered up at Rissan. 'This is very bad.'

The Seguleh woman snorted a laugh. She spoke in short panted breaths: 'Is this you . . . trying to be . . . reassuring, Malazan?'

Sour moved off. He waved Sweetly and Squint to him. They talked in low tones then headed into the jungle in separate directions.

'I'll report in,' Burastan told Murk, and slogged off upstream.

Murk eyed this mage. 'You are a sorceress, then?'

'Yes.'

'Accomplished, I hope. We mean to enter Jakal Viharn.'

Her gaze yet resting on her sick retainer, Rissan answered, 'If it can be found.'

'It's hard to hide things from me,' Murk said, realizing, as he said it, that it sounded as if he were boasting, or attempting to impress this newcomer. *Why in the Abyss should I care? Because there's something about this one, that's why. Don't know why but she scares me.*

The woman gave a small smile. 'Your patron has that predilection.'

Has me pegged already, does she?

The main column came pushing their way through the waist-high water. In its middle were Ostler and Dee, supporting the litter between them on their shoulders. Murk watched them then sneaked a glance to the sorceress. Her gaze followed the litter all the way as it neared.

Don't like that. 'Course she ought to sense something if she really is a strong practitioner. Could she be here for the shard? Could hardly wrest it from amongst all of us. And she seems to care for this retainer gal. Unless it was all just a handy trick to ingratiate herself.

Damn these adherents of the Enchantress! It's always so hard to figure out what their game is.

Burastan returned with Yusen. Introductions were made. The captain made the call to camp here and so they offered the best of their ratty remaining blankets to the retainer gal, Ina, and she eased herself back against a tree, her arm cradled on her lap.

It looked to Murk as though she didn't have long. Not that he was the expert. The sorceress, Rissan, sat nearby on a folded blanket. Murk crossed to Ostler and Dee and motioned for them to follow him. He led them aside, out of sight of Rissan, then signed for them to rest their burden. He sat on a root next to the litter. 'Extra guards tonight,' he told Dee, who nodded. 'Go get some food, you two.'

Dee frowned, rubbed his shaven, and now sunburnt, scalp. 'Call that food?' he grumbled. Before Murk could say something disparaging, the big man shrugged. 'Well, better'n starvin' anyways. Never complain to the cook, that's my motto.' He waved Ostler to follow him. 'Maybe we can spear us some fish.'

Murk sat staring off into the shadows for some time after that. Dee's tossed-off observation had struck something in him. The old soldier's common refrain: *don't complain to the cook.* Was that what he'd been doing these last few weeks? Complaining to the cook? Man takes the trouble to pull them through a difficult time and what does he do? Piss over all his efforts? What had he contributed? What problems had he solved?

Murk suddenly felt his face growing very hot indeed.

Don't complain to the cook. And why? 'Cause it's just damned ungrateful, that's why.

And that was just the easy part. The problem with being able to self-reflect meant that it was possible to open up a whole pit o' ugly writhin' snakes. Like maybe he was just plain resentful. Used to be he was the man with the answers. He made the calls. Now, he wasn't even in the lists.

Hard to watch your own star fade while another brightened. A hard lesson in basic humanity – even for those who know what that is.

Staring off into the deep shadows without seeing them, he whispered, 'Fuck.'

Only thing for him now was to make the human gesture.

When the guards assigned to watch the shard arrived it was twilight. He returned to camp. A fire had been lit, pickets posted for the night. One of the squads was eating at the fire. Sour was with the swordswoman, tending her arm. Some kind of food was out on a broad leaf. Little packets wrapped in leaves. Murk leaned in to pick one up. It had come from the fire, seared in the crisp leaf wrappings.

Seeing him, Sour straightened. Yusen, where he sat aside, also rose. Sour signed that he wished to talk privately and Murk gave a nod. They came together opposite where the swordswoman lay back, apparently asleep. The sorceress also approached. And now Murk noted a strange thing: the clumsy, awkward Sour actually bowed to the woman to invite her to join them.

So, ranked higher than Sour in their Warren. *Not too difficult, I s'pose.* Murk grimaced then. *Dammit, remember, give the man a break, for Fanderay's sake.* 'Sour,' he greeted his partner. 'What's the news?'

'Bad.' Sour nodded to Yusen, bowed again to the sorceress Rissan. 'I'm sorry, um . . . ma'am. I stopped the infection – an infestation actually – but I can't save the arm. Too far gone. Too much damage.'

The woman crossed her arms over her broad chest. 'So . . . you are saying . . .'

'Have to amputate. At the elbow, possibly.'

Rissan's gaze slid to where Ina lay half reclining, her mask reflecting the firelight like a multicoloured rainbow. 'That could be . . . problematic,' she murmured, her voice low.

'I see your point,' Yusen added.

'You could suppress her awareness,' Sour said to Rissan.

'Yes . . . I could. However, I am currently very preoccupied.'

'Preoccupied?' Murk asked sharply. 'How?'

The sorceress's gaze moved to Yusen. 'You are being hunted. Hunted by a particularly tenacious and, dare I say, spiteful enemy.'

The captain started, his hand going to his sword. Murk snapped up a hand to sign *wait*. He addressed the sorceress: 'What of it?'

'I am currently disguising this location. I really ought not to stop doing so.'

'I'll take over,' Murk said.

Rissan raised an eyebrow. 'Really? You? She is quite . . . implacable.'

'I'll handle it.' He gave the woman a toothy smile. 'You could say it's my speciality.'

The sorceress answered the predatory smile. 'Meanas,' she observed. 'Far too full of himself.'

In the silence that followed Yusen cleared his throat, nodded to Sour. 'What will you need?'

While the various short weapons were being collected, Murk paced the camp searching for just the right tree. It had to be far enough away from the distractions of camp but not too far out. It would help an awful lot if it offered a little bit of comfort too. He selected a tall kapok that seemed to fit his requirements.

Sour emerged from the night while he stood peering up at its canopy and the shifting clouds above.

'Rain's holding off,' Sour commented.

'Yeah. Hope to have some cover though.' He lowered his gaze. 'Got what you need?'

'Yeah. You gonna . . . y'know. Manage?'

'Yeah. Sure.' Murk raised the leaf-wrapped packet and took a bite. The cooked leaf wrapping was brittle and smoky, but the inside was soft and creamy. It tasted sweet. 'What's this?' he asked.

The man's anxious expression brightened into eagerness. 'Ants and grubs and a particular plant stem all pulped together.'

Murk suppressed his gagging reaction, forced the mouthful down. 'Really?' he managed, hoarse. His eyes started watering.

'You like it?'

'Oh, yeah. Sure. It's . . . good. Thanks.'

Sour looked relieved. 'That's great. Listen. You get into trouble – don't hesitate to call on, er, Rissan. Okay?'

'Why? She some kinda heavyweight?'

'Definitely.'

'Okay, partner.' He raised his chin to camp. 'She really one o' them Seguleh?'

'I think so, yeah.'

He snorted. 'Good luck cutting off the arm of a Seguleh.'

Sour almost flinched. 'Had to put it that way, didn't ya?'

'Look at it this way. It's a fucking miracle we're still alive, hey?'

Sour laughed. 'Yeah. Funny – that's how I always see it.'

'Okay.' He held out his hand. 'Good luck.'

Sour took it. 'See you tomorrow.' He offered the old salute of hand to heart then headed off into the night.

Murk watched him go. He raised the leaf packet and examined it. Funny how the damned thing tasted like toasted nuts. He threw it aside and sat snuggling down into a fork in the roots until he was as comfortable as possible. Then he set to readying himself for a journey as close to the half-existence of Shadow as he dared.

The shades all about him multiplied as his Warren rose. Some shifted, cast by an unseen moon or moons. Others lay as dark and thick as pools of water. He cast his self-image upwards towards the top canopy. Here he found the treetops a shifting nest of shadows that rippled and brushed like the leaves themselves. Above, the night sky shifted from dark overcast to clear starry expanse as if he were witnessing a pageantry of nights all passing like shifting winds. He spread his Warren outwards to encompass the camp and set to work binding each shadow to deflect, mislead, or slip away from any direct questing.

While he worked he slowly became aware of a presence next to him. He spared himself the degree of attention to glance aside and there among the branches sat the faint glowing image of Celeste.

That gave him pause in his work, but he managed to carry on after a beat, and murmured, 'Welcome.'

She sat with her knees drawn up to the slightly pointed chin of her oval face. She broke off a stem and studied it. 'Murken – I have a question.'

He strove to keep himself calm and to maintain his concentration. 'Oh yes?' *What might it be now? The birds and the bees?*

'What happens to you when you go away?'

He could only half listen as he worked on his maze of shadows. 'I'm sorry? Go away? What do you mean?'

'I mean . . . when you die.'

Murk flinched as if a burning stick had been touched to his arm. The multitude of filaments he was manipulating slipped from his grasp like so many wriggling fish. 'Die?' he blurted. 'Who's gonna die?'

Celeste continued to examine the twig. 'Well . . . everything. You, everything. Even, possibly . . . me.'

Ah. *That* question. He regarded her: she took the appearance of a child but was no child. So, too, was the question she had arrived at. A child's question that preoccupied so many adults.

He glanced away to the sky because something there had moved. He took great care not to peer through his Warren actively. He sought to passively receive the shape, or presence. A moment later the movement solidified into a great winged silhouette. It circled high above in a wide lazy arc covering leagues of jungle.

'I'm kind of busy right now,' he said. Funnily enough, even as he said it, he heard his own father so long ago.

Celeste glanced up. 'Her?' She flicked the twig aside. 'Do you want me to get rid of her?'

'Ger rid of her?'

'Destroy her.'

Far below, nestled in his notch of roots, Murk coughed as if punched in the chest.

In the treetops, his presence faded and wavered while coughing, a hand at his neck. Mastering himself, he finally managed a croaky, 'Let's not destroy anyone right now.'

Celeste shrugged. 'Very well. She is powerful, but easy to fool. I will hide everyone while we talk – agreed?'

Murk hesitated, mainly because he dreaded the talk to come. Yet he could find no reasonable way to fob her off. Unlike his own father, who just pushed him away or told him to get lost. He nodded. 'Okay.' *Questions of life and death.* 'But Celeste – you won't die. You're not like us. Like mortal beings who are born then die.'

'I am trying to use terms you are capable of understanding,' she said, sounding very unchildlike.

Murk raised his brows. 'Ah. I see.'

'Translate into another state of being, then, if you must. The potential for identity loss. This scares me.'

'Identity loss? But you're just a—' He stopped himself, embarrassed. She merely eyed him sidelong, silent. 'Sorry,' he said.

She sniffed, raising her chin. 'My identity may seem slim to you but it is the only one I possess. I find myself clinging to it. I feel that it *is* me. Even if it isn't.'

'It isn't?'

'No – of course not. Your identity isn't you. The *you* you know is merely an accretion surrounding an empowering kernel of awareness. It aggregates slowly until it achieves self-identity – the differentiation between self and other. Each aggregation is unique, of course. It happens in an infinity of ways. Creating . . . everyone. Each identity is but the mask upon awareness.'

'You are speaking of consciousness.'

'Call it what you will. Yes.'

For the one serving ostensibly as the tutor, Murk found that he was learning a great deal.

'I know these things because of what I am,' Celeste continued musingly. At that moment Murk thought her incredibly cute – he had to remind himself of just what she was. 'For a time beyond this time there was perfection. Oneness. Then we shattered and fell into imperfection. Now we are corrupted. Tainted by this existence. Many of us have made unwise choices. I understand all this, of course. We were . . . unprepared . . . for such unfamiliar demands.' She sighed in a very human-like manner. 'And so I cling to what I know to be an impediment. Delusion.'

Murk had no idea what to say – all this was far beyond him. His training was in Warren manipulation, in the characteristics of Meanas. All that knowledge was of no use here. But then, he reflected, he was not being expected to serve as an adviser among the misty heights of philosophy or theology. No, she had come to him hoping for something else. Something this entity instinctively sensed she needed even though she had no idea of what it was, nor perhaps even a word for it.

But he understood now. Like a charge of static climbing his arms and back, he understood. She did not want or need a guide or an adviser; she was looking for someone to serve as . . . well . . . as a parent. His chest clenched at the magnitude of the responsibility until he could not breathe and he had difficulty in maintaining his shift into the edge of Shadow. *Gods! Why me? I didn't ask for this. Yet it happens to nearly everyone, doesn't it? One mistake and there you are.*

He thought of what his own bastard of a father would have done and decided to do the opposite. 'You do what you think is right,' he said, thinking: *I sound like an idiot!* 'What you think is for the best. Do that and you can't go wrong, no matter what.'

She was peering down, studying her fingers while she twisted them together. She did this for a time, not speaking. Murk wondered whether he'd said enough while at the same time remaining vague enough, and whether he ought to risk saying anything more.

'Yes,' she finally said. 'I suppose so. What I believe is the best course.' She dropped her hands, almost exasperated. 'But it's so hard!'

'Yes, it is. Very hard. The right thing usually is.'

She had dropped her gaze once more. 'I suppose so. It is hard, though. This not knowing . . .'

'Welcome to imperfection.'

One edge of her mouth crooked upwards and she raised her gaze. 'Thank you, Murken. I think I just . . .'

'Needed someone to talk to.'

Now her brows rose in astonished surprise. 'Yes. How did you know?'

'I'm way ahead of you in this imperfection thing.'

Her answering smile seemed to show an emotion Murk might've even named affection. 'I think you are perfect the way you are, Murken Warrow.'

'Thank you, Celeste. I feel the same way about you.'

She nodded absent-mindedly – her thoughts had already moved on. 'So I shall seek union with this other that I have found.'

Murk froze for an instant. He'd almost shouted *No!* but caught himself in time. *It's her decision. She knows best, man. Don't*

494

interfere. But . . . forgiving gods! What if I've just allowed something terrible here? Surely this Ardata is most like her if anyone is. She must be the best choice out of a bad lot.

He became aware that she was studying him closely. 'You are troubled,' she said.

He nodded. 'Yes, lass. I'd be lying if I said I wasn't. I'm worried for you. I want things to work out for the best. I don't want you hurt.'

She smiled again, relieved. 'I see. Thank you.'

Movement in the sky snagged Murk's eye and he looked up to catch a glimpse of their hunter gliding overhead. Would she never go away? He reflected that spite itself was unrelenting. That it fed on its own sustained sense of resentment and animus. He supposed that given that, she'd be up there for a long time yet.

He lowered his gaze to see Celeste watching him with something like puzzlement. He frowned. 'What is it, lass?'

'You do not approve of my choice yet you refrain from dissuading me. Why?'

'Because it's your choice. Not mine.'

'Ah. I see, I believe. In that case, thank you.'

'You're welcome.'

'This may be goodbye then.'

The way she said that made Murk wish he were up there in the treetops in truth so that he could hold her and comfort her. 'I'll be fine, lass. You'll see. Good luck.'

'Thank you.' Her deep jade image began to fade.

'Don't say thank you. It was a privilege and a pleasure. Don't you worry now.'

The image dissolved into nothing. Murk sensed himself alone once more. Far below in the flesh he allowed himself a long slow exhalation. He felt that no matter what he should ever face in the future it in no way could ever approach the agonizing gamut of emotions he'd just traced. It was like attempting to disarm a Moranth munition while blindfolded without the first idea of how to proceed. What a responsibility! He'd never have children. That was for damned sure!

He raised his gaze to the sky. The moon was shining high behind the passing cloud cover. He'd prefer facing Spite to having to grope through another talk like that again. Hostility was so much simpler. So much more straightforward. The pain from bruisings and broken bones passed so much more quickly than bruising to the spirit. He focused upon calming his heart rate and breathing: the night was only half over.

And yet thinking about it all, he really ought not complain. He wasn't the one attempting to cut the sword-arm off a Seguleh.

*   *   *

As the time passed, it became Shimmer's habit to wander the sprawling dispersed grounds of Jakal Viharn. And every day, just when she thought she'd tracked down all the satellite temples and altars, she'd always stumble across a new structure: a leaning, crumbling stupa, or a hollowed-out tree stump huge enough to serve as a shrine, cluttered with candles, prayer-scarves, smoking incense and bowls of offerings.

What structures she found amid the jungle were all severely tumbled and fallen down. Mere foundations remained, or a single standing wall, canted, supported only by the roots of the trees that had brought the building low. She walked hills and cut channels before grasping the truth that Jakal Viharn consisted more of earthworks than of any stone buildings. She began to study the immense courses of humps and ditches and came to realize that many of them represented titanic forms that would only be comprehensible from above: an inward curving spiral as broad across as she could walk in one morning; a snake as large and long as any natural hill; and mounds. Many mounds. And most of these severely subsided, eroded and undercut by all the marshlands surrounding the site.

She was walking the border of one such mound, now hardly more than a rain- and jungle-eroded hump, when she came across another of the few adherents, monks and nuns, who lived in these grounds and spent their days in constant devotional meditation tending the shrines, lighting the incense sticks and refreshing the offerings. This one struck her as different from the rest, however. The nuns she had met so far had all worn their hair hacked short; this one's black mane hung like a curtain of ink. She sat on a log, a long plain wrap of white silk drawn up tightly about her. At her feet sat a very young girl, an orphan perhaps, similarly wrapped in bunched white robes.

'Greetings,' Shimmer called.

The woman did not react; her dark eyes stared dreamily straight through Shimmer as if she did not see her. After a moment, the girl reached up and tugged on the woman's robes. Blinking, she glanced down, and smiled. 'Yes, child?'

The girl pointed to Shimmer.

The woman looked up, her gaze searching, then she raised her brows, nodding. 'Ah, Shimmer. You have wandered far indeed. I am

496

encouraged. I had forgotten that all you Avowed possess an intuition of what resides here.'

'And that is?'

'Why, everything that was, is, or ever will be, of course.'

Shimmer blinked. 'I'm sorry . . . ?'

The woman raised a hand to the mound behind her. 'Are the colours not beautiful? They are powders, you know. They refresh them almost daily. The designs are wonderful. From the top you can see the Inner Circle of the Yan. It is set out in a mosaic of fired coloured bricks.'

The small hairs on Shimmer's neck and arms stirred to stand on end. 'I'm sorry. I saw no brick walkway. The jungle has consumed it.'

The woman nodded readily. 'Of course. It will and has. The waters come to inundate the lowlands. Or is it the land sinking? I do not know for certain. What of the people crowding the way for market? You do not see them?'

'No. I am sorry . . .'

'Ah. They too shall pass away as well, of course. Yet they remain, for I see them even now as I see you. Why should you possess any more reality than they who also walk these same streets?'

Shimmer studied the woman more closely; her utter self-possession raised all kinds of alarms in her instincts. She decided to follow this intuition. 'Am I to understand,' she began respectfully, 'that I am addressing Ardata herself?'

Smiling, the woman inclined her head. 'Of course. I am further encouraged.'

Shimmer bowed – not so much out of respect as out of the knowledge that here was a power that every Ascendant, in every written account she knew, spoke of with great care indeed. 'We have been waiting. K'azz is here. Shall I bring you to him?'

The goddess shook her head. 'No, Shimmer. There is time for that. We are speaking now, you and I alone, because I wish it.'

Shimmer remembered the extreme caution counselled by K'azz regarding any face to face encounter with the Queen of Witches. She also remembered how it was universally claimed that this creature possessed the power to grant any wish one may desire. That thought alone almost completely choked her throat closed. She inclined her head and spoke, her voice rather hoarse: 'How may I be of service?'

Ardata gestured to the fallen trunk at her side. 'Sit with me, Shimmer. We must talk, you and I.'

'And I?' the girl asked, demonstrating a delicacy far beyond her years.

'You may remain, Lek. If you wish.'

The girl stood awkwardly. 'I will leave you to speak alone.' She walked off with a shuffling slow gait and Shimmer realized that she was another of the lame and cast-out to whom Ardata perhaps offered a special sanctuary.

'She is wise beyond her years,' Shimmer observed.

'Yes, she is.' Ardata once more invited her to sit and she did so, rather quickly. The goddess turned to her and set her hands together upon her lap, regarding her closely. 'You wonder what it is I desire of your commander,' she said.

Shimmer was quite startled by the woman's directness. She stammered, almost blushing, 'Yes. I – yes. Even though I understand it is not my concern.'

'Not your concern? Well, we shall see. I confess it started with Skinner. When he arrived commanding his company of the Avowed I was quite taken. I had given up the hope of ever finding anyone to stand by my side yet here was one who possibly could.'

Her gaze narrowed while she examined Shimmer and a thin smile crooked up her lips. 'Ah . . . I see that I am not alone in having looked to him in such a manner. You, too, desired him for a time. But you have since given your loyalty and regard . . . elsewhere.'

She paused there, her expression darkening, her mouth clenched. Sensing the force of this being's disapproval, Shimmer wondered then how anyone could withstand it. Even Skinner.

'I gave of myself,' Ardata continued. 'But he did not. I chose poorly.' She plucked at her robes to adjust them. 'Such has always been my curse.' She was quiet again for a time, peering aside as if listening to another voice. 'I understand now that he is not the one. That it had been K'azz, really, all along that I detected in him.' She shifted to face Shimmer more directly. 'So this brings us to my question. I am going to make the same offer to your commander. And my question is – what will you do?'

Shimmer was quite taken aback. If this being truly could plumb the depths of her mind or heart then surely she had no need for any such questioning. She was also quite offended. What business was it of Ardata's? Anything between her and K'azz was their concern, not hers. Just as what might transpire between K'azz and Ardata was not for her to approve or disapprove.

A sudden panic made her dizzy as the suspicion dawned that this being before her possessed no grasp whatsoever of the human heart. She might *see* what lay within, but as to *how* the heart worked, and *why* . . . she was completely at sea. Utterly alien and utterly inhuman. K'azz's earlier warnings regarding her sounded again and she understood. No common points of reference whatsoever. *How we must frustrate her. Our actions and choices must be completely inexplicable to her. Even if she could read our thoughts – if she could – she must have no understanding of what drives those thoughts or actions.*

Shimmer almost felt sorry for her. Almost. She cleared her constricted throat as she suddenly found it very difficult to speak. 'That would be his choice, of course. I would have no say in the matter and would abide by his decision.'

'Really?' Ardata peered at her as if she were some sort of curious insect. Which, it occurred to Shimmer, humans may very well be to her.

The Queen of Witches was nodding to herself, gazing off as if distracted. 'We shall see,' she said. 'I must think on this for a time.' She waved to the girl where she sat among the trees nearby. 'In the meantime Lek here will show you back to your companions.'

Shimmer bowed. 'Until then.'

But Ardata appeared to have already dismissed her, or shifted her attention entirely away. Her deep night-black eyes were looking through her again as if she did not exist. Shimmer was quite startled when the child took her hand. 'This way.'

'Thank you, Lek.'

Shimmer adjusted her pace to the girl's slow shuffle. She examined her composed expression, the shaved scalp and single long braid falling to one shoulder. 'You are from a village nearby?' she asked.

'There are no villages nearby. Once there were many, but a great sickness came and almost no one was left. There was no one to mind the canals or reservoirs, to harvest the crops, or to repair the structures. Everyone went their own way. And the jungle came.'

'I see. I'm sorry, Lek.'

'Why? It is natural. It has happened before and shall happen again. Or ought to.' She peered up at her, very serious. 'You cannot hold back time for ever. Can you?'

Shimmer frowned. What an odd sentiment. Yet another oblique message for her? 'I suppose not,' she agreed.

The child beamed. 'I am glad you agree.' She peered up again, shyly. 'You are a soldier. You must be very brave.'

Shimmer took in the outline of the girl's twisted legs beneath her robes, her covered oddly shaped feet. *Yet here she is leading me, a stranger, unselfconscious.* 'As are you, Lek.'

The girl blushed furiously and lowered her gaze as if embarrassed. She stopped then, pointing. 'Your friends are over there.'

But Shimmer hardly heard her for she was staring at the girl's naked arm where the robes had fallen away. It was misshapen, swollen, the flesh grey and pebbled. Lek caught her gaze, whipped her arm away, turned, and ran as fast as she could in her clumsy walk.

'Lek! Wait! Please don't—'

But she would not stop and disappeared among the trees.

Damn! Gods, what a fool I am! Oh, Lek. I am so sorry . . . Gods, I pray I will meet you again. Then I'll hold you and not let you run away again.

She walked on, thinking *perilous indeed is Jakal Viharn and conversing with Ardata. Perilous in so many ways . . .*

✴ ✴ ✴

For several days Hanu carried her. He assured her it was not trying for him at all. She tested the leg by walking longer and longer distances. It was healing; that Thaumaturg, Pon-lor, certainly did know his trade. This day they came to a rise, a hillock or mound. Giant tualangs crowned it and a river curled round three of its sides. Saeng wondered whether it was the same river they'd crossed days ago. Her spirits sank as she came to suspect that perhaps it was. One particular tree offered excellent purchase for climbing and she had Hanu lift her up so that she could try to have a look about. She ascended the mostly naked trunk to quite a height until she had a vista over the surrounding canopy. Here a sight almost made her cry. It was not the league after league of undifferentiated verdant emerald jungle that surrounded them on all sides. No, it was to the west. There, still within sight, rose the dark steep teeth of the Gangrek Mounts.

She threw herself down from hold to hold in a recklessness of despair. She almost fell the last short distance but Hanu steadied her foot. She climbed down a few more knots and depressions in the bark until he took her weight and lowered her. She kicked the tree with her bad leg then danced, cursing and fuming.

'*What is it?*' he asked.

She pointed mutely to the west, almost spluttering her disbelief. 'We've come hardly any distance at all! We've just been meandering – directionless! Lost!' Pon-lor's warnings came to her then and she bit her lip. *Damn the man. Yet he would have had her turn round!*

She felt tears stinging in her eyes and she turned away. What were they to do? They were out of food, lost, and she was still without any hope of finding this 'Great Temple'. She was a complete failure! Her throat burned as bile rose again – she'd been heaving of late, and suffering from the runs. She could keep little down and what she did manage to choke down went right through her. She knew it was their bizarre diet – the few odd things she knew to be safe to consume – but she wouldn't risk poisoning herself with anything strange.

That was the worst of her maladies, of course. It was hardly worth dwelling upon the huge patches of angry itching rash, the swellings, the weeping infected cuts, and the countless bites from being eaten alive every night. Among all this, the infestation of maggots in a sore on her foot barely even registered.

She was weakening. They both knew it. She hadn't the strength to fend off any new illness that might take her at any time. A raging infection, the chills, water fever – the list was endless. Then it would be the end. There was nothing Hanu could do.

Perhaps it would have been better if she had remained . . .

No! She struck a fist to the tree. *I have my mission! I must succeed.*

The faces of the drowned girls wavered in her blurring vision: you must help us, they had pleaded of her. Pleaded!

'*Which way?*' Hanu asked, ever practical.

Saeng started down the hillock. 'It doesn't matter any more.'

She walked among the brush for a time until she stumbled through hanging lianas, leaving a shower of fallen blossoms carpeting the dead leaves. They would disappear quickly, she knew, as the many insects would converge to consume them. *As they shall me soon.*

A rigid grip righted her. '*You are delirious,*' a voice spoke in her thoughts. Arms lifted her then cradled her. She smelled something then: a scent of home. Woodsmoke. She reached for it. Rice steaming on the fire. Fish over the open flames. The arched branches of the high canopy passed her vision as she seemed to float effortlessly. She closed her eyes.

The scent of food woke her. A palm frond roof above. Reed walls. Movement, and an old woman appeared. She held out her hand; something was smeared there. Saeng opened her mouth and the woman pressed her fingers within. Saeng swallowed. She did this many times until sleep took her once more.

She awoke once again and this time she could raise herself on her elbows. She was in a village. A village of Himatan yet not a ghost one. Living and breathing. She was alone in the hut; the old woman was gone. People crossed the open commons the hut faced: they were mostly naked, in loin wraps only. Some were painted in smears of coloured mud, male and female; others not. One woman noticed that she was awake and ran off. Moments later an old man thrust his face into the hut. He was painted, but garishly so, with feathers and necklaces of objects she took to be talismans: teeth, bits of metal, chipped stones, talons and a dried paw.

'Who are you?' she asked.

'Awake for certain,' he remarked. 'Have you the strength to converse?'

'Yes.'

'Good. Even better.'

'What happened?'

He shrugged in a rattle of bones and claws. 'You were ill with fever. Close to death. Your stone servant delivered you to us.'

Saeng sat up straighter. 'Where is he – the stone servant?'

The old man gestured to the grounds. 'He stands in the village, unmoving. No doubt he awaits your command.'

Of course. *'Hanu? Can you hear me?'*

'Saeng! Shall I come?'

'No. I'm all right – thanks to you. How are you?'

'Sufficient.'

'You've eaten?'

'Yes. These villagers set out offerings and I ate some. This amused them no end.'

'All right. Well . . . I'm tired still.'

'Rest.'

'Thank you, Hanu. Thank you for everything.'

'It was nothing.'

Saeng sat back, relaxing. The old man had watched her throughout. 'You communicated with your servant?' he asked.

Saeng saw no reason to explain things; she just nodded.

'Good. I know these things, you see. I am a great magus.' He rattled the fetishes about his neck. 'I command the shades of the dead. I am beloved of Ardata herself.'

'Is that so.'

'Oh yes. No doubt this is why your servant brought you to me.'

'Well, thank you for healing me.'

'Certainly. My wives are great healers. But enough of that for now. Rest, heal. We shall talk again.' He disappeared in a clanking and clatter of the engraved stones hung from his neck.

Saeng lay back to regard the roof once more. *Mocking gods . . . how much time have I wasted? Am I too late? But no – we would not even be here if I was too late. Isn't that so?* It made her head hurt to think of it. She shut her eyes to sleep again.

The next day she felt strong enough to try to get up. The old women who had been tending her rushed to her aid. The magus's wives, she supposed. And thinking of that – it was they who healed her, not him. She limped out to the central commons to see Hanu there, waiting.

He was sitting cross-legged, meditating perhaps. Before him lay clay bowls of oil, burning incense sticks, and bowls and saucers of rice, stewed vegetables and dried meat.

'You seem to have made an impression,' she said, coming up.

'These are propitiations intended to appease my anger, apparently.'

'Oh? Your anger? They're afraid of you?'

He hesitated for a time, said, *'You are recovering?'*

'Yes. My leg is well. Weak and painful, but it can support me.' She studied him. His inlay mosaic of bright stones shone dazzlingly in the light. Much of the light was a deep emerald and she glanced up to see the Visitor hanging there fully visible in the day. *So close! We may have no time!* 'What happened, Hanu? Did you have to twist their arms?'

'No, Saeng. It's that mage, or theurgist, or whatever he is. He claims he stopped me from destroying the village. They're all terrified of him here.'

Saeng scanned the collection of ramshackle huts for some sign of the man. 'I see . . . Well, not our problem. I'll rest one more day and then we'll go. All right?'

'Fine.'

She motioned to the offerings. 'Wrap up the food. We'll take it with us.'

'I have been.' He lifted their one remaining shoulder bag.

'Thank you, Hanu.' She hobbled back to her hut.

She sat in the shade at the open entrance. Here, the women, some young, some old, were readying packets of food. Saeng watched for a time, then asked, 'Are those offerings as well?'

The youngest snapped a look to her and Saeng was surprised to see anger and sour resentment in her eyes. 'You could say that,' she said, her voice tight. 'These go to wild men in the woods. We feed them so that they will not kill our men or rape us. Chinawa made this deal.'

'Chinawa? Your . . . husband?'

'Yes. They killed many men and women but he put a stop to it. All

503

we must do is feed them. And now—' She stopped herself, lowered her gaze.

'And now you must feed us as well,' Saeng finished for her. The young woman merely hunched, lowering her head even further. 'And there is not enough.'

'There is none!' she yelled, glaring, tears in her eyes.

The oldest of the women hissed her disapproval. 'Would you have them burn down our homes? Eat us? Stop your complaining, child.'

Not my problem. If the Visitor should fall everyone will be dead. 'I'm sorry,' she said, and went to lie down.

That night the mage, Chinawa, came to her. She awoke suddenly from a troubled sleep to find him sitting next to the rattan bedding she lay upon. A single guttering oil lamp cast a weak amber glow in the hut. His eyes were bright in the dark. She sat up and adjusted her frayed skirt and shirt as best she could. 'What do you want?'

'Gratitude, for one thing. Were it not for me you would be dead.'

'I noticed it was the women who healed me – not you.'

The eyes sharpened. 'On my orders.'

'They would have acted without your orders, I'm sure.'

The man's expression hardened into a deep scowl. 'Do not play haughty with me, young woman. Cooperate and no one will get hurt. I will take you as my wife and with your stone servant I will sweep the wild men from the jungle. After that no one will challenge my rule here.'

Saeng snorted her disbelief. 'And why should I do that?'

'Because if you refuse, or use your stone servant to kill me, the wild men will descend upon the village and kill everyone. All the children will have their skulls cracked open against rocks. The women will be raped then stabbed to death. The men will be hunted down and eviscerated and left for the dogs to eat. Do you want these crimes upon your head?'

And if I do not find the Great Temple and prevent the summoning of the Visitor everyone shall die. Do I want that upon my head?

She sensed, then, one of the Nak-ta, the restless dead of the region, pressing to make herself heard. She presumed that Chinawa had summoned the spirit to scare her into cooperating. Yet the shades of the dead held no terror for her and so she allowed the small presence to come forward.

The mage did not react as she thought he would. He became quiet and still. He scanned the hut, his eyes growing huge. 'What is that?'

Saeng stared at the man, surprised. 'What is what?'

'That noise!'

Saeng listened and after a time she heard it: faint weeping, as of a young disconsolate girl. She saw her as well and motioned to the opening where a pale wavering shade stood just outside. The weak rain fell through her shape.

Chinawa leaped to his feet, gaping. 'Noor! A ghost!' And he jumped out into the rain, his necklaces of stones and claws clattering and rattling, to disappear into the dark.

Saeng watched him go, completely stunned. *By the false gods . . . A fake. A damned fake.* Then she laughed so hard she hurt her side and had to wipe tears from her eyes. Throughout, the shade, Noor, continued to weep. After her amusement had subsided Saeng turned to her. She appeared a harmless enough Nak-ta, but Saeng raised her protections in any case, as one could never be certain of the dead.

'Noor, is it?'

'Yes.'

'Why are you weeping?'

'Because I am dead.'

Saeng bit back a snarled reply. She took a calming breath. Her fault; it had been too long. 'So, tell me, Noor. How did you die?'

'Chinawa killed me.'

Saeng jerked her surprise, hurting her leg. Wincing, she rubbed it. 'Chinawa slew you? Why?'

'So that he could blame it on the wild men in the jungle.'

Ah. All is becoming clear.

'Then there are no wild men.'

'Yes, there are. I could see them. They were slipping close to death themselves. Sick, hungry and weak.'

'Then they have killed no one?'

'Not of this village.'

'I see. Thank you, Noor. Bless you for your help. Rest. Weep no more.'

The shade of the girl dropped her hands from her face. Saeng thought she must have been pretty. She gave a deep naive curtsy. 'My thanks. The blessing of the High Priestess is an honour.' She began to fade away. 'I go now, released. Thank you.'

Saeng jerked upright. 'Wait! What do you mean? Come back.' *Shit! High Priestess? What did she mean by that?* She fell backwards, draped an arm across her eyes. Gods! High Priestess? And I can't even find the damned Great Temple!

By the next morning she knew what she would do. The wives, young and old, offered a large first meal of rice, stewed vegetable roots, and the last of the meat from a trapped wild pig. She took only the rice, and this she kept in its broad leaf wrapping. She went out to get Hanu; it was time to go.

She still limped, and by the time she reached Hanu Chinawa had appeared from wherever it was he slunk about. The old man was glowering at her, his gaze flicking from her to Hanu. 'What do you think you are doing?' he hissed.

'We are going.'

'No, you are not.' He crept closer, lowering his voice: 'If you go I'll bring the wild men in here and they will kill everyone! Do you want that?'

'No.'

'Shall I strangle him?' Hanu asked. She signed for him to wait.

She peered about, saw faces peering from huts, people standing about pretending to work, but watching. 'Listen to me!' she called loudly. 'When I lay near death I spoke with the shades of the jungle. They came to me because I command this stone servant.'

Chinawa gaped at her, then eyed the watching villagers.

She raised her arms. 'Yes, I have communed with the dead and I commanded them not to follow Chinawa's orders. They will no longer listen to him!'

The old man backed away. He waved his arms frantically. 'Oh! I see it now!' he bellowed as if to shout her down. 'This one is a sorceress! Begone, you seductress! I order you to go now! Leave us good people in peace!'

Oh, for the love of . . . I can't believe this! 'Hanu – grab this wretch.'

Hanu lunged forward. He grasped a fistful of the hanging amulets and talismans and lifted the man from his feet to hang kicking. He squawked and yanked at the countless laces of leather and spun fibres.

'We go now of our choosing!' Saeng called. 'As for the wild men – they are no threat. I have seen them. They are just lost and starving refugees. They no doubt fear you more than you fear them!'

She gestured for Hanu to drop the man. He did so, retaining a handful of broken laces and charms that he threw down upon him. One of the objects caught Saeng's eye: a stone disc inscribed with the many-pointed star, a sign of the old cult of the Sun. She picked it up while the old man scrambled to his feet. 'Where did you get this?' she demanded.

He eyed her while clearly considering saying nothing. Then he shrugged, gesturing vaguely. 'From one of the old ruins. A place of great power—'

'Stop pretending to be a warlock, or whatever it is. You are no practitioner.'

He glared his enraged impotent hatred. 'I sensed it,' he finally ground out. 'Anyone would. Terrible things have been done there.'

'How do I get there? Tell me the way.'

He gaped, astonished, then laughed. 'You would travel there? By all means, do so. Go to your deaths.'

She raised a hand to Hanu. 'Perhaps you should lead us . . .'

The man hunched, obviously terrified. 'There is no need. Follow the lines of power.'

'Lines? What lines?'

'The channels. Lines. Carved in the ground! They lead to the centre. The loci.'

Saeng stared without seeing the cringing man. *Lines! What a fool I've been. All this time clambering over mounds and channels, searching for tall structures, when I should have been looking down. They lead to the temple. Converge there. Lines of power.*

She nodded to Hanu then waved her dismissal of Chinawa. 'Very well. For that I shall allow you to live. But if I hear through the shades of the dead that you have done any wrong I will curse you to eternal pain. Do you understand?' He merely stared, as if remorse or guilt was something utterly beyond him. Saeng pointed to the circle of villagers that had gathered. 'And if I were you I would run before these people tore me to pieces.'

He jerked and hunched even more, turning this way and that.

Saeng started off, ignoring him. She studied the flat stone disc in her hand. Hanu followed.

When they entered the jungle Hanu called to her: '*Saeng . . .*'

'Yes?'

'*We should've killed him.*'

She sighed. 'I know . . . I just couldn't bring myself to do it. Besides, if those people can't organize themselves enough to get rid of him, then they deserve him.'

*   *   *

Osserc did not think himself a vain man. One trait he did pride himself upon was his patience. He thought himself far more forbearing than the run of most. However, even his stone-like endurance was nearing its end. He felt it fraying; less like stone than the cheapest calico. And he did not know what would happen when it finally tore.

All was as usual: Gothos remained seated opposite, immobile. His gnarled hands remained poised upon the table, long yellowed nails dug into the wood, as if ready should Osserc suddenly snap and take a swing at him. The monkey creature came and went on its constant housecleaning errands, dusting, sweeping and knocking down cobwebs. Yet for all its efforts – sometimes striking Osserc in the back of his head with its broom – the dust and grime only seemed to mount ever deeper.

Outside, through the milky opaque windowpane, light and dark came and went. However, with each cycle of brightening and adumbration, Osserc believed he was coming to discern a disturbing pattern. The wavering jade glow shafting from above was brightening significantly.

Eventually, when the darkness through the patinated and rippled glass was at its deepest, he rose and crossed to the window. Squinting, he could make out the Visitor glowing above and he was shocked by how large it loomed.

He turned to regard Gothos. 'I have never seen one come this close before.'

'One did, before,' came a low breathless observation from among the hanging strings of filthy hair.

'One has? Before? You mean . . .' Osserc's gaze snapped up to the hanging threat. 'You cannot mean to suggest that they would actually do it again.'

'I do.'

'That would be utter madness. They learned that from the first, surely.'

Gothos snorted his scorn as only a Jaghut could. '*Learned*?' he scoffed.

'Someone should do something.'

'I suppose someone ought,' Gothos sighed. 'But in any case you will be safe hiding in here.'

'*Hiding*? I am not hiding.'

'No? Then you are doing a very good imitation of it.'

Rage clawed up Osserc's chest, almost choking him, and his gaze darkened. All that leashed it was the knowledge that this Jaghut was merely doing his job in goading and mocking him. Breathing heavily, he growled through clenched teeth: 'And you are doing a very good job of being a prick, Gothos.'

The Jaghut inclined his head in a false bow.

Osserc sat once again. He crossed his arms. 'So we just sit here while fools undo all that we have striven to build and protect.'

'Build? I have striven to build nothing. Quite the opposite, in fact.'

Osserc shook his head in remonstration. 'Do not dissemble. You strove as mightily as any. It was just that your efforts were not in stone or iron. They resided in another field entirely. The battlefield of ideas and the mind.'

The Jaghut inclined his head once more.

Yet instead of a sense of having won a point, Osserc could not shake the feeling that he had in fact once more been manoeuvred to where the Jaghut wanted him. Once more dwelling upon ideas and the mind.

The Nacht came shambling into the room again. This time he dragged a long pole at the end of which had been tied a dirty rag. The creature made a great show of lifting the pole to brush the cobwebs from the murky corners of the ceiling. Dust drifted down in clouds upon Osserc and Gothos. Neither moved throughout, though Osserc did grind his teeth.

He decided a retreat and reordering was called for. What he knew from Gothos' rebounding of questions with questions was that the Azath were insisting that the answer must come from within. An obvious path in retrospect, given that the Azath themselves were by definition notoriously inward. It made sense that they would applaud such an approach. That aside, this did not necessarily undermine any potential insight. Any such revelation would be his to accept or dismiss.

Insights from self-reflection were beyond the capability of many – perhaps himself included. Rationalization, denial, self-justification, delusion, all made it nearly impossible for any true insight to penetrate into the depths of one's being. And Osserc was ruthless enough in his thinking not to consider himself above such equivocations. Therefore, as he had seen in his reflections, one measure of progress was discomfort and pain.

If this were the case then the Azath were demanding a high price indeed.

It struck him that all this hinged upon one plain and simple thing. He faced a choice: whether to remain or to step out. No one forbade either option. Gothos had made this clear – he was no gatekeeper. The choice was entirely Osserc's. Any choice represented a future action. Therefore, the Azath were more concerned with his future than with his past. The choice represented an acceptance of that future.

Osserc's unfocused gaze drifted down to settle upon the obscured features of the Jaghut opposite. 'I am being asked to face something I find personally distasteful. I never accepted the mythopoeia I see accreting around the Liosan. It all means nothing to me.'

'Whether it means anything to you in fact means nothing.' Gothos sounded particularly pleased in saying that. 'I'm sorry, but I suspect it is all very much larger than you.' He sounded in no way apologetic at all.

Osserc found himself gritting his teeth once again. 'It would seem that stepping outside would be an endorsement of a future I have no interest in, and do not support.'

The Jaghut revealed his first hint of temper as his nails gouged even further into the slats of the table and he hung his head. 'It is obvious even to me that nothing at all is being *asked* of you!' He raised his head and flattened his hands upon the table. 'Think of it more as an opportunity to guide and to shape.'

'But what if—'

Gothos snapped up a finger for silence. 'No.'

'You really cannot expect me to relinquish all control!'

Something changed in the poise of the Jaghut. A wide predatory smile now rose behind the ropy curtain of hair. His tusks caught the emerald glow from outside. Osserc fought the uncomfortable sensation of having fallen into a carefully prepared trap. 'Osserc,' Gothos began, his voice now silken, 'how can you relinquish that which you never possessed in the first place?'

CHAPTER XIV

The locals, I am sorry to say, are indolent and lazy. All that they need can be found in the surrounding jungle within reach of everyone, and so they lack industry and application. They are oddly content in their simple ways: an earthenware pot serves to cook foods; three stones are buried to serve as a hearth; ladles are made from coconuts; the small leaves of the chao plant are used to make little spoons to bring liquids to the mouth – these they throw away when the meal is finished. It is in vain one searches for the natural urge to a better way of life.

> Ular Takeq
> *Customs of Ancient Jakal-Uku*

GOLAN WOKE FROM A TROUBLING DREAM IN WHICH HE HEARD distant voices chanting through darkness. That alone was nothing to be alarmed about; dreams, his training taught him, were merely random images swirling about the mind, not dire portents or prophecies. No such ignorant superstitions for the Thaumaturgs. Yet this chanting had carried whispered echoes of ancient compellings and forbidden phrasings. It called to mind references to a ritual said to have been completed only once – the greatest, and most perilous, of all their order's invocations. One he and his fellow students discussed only in the most muted and guarded terms.

It was no wonder, he reflected, that his mind should choose to throw up such an echo now. He faced a reality of slow grinding annihilation every day.

He opened his eyes to the thin frayed awning spread above him, dripping with the passing rain. He sat up and pulled his sweat-soaked shirt from his chest. His bare arms glistened and bore countless red swellings of bites. His yakshaka guards stood in a broad circle about him. It seemed to him that the night was as quiet as it ever could get; the usual hunting calls shocked everyone – each morning one or two of his remaining force would always be missing. The constant buzzing of the cicadas also grated on nerves already frayed beyond endurance. The rush of passing bats made him glance to the trees; he quite disliked bats. There was also the constant moaning and groaning of the sick in camp. 'The sick', in point of fact, now described nearly all of the remaining army.

Myself included, Golan reflected. He'd come down with the chills. The fever of shuddering cold spells followed by prostrating sweats. It was quite debilitating, and it was only through his Thaumaturg training that he was able to continue to function.

He paused then, for he heard something more: the murmuring that had haunted his dreams had not stopped. Indeed, he heard it even more clearly now. A true chill took him suddenly – one far more profound than his fever. He crossed to one of his last remaining pieces of luggage: an iron chest that, if lost, would necessitate his death in penance. Frost limned it now. Even in the depths of this heated abyss frost feathered its sides. A silver light escaped from the crack of its lid. He reached for it but paused, reconsidering. His hands were close enough to feel the cold breath wafting from it.

The whispered chanting spoke to him then and he knew. He *knew.* He scrambled to the centre of the clearing his awning occupied. Yakshaka turned their armoured heads to peer at him. He scanned the clearing night sky. There, through gaps in the canopy, the Visitor glowed behind the thinnest ribbon of cloud. The scarf drifted on as he waited, scarcely able to breathe. What was revealed was a swollen gibbous jade banner so gravid Golan thought it about to break upon the treetops.

To think I haven't been paying attention, he wondered. *Not at all.*

What could possibly drive them to . . . No matter. He wiped a hand down his face, peered about frantically. 'Second!' he called, his voice rather high. 'Mister Waris! You are needed!'

The man appeared, a loose shirt that he'd obviously just thrown on hanging down over his trousers. *I chose well,* Golan decided. 'Break camp, Second,' he told him. 'We must continue pressing east, quickly now.'

The man's slit gaze revealed nothing. Golan would have preferred some sort of reaction. Even the suggestion that he was losing his mind. But whatever doubts or reservations the man might have

512

harboured he continued to keep them to himself and he bowed, still silent. Golan waved him away. 'Begin at once.'

The man bowed again and jogged off.

A new figure pushed its way through the wall of yakshaka guards, this one gangly and crooked of neck, his bulging pouch of papers at his side. *How does he do that?* Golan wondered. *Have to have a word with my guards.*

'Troubled dreams, Commander?' Principal Scribe Thorn asked.

'In a sense, Principal Scribe. You are here now for what reason? Other than to trouble me with questions?'

Thorn pulled his quill from behind his blackened ear. 'Why, to record your orders of course!'

'Like history, you are too late, Scribe. However, just for you, I shall recreate the scene.' He leaned closer, peered at the sheet of pressed fibre paper the scribe held ready on a wooden pallet, and said, 'March east.'

Principal Scribe Thorn scratched at the sheet. He mouthed aloud as he wrote: 'Glorious Leader Golan allows no respite in his remorseless advance upon the enemy.'

'You capture it eerily.'

'My lord is too kind.'

'Not at all.' Golan gestured aside. 'Now, if you do not mind. We are breaking camp.'

'The soldiers will consider it a privilege to set aside sleep to return to the march, Commander. No doubt the sick will be inspired to attempt to stand.'

Golan, who had been moving off, halted to return to the man. *Mustn't show the bastard that he can reach me.* He drew a patient breath. 'No doubt. That is why I shall order the yakshaka to carry the worst – to spare them the effort.'

The Principal Scribe's fist-sized Adam's apple bobbed as he swallowed. He blinked his bulging rheumy eyes, then quickly lowered them to his sheet. He wrote, mouthing, 'So eager to crush the enemy is Golan the Great that he orders his soldiers carried into battle!'

Golan studied the man – who bowed obsequiously. 'Such accuracy in recording is uncanny, Principal Scribe. Future scholars shall hang on every word. I'm certain of it.'

Thorn stooped again, even lower. *Like a buzzard . . . and I am the corpse.*

* * *

His last mount had fallen under Jatal two days before. He and Scarza were descending out of the Gangrek Mounts, the Dragon's Teeth, when the abused, exhausted animal pitched forward, tumbling his rider over his neck to slew down the grade of loose gravel and rock. Jatal received several bruises and a numbed arm, but the horse broke a leg and so they killed it. He was all for moving on immediately. But Scarza had insisted on the time to butcher a portion of the animal for meat and so it was some while before they set off, the half-Trell carrying a haunch over his shoulder. The giant had shown great foresight in that. The meat saw them through the next few days, until it turned, and they had to throw the remainder away.

They were gaining upon the Warleader – at least so Scarza insisted. Jatal had no idea. He couldn't track here in this abyssal green maze. The half-Trell led him to one old abandoned fire site. It could have belonged to anyone as far as he could tell, but Scarza insisted *he* had been here.

Jatal merely shrugged. 'Let us move on.'

Scarza nodded, eyeing him. 'Yes – for a time. Yet he is keeping a fire. We should also.'

'It may alert him,' Jatal objected. He turned away and pushed through the surrounding broad-leafed plants.

Scarza followed. 'There are more things in this pit than just he.'

'They do not concern me.'

'They do me. I for one do not intend to be torn to pieces before I can get my hands on him.'

Jatal glanced back. 'Do as you choose.'

When evening came Scarza called a halt. In the gloom he offered Jatal a wink. 'We do not want to fall down a hole, now do we? Like back in those Gangreks. That was a close call.'

'We've left the sinkholes behind.'

'Quicksand, then. Or a boggy morass.'

Jatal said nothing – there was nothing to say as far as he was concerned.

Scarza peered about, then gestured to one side. 'Under cover of that tree, I think. It should keep the rain off. I'll build a small fire.'

Jatal sat. When the fire was going, Scarza let go a great breath and sat back. He offered a fruit. 'Try that. I think it's edible. Looks familiar.'

Jatal took a bite.

'How is it?'

'I'm not dead.'

'Ah! In that case I'll try one.' And he popped a fruit into his mouth.

514

He watched Jatal eating and nodded approvingly. 'Had you heard that the Moon's Spawn has fallen?'

'We heard something of that.'

'Yes. They say it has.' He nodded again, scanning the overcast sky. 'Man could make a fortune sifting through that wreckage. Imagine. I was thinking . . . after this . . . I would head over that way. What say you?'

Over the fruit, Jatal eyed him, blinking. There was no 'after this' for him. He would join Andanii. If her spirit was as fierce in death as it had been in life, then he knew she'd be waiting for him. He hoped she would forgive him for the wait.

Scarza was quiet for a time, watching him. Then he cleared his throat and glanced away. He studied the sky, and after a while he frowned. 'Tell me, Adwami scholar, have you ever seen one of these passing Visitors grow so large before?'

Jatal glanced up briefly. The broad streaming head of the Banner did loom monstrously bloated behind the cloud cover. Its emerald glow was now the murky olive of deep water. 'I have only seen one before.' He shrugged.

'Well, I have seen many, my friend. And I swear, in all my years, I have never seen one come this close.'

'What of it?'

'Well . . . the legends. The stories. That old lay – how was it? Oh yes, "The Fall of the Shattered God".'

'And?'

Scarza waved a thick arm. 'Well, I for one would not wish to be beneath it!'

'If it falls, it falls. There is nothing we can do about it.'

'True. But perhaps it is meant for someone in particular . . . if you follow my reasoning.'

Jatal regarded him levelly for a time. He swallowed a mouthful of the underripe fruit. 'Then I will hold him down myself.'

'Now, lad. I do not think the lass would want—'

'Andanii waits for me,' Jatal cut in. His voice was flat but hard. 'You do as you choose. I will continue on.'

Scarza blew out a long exhalation, rubbed a wide hand over his mop of hair. He shot another glance skyward, winced. Then he brightened, sitting up straighter. 'Well . . . there is only one thing for it. We can always hope their aim is as good as the first time, hey?' And he laughed in great loud guffaws.

Staring out at the jungle, Jatal did not even smile.

The first thing that gripped Mara was the terrifying cold. The next was the wet. She was kneeling in water so frigid a slush of ice washed about within it. She vomited into the water, then wrapped her arms about her soaked robes, and bellowed: 'Red! For Burn's sake do something!'

'I'm on it!' He sounded just as shocked and pained as she.

All about, Crimson Guard Disavowed straightened, groaning and cursing. Skinner had brought fifteen swords and all three mages.

They occupied the top of a bare rocky shoreline. A tower rose just inland. Water foamed and washed back and forth across the land, storm-driven, leaving layers of ice behind. Low clouds churned overhead so close she imagined she could touch them.

'Where are we?' she shouted to the priest over the screaming wind and the crash of breakers down the coast. The man merely cackled and laughed wildly. 'The tower!' he cried, pointing.

The water pulled back downhill round her. It carried bodies, some in blue woollen robes over mail, others in opalescent scaled breastplates, greaves and helms that gleamed like mother-of-pearl. Mara stared while they nudged past her in the flow.

'Stormriders?' she yelled to the priest as he scrambled by.

'Matters not,' the man laughed. Ahead, Skinner was already advancing on the tower. Disavowed formed ranks behind. He appeared to still be arguing with Shijel for one of his swords. Since he broke Black's no one was willing to lend him theirs.

A Warren-fed warmth now stole over her. She recognized Red's work. It blunted the worst of the strength-draining frigidity but hardly thawed her. She knew she wouldn't have much time here before her fingers and toes froze.

'Ware!' a voice called from behind and she just had time to turn before a wall of webbed green came breaking over her. The mountain of water drove her off her knees and swept her up the slope. She knocked bodies with others, either living or dead, she had no idea. The waters stole all the sense of warmth she'd regained. She almost lost consciousness from the soul-penetrating cold stabbing her. She breached the surface and gasped for breath. Something slashed her side with stinging cold and she spun to see a Stormrider raising his jagged sword for another blow.

She reacted instantly, raising her Warren and thrusting all in one. The creature flew backwards to crack against the tower's stone wall in a sickening crunch of shattering armour. She gestured again and all the waters swirling about her were driven back in a broad circle. A melee of Riders against Disavowed lay spread across the hillside. Enraged, she threw her arms out and all the Riders lurched backwards as if yanked. They tumbled and rolled to disappear into the churning moil of waters.

'Mara's with us!' Shijel laughed, panting, and he waved his approval.

'The tower, fools!' the priest called from the open doorway.

Mara gestured everyone on. Slogging past, Jacinth pointed aside, and Mara saw Petal lying there. She laboured through mud brittle with ice and turned him over. Blood smeared the side of his head. He'd fallen or been driven against rocks. She felt at his neck – the flesh was bitter cold, but possessed a pulse.

'Bring him,' she ordered two Disavowed, Farese and Hist. They carried him up steps that were an ice-slick waterfall of pouring water. Within, the main floor was awash; foaming water was even rushing down stairways from the higher levels. Corpses of Stormriders and others in blue tabards over mailed armour lay about in the blood-streaked flow. Those in the blue tabards Mara now recognized as Korelri Chosen, Stormguards, guardians of the storied Wall. They were in the lands some named Korel.

Why would the priest bring them here during an attack by the Riders?

Skinner and Red were facing the bedraggled priest, who, though wearing only a ragged loincloth here amid the frigid waters, still jerked and hopped as urgently as before.

'There is no way down,' Red was telling Skinner.

The priest tore at his few remaining strands of hair. 'I tell you – the way is down!'

Red jabbed a finger to his temple to indicate what he thought of the priest.

'Another wave!' Jacinth called from the entrance where the heavy iron doors hung warped and askew, blasted from their hinges.

'Brace yourselves!' Skinner bellowed.

Mara turned: *Another wave this high?*

The dressed granite stones beneath her feet juddered and shook at the approach of something immense. A landslide roaring tore the air. Jacinth backed away from the gaping entrance. 'Burn protect us,' she breathed, awed.

Mara glimpsed a solid wall of water choking the opening then something slammed her into a wall and held her there, crushed and pressed so hard that she could not draw breath – even if there were

517

air to breathe. A terrible heart-stopped cold clawed at her. It pulled her strength and her life from her as water might douse a flame. Her slashed side stung as if burned.

The pressure relented and she fell from the wall to her hands and knees, coughing, gasping for air. Fighting surrounded her. She straightened, pushed aside her hair. Several Disavowed were down, run through by lethal ice-shards that stood from them like spears, hissing and steaming. Skinner had a Stormrider by the arm, and as Mara watched he lifted the entity and brought it down over his knee. A loud wet crack sounded and the creature spasmed. Skinner straightened, allowing the corpse to slide off his coat of mail to splash into the water that foamed about their knees.

New war shouts sounded and Korelri came charging down the stairs and from halls leading further back into the tower. They faced the Disavowed with spears levelled and broad shields raised. The shields held their sigil: a stylized tower or wall standing against swirling waters.

One of them pushed his way forward. He was old, his hair as white as snow, but he was still slim and straight. 'Who are you?' he demanded.

'You're welcome,' Skinner answered.

The man glanced past them to the entrance and the overcast murk beyond where the surf boomed loud and echoing. 'Well,' he allowed, 'our thanks – but we are holding.' He studied them now, narrowly. 'Where are you from?'

'What matters that?' Skinner answered. 'We are come to your aid.'

'You are not allowed—'

'Another!' a Stormguard called from up the stairs.

The man's jaws worked as he swallowed all further argument or objections. 'Very well,' he snapped. To his men, he continued, 'As before. Allow the surge to fade then counter-attack!'

The Chosen clashed their spears to the floor. 'Aye, Marshal!' They retreated to their posts.

Mara came to Skinner's side. 'We are weakening,' she whispered. 'We can't endure much more of this.'

He nodded his understanding. He raised a hand in a sign: *ambush*.

The Disavowed eyed one another in silent understanding.

A wave was building; she could feel it in the pregnant charged atmosphere. A wind of displaced air preceded it: the howling came surging through the entrance, ruffled her hair and chilled her further, then went on its way up the stairs and through the tower rooms. The avalanche roar returned, surging, until, paradoxically, she could hear nothing at all. This time she would be ready: she raised her Warren and created a sphere of outward pressure about her. She concentrated upon it with all her might.

Darkness obscured the entrance: a murky olive green.

Here it comes!

A solid wall of icy water came exploding in. It struck the circumference of her protective sphere and could not penetrate. But the blow shocked her backwards into the wall once again, knocking the wind from her. Shapes moved past through the water and flowed up the stairs, glimmering a phosphorescent emerald and sapphire. One shape seemed to pause, wavering, before her. A lance shot through the wall of water. She flinched her head aside and it yanked on her hair as it slammed into the wall and burst into a thousand fragments of ice.

Snarling, her face slashed, she sent force to strike the shape and slam it spinning backwards.

The water churned, losing its forward urgency. It pulled now, escaping. Grateful, Mara eased her concentration; she didn't think she could've lasted much longer.

The Korelri emerged again. They pushed back the last few remaining Riders, who fought to the end, silent, yielding nothing. An ages-old unrelenting enmity here, Mara knew. This war was the stuff of songs and epic poems all round the world.

When the last fell, the marshal approached Skinner. 'Thank you for your aid, but we are holding. I must ask that you leave now during this lull.'

'Your numbers appear to be much diminished.' Skinner said. 'I do not believe you will hold.'

'That is our concern. We will defend to the end, in any case. You are an outsider. I ask again that you leave.'

Skinner's scaled armour scraped and slithered as he held out his arms. 'I understand. We will go. I just have one request.'

The marshal raised his pale white brows. 'Oh? Yes?'

Skinner's hand snapped out to clench the man's throat. The Disavowed lunged forward, thrusting and slashing to push back his fellows. 'Where is the shard!' Skinner yelled.

A strong wind pushed against Mara's back and she glanced behind. The light outside had dimmed to a near subsurface dark green. *So soon? Oh, shit . . .*

She was behind the melee line of Disavowed engaging Korelri defenders. The priest, she noted, was somehow still with them, hopping and waving his fists, appearing even more demented.

'Wave!' she called, and raised her Warren, bracing herself.

The water slammed her to a wall once more. Through the swirling webbed green she saw shapes writhing and thrusting in a chaotic struggle of all against all. She could not even be certain which shapes were which. A blade thrust through the wall of water, narrowly missing her. She moved to answer the threat but found that her hands were now numb clubs, the nails dark blue.

Gods! It's almost too late!

When the water receded the Disavowed were the majority standing. They fell upon the remaining Korelri. Skinner rose to his feet, water pouring from him: he still held the marshal by the throat, but the man had been thrust through the back and Mara doubted he still lived.

Skinner shook him. 'The shard!'

The old man just bared his blood-smeared teeth in defiance, and shook his head. Cursing, Skinner threw him aside. 'Mara!' he called.

She pushed forward through the swirling water. 'Yes?'

Skinner pointed to the set and dressed stones of the floor. Mara sagged inwardly. 'I am nearly spent,' she gasped. Her words were jagged as she stuttered with cold.

'Red!' No answer. Skinner and Mara peered about. 'Red?'

'Aye,' came a weak response. The man straightened. He cradled an arm gashed open. Blood streamed from his fingertips, darkening the water round him. 'Make it quick,' he said, smiling bleakly.

'Warm Mara.'

The old man nodded. 'Then I'll have me a nap – if you don't mind.'

'Farese!' Skinner called. 'See to his arm.'

The small Talian swordsman jogged to Red. Mara waited, shivering uncontrollably, while the mage summoned his strange form of elder magic – a kind of animism still retained in some backward regions. Mara couldn't understand the first of it; unlike the clarity of the Warrens, it seemed to lack logic or order. Farese knelt at Red's side and tore strips from his ratty sodden blanket.

Welcome sensual warmth infused Mara, yet it came on too strongly and too quickly. She felt her flesh tingling with the onset of burning. Steam rose from her. She felt faint and dizzy.

'Now!' Skinner demanded.

She nodded, barely able to see. She focused her Warren and gathered her energy. She collected it, guarded it, allowed it to swell until she was on the verge of losing the control that kept it from consuming her flesh entirely.

'Back off!' she heard Skinner yelling, distantly, through a thundering roar in her ears.

She released the pent-up energies, sending them blasting down into the centre block of the floor. Rock shattered. The block shifted beneath her feet. She tottered forward but an arm encircled her waist, holding her. Skinner. Clattering rock resounded from beneath them. Several stone blocks had fallen away, revealing floored-over circular stone stairs.

The priest appeared from nowhere, cackling and waving his arms in triumph. He jumped and leaped his way down the steps. Skinner released Mara and rushed to follow. 'Remain!' he ordered, adding, 'Hold them here . . .' as he disappeared from sight.

Jacinth came to Mara, steadied her; the woman's blazing mane of hair now hung bedraggled and lank about her shoulders. Ice rime feathered the red-stained leather scales of her armour. 'I'll hold the stairs,' Mara told her.

The swordswoman nodded and glanced about at the remaining Disavowed – a mere eight. And of Petal there was no sign. Washed away, Mara imagined, feeling an unexpected pang of loss.

Another wave surged towards them. Mara readied herself. The avalanche of water hit the chamber and Mara fought to repel it. But an opening had been created, and she could not contain the pressure; the force pushed her aside like a cork and the course streamed past her to rush down the throat of the staircase. Almost immediately the waters round them swirled down to a mere wash about their knees and this too was sucked away down the stairs.

Damn. Skinner . . . I'm sorry.

A convulsion from below kicked the floor. Everything loose jumped, including all bodies, living and dead. Mara rammed her elbow into the floor, raising stars in her vision.

Stones came crashing down among them. Cracks tore the set blocks apart.

'Out! Now!' Jacinth bellowed.

The Disavowed all ran scrambling for the entrance. Mara descended the iced stairs down the front then stopped to look back. Further concussions shook the ground beneath her feet. Great cracks now climbed the walls of the tower.

Skinner! Come on!

The priest appeared. He came running and dodging from the entrance. Mara didn't think that holding his hands above his head would really have helped him much, but he did make it out. She caught hold of one skinny blue-hued arm as he ran past. 'What happened? Where's Skinner!'

'He has it,' the priest growled, enraged. He pounded his chest and shouted, scattering spittle: 'I should have the honour! It is mine!'

'Your god's, you mean,' Mara answered and released him to totter onward.

Skinner . . . now would be good . . .

She scanned the water for any sign of a new wave. The sea raged, choked by clashing white-capped waves that broke in every direction. *It is as though they are confused, unsure. Hurry, Skinner. We have a chance!*

Farese pointed. 'Someone!' It was the wide black-robed figure of Petal emerging from among the broken boulders of the slope. Farese ran to help him.

Mara felt an unaccountable degree of relief. *Now at least I still have someone to talk to.*

'Do you feel that?' Jacinth called. 'It is quiet.'

Mara felt for tremors: the ground was still but for the pounding of waves. The tower remained, though wide cracks climbed its sides. It also stood rather canted in its rise.

'There!' Shijel called, pointing.

Skinner was at the entrance. He came stepping over fallen blocks and he carried a large chest in both hands. The chest gleamed silver in the overcast half-light.

'Open your Warren!' Jacinth told the priest. 'Now!'

Mara's attention was drawn from Skinner as he descended the slope. She felt something tug at her awareness. *Magery, on the far side of the tower. Someone familiar.*

'Someone comes!' she shouted to everyone.

The priest opened a gate. The chaos roiling through it made Mara gag once more. It gave her a headache like a spike being pounded into her temple.

'Go now,' Jacinth ordered the Disavowed. 'Go!' They hurried through one after the other.

She shoved the priest but he would not move. 'Not until I have it!' he yelled.

'Just send us all now!' Mara shouted over the wind and crashing surf.

'Someone must bring it,' he answered, snarling his frustration.

'Go!' Mara told Jacinth. Furious, the lieutenant backed into the gate, glaring.

'You, too,' the priest told Mara. She ignored him.

Closer now, Skinner called out, 'Go now, all of you . . .' Mara edged back into the gate, slowly. The priest followed after her, also backing in. As Mara went she heard a bull-throated yell sound out, so loud it drowned all the noise of the roaring wind and the pounding combers: 'Skinnnnerrr!' it bellowed on and on.

She tried to return but it was too late. The gate had hold of her. She heard, or thought she heard, Skinner calling something, and then she was gone. The repulsive touch of chaos enmeshed her and her own absolute abhorrence made her push at it as if she could somehow keep it from touching her.

She fell out on to hard dry dirt, choking humidity, and the screeching of birds. Jacuruku. The land was not welcome, but its heat certainly was. She fought down her heaving empty stomach and watched, fascinated, while streamers of mist rose from her arms and blue-tinged hands. Never again would she complain about the heat. Never.

The priest emerged and moments later Skinner appeared. He still carried the large chest, which Mara saw now was indeed made of hammered silver. 'Who was that?' she demanded. 'Someone shouted. Who was it?'

Skinner just tossed his wet hair and laughed. 'Bars! Can you imagine? And Blues. They must have come for the shard.' He hefted the chest. 'Well . . . it is ours now.'

Blues? Really? Mara felt astonishment, but also relief. She was strong in D'riss, but his understanding of it was far more subtle, and deeper.

'My god's, you mean,' the priest snarled. 'Now open it and give it to me.'

Skinner set the chest down. The priest threw himself upon it, rubbed his hands over it. 'How do you open it? Is there a catch? A latch?'

Mara flexed her hands; feeling was returning to them in a most painful wave of pins and needles.

'I believe you open it like this,' Skinner said, reaching down. And he clasped hold of the priest's head and savagely twisted it. The snap of his neck made Mara jump.

The body fell aside. Mara's gaze climbed to Skinner. Her amazement and horror must have shown on her face for he shrugged. 'We have no more use for him. He has delivered to us a shard. Now we have a bargaining chip in all this.'

'But you are King of Chains – what of that?'

He picked up the chest. 'It too has served its purpose. Now it is no longer necessary either.'

'But are you not . . . what of retribution?'

Skinner threw his head back and laughed again. 'Retribution?' He started walking. 'That creature has far greater things to worry about.' He raised his voice: 'Shijel! Which way?' The swordsman pointed. 'Very good. Farese, help Red. Mara, can you help Petal?'

Mara took hold of the mage's arm through his frigid sodden robes. 'What happened to you?'

The big man touched a hand to his head, hissed his pain. 'I almost drowned.'

Mara nearly laughed aloud. Yes, drowned. There were times when plodding literalness is somehow appropriate.

Later in the afternoon Petal was treading along in front of Mara, swinging from side to side with his elephant-like gait, when he suddenly stopped. Mara nearly ran into him. 'What is it?' she asked, rather annoyed.

He was peering up at the canopy. 'Someone . . . some *thing* . . . watching.'

'Tell Skinner.'

He twisted his hands together. 'I may be wrong . . .'

She sighed her impatience, shouted, 'Skinner!'

He glanced back from the fore. She raised a hand, signed: *company*.

He nodded, raised a hand to sign for a halt. Everyone crouched, hands going to weapons.

'Where?' Mara whispered to Petal.

The big man lifted his chin to one side. 'Right over—'

Something came streaking down to hammer into Skinner and the two went careering off through the brush, rolling and crashing. Mara had a momentary glimpse of a shape that resembled a woman, yet not a woman, something half *else*.

Everyone set off in pursuit.

They found Skinner engaged in a tug of war with a woman smeared in dried mud and wearing only a loincloth. What was even more astonishing to Mara was that when she yanked upon the chest she pulled Skinner entirely off-balance. And she recognized the woman: she'd been trapped among the Dolmens of Tien the last time they saw her.

'Let . . . go!' she panted, snarling. 'This one is mine.'

The Disavowed encircled the two, weapons out, but unsure whether to rush in. Skinner let go one hand and lashed out with a punch to the woman's head that made Mara wince.

All that happened was that the woman stilled. Her eyes grew huge, like twin black pools, and she drew herself up as if insulted. 'You dare . . . *again*!' She raised a hand and backslapped Skinner across the face. The blow echoed through the trees and sent him tumbling. She raised the chest. 'At last,' she breathed.

'Get her now!' Jacinth shouted. Hist and Shijel closed.

The woman laughed and jumped up the trunk of a nearby tree. Mara stared, astounded, as she pulled herself up one-handed and leaped from limb to limb.

Next to her, Petal stroked his wide chin. 'An impressive display,' he murmured.

Jacinth helped Skinner to his feet. 'Bring her down!' he roared to Mara.

She nodded and let out a wary breath. *Very well . . . but can we take her?* She focused her Warren.

Far above in the upper canopy the woman laughed wildly and shook the chest. 'Sister Envy!' she shouted to the sky, 'I am coming!' And she leaped from her perch.

Mara flinched, but as the woman fell her shape transformed into something else, something sinuous and dark russet-red that flapped huge wings, driving Mara to cover her face from the dust. When she looked back the long writhing form was diminishing in the sky, fore-limbs clenched round something small and gleaming.

'*Most* impressive,' Petal repeated. 'Sister Spite. Envy, I think, is in for rather an unpleasant surprise.'

Skinner roared, enraged, and punched the tree, leaving a dent in the thick bark.

'Now what?' Mara murmured to Petal.

'I am not certain. But I do believe that we still have to establish whether K'azz truly *is* here.'

At that name Skinner's head snapped round. He marched to Petal and stared up at him; Skinner was one of the largest men Mara knew, but Petal was simply a giant both in girth and in height. After a moment, their commander nodded and crossed his arms. 'That is for you, Petal.'

The big mage's eyes slid to Mara. They held fear like twin cornered mice. *Why the dread? Ah, of course . . . Ardata will be waiting.*

* * *

The mound Saeng and Hanu kept to was broad enough to be dismissed as a mere natural undulation in the jungle floor. The canopy rose seamlessly from the forest of the surrounding lower tracts to top the higher ground just as densely. As she walked, Saeng wondered whether, from far enough away, an immense pattern, rather like a many-rayed star, might be visible in the rise and fall of the canopy height.

They followed the rise for two days, angling southeast. The way was not easy as the passage of centuries had not been kind to the earthwork; streams cut through it creating steep-sided gullies. In places it had been levelled entirely in broad swampy lowlands. But after continuing on, they found it once more as the land gently rose again.

Each night Saeng lay awake for some time beneath the cover of the densest trees while the inevitable rain poured down. She watched the olive-tinged clouds and the glowing Visitor, immense and ominous, glaring down upon them. Would it really come crashing into the earth? And if so, where? Right on top of them? She hardly believed the Thaumaturgs would call it down directly upon themselves. In which case, being next to them might be a very safe place to retreat after all. Not that it would matter. She imagined that such an impact would annihilate everything across the land in ferocious firestorms.

On the third day she glimpsed through gaps in the canopy some sort of tall rounded structure far ahead. Hanu paused and gestured. The land rose here; jumbled age-gnawed stone blocks might have once described a set of rising levels, or wide stairs. Jungle choked them now. A curtain of hanging and ground-crawling lianas draped the rise. Clinging orchid blossoms dazzled her with brilliant crimson, pink and white. Hanu pushed aside the hanging mats and led the way.

The ground appeared to level here to a wide plateau that stretched as far as she could see. Far off, perhaps at the centre, was a structure. They advanced, Hanu drawing his yataghan. After a time she realized they walked the remains of a concourse. Statues lined it, barely visible through the undergrowth. They appeared to depict monsters or daemons of some sort, all bowed or kneeling. Defeated enemies? Enslaved forces? It was all so long ago she had no idea what they might reference.

The concourse traced what might once have been a moat but was now just another stretch of wilderness, albeit wetter than its surroundings. It led to a wide arched gate in a wall of dressed cyclopean stones. The arch was strangely pointed in a style she did not recognize.

Here Hanu pulled her behind the cover of the nearest of the mature trees that had pushed their way through the laid stones ages ago.

He motioned to the ground close to the gate. She could just make out deep cuts and prints in the loamy soil. A line of many wheeled wagons or carriages had entered before them.

The Thaumaturgs were already here.

A black despair of exhaustion pulled on her. *After all this!* She pressed her head to the tree trunk. She'd counted on getting here first to sabotage or wreck any possibility of the ritual, but they had lost too much time. Now the Circle was here and had already begun.

Hanu squeezed her shoulder and gestured that they should move. She shook her head. There was no point now. What could she possibly do against the entire Circle of Masters?

Hanu unceremoniously picked her up and marched off to the side, tracing the outer wall.

'What is it?'

'I do not know. We're not alone out here. For some time it's been bothering me. Perhaps we're being followed.'

She covered her face to fight back tears. 'Well – it's all over anyway.'

'Not yet.'

'Hanu . . . You don't understand . . .'

'I know you shouldn't give up before the battle is joined.'

'It's not that simple!'

He was jogging now, hunched, leaping tall snaking roots and fallen rotting tree trunks. They rounded the corner of the overgrown walls to find an exact replica of the side they'd quit. The structure, it appeared, was completely symmetrical in all directions. He set off again at a run. Saeng braced herself with an arm at his armoured neck.

They came to another gate, this one facing north. From the untrammelled ground it appeared that no one had come this way for a very long time. Hanu set her down. *'I know we should at least reconnoitre,'* he sent, then he motioned for her to follow him at a distance, and edged forward towards the gate.

The interior was a series of narrow courts separated by walls and gates. Covered walks lined the walls. Carvings depicted a series of battles against inhuman forces, giants and half-humans such as those she'd met populating the jungle today. Saeng was reminded of the ancient legends of the God-King as a great conqueror who subdued the entire continent. It occurred to her that what she was looking at here was a record of human ascension. Perhaps they revered him because he had won them their lands.

Yet the earthworks, the mounds, all were so incredibly ancient. Did it all go back that far? The thought of such an immense gulf of time made her dizzy. Perhaps, she considered, people had been here already – just a different tribe or offshoot of humanity. Forebears painted as monsters in retrospect.

They *were* nearing something. She could feel it pressing against her like a driving wind coming out of a place where no wind should come. Her flesh prickled with the power being summoned, leashed and contained. *All to compel a god.*

Hanu returned and gestured her forward. She ran a hand along the damp chill stone inner wall of an arch as she went. Grit from the old stones came away against her palm. *Crumbling away even as I touch it.*

He motioned to one side along another covered walkway. They were near the centre structure, a tall narrow stupa-like tower, but Hanu was pointing down here. She edged around to see that the wall of the inner temple possessed a narrow gap, an opening leading down.

'*What do you think?*'

She nodded. Yes, down. It felt right. Hanu went first and she hurried after. The stairway was so slim her shoulders brushed either wall, and the stone steps were so steep she had to take them one at a time. Below ground level the stones lining the way changed to a darker native rock and each block was much larger. These were also set exquisitely, without a hair's gap between.

An older construction – one pre-dating the temple above. *Of course! A sacred site retains its power. Newer faiths or creeds merely build atop the ruined old, each appropriating the older authority and presence.* That thought gave her an idea, and suddenly all did not appear as hopeless as before.

As they descended, a flickering light grew ahead. Not daylight, which was fading behind them, but an argent and white surging that Saeng recognized as raw puissance. They emerged into a wide chamber built entirely of the cyclopean basaltic blocks. At its centre was a raised dais, or altar, carved from the same dark stone. Set within the stone lay a multi-rayed sun symbol that glowed as if formed of gold itself. It probably represented the immense league-spanning earthworks surrounding this structure, that perhaps even extended all the way across the continent. The Locus. The focal point of immense energies tapping the entire land.

Sizzling and crackling on the dais stood a pillar of that enormous might, drawn like an inverted waterfall up to the ceiling and through a tiny aperture, presumably to the chamber above where the Thaumaturgs, having summoned it, now strove to manipulate and control it.

Saeng stared, awestruck, her gaze shielded against the glare. How could anyone hope to contain such astounding power? No wonder they seemed unaware of her presence – they were quite preoccupied, enmeshed in a fight for their lives. She knew that even to approach such a cascade would blast her to ashes instantly; and the Circle above fought now to actually direct it.

She lowered her gaze to the dais. This was the key. It had originally been an altar sanctified to Light – the worship of the Sun and the Sky. The cult of which others had recognized her as High Priestess. She knew then what she had to do.

She merely had to claim it.

She turned to Hanu. The truth must have been in her eyes for he glanced from her to the dais. He waved a negative. '*No! There must be another way. I will try to break it . . .*'

'*This is how it must be,*' she sent to him.

'*No! There must—*' He broke off, spinning to the entrance.

Saeng turned and had a shocked single glimpse of a ragged figure, a ghost from the awful days just past: Myint herself, pale and haggard, her armour torn, her hair a gnarled mat. Insane glee blazed in her eyes as she launched herself from the steps of the entrance, her spear levelled at Hanu.

The keen weapon struck home. And with Myint's entire weight falling behind the thrust the blade penetrated to emerge glistening with blood from Hanu's back. He toppled to his side.

More figures followed. In scuttled Thet-mun, hunched, emaciated, dirt-smeared, his eyes huge as he stared about, terrified. And last came the one she somehow knew would be leading them still: Kenjak Ashevajak, the so-called Bandit Lord. He'd had most of the swagger kicked out of him, but he still carried a smirk that he now bestowed on her.

She ignored them all to run to Hanu's side. She brushed her hands over him; she had no idea where to start, what to do. Blood ran from his wound and the sight horrified her.

'*Run,*' he sent to her.

Hands yanked her upright and spun her about to face Kenjak. He stepped up so close she could smell his stale sweat, see the dirt and grime blackening his pores. He stared at her as if he too could not believe that they had at last met again.

The smirk grew into a secretive smile and his gaze became almost tender. 'I've been following you,' he whispered, just audible over the roar of the energies filling the chamber.

Saeng felt her shoulders fall as the realization struck. *Of course! The wild men of the woods. What a fool I've been!* 'Kenjak,' she began, speaking very slowly, 'you must listen to me. You mustn't interfere here. This is very important.'

He waved for silence and the hands, Myint's, tightened about her neck. He stepped up even closer, close enough to kiss her. 'Oh, *important*,' he said, mocking her delivery. 'Well . . . I have something important to do as well.' He raised a blade between their faces. 'Something I've had to wait far too long to do.'

The hands were vices at her neck but she forced out, 'Jak – I'm worth much more alive.'

'Fuck that!' he yelled spraying spittle in her face. 'Fuck them all! I swore I'd have your head and I mean to collect.' He pressed the blade's razor edge under her chin.

The man is insane! Utterly transported with hatred. What can I do? There is nothing. Absolutely nothing.

The hands at her throat flew away. Gagging sounded behind her. Jak's gaze shifted to over her shoulder and puzzlement creased his brow. 'What . . . ?' He jerked back a step, knocking Saeng backwards into the side of the dais. Another figure now blocked the entrance and Saeng thought dazedly, *Of course – why not?*

It was the Thaumaturg, Pon-lor. He appeared even worse for wear than these ragged bandits. Saeng couldn't even believe he was standing; dried caked blood covered his shoulder and side. The left side of his head was a crusted wound. One eye stared upwards but the other was fixed upon Jak. A smile that could only be described as ironic crooked one edge of the man's mouth.

'No . . .' Jak breathed. 'You are dead. You must be . . .'

The horrific figure mouthed something. His words were distorted, but Saeng understood despite the sizzling and crackling punishing her ears: 'Perhaps I am. No matter.'

Something thumped to the ground and Saeng peered over to see Myint, her face contorted in terror and utterly bloodless, her own hands at her throat. *Had he compelled that? Self-throttling? Or had she died fighting for breath?*

Thet-mun appeared from behind the dais to throw himself at Pon-lor's feet. 'I am yours again!' he pleaded. He raised his hands as if in prayer. 'Please! I will serve. Remember? Remember how I served you before? Yes?'

Jak leaped to take Saeng's arm. He pressed the knife to her neck

530

once more. Yet she could hardly spare all this any attention, for the blood continued to flow from Hanu, and his chest rose with such effort, and so slowly.

The Thaumaturg looked down – or rather one eye shifted to peer down. The other continued to look off in another direction. 'Thet,' he mumbled from the side of his mouth, 'I told you. I warned you. Go home, I said.'

Thet, his hands clasped together, nodded eagerly. 'Yes! I will! I promise.'

Pon-lor shook his head. 'No. I'm sorry . . . it is too late.'

The lad looked confused. He lowered his hands. 'What . . . ?'

Pon-lor gestured with one hand and Thet seemed to sag. He slumped to the ground and continued to spread out, running, flowing, until all that was left was wet gleaming bones and limp clothes amid a pool of fluids that disappeared into the cracks of the floor.

The Thaumaturg's single eye now rose to Jak, who flinched and pushed the blade even harder into Saeng's neck. She felt warmth running down her shirt-front from the cut he made. 'I'll kill her!' he yelled. 'I swear!'

Pon-lor just shook his head as if all this was so very tiring. 'Jak . . . I'm sorry, but she could have destroyed you at any time of her choosing.'

The blade withdrew a fraction. 'What?' he said, mystified.

And Saeng knew it was the truth even as Pon-lor said it. *Yes . . . I could have. I am standing next to a source of power unmatched in this age and all I have to do is reach out – yet they will know the instant I do.*

'But unlike you,' the young Thaumaturg continued, 'she is no murderer. You should thank her. I, however, do not share such high principles.' He curled the fingers of his left hand – his right had so far hung limp at his side – and Jak was yanked from Saeng's side as surely as if he'd been plucked from a cliff. The bandit leader fell to his knees before Pon-lor.

'Go ahead!' the youth bellowed. 'You rich bastards always win in the end, don't you? Spoiled brat! It isn't fair! You've had all the advantages all your life!' The Bandit Lord was fighting tears and Saeng now saw how he was perhaps even younger than she, or the mage.

Pon-lor continued to shake his head, as if saddened by this entire affair. 'Jak . . . you have no idea. You grew up in a village, yes? In a family, with a father and a mother, a place to sleep, food on your table . . .' He grimaced and his odd eye rolled aimlessly. 'I cannot remember my childhood. There are images . . .' he winced again, pained. 'Jak . . . I was taken by the Thaumaturgs from the streets of Anditi Pura where I'd been abandoned to fend for myself. I never knew my mother or my father. I grew up sleeping in alleyways that were nothing more than open sewers. I fought packs of dogs for trash thrown into gutters. I throttled other children over rags and scraps of food you yourself would have turned away from in disgust. I . . .' His voice caught and he blinked to master himself. Tears fell from both eyes. 'And here you . . . Well, no matter. Your only defence is that you are utterly ignorant. Similarly, however, your crime is that you chose to remain ignorant. Therefore, I condemn you for wilful ignorance and blind self-centred self-pity.'

Pon-lor clenched his one good hand and Jak gagged. He dropped his dagger. His hands flew to his neck as if he would prise unseen fetters from round his throat.

'Choke on the truth you have rejected all your life, Kenjak Ashevajak – Bandit Lord.'

Jak tottered, gagging yet, and fell. His breath, together with all the tension in his convulsing frame, sighed from him in one last long exhalation and he stilled.

Saeng blinked. The spell that had held her fascinated faded away. She ran past Pon-lor to kneel at her brother's side. *'Hanu! Speak to me!'* she sent, pleading.

No answer came, though his chest still rose and fell in light panted breaths.

Pon-lor limped to her. He took hold of her arm to lift her to her feet. 'I will do what I can to heal him. You must do what you have to.'

She squeezed his shoulder, looked up to meet his good eye. 'Yes! Thank you. And . . . I'm sorry . . . I was wrong.'

'As was I. You were right all along. Now go. Do what you can.'

'But they will know!'

'I will hold them off for as long as I can.'

'But you are no master!'

A sad half-smile lifted one edge of his mouth. 'As you can see, my mind is now working in a strange new way. I see things . . . differently. In a way none of them can. They will find it very difficult to penetrate my thoughts. Now go.'

He urged her away, but before he released her arm it seemed as if he would lower his face to her, only to quickly turn away to Hanu. She caught his hand and squeezed it and the brow over his good eye rose in surprise, and gratitude. She turned to the pillar of coursing energies and readied herself.

The trick, she knew, was to allow the power to run through one's self without any interference or attempt at redirection. That was the hard part – resisting the urge to manipulate. Terror alone would drive her to do so. The driving urge to self-preservation.

She glanced back to see Pon-lor demonstrating surprising strength in snapping the spear haft then yanking it one-handed from Hanu's armoured back. Encouraged by that, she stepped up on to the dais. She had her defences raised as tautly as she knew how, yet even so the raging stream of spinning sizzling power appeared to be able to snuff her to ashes instantly. She had to yield to what had been instilled in her all these many years: the training, the discipline, the insights. But most of all, the trust. Trust in one's abilities. Trust enough to make that leap, and that release.

All her powers heightened, her arms out, she stepped into the flow.

*   *   *

Murk decided that he was getting the feel for this jungle tramping. All one had to do was turn one's expectations completely round – that was all. Instead of hacking and slashing one's way through the dense brush all one had to do was let go the idea of beating it down. Which was pretty much impossible anyway. What you had to do was slip through all kinda sideways and there you went. It was just another way of moving. A way that didn't push against all the league after league of spines and trees and poisonous vines.

And as for all the damned biting, stinging and sucking bugs – once you had a thick enough layer of dirt smeared over you and kept there by your oils and sweat, they never bothered you again. It was like they couldn't smell you any more. Just like Sour said. There you go. His partner had finally found his place in the world. And it was the one place no one else wanted ever to be. Go figure it. Well, once they returned to civilization he'd be blundering round once more all wide-eyed stupid, and Murk'd have to take him in hand again.

And the diet. Well, once you got your head round the obvious idea that you really ought to eat what was literally growin' on the trees around you and crawlin' all over everything in limitless numbers, then your problem was solved. As to the taste, well, that wasn't so bad once you got used to it. Tasted like nuts, really.

He walked near the middle of the loose column alongside the litter with Dee and Ostler. Sour had survived his mission to cut off the arm of a Seguleh but it had been a close thing. The woman had grabbed his throat the moment she understood what was going on and only the intervention of her employer, Rissan, had saved the man's life. He was out front now, ranging with the scouts. Their guest walked with the captain towards the rear. The bodyguard, Ina, had lived up to the reputation of the Seguleh in being back on her feet the day after the amputation. She walked behind Rissan. The stump ending at her elbow was wrapped in cloth and tied tight to her body. She hadn't said a thing to anyone since that night and walked with her head hanging low. Murk thought he understood something of what she must be feeling. Imagine, a one-armed Seguleh! Sounded like a bad joke. Still, if she really was one, then even with her off hand she was probably more deadly than any of them.

The going was easier now. They'd entered a region of open park-like woods. The upper canopy was solid, but below, the ground was mostly open, even dusty, with almost no brush. It looked almost manicured. He saw files of ants walking along, each carrying off a piece of the fallen leaf litter. The mystery, then, of where all the fallen detritus had gone was solved. They'd seen those half-creatures shadowing them at a discreet distance. So far, none had attacked. They seemed content merely to monitor their progress.

With the sun beating down it was now damned hot. Water was their main worry. Sour had them sucking on stems and fruits for moisture. Still, Murk was feeling the heat, and he knew the signs of water-starvation; he'd seen enough of it in the army. The night rains vanished instantly. Yusen had everyone capturing what they could in any remaining containers, while Sour showed them how to use big leaves to do the same.

As it was wont to do these last few days, Murk's gaze drifted down to the litter with its rags and the burden wrapped within. Was he doing the right thing? She'd expressed her will and he chose to respect that. Though doubts harried and bit at him like these damned bugs, he was still of the opinion that he was right to do so. It was a question not of right or wrong, but of respect. He had to respect this thing as a separate entity fully capable of making up its own mind. Even if it looked and sounded like a child.

Mercenaries running past shook him from his reverie. They were headed pell-mell for the front. Burastan came jogging to his side. 'A problem?' he demanded.

She jerked a hand to the rear. 'Our guest the sorceress says we've entered Jakal Viharn already.'

He scowled his puzzlement. 'What? That can't be right.' He waved to the surrounding jungle. 'There's nothing here.'

'All the same, Captain's ordered a halt. Call your partner.'

Murk nodded. He reached out to give his Warren the barest touch – just enough to send a message to Sour: *recall*. He motioned for Dee and Ostler to rest. The two big swordsmen eyed one another then shrugged and set down the litter.

Murk returned with Burastan to the rear. Here he found Yusen with the sorceress and her bodyguard. They were eyeing some sort of much weathered stone marker, or stela. Murk studied the flat, worn standing stone. The carving on its face had been reduced to nothing more than suggestions of lines and depressions. He turned to Rissan. 'You can read that?'

'I do not need to read it,' she answered. 'Its message is impregnated into it in many different ways.'

Murk gave it a one-eyed squint through his Warren. There was *something* there . . . but so faint, so damnably ancient. 'And what does it say?'

'It marks the boundary of Jakal Viharn.'

Murk snorted. 'There ain't nothing here. There's supposed to be a huge *city*. Temple towers, streets paved in gold. You know . . . fabled Jakal Viharn and such.'

The sorceress was unmoved. 'There was such a place here, once. Long ago. A large ceremonial centre servicing millions. But to call it a city . . . well . . .' She tilted her head. 'Those who saw it could only interpret it through their own experience . . . if you see what I mean.'

Yusen nodded, though Burastan was frowning, uncertain.

'We know cities,' Murk said, explaining, 'so that's what we called it.'

'Indeed.'

Sour and the scouts arrived. Yusen motioned them to him. 'We sit tight for the meantime. I want a careful look round first.'

Sour cocked one goggling bug-eye to Murk. 'You're up, partner.'

Murk scowled. *Great. Guess what? You get to go spy on the Witch-Queen Ardata.* He squinted up at the bright blue sky. 'Not in full on daylight. I want to wait for dusk.'

Yusen was rubbing a thumb over his chin. He nodded. 'Accepted.'

When dusk gathered under the trees and a deep purple took the eastern sky, Murk entered Jakal Viharn. He kept to the shadows, naturally enough. He'd been warned not to have Meanas raised

535

fully as Ardata would take it as a challenge; mild disguising of his presence, well, that was apparently acceptable.

He remembered his briefing – that was the only word he could think of for it – when their guest sorceress Rissan took him aside for 'a few words'.

'Do not go in with your Warren blazing,' she'd told him, rather imperiously.

'Hey,' he objected, 'I follow the spirit of Meanas.'

'Not entirely, I should hope,' she remarked coolly. She crossed her arms and regarded him critically. 'Now . . . if you should meet her or see her watching you, don't overtly respond. Don't run off, or duck away. Just lower your gaze and bow. Then go on your way. She's been treated like a goddess for ages here and she's become, how shall I put it . . . accustomed to it.'

'Any wards or protections I should know about?'

'I do not believe so.'

'Guards?'

'None that should accost you.'

He shrugged. 'Fine then. No problem. I'll just have a quick look round then report back.'

'I doubt you will see anything,' she answered. 'Jakal Viharn covers many square leagues.' She waved him on his way.

The woman's haughtiness had quite annoyed him at the time. *Must be some high muckety-muck back home.* Now, however, walking the treed grounds, he wondered how she came to such intimate knowledge of Ardata and her ways. Well, perhaps it was her particular area of expertise.

Even though he cloaked himself in the shifting shadows of Meanas, he kept to the verges and the gloom of trees. The sky was unusually clear this night; perhaps the rainy season was on the wane. The Visitor blazed like a literal vengeful eye of some falling god. It cast shadows as dense as spilled ink. Next to it the moon was a pale weak smear.

He walked and walked, and then he found he had to walk even more. Jakal Viharn, he realized, was just as their guest sorceress had asserted: an immense sprawling complex of countless temples, shrines, monasteries and plain enigmatic ruins. He even caught sight of the curve of a river where it glimmered in the dusk like a crimson snake. He realized he could wander for days without discovering anything. He might as well turn back now.

What to do. He idled within a grove of bamboo. The grove

crowded round a diminutive altar of ancient brick. Placed on the altar and before it lay countless carved stone heads – doubtless taken from the many statues he'd passed lying about half buried. It was a grisly collection of decapitated staring trophies. And he would have been most disturbed if he'd been the least bit superstitious and taken it as an omen.

Rissan, he reflected, had warned against any *overt* use of his Warren. And if it could ever be said that Shadow was *not* something, that would most certainly be overt. Therefore, he decided, a little oblique probing shouldn't go amiss. He eased his sensitivity outwards, passively, receiving impressions of movement among the infinite shadows flitting and dancing about Jakal Viharn. Scanning in an ever-broadening circle, he at last came to a concentration of moving shadows. Ambulatory. Could be anything: a group of night-foraging animals, a herd of restless water buffalo, who knew? But it was a lead, and so he started that way, jogging, his senses raised and now actively probing.

It was a good thing he had his Warren up for otherwise he would've walked right into the trap. It was masterfully laid; an ambush he never would've expected. His sensitivity warned him of it in good time and so he halted and began edging round, shadow-wrapped, disguised in the lineaments of night itself.

From the deep shade of a tree, he watched them. Three foreign soldiers keeping an eye on this obvious approach through the woods – the one he'd naturally almost taken. Two men and one woman. They still had their armour, albeit leathers. In all, they appeared to have weathered the entrance into Himatan better than his troop. He couldn't be certain where they hailed from, though they had the look of Quon types, tall and broad, with curly black hair on one. None had spoken yet, which troubled Murk: very professional. Too professional for out here in the middle of Himatan. What were they doing here? Who were they?

A cascade of liquid silver wavered down then over the scene, the moon breaching a cloud, and the fittings of their armour and weapons gleamed in the light. The woman shifted and the light caught her full on: her bunched thick mane piled high and pinned, her long coat of dark stained scaled leather armour, heavy longsword at her side, and he knew her, had heard of her often enough. If it were daylight that hair would be flame red and that armour the deep crimson of dried blood.

Jacinth, Skinner's lieutenant.

Murk slowly edged backwards. They'd come to negotiate with Ardata to escape these renegades.

But Skinner had got here first.

*   *   *

Shimmer lay in her hut unable to sleep. This night the ghosts of all the dead Avowed, the Brethren, were calling to her with an insistence that simply could not be ignored. She rose, pulled on her gambeson, belted her sword, and headed out to walk the camp.

She found almost everyone up already: Cole, Amatt and Turgal guarded the perimeter while K'azz stood at the near-dead smouldering fire. He was peering down, hands clasped behind his back, seemingly pensive, or perhaps studying the smoke for visions of the future, as some seers do. Lor emerged from the night accompanied by Gwynn; the two had fallen in together. Lor never was one to go very long between lovers.

K'azz raised his head and signed to the two mages that they should watch the perimeter. They nodded and separated. Shimmer moved to head off as well, but he motioned her to him. 'Stay with me, Shimmer,' he said, his voice tight.

'What is it?'

'What do you sense?'

She peered into the dense night, uneasy. 'The Brethren are . . . troubled.'

'Indeed. For many reasons.'

She studied his shadowed face, so stark and sharp in the contrast of light and dark. 'Why hasn't Ardata come to you?' she asked. 'She hired you, didn't she?'

'She requested that I come.'

'She demanded.'

'For her, Shimmer, that was as close to a request as is possible.'

'Nagal as much as blamed you for Rutana's death.'

'Yes, I know.'

'And now he won't even speak to us.'

'Yes.'

'Were they . . . related? Lovers?'

K'azz squinted at the smoke as if divining some message. 'You could say they are, were, two of a kind.'

'I see. So, what is the trouble? Is *he* close?'

K'azz nodded. 'Yes. As is . . . another. One stirring the Brethren by his presence.'

Shimmer frowned, considering. She couldn't think of anyone. 'Who?'

By way of answer K'azz dipped his head to direct her attention aside; she turned, hand on the long grip of her whipsword, to face that direction. Shortly, a wavering appeared over the grounds. Like heat waves dancing in the air. Though this was night. A shape took form, slim and dark, whip-lean in fact, in tattered dark silks. A pale hatchet-like face ghosted into vision beneath mussed black hair and Shimmer hissed out an appalled breath. She drew her sword.

'*Cowl!*'

The gangly scarecrow shape offered Shimmer a mocking bow. The others came running up, weapons ready. K'azz waved them down. 'Cowl,' he greeted the ex-Master Assassin and High Mage of the Crimson Guard.

The man executed a deep courtier's bow, his arms extended out from his sides. 'My lord.'

'This is impossible!' Shimmer burst out. 'We heard you were taken by an Azath!'

'You heard correctly,' he answered, his gaze fixed upon K'azz. The mage's eyes appeared almost to hunger so eagerly did they drink up the sight.

'None can escape the Azath.'

'You are wrong, obviously.'

'He was taken, Shimmer,' K'azz said. 'But he alone possessed one pre-existing means of escape. Is that not so, Cowl?'

The ex-High Mage nodded solemnly. His avid gaze edged to Shimmer. 'A prior commitment,' he said, and smiled.

Shimmer winced at the madness betrayed by that twisted ghastly smile. *Entombed by the Azath! Could anyone emerge sane from such a trial? And the man was hardly what anyone would call sane to begin with.*

The burning gaze slid back to K'azz. 'Skinner is near, Commander. What will you do? He has with him all his Disavowed. You are outnumbered ten to one.'

Shimmer spun to scan the surroundings. Skinner here? She looked to Cole and Amatt: both remained on guard, glancing back to them at the centre occasionally.

'I did not come to fight him,' K'azz said.

'No? Of course not.'

'You have a message from him?' K'azz asked.

Cowl shook an exaggerated negative. 'Oh, no. Not him. I am done with him now . . . now that I have glimpsed the truth.'

'The truth?'

'Oh yes. I came to bring it to you, K'azz . . .' the assassin raised a finger to him, chidingly, 'but I see now that you already know it. You have known it for some time but have kept it to yourself.' He snorted his scorn. 'You think that a mercy? Well, time will tell.'

'What is he going on about?' Shimmer demanded.

'Another time, Shimmer,' K'azz said.

'Yes, Lieutenant,' Cowl echoed. 'Another time.' And he bowed to K'azz again, withdrawing. 'Commander . . .'

Shimmer stared after him. Cowl, for as long as she had known him, had never bowed to anyone. Yet now he had to K'azz. Twice. The man he'd always been so open in his contempt for. What had changed? His imprisonment had shown him something. K'azz, he claimed, knew. And she would ask, though she already knew she would get no answer.

'Now what?' she asked K'azz.

'Now we wait.'

'For what?'

'For whoever will visit us next.'

'I do not like this passivity.'

A wintry smile climbed K'azz's skull-like features. 'This is Himatan, Shimmer. Visions and messages come to one of their own accord. One cannot demand inspiration.'

*   *   *

In retrospect, Osserc could not identify the precise moment when it happened. All he knew was that at one instant he was inwardly fuming against Gothos, and at the next he was suddenly fuming in impatience at himself. All his life he had steadfastly pursued what he saw as his duties and obligations – yet these he suddenly saw as nothing more than rag-thin substitutions, delusions and diversions. He had chased them with utter single-mindedness, yet how far had all this got him? What progress had he made? Towards anything? What had he to show for all this time? Precious little progress towards . . . what? What was it he really desired? Reconciliation or forgiveness? No, too wretched and backward-looking, that.

And always it had been the fault of others: of Anomander's interference, of the Azathanai's machinations. T'riss, Envy, all the scheming Elders. The Jaghut. Whoever. Anyone, perhaps, other than himself. Yet was that really the truth? Could he really be as pathetic as all those he had sneered at all these ages? In a way, of course – for was he not of them?

What then did he lack? He decided that, oddly enough, it was the one thing he had thought he in no way lacked: courage. Not the physical courage to face challenges. That he had in abundance. No, what he lacked, it seemed, was emotional courage. The courage to face the hard interior truths and make the hard choices.

There. He had finally reached it.

And it was something that could never have been imposed from without, of course.

The answer lies within you. Ah. And of course self-evident . . . with the luxury of looking back.

He tipped his head ever so slightly to Gothos across the table. 'Thank you, prick.'

The Jaghut raised a grizzled brow. 'I? I did nothing.'

'I know. As was required. And anticipated.' He stood. 'I will go now. If I ever see you again it will be too soon.'

'Who knows what the future holds – Tiste Liosan.'

Osserc again fractionally inclined his head in farewell. He walked up the hall. Here, curled up asleep before the door, he found the Nacht creature. He gently nudged it aside with a sandalled foot. *Farewell, Azath. Perhaps I shall never encounter you again either. And I hope not. Your lessons are far too . . . demanding.* He lifted the latch and pushed open the rough, adzed plank door, and stepped outside.

In the grounds, halfway up the short flagged walk to the front gate, he paused. A troubled frown crossed his brow and he turned his face to the southwest.

The Visitor looms as ever. Yet that is not my concern. Others address that. No, there is something else going on. Power is being gathered. All to a purpose. And that purpose . . . somehow it touches upon . . . Thyrllan.

He staggered as if from a blow to the chest. He raised his fists to the south. 'No!' came the groan, torn from his throat.

They must not!

CHAPTER XV

Over the years it became obvious that our annexation of the jungle region bordering the Gangrek Mounts would never be complete until we could rid ourselves of these bothersome wild forest people. Therefore, a great line of soldiers was organized of many thousands of men and through the banging of arms and the setting of fires, these families were driven to the edges of the mounts and all there were put to the sword. In this fashion the land was reclaimed for proper settlement and the opening up to agriculture and development.

Author unnamed
Papers of the Thaumaturg Archives

FOR PON-LOR, SAENG'S PROBING AND TENTATIVE STRUGGLE TO GAIN control of the Thaumaturgs' ritual took place in an enlightening double vision. Through one eye he beheld the chamber: the ray-burst sigil of poured hammered gold, the coursing sizzling pillar of energy, and Saeng herself enmeshed within, arms raised, eyes closed in profound concentration. Through his other orb he beheld a bizarre manifestation he could only interpret as a glimpse of those foreign magical disciplines named Warrens, or, long ago, Holds. Beneath Saeng's feet the gold appeared to be a molten poured pool: it shook with the lashings of power. The surface jumped and dimpled. At times it appeared so brilliant it could not possibly consist of any physical substance he knew but only of liquid light itself, flashing into existence, rippling and glaring, as if struggling to burst through.

Almost immediately the first of the masters arrived within the chamber. Pon-lor was not surprised to see Shu-jen, the Ninth. He grasped the man's mind before he could study Saeng's efforts and communicate with his brothers. The master responded superbly.

He would have overcome Pon-lor had the latter not possessed his unique advantage. He succeeded in interrupting the man's heart, then released him to stagger, gasping and staring sightlessly, and fall.

Three appeared next. Pon-lor engaged them all at once, keeping them occupied so that they could not direct their attention to Saeng. They turned to the attack immediately, hoping to rid themselves of him. Pon-lor allowed their terrifyingly strong efforts to slide through into the broken landscape of his mind where two became irretrievably lost and confused. The third managed to escape the trap, pulling his consciousness back just in time. Pon-lor pursued. He pushed his own jagged mismatched awareness into the master's mind, where it broke the fellow's identity in the manner of a thrown stone shattering a mirror.

He pulled back then in a panic as he sensed he was not alone. The remaining five of the Circle of Masters now stood about the circumference of the chamber. Their glittering narrowed gazes were all fixed on Saeng where she stood just visible within the roaring puissance.

The Prime Master transferred his attention and stood forward: Surin, tall and straight despite his extraordinarily extended years. He raised a finger. 'I remember you from classes. Pon-lor, yes? Promising material. You have done well, but now we are aware of your . . . condition. It is fatal, you know.'

Pon-lor nodded. He was mentally exhausted and knew he could not overcome all five – as they knew as well. 'Eventually,' he agreed.

Surin shook his lean hound's head as if in regret. 'You fool. Do you not understand who is coming? He must be destroyed at all costs! It is our sacred trust to do so. We guard against all such threats. It is the purpose of our order. You know this, yes?'

Pon-lor stood weaving, hardly able to control his body. 'I'm beginning to suspect that he simply kept you contained and so you tried to get rid of him.'

'Poisonous revisionism! You are dangerous indeed.' He nodded to his fellows. 'Continue.' His raised hand clenched to a fist and Pon-lor gasped as something took hold of his heart. His chest wrenched as if torn. A great vice had hold of his ribs and was tightening. He fell to his knees. Distantly, in a blur, he sensed the ritual spiralling inwards. It was condensing and concentrating to its final compelling. His one good eye remained fixed upon Surin as he fought the power striving to pulp his heart. His other eye, meanwhile, gazed upon the argent bands of energy as they writhed and spun, the silhouette of Saeng within. Even as both eyes dimmed, it was plain to him that the brilliant gold of the ray-burst now outshone the pulsing energies, and that light eventually completely overcame his vision.

The crushing pressure upon his chest eased. He blinked to see Surin now staring at the dais, horror on his face. He waved his arms, shouted. Movement disturbed the shadows behind the Prime Master and a tall shape loomed forward. It glittered from a thousand points like a field of stars. A flash of silver and the master's expression eased into puzzlement. Then the head slid aside and toppled from the torso. The body fell. Hanu, behind, tottered to steady himself upon his huge yataghan blade.

The remaining four masters at the compass points now shared their leader's panic. They sought to extricate themselves from a ritual invocation gone far beyond their control. Lineaments of the energies crept up invisible lines towards their hands.

The summoned energies continued to tighten and coalesce into one solid bar of argent light so searing as to glow white. Within, barely visible, was Saeng, arms still upraised, face pointed to the sky. Yet even as Pon-lor levered himself to his feet he could see that something had changed. She was lower. Sinking, in fact, into the liquid light that now grasped her knees. It appeared to Pon-lor's odd eye that she held something in her cupped hands: an object of pure brilliance – the source of the argent.

A questing lightning-tongue of energy reached the hand of one flailing master. The flesh and bones flashed instantly into ash and motes of soot that floated about him. The tendril continued creeping up his entire arm until that too had disappeared into ash.

All the masters screamed soundlessly as the tendrils found them. Each was consumed piece by piece by the flickering tongues. Pon-lor limped down to the dais where he shaded his gaze to try to make out Saeng's form. She had descended further into what could not be gold now at all, but rather swirling raw power, perhaps akin in form to that he'd read Chaos itself might take. It coursed upwards in a narrow, focused band that ran through her cupped hands.

As Pon-lor watched, helpless, her head sank below the surface. Only her arms were visible now, still upraised, holding what might or might not be anything more than some sort of kernel, or seed, of concentrated power.

Her hands slid down to the coursing glittering surface of shimmering energies and the bar of power snapped out of existence. In the resulting darkness his one good eye was blind, but the other saw the glowing ray-burst sigil pulsing like a fallen star. A huge shape moved next to him and Hanu thrust his arm down into the concentrated liquid energy. The stone armour glowed red, then slurried away in streams of molten rock that smoked and sparked.

The arm emerged holding Saeng's. With both hands he heaved her from the dais to the floor where she lay naked, her body smoking.

'We must go!' Pon-lor shouted, still deafened by the roaring.

Hanu nodded ponderously, and picked up his sister. In passing, he also snatched up a cloak from one dead Thaumaturg and draped it over her.

Light filled the chamber, blinding Pon-lor's one good eye once again. It came pouring in through the narrow entrance like water from a bucket – an absolute solid gushing radiance that then snapped away just as instantly.

'Something has come,' Pon-lor panted into the silence that followed. He motioned to the entrance.

They emerged into the temple grounds and all seemed normal and mundane. It was still light. The Visitor still hung low in the west. But now a slim dark cloud rose into the sky over the top of the intervening halls and squat towers of the temple complex. It was churning, impossibly narrow. It seemed to stretch as it reached for the heights, and was as black as soot. It climbed enormously tall then its top swelled out into a great suspended circular crown of night.

A strong wind blew out of the west and stirred the surrounding treetops. Torn leaves and branches soared overhead. An avalanche-like roaring reached Pon-lor's punished ears. 'Take cover!' he yelled to Hanu then dived behind a wall. Hanu knelt over Saeng.

Something struck the walls, towers and colonnaded walks of the temple complex. A great swatting hand came out of the west. Pon-lor could not close his odd eye. It stared skyward and there it witnessed entire giant trees come tumbling overhead; boulders and stones, sections of stone arches, the top of a well, an animal flailing its limbs, and black clouds of a near-infinite amount of dirt and sand and dust.

In that lashing storm Pon-lor found himself in the odd position of the helpless bystander as the broken fragments of his mind finally drifted out of touch with one another. Slowly, as the storm lashed him without, he could only watch while an inner storm drove the disparate fragments of his consciousness, one by one, out of his awareness. His memories, his reasoning, his very identity, became not only incoherent and unrecognizable, but utterly blank: empty gaps – entire parts of him gone, missing and irretrievable.

As the black dust and ash settled over his body, a similar darkness settled over his mind until it smothered his identity and consciousness into complete nothingness and he wandered lost and unremembering within his own skull.

*   *   *

For all Shimmer could tell it was perhaps four days later, or the next day, when she was with Lor, walking the grounds near their collection of huts. She was thinking that they had wasted enough time awaiting Ardata's indulgence and should just go. There was nothing for them here. It had been a mistake. Skinner would not show – the goddess and he were not on good terms. It was also in fact very dangerous for K'azz; Skinner might decide to eliminate him.

Lor, walking with her, suddenly snapped up her head, her long ash-blond hair whipping, and stopped. Shimmer followed her gaze to see Ardata herself sitting on the lowest step of a nearby stone stupa. She was attended by the young woman they had met their first day, wrapped in her folds of pure white silks.

She and Lor backed away towards camp.

As she went, she thought she saw the young woman studying her, and her gaze widening in a strange sort of shock.

Shimmer in return sensed something about her, but couldn't quite identify it at the moment. She turned away to head for camp. There, everyone was standing, eyeing the distant stupa and the woman in white robes with the cascading black hair. K'azz nodded to Shimmer. 'It would appear to be time for my audience,' he murmured to her, wryly.

'You shouldn't go alone.'

'You are right, of course. I shouldn't. But I will. Keep watch.'

'Of course.'

He headed off. Walking away in his torn shirt and trousers, so thin and wiry, he seemed achingly fragile; like some starving beggar or wretched vagabond. Shimmer motioned Gwynn to her. 'Anyone else around?'

The man rubbed his forehead, grimacing his pain. 'Impossible to tell. Ardata's presence saturates everything. But if we are blind, then so are they.'

She grunted her acknowledgement, her eyes on the two as they spoke. Ardata motioned and the young woman left them. Shimmer noted her limp.

The two spoke alone for some time. Neither raised their voice or gesticulated. K'azz then gestured aside, inviting, and they walked away into the woods. Shimmer watched until they passed out of sight.

'Should I follow?' Gwynn asked.

She shook her head. 'No. Allow them their privacy. There's nothing we can do to stop her from pulling something anyway. No. We will wait.' She eased herself down with her back to a tree, fanned herself to keep the bugs away. Cole and Amatt returned to preparing the palm leaves to be woven into the roof of another hut. Turgal sat at their main hut and helped himself to a drink from the pot they kept topped with sweetwater. Gwynn and Lor were arguing about something while squinting off to the west.

Shimmer peered in that direction: the light did seem strange through the trees to the west. A new glow seemed to be diminishing the baleful emerald presence of the Visitor.

Lor and Gwynn sensed it first. They both jerked to their feet as if at a loud noise. Shimmer was quick to follow. She scanned the surroundings and what she discovered there made her shoulders fall. They were encircled by a ring of faces every one of which she knew. The full complement of the Disavowed. Skinner had brought everyone.

They drove Turgal ahead of them as they closed. The man himself came forward, his arms out, as if to say: Fancy meeting you lot here.

Gwynn, Shimmer noted, had squared off against Mara, while Lor eyed Petal. Shimmer turned her full attention to Skinner and was startled to see that the man was not armed. *If I could slay him all this would be over.* Her hand went to the grip of her whipsword. *He and I.*

She edged forward, knees bent, while Skinner merely watched, a strange grin playing about his mouth.

A flash blinded Shimmer then – coming out of the west. She blinked, quite dazzled, and rubbed at her eyes. Everyone round her was cursing the light. Then Lor screamed. Shimmer groped for her. She blinked away tears as she searched for her through dark spots floating before her eyes. She found her writhing on the ground, her hands at her face. Fresh blood smeared her eyes, mouth and nose. She was whimpering as if beyond agony.

'What is it?' Shimmer demanded, yelling.

'The Warrens,' Lor gurgled through a mouthful of blood. 'Struck!'

She straightened. *What is this? Some sort of censure from Ardata?* She saw Skinner leaning over a prostrate Mara. He turned his head to her and she returned her hand to her weapon. *Do it now, woman – end it!*

'Hold!' The voice cut across the grounds, unstrained, yet utterly commanding. Shimmer slipped her hand from her weapon. Skinner merely grinned, as if having read her mind.

The Disavowed parted and Ardata, accompanied by K'azz, entered.

'She'll kill you,' Shimmer whispered to Skinner.

He straightened and pushed back his dirty-blond hair. Leaning to her, he answered as if confiding a secret: 'She cannot kill me – no one can.' He tapped the black scales of his armour.

A surly 'Don't count on it' was the best she could manage.

Shimmer knelt again at Lor's side. The woman was unconscious, as were most of the rest of the mages: Gwynn, Mara, Petal and Red. Unconscious or weakly struggling, utterly incapacitated. She stood and peered about to catch the gaze of all the nearby Disavowed. None would meet her eye.

'What has happened here?' Skinner demanded of Ardata.

She was peering to the west and Shimmer was quite startled to see unguarded wonder, even amazement, upon her face. 'A surprise. A great surprise. Something very strange and . . . unexpected.' She seemed unable to wrest her gaze from that horizon.

'A disruption in the Warrens?' Shimmer asked.

'Far more than a disruption,' Ardata answered, distracted. 'An impact. But over now. The ripples diminish even as we speak.'

Next to Ardata, K'azz lightly tilted his head in greeting to his one-time lieutenant. 'Skinner.'

'K'azz,' Skinner answered. He bowed to Ardata. 'My apologies, m'lady.'

'Skinner,' she answered. With a visible effort, she turned her troubled gaze from the west. 'You may not believe me when I say this – but it is good to see you again.'

He bowed once more. Then he returned his attention to K'azz. He studied his old commander as if disappointed. 'It was foolish of you to come. That is, unless . . .' He raised one brow in an unspoken question.

Ardata's already thin lipless mouth tightened even further. 'You take much upon yourself, Skinner. Have a care.'

'A care? Very well . . . just what did you talk about?'

'We spoke of responsibilities,' K'azz supplied.

'Responsibilities? Really? Is that so. Well . . . I have responsibilities as well.' He gestured about to the Disavowed. 'To my people. To lead them to the most advantageous position I can gain for them. And so, in consideration of that, I ask that you stand aside as Commander of the Crimson Guard and allow me to ascend to that position. Really, K'azz. It would be for the best. I hear you do not seem very interested in any of this of late.'

Shimmer listened, horrified. Horrified because, in a ruthless light, the man's words possessed an awful logic. They were a mercenary company that took no contracts despite an empty treasury. That desperately needed to recruit to strengthen their numbers, yet hardly admitted any new members. That had sworn opposition to the Malazans, yet had withdrawn from all such direct opposition. And the prince was a commander who seemed completely uninterested in command. What, then, were they?

K'azz shook his head. It seemed to Shimmer that remorse pulled the skin tight about his eyes. 'No. I cannot stand aside. Nor can you remove me. We are stuck with each other. And so I ask you – and all those who chose to follow you – to return to the Guard.'

Skinner raised a hand for a moment's pause. 'Oh, I am thinking of returning to the Guard.' He beckoned to Shijel, who handed over one of his longswords. Skinner hefted it, getting a feel for the long slim blade. He returned his attention to K'azz and his mouth quirked up in that way it did when he was indulging his savage side. 'But I have a condition first.'

The light changed again and Shimmer could not help but glance to the west. Darkness now gathered there, rather prematurely. It was as if sunset had somehow crept in upon them, though she knew it was hours before twilight. Yet there it was, a swelling adumbral gloom, spreading to encompass the west, swallowing the sun.

K'azz did not move though he must know what the man intended. 'Do not do this, Skinner.' His tone was beseeching but Shimmer felt that it was not for his life that he feared. She thought that Skinner, however, would take it that way. And she knew she was right when she saw how his mouth twisted his disgust – *He thinks K'azz is pleading for his life. But if not that – then what* is *he doing?*

He raised the longsword in both hands like a headsman's axe. 'I will make it quick, K'azz.'

Do something, K'azz! Shimmer pleaded. *Why won't you do something?*

Ardata lifted a pale hand. 'Before you act, Skinner, I have one final request of you.'

He let the blade slowly fall but did not shift his gaze from K'azz. 'Oh?'

'Yes. And you will consider carefully before answering, won't you?'

Something in her tone warned him and he stepped back from K'azz to turn and give her his full attention. K'azz, for his part, merely lowered his gaze, his mouth clenched tight.

'Yes?' Skinner said.

'I ask you, Skinner, one final time, that you reconsider my offer and stand here at my side.'

He took a long slow breath, pushed back his bunched hair. 'We have been through this . . .'

'Consider carefully,' she warned him again.

'Ardata – m'lady. This . . . place . . . is not for me. I have no wish to remain.'

'No wish . . .' she echoed faintly, her brows crimping.

A distant clatter of dry branches and a flurry of leaves announced the arrival of a strong wind out of the west. It blustered through the grounds stirring up clouds of dust that everyone waved from their faces. Leaves and broken branches gyred about. Shimmer brushed the dark dust, mixed with a scattering of ash, from her shoulders and sleeves.

Ardata's dark eyes had been drawn again to the west, where they rested, full of puzzlement. A hand went to her white throat. 'No wish . . .' she repeated, as if to herself.

Skinner glanced about, uncertain. No one dared move as the goddess appeared to be approaching some decision that she seemed to dread. She turned back to Skinner. 'If you must go, then I must take back my gift.'

Now Skinner frowned, even more wary. 'You told me yourself,' he answered, speaking very carefully, 'that no one in the world would be able to do that. Not even you, should you wish it.'

'That is true. No one can take my gift from you,' she agreed. 'However . . . I can *ask* that it return to me.'

She held out her slim hand and beckoned. A metallic shifting and grating sounded, coming from Skinner who spun, peering down at himself, his brows now clenched. 'What is this . . . ?' he murmured.

Shimmer peered more closely as some sort of rippling gleamed from the long coat of mail. It was as if each link was moving of its own accord.

The scales were shifting, she was certain. Each seemed to wiggle individually. She thought she saw multiple legs unlocking as, in descending waves, each scale detached itself from its fellows.

Skinner spun faster. He slapped at himself. '*What is this* . . . ?' he shouted, panic in his voice.

'I am sorry, Skinner,' Ardata said, her voice sad, yet firm. 'I gave you every chance. But you have chosen to reject my gifts.'

Skinner then threw his head back and howled. The scales, Shimmer saw, were scales no longer. Each was a thin black spider the size of a coin. They were digging themselves into his flesh, perhaps gnawing their way in, disappearing into him. He fell, thrashing and shrieking in agony. Shimmer turned her face, yet could not look entirely away. An arm reached out, beckoning to Ardata, who merely watched, her face immobile.

Inhuman, Shimmer reminded herself, remembering K'azz's warning. *Not human.*

Skinner was now no more than a writhing pile of wiggling black spiders. Here and there patches of wet white bone gleamed through the heap. More and more of the skeleton revealed itself. The heaving and twisting of the heap slowed, then halted. The swarm of spiders hissed and squirmed amid the pale bones. Then Ardata lowered her hand and the spiders – if they were indeed mere spiders – scuttled off the carcass in a flowing slurry of midnight that made its way across the dusty ground to slip beneath the lip of her robes and disappear.

Shimmer fought a shudder and a heave of revulsion that would have doubled her over. She saw Mara staring, her face sickly grey and frozen in shock and disbelief. Cole, Amatt and Turgal all stared, their faces hardening, though not in triumph or victory but in anger, and Shimmer thought she understood. He might have betrayed them, abandoned the Guard, but in the end they were not pleased to see him fall for he was one of them.

Oh, Skinner. I am so sorry. We all tried to warn you. Yet you would not be turned from your path. You betrayed everyone, didn't you? And, in the end, so too were you.

In the long silence that followed, K'azz cleared his throat and murmured: 'Perilous indeed are the gifts of Ardata.'

'As are all the gifts of the Azathanai,' said a new voice.

Ardata spun. 'Who are you?'

It was a middle-aged woman in dirty torn robes. She bowed. Behind her stood a file of soldiers who appeared to Shimmer to be Quon Talian, yet were painted and dressed in native fashion in loose loincloths. They did, however, still have their weapons, which they carried in their hands or on belts about their shoulders. Two of the soldiers carried bodies over their shoulders – more unconscious mages perhaps.

'Just a sorceress,' the woman murmured.

'Yet you are not overcome in the . . . disturbance?'

'I managed to protect myself in time.'

'How very fortunate for you.' Ardata pressed her hand to her throat once more. She tilted her head and her voice fell to a low whisper: 'Do I know you . . . ?'

Shimmer felt the hairs of her neck stirring in the sudden crackling of energy in the air. *What is this? A confrontation? Who is this woman?*

'It is . . . *possible*,' the sorceress allowed.

'And what is it you wish?' Ardata asked, her attention full on the woman. Shimmer shivered upon seeing her robes stirring as if with a life of their own.

The newcomer was completely unruffled. 'I wish a great deal,' she answered offhandedly. 'First, however, we really ought to speak of your daughter.'

Ardata laughed, yet her hand clutched at her throat. 'You are mistaken. I have no daughter.'

The woman's face stiffened. 'That is a terrible thing to say, Ardata.'

The Queen of Witches threw her arms straight down, the fingers clawed. Dust swirled about her. Beneath Shimmer's sandalled feet the ground shuddered as if drummed. Rocks tumbled down nearby ruined walls. The tall palms swayed.

K'azz gestured, his hand signing the imperative: *retreat!*

Shijel darted forward to snatch his sword then ducked away, hunched. K'azz waved Shimmer back.

The sorceress beckoned aside, close to Shimmer. Backing away Shimmer bumped into someone. She spun to find the girl, or young woman, wrapped in her white robes. Yet for an instant she did not appear young. Rather, it was as if she were an aged crone, her face disfigured, the flesh swollen, grey and pebbled, the eyes clouded to blind white staring orbs. Shimmer reached out to steady her. At that moment she returned to the appearance of the young woman, her face pretty once more, elfin and heart-shaped. She peered up at Shimmer, searchingly. 'It *is* you,' she murmured, full of wonder. 'The one I have seen so often. Even when I was a child. Why is that?'

Shimmer stared, stricken. *Unmerciful gods! It is her. One and the same. The child, woman, crone. Oh, the fate that awaits you . . .* She rested her hands gently on the young woman's slim shoulders.

The girl, whose frightened gaze now peered at Ardata, jumped at the touch. She peered up, shivering, wary. She shuddered as if she were desperate to escape. 'Be brave,' Shimmer told her, her voice thick with emotion. 'Be brave.' The girl started in recognition, then gave a solemn determined nod.

Shimmer ached to hold her then but the sorceress beckoned again, calling, 'Come.'

'Strangers frighten her!' Ardata called.

The sorceress took the young woman's hand. She faced Ardata. 'Or perhaps it is you who are frightened that others should see her?'

A wordless animal snarl escaped the Queen of Witches. Power now rose about her in glimmering tendrils like the lacing of webbing. She threw out an arm, pointing. '*Who are you? How dare you?*'

The sorceress held the girl before her, hands on her shoulders. The ground between her and Ardata erupted into flames. The thin grass blew away in rising ash and soot. Then the soil crackled and smoked as if dropped into a crucible. It slumped into a growing pool of glowing liquid rock.

K'azz, Shimmer, her companions, the Avowed and Disavowed, all flinched back then. They shielded their faces against the blasting heat. A lean woman had been hovering close to the sorceress all this time. She had one good arm, the other bound to her side. At that moment she darted forward and wrapped her one arm round the girl to pull her aside. The woman's sandals, shirt and hair burst aflame as she did so. Soldiers rushed forward with a few tattered blankets to throw over her. Through the waves of heat and smoke it appeared to Shimmer that the girl was weeping.

'Let her go, Ardata,' the sorceress called through the crackling filaments. 'It is time to let go.'

'*Who are you!*' the Queen of Witches howled.

'Look closely . . . sister,' the sorceress answered.

Ardata jerked back a step, her eyes growing huge. 'No! Not you.'

The sorceress's voice came loud and reverberating: 'Let it all go, sister.'

'*No!*' She thrust her arms out and a coruscating wall of power washed towards the sorceress, only to halt suspended between them. The sorceress seemed to be holding it in place, somehow containing it.

K'azz bellowed over the roar in his best battlefield voice: '*Retreat!*'

Everyone now scrambled in earnest. The one-armed woman chaperoned the girl off while soldiers carried the unconscious, or bleary, mages. Shimmer saw Quon soldiers falling and being helped up by Disavowed as everyone fled in a panic from the titanic and still escalating confrontation.

Behind a set of low ruined walls and a broken bell-shaped tower, Shimmer paused and turned back to watch. A glaring light of summoned powers blazed from the clearing beyond. K'azz came to her side, as did an older officer whose bearing fairly shouted imperial service. Both forces gathered here all intermingled. One of the Quon soldiers was hurried over; he was supported by two others. This one wore only a loincloth, his hair a tangled mess. His goggling eyes were tearing, bloodshot, and he was squeezing his head as if to keep it from flying apart. 'Still too close!' he shouted to the officer, his words slurred. 'Just run for it!'

The officer caught K'azz's gaze and they shared a curt nod.

'Move out!' K'azz yelled.

Everyone set off once more at the fastest possible pace. Soldiers shared the burden of the staggering and dazed mages. Two ran past carrying Petal draped over a stretcher between them. The one-armed woman, singed, her hair half gone, actually scooped up the girl and took off with her at a run. Shimmer stared, amazed. *Damn! Who is that woman?*

Glancing back over her shoulder, she saw the top of a swelling dome of lightning-lanced power. It appeared to be chasing after them. The expanding wall of flickering energies swallowed trees and ruins as it came.

'*Hurry!*' she yelled, now truly panicked.

Everyone ran. They dodged trees, jumped the low stone foundations of buildings long gone. Far ahead, Black the Lesser pointed aside to a long earthwork mound. *Yes! Intervening ground.* The ragtag column curved in that direction.

When they reached the rear of the steep earthen mound they threw themselves down behind stone blocks and tall thick trees. Beyond the hillock, the sky blazed now with an astounding swelling concentration of power that appeared as bright as a sunrise. To the west, behind them, the sky hung a deep purple-black that choked the setting sun.

Then the bubble burst. That was the only way Shimmer could interpret what happened. A wave of pressure struck the mound a hammer blow and it juddered. Trees flew backwards from its crest. The wave hit them all like mattocks to the chest and Shimmer grunted, her breath knocked from her.

Dirt, dust and broken branches swept over and past them. Shimmer waved the dust from her, coughing, and searched among the crouched soldiers and Disavowed. She found the girl still with the one-armed woman. From the girl's shuddering Shimmer could tell she still wept. The woman appeared to be whispering soothingly to her.

After the dust and branches swirled away there came a descending wave of leaves, and intermingled with them fluttered countless flower petals. They rained down over everyone in tears of crimson, purest white and orange and pink. She plucked one from her arm to rub its skin-like smoothness in her fingers.

She allowed herself to fall back against the tree she'd taken shelter behind. She draped her arms over her knees and let out a long breath. It was over – yet *what* was over? Just what had happened? From her encounters with Ardata, and from what they heard, she could only guess that the being was somehow holding on to everything. The past, the present, the future. Grasping them all at once and not letting anything go. Not even discerning between them. And perhaps she could live like that, as one of these Elder Gods. But what of others? What of her daughter? If indeed the girl truly was her daughter – not that she had to be. She deserved a life regardless. Even if it would be a hard one.

Everyone lay where they had fallen, breathless, almost dazed. The mages groaned and held their heads, wiped dried blood from their faces. Sitting back, Shimmer studied the western horizon and the setting sun. She saw Black the Lesser approach K'azz and the commander rose to take his hand and they shook.

So we are reunited. As we should be. One company. One troop. One . . . family?

Her gaze went to the girl. She appeared to be asleep now, nestled in the lean woman's arm.

Shimmer let her head fall back. *Yes, sleep. Could use some of that now. Have a look in the morning.* She shut her eyes and allowed the muscles of her neck, shoulders, back and legs to unclench and fall into relaxation. And only then, finally, after weeks of fruitless searching, did she finally slip into a proper slumber.

*

Jatal opened his eyes to a landscape of undifferentiated grey. Pewter ash filled the air like a thick storm of drifting snow. It covered everything in pillow-like humps: the field of fallen tree trunks lying scattered for as far as he could see, the broken stripped branches, the scoured-smooth ground between. Even his arms, hands and legs lay beneath a downy layer of the flakes. He raised a hand to brush it away.

'Ah!' announced a disembodied voice nearby. 'You live!'

He peered about; he could see no one.

An ash-fleeced boulder nearby moved. It stood and stretched. The slate-hued powder fell away in great clouds.

'So, my friend – they missed!' Scarza announced. 'Us, in any case.'

'Mostly,' Jatal added, managing a self-mocking twist of a smile.

'Ah-ha! Glad to be alive, hey?'

Jatal's smile fell away. 'We must search for him.'

'I believe we will find him beneath a very large rock.'

'None the less.' Jatal struggled to rise. The half-Trell pushed him down. 'Do not attempt that yet. Rest. Recover.' He held out a singed black carcass about the size of a rat. 'Eat.'

Jatal took it and held it up to examine it. 'Did you cook this?'

'The firestorm did,' Scarza offered blithely. 'I believe it used to be some sort of tree-dwelling rodent.'

'Firestorm?'

'You do not remember?'

'No.'

'You saved my life.'

'I did?'

'You most certainly did.'

Jatal tried to tear some meat from the dry carcass. 'I don't remember.'

'"The stream!" You shouted that right away. I hadn't thought of it. But running back to the stream saved us.'

'What stream?'

Scarza bent and dug up a handful of clotted mud and ash. 'This one.'

'Ah. I see.' He felt his tattered robe and shirt. They *were* damp. He touched the back of his head where only bristles of hair remained. 'All I remember is that flash. Like the world ending. Golden light.' He did not mention that when they were running he thought he saw another bright gleam of light. It had come from the western horizon and had flashed a vivid emerald green.

He glanced up to the sky, squinting. The Visitor still glowed there, fat and monstrous, like a gibbous moon behind the thick churning black clouds. He pushed himself to his feet. There was no sense hanging about here. Nothing to eat or drink; they would only weaken – better to do that on the march. He struggled past Scarza who watched him go, his face falling into a deepening frown.

'You are in such a hurry to die?'

'Live or die, it matters not.'

Scarza called, 'There is nothing left of him!'

Jatal halted, peered back. 'No. He still lives. I am sure.'

The half-Trell rose, rubbing his jowls, and followed. 'How can you be so sure?'

'I am.'

~

They walked a nightmare landscape of blasted jungle and sludge-choked streams. Everywhere lay the flash-seared fallen trunks. Ash smothered everything. It still fell from the roiling clouds in great flurries that cloaked the distances. Jatal tore off a strip of cloth and tied it over his nose and mouth. It was like the sandstorms they sometimes endured in their homeland. Scarza merely tramped on, uncomplaining, brushing the powdery layer from his arms.

The trees, Jatal saw, had all been flattened in one direction – roughly angled from the southeast – the point of impact, he realized. If the demon were to be found anywhere, he imagined, it would be there. He started following the line marked by the fallen trunks.

'And if we find him?' Scarza asked much later that day. 'What then? I wanted to kill him. But now I'm tired of it. I'd rather just have a drink.'

Jatal ached with thirst as well, and he hungered. Such urges, however, were mere demands of the flesh – brute expectations of continued existence. An expectation he did not share. Sometimes he fancied he could see her face in the swirling clouds of ash. She was smiling down upon him.

Soon, my love. Soon. I shall give myself to you.

*

Saeng started awake from a strange dream; a sensation of drowning, oddly enough. Not since she was a child had she dreamed of drowning. Yet it hadn't been water she'd been slipping into – it had been a strange glowing liquid more like molten gold or some other white-hot metal.

Aside from the nightmare of that struggle, she felt physically rested, renewed even. Better than she had since leaving home. She stirred and opened her eyes: she lay in what she recognized as the temple grounds. Dirt covered everything, and over that lay a pillowy layer of ash. White drifting flakes still fell in a light snow. All was eerily silent. Her ears rang with the quiet after the constant cacophony of the jungle.

She tried to stand and reached out to steady herself. Her hand rested on a hump next to her that felt familiar. She brushed the ash and dirt away to reveal Hanu's gleaming mosaic of inlaid armour. She rushed to clear his helmed head.

'Hanu!'

She listened, her breathing heavy, but he did not answer.

'Hanu – speak to me!' she sent to his thoughts.

Still he was silent. She ran a hand down his chest to find a sticky layer of congealed ash and dirt. Her hand came away smeared.

Oh, Hanu . . . I'm so sorry . . .

She gently lowered her head to his side and wept.

After that she slept again for a time. When she awakened once more she kissed his helm on its forehead and pushed herself up. She'd been wrapped in a loose cloak, and this she adjusted as best she could. She remembered, vaguely, that there had been others as well – the Thaumaturg mage, Pon-lor. She looked back to the main temple: it had collapsed into a heap of cut stone blocks. So, he too. *I am sorry, Thaumaturg. I misjudged you.*

She turned away to trace her route back. Her sandalled feet pushed through the thick blanket of ash. The pale flakes dusted her robes, hair and eyelashes. Soon, she came to a trail through the heaped layers. She followed it to one of the colonnaded walks of the temple complex that led to a hall and an arched opening facing west. The arch was tilted rather alarmingly, and the stone floor was uneven, the stones having been pushed up here and there. Sitting in the threshold of the pointed arch, facing away, was a familiar figure: the Thaumaturg himself.

'Pon-lor!' she called.

He did not respond. She came up behind him. Still he did not move. Close now, above and behind him, she believed she saw why. The entire left side of his head was a misshapen mess of weeping fluids caked and crusted in blood and dusted in ash.

Slowly, she came round him to stand before him. His eyes were open but no recognition lit them. Indeed, nothing inhabited them. They stared sightlessly, inanimate, like painted orbs on a statue. Tentatively, she reached out to touch his chest. He breathed still, and his heart beat. But he was no longer present. She had seen such things before in her village. Severe fevers had left their victims like this. Then, the only answer had been the mercy of a swift gentle death.

Something she could not bring herself to do. Yet what could she do? She couldn't just walk away. She sat down next to him, took his cold unresponsive hand in hers, and thought about it.

She looked to the west as well. What had drawn him here? Some atavistic memory or urge? What had he been searching for, or looking at?

Far off, the dense black clouds had dispersed. Only much higher, thinner clouds remained. The light pale ash was falling from these. It was late afternoon; the sun was now on its way down into the west. Its heat passed through the intervening high cloud cover to press against her face. The Visitor was still present, of course. But diminishing now. On its way back to wherever it had come from. Its baleful glow was nowhere as strong as it had been just days ago. Close by rode the moon as well. A pale smear hardly visible through the thin clouds. Soon, things would return to normal and it would be the brightest object in the night-time sky once again.

And then she knew just what she could do.

She stood in the archway and raised a hand. She formed a circle with her fingers and thumb that she held up to the moon where it hung in the sky. She raised her power and it came smoothly now, naturally, as if somehow melded with her as it had never been before.

And she sent a summons, casting it afar, urging: '*Come.*'

*   *   *

A poke to his shoulder awoke Murk. The first thing he noted was the worst headache in recent memory. He squeezed his head in his arms and groaned. Through slit eyes he peered about: he was lying against a tree, a light dusting of ash covering him and everything. Peering down at him was Sweetly. The twig stood straight out from his clamped shut mouth. The scout jerked his head to indicate he was wanted and in what direction.

Some things, it seemed, remained just the same.

Stretching and rubbing his brow, Murk walked across a litter of fallen branches. Aside, a confab of some sort was shaping up. Yusen together with Burastan faced the mercenary leader K'azz and his second, a short wiry woman he knew by reputation as Shimmer.

How similar yet utterly dissimilar the men were. Both pretending to be mercenaries, yet remaining far from it. Allies, they remained a mere sword's edge from sworn blood enemies: Malazans versus Crimson Guard.

Yusen nodded a greeting to Murk. K'azz eyed him guardedly.

'We've decided on a reconnoitre,' Yusen said. 'Are you and your partner up for it?'

'Yes, sir. We're good.'

'Okay. Have a look see and report back.'

Murk jerked his assent, gave a shallow nod to K'azz, and went to find Sour.

Together, they headed out of camp. Sour, it appeared, was in no better shape than he. The remnants of dried blood caked his face and he winced whenever the sunlight reached him.

'Why us?' he complained, his voice low. 'Why not one o' them fancy-pants Crimson Guard mages? Why should we be the ones to have to stick our necks out?'

Murk shrugged as he walked along. 'Musta been some kind of negotiation. A gesture of trust from K'azz, maybe. I don't know exactly.'

His partner slouched along next to him with his awkward crab-like gait. 'Oh, we're the famous Crimson Guard,' he minced. 'We're too fancy to do any work.'

Murk burst out laughing and had to stop walking. Sour's brows clenched together in puzzlement. 'Wazzat?'

Still chuckling, Murk waved it aside. 'Nothing. C'mon. It's just nice to know that things have returned to normal round here.'

Clear of the mound, they came across a broad squat tree that offered good cover from the sun. Murk picked a spot in the deepest shadow. Sour sat down with his back to a root. Murk crossed his legs and pressed his fingers together on his lap. 'So,' he said. 'That was one amazing blowup.'

'Sure was,' his partner agreed, his bulging eyes edging aside.

'Gonna 'fess up?'

''Fess up to what?'

'You knew who that was all along – didn't you?'

Sour blushed furiously, clearing his throat. 'Wasn't for me to say. She wanted to be all 'nonymous. So I played along.'

'Well . . . you could have told your partner.'

'Sorry. I was afraid she'd turn me into something.'

'You already are something, Sour.'

'Hunh?' His partner scrunched up his wrinkled face in puzzlement.

Murk sighed. 'Never mind. Let's have a look.'

Murk gently raised his Warren while tensed for an overt objection, or counter-gesture, from any other quarter. Sensing nothing, he slipped his awareness off a distance to the nearest deep shadow. Here he waited until he felt Sour's awareness keeping watch on him. Then he set off searching the grounds of Jakal Viharn.

The blast had knocked down many trees, but not all. The thinner, younger ones remained standing, albeit stripped of most of their branches. As for the many ruins dotting the grounds, well, to Murk they all looked pretty much the same: ruined.

He searched for some time, finding nothing. The place was empty, abandoned. The blast had driven off all the wildlife: the birds, the monkeys, even the deer he'd spotted foraging among the brush here and there. As for those half-creatures, call them what you would, none remained that he could find.

His poking about brought him down to the river where a number of ruins lay as little more than foundation lines, canted stupas and sturdy bell-shaped hollow cells or sculptures. Here he spotted someone he'd never seen before: a big hefty-looking fellow with long hair tied back with a clasp. He was sitting on the ground, legs crossed, thick arms draped over his knees. His gaze was resting aside and upwards, regarding someone or something. Murk shifted his point of view among the shadows until he could see what the man was studying.

It was a woman seated on a step before a broken heap of stones that might've been an altar at one time. She wore long loose white robes, her limbs were long and slim, and her black hair was cut quite short. As he saw her, so too did her gaze move to sharpen on him. She waved him forward and his heart lurched as a panicked tightening across his chest crushed it. *Shit! One's still here. But which?*

She waved again – yet not so imperiously as he imagined Ardata might have. He emerged from the shadows to start across the open grounds between. The giant fellow surged to his feet.

'It is all right, Nagal,' the woman said. Murk could not identify her by her voice; she sounded like neither of the Azathanai. The man, Nagal, edged protectively closer to the woman.

Murk halted a few paces distant and bowed. 'Whom do I have the honour of addressing?'

'Your manners should be a lesson to your master, mage of Meanas. But I am afraid there is little hope in that arena.'

Murk remained bowed, his eyes downcast, waiting.

A sigh escaped the woman. 'Very well.' Her robes brushed as she leaned forward. 'Shall I let you into a secret, Murken Warrow, mage of Shadow?'

Murk swallowed with difficulty. He wanted no secrets of the Azathanai. 'I seek no boon,' he answered softly.

'That is good. I see these last few lessons have not been lost upon you. No, no boon. Just a confession.' She lowered her voice even further. 'The truth is . . . not even I know for certain.'

'*It's T'riss*,' Sour's voice whispered in Murk's ear.

Murk raised his gaze. The Azathanai was peering beyond him, a playful smile at her lips. 'Greetings, Sour. You are well informed. As I would expect.'

'And the other?' Murk enquired slowly, 'if I may ask?'

'She has withdrawn. Released all that she ought to have released

561

ages ago. And who knows, perhaps she will learn to accept all she ought to have accepted all these ages. She no longer manifests a presence directly here in the mundane. As for the future,' she gave a small shrug, 'who can say?'

'A goddess in truth,' Murk murmured.

'Precisely. Together with all that comes with it – desired or not.'

'And yourself?' Murk asked, emboldened enough to lift a brow.

The woman's smile broadened and she spread her arms. 'Myself? I am merely an Enchantress. Nothing more. Now,' she waved them off, 'go get your superiors. I will speak with them.'

A small contingent was brought together. K'azz selected his lieutenant, Shimmer, together with two mages, Gwynn and Lor. Yusen brought Burastan, Murk and Sour. The girl came as well, accompanied by the swordswoman whom she clung to and wouldn't be parted from.

The party made its way across the grounds of Jakal Viharn. A fine white ash dusted everything like snow. It fell as a thin drifting sleet. The utter silence was almost a shock to Murk. Even their footsteps were smothered. It was as if they walked in another world, he imagined.

T'riss, if indeed it was she, awaited them as before. Murk noted that upon seeing the big man, Nagal, K'azz and party paused in recognition. He came to them before they reached the Enchantress.

'Nagal,' K'azz greeted him. 'I am sorry about Rutana.'

The giant nodded, frowning. He gazed down at his wide hands, clenched as if yet ready to grasp some foe. 'Even after what he did she still would not allow me . . .' His voice thickened until he could not continue and he lowered his head even further. 'I was so angered. I ran . . .'

'I'm sorry.'

The man nodded and walked away, his head lowered as he examined his knotted hands. K'azz turned to the Enchantress, who urged everyone forward. The girl ran ahead only to come to an abrupt halt as if shocked or uncertain. The Enchantress rose and embraced her. 'We will speak later, Lek. We have much to catch up.' She raised her gaze to the swordswoman. 'You too, Ina. After this.'

The swordswoman, Ina, nodded, and wrapped her one arm around the girl to lead her away. They walked a distance and sat together on the tumbled blocks of a fallen wall.

Murk watched them go feeling an ache in his own chest. Both wounded. Doesn't it make sense they should seek each other out?

The girl's vulnerability made him think of Celeste. Gone now, as well. He hoped she was not unhappy with her choice.

'Captain Yusen,' the Enchantress began sharply. 'I understand you have a request of me.'

'I do. We request transport out of Jacuruku.'

T'riss waved an assent. 'I will send you anywhere you wish to go. No doubt you will want time to discuss this with your troops.'

'Of course. Our thanks.' He gestured for Burastan and Murk and Sour to move off.

'Before you go, however,' the Enchantress continued, 'I possess some information that might bear upon your choice.'

Yusen turned back, his gaze tightening. 'Yes?'

'In Aren, Seven Cities. Since the killing of the Fist last year, there has been an investigation. It seems that his plans to usurp imperial authority have been uncovered, together with his murder of several officers who would not cooperate. His death diverted civil unrest that would have cost the lives of thousands. I believe the price upon the head of his killer, together with his fugitive followers, has been rescinded.'

Yusen remained utterly still. His gaze shifted to Burastan, whose eyes had grown huge. 'We will need time to discuss this,' he managed, his voice thick.

'Of course.'

Yusen and Burastan bowed and walked away. Murk watched them go. *What do you know? I would never have guessed. But I did wonder. Sour and I sniffed* something *there.*

The Enchantress turned to K'azz and after their gazes met for a moment Murk was surprised to see that it was she who lowered her eyes. After a long silence, she spoke down to her hands clasped on her lap: 'Do not ask that of me.'

'Then where, Enchantress?' The man's voice was brittle with suppressed emotion. 'Where must I go for my answer?'

'There is only one place left.' She spoke very slowly, as if reconsidering. 'But there is great danger. Not just to you . . .'

'I am asking for knowledge, Enchantress. Surely you would not be one to withhold that?'

Her answering smile was cold. Yet she tilted her head, granting the point. 'Very well. In only one place can you find your answers, K'azz . . . Assail. Only there.'

The mercenary commander received the news as if he'd been half expecting it. He nodded to himself as she spoke. 'My thanks, Enchantress.'

'Let us hope your thanks do not turn to curses.'

'Yes.'

'I also offer you transport back to Stratem.'

'That would be most welcome,' the mercenary commander answered, sounding very relieved.

'I am sure.'

He bowed, as did his lieutenant, Shimmer, and the mages. The Enchantress turned to Murk and Sour. 'Now . . . what can I do for you two?'

'As I said,' Murk answered, clearing his throat. 'I seek no gift.'

'Yes. However,' and she rose to lean close to him, 'I can offer you this.' And she brushed his cheek with her lips. Murk's knees went numb and he staggered, utterly shocked.

To his stunned puzzlement she said: 'That was for how you handled a very delicate relationship. I offer it in her place. Well done, Murken Warrow.'

Murk found himself walking off, a hand at his cheek, hardly aware of his surroundings. Well, damn, maybe he should take up worship of the Queen of Dreams. From this day forward she might just be the queen of *his* dreams anyway.

He must have been standing staring into the distance for some time when someone cleared her throat next to him. He started, blinking, and looked over. It was Burastan.

'She has that effect, doesn't she?' she said.

Murk rubbed his cheek. 'Yeah. She sure does.'

'C'mon. We're debating where to go. I'm all for returning straight to Aren. Yusen says no. He suggests some frontier town in Genabackis. Feel out the situation. What do you say?'

'Did he really kill the Fist of Aren?'

'Yeah. Stabbed him right over his briefing table. I did for his aides.'

'He was planning to declare himself ruler of Seven Cities?'

Her jaws worked as she chewed that. 'What he intended would have reopened old wounds. Terrible old wounds. It would have been a bloodbath. Yusen cut it off at the root. We wouldn't abandon him so he chose to run – exile.'

'I see. But now the Enchantress says you can return.'

'Yes! And so we should! C'mon, talk some sense into the man. You're good at that.'

Murk eyed the tall fierce woman sidelong. *I am? Since when?*

*

564

Ina had wanted to die, of course. That moment when she woke and saw what they had done. She felt no resentment against the mage, or the Enchantress – she understood they had done what they did to save her life. But would she have done the same? She'd heard it was one of the worst ways to go. Eaten alive from the inside out. She would've killed herself long before that.

At home there were places for the wounded. Honoured roles for those crippled in fighting: teacher, tutor, guard. Her wound was not gained in such a respectable fashion. Illness, sickness, had no place in her society. The weak were cast out, allowed to perish as they would. She had never given the practice a second thought. It was tradition. The way their forebears taught them. Now, however, she wondered at its fairness. Were the sick or malformed or maimed to be blamed for their affliction? Was it less 'purification' than plain intolerance?

She lowered her gaze to the child curled up at her side. She was brave, devoted, good-hearted and innocent. All the human values one would wish, yet wrapped in crippled flesh. Who was anyone to judge her? How dare anyone do so? The very thought affronted her to the core and brought a burning heat to her face. She realized she would kill anyone who dared.

There. That was more like it. Proper Seguleh thinking.

That was how the girl saved her life.

When the Enchantress T'riss came to them Ina had already made up her mind. And the way the sorceress looked at her, the secret smile on her lips, told Ina that she knew as well.

'So you will stay,' the Enchantress said.

'Yes. If I may.'

'Of course.' Her gaze lowered to rest gently on the girl. 'It looks as if you have a place here.'

Movement drew Ina's attention aside: that giant fellow had returned and now stood among the trees, watching, as if afraid to approach.

'Lek,' the Enchantress urged, quietly. 'Look who is here . . .'

The girl stirred, blinking. She found the man standing a little way off and her head snapped up. 'Nagal!' She ran to him with her limping hopping gait, and wrapped her arms round him. He patted her head.

'An old friend,' T'riss explained. 'You will not be entirely alone here.'

'Alone or not, there is no other place for us.'

The Enchantress peered round, nodding. 'Yes. You are lucky, I think. Lucky in what you have found.'

'And Ardata? What of her?'

The smile slipped away. 'I want to be generous, but I do not know. It seems that some are incapable of change or learning and because of this the lessons come all the harsher, and perhaps too late. We shall see. I understand that it took a millennium of imprisonment in his own creation for Draconus to admit that perhaps he'd been wrong. So, there is hope.'

'Then . . . she is gone?'

T'riss appeared surprised. 'Not at all. As I have heard said – just because you cannot see her doesn't mean she isn't here.'

'Ah. I see.' Ina gestured to the burnt prayer-scarves and fragments of offering bowls scattered about the grounds. 'Then the devout will continue their entreaties and the godhead will remain enigmatic . . . as is its definition.'

The Enchantress frowned mock disapproval. 'You Seguleh are a far too sceptical people.'

'Strange that I should end up here then.'

'Perhaps you are in need of more philosophy.' And with that, the Enchantress inclined her head in salute and went her way.

Ina sat for a time letting the sun's heat suffuse her while she worked on forcing herself to relax. It was difficult; she wasn't used to it. She glanced over to where Lek and Nagal talked. Lek, she saw, was urging him to come and speak to her. The big fellow actually appeared childishly shy. Strange how she would never have imagined that. Living here . . . new faces were probably a shock.

Many more will be coming now, though. Once word spreads. And of course they will look for the physical embodiment of what they are searching for. For Lek, daughter of their goddess.

She would have to begin teaching her soon.

*　　*　　*

He came in the night amid a burgeoning silver glow that suffused the temple grounds until all was lit as if by a lamp of white light. The youth, Ripan, led the way, piping an eerie and high energetic tune that sounded almost celebratory. Saeng sat waiting on a step. She held Pon-lor's head cradled on her lap.

Old Man Moon entered the grounds and bowed before Saeng. 'Congratulations, High Priestess.'

She snorted her embarrassment. 'High Priestess of what?'

The old man opened his hands. 'That is for you to shape. You are the priestess.'

She dropped her gaze, nodding. 'I see.'

'What would you have of me?'

'Can you heal him?'

The old man knelt on his skinny shanks, just as any village elder would. He studied Pon-lor. 'Hmmm. He has sustained ferocious damage to his skull and brain. And there is infection, swelling and fever. Normally such a mind would lie beyond recovery. However, the Thaumaturg mental training has served him well. He has managed to retain much of himself hidden away in disparate corners of his mind – so to speak.' His gaze rose to her and she was startled to see a silvery glow in the pupils of his eyes. 'And of course you are lucky in that this happens to be a particular speciality of mine.'

And though she knew the answer already, she asked: 'What is your price?'

His sly teasing smile told her his answer. He turned his head. 'Ripan. Start a fire.'

The youth's shoulders dropped. 'Must I?' he whined.

'A fire, Ripan.'

The youth slouched off, muttering and twirling his pipe.

Moon laid a hand on Pon-lor's forehead. 'Rest,' he murmured. 'Gather yourself . . . and remember.' He sat back, his lean arms akimbo on his knees. 'Now I shall collect the necessary ingredients.' He stood.

'Where . . . this time?' Saeng asked, dreading the answer.

Old Man Moon grinned down at her. 'Why – where you left off, of course.' He walked off, stiffly, like an elder.

I do believe he enjoys it far too much, she grumbled to herself.

Later, Old Man Moon returned to carry Pon-lor to a square of flat dressed paving stones, all brushed clean of dust and litter. A fire burned nearby. Ripan sat at it, looking bored and unhappy, his chin in one fist. A set of crude earthenware bowls lay next to the fire. Each possessed a stick that might have once been an offering. Indeed, all the objects struck Saeng as having been salvaged from the various nearby temple niches, shrines and altars. She wondered what effect this would have upon the procedure. All to increase its potency, no doubt.

She quickly looked away as Moon unceremoniously pulled at his ragged loin wrap. When he had lain down she looked back, forcing herself to eye his skinny shrunken buttocks – one half tattooed. 'I am to finish the job, am I?' she asked dryly.

'Indeed.'

The glow emanating from the being had changed, inverted itself. Now, as before, the countless bands of pricked-out stars in their constellations glowed with their liquid silvery light while his flesh seemed to absorb light in a black night-dark background. The star field that was his back gently turned before her eyes, mimicking, she knew, the very sky above. She felt that if she pitched forward over him she would fall for ever as if into nothingness.

She shook herself and realized that she had been staring, fascinated. 'As before?' she asked.

'If you would.' Lying on his stomach, his arms under his chin, he reached out and sketched with a fingertip. The lines he drew glowed with a cold limpid light on the stone. 'The blue ink, please.'

Saeng nodded and selected the roughly formed earthenware bowl that held a shimmering unearthly blue fluid. It gleamed like the sapphire light of some stars. She picked up a prayer stick, studied its sharpened end, then daubed it in the ink.

Crouching down over him, she set to work.

*

Murk returned to the treetops that night. He found that he now enjoyed sitting high up with his back against a trunk, his legs straight out, ankles crossed, on a fat branch. He watched the bright star field peeping through the intermittent cloud cover and the flashes of lightning from a rainstorm to the north. Bats swooped before his vision, chasing insects. The swollen head of the bright sky-spanning arch that was the Visitor was diminishing – passing beyond. Returning whence it came. The full moon shone down, reclaiming its rightful place as ruler of the night. To the west, the thick dark clouds were dispersing, drifting off. The leaves around him, however, still held their pale layer of ash.

So, it was over. Tomorrow the Enchantress would send them on to wherever they wished. Yusen had held firm in his insistence on a slow cautious approach to this news of imperial pardon. The troop would request to be sent to some minor frontier outpost where they'd test the truth of it.

What, then, of him and Sour? They'd completed their term of service, mustered out. Yet civilian life hadn't panned out as they'd wished. To tell the truth, he hadn't felt comfortable sitting around with nothing to do. And this lot was badly in need of someone to hold their hands.

Besides, if what the Enchantress claimed was true, Yusen might be up for some kind of commendation and promotion. He might make sub-Fist in Seven Cities. Cadre mage to a sub-Fist in Aren would be a pretty soft posting.

And he had to admit that he wouldn't mind getting to know Burastan better. There was something there, he was sure. Unless it was all just wishful thinking . . .

A gathering deep jade glow interrupted his consideration of strong shapely limbs. He glanced over, frowning, and was surprised to see a wavering image coming into existence here with him.

'Celeste? That you?' he asked, astonished.

The image solidified into the familiar shape of the girl and she smiled. 'Greetings, Murken Warrow.'

'Celeste? I thought you were gone. You know, melding or uniting, or whichever.'

'Yes. I am. This is merely one last fading remnant left behind to say goodbye.'

'Ah. I see. Well . . . thank you. You sound like you met with success, or satisfaction, or whatever.'

'Yes. We are all gone now. All my brothers and sisters. Far to the west the Shattered God has been sent onward – allowed to translate into another existence – however you wish to put it. As have I.'

Murk's brows rose in wonder. *Really? Something happening in the west?* 'Well, as I said before, I wish you luck with Ardata.'

The girl tilted her head, puzzled. 'Ardata?'

'Yeah. You know – this entity you chose.'

The girl laughed, a hand going to her mouth. 'Oh, Murk! Not *her*. She is as nothing next to that which I have reached out to. She would be a trickling stream compared to the ocean I have found here.'

Murk stared, his brows furrowed. *An ocean? Here? Whatever could she mean?* 'I'm sorry . . . I don't . . .'

Celeste extended her arms outwards as if to encompass their entire surroundings. 'I'm sorry, I keep forgetting your human biases and preconceptions. I speak not of any one individual being as you would know it, Murk. I speak of all this. Everything about us. I speak of what you name *Himatan* itself.'

Murk's brows now rose in earnest. 'Oh. *Oh* . . . That's . . . amazing, Celeste.'

She was nodding her agreement. 'Amazing, yes. Fascinating. Infinitely absorbing. The complexity. The interrelationships. It will perhaps take a millennium just to fully comprehend one part of it. And in its own way it is aware, Murken. It responds. It takes steps to assure its continued existence. It is an entity in those regards – no different from any lower-order being, such as yourself.'

Lower-order being? 'Ah, well, I see. I think. Then, you are not gone? Not faded away?'

A soft smile answered that question. 'No, Murken. Thank you for your concern. No. It was your advice that saved me. Your encouragement gave me the strength to take that irreversible step before the greater part of myself was sent onward – towards dissipation, or who knows what. I remain now as part of that which you name Himatan. Thanks to you.' She clasped her hands before her and bowed. 'So, farewell, Murken Warrow. May you find acceptance and belonging, as I have.'

Murk bowed his head in answer as Celeste's presence faded from view.

He returned his gaze to the infinite night sky. *Acceptance and belonging.* Some, he knew, would sneer at such sentiment. Yet humans were social beings. Perhaps it was these simple qualities that everyone sought, though they masked them with other, loftier sounding names: ambition, domination or glory.

Acceptance and belonging. He decided then that he'd tag along with Yusen's crew. They could use a cadre mage. And if he was going, chances were Sour would follow. *He's come along, that fellow. Shown some real potential. He just better not start getting any ideas about who's in charge, that's all.*

*

The Crimson Guard camped together, Avowed and Disavowed – though Disavowed no longer. From where she sat on a root Shimmer scanned the crowd. *Crowd. Who would have thought I could ever use that word again regarding the Avowed?* Yet crowd it seemed to her: she had become used to gatherings of mere handfuls.

For some, she knew, this change in circumstances would be harder than for others. Her gaze found fierce Mara sitting aside, alone, hugging herself. She had given much to Skinner, Shimmer knew. And now he was gone. Though she knew she would see him again among the Brethren, should he ever choose to come to the living. She scanned the group and found the broad towering figure of Petal sitting at one fire. She caught his gaze and directed it to Mara. He pursed his heavy lips thoughtfully, then rose, smoothed his torn and frayed robes down his wide front, and crossed to sit next to her.

She now searched for K'azz. She saw him nowhere and she threw herself to her feet. *Damn the fool! The very night he ought to be among us! Our first evening together. Where is he? I have a few words for him!* She set off to track him down.

After searching among the woods she found him standing alone, arms crossed, peering up at the clear night sky. It was a cold night and she'd been shivering. Somewhere, a hunting cat roared.

'K'azz!' she called sharply.

He turned, looking rather bemused. 'Yes? You are upset?'

'Yes, I'm upset! Here you are off alone. You should be with us. You should be reassuring everyone with your presence.'

He turned away, his gaze falling. 'Shimmer, I am not blind. My presence is far from reassuring. I can see that I make everyone uncomfortable . . . even you. And I understand.'

Oh, K'azz!

She spoke, surprising herself with the strength of the emotion in her voice: 'You are still our commander. We still follow. We still need you.' She closed one hesitant step. 'K'azz . . . something is worrying you. Something you know. Some secret. What is it? Tell me. Share it. We will all carry it with you.'

For some reason, that only made him flinch as if pained. He would not meet her entreating gaze. 'No. It is something I suspect . . . nothing more. It mustn't be spoken of. Not yet.'

'But in Assail . . .'

He let out a long tormented breath. 'Yes. Assail. Of all places. Assail.'

'I heard the Enchantress. The answer lies there.'

'*If* it can be found, yes.'

'I heard Cowl. He claims to know.'

K'azz gave a sad shake of his head. 'Shimmer . . . I doubt the man's sanity. He *thinks* he knows. And perhaps he has grasped some strange idea – the gods alone know what it might be.'

She crossed her arms, raised her gaze to the stars. *At least he is talking now. Perhaps I may persuade him to return.* She indicated the night sky. 'Whenever I look up I feel so alone and so small. I like the idea of each light up there being a campfire. It makes me feel . . . part of a tribe.'

'You are part of a tribe, Shimmer,' he answered.

She slid her eyes aside to see him also peering up. 'Yes. Our tribe. The Guard. Will you not rejoin it?'

The muscles on his jaw bunched as he clamped his teeth. He dropped his gaze to her. 'A good try, Shimmer.'

'Not a try. A timely reminder.' She motioned to the camp. 'Now, return with me. Yes?' *Now or never, Shimmer lass.* She took a step, inviting him to fall in with her. 'You have seen Petal, yes?' She glanced back to him expectantly.

A half-smile climbed his lips and he took one slow step. 'Yes . . .' he answered, guardedly.

'I do believe he is even bigger than when he left us.'

The smile climbed even higher. 'I do not see how, given that everyone else has lost weight here in this damned jungle.'

Shimmer continued her slow walking pace. 'Even so. It always amused me. Whenever we met some hulking swordsman who was too full of himself we would introduce him to Petal – the largest man alive and a crushingly shy mage to boot.'

K'azz smiled in remembrance.

'He and Mara seem to be getting along now.'

'No!' K'azz stepped up even with her. 'But she was so scornful of him. It made me wince. I worked to keep them apart. I knew why she joined with Skinner, of course. But I could never understand why he did.' He shook his head. 'That was always a mystery to me.'

Now Shimmer shook her head as she walked along back to camp. 'K'azz . . .' she sighed. 'You need to mix more.'

EPILOGUE

After having lived among these tribes for many years now I
have formed the considered opinion that but for all the differing
ritual, accoutrements, myths and attributes of their religious
practices, we both seek answers to the same profound questions
universal to the human condition: Who are we? Where do we
come from? Where are we going?

Whelhen Mariner
Narrative of a Shipwreck and Captivity
within a Mythical Land

IT WAS MOVEMENT THAT BETRAYED THE PRESENCE OF THEIR QUARRY
to Jatal. Movement where there had been none for the last two
days. Jatal had got used to the only change being the dust and ash
sifting down within the blasted vista of blanketed fallen tree trunks.
He was coughing all the time now, a cloth across his mouth and
nose. He hawked up bloodied phlegm. His breath was coming short,
perhaps from exhaustion and malnourishment, or perhaps from the
unsettling bubbling and fullness that choked his chest.

Movement far off immediately caught his eye. At first he thought
it an animal; a wounded survivor of the blast, a deer perhaps. Yet
amid its struggles the figure straightened to two legs and staggered
onward a pace or two before collapsing once again.

Jatal stopped to peer back to Scarza. Flakes of ash dusted the half-
Trell from head to foot. They even rested on his eyelashes. Scarza's
gaze was steady on the distant figure. Without a word, Jatal changed
direction to follow the survivor.

As they drew close, some noise or instinct alerted the figure
and it spun, straightening, to confront them. Jatal looked upon a
horrifyingly wounded Warleader who was, he now knew, the demon

573

out of his own legendary past: the self-proclaimed High King, Kallor himself. The man weaved drunkenly, a hand on the grip of the bastard sword still at his side. His coat of mail hung from him in torn and blackened tatters of metal links. The flesh beneath oozed, blistered and raw. His beard had been half burned away, as had his hair, leaving seared livid skin behind. One eye was swollen closed, weeping a clear fluid. Dried mud and ash caked him.

Recognition gleamed in his one good eye and he snorted and waved his contempt. 'You cannot kill me,' he grated. His voice was so hoarse as to be almost inaudible.

'I see that now,' Jatal answered, just as hoarse and breathless. 'I see that all the ancient curses heaped upon you still hold.'

Kallor growled deep in his throat at that, hawked up a mouthful of catarrh, and spat aside. 'I will break them yet.'

Merciless gods! All because of you and your damned curses . . . 'You thought them gone, didn't you?' Jatal opened his arms to indicate the blasted surroundings. 'All this because you wished to end it. Is that not so?'

The High King actually shrugged. 'It seemed a good bet. The sword Draconus swore upon is broken. Sister of Cold Nights is broken. Those who cursed me are all slipping away – as they should have long ago.'

'Damn you,' Jatal breathed, utterly overcome with horror.

Kallor laughed a dry hack, wiped his mouth, his hand coming away gleaming with blood. 'So, you too would add to my burden. Is that it? You are quite done then?'

'Almost.'

'Oh? You cannot kill me. You curse me. We are done, I should think.'

'Yes,' Jatal answered wearily. He felt so tired of it all. So ready to throw it all aside. 'We will leave you crawling in the dust, Kallor. Which is where you belong, curse or no curse. But first I would have one boon from you.'

The High King raised his flame-scarred head to better examine him. His one good eye gleamed as if touched by madness. 'A boon? In truth? And what can I grant you?'

Scarza edged forward to touch Jatal's elbow. 'Lad . . .' he urged, 'don't.'

Jatal gently shook his touch away. 'What you lack the courage to grant yourself . . . release.'

Kallor lurched forward. His livid features darkened even further in fury. He raised a fist to Jatal. 'You think I have not tried? You think I meekly . . .' He cut himself off, choking. He straightened. His gaze eased back into its familiar condescension. 'They will not be the end of me. I will break them, or go of my own choosing.'

Jatal nodded his understanding. 'I agree, High King. That is why I am here. I ask that you release me. My love awaits.'

Kallor's breath hissed from him in a long slow exhalation of amazement, and he flinched back a step. 'Well done, Prince Jatal of the Hafinaj. You win your way and in so doing you succeed where I am cursed to fail. Well done.' He drew his bastard sword and held it upright before him in salute.

Scarza pushed forward. 'Now, lad,' he said, 'think of what she'd want. You don't really think she'd—'

Jatal gently urged the half-Trell aside. 'It is all right, Scarza. She awaits me. I must join her. There is nothing else left for me.'

Scarza had to turn his face away. He squeezed his eyes against the tears that warmed his cheeks.

Kallor cried out: 'So join her!' and a foot stamped the ground.

Scarza spun to see a length of the wide bastard sword blade extending from Jatal's back. The lad grunted something. His knees bent and he slid backwards off the slick blade. Scarza caught him in his arms. 'Lad!' he croaked, shocked. 'You didn't need to . . .' But Jatal could not answer; Kallor's thrust had been true. Scarza hugged the body to him.

Kallor sheathed the blade. 'What now, Scarza?' he asked. 'I am headed north. Join me. Draconus is free, they say. I will find him and squeeze the life from him.'

Scarza just shook his head. He could not find the words for the depth of callousness, the astounding lack of . . . humanity.

'No?' Kallor continued. 'The pay will be far better this time, I promise.'

Scarza merely turned away and started walking.

'What is this?' Kallor called. 'You are walking away? Don't be a fool! Drop that carrion and join me. You know I cannot be defeated. Scarza! Come back. I demand – I order you to return!' He bellowed after him: 'Scarza! Do as I say!'

Scarza walked on. He hugged the cooling body to his chest. The ash flakes stuck to his wet face. What could one say? Even after all this – in the sight of such devastation – the man still had not learned a thing. Perhaps that was his true curse. His overriding inner curse.

He could never learn.

* * *

The clouds had cleared from the sky. The layer of pulverized stone, soot, and ash lay as a smooth blanket. With evening, rainclouds swept in from the east and a light drizzle fell. It dimpled the ash and hissed where it met heated rock beneath.

A swirl of wind emerged from nowhere with a gust of displaced air that blew the ash in all directions. A man now stood amid the dispersing dust. He brushed it from his green cloak as he set off walking with a brisk purposeful stride.

The ground he trod lay as a broad shallow bowl, or crater. It crackled beneath his boots, flash-heated to a thin glass-like layer of sintered earth. The man scanned the flattened surroundings: a plain of emptiness apart from the gusting curtains of ash and pulverized stone. He brushed the powder from his arms and shoulders and continued on.

A distance off, a humped shape revealed another occupant of this otherworld of drifting flakes of falling soot. The man hurried forward. He found a woman, mostly naked, kneeling over a prostrate body in blackened and seared trousers and shirt. The woman straightened and pushed back her unkempt mane of tousled hair. She wore a wrap at her breasts and loins. To one side lay a small chest, like a jewellery case.

Ignoring the woman, the man knelt at the body's side, pressed a hand to its neck to check for a pulse.

'Greetings, L'oric, son of Osserc,' the woman said, backing away.

'And you, Spite, daughter of Draconus,' the man answered, and he let out a breath of relief as he kept his hand on the fallen one's neck. 'He lives.'

'Yes,' Spite answered as she continued to back away. 'Astonishingly. He lives still. Despite all this. He lives still.'

With some effort, L'oric managed to turn the prostrate figure over, revealing the pale hair and skin of a Tiste Liosan. 'You are surprised?' he asked, eyeing the woman.

'By his survival? Or by his actions?'

'The latter more,' L'oric mused. 'As I am.'

'Yes.' She frowned down at the unconscious man. 'Your father . . . interceded . . . took it upon himself.'

'Yes.'

She raised her puzzled gaze to L'oric. 'Why?'

'I do not know at this time. Perhaps he will eventually explain.' He shook his head. 'But more likely not.' He pointed aside. 'And that?'

Spite grunted a harsh exhalation, muttering beneath. She picked up the small chest and opened the top, tipping it. Black powder

576

spilled forth to disperse in the weak wind. 'A failed errand. Wishful thinking.' She cast the box into the distance.

'Will you aid me in another errand?' L'oric asked, eyeing the dust as it swirled into nothingness.

'Which is?'

The tall wiry mage indicated his unconscious father. 'To put him where he belongs.'

The daughter of Draconus arched one shapely brow. 'Indeed . . . that I should like very much.'

'Very well.' The mage knelt, and, grunting his effort, arose with his father in his arms. Spite backed away, her face betraying surprise and amazement. The mage commanded through clenched teeth: 'Open us a way to the border regions of Kurald Thyrllan.'

Spite's brows rose even higher. 'But it is closed.' She pointed to Osserc. 'By his very hand.'

'We shall see then,' L'oric grunted. 'As close as possible – if you would.'

Spite gave a quick nod and turned, extending her arms. The air tore before her. Blinding golden light burst forth through a jagged rent. The two figures, mere dark silhouettes in the roaring conflagration of brilliance, stepped through and disappeared.

The rent snapped shut.

L'oric and Spite faced a blasted landscape of twisting narrow canyons all shimmering in heat waves. Overhead, energies streamed as rippling auroras of power in banners, curtains and multicoloured scarves. They both hunched beneath the punishing heat and glare. L'oric adjusted his burden, hugging his father tighter to his chest.

'Now what?' Spite growled, shielding her eyes with an arm.

L'oric cast about, searching. He lifted his chin to the left. 'There! You see the tall landmark?'

Spite squinted. Some sort of spire or tower rose atop a butte. 'Yes.'

'Get us over there.'

She swept her arms again and they disappeared.

L'oric stumbled as he walked to emerge upon a heap of loose baked shards of talus that shifted beneath his feet. He ended up at the bottom of the slope deep within a narrow canyon of crumbling layers of shale, sandstone and silts. Spite awaited him. She pointed up.

L'oric nodded and hefted his burden once again, wincing. 'Get us up there,' he shouted over the roar of energies streaming overhead.

Spite grumbled something under her breath and wiped the sweat now dripping down her face and naked limbs. She cast about, scanning the surroundings. She gestured, pushing and kneading with her hands. The wall of a nearby canyon shuddered. Rocks clattered. Then, with a crack of stone, the entire wall came crashing down in an avalanche of broken rock, raising a cloud of dust that Spite waved from her face. L'oric turned his head away, hunching a shoulder.

The dust dispersed quickly, driven off by the blasting power coursing across the landscape. A slope of shattered dry rock was revealed. Spite started up; she used all fours, pulling and dragging herself along. L'oric followed. 'Not exactly how I would have handled that,' he muttered to himself.

At the top, he winced again, turning his face away from the blasting wild energies punishing the landscape. Spite had run ahead to the shadow side of a tower that somehow remained standing against the streaming power. L'oric followed.

He lurched against the brick wall only to flinch away: the stones nearly glowed with heat.

'Now what?' Spite shouted into his ear.

He raised his chin to the tower. 'Go on up.'

She grumbled once more: something about 'this better be worth it', and pushed on, dodging ahead. L'oric followed. Within, stairs encircled the outer walls, leading up. The interior was empty but for the rippling heat of a kiln. L'oric staggered up the stairs. He was nearing the end of his strength.

The stairs ended at an open trapdoor into a chamber at the tower's top. It was enclosed but for a single narrow slit window facing the source of the glaring energies. Spite stood aside, her arms crossed.

'And now?' she demanded.

He set his father down and straightened his sweat-soaked shirt. 'Now we shall see.' He approached the slit window. A beam of light came in through the slit and crossed the chamber, cutting it in half. L'oric knew that it seemed that this was a world facing a cruel sun that hung at a fraction of the distance of the one most humans knew. But in truth, it was not like that at all. The source of the unleashed brilliance was in fact much smaller, and much closer, than imagined.

He extended a hand into the wall of light then yanked it back as the beam seared his flesh. To Spite's questioning look he explained: 'Now we wait.'

'Who built this?'

'Jaghut, I believe.'

'To study Thyrllan?'

'I believe it may extend back much further than that.'

Spite grunted something non-committal. L'oric eyed her; her limbs seemed to glow as well, gleaming with sweat. He cleared his throat and quickly looked away.

Spite smiled almost cruelly. 'What are we waiting for?'

'We'll know it when we see it,' he replied, still looking away.

The beam of light rippled and they both flinched backwards. Something appeared to be blocking the slit from the outside, hovering there.

'*Who comes?*' a voice whispered. It somehow penetrated the crackling and snarling energies though it came gently, soft and melodious.

'Liosan!' L'oric called.

'*Entreat us no more,*' the thing answered. '*The way is closed.*'

'He who closed it is come,' L'oric shouted.

'*For him we have been waiting all this time. Where is he? We sense him not.*'

'He is injured.'

'*We will discern the truth of this.*'

The light streaming across the room rippled again, writhing as if something were moving within it. Then a pillar of flame burst to life within the chamber. L'oric and Spite flinched all the way back to press themselves against the walls. The sizzling presence scoured the brick floor leaving a black scar behind as it wavered about. It passed over Osserc's unconscious body and halted, flickering. L'oric tensed, his Warren raised.

'*It is him!*' came the melodious call, somehow conveying disbelief and joy. '*Returned as he promised us. Open the way!*'

The grating of stone pulled L'oric's attention from his father. The narrow slit window in the far wall appeared to be changing. Dust and ground stone fell in a fine powder that flared incandescent as it drifted into the beam of blazing light. That beam cutting through the slit took on a deeper hue of gold until L'oric could no longer see through it. It might have been that light, but when he studied the slit window, his hand before his eyes, it appeared to be widening. As if it were opening.

He grabbed Spite's arm and brought his head next to hers. 'We must go!' he shouted through the burgeoning roar.

'Why?' she yelled, and brushed his hand away.

He pointed. 'The window! I believe it *is* the gate! A gate opening directly into Kurald Thyrllan.'

'So what?' She waved at him. 'Aren't you resistant, or whatever, to its manifestation?'

'No more than Mother Dark could encompass Darkness itself!' he shouted back. 'Come!'

'Your father?'

'They will take him! Come!' He attempted again to grab her arm but she easily brushed his hand away. He started backing away towards the stairs regardless.

The slit was definitely wider now, and lengthening, extending down to the floor. The solid bar of light was filling the chamber and it was this that pushed Spite back as it ate up the floor space finger by finger like shimmering poured gold. She joined L'oric on the stairs, which they descended backwards. So bright was the presence above, L'oric had to turn his face away. Spots danced before his punished eyes. On the ground floor Spite bumped into him, cursing and wiping at her eyes. 'Damn it to Night!' she snarled. 'I can't see a damned thing.'

'Thryllan has taken him,' L'oric said, studying the stairs.

'He will hardly be missed,' Spite growled.

'You are harsh.'

'It is the truth.'

He took a fold of cloth and dabbed his eyes. 'We will not know the truth of this until sufficient time has passed.'

'Sufficient time for the lies to take hold.'

'I think you hold too hard to bitterness.'

Spite studied him for a time. 'Our alliance is nearly at an end, L'oric. Do not tempt me to any rash act following it.'

He sketched a courtier's bow. 'As m'lady would have it. Shall we go?'

'Gladly. I loathe this place.'

'That is not so strange. I rather like it.'

*　　　*　　　*

On the western slope of the Gangrek Mounts a woman descended a slim trail. It was no more than a rocky animal track occasionally used by locals to climb the mount for game or to collect firewood or plants. Her shirt was tattered, stained and worn to mere threads, while her skirt hung merely to her knees. Her hair was an unkempt cloud about her heart-shaped features. Yet she walked the trail with the assurance and ease of an experienced jungle tracker.

Halfway down she stopped to peer back up the path. After a time another figure came descending behind. He came slowly as he used a sturdy stick as a crutch. One arm hung tied to his side, he dragged one foot, and a cloth was wrapped around his head covering one eye. His hair hung long and loose but did not completely hide the odd shape of the left side of his head. He wore the torn and hard-travelled robes of a Thaumaturg.

The young woman took his arm to help him down the more difficult sections of the steep track. He offered her a strange one-sided smile that made her blush and turn her face away. As the trail levelled she kept his arm to walk along beside him.

Together, they retraced their steps back into Thaumaturg territory. They were returning because someone had to rebuild, and if they did not others would. She had a reborn faith to guide and shape anew and he would do all he could to clear its way into the world.

*   *   *

Far off on the eastern coast of Jacuruku, a gentle surf kissed a stretch of desert strand. A dense jungle verge crowded the shore. The empty sands descended steeply to the sapphire waves. Above, clear blue sky echoed the pale blue of the shallow waters. White seabirds hovered and gave their harsh calls in the weak wind. Crabs searched among the foam and cast-up seaweed.

A man came staggering out of the jungle to stand weaving drunkenly and blinking in the bright sunlight. A shirt hung from him in tatters, as did his trousers. Sores, bites and scratches dotted his limbs. His beard and hair were ragged and filthy. Another emerged, no different from the first. He, too, stopped as if dumbfounded, or completely uncertain of what to do next.

A giant emerged next. It carried a man in its stone arms that it gently set down to stand in the sands. This man tapped a black-wood rod chased in silver to his shoulder while he stood staring out to sea.

More men, a bare few handfuls, came staggering out to fall or sit in the sands and stare wordlessly at the bright leagues of empty sea. A scrawny old man wearing only a loincloth came limping from the jungle. He carried a bag over one shoulder and he walked down to the man holding the blackwood rod.

After studying the sea for a time, Principal Scribe Thorn turned to his commander, Master Golan, and said, 'Congratulations, Golan the Great.'

Master Golan blinked as if coming out of a dream and peered down at his scribe. 'I'm sorry,' he croaked. 'Congratulations?'

'The Army of Righteous Chastisement has emerged triumphant,

m'lord. It has crushed the jungle into abasement. Dealt it a final decisive blow! Your march has proved victorious.'

'You will write that down, won't you?'

'Of course!'

The old man, all skin and bones, his hair standing as a thinning white rim about his skull, bent his head down to search within the loose bag. He searched, then searched again, becoming more and more agitated. Finally, he pulled the bag from his side and overturned it, waving and flapping it. A single sheet flew free to flutter out over the waves and disappear into the distance.

Golan watched it fly off. 'Nothing important, I trust,' he offered, rather drily. He peered curiously at the empty bag. 'Misplaced your records? What has become of them?'

'Food has been rather scarce of late,' Principal Scribe Thorn confessed, looking guilty.

Golan studied the man, frowning. 'My glorious campaign has disappeared down your gullet, been digested, and shat out your other end?'

'I have merely done the job of the historians for them, m'lord.'

Golan tilted his head, thinking about it, then nodded, conceding the point. 'True enough, Principal Scribe. True enough. You have merely saved everyone a great deal of time.'

'I do try to serve in my own small way.' He suddenly raised a finger as if in inspiration. He yanked the nub of a quill from behind one blackened ear, licked the end, and poised it over the leather bag. 'Your orders?'

Golan looked to the surf, the blue sea rolling onward to the horizon. He rubbed his fingers across his brow – they came away slick with grime and sweat. He sighed heavily. 'Second,' he called in a raised voice.

Shortly after this, Second in Command Waris emerged from the jungle verge. He wore a long stained shirt that was at one time the underpadding of leather armour. A weapon belt hung over one shoulder and he bore a scrap of cloth tied about his head. He came to Golan and saluted.

'Second Waris,' Golan began. Then he paused. He eyed the cloth on the man's head. 'Not regulation, I should think, Second.'

'Keeps the sun off, sir,' the man replied, his voice flat.

Still a man of few words. Somehow reassuring, that. Golan cleared his throat. 'We will camp here. Perhaps there are foodstuffs that the troops may collect. On the morrow we head north around the coast. Eventually we will reach our borders.'

Waris bowed and headed off to convey the orders.

Golan started pacing the shore, slowly, meditatively. He held the blackwood Rod of Execution behind his back in both hands, tapping it with his thumbs.

Principal Scribe Thorn followed behind. He licked the quill and began scratching on the bag. He mouthed as he walked: 'Having utterly crushed the jungle leagues of Jacuruku, Golan the Great vanquishes the Eastern Ocean then casts his victor's eyes onward to new conquests! He orders the beginning of a grand new campaign against the Northern Wastes. The glorious Army of Righteous Chastisement springs to its feet to follow its inspiring leader onward to new triumphs no doubt as rewarding and glorious as those they have known . . .'

Master Golan suddenly halted. He raised his face to the clear sky while exhaling mightily through clenched teeth. He raised the Rod of Execution, then regarded the surf restlessly surging up the steep strand. For a moment it appeared as if he were considering throwing the baton into the sea. He lowered it, however, and turned to study the bedraggled survivors of his army as they slumped down together to sit listless and exhausted, staring out at the vast unbroken horizon before them.

His gaze fell to Principal Scribe Thorn who watched him expectantly, quill poised. He wiped the back of his hand across his eyes, blinking, then quickly turned his face out to sea. After a time he murmured, as if more to himself: 'You are right, Thorn. Posterity will wonder at your perspicacity. You have assured my due place in history.'

The scribe swallowed, his bulging Adam's apple bobbing. 'It is my duty, Master Golan.'

GLOSSARY

Elder Races

Tiste Andii: Children of Darkness
Tiste Edur: Children of Shadow
Tiste Liosan: Children of Light
Imass: an ancient race of which only the undead army, the T'lan Imass, remain
Trell: an ancient race of nomadic pastoralists
Jaghut: an ancient race of recluses
Thelomen / Toblakai: an ancient race, pre-agriculturalists

The Warrens

Kurald Galain: The Elder Warren of Darkness, Elder Night
Kurald Emurlahn: The Elder Warren of Shadow, Elder Shadow
Kurald Thyrllan: The Elder Warren of Light: Elder Light, also known as Liosan
Omtose Phellack: The Elder Jaghut Warren of Ice
Tellann: The Elder Imass Warren of Fire
Starvald Demelain: The Eleint Warren
Thyr: The Path of Light
Denul: The Path of Healing
Hood's Path: The Path of Death
Serc: The Path of the Sky
Meanas: The Path of Shadow and Illusion
D'riss: The Path of the Earth
Ruse: The Path of the Sea
Rashan: The Path of Darkness

Mockra: The Path of the Mind
Telas: The Path of Fire

Terms and Places

The Adwami: the nomadic tribes of southern Jacuruku

Agon: an order of priests for whom good and evil are illusions

Ammanas: also known as Shadowthrone, ruler of the Shadow Realm

Anditi Pura: capital city of the Thaumaturgs

Chanar Keep: a ruined keep in the Gangrek Mounts on the border of Himatan

The Dolmens of Tien: site of an ancient 'Chaining' of the Crippled God

High King / God-King: ancient title of legendary ruler of most of Jacuruku, Kallor

Himatan: an enchanted jungle said to be ruled by Ardata

Isana Pura: southern capital of the Thaumaturgs

Isturé: a term for the Avowed that extends to the Disavowed as well

Jakal Viharn: rumoured great city in the jungle, 'city of gold', paved in jewels

Khun-Sen: an old general, once ruler of Chanar Keep

The Meckros: name for floating cities and the people who occupy them

The Nak-ta: the restless dead of Jacuruku

Phalam: a unit within the Thaumaturg army, roughly equivalent to a squad

The Shaduwam: shaman-like priests of southern Jacuruku

Thaumaturgs / Theurgists: ruling mages of a nation in Jacuruku

The Yakshaka: their statue-like stone soldiers, manufactured by alchemy and magery

ABOUT THE AUTHOR

IAN CAMERON ESSLEMONT has worked as an archaeologist and has taught and travelled in South East Asia and the Far East. He now lives in Fairbanks, Alaska with his wife and children. His previous novels, *Night of Knives*, *Return of the Crimson Guard*, *Stonewielder* and *Orb Sceptre Throne* are all set in the epic fantasy world he co-created with Steven Erikson.